Harlequin
Omnibus

The second collection of 3 Great Novels by
Elizabeth Hoy

Harlequin Books

TORONTO • LONDON • NEW YORK • AMSTERDAM
SYDNEY • HAMBURG • PARIS

These books by Elizabeth Hoy were originally published as
follows:

SO LOVED AND SO FAR
Copyright © 1954 by Elizabeth Hoy
First published in 1954 by Mills & Boon Limited
Harlequin edition (#903) published March 1965

FLOWERING DESERT
Copyright © 1965 by Elizabeth Hoy
First published in 1965 by Mills & Boon Limited
Harlequin edition (#1031) published July 1966

HONEYMOON HOLIDAY
Copyright © 1967 by Elizabeth Hoy
First published in 1967 by Mills & Boon Limited
Harlequin edition (#1226) published August 1968

ISBN 0-373-70393-7

First **Harlequin Omnibus** edition published June 1978

Contents

So Loved
and So Far

Gail had once been in love with Major Rodwell Sterne. But if Rod had ever been attracted to her, it was plain that he was cured now.

"Nothing is as stale and unprofitable as a past that is dead," he said, his look at Gail emphasizing his meaning. "It is a mistake to try and revive it."

So Gail decided to put him out of her mind. That, however, proved to be much more difficult than she had imagined!

CHAPTER ONE

"If I send you to Ireland," Miss Chatsworth said, "you won't be available if they should want you to help at the Horse Show Committee again this summer."

Gail sat very still on the hard little office chair, her hands on her lap clasped so tightly that they hurt. "I can't work at the Horse Show this year; I *can't!*" her heart cried within her, and it was as though the bright oval of grass was there before her once more, the flags flying, the band playing, the spectators, tier upon tier of them, rising in their seats to cheer, while a man on a shining ebony horse rode slowly round the ring: Rodwell Sterne on Connaught King.

"But the work at the Horse Show Committee is something anybody could do. I mean, I don't suppose they'd ask specially for *me*," she said, trying to keep the eagerness out of her voice. There was a perverse streak in old Chatty that made her likely to withhold a job if she thought you were too keen on having it. Not that she *was* all that keen, Gail told herself. It might indeed turn out to be rather a dull assignment; an elderly crippled lady who sounded as if she needed a nurse-companion rather than a Chatsworth-trained social secretary. Even if there was a nineteen-year-old niece in the background, and she was going to be married in August, there wouldn't surely be much social life to organize in a place called Laheen, lost in the wilds of the Irish mountains. It was the sudden unexpected prospect of getting away from a routine gone grey and dull beyond endurance in the past dragging months that brought the desperate sparkle of hope to Gail's gold-flecked hazel eyes. Freckled eyes, Rod had once called them.

"Personally," Miss Chatsworth was saying, "I'd rather have sent someone older. But Miss Ross O'Donnel specially asks for one of the younger members of my staff." Peering at the letter spread before her, she began to read aloud:

9

"My niece, Shelagh, has had so little young company of her own sex that I feel it would be of great benefit to her to have the companionship of some gently nurtured girl not too far from her own age. She needs guidance in matters of dress and deportment, and skilled help in the choosing and ordering of her trousseau—all of which I am too much of an invalid to attend to myself. So I must throw myself on your mercy, and I am assured by Lady Starforth, who told me of your comprehensive organization, that the members of your staff are qualified, not only in secretarial work, but in so much else besides. Table-decoration, dressmaking, beauty culture, ballroom dancing, household management, conversation, are among the accomplishments Mary Starforth mentioned. My dear Miss Chatsworth, at the thought of the paragons you produce my heart fails me! How do you do it?"

Gail suppressed a desire to giggle, as the dry voice went on reading:

"To teach conversation, for instance! An art I imagined to be almost extinct in a busy, progressive, mechanically minded world. Here, of course, where we are neither progressive nor mechanical, people talk all day, and half the night, with the least encouragement. . . ."

Gail's lips quivered as Miss Chatsworth shot her a repressive glance. Was this Miss Ross O'Donnel person making fun of her? her small angry eyes seemed to demand. A sense of humor was not one of poor Chatty's stronger points. "You can inform Miss O'Donnel—*if* I send you to Laheen—that our conversation course at Chatsworth House is most carefully planned," she declared fiercely. "And that it includes not only a grounding in general knowledge, but a debating society, a drama section with lessons in voice production, and that I encourage all my students to read through at least two of our greater national daily newspapers each morning so that they may be kept in touch with current events and be able to discuss them intelligently."

"Yes, Miss Chatsworth," Gail murmured with deceptive meekness. "I'll do my best in every way, if you decide to send me."

Miss Chatsworth gave her a final searching glance. "Well, you'd better go home and talk it over with your parents," she conceded grudgingly. "If they are agreeable, I suppose I may as well let you see what you can make of these Ross O'Donnels. It won't be an easy post . . . a crippled employer, and a wedding to arrange: you'll need plenty of initiative, common sense . . . and dignity." The last two words held an admonitory note. "I could wish you were a little more than your . . . what is it? Twenty-one years?"

"I'll be twenty-two in October," Gail supplied, trying to hide her elation. Laheen was hers . . . if her mother and father were willing to let her go. And she was quite sure they would be. They'd known when they sent her to Chatsworth House to train that it was something more than an ordinary secretarial bureau; its graduates likely to be whisked off to any corner of the earth where skilled temporary secretarial or social help was needed. There was Joan Frene, she reminded them when they discussed the matter that evening, who had been sent to Persia to assist some oil tycoon at an international conference; Anne Benson summoned to the Bahamas by a famous novelist whose typist had fallen ill in the midst of a specially urgent spate of work, and Cynthia Smith who'd spent an enviable winter on the ski slopes of the Swiss Alps with a winter sports organization.

"I might have been sent anywhere," she pointed out. "Ireland is nothing."

Mrs. Darnley's shrewd and motherly ear caught the note of eagerness in her daughter's voice. It was months since she had seen Gail so animated. The sudden unaccountable listlessness that had come over her last summer —round about the time of her job with the Horse Show Committee—had persisted all through the winter and spring. A few weeks in Ireland might be very good for her. "It will be nice for you to have a complete change," Mrs. Darnley said; "get right away from all of us for a spell. It

11

has been rather a . . . restless year for you, dear, hasn't it?"

Good old Mother, Gail thought wryly, who never asked awkward questions . . . and yet seemed to know all the answers! A restless year. Well, perhaps that was as good a way as any other of describing the emotional upheaval that had wrecked the neat little pattern of the life to which she might so easily have settled. Work for a year or two at the Chatsworth Bureau, by which time Jimmy Hansen would have obtained the science degree for which he was now studying at London University. And as soon as he had got a post she would no doubt have married him. Dear, nice, familiar Jimmy whom she had known all her short life. He lived in the same pleasant suburban road as the Darnleys, and Gail had drifted almost inevitably, as school days were left behind, into the comfortable rather than romantic friendship which she had found satisfactory enough. Until Rod Sterne flashed like a meteor across her tranquil horizon . . . destroying tranquillity for all time!

She'd known then she could never marry Jimmy and, without mentioning Rod, she had told him so. None of her family had known about Rod. There was, after all, so pitifully little to know! Sometimes she wondered if it wouldn't have been fairer to have told Jimmy at least the whole humiliating story. As it was, he persisted in regarding her altered attitude towards him as a prolonged attack of feminine whimsy, and obstinately refused to be sidetracked. Getting away from poor, loyal, silently reproachful Jimmy was one of the things that made the thought of Ireland so attractive!

He came to Euston on the bright May evening the family assembled to see her safely installed in the Irish Mail train; her mother and father, Debby, her seventeen-year-old sister, Clinty, her nine-year-old brother.

"I could perhaps run over and have a look at you in your wild western lair during the long vac?" Jimmy suggested hopefully, as they all stood bunched round her compartment door, caught in that nervous hiatus which makes last-moment conversations in railways stations so jerky and unreal.

12

"Oh, Jimmy, please don't!" Gail cried in horror. "There's nothing more demoralizing than to have relations and friends cropping up when one is battling with a new job. Besides, I shan't have very much free time."

"And no followers allowed," Debby put in with a giggle.

"Well, as long as you have time to discover how much you miss me!" Jimmy said wistfully. And suddenly porters were banging compartment doors, whistles were sounding. Gail turned to her mother, the unexpected sting of tears in her eyes. Now that the moment of parting was actually upon her, Laheen seemed very far away. There was a last flurry of embraces, Jimmy taking advantage of the emotional atmosphere to press his lips hard against her quivering mouth. The great express shuddered and stirred. It was incredible how quickly the little group on the platform was left behind!

For a moment or two Gail stood dazed by the open window, feeling as though some vital part of her had been lopped off. Then she sank down into her reserved corner seat and a little shyly, conscious of the tear-stains on her cheeks, surveyed her fellow passengers. Absorbed in their papers and magazines, they seemed totally unaware of her, so she dabbed at her short straight nose with a powder puff, opened a magazine on her own account and forgot about them.

Slowly, intoxicatingly, the sense of freedom began to work in her veins. She was off. Alone. On her way to face a new world where everything would be fresh, stimulating. This was her chance to cut her losses and move bravely forward. It was almost a year now since she had said goodbye to Rod. It was crazy to go on letting him matter to her . . . a man she'd known little more than a week!

Dropping the magazine, she tried to concentrate on what lay ahead. But the Ross O'Donnels refused to take substance and Laheen was no more than a name, without meaning. A cloud of unreality seemed to descend upon her, that hypnotized state induced by a long journey to an unknown destination. She was a nameless nonentity shut up with four other equally nameless nonentities in a brightly lit, plush-lined box flying westward through the gathering darkness. It was a faintly irresponsible sensa-

13

tion, pleasantly relaxing. Suspended in time and space she closed her eyes.

And instantly it was last August again. Into the emptiness of her heart the past came flooding.

It was the second morning of her fortnight with the Organizing Committee of the great International Horse Show and she was sitting in the little white-painted office behind the Show Ring, waiting for Miss Crump, the honorary secretary, to come in and dictate the day's letters. There was a mirror on the wall beside her desk and she could see herself sitting there, looking very young and a little apprehensive—because this was the first important job Miss Chatsworth had sent her to. She was wearing a new dress, she remembered, a soft navy linen with crisp snowy collar and cuffs. Absently she surveyed it, and the girl in the mirror stared back at her; a girl with thick, short-cut, glinting, goldy-brown hair and a freshly colored oval face—that was looking unusually serious with its blunt straight nose, sweetly curved lips, and rounded firm little chin. A face so familiar that she turned away from it in boredom and began to go through the list of show entries once more to make sure that all the names of the competitors had been correctly spelled. In the first rough proof of the list, the name of the star entrant had appeared disastrously without its final "e". But now the mistake had been corrected. Vaguely Gail wondered if its owner would have been greatly annoyed if it had not been. The legendary Major Rodwell Sterne who made news wherever he went with his magic mount, Connaught King. And he went, it seemed, plenty of places, scooping the pool in all the big international jumping contests . . . Helsinki, America, Canada, Madrid. Miss Crump practically genuflected when she spoke of him. But her enthusiasm left Gail unmoved. Major Sterne was no more than a name to her, a troublesome name that got itself wrongly spelled in important lists.

The telephone rang at her elbow. It was Miss Crump speaking on the inter-departmental connection. She said, "Oh, Miss Darnley, Major Sterne is here and I want you to meet him. You'll find us in the ring by the Judges' enclosure."

Gail, mildly surprised at the summons, hung up the receiver. Why had Major Sterne turned up almost a week before the contests were due to begin, and why did Miss Crump want her to meet him?

She went out into the brilliant August sunshine. The grass of the ring was a blinding green and workmen were busy erecting the formidable-looking jumps. The man standing with Miss Crump before the ornate façade of the Judges' box might, at a first glance, have been any man whose life is devoted to horsy pursuits. A little over middle height, lightly built, wide in the shoulders, narrow in the waist, with that suggestion of perfect muscular control in his easy stance that only a trained athlete can achieve.

"This is Miss Darnley," Miss Crump said.

Gail's fingers were enveloped in a brief, steel-strong clasp and she found herself looking up into a lean, deeply tanned face touched with an arrogance that could have been intimidating except that it vanished suddenly in an unexpected smile, the strong, even teeth showing with an almost startling whiteness against the golden tanned skin. He was facing the rays of the powerful midday sun and it gave him a curiously lucent quality, as though he were all made of gold; even his jet-black hair had a bronze glint in it and his eyes were like twin flames under the level dark brows; agate-colored eyes of a tigerish yellowness, with a strange knack of remaining steady and unblinking in the strong light. Meeting their penetrating gaze, Gail found that her heart was beating faster than usual. There was something a little frightening, faintly inhuman, in the quality of that unwavering glance. He is like an eagle, she thought, remembering that she had read somewhere of the eagle's power to look undazzled into the full blaze of the sun.

"Major Sterne," Miss Crump was saying, "is in difficulties over an article he has promised to write for *The Horseman's World*, and we were wondering if you could help him out?"

"Miss Crump tells me you are formidably efficient!" The white teeth flashed pleasantly.

"But not at . . . journalism," Gail murmured diffidently.

15

"This effort of mine will hardly rank as journalism." The smile widened into a boyish grin. "At the moment it amounts to nothing more than a pocketful of scribbled notes. If you could sort them out for me a bit . . . type them perhaps . . . ?"

"But of course," Gail agreed a little breathlessly, aware once more of the compelling quality in those agate-gold eyes—that no smile could altogether soften. It was as though the whole of the man's considerable personality was centred there; dominating, inflexible, capable of ruthlessness. Eyes that would give no quarter and ask none. And yet in their sheer electrical vitality they conveyed a warmth that made Gail feel suddenly tinglingly alive. Walking by his side back to the office she wondered why she had imagined the August day to be languorous and airless. It was a sparkling day, a lightly-dancing, spring-like day that lifted the heart on wings!

And that had been the beginning of it.

Recalling herself to her surroundings, Gail saw that her fellow passengers were all asleep. The lights had been dimmed now and in the faint blue glow of the single ceiling lamp their faces loomed pale and ghostly. Beyond the night-blackened windows the world lay dead, a hollow cavern through which the great express rocked and thundered. With a shiver of loneliness Gail gave herself up once more to the memory of those strange, bright, painful days, which after tonight she would blot out of her mind for ever.

Because she could not devote a great deal of time to the Horsemanship article during the office hours of that August day, she had stayed on in the evening to work at it. Major Sterne, grateful, concerned for her, had insisted upon driving her home to her distant suburb. The second evening she had worked on the article again, and he took her out to dinner. At first she had been a little in awe of him, but his easy charm of manner had quickly broken down her restraint and their conversation had gone easily. He told her about his years in the show ring, of the weeks of grilling preparation before a contest, and of the difficulty of handling a temperamental thoroughbred enduring the strain of world-wide travel. She began to understand some-

16

thing of the circumstances which had produced in him the quality of tempered steel. He had, he told her, been in the saddle since almost before he could walk, and had held a short service commission in a famous cavalry unit.

It was when they had arrived at the coffee stage that he said, "Now we've had enough about me and my affairs. Tell me about *you*."

She said, inevitably: "There isn't much to tell." But his quick, penetrating questions held a note of genuine interest and she found herself talking easily, even amusingly, about Chatty's, about her home in Hampstead, about Debby and Clint.

He said, "Your parents seem to go in for unusual names for their children; what did they call you? I've been trying to imagine to myself what would go well with your musical surname."

She colored a little at that, wondering with a sudden swift hungry pang if it were really true that he had been speculating about her name in his mind. "My parents named me Gabrielle," she told him, saying it the French way.

"But that's charming . . . Gabrielle Darnley."

"It's not really so good," she told him, laughing. "People never seem to know how it should be pronounced, and make me sound like the Archangel Gabriel. So for convenience sake we've shortened it to Gail."

"Gail," he repeated softly. "The perfect diminutive . . . as crisp and fresh and honest as its owner!"

He admitted then that he found his own given name rather a mouthful. "But if anyone shortens it to Roddy I'm apt to become murderous," he warned her, "so you'd better make it Rod . . . as all my friends do."

Glancing at him shyly across the softly lit restaurant table, suave, sophisticated, so many years older than herself, she didn't think it possible that she would ever have the courage to address him by his Christian name. But it was nice of him to have said she might.

She discovered that he lived—as of course he *would*—in the Quorn hunting country, with a brother who was a Master of Hounds, and that for the period of the London Show he was staying with a married sister in Kensington.

17

There was no Mrs. Rodwell Sterne, she gathered, wondered a little about that . . . and was glad!

By the time the jumping contests began they were on a casually friendly footing that filled her with incredulous pride, and the first time she saw him riding into the ring on his great ebony horse, in his coat of splendid scarlet, she knew that she was hopelessly in love with him, and that, compared to the emotion which had now taken possession of her, her whole life was shadowy, unreal as a forgotten dream.

The days that followed were dazzling with glory; vicarious glory for Gail, for Rod filled with the acclaim of the multitude as he won round after round in the International Tests. She had thought that in the heightened tempo of that week of triumphs he would forget her, but, incredibly, time after time he sought her out, introducing her to friends and acquaintances who thronged about him, insisting upon including her in the sherry parties or gay impromptu dinners with which the festive days so often ended. One night there was a riverside party some miles out of town, and he danced with her on a Thames-side lawn lighted with rainbow-colored paper lanterns. When he held her close she looked up at him, her hazel eyes suddenly wide and troubled. Swept for a moment beyond the barriers of her natural shy reserve she heard herself say breathlessly: "What are you doing to me, Rod? Why are you making this week so wonderful for me? I shall never be able to forget it!"

"I don't want you to forget it," he had answered her gravely. "For me, too, it will be memorable." His clear glance kindled as he looked down at her, the flame in his amber-gold eyes palpable as a tongue of flame touching her heart. "Is it so strange to you that I should find your company enchanting?" he asked softly.

"Yes, I think it is," she answered, utterly without coquetry. "I am not of your world. I cannot talk to you as these other women of your acquaintance do of hunting and riding and travelling."

"But that is what is so refreshing about you."

18

She shook her head, unconvinced. "I am young, insignificant; I've been nowhere, done nothing. While you are . . . famous. . . ."

"In a very mild way," he put in. "I take my Connaught King over the sticks a little more deftly than the next man, and what in the end does that amount to? Prizes, popularity of an ephemeral kind; in a few years' time it will all be forgotten. It's an unreal kind of life, Gail, and it seems pretty empty as the years go by. I'm thirty-two now and I'm beginning to find it a bit unsatisfying, hurrying from show to show all over the world; rootless, in a sense homeless, and"—his voice dropped—"when the applause dies down . . . just plain lonely."

She found herself thinking on a swift surge of elation that was half terror: This isn't the way a man talks if he is just . . . flirting; these things he is saying to me are true, straight from his heart. A great wonder filled her spirit, and, though she did not know it, the glow of it spilled over into her candid lovely eyes, her vivid, sensitive face.

The invitation in her vulnerable quivering lips was too much for him. Stooping, he kissed her, briefly but with a passionate intensity that left her breathless and dazed. "There isn't anything unreal about *you*, sweet Gail," he whispered. "You're the loveliest, freshest, most honest thing I've met in a long, rather dusty journey."

The ending of the dance number had separated them, Rod's sister Sonia claiming him a little ostentatiously, reminding him of the list of duty dances awaiting him. And on an impulse she couldn't quite explain Gail had slipped away, accepting the offer of a lift from some people who were leaving the party early, driving back to town. To have hung about waiting for Rod to be free would have been humiliating, and to dance with any other partner seemed utterly impossible. She had touched the heights in her moment with Rod and she wanted to go away by herself and think about it.

During this strenuous week of the Show she was not returning at nights to Hampstead, but sleeping at the more centrally situated Chatsworth House Hostel. But that night there had been little sleep. Lying in the narrow, neat

19

unfamiliar bed, she had given herself up to the thought of Rod. At the memory of his kiss such a rapture possessed her that it frightened her. She had not dreamed it was in her to feel like this! How could she, she asked herself, ever have imagined that the mild excitement which was her reponse to Jimmy's tentative, boyish caresses had anything to do with love? There was nothing boyish about Rodwell Sterne; he was a man, adult, dominating, strong, very sure of himself. And tonight he had held her close in his arms and told her she was the loveliest thing he had ever met in a long, rather dusty journey. Had he come to the end of his journey in his meeting with her? Was that what he had meant? It seemed impossible . . . and yet something of the assurance that had looked at her out of his strangely compelling eyes found an echo in her heart. But in the very first moment of her earliest meeting with him—that day when he had stood by the Judges' enclosure and she had met his clear, inexorable look—something vital within her, recognizing destiny, had surrendered.

And now, almost a year later, as the great express carried her through the soft spring darkness, she knew that what she had lost in that surrender had gone from her for all time. Tears stung her lashes, but impatiently she brushed them away. She had wept enough in secret bitterness over Rodwell Sterne. If she wept now, let it be for her own foolishness!

It was on the final day of the Show that Glenda Grayson had come upon the scene. And here, in the stuffy darkness of the compartment, Gail only had to close her eyes to relive that moment. All afternoon she had watched the jumping contests from the Committee's box, busy with her record-keeping. Every time the voice from the Tannoy announced Rod's entry into the ring it was as though trumpets of glory sounded for her. The memory of the riverside evening before was a glow that pervaded every nerve in her body. They had not yet had an opportunity of speaking to one another, but once as he cantered to the exit after a particularly brilliant and flawless round he had raised his eyes to the Committee's box, his clear direct glance so obviously a salute to her that the blood leaped to her cheeks. Then when she was fetching Miss Crump's tea

20

at the mid-afternoon break she ran into him just outside the canteen. "Gail!" his voice halted her, and she swung round with the tea-tray in her hand, her heart racing. There he was like a prince before her in the scarlet splendor of his "hunting pink" and feather-weight, fine suede breeches, but his eyes under the visor of his velvet cap held a hungry glint and his brown face wore a look of strain. That brilliant exhibition of jumping just now didn't happen of its own accord, Gail thought, it had taken its toll of nerves and endurance. She began to speak of his performance, congratulating him, but he did not seem to hear her, breaking in almost roughtly to say: "You vanished from the dance last night . . . what happened to you?"

The hint of ownership in his tone thrilled her, but it was no moment for the explanation of last night's tender mood. Here, with the crowds jostling them, she could not tell him she had run away because her heart was overflowing. So she said prosaically that she had had the chance of a lift back to town and had thought it best to take it. "You were busy with your sister and her friends and . . . I was a little tired," she ended lamely.

He gave her a brief unsatisfied glance. They were calling his name on the Tannoy again and there was only time for him to remind her as he hurried away that they were expecting her at Regency Gardens between six and eight. His sister's cocktail party. It was Rod's doing, of course, that she had been invited to it. Gail had no illusions about the way Sonia Treacey regarded her, and had indeed overheard that young woman describe her earlier in the week to a woman friend as "Some little typist connected with the Show personnel". She was, clearly, both puzzled and annoyed that her famous brother should find it necessary to put himself out to be charming to anyone so insignificant. And Gail couldn't really blame her. She herself found it puzzling. Or at least she had done until the night before. Rod's kiss seemed to have changed everything—given her a new glad confidence in herself that Sonia's scorn had no power to touch.

There were about twenty guests assembled in the drawing room at Regency Gardens that evening, most of them in dinner frocks and jewels because it was to be a gala

21

night for the Show's finale, with a supper party afterwards at the Savoy. Sonia in a Dior white satin gown, and diamonds, greeted Gail coolly. Because she was still on duty at the Show she was wearing the neat dark frock without ornament that Chatty would have expected of her. Feeling something of a Cinderella among the glittering guests, she shrank into a corner with the glass of sherry Rod had brought her. They had barely had time to exchange a word before Sonia called to him that the cocktail shaker was almost empty. Watching him measuring out gin for a fresh round of Martinis, Gail thought that the strain of the afternoon still showed on his lean, taut face, and a wave of anxious, almost maternal tenderness surged in her heart.

She heard Sonia say: "I've got a surprise for you, Rod. Glenda has arrived."

Rod looked up sharply. But his quick: "Oh, good show!" seemed warmly enthusiastic.

"She's upstairs having a bath," Sonia went on. "It's a gritty journey from Paris even on the Golden Arrow!"

The drawing-room door opened at that moment. The woman who halted a perceptible and dramatic instant on the threshold was tall and slender and dazzlingly blonde, with the sort of breathtaking Parisian chic which is even more effective than natural beauty. She was not perhaps strictly beautiful, but she had poise, sophistication, assurance. "Rod, darling!" she cried, ignoring everyone else in the room as she fluttered over to him, her arms held out.

As she watched them embrace Gail's throat tightened. Glancing hurriedly away, she met Sonia's dark eyes. There was a distinct glitter in them. Was it malice? Triumph? Before Gail had time to decide she became aware that Rod was approaching her . . . the blonde woman at his side, his hand lightly cupping her elbow. "Gail, this is Glenda, Miss Grayson. She has come over from Paris specially to be in at the kill tonight . . . I wonder if you could do anything about finding her a ring-side seat?"

"Why, of course!" Gail found herself answering, with an exaggerated nervous effusiveness that even in her own ears sounded false. Every available seat, she knew, was taken. Mentally she battled with the dilemma while Glenda murmured graciously in her ear the conventional words of thanks.

"I'll go straight back and see Miss Crump about it," Gail said. Rod's protests, she felt, were polite rather than sincere, his real concern now for Glenda who had come all the way from Paris to share in his triumphs this last night of the Show. Who was she? And just what part did she play in his life? She didn't look the type to play a minor role in any man's concerns . . . and Rod had seemed glad enough to welcome her.

Fighting back a sickening sense of foreboding, Gail tried to throw herself into the excitement of her last session of record-keeping. Through a mist of abstraction she watched the scarlet-coated figures of the horsemen under the great arc lights, and once more it was Rod's evening, his points mounting with every round, his "faults" almost negligible. But now, if in riding past he glanced up at the Committee box, it was Glenda who waved to him and smiled. For it was here Miss Crump had made room for the distinguished late-comer: Major Sterne's friend from Paris. Sonia and her husband too had been squeezed in. So that they were quite a family party, Gail thought with the wistfulness of an outsider, and she was careful to keep in the background, concentrating on the figures Miss Crump dictated.

At last it was over, Rod riding round the ring for the last time to a thunder of applause, the glittering silver cup that was the crowning trophy held high in his hand. The band broke into the National Anthem and the spectators began to surge towards the exits.

In the narrow passageway from the Committee box Gail found herself wedged with Sonia as they made their slow progress. Glenda had somehow forced her way on ahead, eager to be the first to congratulate Rod. In the distance, caught at the main exit from the ring, Gail could see him standing with his hand on King's bridle while admirers thronged about him. A girl with a mop of dark curly hair had just hurled herself at him, flinging her arms about his neck, and he was laughing down at her. Gail could only see the girl's back. She looked very young, very slender. Sonia said: "Well!" in a mildly shocked tone and laughed lightly. "Poor little Lalagh," Gail heard her murmur, apparently in recognition. Then she turned to Gail and added with unmistakable intention: "*Another* victim of Rod's unconscious charm . . . even if she is still practically in the schoolroom! The sooner Glenda takes him in hand the better. He doesn't know how devastating he can be to all you young things!"

With a sudden access of friendliness she took Gail's arm. "They will probably be married quite soon," she confided. "Rod and Glenda. It's something I've been expecting for a long time, and now Rod is speaking of giving up show jumping. He is tired of it, he says, anxious to settle down. . . ."

Just what comment she made at that juncture Gail never knew. But somehow she had forced her lips to utter the conventional phrases the moment demanded.

There wasn't very much to remember after that . . . the Committee room packed to suffocation with Rodwell Sterne fans . . . Rod laughing, joking, signing autographs, Sonia and Glenda never very far from his side. They were there when Gail said goodbye to him, her head held high, her stiff lips smiling.

"But you're coming on to the Savoy with us?" he had exclaimed.

"I'm not dressed for a Savoy supper party," Gail pointed out.

"Then when am I going to see you again?" Rod asked, with the eagerness that could mean so little!

Gail stared at him in aching confusion, hardly seeing him. "Why . . . I . . . don't know . . ." she stammered. "Never . . . I suppose."

"Unless he applies to Miss Chatsworth for a clever little typist to help him with his correspondence some time," Sonia put in with so insufferable an air of patronage that Gail's spirit stiffened. It was wounded pride, the sudden overwhelming desire to be even with Sonia Treacey, that made her say, "I don't suppose I shall be very much longer at the Chatsworth bureau . . . I'm leaving shortly to be married."

Did she really believe it as she said it? Had the memory of Jimmy Hansen's devotion seemed to her like a hand held out to her in the engulfing misery of that moment? Afterwards it seemed a fantastic statement to have made—but it got her out of the Committee room, out of Rod's life with a semblance of dignity left to her.

There were harbor lights now flashing against the polished darkness of the carriage windows. Someone had opened a corridor door and the sharp pungent smell of the sea came into the stuffy compartment. Gail began to gather up her things, glad to be done with the long train journey, eager for the sea. Like a portent it beckoned to her—the clean, wide, rolling water she would put between herself and her youthful foolishness. Why had she wasted so much of her spirit on so trivial a matter as her encounter with Rodwell Sterne? she could ask herself now almost with detachment as she emerged into the cold salty night. Because it had seemed to her, in spite of its tenuous quality, *not* trivial, but touched with destiny. Beyond good sense or reason had lain the feeling of inevitability in their meeting. Rod had held out his hands to her and she had gone to him, caught by a force too mysterious even now to be assessed. With her conscious will she could put it behind her, but the queer questioning echo would remain, the intimation within her of something begun, and left unfinished . . . a queer intuitive waiting. She couldn't have defined this feeling, for it was barely articulate. But it was *there*, and it would take a lot of living down.

On the boat she slept deeply, and woke refreshed to find the new land spread before her . . . an outline of gentle blue hills against a morning sky that held in its greyness the iridescence of a pigeon's wings. As she came ashore and heard the soft Irish voices all about her, felt the mild sweet air on her face, the tenseness of her spirit relaxed. Everything seemed so leisurely here; nobody hurried. Even the business of disembarking the big cross-channel steamer was something that could be done at an easy pace with time to wonder and observe. For although the tempo applied to a task might be leisurely, the interest displayed in it seemed to Gail nothing short of passionate. To the porter who escorted her to the waiting

25

jetty-side train, her luggage, her self, her destination appeared to be matters of dramatic importance. Frankly he studied the labels pasted on her tunk. "Laheen," he read aloud. "That's a fine Castle they have there, I'm told —would it be to the Castle now you are going?" And when Gail told him it was not to the Castle but to a house called Kildoona Lodge, he could scarcely hide his disappointment.

But the whole day was an enchantment; the sauntering progress of the little train across miles of heatherclad bogland, through small grey stone towns and whitewashed villages. Everyone who entered her compartment spoke to her with an instant simple friendliness, as eager to discover where she was bound for as the harbor-side porter had been, their curiosity so warmhearted that it couldn't possibly be offensive. And when they left her—for the train was picking up and dropping its passengers at every wayside station—the women would bless her with a soft Gaelic prayer, the men doff their hats, their parting glances quick with homage for her youth and comeliness. The charm of the Irish. She'd heard of it . . . vaguely . . . without conviction, but here it was right away spreading its gentle welcoming allure, a balm to her bruised and weary spirit. Would the same simple welcome await her at Kildoona Lodge? she wondered, her nervousness increasing as she approached her journey's end.

She had been told to alight at Ardossa, which proved to be a lost little station set under the shadow of a towering granite-sided mountain. There was a battered hackney car to take her the remaining five miles of the way. A little dazed by her long travelling, she found herself being whisked at an unbelievable rate through vistas of loveliness; may trees and beech trees and misty green larches swam before her eyes, rivers and streams, thatched cottages and church towers, the recurring glimpses of a lake that seemed wide as an ocean . . . and there were bluebells everywhere.

There was a great Italian ironwork gateway then and a mile of curving drive, honey-sweet with the perfume of azaleas. On either side the flowers were banked, rosy and gold in the clear May evening; there seemed no end to them, for they stretched as far as the eye could see with

26

the tall silken beech leaves quivering above them, a tide of sweet color washing right up to the walls of the big square white house with its Palladian portico and plain sash windows.

Standing on the threshold of the open door, Gail saw the pleasantly spacious hall, awash with the late afternoon sunshine. Here too there were azaleas in porcelain Chinese vases, their flowering branches sprayed against the cream-washed walls. The maidservant who appeared in answer to her ringing wore the conventional uniform of a smart parlormaid; a frock of violet poplin set off by a frilly ecru apron. But there was nothing conventional about her wide smile of greeting. "You'll be the young lady from London," she declared rather than enquired in her rich, sweet brogue. "If you'll step in here a minnit, Miss, I'll tell Herself you're after arriving."

Herself. There was a majestic ring about the quaintly spoken title. With a quiver of awe for the unseen Miss Ross O'Donnel, Gail moved through the door held open for her, finding herself in a long narrow apartment running the full length of the house, obviously a drawing-room, furnished with an eye to cosiness rather than elegance. The pungent smell of the turf fire burning on the hearth mingled pleasantly with the scent of the spring flowers that stood in bowls and vases on every available table or shelf; violets and potted hyacinths, pale wild primroses and golden-eyed narcissus. The deep, comfortable armchairs were covered with rose-patterned chintz and the fitted Aubusson carpet was rose-colored too, so that the entire room seemed to glow with its warmth. The whole effect was so simple and harmonious that the immense oil-paintings on the walls came as something of a shock. Overpowering in their heavy gilt frames, they would have needed a sizable gallery to do them justice. Here they were out of proportion. They were mostly portraits: Ross O'Donnel ancestors all through the centuries, Gail decided, her attention caught by the canvas hung over the white marble chimney-piece. It was the painting of a young woman with dark, softly curling hair and very blue eyes. The face was exquisitely modelled, exquisitely young, touched with an innocence that seemed to belong to an earlier, more unsophisticated age, and the court dress too was dated with its tiny nipped-in waist, frilled lacy sleeves and head-dress of ostrich plumes.

" 'Tis a picture of Herself when she was young," the soft voice of the maid supplied, and, turning, Gail saw that the girl had returned and was standing close behind her, her eyes lifted to the painting; wide, sorrowful, curiously tender. "Isn't it a hard thing to see her there looking so lovely, and she not knowing the life of pain that lay before her?" she whispered.

"She was not always a cripple then?" Gail whispered back. After her friendly contacts in the slow little country train there seemed to be nothing extraordinary in this confidential, almost emotional exchange. That was how it was in Ireland. People's hearts opened to you quickly, spontaneously.

" 'Twas a hunting accident that made a lifelong invalid of her," the girl explained. "Soon after that picture was painted it happened." With a sigh for a past she could only have known through hearsay, she recalled herself to her duties, her wide, kindly smile reappearing. "I'm to take you up to your room, if you please, Miss," she said. "Herself is resting at present, but she'll see you at tea in about half an hour, she bid me tell you."

They went up the wide shallow staircase to a small, prettily furnished room which Gail hardly saw, for the window instantly drew her glance, framing a view of such arresting loveliness that it made her catch her breath. Leaning on the broad low sill she looked out at the vista of shining water with the crumpled line of a mountain range beyond it. This was the lake she had glimpsed in her drive from the station and she could see it now in its fullness, a measureless silvery expanse dotted with islands, its wooded shores stretching away into hazy distances. But the dramatic note of the picture was the great turreted castle that stood where the shores curved, almost opposite Kildoona House, its pale limestone walls and battlements strangely ethereal in the golden May evening, so that it seemed to float in the quiet air with no more substance than the reflection which dreamed beneath it in the calm lake water.

"Oh, but it is beautiful," Gail breathed in awe. "Is that Laheen Castle?"

"It is indeed, Miss." There was a ring of pride in the girl's young voice. "The home of the Ross O'Donnels before the hand of misfortune fell on them."

Gail's eyes widened with interest.

" 'Twas there Herself was reared, and a great establishment it was in the time of her childhood. My own grandmother was an under-housekeeper in it, and many is the story I've heard her tell of the balls and the parties that used to be given there, the Kings and Queens of the whole world coming to stay for the salmon fishing and the pheasant shooting. There wasn't a place to equal it in all Ireland . . . until Himself (God rest him), Miss O'Donnel's father, lost it in a wager with some English Duke and they having a game of cards."

Gail sank down on the window-seat, the better to digest this saga. "You mean he just gambled it away . . . like that . . . quite casually; the entire Castle!"

"He did indeed. He was that sort of a gentleman; always out to take risks whether it was in hunting or wagering. It was a terrible blow to the family, with nothing left to them but this lodge, Kildoona, and the small part of the estate that goes with it."

"You'd think the Duke, whoever he was, would have been ashamed to take advantage of such a situation," Gail said indignantly.

The girl shrugged. "Small shame he had, then, but only too eager to get his hands on such a fine property, for he was very near bankrupt himself, by all accounts. He put the Castle up for sale right away and it was bought for a big price by an Englishman, Sir Charles Bowfort, who made a fortune out of cotton mills in Manchester."

Gail took a long breath, an odd little thrill of exhilaration running through her. What a fantastic world she had stepped into! Kings and Queens and Dukes dancing, hunting, gambling . . . and a castle that looked like a fairy palace changing hands over a gaming table. She was glad she had come to Laheen. London and home and the prim Miss Chatsworth seemed very far away. Even the thought of Rod now seemed a little overshadowed . . . an old, stale, foolish ache to be lost in this fresh, wild world where everything seemed just a bit larger than life. A place in which anything might happen!

The sound of laughing young voices drew her glance to the window once more, and looking down into the paddock that lay directly beneath she saw a girl mounted on a spirited horse which she was trying to control, a young man riding beside her on a great prancing grey, that, as he reined it to a halt, rose with its forelegs alarmingly in the air.

There was no mistaking the identity of the girl. The face under the wind-blown tangle of dark curls was a replica of the painting over the drawing-room mantelpiece. In her modern way this child was perhaps even more beautiful, for her porcelain, delicate features were lit with a fire missing from the more decorous young woman downstairs, and her very blue eyes were vividly alive with her laughter.

"She's mad on horses, Miss Shelagh; never out of the saddle," the communicative maid murmured tolerantly. " 'Tis well for her she is marrying a man of a like mind."

"He certainly knows how to handle that fearsome-looking grey!" Gail agreed, with a glance of admiration at the easy manner in which the quite strikingly handsome young man was sitting out the tantrums of the beast who seemed determined to throw him.

"Is it Pat Crampton?" the maidservant demanded, sounding faintly shocked. "Sure that's not her fee-ansay, Miss, that's the trainer from Ardrossa. Miss Shelagh is marrying Sir Charles's nephew and heir—a grand man, he is, famous all over the world for his horsemanship. Major Rod Sterne. Maybe you've heard tell of him?"

CHAPTER TWO

THERE was a tap at the door and a red-headed youth in shirt sleeves, wearing the green baize apron of a pantry boy, appeared with Gail's suitcases. Automatically, Gail thanked him.

"Would you like me to unpack for you, Miss?" the maid offered.

"No, thank you, I prefer to do it myself. What time does Miss Ross O'Donnel expect me downstairs?"

"Tea is at five o'clock, Miss," the girl said.

When the door closed behind her Gail sank down weakly on to the edge of the bed. Shelagh Ross O'Donnel was going to marry Rod. *Rod!* And she was here to help with the arrangements for their marriage. If she could only bring herself to see it that way it was really terribly funny. Fate, or whatever power it was that played these tricks with people's lives, certainly had a pretty sense of humor. She ought to be laughing herself sick over it. Her new world, her wonderful fresh era in which all the youthful foolishness of the past was to have been forgotten!

For an instant sheer panic assailed her. If she hadn't been five miles from a railway station she would have been tempted to pick up her suitcases, rush out of the house, and take the first train back to Dublin and the Channel boat!

With a trapped feeling she looked round the pretty room. Beyond the looped muslin window curtains she could see the turrets of the Castle etched delicately against the tender sky. Was Rod there at this moment? The thought of meeting him took all the strength from her limbs. And yet it was bound to happen sooner or later. Restlessly, she stood up and began opening her suitcases, searching for a frock to replace the crumpled suit in which she had travelled all night. The Bowfort Cotton Millions. So that was Rod's family background. When his uncle died he would be one of the richest men in England. And she had been credulous enough to imagine for a brief insane interval that he was interested in her! The insignificant little typist to whom it had amused him to be kind. All that nonsense about destiny, inevitability! Persistently it had lurked somewhere just beneath the level of consciousness, not even the thought of Rod marrying Glenda Grayson had entirely destroyed it. But Rod—for whatever reason— hadn't married Glenda Grayson. He had come instead to this green and flowery valley that would one day be his kingdom . . . where Shelagh, young, patrician, exquisitely lovely, waited for him. The daughter of the dispossessed

31

Ross O'Donnels. As his bride she would go back to the Castle that was her ancestral home. There was destiny indeed, there was inevitability!

Washing, changing, brushing her gold-brown hair, creaming and powdering her travel-weary face, Gail worked with a savage energy. Pride must be her armor now . . . and her own good common sense. It was, after all, a good thing that she had come to Laheen, she told herself fiercely. To see Rod in this fabulous setting, with Shelagh at his side, would cure her of the last dregs of her foolishness.

With her head held high she went downstairs, her eyes bright with a new, defiant courage. She was wearing a simple pastel green jersey frock—the only item of her wardrobe that had travelled uncrushably. The color suited her, emphasizing the golden glint in her hair, bringing a greenish tinge into her hazel eyes under their heavy dark lashes.

In the drawing-room Miss Ross O'Donnel awaited her, a tall emaciated woman with her back to the hearth, her haughty bearing undefeated by her dependence upon the two ebony sticks on which she leaned heavily. Gail couldn't resist a quick glance at the portrait beneath which she stood, and a little shiver of pity ran through her. Time and suffering had wiped out so completely the fresh young beauty which had once inspired an artist's brush. The soft dark hair was touched now with grey, the pink and white face was ivory pale, set into lines of proud endurance. A beautiful face still in its chiselled perfection, and the speedwell eyes were as blue as ever they had been under the delicate brows. But innocence had gone from them. An infinite, weary wisdom looked out of their sunken depths.

"Ah . . . Miss Darnley. I am glad to see you. I trust you have had a pleasant journey." With a curiously old-fashioned queenliness she inclined her head in greeting, and Gail had a ridiculous impulse to drop a curtsey in response. But instead she found herself smiling a little nervously, saying, thank you, she had had a very pleasant journey indeed.

"If you will press the bell, Bridget will bring tea; I expect you will be glad of it." The order was given with the unconscious assurance of one born to command.

Gail found the electric button by the chimney-piece and as she touched it was aware of Miss Ross O'Donnel moving painfully to the couch drawn diagonally across the white fur hearthrug. Should she offer to help or not? she wondered a little awkwardly. The matter was settled for her by the rich musical voice that demanded her arm. "You may place my canes on the floor behind the couch," Miss Ross O'Donnel declared when she was settled. "Bridget has a knack of falling over them if I am not careful to put them away." There was a sudden gleam of laughter in the blue eyes, the whole face softening charmingly. Beneath the mask imposed by suffering a ready humor lurked. Gail could feel it like a burst of sunshine, thawing the cold little sense of awe that her meeting with Miss Ross O'Donnel had engendered.

"We have an almost inexhaustible supply of domestic help available in Laheen," she was saying, "but they are untrained country girls . . . in a certain way untrainable. The Irish do not make good servants in the accepted sense of the word. They are loyal, devoted, hardworking, but incurable individualists, irrepressibly friendly. In the old days, at the Castle, all our upper servants were English or Continental . . . silent people, self-effacing, colorless." Miss Ross O'Donnel's surprisingly whole-hearted laughter rang out. "I cannot imagine any circumstance reducing my present batch of Bridgets and Marys to a state of either silence or self-effacement. I hope you will not be shocked at their easy ways."

The door opened and Bridget in her violet uniform appeared, tottering a little under the weight of the heavy salver she carried. She was followed by the red-headed boy bearing a cake stand and a small copper kettle.

"Put the kettle there on the hearth, Thady, and be off with you," Bridget breathed gustily. "You've no right to be coming into this room at all. I told you to bring them things no further than the door."

"That will do, Bridget!" Miss Ross O'Donnel interposed icily.

33

Bridget, quite unmoved by the rebuke, gave Gail a wide, companionable grin and retired.

"You see how it is?" Miss Ross O'Donnel said with a resigned shrug, and becoming aware of the twinkle in Gail's eyes, added: "I know it's amusing, but there are times when it can be vastly irritating; and it's not the right atmosphere for Shelagh. She is far too inclined to play about with the younger maids, enjoying their fun, besides which she spends too much time in the stable yard and the paddocks. She'll have to learn to handle her staff on a much more formal level when she is mistress at Laheen Castle. I'm hoping you will be able to help her to see things more conventionally." The blue eyes gave Gail a keen, assessing glance. "You are very young, but you have, I can see, been carefully taught by this wonderful Miss Chatsworth. Forgive me if I am frankly personal, but I like your quietly assured manner, your very proper concern for appearances. Though you have just completed a long overnight journey you have taken the trouble to make yourself look fresh and charming before coming down to tea . . . and you know how to dress. If I mention these things it is because they represent qualities Shelagh almost entirely lacks. . . . You will, I am sure, be able to influence her."

"I will do my best, Miss Ross O'Donnel," Gail murmured, trying not to sound smug, inwardly a little appalled at the thought of herself in the role of mentor to a girl not quite three years younger than herself.

"I am sure you will. And you may call me Miss Ross . . . as everybody else does. The double-barrelled name is a bit of a mouthful!" The humorous smile flashed briefly as Miss Ross set herself to pouring tea from the immense silver teapot. "I don't want you to feel you have to preach at Shelagh . . . just be yourself with her. Remember you are here to lead her . . . not to follow her, and it will all work out quite well. She is very anxious to make herself worthy in every way of the considerable responsibilities that will come to her with her marriage. Her fiancé, Major Sterne, is the nephew and heir of my old friend Sir Charles Bowfort, the present owner of Laheen Castle." As she spoke she held out the delicate Rockingham cup and

34

saucer and with a hand held rigidly steady, Gail accepted her tea. Thank goodness for Bridget's talkativeness! she thought. Thank goodness she already knew about Rod and had not had to meet this moment with defences unassembled.

Even so it was with the utmost difficulty that she kept her expression impassive as Miss Ross went on: "Sir Charles has never married. A devoted sister kept house for him until recently, when the threat of arthritis warned her it would be safer for her to live in a drier climate, and she moved to the South of France. But she had never been strong. It was a quiet household under her management." Miss Ross helped herself to a wafer of bread and butter with a musing air.

"Laheen was my childhood home, I had better explain. So that everything that happens there is of an almost painful interest to me. In the time of my parents, and even more so in the time of my grandparents, it was famed for its lavish hospitality. As a young girl I moved in a world of elegance, of brilliance, my home so constantly filled with the most interesting figures of the day that it has grieved me to see the Castle in the years that have elapsed faded into social obscurity, its beautiful entertaining rooms shut up and wasted. But now . . ."—the blue eyes held a sudden avid light—"I am hoping everything will be altered. As soon as they are married Shelagh and her husband will occupy Laheen—it is Sir Charles' wish. Life will return to the great halls and galleries and banqueting rooms. There will be house parties again for the shooting, the hunting; parties, balls. It will be like old times once more."

She fell silent, gazing into the fire with a far-away look, and watching her Gail felt an odd little stab of pity. It was as though ghosts stirred in the bright comfortable room . . . ghosts of youth . . . of hope. But her heart, heavy with apprehension, filled the silence with its own more vivid images. Shelagh at Laheen queening it . . . with an adoring Rod at her side. Was he there now? Would he be coming to Kildoona Lodge today . . . tomorrow? If only she had the courage to ask! But such questions from the newly arrived secretary-companion would be peculiar, a little impertinent. And even if it were not so, she could not have trusted herself to utter Rod's name. She must wait with patience for things to take their course.

If he should come in now . . . suddenly, unannounced, she thought on a wave of sheer terror, and saw, with her breath held back, that the door was actually opening. But it was Shelagh who appeared, her entry so explosive, so young, impetuous and urgent that ghosts and terror went flying before it.

"I'm so sorry I'm late for tea, Aunt Dodie!" Light as a blown leaf she was running across the room, dropping a penitent kiss on her aunt's impassive brow. "I've been riding Finnmacool all afternoon. We got a halter and bridle on him and I went up for the first time barebacked, then he gave in and submitted to a saddle. He's an angel, Aunt Dodie, wild as a steer and swift as a panther. I didn't dare to let him jump, but he wanted to. Pat says . . ."

"Shelagh, Shelagh!" Miss Ross broke in. "Angels are not usually connected with either steers or panthers . . . and we have a visitor with us. . . ."

"Oh, Aunt Dodie, I'm sorry," Shelagh burst out again, and swinging round held a slender, brown, rather dirty hand out to Gail.

"Miss Darnley," Miss Ross murmured with an exaggerated air of correctness. "My niece, Shelagh O'Donnel."

The two girls measured one another in a swift, secret glance. Rod's love! Gail's heart whispered to itself bleakly. A child with the long-limbed grace of a gazelle, thin as a boy, wild as a boy in her loose torn shirt and shabby jodhpurs. There was a reek of stables from her mud-stained, scuffed shoes, but her face was lovely as a flower under its mop of dark curling hair.

"I'm so glad you've come, Miss Darnley," she was saying, a trifle mechanically, her mind obviously on other matters . . . horses that jumped like panthers perhaps . . . or her dark grave lover. "Was it a hateful crossing?"

"Not at all. I slept all the way over."

Shelagh sank down into a convenient chintzy armchair and reached out for a buttered crumpet.

36

"Your *hands!*" sighed Miss Ross.

"I know. But if I'd waited to wash tea would have been over and I'm starving." She bit into the crumpet generously, her blue eyes dancing with mischief, with zest, with the sheer joy of being alive.

"Wasn't Pat ready for some tea, too?" Miss Ross was asking.

"He had to take Finn to the farrier's before it was shut. You know he has never yet been properly shod. Finn, I mean. But he let me groom him today. Pat says . . ."

"Lalagh dear, must we talk the entire time about horses? It's not very amusing for Miss Darnley . . . she may not be interested in endless stories of Finn."

Lalagh! The name rang like a bell in the corridors of memory. That last night of the London Show, Gail thought, a girl with a mop of dark hair throwing her arms round Rod's neck and Sonia's gently breathed, half scornful . . . "Poor little Lalagh!" So this was the end of it— the loose ends of the pattern knitting up. And Lalagh wasn't poor. Lalagh was young and triumphant and so lovely even in a raggedy shirt and rubbed old jodhpurs that it was no wonder Rod had forgotten Glenda Grayson and whatever plans he might have been making to link his life with hers. On the crest of the wave of his fame and glory that hot August night Shelagh O'Donnel had come to him, her eyes as blue as the lake of his own Laheen, her soft Irish voice talking to him in a language he understood, sharing with him every detail of his triumphs as Glenda the Parisian never could have done. A girl who could control a half-broken colt with steely strength and an airy grace . . . who would ride at his side through the long hazards of life, gallant as a boy, but with her own sweet feminine allure. Oh, but she is *made* for him! Gail summed it up in quiet, bitter resignation as she heard the lilting voice enquire coaxingly: "*Aren't* you interested in horses, Miss Darnley?"

"I don't know very much about them," Gail said.

"Haven't you ever ridden?" Shelagh sounded faintly shocked.

"I did have a few riding lessons just after I left school." Tired, spiritless old hacks jogging round a suburban park.

Not riding as Shelagh O'Donnel understood it. But the answer pleased her.

"We must ask Pat to find you a mount," she said. Then turning to her aunt: "He'll be glad to come to dinner to-morrow night, by the way. The back axle of his car is a bit shaky but he thinks he can patch it up . . . ."

Miss Ross glanced across at Gail. "Major Sterne is arriving at Laheen Castle tomorrow, and I'm giving a small dinner party by way of celebration. Just a few intimate friends . . . nothing very formal. You'll join us, of course."

"Thank you, Miss Ross," Gail breathed faintly. So she had twenty-four hours' grace. One short swift day and night to steel her heart, steady her defences. How would Rod treat the encounter? Ought she to mention now that they had already met? But while she hesitated the opportunity was lost.

"I was going to ask you," Miss Ross was saying, "if you could suggest a savoury for the ending of my dinner menu. My cook monotonously serves sardines on toast, or stuffed eggs, or a cheese soufflé. You did take a course of cookery, didn't you, at Chatsworth House?"

"Why, yes," Gail agreed, a little flustered, her thoughts so far away from Chatty and her rather sketchy cookery classes that it was difficult to recall them. "A savory," she murmured musingly and suddenly the curried anchovies floated into her mind, hot and pungent on a little silver dish, and she could hear Rod's deep leisurely voice explaining just how they were produced. It was the first time he had taken her out and they had eaten in a small exclusive French restaurant in Soho; a restaurant where Rod was well known, his tastes catered for by an obsequious proprietor. They had finished their carefully chosen meal with the savory that was Rod's favorite.

Would it be wise to suggest it now? But Rod, with his mind and heart full of Shelagh, would never remember that Soho evening. And it was too good a piece of culinary artistry to waste. The question had so obviously been put as a sort of test of the new employee's ability.

Curried anchovies. Miss Ross looked pleased as Gail listed the few simple ingredients: tinned anchovies mashed with fresh butter, paprika, a pinch of curry powder, the whole to be sprinkled with grated hard-boiled eggs and served on strips of crisp buttered toast.

"It sounds delicious," Miss Ross pronounced. "And if Mrs. Murphy hasn't any anchovies in her store cupboard we can get them from Whelan's, our grocery store in Ardrossa." She turned to Shelagh. "That's a recipe you'd better put in your household notebook, Lalagh," she suggested.

Shelagh giggled. "Darling Dodie!" she murmured indulgently. "My household notes," she explained to Gail, "are something of a family joke."

"A very melancholy joke," Miss Ross said grimly. "I've been trying for weeks to arouse my niece's interest in household management in view of her coming responsibilities."

"Only that it won't be household management at Laheen . . . it will be castle management," Shelagh put in irrepressibly. "They are totally different things, I tell Aunt Dodie. I shall have a French chef and an English housekeeper and they will be so busy squabbling with one another, or falling in love with one another, or both, that they won't let me near the kitchens." She nodded her wild dark head impressively. "Yes, it's kitchens in the plural in that great barrack of a place. Me and my poor little anchovies . . . we should be utterly lost!" She was out of her chair and across the room in one swift graceful swoop, one hand on the painted china knob. With the back of the other she brushed crumbs of seed cake from her lips. "I've gotta go down to the stables a minute," she announced. "Gay Lady was a bit lame today when I cantered her. I think it's that left fetlock of hers again. Micky Mulligan is coming out at six to have a look at it."

As the door closed behind her a heavy silence fell. Gail drew in a long breath compounded of hyacinths, peat-smoke, toasted crumpets and perfumed China tea.

"Micky Mulligan is a disreputable old drunkard with a genius for horse-doctoring," Miss Ross said at last. "She'll be perfectly happy pottering about the stables with him for the next hour and as likely as not forget to come in for dinner. What am I going to do with her?"

39

"But she's . . . enchanting!" Gail cried on a strange note of despair.

Miss Ross' grim white face softened. "She's a dear child . . . and I've spoiled her, I expect. How could I help it? She came to me a lost, frightened baby of five when her parents were killed in a plane crash fourteen years ago. There was nothing we would not do to try to make up to her for that dreadful loss . . . her devoted Nannie and I. We felt she had to have love unstinted."

"And I am sure you were right," Gail offered shyly.

"But now she has to grow up . . . face a life so totally different to the easy years she has known here."

"I am sure it will all work out," Gail said, feeling more and more inadequate. The blue eyes, disregarding her, looked towards the window to the shining lake and hills that lay beyond.

"She is very much in love," Miss Ross said softly, as though she mused aloud. "And love must be her guardian now . . . as it has always been."

Rod's love, Gail thought with a swift, bitter pang, and saw Miss Ross with a wince of pain draw herself up, the mask of endurance rigid once more on her white proud face. "If you will hand me my canes," she said, "I will go to my room now. And I expect you would like to go to yours; you will have unpacking to see to. The maids will help you. Call upon them for anything you need. Dinner is at eight. Sherry, in here, at seven-thirty."

Seizing her silver-topped ebony sticks, Miss Ross began her halting journey. Her bedroom, it emerged, was on the ground floor across the wide hall opposite the drawing-room. Wide-eyed with sympathy, Gail followed her, her offer of help coldly ignored, perhaps not even heard in the anguish of that struggling progress. But unmistakably she was dismissed, the moment of condescension over. There would not often be confidences such as she had listened to this afternoon, Gail guessed as she went upstairs.

She was busy shaking out tumbled frocks, laying neat piles of underwear in the drawers of the mahogany tallboy, when Shelagh, after a perfunctory tap, came in. "Micky Mulligan is blotto," she announced patiently and without preamble. "I can't get a word of sense out of him. He has

40

been getting potheen from somewhere or other; has a bottle of it in his pocket. I've left him hanging over the loose-box door singing a bawdy song to Gay Lady . . . and she seems to be liking it. I'll have to get the vet to her fetlock in the morning. Nuisance!"

Going over to the low window-seat she curled herself up, hugging her knees with two slim brown arms. "Mind if I stay a minute and talk to you before I have my bath?" she asked. And without waiting for an answer went on to explain that there were three bathrooms in the house. "One on the ground floor for Dodie, one over the kitchen for the maids, and the third right here at the end of the corridor for you and me. Sometimes there isn't enough hot water to go round, specially when Thady forgets to stoke the boiler."

Gail smoothed out the sapphire velvet housecoat that had been her mother's going-away present to her and hung it in the wardrobe.

"You're very tidy, aren't you?" Shelagh remarked with a hint of disapproval, eyeing the orderly array of brushes and cosmetics on the dressing table, the neat layers of tissue paper protruding from the opened suitcases.

"Well, I am to start off with . . . when I find myself in a nice fresh bedroom like this," Gail said, hoping it didn't sound apologetic, remembering Miss Ross' injunction to her to lead Shelagh rather than follow her.

"All English people are tidy," Shelagh sighed. "Rod is English, of course; Major Sterne. Aunt Dodie says he'll hate it if I'm not . . . tidy, I mean."

"Men are never really tidy, not over domestic affairs," Gail offered consolingly. "My father is absolutely hopeless when it comes to things like arranging ties and socks and hanging up suits. He usually leaves his garments in a heap on the floor when he takes them off."

"Oh, does he?" Shelagh said, sounding comforted.

"But I expect Major Sterne will have a valet to see to all that sort of thing for him."

"Oh, yes, he has got a valet. And I shall have a maid to pick up the pieces after me, so I daresay we'll get along!" She put her head back against the window embrasure, exposing the long slender column of her throat. Her eyes

41

were dreamily half-closed under their dark curling lashes, her red lips a little parted, innocently voluptuous. "Funny," she said, "the tiresome details that come crowding in on you when you begin to plan a marriage. First it's just . . . a vague heavenly feeling, like living in a shining golden cloud. You fall in love and it's all wonderful. And it was so unexpected . . . my falling in love with Rod, I mean. I'd known him in a way for a long time, seen him here visiting his uncle at Laheen on and off, and of course I'd liked him awfully, but I wasn't romantic about him, until last summer when I was in London and I saw him riding in the International Horse Show . . . winning all the prizes . . . making the other horsemen look somehow so ordinary. He was like a king on his great black horse, so proud and sure and strong!"

Gail bent over the chest of drawers to hide the pain in her eyes. Like a king! So she had not been alone in her adoration of Rod that memorable, stirring week.

"It was all so thrilling," came the soft voice from the window-seat.

"I know. I was there," Gail found herself blurting, wondering at once if it were wise; only that it would probably have to come out some time. It was silly to make a mystery of her connection with the Horse Show Commitee. Rod might so easily mention it casually—and then she would look foolish. "I was typing and answering telephones for the Secretary of the Committee that week," she added.

"What an extraordinary coincidence," Shelagh commented politely but without much interest. "Then you will have seen Rod ride. Connaught King is a super animal, isn't he?"

"I wouldn't really know," Gail offer d humbly. And as though suddenly bored with the conv rsation, Shelagh uncurled herself and stood up saying abruptly that she must see about her bath.

She appeared at dinner in a flowery, voile frock, skimpily cut, obviously much worn. It made her look like a leggy, overgrown schoolgirl. Miss Ross, impressive in maroon velvet with a marabou shoulder cape, gave Gail an approving glance as she took her place at the oval

Chippendale dining table. She was still wearing the green jersey frock but she had added a chunky necklace of carved wooden beads to the plain neckline, and wore a bracelet to match.

"You must go through Shelagh's wardrobe with her tomorrow," Miss Ross said later as they planned the next day's duties. "She is hopelessly understocked, but perhaps you can find something suitable for her to wear at our little dinner party. Later, next week perhaps, I want you to take her up to Dublin for a really serious onslaught on the necessary shopping for her trousseau. Chardin is designing the wedding gown, but all the other items we must see to ourselves, and time runs on so quickly!"

Chardin the great French dress designer! Gail opened her golden eyes in awe. "When is the wedding to be?" she asked.

"Late July or early August; it isn't quite decided. It depends upon Major Sterne's plans."

"And on the bride's whim," Shelagh put in pertly. "Brides always choose their own dates. I know because I read it in a book of Victorian etiquette I found in the library. I might put the whole thing off until September."

"Shelagh, don't be tiresome!" Miss Ross exclaimed, exasperated.

"Well, I should miss the August gymkhana if I had to be away just then on my honeymoon. Pat would be so disappointed. We want to put Finnmacool in for the jumping. But if my honeymoon was in early September I could work in the gymkhana perhaps, and still be back here in time for the end of the cubbing."

"Dear child!" Miss Ross sighed patiently. "It is Rod you have to consider now, not Pat Crampton and Finnmacool. And you'll probably be far too busy looking after your first big house-party at the Castle to do much about the cubbing season this year."

Gail had nervously dreaded the hours that must intervene before her meeting with Rod, but the next day was so filled with work that she had little time to think about the evening. Immediately after breakfast she was summoned to Miss Ross's pleasant room, half bedroom, half boudoir. Mrs. Murphy, the cook, was sent for and the menu for

43

dinner discussed, including the savory. There were no anchovies in the house, so Gail had to take the rather ancient but well-kept car into Ardrossa to pick them up from Whelan's surprisingly well-stocked grocery shop. After lunch there were two hours' secretarial work to be tackled, flowers to be picked and arranged on the dinner table. It was almost tea-time before she was free to go through Shelagh's wardrobe, a haphazard collection of shabby tweed suits, outgrown girlish summer cottons, a faded flimsy georgette dance frock, a velvet afternoon frock and a startlingly vivid blouse of jockey silk.

"That's the shirt I wore when I rode in the Ladies' Steeplechase at Ardrossa Races last year," Shelagh explained proudly. But she didn't pursue this no doubt epic story, her interest for once centred on more feminine matters. She seemed almost nervously anxious to look her best that evening. "I want to look beautiful for Rod," she said on an odd little note of wistfulness. "It's a whole long empty week since I have seen him. I want him to be really . . . proud of me when he comes back from London this time. Sometimes I feel so horribly . . . young and sort of raw, compared with the marvellous, sophisticated smartly dressed women I know he must meet in London and Paris."

"And there isn't one of them, I'm certain, who wouldn't give her eyes to be nineteen again," Gail offered consolingly.

But Shelagh ignored the sop. "Rod is exactly thirteen years older than I am . . . unlucky thirteen. Do you think it matters frightfully?"

"Not in the least," Gail returned briskly. "Men's ages never matter . . . not within reason."

"As long as they're not over seventy!" Shelagh giggled. "Pat Crampton is twenty-three," she added with apparent irrelevance.

Gail held out a crumpled, frilled organdie, which she had just discovered at the back of the wardrobe. It was a heavenly deep blue and when she tucked it experimentally beneath Shelagh's chin it made her eyes look like twin sapphires. "What about putting this on for dinner?" Gail suggested.

"I could wear my garnet necklace with it," Shelagh said, with a surprising touch of artistry.

"And one velvety red rose in your hair. I saw some today in the greenhouse when I was doing the flowers." Gail whisked the frock under her arm. "I'll take it away and iron it," she offered.

It was very late by the time she got around to her own dressing, hastily slipping into a ballet-length, full-skirted black velvet frock, the bodice tight and cut with a low scooped neckline. Plain enough to be suitable for the secretary-companion, she thought wryly. She must not try to compete with Shelagh. But she fastened a slender gold chain round her slim white throat, bearing a heavy cross of pure gleaming amber; an old-fashioned ornament that had belonged to her grandmother. Above the single gleaming jewel her hair was a smooth burnished bell of chestnut-brown and her eyes had points of golden light in them.

Turning to leave her room she was aware of the crimson spots of color burning on her cheekbones, and her heart beat unevenly. The dread moment was upon her now and there was nothing to do but plunge forward and meet it. They would be in the drawing-room drinking sherry, she thought as she went downstairs, and did not notice that the murmur of voices which indicated that the guests had arrived—Sir Charles and Pat and Rod—came from Miss Ross' boudoir on the other side of the hall. Steeling herself, she opened the drawing-room door and for an instant stood hesitant, with a feeling of anti-climax, for the room seemed to be deserted. Someone had lighted a single tablelamp and in the cool twilight it glowed beside a bowl of hyacinths like a big yellow flower. On the hearth the burning peat was piled dangerously high and as she slowly advanced Gail became aware of the figure stooped over it, tongs in hand, adjusting one toppling square of flaming turf. A man in evening black, cut to the lines of his narrowing waist and athlete's shoulders.

Straightening himself, he turned towards her, a look of almost comical astonishment spreading over his lean dark face, his topaz-colored eyes widening.

45

"Gail!" he exclaimed in a tone that seemed to be one of annoyance as well as surprise. "How on earth did *you* get here? What are you doing at Kildoona Lodge?"

CHAPTER THREE

GAIL drew in a long steadying breath. To her dying day, she thought, the sweetish, sickly scent of hyacinths would bring this moment back to her. But her voice was quiet, almost wooden as she answered: "Chatsworth House sent me. I've been engaged to help Miss Ross O'Donnel for a few weeks . . . until the wedding."

Rod's face seemed to close up, grow guarded. If there had been any emotion behind those unwinking tigerish-yellow eyes it was gone now. He said: "Shelagh did say something about a Miss Darnley having arrived. But it didn't occur to me it might have been you; the idea never crossed my mind."

Why should it? his hint of a shrug seemed to add. Why indeed should he have remembered that she existed? He turned to pick up a silver cigarette box from the low table by the hearth. "I thought you were leaving Chatsworth's. Didn't you tell me you were going to be married?"

The swift startled color swept up into Gail's cheeks. So that much at least he had not forgotten! "It . . . it fell through after all," she stammered.

"I'm sorry to hear that."

You needn't be; it doesn't in the least matter, she wanted to cry out defensively, but something that might have been derision in his look kept her silent. For a few moments they stood facing one another in the scented, lamp-lit room, their glances locked. The sense of tension was almost palpable, like the tingling of an electric current between them, but it was, Gail knew, no more than her own nervous response to the sheer physical demand of meeting those curiously powerful eyes. Did Rod guess the effect they could have on her? There was a hint of impatience on his lean dark face as he turned away, quite clearly bored already with the improbable encounter. "I suppose it's not really such a very extraordinary coincidence . . . your turning up here," he said. "If Miss Ross was in need of temporary help of the more ladylike kind, Chatsworth's was the obvious place for her to apply."

With the air of having settled an unimportant matter to his satisfaction he went to the door. "They'll be waiting for these cigarettes which I came to fetch," he said. "We're having sherry in Miss Ross' room across the hall." With his hand on the flowery china doorknob, he hesitated, obviously wondering a little about Gail's position in the household. "Do you join us? Or shall I see you later at dinner?" he asked.

But before she had time to answer Bridget appeared, hurrying urgently through the baize-covered door at the far end of the hall. Catching sight of Gail she beckoned violently. "Will you come down to the kitchen for a minute, Miss? Maggie Murphy wants you," she demanded in a gusty stage whisper, much louder than her normal speaking voice.

With a sense of escape Gail slipped away.

"It's them little fish she's doing for the savory," Bridget confided as they went down the long flagged passage.

By the time the matter of the curried anchovies had been satisfactorily settled the silvery echoes of a Chinese gong were announcing that dinner was served. Going to the dining room, a pleasant room at the back of the house, with windows overlooking a glimpse of lake frinzed by towering azaleas, Gail found the company already assembled. Miss Ross, leaning painfully on her canes, was standing at the head of the oval table that was lit tonight by tall candles in sconces of Georgian silver. In the lingering western twilight their flames were pale and cool as lily petals. Gail had arranged low Lalique bowls of yellow roses in between them, the color of the flowers toning with the creamy lace mats which were the table's only covering. The silver set at each place was solid, heavily monogrammed, flanked by the sparkle of cut crystal wine glasses.

"Ah, Miss Darnley!" Miss Ross exclaimed a little reprovingly, as though they had all been kept waiting. "I thought you would have been with us at the sherry stage . . . and now here you are, not knowing anybody. Let me see; Charles, this is Miss Darnley. Miss Darnley, Sir

Charles Bowfort." A large florid gentleman, with the kindly, ingenuous pink face so often to be found in the shrewdest of business men, bowed graciously. Gail, a little flurried, bowed in return. And the faintly peevish introductions went on.

"Miss Darnley, Mr. Crampton . . . whom you will sit beside if you please. Major Sterne, Miss Darnley. . . ."

"Miss Darnley and I," Rod murmured, "encountered one another while I was fetching the cigarettes." And left it at that. In the general commotion of seating and arranging themselves it was adequate. But he added no further explanation to it as the evening went on. Those days of contact a year ago were apparently too unimportant to be mentioned now! A casual impulse of friendliness towards a very insignificant member of the Show Committee staff. Hadn't she already realized in long bitterness that that was all his kindness had amounted to? Why then should his tacit denial of that earlier meeting hurt her so much now?

As she glanced at him across candlelight and roses, Gail's heart contracted. If only he had been less attractive than she had remembered! But tonight there was a new quality in his rather saturnine good looks, a gentleness, an air of half-amused tenderness as he talked to the lovely child at his side, his manner towards her touched with a courtliness that was faintly old-world. If he passed her the salt, or stooped to pick up her fallen table napkin, it was as though he laid his heart at her feet. When the tulip-tall hock glasses had been filled with the Riesling that was served with the salmon Gail saw them drink to one another, a swift, secret lovers' toast.

With her own dinner partner, Pat Crampton, the trainer, she had exchanged but the briefest platitudes. How was she enjoying her first visit to Ireland, he had enquired with a scarcely veiled boredom, and she had answered, equally bored, that she was enjoying it very much indeed. Miss Ross, on his other side at the head of the table, claimed his attention then, but their conversation did not go very much better. Before they were half-way through the soup course Gail guessed that most of Pat's interest, like her own, was centred on the two people opposite. He could not take his eyes off Shelagh, and indeed it was hardly to be wondered at, for she seemed all made of fire and light this evening, her cheeks delicately flushed, her blue eyes brilliant.

"Rod brought my ring back from London, Gail," she said presently, holding a slim left hand out in the candle-light. The heavy, diamond-encrusted sapphire that sparkled on it was not more blue than her eyes.

"It's beautiful!" Gail exclaimed softly. "But it would have to be sapphires, with your lovely Irish coloring, wouldn't it?" She glanced swiftly, shyly, at Rod, wondering if the moment demanded any more of her . . . some formal little word of congratulation. But, unaware of her look, he had turned to Sir Charles who was seated at the foot of the table.

"It doesn't really go with my garnets." Shelagh's eyes rested lovingly on her ring. "But Rod put it on to see if it fitted and I couldn't bear to take it off again." She held it out once more, turning it about the catch the candle-rays, like a pleased child. "It's made a sort of engagement party of our little dinner, hasn't it, Aunt Dodie?"

Miss Ross said: "But we must have a more adequate engagement party than this!"

"At the Castle," Sir Charles put in from his end of the table. "Let's do it together, Dorothy . . . on a grand scale, give a ball in our poor neglected ballroom and invite the entire South of Ireland."

"Which means, of course, that you'd try as usual to shoulder the whole cost, my poor Charles!" Miss Ross said, giving the big, beaming man a look of gratitude and affection. "But that's something we shall have to talk about later! If we do give a ball it must be on a fair-shares basis."

"It would be an opportunity to introduce Rod to his neighbors . . . and we could work in a little useful preliminary publicity for the fabulously expensive stud farm that is to carry the Irish race horse a step further in the evolution of the thoroughbred." Sir Charles shot at his nephew a whimsical, half-rueful glance.

Then, politely including the rather neglected Gail in the conversation: "Did you know, Miss Darnley, that Major

49

Sterne has retired from the Show Ring to devote his time to founding a breeding centre for bloodstock racers here at Laheen? We've already started building the new and very up-to-date stabling."

"How very interesting," Gail murmured, a little out of her depth. "I am sure it will be an absorbing and fascinating occupation." Once more she glanced in Rod's direction; once more he flatly ignored her.

He had picked up a French brood mare during his week in London, he was announcing, and instantly a passionate discussion broke out. It went on through the meat course, flamed with a new zest over the dessert; it was amazing how much they all knew of the science of horse-breeding, how knowledgeably they reeled off pedigrees. And the French mare it seemed didn't please Pat at all, even though her progeny included two winners of the coveted Paris Grand Prix.

"You ought to have kept to Irish stock," he flung across the table, looking like an angry Greek god. He really was extraordinarily handsome, this clear-skinned, blond young Irishman, his golden hair curling tightly on his narrow, beautifully shaped head, his dark grey eyes flashing with a recklnessness that hinted at a temper only just kept in check. Sitting beside him, Gail could feel his tenseness . . . an energy held back, like a coiled spring too dangerously taut. He seemed to be laboring under an emotional strain too great to have been caused by this technical disagreement on the relative merits of breeding stock. The knuckles of the hand clenched on the table before him were white and his voice rose to a shout as he cried out with more heat than courtesy: "I thought the whole idea was to produce a pure-bred Irish strain. And here you go bringing in some flibberty-gibbet of a French dam!"

"But the French horses seem to have all the speed nowadays," Miss Ross offered in conciliation.

Pat flung out his hands in a gesture of despair. "Well, if it is speed at the price of stamina you want! The world has gone mad on speed. Throw all your best two-year-olds into the big classic races, lash them on, over-race them, pick up your winnings and hurry the winners, half-blown,

50

into retirement before their stud value drops. I thought it was to be form—and by that I mean staying power—rather than big money, we were after at the Laheen stables."

"Form every time," Rod agreed mildly. "But there's no reason why I should keep exclusively to Irish blood-stock dams. I can breed my pure-bred Irish strain and keep Midinette on the side-lines."

"You'd have done a damn sight better to buy up Captain Darcy's Red Mary."

"I hope that's a pun, Pat, though it's a very poor one," Miss Ross interposed in mild rebuke.

Pat flashed her a harried glance. "I'm sorry, Miss Ross, darling, I apologize."

"Dam sight. Ha, ha! Very good." Sir Charles laughed gustily but nobody else seemed amused. Horses, Gail thought, were a subject you didn't *joke* about over an Irish dinner table.

"I'd like to buy Red Mary," Rod was declaring seriously. "In fact I've every intention of buying her . . . if she's as good as you say she is, Pat. We could ride over and have a look at her tomorrow."

"All of us," Shelagh put in eagerly. "Gail, you'll come too, won't you? It's a heavenly ride round the lake road to the Darcys' place. Pat will mount you. . . ."

Pat turned on Gail his blind, wild look. "You can have Tara Lad," he offered absently.

Gail said unhappily: "But I'm not very good. I've only ridden a little—and then it was only on ponies from a London livery stable. I couldn't handle anything . . . too large or fearsome!"

"Tara Lad is no more than fourteen hands," Pat assured her. She had no idea how high a fourteen-hand horse might stand—and feared the worst. But there was, she could see, to be no more discussion of her fate, for Pat was launching a fresh attack on Rod. . . .

"I'm told you're thinking of rebuilding the Leahy's old farmhouse as your chief trainer's quarters," he said disapprovingly.

Rod looked annoyed. "What's wrong with that?"

"A lot," Pat said tersely. "You'll stir up a hornet's nest if you pull that old place down. Leahy still cherishes the

51

illusion that he will be going back to live there one of these days."

"An illusion indeed," Sir Charles commented dryly, his air of geniality suddenly vanishing. "I compensated him lavishly for the house when I moved him out of it fifteen years ago."

"Fifteen years!" Rod echoed. "Is it as long ago as that? I should have thought Leahy would have put down roots on his new smallholding by this time."

Pat shook his burnished curly head. "Takes longer than that for a dispossessed Irishman to forget the home of his fathers."

"And very troublesome fathers they were too," Miss Ross added. "The Leahy family have been a thorn in the flesh of the Laheen estate as long as I can remember. It was simply because this Leahy's grandfather was coachman to the Castle that they got dug in so firmly at Teacht-an-Gail. My father often regretted they had been given the house, for it was one of our more comfortable fishing lodges."

"With a most outlandish name which I refuse to use," Sir Charles said, "even if I could get my tongue round it. We call it simply Creek Cottage."

"Teacht-an-Gail," Shelagh said. "But that's extraordinary, I hadn't noticed the coincidence before. It means Gail's House."

"Or, more correctly translated, 'The House of the Stranger'," Miss Ross added a little crushingly. "Gail, or ghoill, being the old generic term for foreigner. Miss Darnley's rather unusual Christian name is Gail," she explained to Pat, who was looking a little puzzled.

He turned to Gail, smiling. "Isn't that a shame, now," he said with a sudden friendliness that warmed her heart, for she had been feeling rather neglected. "But never mind, Miss Darnley, you won't be a stranger among us for long, name or no name. We don't make strangers of our visitors in this country."

"I've felt that already," Gail told him gratefully.

They had arrived at the savory now, and Rod looked up from his plate to say contentedly: "Curried anchovies,

52

and perfectly done! My congratulations to your cook, Miss Ross."

"It was Gail who was responsible for them," Shelagh put in loyally.

Gail went crimson, and across the table Rod threw her a quick inscrutable glance, one sardonic black eyebrow lifted. But he didn't extend his congratulations, and turning his attention to his savory once more murmured rather strangely: "I hear a voice, perchance I heard . . . long ago, but all too low. . . ."

"Rod, what *are* you talking to yourself about?" Shelagh demanded in mild alarm.

"I'm quoting poetry," he said. "That's the effect curried anchovies invariably have on me."

She gave him a blank young look. "Darling, you're absolutely bats sometimes. I hope you're not going to turn into one of those old men who go all goofy over food."

"I'm not going to turn into an old man of any kind for a long time," Rod said, sounding rather offended.

"And when you do, you'll be much more likely to go goofy over drink," Pat contributed cheerfully. "All Irish horse breeders end up that way. Look at our friend Micky Mulligan! Sober one day out of seven."

"He was here to look at Gay Lady last night," Shelagh sighed. "Drunk as a lord. It was sheer waste of time sending for him."

"What's wrong with Gay Lady?" Rod asked in the tone of passionate concern the matter inevitably demanded.

They were off on the subject of horses again then and the vagaries of Gay Lady's fetlock occupied them until the end of the meal. "You'd better come out and have a look at her presently," Shelagh said to Rod, and as soon as their coffee—served in the drawing-room—had been hurriedly disposed of they went off to the stables, rather pointedly omitting to invite Pat to accompany them. His handsome face sulky and bored, he fidgeted about the room, his eyes constantly turning towards the door, and when the ormolu clock on the mantelshelf struck a musical half-hour after nine and Shelagh and Rod had still not returned, he said rather more abruptly than politely that it was time he was going home.

53

When, after the most cursory of farewells, he had departed, Gail too excused herself and slipped away, leaving Miss Ross and Sir Charles to their *tete-à-tete*. It was too early for bed, but she could write a letter home. So far she had had time only for the telegram announcing her safe arrival at Kildoona. But when she reached her room a sense of restlessness came over her. To sit down at the neat little writing desk seemed suddenly impossible. The evening had been a greater strain than she had realized, and now that she was alone she felt shaken and unnerved.

Going over to the window she sat down on the low seat and drawing the curtains aside looked out over the lake. It was still light enough to see the outlines of the hills that circled the great curve of silvery water, for the endless summer twilight persisted, a wash of faint rosy-blue turning to palest primrose in the west where the sun still travelled across the wastes of the unseen ocean. In the garden beneath her the trees and grass were full of lilac shadows, the pathways showing white and glimmering. Somewhere down there among the ghostly sweet-scented azaleas Rod and Shelagh were together.

Digging her nails into her palms, Gail closed her eyes and instantly Rod's face was there before her—more vivid than life; dark, sardonic, one eyebrow lifted. Those odd lines he had quoted when they were talking about the anchovies. "I hear a voice, perchance I heard . . . long ago, but all too low." What did it mean? It was impossible to know. But at least it seemed to indicate that he had not forgotten their dinner together in the little Soho restaurant that hot August evening. How adroitly he had avoided any mention of that week in London when Miss Ross had introduced them. But she was thankful he had avoided it, Gail thought. As she herself had not spoken of their encounter at the Horse Show, it might have been awkward. Their brief friendship, such as it was, must remain a secret between them. An annoying secret for Rod, no doubt. It would be irritating for him that she had turned up at Kildoona Lodge.

With a small shaken sigh she stirred herself, and lifting a hand to draw the curtains together again saw between their looped folds the pale ribbon of pathway that emerged

54

from the dark blur of the shrubbery. In the shadow of a whitely blossoming cherry tree Rod and Shelagh were standing motionless, locked in each other's arms.

CHAPTER FOUR

TARA LAD looked terrifyingly large when Gail saw him the next morning waiting for her on the neat circle of gravel before the Palladian portico. He was a barrel-chested piebald, like a rocking horse, Pat said, and just about as safe. He helped her up into the saddle, and she sat rigid with fright, feeling as if she were astride a billiard table, her feet nosing helplessly for the stirrups.

It was Rod who adjusted the leathers for her. "Are you sure you'll be able to manage?" His thin brown face had an anxious look as he put the reins into her nerveless hands. But his concern for her, while it warmed her heart, had the effect of increasing her inward panic. She would at that moment have given everything she possessed to get out of this ride to the Darcys'. Only pride made her answer brightly that of course she could manage.

"It's just that I'm a bit out of practice," she explained. "And Tara Lad is bigger than any horse I've ridden before."

"Keep him on a short rein for a bit," Rod advised. "Sit well forward and let him feel you are really in the saddle. You're a good deal lighter than the weight he is accustomed to, but he is an even-tempered animal and he won't give you any trouble."

It was just at that moment Shelagh came spanking round the corner from the stables on Finnmacool, riding with the loose-limbed ease of a cowboy, and Rod turned to watch her, his face kindling with tenderness and pride, Gail's problems apparently forgotten.

A moment later the little cavalcade was on its way, Shelagh with her flighty Finn and Rod on Connaught King leading, Gail and Pat bringing up the rear. It had been decided that because of Finn, who was newly broken, they had better keep to a bridle path through the larch woods for the first part of the journey. Gail, concentrating

55

on her riding, was only vaguely aware of the fresh spring loveliness all about her. The grassy track was soft as velvet under the horses' feet and they were going at a gentle canter, which dropped to a leisurely walk as the track narrowed amid drifts of bluebells. Very soon, as she began to get the "feel" of her mount, her confidence increased. Old Tara's responses to her touch were sensitive and immediate and it was quite obvious he wanted to please his rider. Leaning forward with a growing courage, she fondled the side of his long muscular neck and spoke to him reassuringly.

"That's the way!" Pat at her side encouraged her. "Treat your horse humanely and you'll get far more out of him than if you start bullying him. But I can see you know that already."

Gail glowed at this mild commendation. Her nervousness subsided and she began to enjoy herself. It was a perfect morning for a ride, the sky high and blue with cool, little white clouds scudding across it, blown by a fresh southerly wind that smelled of dew-wet bracken, moist peat and sun-warmed resinous larch boles. Rod and Shelagh had moved on so far ahead by this time that they were almost out of sight, half-hidden by the pale green veils of the hanging feathery branches.

"Oughtn't we to be catching up with them?" Gail suggested presently, but Pat shook his head sombrely.

"Mustn't be spoilsports," he said darkly. "They won't really want us tagging along too close behind."

For a few moments they rode on in silence, and then Pat said suddenly, with a sort of goaded quietness: "Takes a bit of getting used to—this new role of Shelagh's."

"You mean her engagement to Major Sterne?"

He nodded, his young face grim. "Sometimes I wonder if she knows what she's doing . . . or if it's all just some wonderful game of make-believe she's playing."

"Why should it be?" Gail asked a little uncomfortably. She didn't want to discuss the subtleties of the situation with Pat Crampton of all people. There was something a little frightening about this boy with his smouldering tempers and reckless grey eyes. It had not taken her long to guess at his hopeless love for Shelagh, but all the same

56

she was startled by the passion with which he burst forth now. "She is like someone bewitched ever since the time she went off to that confounded Horse Show last August. It was old man Bowfort's doing. He got himself worked up reading of Rod's triumphs that week in the papers and suddenly decided to fly over for the final day of the Show. And he took Shelagh with him. Something happened to her then . . . something that changed everything she was before."

"She fell in love with Rod," Gail whispered.

"Whom she had known nearly all her life," Pat exploded. "Why didn't she fall in love with him long ago if she were going to? What made him so attractive to her suddenly?"

"The Show Ring," Gail said. "The glamor of his success, the music, the applause . . . oh, the whole dramatic set-up."

Pat shook his head. "That kind of little-girl infatuation would have worn off, burned itself out harmlessly enough, if Sterne hadn't deliberately seized on it . . . cashing in on it."

Gail's anger flared, but she held it back. She mustn't join in this emotional discussion on Pat's too personal level, must remember that she was supposed to be no more than the merest onlooker. She said temperately: "How can you imagine anything so fantastic! He's . . . crazy about her, anyone can see that." If there was a touch of bitterness in her tone it was quite lost on Pat.

With a brief mirthless laugh he turned to her. "Crazy about her! That cold-eyed Englishman?" His own eyes glittered dangerously. "I've known Rod for years. I like him. But I've got no sentimental illusions about him. He's far too sophisticated to lose his head over a slip of a girl like Shelagh. He's hard-headed, calculating and ruthless; if he's going into this marriage it is because he is getting something besides . . . well, moonshine . . . out of it. I wish I knew what it was."

It was as though he had forgotten his listener then, as though he mused aloud, his face in classic profile turned aside, his beautiful head flung back, the grey eyes drunk with their dreams of love and hate. "But this I do know,"

Gail heard him say with a deadly quietness, "and that is, if there is any treachery going on I'll find it out . . . put my spoke into it. I'd rather," he said, his voice dropping to a tense whisper, "kill Rodwell Sterne with my two bare hands than that he should cause my darling girl one moment's pain!"

With a sudden movement, he kicked at his horse's flanks, urging it on, not caring now, it seemed, if he overtook the riders ahead, if indeed at that moment he remembered their physical existence. It might have been that they were no more than the menacing phantoms that drove him, as, lost in his bright and terrible fantasy, he went galloping under the feathery green branches.

*　　*　　*

Carna House, the Darcys' place, was a square stone building, fashioned for strength rather than beauty, its grim outlines softened by the climbing rose vines and budding creepers that sprawled over its weathered façade. But its setting was arrestingly lovely, for it was situated on a wooded spur of land that descended in a sweep of flowering meadow to the shores of the lake. When the rest of the party had retired to the stable yard to talk endlessly about Red Mary, the brood mare, Gail walked down to the water's edge.

It was a relief to be alone . . . and out of the saddle a while, for her unused muscles were already aching, and she was still a bit shaken by Pat's outburst. Though in retrospect it didn't seem quite so alarming. His mood had changed so quickly. By the time they had joined Rod and Shelagh at the end of the larch wood he seemed to have forgotten all his wild threats, and talked away to Rod quite naturally, discussing Red Mary's points and pedigree.

Sitting on a wide, flat slab of sun-warmed limestone, listening to the dabchicks twittering in the reeds at her side, Gail wondered if the whole thing hadn't been more or less hot air. That fatal Irish intoxication with words, which could distort the most ordinary statements, making everything a little larger and more colorful than life. It was impossible for Pat to say simply that he wanted Shelagh to be happy; he had to exaggerate everything, working himself up into a frenzy about what he would do to Rod if

58

she were not. And his notion that Rod wasn't utterly in love with her was of course no more than wishful thinking. It would be silly to take him seriously, Gail told herself, as she stretched out to bask in the mild sweet sunlight.

Through half-closed lids she gazed at the milky-pale expanse of the lake, half hypnotized by the glinting lights on its surface. A family of swans drifted far out, majestically. There was a murmurous sound of water lapping about the smooth shingle at her feet. Tired after her unaccustomed exercise in the saddle, she gave herself up to the drowsiness that crept over her, and soon she was asleep.

When she awoke after a timeless interlude Rod was sitting at the other end of the limestone slab, contemplating the landscape, a cigarette held slackly between his lips. At her movement he turned his head and she started up, aware of her dishevelled hair and ruffled appearance. Foolishly, she had not thought to bring her riding kit to Ireland with her, but had asked her mother to send it on— in the letter written last night. Meanwhile she was making do with an old pair of navy serge slacks and the jacket of a new tweed suit, a serviceable dun grey, so she had twisted a scarlet gypsy handkerchief about her throat for the sake of its color. As she groped in her pocket for a comb she was aware of the mild amusement in Rod's eyes.

"The swans have been singing to you," he said, and he began to relate the ancient legend of the two swans who sang so sweetly that those who heard them slept for three days and nights. "They were," he told her, "enchanted lovers." But there were many stories in Irish mythology of unhappy lovers who escaped from the complications of life by becoming swans, he said.

For a moment they watched the graceful white birds, who had drawn nearer to the shore in their search for food, and Gail wondered a little uneasily if they ought not to be going back to the house. Rod, however, seemed in no hurry. How long had he been sitting beside her watching her sleep? Stretching himself out on the big sunny stone he folded his hands comfortably behind his head and began again about the swans, saying that it was on this very lake they had sung their magic song and that it all

59

happened two thousand years ago, when Aengus, the son of a god, fell in love with Caer, a beautiful mortal girl.

"She ran away from him before the affair had time to come to anything," the deep, faintly sardonic voice went on, "and the story tells how he searched for her all over the land, heartbroken. He had of course a great many terrible adventures of the kind pagan gods seemed to thrive on in those days and in the end he found his beloved here, on the lake, having been bewitched and turned into a swan. Without a thought for his life Aengus plunged into the deep water to reach her and was apparently drowned, but soon he was seen also in the form of a swan by the side of the bewitched Caer, and they flew together over the water linked by a silver chain, singing their wonderful song."

"What a lovely story," Gail said softly. "I wonder what it means?"

"Perhaps that even two thousand years ago there were star-crossed lovers in the world," Rod answered, "and that to straighten out their affairs they had to sacrifice all merely wordly considerations. It's just an old piece of folk widsom, poetically preserved, I expect." Picking up a handful of the little flat stones he began to send them skimming across the smooth pale water.

In silence Gail watched him, a strange sense of peace pervading her. It was so quiet here by the wide waters; in the distance the mountains were little more than a blue haze. Tranced in the noonday stillness, the whole scene held a dreamlike quality; even the soft southerly airs that moved against her face seemed enchanted. Rod's presence did not disturb her now; she felt curiously at ease with him. Perhaps I am not quite awake, she thought. Perhaps I am still asleep, hearing the magic singing of the swans who were lovers. And suddenly there were tears in her eyes.

But in a moment everything was safely mundane again. He had really come, Rod said, to ask her if she felt equal to riding the long way home. "I've bought Red Mary, and I'm taking her back to Laheen. I've suggested you should all come and have lunch at the Castle."

"That would be lovely," Gail agreed, jumping up. "But won't they be expecting us at Kildoona Lodge?"

"Shelagh is phoning her aunt," Rod explained.

By the time they reached the Castle after a four-mile ride on the hard macadam lake road, Gail felt as if every bone in her body was more or less dislocated. Tomorrow she wouldn't be able to sit down! But she had vindicated herself as a horsewoman, keeping up with the others, trotting when they trotted, cantering when they cantered. Now they were trooping up the wide shallow steps that led to a great old door of unpainted oak, so weathered with age that its timbers were white and flaky and seemed to be only held together by the outsize hinges of iron that stretched half-way across them. Beyond the door was a vast soaring hall with a green marble floor, like frozen lake water, and a domed ceiling all painted over with cherubs and little rosy clouds. It was more like the entrance to a museum than a home, Gail thought, but kept this piece of heresy to herself.

Sir Charles was waiting for them in the library and a servant in livery brought in sherry which they didn't linger over because lunch was waiting. The dining room, a long, galleried, imposing apartment, had the same sort of marble floor as the hall. Shelagh told Gail when she admired it, that the marble came from a quarry in the mountains the other side of the lake, and that it was considered so beautiful it was sent all over the world, even to Italy, the land of marble. It was a little pathetic, Gail felt, the way Sir Charles deferred to Shelagh when they spoke of anything concerning the Castle; as though she were the resident and he the guest. Sitting at the head of the immense polished table he had a lost, almost diffident air as he listened to Shelagh, drawing her out. His own feeling about the marble, he said, was that it was a bit cold and unhomely, but when he suggested covering it up with a nice thick red carpet Miss Ross had been shocked.

"When Shelagh and Rod take over," he told Gail, "I'm moving into a suite I've had re-done for myself on the first floor. A humble bachelor hide-out where I can potter about and be as Philistine as I please, with my fishing rods and all my tackle and clobber about me."

He was fanatically keen on fishing, Gail discovered. It was that which had first brought him to the lake country away from the bustle and grime of Manchester. Gail tried to picture his life here in the great empty echoing rooms of the Castle. How could he have borne the loneliness year after year? Was it simply for the sake of the excellent fishing he had endured it? It seemed a pointless kind of existence. It was no wonder he had arranged matters now so that he would have Rod and Shelagh to keep him company. Already Shelagh appeared to be completely at home in her imposing surroundings. But then in a sense the Castle *was* her home, for the inherited memories of the generations of O'Donnels who had lived here lay behind her.

There was a quaint little air of queenliness about her as she showed Gail round when lunch was over, Rod at her side, his thin, dark face inscrutable.

There were drawing-rooms, a whole series of them, their furniture shrouded in dust sheets, a banqueting hall, a ballroom hung with glittering chandeliers. Sir Charles began to talk about the ball he was planning to give for Shelagh and Rod. He and Miss Ross had, it seemed, already drawn up a list of the people who were to be invited.

"We have decided to keep it a more or less informal affair so that we can have it quite soon," he said. "Later, after the wedding, when the honeymoon is over, would be a better time for a gathering on a grander scale . . . when the hunting crowd are in residence. This time we shall have only about a hundred guests, most of them more or less local." He turned to Gail. "Miss Ross will be asking you to send out the invitations within the next day or two, I expect."

Shelagh gave a young whoop of delight and went pirouetting across the glassily polished floor with an airy grace quite unhindered by riding boots and breeches. Humming a popular dance tune, she held out her hands to Rod. Laughing, he gathered her into his arms. Pat's handsome face was sullen as he watched them, and with a stab of pity for him Gail drifted over to one of the long uncurtained windows and stood looking blindly out at the paved terrace beyond, remembering the riverside party last summer near London, when she had danced with Rod on a lamplit lawn, and under the thick murmuring trees he had kissed her.

pounding of hoofs was like the sound of thunder in her ears. There were no stirrups under her feet any more, no reins in her hand. She was clutching desperately at Tara Lad's clipped mane when she saw the loose stone wall rearing up before them. She could feel the horse gathering himself beneath her to take the jump and then she was clear of the saddle, sailing high in the air, describing a graceful, slow parabola. It seemed an incredible length of time before the end came—the dull thud of impact as she hit the ground, and everything went blank.

CHAPTER FIVE

How long the blessed sense of nothingness lasted Gail never knew. It was the coldness of water penetraing the back of her tweed jacket that she felt first, and then someone began to chafe her hands. Reluctantly opening her eyes she saw Rod kneeling beside her. The expression on his face surprised her mildly—for everything was still a little vague. He was very white under his tan, his eyes blazing with what might have been a very passion of concern, though it was more likely that he was angry with her for riding so badly and frightening them all.

When she tried to sit up, his arms came about her, strong and hard, folding her tightly. She rested her head against his shoulder and heard his heart pounding against his lean hard chest. When presently he relaxed his hold a little she drew away from him, looking up at him in bewilderment. So grim and white-lipped he was! Could it possibly matter so much to him that she had for a little while been in some danger?

"Are you hurt, Gail?" he whispered.

She shook her head, her wide clear glance still questioning him. Suddenly she couldn't fight it any longer. Weak with the shock of her fall, she was off her guard, and she could feel the tide of her love for him rising within her, sweeping all caution before it. With a little sigh she leaned against him. Just to be here in the circle of his arms was an almost unbearable joy. Humbly she was grateful for this strangely stolen moment. With one hand he caressed her tousled head, rumpling the soft curls, holding her close, then abruptly he released her, his fingers running lightly down her aching shoulders. "Not even a collarbone damaged!" he said, not quite steadily. "You've had a lucky escape, young woman!"

As he helped her to her feet she shivered, feeling the water in which she had been lying trickling down her back. "It seems that I was wise enough to fall into a nice soft ditch of bog water!" she laughed ruefully. She looked down at the cushion of squelching moss that had, Rod pronounced gravely, saved her anything up to a broken neck.

It was a dreadful journey back to Kildoona Lodge after Rod had rounded up the trembling, penitent Tara Lad, and untied Connaught King from the convenient tree-stump to which he had been tethered. It was best to mount again as quickly as possible after a bad fall, Rod said. That way confidence was more likely to be restored to both horse and rider. But Gail, aching in every wrenched muscle and limb, hardly cared whether she had confidence or not. She could only grit her teeth and grimly endure the jolting progress, listening to Rod's little homily on the meeting of such emergencies as the bolting of one's mount and the jumping of Irish stone walls.

"You've got to have some lessons in jumping," he said, "if, as you say, you've never progressed that far. I thought you were a bit more experienced. You ought to have told me you were not . . . it was foolish, and very brave, to have undertaken today's trek with so little knowledge of what you might be in for." He gave her a quick, glowing look that took the sting out of the reproach. "If I've the time I'll give you a little coaching in horsemanship myself," he promised then.

She thought: That would be a wonderful thing to hear him say if I hadn't got about five hundred wrenched and bruised bones banging about inside my body! Later on perhaps I'll be able to be glad about it.

There was no sign of the vindictive farmer and his geese when they reached the high road. Shelagh and Pat too had disappeared, and Gail realized with a pang that she had forgotten that they existed! Finnmacool had made for home, hell for leather, Rod said. But Shelagh had been in perfect control of him and he wasn't worried about her. Besides, Pat had gone after her and would have kept an eye on her.

When they reached Kildoona Lodge, Rod advised bed after a long soaking in a very hot bath. "I'll make it all right with Miss Ross," he promised with a nod in the direction of the drawing-room where they could hear the clatter of tea cups and the sound of young voices. Pat and Shelagh, it seemed, were safely home.

The next morning Gail was little the worse for her accident apart from the aching bones. Shelagh and Miss Ross were very kind and concerned for her, but she insisted upon getting up, saying she was sure it would be best for her to move about and overcome her stiffness. Pat came round to enquire for her before lunch and she remembered to ask if Tara Lad was all right, and to apologize for failing to hold on to him when he ran away.

"He's as right as rain, the old warrior!" Pat laughed. "But Leahy's geese gave him the fright of his life. I've never known him to bolt like that before."

Leahy. Wasn't that the man whose family had been turned out of the house with the queer name? Gail's House. With an inward shiver Gail remembered the flood of threats she had only half-heard yesterday, but there was a sinister significance about them now that frightened her. The man certainly seemed to feel he bore a grudge against the owners of Castle Laheen. He had cursed Rod by name.

"He struck out at Tara Lad with a stick," she said. "That horrible Leahy creature! I thought he was just angry because his geese were under the horses' feet."

"So he was," Pat agreed. "But he was glad enough of the excuse to let loose at Rod. I expect it was Rod's mount he was trying to hit when poor old Tara got in his way. And he isn't a horse you can beat. The touch of a whip always angers him."

"I ought to have been able to quieten him, but I lost my head," Gail confessed. "I'm afraid I'm not much of a rider. I don't suppose you'll ever lend me Tara Lad again."

"Indeed, I will then," Pat assured her generously. "I'll take you out on him any time you have an hour to spare. Rod says I'm to give you a few lessons in jumping."

Gail's heart sank. So he hadn't meant it when he said he would coach her himself. The disappointment was crushing, so utterly devastating that she was inwardly furious with herself. Would she never learn to accept the inevitable? She was nothing to Rodwell Sterne; an insignificant employee to whom he offered the mildest of courtesies when circumstances demanded them. Naturally he had been concerned about her yesterday when she fell off Tara Lad, but it was sheer lunacy to imagine the incident had disturbed him unduly.

She spent the rest of the day filling in the gilt-edged cards that invited the selected guests to a ball at Laheen Castle on an evening in early June, working in a comfortable little book-lined study behind the drawing-room.

Rod came to the house during the afternoon. She could hear his voize, lazy and amused, talking with Shelagh in the hall. But so utterly had she vanished from his consciousness that he did not seek her out to ask her how she was after her adventure, even though he passed the half-open door of the study and must have heard the tapping of her typewriter as she addressed the pile of envelopes. Her tea was sent in to her on a tray so that she need not interrupt her work. Miss Ross wanted the invitations to catch the evening post and by the time Gail had despatched them Rod had gone.

"He enquired after you most tenderly," Shelagh relayed lightly, a little later across the dinner table. "And I told him you were sitting up and taking nourishment . . . though the *sitting* was still something of a problem!"

Bridget, handing soup, giggled appreciatively at this sally, and Miss Ross, assuming her most severe air, began to talk about the trip to Dublin. "You'd better get off first thing on Monday morning," she said, as they discussed all there was to be done in the city and how long it might be expected to take.

"I'm going to have the most wonderful hair-do," Shelagh announced. "And buy the loveliest frock in all Grafton Street for the ball."

"The main object of this journey is that you should get what you need for your trousseau," Miss Ross reminded her.

"A round dozen of everything," sighed Shelagh. "It really is extraordinary when all my life I've done with two of everything—and none of a good many things—that I've suddenly got to have all these fal-de-lals! I am sure I shall never wear the half of them! Day dresses, and nightdresses," she said, with a mischievous glance at Bridget. "Hostess gowns, dinner gowns, afternoon ensembles, town clothes, country clothes . . . and *hats* which I abominate. Do I really have to wear hats when I become Mrs. Rodwell Sterne, Aunt Dodie?"

"As the chatelaine of Laheen Castle you will naturally be expected to present a suitable appearance on all occasions," Miss Ross said primly.

Shelagh sighed. "Rod won't know me! He's never seen me in anything but me ould duds. It will be like Micky Mulligan's story of the very inebriated bridegroom who woke up the morning after his wedding and looked over at the face on the other pillow to cry out: 'Bedad, it's the wrong woman I'm after marrying!'"

With a scarcely suppressed explosion, Bridget fled from the room.

The next day was Saturday and there was some household shopping to be done. Gail took the car into Ardrossa soon after breakfast and found the streets of the little town congested with turf lorries and country carts. There were cattle-pens in the central square, and stalls set out with the wares of itinerant tradesmen. Donkeys with panniers slung across their backs made their leisurely progress in the centre of the road. Animated groups thronged the pavements, big raw-boned mountainy men in homespun tweeds and the white flannel jackets known as bawneens, their womenfolk more stylishly attired in up-to-date garments, though here and there an older woman could be seen wearing the soft brown shawl and voluminous red petticoats of an earlier generation.

Quite obviously it was market-day, and, enjoying the novelty of the scene, Gail drove carefully, dodging donkeys and children and an occasional flurry of harassed cattle. Mrs. Murphy had asked her to pick up some groceries at Whelan's and she left the call till last, pushing her way into the crowded shop that was, she realized for the first time, a public house as well as a grocery. The ill-lit bar at the far end of the shop was dense with the swaying forms of the big tweedy men. The air was blue with tobacco smoke, loud with the thick burr of the Gaelic tongue, a language that seemed to Gail's unaccustomed ears to be filled with emphatic, argumentative cadences. It sounded as though the speakers were quarrelling with one another violently. But no doubt they were merely enjoying themselves in their own exaggerated Irish fashion, making dramatic mountains out of the mildest conversational molehills.

As she stood by the grocery counter waiting for the assistant to parcel up the Kildoona Lodge goods, one of the big tweedy men drew near and, leaning over the piles of bacon and butter, whispered something in the assistant's ear. The young man nodded mysteriously, and turning to Gail said: "If you are going back by the Laheen road, Miss, I wonder would you mind giving this man a lift? He's after missing the only bus that does be passing this way in the day and he has a sick cow at home waiting on him."

Hurriedly sorting out this jumble of information, Gail glanced at the tweedy giant who stood beside her. He took off his visored cloth cap and bowed ingratiatingly. She didn't much like the look of him, but he seemed sober enough in spite of the reek of porter that emanated from him, and he certainly had courtly manners. The sick cow, he began to say, was in severe pain. "I have a drench here I got from Micky Mulligan to relieve her. It's a pity for her to be waiting on it and she racked with the spasms!" Plaintively he held out a dirty bottle filled with a thick, greenish liquid and Gail felt her defences weakening. It would be unkind to refuse to help the sick cow!

Presently she found herself going out of the shop, the big man carrying her parcels behind her. While they drove through the town he sat in silence, and it wasn't until they had come to the lake road that he asked her if she didn't find Laheen a pretty quiet sort of place after London.

A little surprised that he should know where she came from she turned to glance at him, and the first faint twinge of recognition stirred uncomfortably.

70

"I hope you were none the worse for the toss you took when my geese sent Crampton's horse bolting with you the other day?" he said, a hint of malice in his smile.

Gail's heart turned over. So it was Leahy here beside her in the car! In the turmoil of their earlier encounter she had not seen him very clearly, but now he had settled the question of his identity beyond all doubt.

"It wasn't your geese that made Tara Lad bolt, but the blow you struck him with your stick," she said indignantly.

"So it was the horse under you I hit?" He put a hand to his head with an exaggerated air of bewilderment. "I'm terribly sorry, alannah! It isn't a thing I would have done if I'd been in my right mind, but there are times when the sight of gentry from Castle Laheen makes me forget myself!"

Involuntarily she accelerated, glad that Kildoona was no more than five miles away. She would drop this queer Leahy person as soon as she decently could. But even as she stretched out to change gears his hand came down heavily on her arm.

"Don't be in such a hurry, like a good girl," he murmured familiarly. "There's a few little questions I want to ask you, that it won't be hurting you to answer with civility." The greasy smile he bestowed on her held a menacing leer. " 'Tis lady's maid to old Miss Ross you are, I believe?" His fingers tightened about her wrist. "Working there at Kildoona you'll be hearing a lot of talk, I'm thinking. Thady was telling me the way you do be having your dinner with the whole of them, and Sir Charles and his nephew from the Castle along with you. Did you ever hear them mention a house called Teacht-an-Gail?"

Too angry now to be alarmed, Gail shook his hand from her wrist. "I am not Miss Ross O'Donnel's lady's maid, but her confidential secretary," she said coldly. "I do not like your manner, Mr. Leahy . . . or your questions."

" 'Tis only that I was wondering if there was any truth in the report that Major Sterne is going to pull the old house down and build another in place of it for some English trainer?" Leahy muttered sullenly. "There's no call for you to be annoyed with me! All I want to know

71

from you is whether you heard any word of a surveyor being brought down from Dublin to go over Treacht-an-Gail, or Creek Cottage, as they call it now?"

Gail ignored this, and, her foot hard on the accelerator, covered a straight mile at a reckless rate.

"Glory be to God, do you want to kill the two of us!" she heard Lahy cry out.

"I thought you were in a hurry to get back to your sick cow," she couldn't resist reminding him as she slowed down to negotiate a series of hairpin bends.

"Ah, sure she is dying on me!" Leahy began in a moaning whine. "I'm a poor unfortunate man, thrown by the roadside to make a living out of a patch of bog and stone. No wonder the cow is sick, with nothing but the sour grass of the waste land to put in her stomach. Time was when the Leahys owned the best pastures on the shores of Laheen Lake. Tenant farmers on the Castle estate we were since the days of Cromwell . . . until Sir Charles took a whim and evicted us. Evicted! Have you any notion of the cruelty contained in that word? No more than a child I was at the time, but to my dying day I will remember the sight of my mother weeping on the roadside, her furniture strewn around her. My old grandmother that was a helpless cripple, taken from her bed to lie under the open sky . . ."

Did the man really believe the nonsense he was talking? Gail thought of the solid, prosperous-looking farmhouse from which she had seen him come the other day. They had reached the open gates of Kildoona Lodge by this time and with a surge of relief she stopped the car. "This is as far as I can take you, Mr. Leahy. I hope your cow will be better for the medicine you are bringing her."

He got out with a reluctant air and standing with his hand on the door of the car gave her a long hard look. "You've no news for me then?" he persisted. "If you were to tell me whether it is this coming week or the week after that the surveyor is due to arrive, I'd be satisfied."

"I've no idea, and if I had I shouldn't discuss it with you. I don't talk to outsiders about the affairs of my employer . . . or her friends. Why are you so anxious to know about this surveyor?" Gail asked

72

A crafty expression came into Leahy's bloodshot eyes. "A fellow that will be nosing about, probing here and there, going down to the very foundations of the place . . . measuring it!" He turned and spat suddenly into the dust of the road with a queer, hissing, snake-like sound. " 'Tis nothing to me, of course, Miss," he resumed, shrugging his shoulders. "I was only thinking that if there was going to be a job of building in it, there might be work for a young nephew of mine that is learning the trade. A bricklayer, he is." This had a hstily improvised sound and was somehow unconvincing.

"You should speak to Sir Charles about that. It is no concern of mine," Gail said crisply, and, without waiting for any more, restarted the car.

CHAPTER SIX

As she drove up the avenue of azaleas she wondered if she should say anything of the odd encounter. But when she reached the house there was no one about and she remembered that Shelagh had gone with Rod to a race-meeting the other side of the county. She would not be home until the late evening. Miss Ross, who slept badly, never appeared until after lunch, and by the time she sent for Gail that Saturday afternoon the queer conversation with Leahy had more or less passed from her mind. In any case it was hardly the kind of thing she could imagine herself relaying lightly to her rather forbidding employer. Though she was kindly enough, there was a regal dignity about Miss Ross O'Donnel that made casual conversation impossible. Like Royalty, she conveyed the impression that she expected you to speak only when spoken to, and the topics discussed would always be chosen by herself.

That afternoon she was absorbed in a survey of the forthcoming Dublin shopping expedition. When an exhaustive list had at last been compiled she instructed Gail to take a cash-box from the wall-safe half-concealed by the draperies of her large four-poster bed. Most of the purchases, especially at the larger shops where the family was known, could be charged to the household account, but they would need cash for their travelling expenses and the many inevitable incidentals.

The two girls were to stay at "Avonlea", a guesthouse kept by a retired hospital nurse who had at one time—during the early days of Miss Ross' disability—been employed in her professional capacity at Kildoona Lodge. "Nora Quinn is a good soul," Miss Ross expanded. "She will take care of you both . . . act in a way as chaperon. In fact I should hesitate to send you on this trip at all if she were not there to look after you and provide you with a seemly lodging place. With all your good sense, my dear, I should not feel it altogether suitable for Shelagh to stay at one of the larger Dublin hotels with so young a companion."

Feeling a little diminished by this pronouncement, Gail pored over the lists she had typed out, ticking off items as she read them aloud.

"Those slips and night gowns and the négligés, they ought really to be hand-made," Miss Ross sighed. "But hand-made underwear when purchased in the city is a prohibitive price. If we'd thought of it all earlier . . . if Shelagh had been interested enough, we might have had a needlewoman in . . . someone from the convent. The nuns teach the local girls such exquisite handwork. But it is too late for anything like that now."

She would have handed the entire trousseau over to the House of Chardin, she said then, if she could have afforded to do so. "But I have to be very careful," she explained. "For most of my life I have been trying to accustom myself to the idea that I am really a very poor woman. It is not easy, for I was brought up so differently."

Glancing round the pleasantly furnished boudoir in which they were sitting, Gail couldn't help reflecting that if Miss Ross was poor it was a pretty comfortable sort of poverty. Her glance took in the gold and tortoiseshell fittings on the dressing table, the rug of deep white fur beside the bed, the original Orpen in a vast gold frame on the wall. On the low mother-of-pearl inlaid table by Miss Ross's chair there was a photograph of a handsome, portly, bearded gentleman in out-dated shooting clothes. The flourishing signature in the bottom right corner of the picture bore a royal cipher. Had he been one of Bridget's cohort of visiting kings and queens? It seemed very likely, for he appeared again in a larger photograph on the mantel-shelf, in the centre of a group of be-whiskered gentlemen and neat-waisted ladies in immense hats, seated on the terrace of Laheen Castle. Gail recognized the pale oaken doors in the background. The little girl in a frilly frock curled up at the feet of the august personage bore an un-mistakable likeness to Shelagh, and was probably Miss Ross herself. It was clear at all events that she had enjoyed a glittering childhood and early youth. Life at Kildoona Lodge, for all its comforts, would no doubt seem very mean and constricted in comparison with those golden, vanished days.

* * *

Early on Monday morning the two girls set out for Dublin by train. It was arranged that Rod should join them later in the week, staying a night or two at his club before driving them home in the car, a capacious tourer with sufficient luggage space to take the spoils they would by that time have collected.

The weather was still brilliantly fine and Gail was en-chanted by the old grey city with its spacious streets and lazy wide green river. The may trees peeping over the high walls of Trinity College were tufted with tight red blossoms that filled the air with their perfume. Stephen's Green was a forest of flowering shrubs and lofty beeches and in O'Connel Street Nelson looked down from his fluted column on to an avenue of budding green. It seemed a little odd to find the great English sailor so honored in this Republican city, Gail couldn't help pointing out. Shelagh laughed and said the Irish were a tolerant people. "But Nelson hasn't got the street to himself," she added. "That was the Parnell Monument we passed just now, and if you wait a while I'll show you Dan O'Connell stuck up on his rock of Galway granite by the river, Dark Rosaleen beneath him waving the Act of Emancipation in her hand."

A moment later their taxi was crossing the vast span of O'Connell Bridge and turning eastwards through a maze of narrowing streets came to a quiet square of Georgian houses built around a patch of railed-in green, where "Avonlea" and Miss Quinn awaited them. Greeting them with as much fervor as if they had travelled half-way across the world, she showed them up an immaculately kept staircase to the almost aseptically stark, double bedroom they were to share. The linoleum-covered floor was polished to glass-like brilliancy and the spotlessly white quilts on the twin beds were so tightly drawn that Gail couldn't imagine herself ever daring to disturb them. There were bare glass-topped lockers beside each bed.

"It's a bit like a nursing home," Gail said when Miss Quinn had left them. "It even smells like a nursing home . . . that faint tang of boiled cabbage mixed with soft soap. . . ."

Shelagh giggled. "I believe it was a nursing home at one time. But Quinney got tired of sick people and turfed them all out and decided to take paying guests instead. She adores bank clerks and medical students. I expect we shall be surrounded with goggle-eyed young men at meal times," she ended with a touch of relish.

Rather to their disappointment, however, they found they were to eat with Miss Quinn in her own private room. It was clear that she was taking her duties as chaperon very seriously. Her attitude towards Shelagh was a mixture of sheer adoration and the gentle but adamant bossiness so often assumed by hospital nurses to their patients. And when she spoke of Miss Ross it was in a tone of veneration amounting to awe. "I told her I'd be responsible for the two of you," she said anxiously when they insisted they were perfectly capable of tackling an afternoon of shopping alone. Following them to the hall door she poured out instructions and warnings as though she expected them to encounter a whole series of dangers the moment they were out of sight. But for all her fussiness Gail couldn't help liking her. She was a woman of perhaps fifty-five with round, child-like blue eyes (that could on occasion hold a glint of shrewdness), and dimples still lurked in her firm apple-red cheeks when she laughed—which she often did.

As the week went on Gail was increasingly glad of her cheery good humor, for Shelagh seemed to grow progressively more moody. "The truth is I hate cities and shopping," she confessed one warm, airless morning when in an interval between appointments they sat eating strawberry ice-cream in Grafton Street's most delectable *patisserie*. For an hour she had submitted with obvious boredom to the ministrations of the fitter who was altering the pastel blue coat and frock which she was to wear when she set out on her honeymoon. It was an exquisite ensemble with the touches of dressiness permissible in a bridal outfit. But Shelagh suddenly hated it. "It makes me look like a fluffy doll," she complained now.

"Then why did you agree to have it when we looked at it yesterday?" Gail asked, dismayed.

Shelagh made a small grimace. "I wasn't really thinking about it. Oh, Gail . . . I just don't care! Don't take any notice of me. You choose the things you would like to wear yourself if it were *you* that were going to marry Rod . . . and I'm sure it will all work out."

Gail felt the swift painful color surge up into her cheeks. It was amazing how sharply the unthinking remark could hurt. If it were she who were marrying Rod! The very sound of the wild words echoing on the vanilla-scented air of the little *patisserie* could make her heart turn over sickeningly.

But Shelagh, blindly unaware of the turmoil she had caused, scraped the last creamy mouthful from her glass plate with an appreciative air. "Real fresh strawberries!" she pronounced on a note of satisfaction. And then, sitting back with a long sigh, added with seeming irrelevance: "I wish to goodness it *could* be the way Pat said the other day when we were looking at Laheen Chapel. . . . The wedding, I mean . . . Rod whipping me up on to the pommel of his saddle and away with us to the nearest priest."

Only that it wasn't *Rod* Pat had seen in the leading role of this spirited display, Gail could have reminded her. But she kept silent.

"It's the thought of the functions all these fussy garments are intended to grace that worries me," Shelagh went on. "Dinners and at-homes, garden parties and house parties. I'm so *bad* at all that sort of thing. The prospect of my first batch of house guests scares me stiff. Aunt Dodie already has them all picked out for us. She wants us to

77

have about thirty people for the autumn shooting, most of them rather on the ancient side. Hangovers from the old days when she herself lived at the Castle. A peer and peeress, a Cabinet Minister with a frightfully snooty wife who went to finishing school with Aunt Dodie when she was a girl. There's an Anglican Bishop, a couple of minor royalties." She ticked the august names off on her finger-tips. "And as a concession to my youth, a pair of newly-weds with pedigrees longer than Finnmacool's. In fact if they weren't well and truly in the stud book they wouldn't be invited to Laheen."

"I expect they will all turn out to be charming . . . just a lot of nice friendly human beings as keen on having fun as you are yourself," Gail offered consolingly.

"Fun!" Shelagh hooted. "A fat lot of fun I shall have being hostess to that stuffy crowd . . . sitting at the head of that terrific great table in the banqueting hall through endless dinners, wearing the family diamonds, trying to think up intelligent topics of conversation . . . and I'm not intelligent, except about horses. You can't talk to Bishops about horses! Oh, it is lost I will be!" she moaned, lapsing into the exaggerated brogue she sometimes affected. "Not a hair of me head out of place, wearing one or other of those glittering dresses you are after ordering for me, a fixed grin nailed on me face and me tongue stuck to the roof of me mouth with the fright!"

Gail couldn't help laughing at this woeful picture. But there was genuine panic behind it. Her voice was warm with sympathy as she said: "You'll find when you come to it that it won't be a bit like that. The Bishops and Cabinet Ministers will adore you, whatever you talk to them about . . . and Rod will be so proud of you!"

"Oh, Gail, I hope he will!" The vivid, lovely little face softened, the sapphire-dark eyes were suddenly bright with dreams. "It is only the thought of him that makes it all bearable. I know it will be good for him if we have what Aunt Dodie calls an adequate social life at Laheen. Even though he says he'd be quite content to live in any old cottage with me, thinking and talking about nothing but horses . . . it wouldn't work out. He's such a man of the world, his whole life has been spent in travelling; meeting

78

and mixing with famous people. He'd miss all that terribly. He'd get bored in time . . . even with me. Sometimes I think he gets a bit bored with me even now."

"Shelagh!" Gail cried in horror. "What utter nonsense!"

"He's so terrifically clever, Gail. If you only saw the books he has in his own special den at Laheen—whole shelves of them, biographies and histories and poetry, fearsome tomes on things like military strategy and philosophy. He knows all about art too, and antique furniture and architecture. He has lived in all the capitals of Europe and can talk about them interestingly. It makes me feel so silly and empty-headed." She drew in a long quivering sigh. "If only I could be sure I wouldn't be a disappointment to him! I'm so afraid of failing him."

"You won't fail him," Gail whispered a little unsteadily, "You love him too much to fail."

* * *

It was the following day that Rod arrived at "Avonlea". Gail was alone in Miss Quinn's small back sitting room, making entries into the account book she was keeping for Miss Ross when he was shown in. Foolishly startled, she jumped up from the bureau in the window recess. They had not expected him until later in the day. He had telephoned Shelagh that morning before leaving Laheen, saying he would turn up in time to take her out to dinner. And now it was barely tea-time. That, however, was no excuse for the way Gail's heart plunged as he walked into the room. He was wearing a rather pale, impeccably cut grey lounge suit which made him appear more bronzed than ever—and in some way slightly forbidding. It was so much more usual to see him in riding kit or country tweeds. For a moment she was quite unable to speak and left his casual "Hello, Gail!" unanswered. The room seemed to fill up with a queer electrical tension as they looked at one another in the awkward little silence. In his deeply tanned face Rod's eyes were hard, alert and curiously light in color.

"Shelagh is in the garden," Gail managed to bring out at last. He came over to the window, standing by her side, and together they looked down into the little walled-in

79

patch of green some feet below the level of the room. Shelagh was lying half asleep in a deck chair dragged carelessly into the middle of a bed of forget-me-nots in the shadow of a plum tree. Petals from the plum blossom had fallen on to her dark hair. There was a tranced quality in her absolute stillness. But there was something faintly artificial about the whole scene, bathed in the strong afternoon sunshine. It was like looking down through a wall of golden glass that emphasized and distorted everything. The grass was unbearable green. Every leaf and twig and flower in the tiny enclosed space seemed caught and fixed, touched with an unnatural polished brilliancy.

Making no attempt to attract Shelagh's attention, Rod turned away, and began to move about the room restlessly. "How are the bruises?" he asked. It was the first time he had seen her since her accident with Tara Lad, and remembering with a sudden uncomfortable vividness how he had held her in his arms that day, Gail felt her cheeks grow pink.

"Oh, I have quite forgotten them!" she laughed.

"And how are you enjoying Dublin?"

"I'm loving it!" Her self-consciousness suddenly vanished. For days she had been storing up impressions and had had no one to share them with. Shelagh, who seemed to have left her whole heart and soul at home with Finnmacool and Pat . . . and of course Rod, wasn't interested in her reactions to this her first glimpse of a foreign city. "Because it is a foreign city," she found herself enlarging. Something in the way Rod was listening made the eager words come pouring out. "It is quite unlike an English town; all the wide streets with their trees and air of gaiety, the way I've always imagined the Parisian boulevards to be. And the quays by the river exactly like the paintings I've seen of the banks of the Seine, even to the bookstalls. That terrific Bank of Ireland, too, like a Greek temple flowering in the middle of College Green."

"The Parthenon of the Liffey," Rod said, smiling. "Some day you must see the Parthenon on the Acropolis. A ghost in white marble, more than two thousand years old."

80

Gail nodded, her gold-flecked eyes bright with interest. "I've seen pictures of it. Those *wonderful* soaring columns, like . . . like frozen music," she ended, with a small apologetic laugh for the fanciful simile.

But Rod's dark face kindled. "You have the true traveller's instinct for spotting the essentials, haven't you? And you're so right about Dublin being a foreign city. Most visitors fail to realize it simply because English is mostly spoken here. Though it's not at all orthodox English."

"It's more vivid and poetical than the way people talk at home," Gail mused. "I wonder why?"

"Because it was evolved by a Gaelic-speaking nation. There's a completely different culture behind it. Have you seen any of the collections of Celtic antiquities, since you came?" Gail shook her head regretfully, and he was still telling her about the golden bell of St. Patrick in the National Museum, the cloak pins and ear-rings and brooches of exquisite workmanship dating back as far as the Bronze Age, when Miss Quinn came bustling in in a flurry of greeting and shocked tut-tuts.

"Mary tells me you are here for the past half-hour, Major!"

She turned to Gail, her round eyes fierce with reproach. "Why didn't you call Shelagh, Miss Darnley?" Running over to the window she flung it wide, crying in a voice throbbing with romantic feeling: "Shelagh, Shelagh, Major Sterne is here looking for you!"

Gail gathered up her bills and receipts and slipped away to her room to finish her accounts. When she came downstairs to the sitting room again tea had been brought in. Shelagh was sitting on a low stool by Rod's side, leaning against his knee. The petals of plum blossom still rested like confetti on her dark hair and she was fastening a sprig of forget-me-not in the lapel of the severe lounge suit. All her moodiness had vanished. Her lovely face had the delicate glow of a wild rose as she laughed up into Rod's eyes. Not hard or alert any more but filled with the tender amusement Gail had so often noticed in his glance when it rested on the child who was so soon to be his wife. Throughout the meal she plied him with questions about Kildoona and Laheen. Had he been over to see Finnmacool? Was Pat putting the young horse to the jumps yet? How was Red Mary settling down? It was as though she had been away from home a year instead of a few days.

"But what about the shopping?" Rod interrupted her at last. "Have you almost finished buying up Grafton Street?"

"I've got a jewel of a frock for the ball next month," she told him. "It's pale pink tulle and there is at least a hundred yards of stuff in the skirt. I feel like an evening sky in it . . . trailing clouds of glory."

It was the only frock she had shown any interest in, Gail reflected, refusing the white version of it that would have been more suitable for a bride. "I'm not going to be a bride on the night of the fifth. I'm going to be myself . . . for one last glorious binge!" she had said on a queer note of desperation, her young voice taut and harsh.

"By the way, Sonia . . . Mrs. Treacey, may be flying over for the ball," Rod announced, looking across at Gail.

Shelagh turned to stare at her in an arrested way. "Does Gail know Sonia?" she marvelled.

"She met her when some of the Horse Show Committee people came to Regency Gardens one evening for cocktails," Rod put in before Gail could speak. She was aware that she had changed color nervously . . . was aware too of the odd, almost warning glance Rod shot at her, as he added: "Gail had been sent along by the Chatsworth Bureau that week to help the Show secretary."

"Oh, yes, you did tell me that," Shelagh said to Gail, her face clearing. "But I didn't realize you knew Sonia."

"You could hardly call it 'knowing her'," Gail amended in a carefully casual voice. "She would barely have been aware of my existence that evening, there were so many people milling about. I was very much in the background." That was true enough at all events.

"Didn't she introduce you to Rod?" Shelagh asked.

"Oh, no!" Gail laughed. "I wasn't in the house more than a few minutes. I had to go back to the Show to organize seats for the evening performance."

"That was the night I was there," Shelagh mused. "Funny we were all three there, you and I and Rod . . .

and we didn't know you, and you didn't know us . . . and now here we all are. . . ." The involved sentence trailed away into silence and when she spoke again it was to change the subject.

"Isn't it lovely to see them so devoted to one another!" Miss Quinn fervently remarked later in the evening, when the lovers had departed and she and Gail sat over supper. Rod had gone back to his club after tea to change, returning in his car to collect Shelagh, who had put on her frock of rosy tulle. They were going to the Shelbourne to dine and dance. Gail tried not to envy them as she plodded through her own prosaic meal of cauliflower cheese followed by a mysterious confection which Miss Quinn called "cold shape", but which tasted suspiciously like boiled ground rice.

"History repeating itself," Miss Quinn murmured reflectively, a spoonful of cold shape arrested in mid-air, her round blue eyes dreamy. "The heartbreak of one generation healing itself in the next. Mr. Rod marrying little Shelagh! It's so simple and beautiful a sequel . . . and one I'd never have thought of with the big difference there is in their ages. But it's happening . . . the wish of Sir Charles' life coming true and a Ross O'Donnel going back to Laheen. Much as this marriage may mean to the young ones it will mean more to Miss Ross and Sir Charles, for planning it all they will be living their own love story over again. Their poor love story that came to naught!"

Gail looked up, startled. Sir Charles and Miss Ross! "Living their own love story over again." The romantic phrase seemed incongruous.

"She wasn't always a cripple, you know," Miss Quinn said, smiling a little pityingly at the incredulous young face across the supper table. "You won't believe me, perhaps—for youth never does see farther than the end of its nose! But they must have been a strikingly handsome couple in those dead-and-gone days. I never saw my poor Miss Dodie, save as an invalid, but Sir Charles, when I first came to Kildoona, was a blond giant of a man, very handsome in his English way. Not an aristocrat like herself, it's true, but a merchant prince with the Bowfort millions behind him. That gave him an entrée into the highest society. He was a friend of the Duke of Westchester; who sold him Laheen Castle, having acquired it—rather doubtfully to my mind—over a game of cards."

"So it is true . . . that strange wild story!" Gail exclaimed.

"Aye, indeed, true enough. But maybe neither so strange nor wild as it sounds, for Mr. Clarence, Miss Dodie's father, must have known years of desperation before ho let the old place go. It was mostly debts he inherited from his own father, Valentine, an old rake if ever there was one! And Mr. Clarence wouldn't have been brought up to practise the mean little stints of economy. The family traditions had to go on; the balls, the parties, the comings and goings of half the nobility of Europe. A lavish life they led in those days, the O'Donnels, and in the end there was little left to them but the roof over their heads . . . and it takes more than a pittance to keep the roof of a castle intact. So there it was: ruin, like a death's head, grinning over poor Mr. Clarence's shoulder the night he staked Laheen against the Duke's cool fifty thousand. It was a justifiable risk he took in my opinion. But it didn't come off."

With a reminiscent sigh, Miss Quinn fell silent. In the plain, orderly little room the fabulous echoes lingered . . . the rattling of ghostly dice. Tragedy played out gallantly to its bitter end.

"It was all over and done with when I came on the scene," Miss Quinn was saying then, banishing the echoes, turning her square sensible back on that chapter in profligacy. And it was of a later tragedy she was speaking now, of Miss Ross when she was little older than Shelagh, as lively, as beautiful . . . but condemned to perpetual pain. "I nursed her for five years after her accident," the lilting Irish voice went on. "I saw her through fever of mind and body, through heartbreak and long despair. I . . . lived it out with her as though it was my own sorrow. In the endless nights when she couldn't rest in spite of all the drugs that were poured into her she would talk to me in that dreamy mood induced by drugs that is neither sleeping nor waking. And what she didn't tell me I could read between the lines. There's no breach of confidence in

84

speaking of it now . . . it's too old a tale to be a secret, and you're there with her at Kildoona, watching the last act in the drama. It won't hurt you to know what has gone before!" Gail caught the purposeful inflection in the gentle voice—and wondered at it a little.

"It was for my lovely Miss Dodie Sir Charles bought Laheen back from the Duke," Miss Quinn said.

Gail stared. Was there no end to the extravagances of this old history?

"Aye, indeed, you may well open your eyes!" Miss Quinn nodded her grey head with an air of satisfaction. "He fell head over heels in love with her the first time he saw her, and swore to himself then and there that he would right the wrong the Duke and her own father had done to her. It wasn't hard for him to get Laheen, for he offered the Duke twice what he had wagered for it. He took the deeds over to Kildoona and laid them, along with his heart, at Miss Dodie's feet. She wouldn't listen to him at first, not daring to let herself think about his love, resenting his pity. Proud as a queen she was!" Miss Quinn drew her plump shoulders up in quaint imitation of Miss Ross' regality. It was as though she were acting the old sad drama out in her mind.

"He set himself to woo her. It was the night of the Hunt Ball that she finally said 'yes' to him. They danced until the dawn together, and with the music still in their ears, their hearts wild with their new-found joy, they went out . . . leading the hunt. That was the day she broke her back . . . and her own heart and his along with it. To marry him as a hopeless invalid was something her pride would not allow. Penniless she could have faced him . . . but not crippled."

Gail's eyes were not quite dry. "What a tragic ending!" she whispered.

"But it was not the end," Miss Quinn declared softly. "From that day to this he has watched over her . . . living in solitude in that great lonely Castle just for the sake of being near her: as near as she would permit, for her pride increased as the difficult years went on. His friendship she would accept, but not his pity, and never the material help he would have been glad to give. And now this miracle of Rod and Shelagh has happened. You can imagine what it must mean to Miss Dodie and Sir Charles!"

Gail nodded, a faint uneasiness stirring within her as suddenly she remembered Rod's outburst in the chapel at Laheen; when he had cried out to Shelagh in exasperation: "Sometimes I wonder if it is Aunt Dodie's wedding or our own that is being arranged!" Was it possible, as Pat had hinted—in an even wilder outburst—that Rod had in some way been dragooned into the whole affair? "Arranged" was such a hard, horrible word, utterly alien to the lovely, spontaneous flowering of true romance. And yet surely, surely Rod was truly in love with Shelagh! You only had to see them together to realize how happy they were. . . .

"It would kill Miss Ross, I believe, if anything were to hinder this coming marriage! She wouldn't be able to bear a second disappointment," Miss Quinn suddenly cried out, her voice trembling.

"But what *could* hinder it?" Gail asked, mildly amused at the state of emotion into which Miss Quinn was lashing herself.

The round blue eyes were suddenly shrewd and hard. "There's many a slip 'twixt cup and lip. He's a very attractive man, the Major, and a very rich man. It is not hard to imagine the appeal he could have for the opposite sex . . . even now, engaged and all as he is. And Shelagh is a child . . . with no guile in her heart . . . nor perhaps a great deal of self-confidence. It wouldn't be difficult for a girl a little older than herself, a little more sophisticated, to hurt her a very great deal by . . . appearing to compete with her for the Major's interest."

Gail colored. The implication was unmistakable. So there had been a definite purpose in the spate of confidences! That unthinking half-hour Rod had spent in the house this afternoon before seeking Shelagh out . . . it had not been lost on Miss Quinn. Had she read her own meaning, too, into the cautious exchange at tea-time when Sonia's name had come up?

Steadily and with a mounting indignation Gail encountered the penetrating round blue eyes. "I think you are worrying yourself quite unnecessarily," she said crisply.

"You do? I'm glad! That's all right then." A dimple appeared in the apple cheeks. "I can comfort myself with the thought that you are to be at Kildoona during the coming weeks. They won't be easy for Shelagh with her nervous over-sensitive heart. But she thinks the world of you, my dear. You'll stand by her, won't you?"

"Of course I shall!"

It was as though a promise had been demanded—and given.

Miss Quinn stood up with an air of one who has successfully weathered a small crisis. "We'll have our coffee in the garden," she said, as she touched the bell.

* * *

It was on the drive back from Dublin that Shelagh announced she had invited Miss Quinn to the ball.

"Think she'll fit in?" Rod offered a little doubtfully. They were all three sitting in the capacious front seat of the big car, and Gail could feel the little wriggle of impatience from Shelagh at her side.

"Don't be tiresome, darling; of course she'll fit in! It's going to be a comfortable sort of party—quite unblessed by Debrett, apart from a few of the county die-hards. We'll keep the peerage out until after we're married, if you don't mind."

Rod laughed. "I wouldn't mind if you kept them out for ever!"

"Charles says it is to be *my* party," Shelagh persisted. "And I'm to invite whom I like. So I'm having all my best friends. Gail"—she put a hand on Gail's arm affectionately—"and Pat and his mother, and Miss Quinn and her young man."

Gail, who hadn't until that moment been certain that she was to be included in the forthcoming festivity, felt a small thrill of very natural pleasure, and began mentally to plan what she would wear. Tempted by the orgies of shopping which had filled the past week she had bought for herself a handsome shot taffeta, shading from bronze to green. Sophisticated. Would it be "competing" with Shelagh to appear in so striking a frock? For the past two

87

days, uncomfortably aware of Miss Quinn's words of warning, she had steadily refused to be included in the expeditions Rod had organized, visits to museums and art galleries, a drive through the Wicklow glens, an evening at a small private theatre where an Irish company were giving Yeats' *Countess Cathleen*. With his air of casual, almost absent-minded kindliness Rod had assumed she would like to make the most of her week in the new city, but he had seemed completely unmoved when she refused his invitations, his strong dark face inscrutable.

She heard him say now, puzzled, "Miss Quinn's young man?"

"An osteopath," Shelagh giggled. "You know how she is always trying to get Aunt Dodie to see her latest discoveries in the way of doctors and surgeons? Now she has fished up some Welsh wizard—Tom Darnow, says he has a magic way with spinal injuries. She wrote to Aunt Dodie about him a few weeks ago, and Aunt Dodie flaty refused to have anything to do with him. So we've conspired together, Quinney and I, and we're going to spring him on her."

"In the middle of a ball?" Rod enquired mildly.

"He'll be staying the weekend."

"Well, I hope you know what you're doing!"

"Oh, I do!" Shelagh declared fervently, and for the next twenty miles or so enlarged on Tom Darnow's credentials. He was an uncle of one of Quinney's medical students, and had worked with the famous osteopath Sir Trevor Harthrop in London for many years. Now he had a fashionable practice of his own in Merrion Square. People were flocking to him. He had, according to Quinney, already achieved a sufficient number of cures to set the orthodox faculty by the ears. "Charles will believe in him, even if you and Dodie don't!" she cried impatiently at last, exasperated by Rod's cautiously maintained silence.

Poor Sir Charles with a lifetime of empty hopes behind him! Thinking of him pityingly in the light of her new knowledge, Gail lifted her eyes and saw on the far horizon the glitter of lake water, the blue bastion of a line of hills. They were nearly home.

CHAPTER SEVEN

It was a week later that Gail had her first riding lesson with Pat. He took her to the wide green paddock that he used as a training ground for the yearlings and colts it was his job to break. It lay on the outskirts of the little town of Ardrossa, a green sickle of land with a foam-flecked river, all shallows and rapids, roaring along one side of it. For an hour, with the patient Tara Lad beneath her, Gail tackled the graduated jumps of brushwood and was thrilled to find her skill, and her nerve along with it, growing more assured.

"We'll have you following the hunt with the best of them if you stay here till the autumn," Pat commended her, as they trotted back to the stables. Her heart knew a sudden curious hollowness. In the autumn! She would be back in London long before the trees under which she now passed had turned to gold. The thought brought a desolation that frightened her. She felt so oddly . . . permanent here, so settled, so at home! But it was not her home. The life that waited for her far away, when this halcyon summer ended with the knell of wedding bells, stretched before her—a grey and endless wilderness. She would never see Rod again. And suddenly, her heart betraying her, she saw the magic of this smiling summer for what it was. A treasuring of the trivial kindnesses that came her way; looks, tones, glances . . . the brief casual encounters on which she was feeding her hungry heart. How could she ever forget, even for an instant, that she was here to help—not her own love—but Shelagh's, to its bright fulfilment! Was there no end to the madness that obsessed her? she wondered in dull pain, as she heard Pat saying they would drop in at his house for a cup of tea before he drove her back to Kildoona. "I would like you to meet my mother," he said, adding a little oddly, "I don't suppose you've ever come across anyone quite like her!"

They drove in his rather battered car through a network of back streets behind the main street of Ardrossa's little shops. Gaunt shuttered mills they passed, half-ruined indefinable warehouses, rows of whitewashed cottages. And there were rivers everywhere, a spate of loud brown waters rushing to lose themselves in the vast invisible lake. They came to an island which they reached by a bridge, and here, set apart, stood a tall house of stone with water of the many rivers rushing from its very foundations.

Pat pushed at a front door, unlatched, and they went into a dark narrow hall breathing of dust, neglect; the sudden silence held a strange enchantment. But when they passed on into an adjoining room the noise of the rushing water was all about them again. A room that seemed at a first glance to be all windows, and beyond the windows lay the brightness of the flashing water so that the effect was blinding, the interior filled with the green reflections of the sun-dappled river—like ghostly water dancing on walls, on ceiling.

Dazzled, Gail peered about her, seeing dimly the woman who sat by the wide fireless hearth, shadowy as a figure in some heroic tapestry . . . her head bowed a little, her left hand fingering the strings of a great golden harp. The music she made was almost lost in the sound of the rushing river—which had deadened too the sound of their entry. Standing motionless just inside the door, they watched her in silence. Then, as though some vibration of their presence reached her, she turned slowly and saw them.

As she rose to greet them Gail's vision cleared and she drew in her breath sharply at the strange beauty of the woman coming towards them. "This is my mother," Pat was saying. "I've brought Gail Darnley over from Kildoona to see you, Mother. We have been riding in the paddock all the afternoon and we're dying for a cup of tea."

Mrs. Crampton held out her hand and murmured kindly-sounding, though, to Gail, quite meaningless words, for she was speaking in Gaelic. But it scarcely mattered, for in her flowing robe of deep blue with its archaic gold embroidery of Celtic designs, she was so completely a figure from some other world, some other era, that ordinary communication with her might well be impossible. She was strikingly like her son, as strikingly handsome, the classic

90

features softer, the eyes shadowed with sorrow, experience. Though the lovely oval of her face was unlined, youth had in some way gone from it. A brooding, tragic face. Her hair, rich, honey-gold, was drawn back from a central parting and fastened in a heavy knot in the nape of her neck.

The hand that held Gail's fingers briefly was strong; a harpist's hand. Relinquishing her grasp, Mrs. Crampton smiled, and the strange soft alien words came pouring out again.

"Gail is English, mother," Pat said. "You've got to make an exception of her . . . she cannot possibly understand our language."

"My mother," he explained, turning to Gail, "is an Irish-speaking fanatic. She has an oath taken that she will never use any other tongue unless necessity forces it upon her."

Gail was aware of Mrs. Crampton's smiling nod of agreement. So at all events she understood English—even if she disdained to use it. Urgently she spoke to her son, answering perhaps his argument. He shrugged as she went out of the room, moving with a statuesque grace in her strange, loosely-belted robe.

"She has gone to make the tea," he said, and pulling a chair forward for Gail threw himself down on an uncomfortable-looking couch covered with cheap black oilcloth. But everything about the room was cheap, ugly, tasteless; little bamboo tables, Victorian whatnots, wicker armchairs; the faded green carpet on the floor was threadbare, grey with dust. A room that made little concession to comfort, none at all to feminine daintiness, as though its owner lived on a plane remote from such human weaknesses. Incongruous as an angel, the harp stood on the tatty rag rug before the unswept fireplace. On the damp-stained walls hung the portraits of three generations of Irish patriots. "Wolfe Tone," murmured Pat, following Gail's exploratory glance. "O'Donovan Rossa. Parnell. And that's Padraig Pearse over the mantelpiece."

Gail shook her head. "Means nothing to me, I'm afraid," she confessed. "I'm woefully ignorant of Irish history."

91

"My father went to Pearse's Irish School," Pat said. "He was one of the principal figures in the Gaelic revival . . . Pearse I mean; and my father made a great hero of him. But they were all in the Movement, my mother's family and my father's. My mother's grandfather was killed fighting with the Land League in the old troubled days that followed the great Famine. . . ."

The door opened and Mrs. Crampton appeared with a laden tea-tray, which she put down on a bamboo table that rocked dangerously under the weight. Happily ignoring this, she began to pour tea from an immense brown shiny teapot into the thick delft cups. There was a plate of clumsily cut bread and butter, a pot of shop jam, and a rather stale seed cake on a tarnished silver platter. "Pat is quite right, of course," she said, speaking now in soft lilting English, "it wouldn't be polite to talk Gaelic at you and you not having a word of it. But it is a great sorrow to me that you are not forced into learning it for your contacts in this country—as you would learn French, for example, if you were to make yourself at home in Paris. If only it were still the everyday language of our land, instead of being the half-forgotten, wholly neglected thing it is! A country without a language of its own is . . . a country without a soul."

"It has such a beautiful softness when you speak it," Gail offered shyly. Mrs. Crampton beamed at this commendation, and abandoning the tea-table with a sudden impulsive movement, jumped up and seated herself before the harp. "Listen to this," she cried, and began to sing in a rich contralto: *"Grama-chree ma cruiskeen, Slainte geal mavourneen . . ."*

"What does it mean?" Gail asked when the rollicking chorus ended.

"Never mind what it means . . . just get the *blas* of it into your ears . . . the rhythm. It's a young man extolling his love, not very originally and with many repetitions. Come on now, sing it along with me!"

Laughing, Gail tried to join in the words and found them easier than she had expected.

"I'll teach you a few simple greetings you can call out to the country people when you meet them on the roads,"

Mrs. Crampton offered, coming back to the rocking wicker table.

"You'd better rope her in to your evening classes," Pat laughed.

"I'll lend you O'Growney's Irish primer," Mrs. Crampton told Gail, her beautiful grey-blue eyes sparkling with enthusiasm for her latest convert. "Or you could borrow the whole series from Shelagh. She hasn't been near me for ages, the little scamp. Time was when she came to her Irish lessons three times a week, but that was before she got herself into this unfortunate engagement."

There was an odd, tense silence for a moment, and Gail saw Pat's face darken. "Unfortunate?" she murmured, on a rising inflection.

"She ought to be marrying one of her own people," Mrs. Crampton declared in her forthright way. "I've nothing against Major Sterne personally. He's a fine man. But Shelagh is a Ross O'Donnel. A direct descendant of the Earls of Tirconnell, and they, as everybody knows, were descended from the ancient Irish Kings."

"But she will be going back to Castle Laheen, the home of the O'Donnels, when she marries," Gail pointed out, a little amused at this excursion into the dim ages.

"Our lovely Castle in the hands of a foreign owner!" Mrs. Crampton burst out passionately. "And I'm invited to go there!" She waved a strong white hand in the direction of the mantelpiece and Gail saw propped up beneath Pearse's photograph the gilt-edged invitation card to the forthcoming ball. She remembered now addressing it.

"I'll not put a foot in the place!" Mrs. Crampton cried. "Me . . . the granddaughter of a man who was jailed with Parnell at the time of the land agitation, who helped to draw up the 'No Rent' manifesto and was later killed by the bullet of an absentee landlord's bailiff!"

"After being pretty handy with the trigger-finger himself," Pat put in proudly. "He was a great old boy for taking a pot-shot at the landlords."

"And I wish there were a few more like him alive today!" exclaimed the formidable Mrs. Crampton, with such venom in her tone that Gail shivered inwardly. Pat caught her startled glance. "You're scaring the life out of our English guest, Mother," he said quietly.

Mrs. Crampton turned, her glance blind, unseeing. A look Gail had seen on Pat's young face at moments of emotional tension. As though the outward world was nothing . . . the inward passion all."

"My dear child, don't mistake me." She touched Gail's hand lightly, reassuringly, and suddenly her smile was very sweet. "Sir Charles is a grand person. I'm really devoted to him. And though I don't know the Major so well, I have a great regard for him, too. They are here in our country—our honored guests. We are glad to have them living among us. But intermarrying with them, or any other foreign race, is another matter. The old Celtic families should keep their strain pure. If our culture is ever to be revived—take its old proud place in the world once more—we must guard it, not fritter it away by thoughtless unions with those of alien blood. I'll have no part in this step Shelagh is taking. I feel it is a tragic mistake. I'd do anything in my power to stop it. Anything!" There was a frightening intensity in her tone.

"But the ball has nothing to do with the wedding," Pat said. "It's just a bit of a *Ceilidhe* Shelagh is giving as a kind of farewell to all the old crowd, and she'll be hurt if you refuse her invitation to it."

"Do please come," Gail urged, anxious to smooth the situation over.

"A *Ceilidhe!*" Mrs. Crampton mused, her lovely face growing dreamy, as though the term were a magic incantation. "If only we could make it that indeed; a true Gaelic evening with the old dances, the old songs. That is the meaning of the word *Ceilidhe*," she said, turning to Gail.

"You could bring your harp and sing to us," Gail suggested, her imagination kindling.

The long lashes drooped over Mary Crampton's eyes, slyly, secretively. "If I sing it may be that my songs may not be to the liking of the strangers," she said. "And the song that I have in mind for the ears of Major Sterne might be the hardest of all for him to hear."

"What song is that, Mother?" Pat demanded sharply.

94

His mother gave him an inscrutable look. "You'll see when the time comes!" she declared, and try as he would that was all he could get out of her.

"She's up to some mischief or other," he said a little later as he drove Gail back to Kildoona. "Maybe it's a pity we coaxed her to agree to come to the ball. The Lord knows what she'll do when she finds herself in the Castle— stand up and denounce the Major, as likely as not!" He laughed, not altogether ruefully.

"Why is she so against Rod?" Gail asked, suddenly indignant. "All that stuff she talked about alien blood sounds absolutely fantastic. Being English is surely not so very different to being Irish?"

"It is to my mother. She thinks it's patriotism, but it's really a kind of chasing after rainbows, searching maybe for something she lost in her youth, when she and my father and Pearse and the whole lot of them saw Ireland as a kind of Utopia, a self-contained heaven shut away from the rest of mankind. She won't realize that you can't shut it away, or that the new Ireland belongs to a generation that is more interested in the future than in the twilit past. But they're all the same, the older people." There was an edge of bitterness in his tone. "Miss Ross mooning away there at Kildoona over the vanished grandeur of Laheen, getting a vicarious kick out of the fact that Shelagh is to bring the old times to life again for her. And with Sir Charles it's something else again. . . . Rod getting the Ross O'Donnel bride he himself missed, perhaps. But whatever it is, it is always of themselves it seems to me the last generation is thinking, groping about amid the ashes of their lost hopes. . . ."

In the long drive the last of the azalea petals ran like scraps of crumpled paper before the rising breeze. Suddenly it was cold and Gail shivered. The ashes of lost hopes. How terrible it must be to grow old in loneliness and frustration! Like watching doors close slowly and for ever, one by one, shutting out life.

She was very patient with Miss Ross that evening when they dined alone—for Shelagh was over at Laheen with Rod and Sir Charles. The conversation drifted inevitably to the ball, so soon to be held, merging imperceptibly for

Miss Ross into the memory of other more glittering functions held in the same great banqueting rooms. In the interminable summer dusk ghosts jostled; Grand Dukes, German Princes, a Balkan King—who had ended up as the victim of an anarchist's bullet; even as Mary Crampton's grandfather had ended, if more humbly, at a charge from a bailiff's gun.

In the garden beyond the darkening windows the slow warm Irish rain streamed down, drenching lilacs and roses.

Pat is right; they forget nothing, these older people, Gail thought. The past, more real than anything contemporary could be, held them in thrall. But at least the memories of Miss Ross and Mrs. Crampton were colorful, dramatic . . . stirringly linked with history. With young unhappiness and a sudden sense of dread Gail peered down the corridors of her own waiting years and saw only emptiness. Her life could never be eventful as these other lives had been. When it came to her turn to be old would there be anything for her to look back upon? She would remember perhaps this one bright summer, sharp with its inescapable pain . . . and that would be all!

Tears were not far from her eyes as she stooped under the table to pick up Miss Ross' ebony canes. Dinner was disposed of now and they would linger another endless hour over coffee in the drawing-room. Then perhaps Miss Ross would ask her to read to her from the big volume of Edwardian memoirs which was her favorite book. And after a time she would cease to listen, her head nodding drowsily, her blue eyes closed, the old dreams blurring, even heartache forgotten in the rising tide of weariness and sleep.

CHAPTER EIGHT

THERE was a rosy afterglow in the sky three evenings later when Gail, with Miss Ross and Shelagh, drove to Laheen Castle on their way to the ball. A perfect evening after the first day of real summer warmth, and now the June twilight lingered. But in this western land darkness would barely touch the hills throughout the short night, while in the glittering ballroom chandeliers sparkled behind drawn silken curtains and the fiddles laughed and sang.

Sir Charles had sent a vast old Rolls to fetch them—with a feather-bed interior, kind as a cloud to brittle bones. The chauffeur, carefully briefed, drove slowly, even on the smooth lake-side road, while Miss Ross, ignoring her aching spine, sat proudly upright in her cushioned corner, regal tonight in silver brocade and diamonds. Like a ghostly bride in her silver and white, Gail thought; the colors that ought to have been Shelagh's—who glowed at her side in the rose-tinted tulle, wearing flowers instead of jewels—the blush pink rosebuds Rod had sent from the Castle gardens. Her cheeks were roses, too, untouched by make-up. She was unutterably lovely in her mood of gay anticipation—heart-rendingly young.

Sitting opposite her in the greeny-bronze taffeta Gail felt the swift, familiar pang. It was hardly envy, she was too generous for that. But it was impossible to help thinking that Rod would have eyes for no one but Shelagh tonight. How could he have? And yet—as though it could matter—she had taken special pains with her own dressing for the occasion. Under the loose dust coat of tussore-colored dupion that served as a wrap, the new frock was a success. In her bedroom mirror she had watched it transform her, bringing green lights into her hazel-gold eyes, an emphasis to the bronze sheen of her hair.

Cars already thronged the sweep of gravel before the Castle when they drew up. The great oak doors stood open and early guests filled the green marble hall. But in spite of the confusion Sir Charles was aware of their arrival almost before the Rolls halted, and came hurrying out to greet them, his pink face eager, oddly boyish. With scarcely a glance to spare for the girls he helped Miss Ross to alight, and then—before she had time to protest—he had lifted her in his arms and carried her up the steps. Gail, following with the ebony canes, realized afresh how helpless a cripple she was. She would never have been able to negotiate that flight of shallow steps unaided. Sir Charles, broad-shouldered, immense, seemed to feel her fragile weight hardly at all, laughing down into her lined, proud face, rallying her. As he swept her across the threshold in

97

her floating silver brocade, Gail was irresistibly reminded of brides once more. But how tragic a travesty this was of a bridal homecoming! Life could be unendingly, relentlessly cruel. The thought came to her young heart with the frightening force of a fresh, unwelcome discovery.

Then Rod was there, crying: "Here you are!" His eyes —the bright points of yellowish flame in them very noticeable tonight—slid away from her almost at once to rest on Shelagh in her cloud of rosy tulle.

"Miss Quinn and the Wizard have arrived," he told her, tucking her arm into his own. "Charles has offered to put them up for the night, for the entire weekend if things don't go well with your aunt."

"Oh, Rod, that's sweet of Charles! Does he like Mr. Darnow?"

"Dunno," Rod grinned. "Don't think he has had time to find out."

They drifted away and Gail stood feeling a little lost— with the ebony walking sticks in her hand. Sir Charles and Miss Ross had vanished.

"They are in the library, Miss," a watchful footman murmured in her ear. She hurried to join them. Miss Ross, tired after the short drive, was in an exacting mood. "If you will take my wrap, Miss Darnley . . . pass me my bag, my smelling salts. . . . Presently, when I have finished this sherry and rested a few moments, I shall be glad of your arm into the ballroom. Charles, you must not wait. You must go to your guests. Miss Darnley will look after me."

But that was what she was really here to do, Gail thought. Not so much a guest as a kind of upper servant. A lump thickened in her throat. She felt childishly dashed. She had put on her beautiful frock with such a sense of excitement; set out so hopelessly. But in heaven's name hoping for *what!* she asked herself as she and Miss Ross made their slow painful entry into the ballroom, where already the dance band—imported from Dublin—was playing the opening bars of the first number. A waltz from *The Pink Lady.* Was that Rod's doing? A pretty little tribute for his love in her rose-colored frock.

98

Against walls banked with smilax and carnations guests stood, expectantly. More, surely, than the hundred or so who had had the little gilt-edged cards! Shelagh, it seemed, had been busy, taking advantage of the good-natured *carte blanche* Sir Charles had given her . . . rounding up contemporaries. Those youngsters milling around her would be the girls and boys from the pony club. But it was a handsome, distinguished gathering; they hadn't quite succeeded in keeping out Debrett! The county neighbors were by no means the simple rustics they might have been. Gail recognized a much-photographed Society beauty, daughter of an Earl, and the man with the medals on his breast was a famous General. Had Sonia Treacey arrived? she wondered, with a pang of uneasiness.

There was Mary Crampton . . . in a green robe to-night, heavy with the unmistakable Celtic embroideries. A scarf-like drapery hung from one shoulder, fastened by an immense Tara brooch, and she had bound a fillet of silver medallions about her brow. Rather startlingly, her hair fell loose to her waist, a cascade of rippling gold. She might have been a medieval queen, seated on a little gilt chair, her harp beside her, her courtiers the group of young men in saffron-colored kilts who stood around her.

"To you, beautiful lady, I raise my eyes!" sang the band leader soulfully as Rod and Shelagh swept out across the floor. Instantly, as though a signal had been given, the great shining expanse was a whirling kaleidoscope of colored frocks and flying coat tails. With no interval at all for warming up the party was at fever point. Laughter was everywhere, voices soared, taking the song from the band leader. Shelagh's song.

"Dance, dance, beautiful lady, on light, bright wings
While the rapture of music around us swings.
Dream, dream, dream and forget
Care, pain, useless regret . . ."

Almost without warning then, the violins changed their rhythm to a rollicking air that made Gail's toes tingle inside their little gold slippers. A square dance got under way, the caller, a huge young man with red hair and a glorious brogue, bellowing into a megaphone. Now the fun was fast and furious. Gail had never known so vigorous a start to an evening's dancing. They wasted no time, these Irish folk! A very passion of merriment seemed to blow through the great solid room, shaking it to its foundations. If there were ghosts here for Miss Ross sitting rigidly patient by the flowery wall, this sheer exuberance of life would surely send them flying!

"But you must dance too," she said to Gail kindly. "We must find you a partner!"

Blinking in astonishment, Gail watched a tall calm blonde go by on the arm of Sir Charles. Glenda Grayson! What on earth was *she* doing here? Had Sonia brought her? And if so, why? And where was Sonia herself?

She heard Miss Ross at her side give a small gasp and, turning, saw Miss Quinn, almost unrecognizable in a new hair-do and black lace and pearls. There was a cadaverous, sallow young man at her side.

"Miss Ross, *dear*!" With little cries of joyful greeting she bore down on them, kneeling dramatically to clasp Miss Ross' limp hands to her bosom. " 'Twas Shelagh's idea, the sweet child, that I should be here at her party tonight . . . as a wee surprise for you!"

"Look, Gail, *asthore*." She turned to Gail. "Take Tom dancing while I talk to Miss Dodie for a few minutes. Tom, this is Miss Darnley, Miss Shelagh's companion. . . ."

Gail found herself being led away by the tall, sombre osteopath.

"Come and have a drink," he invited. "I'm no good at dancing, and anyway we can't crash in on these sets."

They went into an adjoining room, where a lavish buffet awaited them. It was deserted for the moment save for a slim figure in wine-colored velvet. Sonia Treacey. She nodded casually, seemingly quite unsurprised to see Gail. Perhaps Rod told her I would be here . . . warned her! Gail thought, and was instantly ashamed of the dramatic implications. The explanation was so much more simple when it came. Sonia had run into Miss Crump at a recent race-meeting in England. "We happened to speak of you," Sonia said. "Miss Crump had been trying to get you from that bureau again to give her a hand with some

100

gymkhana thing she'd got involved with, and she learned you'd been sent over here to help out with Shelagh's wedding."

"I had no idea when I accepted the job it was to be Major Sterne's wedding, too," Gail blurted, and was instantly sorry. Whatever had made her say such a thing!

Sonia's eyebrows went up. "What difference would it have made if you *had* known?" she demanded sardonically.

"None, of course . . . it was just . . . a little odd running into him in Ireland. I hadn't known of his connection with Laheen."

"How could you know? You, naturally, know nothing about . . . any of us," Sonia said witheringly. "But as long as you earn your living as a social secretary you must expect to find us cropping up. We are very active socially, my brother and I, and Rod, of course, is overwhelmingly popular, very much sought after."

Gail nodded, feeling thoroughly snubbed.

Sonia started on a second lobster patty. "We've just arrived by air," she explained between mouthfuls. "And I haven't had any dinner. I never dare eat a thing when I'm flying."

"Are you staying at Laheen for long?" Gail ventured to ask.

Sonia gave her an icy, rather affronted look, and after a moment's hesitation answered curtly: "We are driving down to Shannon airport tomorrow, Glenda and I, flying on to Paris—this is really a call *en route*." Firmly, then, she turned a smooth bare shoulder and, realizing she was dismissed, Gail drifted away. Mr. Darnow, it seemed, having provided her with a champagne cocktail which she didn't want, had abandoned her.

On the threshold of vast, connecting folding doors, flung wide tonight, she stood watching the dancers. Desolation crept about her heart; she knew nobody! She would never join that gay whirling throng. She might just as well have stayed at home.

"Oh, Gail, there you are at last! We've been looking everywhere for you. . . ." It was Shelagh hailing her, running, skidding, sliding across the slippery floor, dragging a panting young man behind her. "This is Derry, other-

101

wise Dr. Fitzderwent. He's been crazy to meet you ever since he saw you coming in with Aunt Dodie . . . pestering me. . . . There she is for you now, Derry!" As breathlessly as she had appeared, she vanished. Derry Fitzderwent, six feet of bronzed, tough, handsome masculinity, grinned down at Gail.

"Why wouldn't I be crazy about you?" he demanded imperturbably. "You're the loveliest thing I've ever seen, in your gown of green and gold!" Without more ado he folded her expertly in his arms and whisked her away into the ballroom.

After that she danced without respite. There was no more hanging about waiting for partners.

It was after the supper interval that Rod came to her. Perhaps because Shelagh was romping through this particular number with Pat, he had sought her out, beating by a hair's breadth the muscular young priest who had been about to claim her.

"You're very much sought after, aren't you?" he offered dryly as he put a firm arm about her. So he had noticed her little triumph this evening! Had spared that much of his attention for her.

"Father Duggan dances like an angel," she said.

He laughed. "That's surely as it should be. If angels can be adepts at the Conga! I saw him pilot you through that last uproar with commendable . . . celestial . . . skill."

Gail giggled. "Look at Mrs. Crampton and her queer immovable young men!" she said a little breathlessly, trying not to be too tremulously aware of Rod's nearness as he put an arm lightly about her.

"They're waiting for the bagpipes to arrive."

"Bagpipes!" Last time they had danced together . . . on a river bank scented with lime trees, lighted with fairy lanterns . . . he had not held her in this fashion; stiffly correct. Last time . . .

"Micky Mulligan, who is an expert piper when he isn't doctoring horses or drinking himself into a stupor, is due to arrive any minute. Shelagh arranged it. It seems Mrs. Crampton insists upon a purely Gaelic interlude and she won't take any part in the proceedings until it happens.

The young men are a team of . . . I suppose you would call them . . . folk dancers."

They passed Miss Ross, leaning back, in the deep arm-chair that had now been found for her. Miss Quinn was still kneeling at her feet. Had she been there all the evening? Anything was possible in this intense and passionate country! Miss Ross looked flushed, defensive, Sir Charles sitting on her right, Mr. Darnow on her left. They were all talking to her at once.

Shelagh and Pat had vanished from the floor. On the tall french windows silken curtains billowed as the soft night air flowed in. Glenda Grayson was dancing with the General. She flicked an airy finger-tip at Rod in greeting as they passed. Gail glanced up at him enquiringly; a hurried, rather furtive little glance. Would he make any comment on Glenda's visit to Laheen? But his answering look was wooden, uncommunicative . . . bored. The face of a man getting through a duty dance with what grace he could muster? Her heart shrivelled within her, tears ached in her throat. It would have been better if she had kept to Father Duggan and Dr. Derry. To be in Rod's arms with this cool wall of indifference between them was almost more than she could endure.

It was a relief when the number ended and she could make her escape, slipping out through the billowing curtains on to the terrace. Lifting her hot face, she breathed in the fresh, sweet air. A faint wash of pearly light made the stars small and faint; somewhere the moon was hidden, a waning moon that rose late. Slowly she moved down the terrace steps and presently she could feel the grass of the lawn soft under her feet. How peaceful it was out of doors after the noise and glitter of the ballroom . . . how utterly still! The dance music came to her muted by distance; strangely sad and far-off it sounded. She could smell the dew-wet flowers that glowed with a ghostly pallor in the darkness; lilac and night-scented stock, massed roses and waxen syringa. The flutter of something that moved—just beyond her in the shadow of shrubs—caught her eye. A cloudy tulle frock. She saw then . . . could not help seeing; Shelagh and Pat locked in a motionless embrace.

103

Her impulse was to turn and flee—as silently as she had come. But for a moment sheer amazement kept her rooted where she stood, hearkening in horror to Pat's reckless, broken young voice: "You can't marry him, Lalagh! You're mine . . . my *cailin dubh*! You always have been mine . . . you always will be. This other thing is no more than a bad dream bewitching you. . . ."

"Ah, Pat, you're sweet!"

That throaty, throbbing little laugh . . . like blackbird music!

Cautiously Gail began her retreat, her heart hot, shamed, bewildered. How much did it mean, this scene upon which she had stumbled? Little enough perhaps. Shelagh humoring a Pat intoxicated with the evening's excitement. . . . The lavish flow of buffet champagne, too, might well have played its part, unloosed his tongue. Probably not for the first time. It would be no secret to Shelagh that Pat felt that way about her. But that embrace!

A sword of light fell across the terrace as curtains parted. Someone was coming out. With a stab of terror, Gail saw that it was Rod. There was no time to think about it; she must head him off somehow. He must not find those two in the shrubbery . . . must not see what she had seen. Soundlessly over the thick wet grass she ran to him.

"Have you seen Shelagh?" he demanded. "She came out here with Pat just now. . . ."

"I know," Gail nodded, her pulses stampeding. "They will have gone round to the back of the house, I expect, to see if Micky Mulligan is held up in the kitchen." She had no idea where the glib improvisation had come from, and the moment it was out she knew it was a strategical mistake. To reach the kitchen they would have to pass through the shrubbery. Hardly knowing what she did, she put a hand on Rod's arm. "The moon," she said crazily. "Look, it is rising over the lake. I was just going down to watch it . . . will you come with me?"

In the midnight dusk his face was all shadows, the bone structure emphasized, the eyes dark hollows lit by their strangely pale, yet burning irises. A face touched unbearably with pain. But that was a trick of the half light. She saw the line of his jaw whiten. He walked by her side in silence down the long green lawn. There was the drive to cross then, and a patch of rough ground where the rocky shore of the lake intruded. He took her arm as her foot slipped on a loose stone and he did not relinquish it as they stood by the lapping water, his fingers hard on her wrist.

"You will be cold in your lovely frock," he said.

"Oh, no, I am not in the least cold," she answered, shivering. They will be back in the ballroom now, Pat and Shelagh, she was thinking. Surely they will be back! It would be safe for Rod to return. But they did not move. Scarcely they seemed to breathe in the night's vast stillness. Beyond the lake which stretched before them the line of the hills was etched against the brightening sky. Dark mountains edged with silver, that turned to gold as the disc of the moon appeared. And all at once the whole valley was filled with the clear, unearthly radiance. Somewhere a nightingale, watching the moonrise even as they watched, poured out its cascade of song. Wild as the very voice of love unbridled, the rich notes bubbled up, spilled over, heartbreak and triumph blending.

There were tears in Gail's eyes, tears, wet on her cheeks. "Oh, Rod, it's so beautiful!" she whispered, hardly knowing that she spoke aloud. She felt his fingers tighten about her wrist—painfully—as he swung her round. And suddenly she was in his arms, his lips hard and purposeful on her quivering mouth. Savagely he kissed her . . . again and again. Kisses without tenderness. She was bruised, breathless, outraged, pushing him away from her, crying out: "How dare you do that? Oh, how could you?"

She saw him pale, dishevelled in the greenish moonlight, his eyes blazing, as breathless as herself, seemingly as angry. "That's what you wanted, wasn't it? That's what you were asking for?"

She covered her face with her hands, shaken, sickened, utterly bewildered. "I don't understand you!" she moaned.

"But I, unfortunately, understand you all too well."

"You're not unique, Gail," he added after a moment's silence. His voice was flat now, unutterably weary. "There are a good many of your sort in a man's lifetime, you know," he said.

With a blind stumbling movement she turned from him, hurrying up the rough sloping ground, reaching the drive.

"Where are you going?" he called after her. She did not answer him, fleeing like a wounded creature driven by the instinct that bids it hide its wounds. For a time it seemed as if his footsteps followed her and then he was not there any more and she was running under dark trees, deeper and deeper into the woods. Intuitively she had chosen the direction that led away from the Castle. But she had no idea where she was going, nor how long she kept on her blind way. Only longing to lose herself, hide for ever, here in the thick gloom of trees. Moss-covered rocks loomed up in the shadows, like crouching beasts. There was a strange, moist, earthy odor. Wild garlic. She had left the pathway now, was crushing the pungent herb under her feet. The ground rose steeply. She stumbled on, climbing, briars catching at her silken skirts, but she did not care. There were briars catching at her heart, lacerating it! Why had Rod treated her so . . . horribly? Those scornful, cruel kisses. "That's what you wanted, wasn't it? That's what you were asking for!" Oh, how could he think of her like that! Imagining that she had lured him down to the lakeside in the moonlight like any cheap little flirt. Was that how he had always seen her?

Panting, she reached the top of the incline, and here the ground fell sharply away, halting her crazy progress. It was a sheer precipice that lay before her, a drop of some hundred feet, perhaps. She looked down into a hollow, clear of trees, filled with the sharp silver tones of moonlight that picked out rocks, thorn bushes, a stretch of grass that might have been a neglected lawn, the gable-end of a house covered in creeper. Dully, she took it all in, tired suddenly with her hurrying, scrambling journey. Leaning against a boulder rock she waited, even then the

106

troubled intimation stirring in her, the knowledge that she was not alone in this seemingly deserted wilderness.

She was not afraid at first, only curiously alert—as a hunted animal might have been. It was almost as though she had been expecting them when she saw the furtive figures coming round the gable-end of the house to move across the moon-bright sward beneath her; like actors making their entrance on to some shadowy stage. Young men walking in single file as though in some weird ritual march. Curiously fragile and without substance they appeared in the greeny twilight. But there was nothing ethereal about the glint of steel that went with them. Evil as murder, the rifle barrels poised on their shoulders.

Gail caught her breath. Men marching with guns . . . here in Laheen Woods, in the middle of the night, not a mile from the Castle! What could their purpose be? Nothing lawful, it was quite obvious! Her heart froze as she watched the final figure emerge from the shadows of the house. Big, burly, lumbering, familiar with its hint of menace. It was Leahy who stepped forth now into the moonlit arena, a pistol in a holster strapped to his side.

CHAPTER NINE

THE way back to the Castle seemed endless. Not until she reached the drive did Gail dare to run openly. Creeping stealthily down the boulder-strewn hill, she had halted at intervals to listen. Had the gunmen seen her? Were they following her? Or could they be making for the Castle by some other route?

Fragments of half-remembered Irish history floated to the surface of her distracted mind. Wasn't it true that the peasantry had always loved organizing secret societies? She thought of a film she had recently seen in the peaceful suburban cinema at home: *Captain Boycott*. It had meant little to her at the time, but now she remembered that it had dealt with the long struggle of the dispossessed for land. Mary Crampton's Land League had had the same object. Her grandfather had lost his life fighting for people like Leahy. Was Leahy reviving that old conflict . . . preparing to defend his imagined right to his old home with violence? If so, Rod's life was—at this moment— in danger!

Panting, exhausted, her frock torn, her golden shoes in ruins, she reached Laheen at last. The great front doors stood open and the sound of music and laughter floated out to meet her as she entered the hall. How easy it would be for half a dozen armed men to walk in by this unprotected entry!

Her eyes wide with her wild, half-formulated fears, she stood on the threshold of the ballroom searching for Rod. The Dublin orchestra had disappeared and a shabby little man, his red cheeks puffed out to bursting point, was strutting up and down the dais playing a lively air on a set of bagpipes. The famous Micky Mulligan, Gail decided, not really caring. On the dance floor just in front of him, the young men in saffron kilts were going through the mazes of an intricate jig with a solemn concentrated energy, their faces wooden, their arms held stiffly to their sides, their feet flying back and forth soundlessly and with incredible lightness. Suddenly a mouth opened in one of the wooden faces and a wild "Wa-hoo!" rent the air. It was so unexpected that Gail, her nerves on edge with strain, almost jumped out of her skin. The Irish war cry. She had never heard it before and did not recognize it now, but its primitive savagery added the final touch to her terror. Where was Rod? Supposing he had not come back from the lake yet? Supposing the desperate young men with their guns encountered him out there alone in the moonlight? With renewed urgency she pushed her way through the groups of guests that clotted the sides of the dance floor.

The jig had ended now and applause broke out; cries of "Arish! Arish!"—the Gaelic encore. Laying his bagpipes aside Micky Mulligan sat down on one of the bandsmen's chairs, an accordion opening like a big solid fan upon his knees. In her green, embroidered robe, her golden hair flying, Mary Crampton appeared at his side. Flinging her arms dramatically aloft she began to make a speech in Gaelic.

108

"What on earth is it all about?" Gail heard a girl in a sophisticated frock say to her escort.

"She's telling us we've had American music, English music, Negro music all the evening," the young man explained. "And now we are to dance to our own good wholesome Irish airs. Got some pluck, hasn't she? Here right in the stronghold of the Philistines! She's sent the imported band packing, I believe."

"She's . . . wonderful!" the girl murmured on an oddly wistful note. "I wish she'd give us one of her songs, with the harp. I heard her singing at a *Ceilidhe* in Ardrossa one night; I'll never forget it."

"She says there's only one thing she'll sing in this place tonight," the young man replied. "A song for Shelagh, she called it."

Desperately, Gail broke in on them. "Have you seen Major Sterne anywhere?" she asked.

The girl gave her a startled glance, and suddenly Gail realized how wild her manner must seem, how dishevelled her appearance. But she did not care. "Major Sterne is just over there with Shelagh," the girl was answering her in a mildly surprised way.

With an almost unbearable surge of relief Gail saw him then, but before she could reach him Micky Mulligan's accordion was filling the room with a great volume of sound and as the opening bars of "The Little Red Fox" flowed out the dancers began to form figures for some kind of reel. Rod and Shelagh, Gail saw, were already dancing.

She drifted over to the doorway that led to the buffet, baffled, suddenly exhausted. The evening stretching behind her seemed now like some long protracted dream. That searing scene with Rod on the shores of the lake! For a little while she had almost forgotten it in her anguish of concern for him. But now it came back to her, bitter, hurtful. How could she possibly approach him after that humiliating kiss? What could she say to him? The memory of the drilling men in the moonlight seemed to her all at once fantastic . . . part of the strange, agonizing dream through which she was moving. Rod would laugh at her, perhaps. Or worse still, think that she was concocting

109

the whole thing in order to thrust herself once more upon his attention. Tears glistened on her lashes and the ball-room on which she looked swam indistinctly, a great whirling rainbow of colors and lights. She did not see Pat until he was close beside her.

"Don't you want to try this reel with me?" he asked.

She looked up at him through her wet lashes, wondering at his suave unruffled air. Had he already forgotten that heartbroken embrace in the shrubbery? But that too was only a part of her dream, Gail thought crazily. If she had not seen Shelagh and Pat in each other's arms . . . if she had not, in all innocence, led Rod away in an opposite direction. . . .

"What's up?" she heard Pat demand with more sympathy than elegance. Gruff now, uneasy at the sight of her tears, he was awkward as a boy looking down at her, seeing her distraught, bedraggled. "What on earth have you been doing to yourself, Gail?" he murmured, shocked. "There's blood on your cheek!"

She put her hand to the small dried scar where a briar had caught her. She had not felt it at the time. She gave a little laugh that was half a sob. "I was running through the woods . . ." she said. And suddenly her terror was clear and sharp again. She put a hand on his arm. He would help her . . . warn Rod for her. Why hadn't she thought of it before? Pat of all people would understand the significance of the strange drama she had witnessed played out by the old house in the moonlit hollow. Hurriedly, she began to pour out her story. She saw his face change, grow wary.

"You were away off there by yourself!" he broke in, as if playing for time. Her flight through the woods would seem to him extraordinary . . . she had overlooked that. A faint color washed over her wan, frightened little face.

"I went out for a breath of air," she offered stumblingly. "The moon was rising over the lake and I suppose I was fascinated, watching it; anyway, I went on and on, going farther than I realized."

"And you came to Creek Cottage," he prompted.

"I suppose it was Creek Cottage. A house in a hollow about a mile from here. I was looking down at it from the

110

high part of the woods and I saw these young men with rifles, and Leahy—giving them what sounded like orders, in Gaelic. He was carrying a great beastly revolver in a holster!"

The reel was at its height now, the air filled with the sound of stamping feet and shouting, laughing voices.

"What were they doing, Pat?" Gail begged. "We've got to tell Rod . . . Sir Charles . . ."

"No, we haven't, Gail!" Pat's voice was steely. "If you mention a word of this to Sir Charles or Rod you'll be doing more harm than good. Come over here until I talk to you!" He took her arm and urged her purposefully into the buffet where it was quieter. "I'll get you a drink. You look all in. Sit here now and take it easy for a minute. I'll be right back."

She sank down on to the deep couch he had indicated, aware all at once that she was dizzy with fatigue . . . with hunger. All evening she had been too distraught to eat and it was with absent-minded gratitude she saw the tray Pat was presently setting on a low table before her. Hot soup as well as sherry, an assortment of canapes and sandwiches.

" 'Tis practically breakfast time," he announced, and sitting down beside her he began on the sandwiches while she waited nervously for what he had to say.

"Listen to me now," he ordered presently, and quite unnecessarily, for she was only too eager for him to begin. "And for heaven's sake eat while you're listening! There's a wispy look about you, as though the wind would blow you away!" He pushed the bowl of soup towards her and waited until she had taken a spoonful or two. Then he said quietly: "You've walked into a nice mare's nest to-night, my child . . . but it will easily turn into a nest of stinging adders if you go stirring up things that don't concern you. Leahy has been using the cellars of that old house as a storing place for the goods he is smuggling."

"Smuggling!" Gail stared at him, and for a blissful instant it seemed as though the unexpected word settled everything, wiping away all apprehension.

"There's an inlet on the lake on the other side of the house," Pat went on. "And it is there Leahy keeps the turf barge he loads up with contraband. Turf on top, do you see, and under the turf the butter, whiskey, potheen, bacon, nylons . . . all the things that are scarce or rationed over the border."

"But the border is miles away, surely?" Gail protested.

"Not so far from the other end of the lake, which runs a good thirty miles up into the mountain country. Lorries pick up the stuff there and take it over into Fermanagh. Leahy has been making a good thing out of his little racket for a couple of years now; that's the main reason, I believe, he's so mad with Rod for planning to rebuild Creek Cottage. It will queer his pitch good and proper. I suppose he was clearing his stuff out tonight because he's got wind that there is a surveyor coming shortly to take over the job of demolishing. . . ."

"But . . . the guns?" Gail whispered, her uneasiness returning.

Pat shrugged. "Looks as if he was ready to shoot if anyone disturbed him. He's a fool," he murmured somberly. "And a dangerous fool. He's got those lads that have been helping him well under his thumb . . . a wild-headed gang of youngsters who are in it just for the devilment of the thing." For a moment he was silent. Then he took out his cigarette-case and offered it to her. As he held the lighter for her she saw that his hand wasn't quite steady.

"But surely Rod ought to know all this, Pat! Or the police?" Gail urged.

"The police!" He looked at her pityingly. "If you knew the first thing about your friend Leahy you wouldn't suggest that! Leave him alone and the whole thing has a chance to fizzle out. He'll find some other hide-out for his merchandise and that will be that. Soon enough, with rationing very nearly at an end and goods everywhere coming into sufficient supply, the racket will die a natural death. But . . . let Leahy in his present mood meet resistance from the Castle or the police and . . . there might well be a couple of deaths that wouldn't be natural

at all!" He laughed hollowly at this ghastly little witticism. In the warm bright room Gail shivered.

"But I don't see how I'm *not* going to tell Rod . . . Sir
Charles. . . . It seems so terrible that all this should go on
. . . unknown to them!" From some fresh depth of
anxiety the cry was wrung from her. How far could she
trust Pat Crampton? How was it he knew so much of
Leahy's lawless enterprise? His hand closed like a vice on
her wrist and she saw the beads of moisture that gathered
about his lips.

"For God's sake, Gail!" he whispered thickly, "can't
you realize the way things are! Give the least hint of this
to Rod and you put him and his uncle on the spot . .
absolutely. Charles is a magistrate. Did you know that?
It would be his duty to prosecute Leahy and being Si
Charles and a stickler for duty . . . he'd do it. Send
Leahy to jail with a fine that would bankrupt him."

"And why not?" Gail persisted.

Pat made a small despairing sound. "You don't know
the first thing about the Irish peasant mentality, do you?
Here you have Leahy . . . already nursing a grudge
against Sir Charles . . . because he terminated his
father's tenancy of Creek Cottage and made him the
outright owner of a fine farm instead. Oh, I know it
sounds mad to make a grievance out of such a generous
transaction . . . but that's the class of a lunatic Leahy is!
And then . . . on top of all that you suggest that Charles
should step in and smash up his little smuggling game.
Surely you can see the kind of vendetta that would
light up?"

Gail shook her head in unhappy bewilderment. "I . . .
just don't understand, Pat!"

"Then for heaven's sake leave it to someone who does.
I'll handle this. I'll watch out for the safety of the Major
and Sir Charles."

"You promise?" Her eyes were black-centred with
agonized indecision.

"If you'll promise me to keep your mouth shut."

"All right." It was little more than a whisper . . .
dragged from her. "I'll say nothing . . . for the moment.

113

But if I come across anything else that seems to me alarming . . ."

"You'll tell *me*," Pat broke in.

In the archway that separated buffet from ballroom a figure appeared, waving, gesticulating. Miss Quinn. "Ah, Gail, my dear! There you are!" she called with the triumph of a searcher rewarded. The talk with Pat was over. No more chance just now for the arguments, doubts, terrors that still seethed . . . and wouldn't be altogether allayed. Least said, soonest mended . . . she could see the point of that advice, and . . . Sir Charles sending Leahy to jail? Yes, she could well imagine the bitterness that would foster. But those guns! Those slinking, furtive figures on the moonlit grass!

Suppressing a shudder, Gail stood up. Miss Ross was very tired and wanted to go home. "I thought maybe you'd like to go with her," Miss Quinn smiled, heavily tactful, reminding Gail of her duties. But there was no sting now in the thought that she was not quite as these other young people who would dance until the sun rose. She was glad to be getting away from it all . . . had had more than enough of this evening of strangely mingling dramas. Shelagh and Rod . . . Shelagh and Pat . . . Pat and Leahy. Was there somewhere a sinister pattern in the interweaving strands?

She'd have gone home with Miss Ross, herself, Miss Quinn was explaining, as they skirted the ballroom arm in arm, only that Sir Charles had so kindly arranged for her to stay at the Castle for what was left of the night. "But we'll be coming over to Kildoona tomorrow, Mr. Darnow and I," she exulted. "Miss Ross has taken to him, praise be . . . and that's half the battle. And Sir Charles has been a jewel . . . talking her round, persuading her. . . ."

He was waiting with her in the hall when Gail came to them, and the old comfortable car was at the door. Lightly as he had carried her up the steps some five hours earlier he now carried her down, a weary, pain-worn woman in a silvery bridal gown. As Gail followed them she was aware of the sudden silence in the crowded glittering rooms behind them, and out of the silence, soft as the sound of weeping, came the throbbing music of a harp.

* * *

The next day was Saturday and well on into the morning Kildoona Lodge was somnolent, its occupants resting after the exertions of the night before. About eleven o'clock Gail got up and had breakfast alone. She told Bridget about the rooms which must be prepared for Miss Quinn and Mr. Darnow and then took the car into Ardrossa for the usual weekend shopping. It was a tranquil, grey morning with a warm southerly breeze flowing in gently across the lake. The mountains were vividly blue and seemed to have drawn nearer, which was generally a sign of rain to come.

Driving along the pleasant, winding road, Gail wondered at the curious flat peace which pervaded her. As though she were not yet wholly awake. But she had lived through the events of last night so intensely that for the moment her capacity for feeling seemed exhausted. Even her terror over Leahy was a little unreal now as she looked back on it. But when she saw him, drinking with a crony in the shadowy bar at the back of Whelan's shop, her heart missed a beat. If he asked her today to give him a lift, she would flatly refuse, she decided. However, he did not ask her, did not as much as turn to look at her as she hurried out of the shop, the assistant behind her carrying the Kildoona groceries. As she drove home she tried to think about him, calmly, objectively. He had seemed so . . . ordinary there in the village shop, a man moving at ease among his neighbors with no sinister purpose on his mind. Probably they all knew about his smuggling activities, helping him even, sharing in some small way the profits and excitements of the game. And, to the Irish, it was the excitement that would be the most important factor.

If the whole thing had not been more or less an open secret Pat wouldn't have known about it, Gail told herself, finding in the thought a comfort she was careful not to define. She didn't want to remember her momentary doubts of Pat's integrity. He had taken the smuggling calmly, but had pointed out to her how dangerous it might be if Rod or Sir Charles were roused to take any action

115

against it . . . and in that, she could see, he had been perfectly right. He had said he would keep an eye on the situation . . . watch out for the safety of Sir Charles and Rod. She must trust him, and try not to worry. It was quite true that she was completely out of her depth in this affair. She didn't understand this country or its ways. Things that would have been absolutely outrageous in England might be quite differently regarded here. It was all, no doubt, a matter of custom.

The reasonable thoughts ran on. Pat had been convincing . . . and yet, she wasn't, she knew, altogether convinced. But she was too tired to think about it clearly just now, suppressing the disturbing memory of Pat last night with Shelagh in his arms . . . crying out: "You can't marry him, Lalagh . . . you're mine . . . you always have been!" So easily it could all link up into a pattern too terrifying to contemplate!

That day they had ridden over to Carna—prompted her uneasy mind—and Pat had talked so strangely of Rod, insisting that he was marrying Shelagh for some material reason that had nothing to do with love; hinting at nameless treacheries, saying he would rather kill Rod with his two bare hands than have Shelagh hurt by him. Wild, exaggerated statements she had decided at the time not to take seriously. But now!

With a feeling of utter helplessness her thoughts reached deadlock. Would Pat keep his promise and watch over Leahy's very odd activities—with an eye to Rod's safety? She must try to believe that he would. To think anything else was intolerable. Pat was young, impetuous, madly in love with Shelagh, but he was not a cold-blooded villain, capable of planning or conniving at some indefinable violence against Rod.

Firmly she told herself this as she drove along the quiet lakeside road. But at the bottom of her heart the doubts remained. There was nothing she could do about them, however, only wait with sharpened awareness for any fresh developments that might arise.

116

CHAPTER TEN

WHEN she got back to Kildoona it was almost lunch time and Bridget was coming through the baize-covered door into the hall with a tray of tea-things in her hands.

"Miss Shelagh is dead after the ball!" she announced with simple relish. "She's not getting up yet and doesn't want any lunch, only this drop of tea I'm bringing up to her."

"Give it to me and I'll take it," Gail offered, with a sudden desire to see Shelagh, and talk over last night's party . . . omitting its more uncomfortable undercurrents. A young, lighthearted discussion of frocks, guests; all the small foolish matters that are such fun to go over afterwards. And she wanted to know if Mary Crampton had sung the promised song that was to be for Shelagh alone. There was something a little mysterious about that song!

She found Shelagh sitting up in bed tousled and curiously puffy-eyed, as though she had been weeping, not recently, but with a violence that had left its mark through all the hours of her sleep. Her room was in wildest disorder, the lovely pink frock thrown like a rag upon the floor, shoes, diaphanous undies and stockings, the dead pink roses strewn around it.

Gail put the tea tray on the table beside the bed. "I hope you've brought me what Micky Mulligan would call a corpse reviver!" Shelagh greeted her, with a rather forced little laugh. "The soles of my feet are destroyed!" She stretched her thin, childish arms above her head with a vast yawn. "I danced nearly every dance . . . !"

"It was a terrific party," Gail agreed, seating herself at the foot of the tumbled bed.

"It was a horrible party!" Shelagh said with sudden passion, her speedwell blue eyes welling up. Angrily she dashed the tears away. "I had a row with Pat," she explained.

Gail picked up the teapot. "Have a cuppa," she offered. "It will make things seem a little better maybe."

Shelagh took the tea in silence. So the scene in the shrubbery had ended with a snub for Pat, Gail was thinking. Well, he had certainly earned it. And yet she couldn't help remembering the caressing note in Shelagh's voice, murmuring, "Ah, Pat, you're sweet!"

"He has always been like . . . a brother to me," she was saying now. "Maybe a bit more than that." She laughed shakily. "I proposed to him when I was ten . . . and he accepted me. It was all just nonsense of course, though maybe I didn't think so at the time. I remember feeling that I simply had to make sure of him, that if I waited until I was grown up to mention my devotion some other girl might get in first!" She laughed again. "But it was all kid stuff, of course. The awkward thing is that some of it seems to have stuck . . . with Pat. He can't get used to the idea of my being in love with Rod. He hates Rod!" she whispered.

"I suppose that's natural enough," Gail said, trying not to notice the queer cold feeling the whispered words brought to her. "Did Mrs. Crampton sing you your special song?" she asked.

Shelagh nodded, sipping contemplatively at her tea. "That was another not so good moment. It was the old song about the twisting of the rope. Everybody knows the story . . . it is done as a play sometimes. She sang it in Gaelic of course and then in case its significance might be lost on Rod and the other English people present, she translated it. It's the story of a foreigner who fell in love with an Irish girl. When he came to her home to claim her, her mother, set on saving her daughter from marrying a man not of her own blood, determined to get rid of him. She was twisting a rope of straw for the thatching of the house and she asked the unwanted suitor to hold one end of it. He had to keep stepping backwards as the rope lengthened and as soon as he was over the threshold of the house door she slammed it in his face." Shelagh shrugged. "You can imagine what dear Mrs. C. made of *that* little allegory. Oh, she was *awful*, standing up there on the dais with her great eyes blazing, saying the old wisdom was the only wisdom. You couldn't possibly mistake her meaning! She might as well have said straight out that she thinks my engagement to Rod is a terrible mistake—a piece of treachery to Ireland and her queer fanatical faith. People tittered, and Rod . . . well, naturally he was furious. But he was in such a strange difficult mood all the evening!"

Gail's heart lurched. "I'm sure he wasn't. You're imagining things," she said firmly.

"Do you think I am? Sometimes I feel so . . . unsure about everything. Rod is always wonderful to me, kind, tender, perfectly sweet, but I get a feeling now and then that he doesn't feel quite the way about me that I do about him."

There was something so pitiful in the small white face under its mop of sleep-tousled curly hair that Gail turned sharply away. Going over to the window she stood looking down at the still grey lake. Last night it had shone under the moon, a floor of ebony and silver. Last night!

She said in a rather muffled voice: "I'm sure you're worrying yourself without cause. Perhaps people do sometimes when they are engaged. I've never been engaged, so I wouldn't know. But I understand it's quite in order to have attacks of jittering and doubt. Not that you need have them. Rod adores you. It's so obvious!"

If there was a note of bitterness in her voice Shelagh didn't seem to be aware of it, intent on her own unhappy thoughts. "What seems to be obvious to Glenda Grayson," she said, "is that Rod is marrying me to please Sir Charles!"

Gail swung round. "Glenda Grayson!" The exclamation was out before she could stop it, but Shelagh, taking it for a question, answered: "The tall fair woman who came with Sonia yesterday. I don't know if you noticed her, terribly chic, wearing slinky black and pearls. She's a third cousin of Rod's. Lives in Paris with her brother who is something in the Embassy there. Rod always stays with them when he is in Paris and Glenda is more than a bit fond of him. In fact I think she'd decided to marry him herself and it must have been a bit of a jolt for her when our engagement was announced."

"Well, in that case, I shouldn't take any of the more catty things she says to you too seriously," Gail offered sensibly. "She's probably wild with jealousy. As for Rod

119

marrying you to please his uncle, I never heard anything so fantastic . . . !"

"It didn't seem fantastic the way Glenda put it last night." Shelagh's voice quivered ominously. "Very clever it was, all tied up in laughing hints and gay little innuendoes. But I got her meaning all right! I knew of course that Charles was pleased when Rod and I fell in love that week after the Horse Show last year . . . when I was staying at Sonia's. And I knew Charles promised then that he would make Rod's inheritance available to him right away instead of leaving it to him in his will . . . as a sort of wedding present. But I never regarded it as a bargain . . . a payment for marrying me!"

Gail's cheeks went hot. "What a beast this Glenda woman must be to even suggest such a thing!" she cried on a surge of sheer healthy young anger.

"She's a very clever beast," Shelagh said in a tight goaded voice.

Pushing the bedclothes back she jumped out of bed and began padding about the room, picking up last night's discarded flowers and finery. Like a lost Ophelia she stood with the withered flowers in her hands, her face drawn, strangely old suddenly, all the light gone from her eyes under their swollen lids. "I know it's silly of me to get so worked up about it. I wouldn't if I was a hundred per cent certain of Rod . . . but I'm not. I don't think I ever have been. I've always felt he must have known so many women far more clever and amusing than I am . . . and last night Glenda was throwing out dark hints about someone he was supposed to have been very much in love with, someone completely impossible but I expect frightfully attractive. A typist or shop girl or something. Glenda didn't really seem very sure about her and didn't know her name. Sonia told her about it after my engagement to Rod was announced, saying she was so thankful I'd come along in the nick of time to save Rod from making a fool of himself."

Gail stood motionless, her face carefully blank, the palms of her clenched hands wet. But in that instant of electrified silence her heart soared . . . and fell, lay in

120

her breast very still like a winged bird. "He was . . . in love with her!" she whispered.

"The typist person?" Shelagh retrieved a rosy taffeta petticoat from the floor and hung it on the back of a chair with an air of desperate concentration. "So Glenda seems to think. At all events Sonia was pretty worried about the affair, so I suppose there must have been something in it." She brushed the back of her hand across her eyes; a childish, defenceless gesture that smote Gail's heart. "I can see now on looking back," the troubled young voice went on, "how avidly Sonia seized on me! Not that I was really the sort of person she'd have wanted for Rod; she was very ambitious for him. But Charles was staying at Regency Gardens too that week and he'd have talked to her perhaps. She'd have liked the sound of the Bowfort millions! In fact they may have planned the whole thing together, more or less, throwing me at Rod, making this bargain with him about the inheritance so that he'd marry me instead of the typist or whoever it was."

"Did Glenda put it like that?"

"She hinted at it."

Gail drew in a long steadying breath. "I've never heard anything so absolutely . . . foul!"

Shelagh shrugged. "Well, it all does rather tie up, doesn't it? Charles suddenly discovering I was grown up enough to be in love with Rod and thinking what a good idea it would be for me to come as his wife to Laheen Castle . . . you know he has always wanted us to have our old home back . . . he's so fond of Aunt Dodie! And Sonia, anxious to save Rod from the siren, and of course overjoyed when she found Rod was to come into his uncle's fortune right away. . . . Naturally, they both did quite a bit of clever managing, forcing the situation along. While I, like a fool, thought it was all my own work! Believed Rod was as much in love with me as I was with him . . ." The words trailed away brokenly.

"And you were right. I'm sure you were!" Gail took the dressing gown flung over the end of the bed, and with a motherly little air wrapped it about Shelagh's thin, bare shoulders. "No matter how many sirens there were in the offing before you came on the scene they wouldn't have

121

mattered to him a hoot as soon as he found you in your . . . new mood. You must see why Glenda tried to put all these horrid ideas into your mind; she's just beside herself with jealousy."

Somehow she made herself meet steadily the questioning look in the very blue eyes turned to her. "Oh, Gail, you're so comforting! Perhaps I am making mountains out of molehills. But I can't help wishing Charles hadn't decided to give Rod that kind of fabulous wedding present."

"Rod isn't the sort of man who could be . . . bought," Gail declared loyally. Suddenly her hands on Shelagh's shoulders went rigid and she was remembering that day by the lake at Carna House when he had told her the strange old folk-tale of the singing swans, Caer and Aengus. The star-crossed lovers who in order to straighten out their unhappy story had had to sacrifice what he had called "all worldly considerations". Had he been thinking then of his great future? And of her own humble self who could have no part in it? She thrust the wild surmise away from her, but the tumult in her heart would not be quite controlled, frightening her by its intensity. This extraordinary conversation! It was so unexpected and she had not yet found the inner armor with which she must meet its implications. In a dazed way she watched Shelagh fastening the silken dressing gown about her slim waist, stooping then to search for slippers kicked under the valances of her bed.

She said musingly: "I imagine if Rod had really been in love —in the only way I'd mind him being in love— with that unsuitable girl, it would have taken more than me to upset the apple cart. Even if I was offered to him with the Bowfort money tagged on. I mean, he isn't a person it would be easy to change if he had once made up his mind about anything."

"He certainly isn't," Gail forced herself to agree. And yet, she thought, how cleverly Sonia had circumvented him! Utilizing Glenda's arrival that evening to shatter a heart too young, too unsure of itself and its heady dreams. Oh, she had summed up the situation brilliantly, moved swiftly, ruthlessly and with complete success.

If I had refused to believe her that night, seen through her ruse, if I had ignored Glenda, gone on to the party at the Savoy after the Show . . . Gail brushed the useless speculations aside. It was too late for might-have-beens. Whatever Rod might have felt for her last year it was quite clear that he despised her now. Those cruel kisses last night by the lake had told her all she needed to know. And he was promised to Shelagh, sweet, beautiful, adoring enough to heal the wounds in any man's heart. In a few weeks' time they would be married. On a surge of pain she heard herself cry out: "I don't know why you are tormenting yourself; you've got so much. You've got everything! Rod is marrying you . . . not for castles and fortunes, but because he loves you. It's so obvious," she reiterated, ignoring her own pain, "that it is more than that jealous fiend Glenda can bear. You ought not to give her another thought."

"Perhaps I am being an awful little juggins," Shelagh agreed with a small uncertain smile. "But so many things went wrong last night: Pat's tantrums, and Rod being in one of his moods and then Mrs. Crampton singing that crazy song at me . . . making me feel somehow as if she was putting a curse on me. Like a beautiful green witch sitting there with her harp . . . twisting a rope of words to send Rod away from me. And on top of all that Glenda . . . with her spiteful insinuations; I began to feel as if everyone was against me . . . trying to break up my engagement."

"Outsiders can't break up engagements," Gail said softly.

Drawing her thin silken robe closer about her, Shelagh shivered. "That's true enough. But things can go wrong. Sometimes I get the queerest feeling that I'll never marry Rod. . . ."

"You're just imagining things because you're tired," Gail said.

"Well, I'll go and have that bath." Shelagh padded across the room. "Rod's coming to tea when he gets back from taking Sonia and that snake Glenda to the airport, and I can't let him find me looking the wreck I am. That *would* be the end of everything between us!" With a

123

shaken little laugh she was gone and Gail began to tidy the littered room with a furious energy, her mouth set in a hard line, her eyes wide and dark in her white face. Like a hunted thing she was, moving blindly, frenziedly, putting away the tumbled pink frock, pink slippers . . . pink roses, withered now. The roses Rod had sent to Shelagh last night. With a little cry she buried her face in them and felt their wilted petals cold against her lips.

CHAPTER ELEVEN

The following afternoon Miss Quinn invited Gail to go for a row with her on the lake. "The people in this place," she declared, "are so taken up with their old nags and horses and endless riding here and there that they never lift an oar in their hands. But I love the water and to me Laheen is the most beautiful lake in the whole world. I'm not going back to Dublin tomorrow morning without my little row round. Would you like to come with me, my dear?"

They found the rusted keys that fitted into the lock of the neglected boathouse—half hidden by rushes and climbing weeds, and now they were moving slowly across the milky-pale expanse, Miss Quinn handling the sculls with surprising energy, while Gail steered. A special Sunday quietness seemed to enfold the far blue hills and somewhere a church bell was ringing. Shelagh had ridden off on Finn after lunch to join Rod for some unspecified expedition. Miss Ross was resting, still weary after the ball and with the ordeal of a morning spent under the hands of Mr. Darnow the osteopath—whom they had left dozing in a deck chair on the lawn.

"But he is always exhausted after examining a patient," Miss Quinn was explaining, as she bent back and forth over her oars. "He is more of a healer than a doctor," she added with unconscious irony. "Some virtue goes out of him when he touches a patient. I was watching him this morning with Miss Ross; it was as if he was drawing the pain out of her into himself. I saw his face go white with the strain of it, and there she was afterwards moving across the room with almost no effort."

"But surely he hasn't cured her as easily as all that!" Gail exclaimed incredulously. Sometimes it was a little difficult to disentangle the truth from the dramatic trimmings of Miss Quinn's statements. But then, Gail had discovered, most conversations in Ireland were like that.

"No, he hasn't cured her yet," Miss Quinn was saying. "But it is my belief he has a good chance of success. What he did this morning was to find the root of the trouble, the place in her poor spine where the bones are grown together in the scar of the old injury. If they could clear the thickened tissue away she would be able to walk without pain, he says, and he wants her to come up to Dublin to his own nursing home for the initial treatment. She'd never regain her old suppleness, of course, it's too late for that; but at least she wouldn't be the total cripple she is now. But it's not going to be easy to persuade her. Doctors have raised her hopes before now. In the beginning she had operation after operation but they did her no good."

Gail looked out over the bright smooth water, her eyes soft with pity as she thought of the long years of pain . . . and hope deferred. "What makes you think Mr. Darnow can succeed where the others have failed?" she asked.

"Well, it would be something new . . . and nothing to do with surgery. He'd be treating her by radiation, massage, remedial exercises. It would take time and patience, but I think maybe she'd agree to go through with it if I could be with her. I'd have to hand 'Avonlea' over to a friend of mine for a few months," Miss Quinn mused. "But I wouldn't make a trouble of *that*. Indeed I'd give the place up entirely if I thought it would help my poor Miss Dodie to regain her health," she ended with simple devotion.

They rowed on for a while in silence and presently the water about them narrowed and they were turning down a long shady inlet. "This is the way to Creek Cottage," Miss Quinn said. "It's a pretty little place—you ought to see it, though it's a bit dilapidated as nobody has lived in it for years. Some people called Leahy rented it in the old days and then Sir Charles had the idea of turning it into a fishing lodge again—which was what it was designed for. But it never came to anything. Now Major Sterne is taking it over, I believe, having it rebuilt for some English horse trainer he is bringing over."

They slid round a clump of overhanging willows and suddenly the lake had widened out again, so that the house set on rising ground with the beech woods soaring behind it looked out over a great expanse of water to the hills beyond. Gail caught her breath. It was hard to believe that this long rambling stone house with its draping of roses and wistaria was the same place she had seen from the wooded side on the night of the ball. There was nothing sinister about it in the clear afternoon sunlight. It looked homely and welcoming with its wide stone porch and open front door.

"Someone is here before us!" Miss Quinn exclaimed, and just at that moment Rod and Shelagh came out of the open door and saw them. Shelagh waved to them enthusiastically. "She wants us to go up to her," Miss Quinn decided happily and with an expert movement seized the painter and tied it to an overhanging branch.

Climbing the grassy slope to the house Gail felt her heart contract. She had carefully kept out of the way when Rod came to Kildoona yesterday. Not since that nightmare encounter in the moonlight on the evening of the dance had she found herself face to face with him, but there was no avoiding him now. On the steps of the porch he awaited them, his arm lightly about Shelagh's shoulder. There were no tear stains on her lovely little face today. She looked utterly happy.

"Are we intruding?" Miss Quinn called archly.

Shelagh's whole-hearted laughter rang out. "You're just in time to help us to decide on the drawing-room furniture," she said. "We've been going over the whole house, deciding we'd much rather live here than at the Castle."

So that was the reason for her happiness, Gail thought. Rod didn't want castles or fortunes after all . . . just love in Creek Cottage!

They were all trooping into the rather musty-smelling hall then. The tiled floor was broken in places. Paper hung damply from the walls in discolored strips, but the staircase sweeping up to the balustraded gallery that was the

126

first floor landing had nobility of line, and the twin newel posts were beautifully carved.

"Solid bog oak," Rod said, as he touched them in passing, "as sound now as it was the day it was dug out of the mountain-side a hundred years ago. The old house is full of it, it has been used for floors, stairs, doors . . . it would be a shame to discard it."

"We won't discard it, we'll build round it," Shelagh declared. "It would be absolute vandalism to pull Creek Cottage down and put up some horrible modern concrete thing instead. All we shall need is a fresh roof and a lick of paint and the new wing Rod is planning to take the place of the dark, tumble-down kitchen. We're going to have a lot of those trees at the back cut down to let in light and air."

They went into the room Shelagh called the drawing-room, a long oval apartment with large windows on two sides of it. "Imagine having curved walls!" she exulted.

"It's pure eighteenth century," Rod said. "And that's an Adam fireplace if I'm not very much mistaken."

"Well, you'll have plenty of Adam fireplaces at the Castle," Miss Quinn reminded him, not quite approving of this game of make-believe the lovers were playing. "Living at Creek Cottage indeed! You'd soon tire of it."

She led the way firmly out into the hall again and, penetrating the darker regions at the back of the house, exclaimed in disgust at the dust and dirt of the kitchen and scullery and pantries. "Will you look at those cobwebs on the cellar stairs!" she cried, and seeing the cavernous descent into inkly blackness Gail thought uneasily of Leahy. Had he succeeded in removing all his illegal stores? she wondered. She wished she hadn't found out about his smuggling activities—knowing it and not being free to speak of it made her feel sly and dishonest.

When they came out into the courtyard under the over-hanging trees she looked up at the place where she had stood on the night of the dance. There was the stretch of greensward on which the young men with guns had gone through their strange clumsy ritual of drilling and marching. Drifting over the damp, too densely shaded grass she saw a white square of card tacked to the smooth grey bole

127

of the soaring tree which stood alone at the table end of the house. There were scrawled printed words on it . . . crazy words . . . threatening. With a tremor of fear in her voice she called: "Shelagh, come here a minute!" But it was Rod who presently stood at her side reading aloud the strange notice: "The Curse of Balor of the Evil Eye on him who cuts this tree!"

"Looks like one of Leahy's tricks." Impatiently Rod tore the white card from the tree and threw it on the ground. With a little cry of protest Miss Quinn picked it up, her plump face filled with concern.

"Who is Balor when he's at home?" Rod laughed.

Miss Quinn gulped. "The ancient God of Life and Death. Nobody believes the old pagan tales about him now, of course, but superstition dies hard in country places and there are still villages out West where the feast day of Balor is kept on the first of May. Branches of green are hung all over the house doors to protect the occupants from the Evil Eye." She looked up at the green canopy above them. "This it would seem is regarded as a fairy tree. There are lots of them about and it's supposed to bring bad luck if they are cut down."

"Was this one of the trees you'd marked for destruction?" Shelagh asked Rod.

He nodded. "It's right in the way of that new wing I'm having put on at this end of the house."

"You'll upset Leahy if you do cut that tree," Miss Quinn warned. "These old beliefs go pretty deep."

Rod shrugged. "Leahy is too tough a specimen to fall for old wives' tales. And if he thinks I'm that easily scared he's got another think coming to him. The whole of it is, he's annoyed because he can't use Creek cottage any longer. My uncle allowed him to store turf here—peat that he cuts from bogs on this side of the lake. He'd keep it here a while and then take it over to Ardrossa by boat."

Did Rod know there had been other things beside turf stored in the old cellars and taken across the lake? Sharply Gail glanced at him. For an instant their eyes met. She saw the queer little points of flame that kindled in the light yellowish pupils, a flicker of scorn darting out at her, a momentary unwilling awareness of her existence. She turned away, her color changing, Leahy forgotten. Rod actively disliked her, couldn't stand the sight of her, she told herself bleakly. It was inevitable perhaps that it should be so, but it was going to make her remaining weeks at Kildoona pretty uncomfortable.

As they walked back to the boat Miss Quinn was telling a long rambling story about a peasant farmer she had known in her youth who had moved from his two-roomed cabin to a new house he had built, cutting down a fairy tree that had stood in the way. "Before a year was out his wife and his two fine sons were dead," she recounted. "The poor man, left only with a daughter who was soon stricken with consumption, moved back to the cabin and the new house was left empty to rot quietly away. There was no one who would set foot in it from that day."

"And you think the poor farmer's misfortunes were all the doing of this gentleman with the Evil Eye?" Rod mocked her gently.

"It was probably sheer coincidence," Miss Quinn murmured a little uncertainly. "I'm just telling you the story as it happened. I was young at the time and it made an impression on me."

"Perhaps we could fool Mr. Balor by changing the name of the house," Rod teased. "Go back to the old name which is so much more impressive."

"Teacht-an-Gail," said Shelagh. "The House of Gail." She laughed, her blue eyes mischievous. "If it's called that, Gail would have to come and live in it. She could fall in love with the English trainer and marry him, and I would be stuck over there in that great barracks of a Castle envying her for the rest of my life." There was a sudden desperation in her young voice which was not lost on the shrewdly observant Miss Quinn .

"It wasn't all joking, that talk against the Castle," she said to Gail as they were rowing home. "I've heard her at it several times this weekend. The trouble with Shelagh is that she hates the thought of growing up. Picnicking with Rod in a cottage, playing at life, would suit her down to the ground, but she doesn't want the responsibility of being a great lady."

"She's very young," Gail said.

129

"And very silly in some ways," Miss Quinn amended sternly. "Love and marriage isn't something to be looked at through an impossible golden haze. It's a settling down to the full life of womanhood, and believe me that entails hardships whatever the background. You go through a door into the world of reality when you put that little gold ring on your third left-hand finger!"

She caught the twinkle in Gail's hazel eyes. "Oh, I know I'm just an old maid talking," she conceded. "But I've seen plenty of life in my time. Nurses do, you know! Men are men all the world over and there isn't one of them that is altogether easy to live with. But that's a little aspect of the matter that poetry and story-books and films leave strictly alone . . . more's the pity!"

Would Rod be easy to live with? Trailing her fingers in the mild lake water Gail felt a queer little thrill of exaltation run through her veins. Like a call to battle.

"Major Sterne now," she heard Miss Quinn say, "he'll need pretty careful handling. Autocratic, not over-patient, used to his bachelor freedom, he'll not take to running in harness any too smoothly unless it's with the right woman."

"And you think Shelagh is the right woman?" For the life of her Gail couldn't keep that question back, though she colored up as soon as it was out.

Miss Quinn gave her a shrewd quick glance. "Almost any woman who is really in love with her man is the right woman."

Something in her tone made Gail say hurriedly, almost defensively: "That puts Shelagh in the clear then."

Miss Quinn nodded, her round blue eyes gazing blindly out over the wide water. "Oh, Shelagh is in love all right," she said after a long musing pause. "In love with her own easy dreams. She's like hundreds of starry-eyed young brides before her and, like most of them, I daresay she'll wake up . . . and grow up . . . without undue fuss when the time comes and make a thriving success of being the Lady of Laheen.

"We were all young once," she added presently with a reminiscent sigh. A wistful remark that seemed to include Gail, making her feel old and lost and curiously lonely.

Could life be over at twenty-one? she wondered and caught the glint of amusement in the round blue eyes watching her. "Cheer up, me dear," Miss Quinn laughed cryptically. "You're not on the shelf yet, by a long way—and if it's a trite saying it's a true one . . . there's as good fish in the sea, or Lake Laheen for that matter, as ever yet came out of it!"

Gail went crimson. Was she really as transparent as all that, she wondered, or was Miss Quinn a thought reader? There was something disturbing about this plump little Irish woman with her acute perceptions. But Ireland was a disturbing country with its sacred trees and evil-eyed gods, its mixture of shrewdness and credulity, of mysticism and sheer hard common sense.

The next day Miss Quinn and Mr. Darnow went back to Dublin. Gail drove them to the station. Sir Charles had spent a persuasive evening with Miss Ross the night before and she had at last agreed to try Mr. Darnow's treatment. At least, she had declared, it could do her no harm. And it was odd, almost unbelievable, how much her pain had eased even after one manipulation from the osteopath's hands. It was that factor perhaps as much as Sir Charles' arguments which had made her agree to go to the Dublin nursing home as soon as it could be arranged. But the wedding preparations must not be hindered. Late into the night Miss Ross had sat, propped up on the pillows of her great silk-curtained bed, ordering her household. She sent for Mrs. Murphy, for Gail, and Shelagh in turn. The wedding date, she had insisted, must now be fixed. Argumentative, a little tearful, Shelagh had agreed to the last week in July. "That will give us almost seven weeks," Miss Ross told Gail. "I shall not be away more than a fortnight, Mr. Darnow assures me, and during that time Miss Quinn will be here with you and Shelagh."

"I'll be right back," that devoted soul said now to Gail as they drove along the lake road, "as soon as I have my affairs at 'Avonlea' fixed up. And I'll stay on then through the summer. There'll be a resident masseuse with Miss Ross for weeks after she comes home, I expect, but she'll need me as well." From the back seat where he sat in a state of Buddha-like calm Mr. Darnow made a small

131

sound of assent to this remark. He was a man of singularly few words, but when he did speak it was with authority. He seemed completely sure of himself.

When she had seen the rather oddly assorted couple safely into the Dublin express, Gail drove back through the streets of the little town. Shelagh had asked her to deliver a note to Pat Crampton. "It's about entering Finn for the Ardrossa Races in July," she had explained unnecessarily and somehow a little guiltily. "Even if it is due to take place the day before my wedding, I'm going to ride in the open race," she had added defiantly. "It's the most amusing event in the whole meeting, people turning up on every imaginable mount from thoroughbreds to cart-horses; even donkeys have been known to join in—unofficially! I wouldn't miss it for anything."

Gail wondered now if Miss Ross knew of this decision. It was unlikely that she would approve. The weeks before the wedding were already full enough and there would be little time for Shelagh to get Finn and herself into training; for even though the village races were hardly to be taken seriously, Finn was scarcely yet broken. Gail thought of her own accumulation of duties, the wedding invitations that would have to be sent out, the sorting and listing of the household linen Shelagh would take to the Castle with her—Miss Ross' lavish gift. Every article was to bear its hand-worked monogram and this was to be done at the Convent, Gail being responsible for taking the stuff there and seeing it was back in good time. Then there was the July house-party at the Castle, including Chardin the great dress designer, who would bring with him Shelagh's wedding gown and supervise its final fitting.

But by the end of July I shall be finished with all of them, she reminded herself as she turned into the street of the rushing rivers that led to the Cramptons' house. Sonia, Miss Ross, Miss Quinn . . . even Rod and Shelagh; soon they would be no more than memories. Somehow the thought was not so consoling as it ought to have been, and it was with a queer hollow sense of loss that she got out of the car and knocked at the half-open door before her. Would her heart never learn its grim lesson? she wondered. She meant so little to these people who employed her . . .

nothing at all to Rodwell Sterne, in spite of Shelagh's revelations on the morning after the ball. Endlessly Gail had thought over Glenda Grayson's spiteful hints of his preoccupation with the "unsuitable typist person". A story that could mean so much, or so little. If he had really loved this unknown rival, Shelagh had wisely pointed out, he would not so easily have let her go. And of course she was right; Rod was a tenacious man, and a very determined one. But however that might be, it was too late now for speculations. If Rod had ever been attracted by her it was abundantly clear that he was cured now, Gail told herself bitterly and for the twentieth time, as she stood waiting at the Cramptons' door.

There had been no response to her knock and after another moment or two, remembering how the roaring of the rushing rivers could drown all sounds within the house, she went into the hall and tapped on the drawing-room door. She could hear voices within and presently Pat appeared. At the sight of her he seemed a little confused and he did not invite her in. Stepping out into the hall, he murmured something apologetic about a visitor who had come to see his mother on a bit of business. But she had only dropped in to bring a note from Shelagh, Gail explained, handing Pat the envelope. As he took it, her glance went involuntarily to the crack of the door he had left ajar behind him and she saw that it was Leahy who was in the drawing-room, seated on the black oil-loth couch deeply engrossed in conversation with Mrs. Crampton.

CHAPTER TWELVE

ALMOST unseeingly Gail drove back to Kildoona Lodge that blue and gold June morning. Pat and his mother and Leahy closeted together. Was there any significance in their meeting, any reason for the fresh uneasiness that now assailed her? She had tried to put the business of the armed men and their smuggling out of her mind. But yesterday there had been the threatening notice on the

133

beech tree at Creek Cottage. And now this. Was there a link-up anywhere in this series of rather odd happenings? Probably not. It was fantastic to imagine dangers to Rod at every juncture. Just because the thought of him haunted her . . . was for ever in her heart! Mrs. Crampton could quite well have been ordering her winter supply of turf just now . . . and Leahy was no doubt a life-long acquaintance. One did business with old acquaintances in Ireland, even turf cutters, on a social basis. It was a courteous and hospitable country, Gail reminded herself. A country she did not yet altogether understand. It was foolish to worry over things one did not understand, foolish to jump to wild conclusions, seeing not only Pat now, but his mother as accomplices in some fantastic plot!

And indeed in the days that followed there was little time for worrying. Gail was kept hard at work helping Miss Ross to prepare for her departure to the nursing home. Every day there was a fresh spate of instructions relating to the duties to be performed in her absence. The printers must be telephoned daily until the cards for the wedding invitations were delivered. They were already overdue. A dozen times Miss Ross went over the list of guests, adding fresh names. The decorating of the little chapel at the Castle was to be left to Gail. A great honor, Miss Ross indicated, and a greater responsibility. Gail must go over to Laheen at once and confer with the head gardener, presenting her scheme of flowers for his approval, finding out if he could supply all she would need. If not a Dublin florist must be enlisted.

The wedding reception was to take place at Kildoona. Miss Ross, a stickler for etiquette, had insisted upon this, refusing all Sir Charles' offers of the more spacious accommodation at Laheen. A bride must be married from her own home. So to Gail, too, would fall the arranging with caterers, the checking over of menus, wine lists, the selection of a suitable marquee to be erected on the lawn.

"Shelagh will help you with all this, of course," Miss Ross declared in happy innocence, while in the paddock beyond the azaleas her niece rode hour after hour on the skittish young Finnmacool, putting him to the jumps which Pat had set up—an eager-eyed, ever-present Pat who alone with Gail shared the secret of the enterprise that loomed. Miss Ross, Gail discovered, had not been told of the race in which a bride would compete (to the horror and delight of the County no doubt) the day before her wedding. And the jumps in the paddock were but a preliminary, it seemed. Later there would be gruelling cross-country tests, when more dangerous and exacting stone walls, thorn hedges and murderous ditches would be negotiated.

"It's my last little fling," Shelagh argued—with herself as much as with Gail. "Aunt Dodie needn't know about it until it's all over. I'll tell Rod nearer the time, when it is too late for him to make me draw back. Maybe he'll be wild with me, but I don't think so. He's too much of a sportsman and a horseman not to get excited at the idea of any race . . . and this steeplechase is quite a test, even if it does take place at a small country race-meeting."

Doubtfully, Gail had to leave it at that, sworn to uneasy secrecy.

On a morning veiled in swathes of fine, warm rain the old comfortable car with the feather-bed interior came over from Laheen to take Miss Ross to Dublin. Miss Quinn, who had settled her domestic problems and returned to Kildoona within a week, was accompanying her, coming back by train the same evening. But Sir Charles would stay in Dublin for a few days, ostensibly to see about the purchase of additional fishing tackle for his summer guests, but actually, Gail suspected, that he might keep an eye on his old friend's reaction to her new surroundings. If she were unhappy, if that fellow Darnow worried her, Sir Charles would be at hand to comfort and advise . . . to bring her straight home again if need be.

As she carried out rugs, cushions, the travelling basket with its Thermos of hot coffee and flask of brandy, Gail found him bare-headed in the rain, conferring with his chauffeur, peering at gauges, testing tires. Immense, solid, dependable in his well-cut tweeds, his kind pink face glowing with health and, oddly, Gail thought, with happiness. Was it the thought of the small service he was doing for Miss Ross today . . . or the fresh glimmer of hope implied in this questing journey that gave him hi[8] air of almost youthful zest?

"A fine, soft morning!" he greeted her enthusiastically —the local salutation employed on rainy days that provided anything less than a downpour. Taking the cushions from her he began to pile them inexpertly but earnestly on to the back seat of the car. It was a perfect day for salmon trout, he said. They were rising all over the lake— you could almost see them if you looked out over the water.

But he was turning his back on the best fishing week that had happened in a month—for the sake of . . . what was it? Love? Could you be in love rising sixty? Suddenly Gail found herself liking him a lot—this man who had spent the best part of his life in pursuit of an impossible dream. Sentimental perhaps, but there was a single-mindedness about it that was very close to nobility. Only once in all the years since Miss Ross' accident had he been away from Laheen for any length of time, and that was during the war when he had returned to Manchester to work as a humble Air Raid Warden in his own factory. Apart from that he had endured his voluntary exile in the empty Castle, wifeless, childless, faithful to the woman who could be no more than a shadow in his life. Was it idealism . . . eccentricity . . . some quality not quite intelligible to a later, more realistic generation?

You couldn't imagine Rod in the same lonely, frustrated role! An idealist he might be, Gail thought, as she helped Miss Ross into the nest of cushions and listened to Miss Quinn's running patter of admonition and advice. That lost enchanted week in London; it was an idealistic Rod who had talked to her for hours over a rosily lit table in a Soho restaurant. But he was no sentimentalist. Hard, uncompromising, with an integrity that would give no quarter. He would have no use for the second-rate. If he rode in a Show Ring it would be flawless riding . . . on a flawlessly trained mount; if he ran a stud farm it would breed only the most perfect of thoroughbreds. And in the life of his spirit? He would demand a love that was whole, complete; he would have all love could offer, or leave it alone. There would be none of the half-a-loaf philosophy

136

by which his uncle seemed to exist. Everything, or nothing. That was Rod's way. A difficult man. For the first time Gail felt a faint uneasiness for Shelagh, a stirring of pity. Would she be able to live up to all that Rod would expect of her? Were the qualms she sometimes spoke of a premonition of the failure that could so easily lie ahead? Oh, Miss Quinn had been right enough when she said marriage had much better not be seen through an impossible golden haze. You wanted all your wits about you to face it clear and whole. Adventure on a high scale . . . any marriage. But marriage with a Rodwell Sterne!

With a shiver Gail realized she was standing on the steps in the softly drifting rain, staring at an empty driveway—the big, smoothly moving old car had long since disappeared. She went back into the house to face the assortment of tasks that had been left to her. In the little study at the end of the hall there were letters to be typed—Miss Ross had cleared off every possible arrear in her correspondence before her departure. Later there was the drive over to the Convent for a preliminary talk with the Mother Superior about the embroidered monograms. And Mrs. Murphy would be waiting for orders about the day's meals. Rod was coming to dinner.

"I shall expect you to preside at the table on this occasion," Miss Ross had told Gail in her usual formal fashion. "Miss Quinn will take my place as a rule, but she cannot possibly get back to Kildoona before midnight tonight."

So there was no chance of slipping away, leaving Shelagh and Rod to eat together—a course Gail would have been quick to seize on if it had not been for that autocratic order. All day it haunted her. To be anywhere near Rod in his present mood of obvious antagonism was sheer misery. And yet as she bathed and changed after her day's work that evening she found herself taking special pains with her appearance, brushing her hair until it shone with bronze-gold lights, touching her lips and cheeks with color, tipping her long lashes with a soft brown mascara, smudging a little eye-shadow on her lids. All very subtly applied, with a skill that was indeed professional. There had been lessons in beauty culture at Chatsworth House,

137

and though she didn't often bother about really serious make-up, tonight it seemed to her a necessary armor. She put on the full-skirted frock of apple-green jersey silk—and very nearly took it off again. On this grey, rainy evening it looked a little cold in color. But she remembered a scarf of deep soft crimson tucked away among her things and when she had knotted it about her shoulders saw with a small pang of pleasure how perfectly the warm rich tone became her.

There were flowers of the same shade on the dining table when presently they sat down to eat, a great crystal bowl of glowing damask roses that filled the room with their perfume. A little nervous in her role as Miss Ross' deputy, Gail had already dispensed sherry in a drawing room warmed tonight by a heaped peat fire. Rod, in an abstractedly genial mood, had made it easy for her . . . And Shelagh was all quicksilver tonight, laughing, sparkling, her eyes two burning sapphires under their dark, innocently curling lashes. Still wet from the rain, her black hair curled closely about her small, shapely head. She was wearing a nondescript georgette, patterned with pallid indefinable flowers. But it didn't matter, the very drabness of the frock seeming to enhance her strange luminous beauty. Lit up, a firefly of a girl. Drunk with rain and Finnmacool, she said. All day she had been riding, rushing in from the stable yard so late that she had had barely time to change for dinner.

And now as they ate she glowed with triumph; it had been a good day. She could not stop talking about Finnmacool. He was terrific, she exulted; those muscular quarters, like steel springs to carry him over the wildest jumps. "He could tackle Becher's Brook without turning a hair," she said, "and his speed is fabulous . . . if his staying power matches it and I think it does; that's what we've been finding out today; he'll walk away with everything at the Ardrossa Races." She laughed at the flicker of warning in Gail's glance. "It's all right," she explained, "I've told Rod we're entering for the race, Finn and I, and he is being an angel about it, in fact he's quite sold on the idea, thinks of joining in the fun himself, with Connaught King, and we could rope Pat in as well. It would be quite

138

a sensation, wouldn't it? Bride and bridegroom and best man all haring over the sticks less than twenty-four hours before the wedding feast, competing against one another!"

Amusement . . . a touch of malice on Rod's dark face now.

"Miss Ross will be shocked," Gail blurted out before she had time to stop herself.

"That's rather the idea," Shelagh laughed. "This is just the opening shot in the little rebellion we've decided upon, Rod and I . . . a declaration of independence."

"I'm a worker, not a socialite; horses are my job," Rod said quietly, apparently absorbed in the contemplation of the excellent grilled salmon before him.

"Aunt Dodie can have everything the way she wants it on our wedding day," Shelagh took it up, "but after that we're running our own lives. That dreadful post-wedding house-party that I told you about, full of bishops and princelings . . . we're cancelling it."

"So sweet of her to plan it for us," Rod murmured to his salmon, "but I shall be too busy inaugurating my stud farm in the autumn to have time for elaborate shooting parties of the kind people went in for when Aunt Dodie was a girl. We cannot revive the old echoes for her, I'm afraid; conjure up the vanished ghosts. We must choose our own friends. If Laheen is to live again it must be with new life . . . not old, outworn codes."

The brilliant, tigerish-yellow eyes flashed for a moment full at Gail. "There is nothing so stale and unprofitable as a past that is dead; it is a mistake to try to resuscitate it."

"It is also a mistake to order one's life to the pattern someone else has chosen," Shelagh chimed in.

"Absolutely," Rod agreed.

Shelagh regarded him with a sudden new air of interest. "Do you really mean that, Rod?"

"Why, of course! What makes you ask?"

She drew in a long breath—color flamed in her cheeks as she said recklessly: "You wouldn't let anyone, for example, choose your wife for you?"

"Good heavens, no!" Rod's laughter was easy. "And who, might I ask, do you think chose *you* for me?" It was

139

all light-hearted so far—a ripple of badinage across the dinner table.

"Glenda Grayson says Sonia did."

His face darkened dangerously.

Gail's heart faltered. Careful! she wanted to cry out to Shelagh. Go carefully with him, you are treading on dangerous ground!

But Shelagh, having shot her little bolt, was enjoying the sensation it caused. And courage was wine in her veins. She would take this ditch now she was headed for it, in the same high spirit with which she rode Finnmacool over the soaring stone walls of the Laheen bog-lands. She lifted her wine glass in her slim brown hand and looked at Rod over its rim, smiling.

"Poor Glenda who loved and lost you!" she teased. "Maybe she could not bear to believe that you could turn from her distinguished self to a teenage nobody like me. There had to be some great dramatic reason goading you on. . . ."

"So she invented one," Rod prompted dryly.

"A girl . . . who wouldn't have done at all for you . . . oh, most unsuitable! Sonia had to save you from her somehow. . . ."

Gail clasped her hot hands together under the table. If only Bridget would come in to change the plates. Bridget or an earthquake! Anything to interrupt this insane conversation.

"Was there such a girl?" she heard the cool young voice pursue.

"That week of the Horse Show? There were dozens of girls." Rod was laughing again now, back safely on the plane of badinage. "Didn't Glenda give you any more details of this siren who was to wreck my life?"

Shelagh shook her head. "She only seems to have existed in hints from Sonia. Glenda didn't know many details about her."

"It would have been difficult for her to know much about someone who existed only in Sonia's imagination . . . which has been inventing dangers of the same kind for me ever since I can remember." He shrugged, looked straight across the table at Gail. "Poor Sonia," he said,

140

"she ought to have discovered long ago that a Show Ring rider is something like a circus star—there will always be girls of a certain type tagging after him, silly little moths dazzled by the arc lights, the lamplight, the cheap notoriety. . . ."

The door opened noisily, blessedly. "Are ye ready for the pudden?" enquired Bridget, cheerfully uninhibited in Miss Ross' absence. Somehow Gail got through the rest of that dreadful meal, watching Shelagh's gaiety and air of confidence increase. The ghost conjured up by Glenda Grayson's spite, if it had ever seriously haunted her, was laid now. And so many other spectres besides. Rod didn't want Debrett at Laheen. Rod didn't give a hoot for convention—and would spend his wedding eve flouting it. Rod was tender, attentive, amusing, deferring to his love in every word and gesture, so openly ignoring the third person at the table that it could not help but be heartwarming.

They didn't want her, were scarcely aware of her, Gail decided, when the coffee tray had been carried into the drawing-room. With a murmured excuse she slipped away. Upstairs in her room she surveyed the litter of cosmetics on her dressing-table—mute reminders of the strangely expectant half-hour when she had dressed with such care. Dressing to impress Rod! Oh, fool that she was! Over the apple-green frock and crimson scarf she fastened her old riding mackintosh and went out into the darkening evening. It was still raining—that endless, gentle Irish rain that drifted in straight from the Atlantic and tasted like sea-spray on her lips. But it was a relief to be out of the house, to walk and keep on walking, seeking to escape from the tight knot of pain in her heart. She took, by force of habit, the road that led by the lake to Laheen. Across the grey water the turrets and towers of the Castle were soft as a pencil sketch against a shadowy background of trees.

A group of whitewashed cabins then, a madonna-faced woman leaning over a half-door who greeted her with a smile and the softly-spoken customary blessing: "God go with you!" Gail would have liked to stop and talk to her awhile—as Shelagh, who knew every cottager for miles around, would have done—but shyness prevented her. Hurrying past the little houses with their glimpses of firelit interiors she felt lonely and alien, a stranger in a strange land. A sharp wave of homesickness assailed her, and suddenly she remembered the letter in her pocket which had come that morning. Her mother's weekly screed. She had barely had time to read through it during the long busy day. But now she was hungry for its snippets of news and homely gossip. A sharp turn in the road brought her to a thick coppice of nut trees and sloes, their interlaced branches making a canopy over the low stone wall that bounded a stretch of moorland. She could sit here and be dry while she read her letter.

It was very quiet as she turned the closely-written pages. Away in the heather and gorse behind her curlews uttered their lonely cries, and she could hear the tiny sounds made by the rain in the leaves above her. Jimmy was sitting for his finals next week and sent his love. Clinty had had a pair of cricket pads given to him for his birthday and was so thrilled with them that he wanted to wear them even in bed. Debby hoped Gail wouldn't mind, but she was using her tennis racket while her own was being re-strung. She was playing every evening at the club now, practising for the summer tournament.

Anyone would think it was the Wimbledon Centre Court she was preparing for! (wrote Mrs. Darnley). When she's not at the club she is hitting up balls here on the lawn, roping in Dad or me or even Clinty to partner her, though none of us ever survive more than a moment or two of her ferocious service. I have been busy with fruit bottling; we have a wonderful crop of gooseberries this year. Jimmy has just come in and asks me to say that he will be writing you next week when he is clear of his exams. . . .

It was almost too dark to read any more; the letter went slack in her hands. Poor Jimmy; he had already written to her more than once and she had not troubled to reply. He seemed unreal as a wraith as she sat there under the thick trees looking out over the rain-dappled lake—

where a little light still lingered. Clinty with his cricket pads, Debby and her tournament. She could see the garden at home, a straight narrow strip, very neat and suburban, the patch of lawn near the house where the tennis net had been put up, and then a rustic screen covered with rambler roses and behind it the cabbages and lettuces and fruit bushes. There were gardens exactly like it on either side, a railway line running along the far end of them. In a few weeks' time she would go back to all this . . . home to Debby and Clint . . . to Mother and Father . . . and the faithful Jimmy. A thought that ought to have been comforting on this desolate Irish evening, but suddenly her eyes were full of tears.

The curlews were still crying to one another over the twilit bog, drawing nearer. Strange that they should fly so late . . . the last quavering "pee-wit" turning into something curiously resembling a human whistle.

"Is that yourself, Leahy?" she heard a voice whisper cautiously in the tangle of sloe bushes behind her. There was an answering hushed: " 'Tis so, Paudeen. I thought you were never going to get here!"

The bushes rustled with movement. Utter silence then. Her heart pounding, Gail listened. Not the voices or the movement but the silence that had followed them frightened her. Leahy and someone called Paudeen. What were they doing crouching here by the roadway at the fall of night? The small sharp clatter of metal striking metal came to her. "Keep your finger on the trigger now, man . . . it won't be long!" one of the men urged the other. They had guns with them then; She remembered rifle barrels gleaming in the moonlight on the night of the ball and it was as though she were seeing them again here and now; only this time they were not harmlessly poised on the shoulders of drilling young men, but concealed in undergrowth behind a stone wall . . . trained on a sharply curving road where a car would inevitably slow down as it came into sight.

Rod's car!

This was the road he would take when he left Kildoona. She didn't wait to work it all out, the whole thing added up instantaneously in her mind . . . all the waiting bits and

143

pieces falling into place like a ghastly jig-saw puzzle. Suspicions she had repressed, suspicions she had scarcely been aware of became sudden hideous certainties That threatening notice on the fairy tree. They had cut the tree down today, Rod had said. The purposeful moonlight gun practice. Hatred, naked as a knife in Leahy's eyes the day Tara Lad had bolted. Hatred in Pat Crampton's heart. That odd triangular conference she had interrupted at River House a week ago. Oh, God! how much had Pat and his mother to do with what was afoot tonight? An ambush. In a spot so carefully chosen. Shots ringing out in the twilight . . . splintering the windscreen of the approaching car. *They were going to shoot Rod.* She was quite sure of it.

How long she sat there in frozen terror she did not know. If she moved, the men would become aware of her . . . and indeed she had no power to move, even her ability to think now deserting her. Hypnotized, she waited. There was nothing in the whole world but the terrible silence filled with the tiny rustlings of the rain, the faint lapping of the lake on the stony shore the other side of the road. Not a sound from the crouching creatures so close to her in the bushes. How *could* they keep so still? The tumult of her pounding heart would surely reach them!

The car was a dull throbbing in the distance at first. She listened to it stupidly. Did she imagine the sudden galvanized stir in the bushes beside her, the sharp intake of a breath? But even then there was no clear plan in her mind . . . nothing but the mounting terror that forced her blindly to her feet. Terror for Rod. She'd got to stop him. Warn him. Of her own danger she had no thought, though in a vague uncaring way she was ready for the bullets that might rip the darkness about her as she fled.

She was running round the bend of the road then, right into the spreading cone of the approaching headlights, her arms outstretched. Brakes crashed, tires dragged and screamed. Not an inch away from her the great car stood shuddering.

"Gail! What on earth are you doing . . . flinging yourself under my wheels!" Strained and angry Rod's

144

voice came to her as she tottered round the long bonnet to reach his side.

When he switched off the engine it was very quiet . . . so absolutely still that the impact of a flying beetle hitting one of the headlamps made her start violently. A beetle instead of a bullet! A feeling of anti-climax came to her, and as she began to stammer out her strange story she could see the disbelief on Rod's set face, stony and implacable.

"But what makes you think it is Leahy lurking there in the bushes?"

His voice cut coldly across her eager spate of words, bringing her up short. She hadn't said anything yet about her fear of an ambush, nor could he realize that she had rushed forward to save him from what she imagined to be a threat to his life. The way he was looking at her made the whole thing suddenly begin to seem melodramatic and impossible. Perhaps she had been mistaken. Why hadn't the two men tried to stop her as she raced up the road?

She said a little uncertainly: "I'm sure it was Leahy. The man who was with him spoke to him by name. They have guns, Rod! I heard them making the triggers click. . . ."

"A couple of poachers probably . . . after our pheasants, or doing a little quiet rabbiting. Let's go on and see if they are still there."

She was so deflated by his matter-of-fact manner that she got into the car beside him without protest. As they approached the sharp bend in the road she held her breath. But no bullets greeted them, and in a faintly bewildered way she accepted this as somehow inevitable. The headlamps flooded the low wall and the sloe bushes with light. There was no sign of any lurking gunmen. "But they were here a moment ago," she said shakenly. "I *heard* them. I was sitting on that wall reading a letter—and suddenly they were crouching behind me . . . and then I heard the little sound of the triggers being cocked. I . . . was terrified. . . ."

Rod gave her a withering glance. "If you scare as easily as that you'd better not wander about the country-

145

side in the dusk! Leahy taking an evening stroll with a rabbit gun!" He laughed. "Honestly, Gail, I'd have thought you'd have had more sense! What did you think he was going to do . . . murder you?"

Gail stared at him helplessly, feeling more and more of a fool. Perhaps Leahy *had* been merely poaching. If he had been after the valuable and strictly preserved pheasants, that would account for the stealthy way he had behaved, and the way too he had melted away when he realized he had been observed. All her suspicions seemed now quite fatuous. How *could* she have been so silly as to have imagined Pat and his mother having anything to do with . . . planning a murder? For that was what it amounted to. It was a crazy idea. She'd die rather than let Rod discover what had been in her mind. Pat . . . who was one of his trusted friends. Leahy was different. Leahy, she felt, was capable of anything, but murder was a dangerous enterprise for the murderer. Besides, he'd been at logger-heads with the Bowfort family for years . . . could have taken a pot-shot at Sir Charles or Rod ages ago if he'd wanted to.

"Well?" Rod prompted impatiently. "Just what was it that made you hurl yourself in front of my car in that suicidal fashion?"

"I don't <u>know</u>," she murmured in a small shamed voice. "I was scared . . . and then I heard you coming. . . ."

"And you decided you'd like a lift back to Kildoona," he said with a short laugh. "You don't think I'm really taken in by all this poppy-cock about lurking villains, do you?"

So he thought she had—literally—been trying to hurl herself at him, cadging for his attention . . . and the lift. She was so angry she felt she was going to choke.

Blindly she groped for the catch of the car door. She only wanted to get away from him now . . . lose herself in the kind, dark night . . . escape from a situation that was becoming more distorted every moment. But his hand was hard on her shoulder, forcing her none too gently back into her seat.

146

"Stay where you are," he ordered curtly. "It's close on midnight and all of two miles back to Kildoona. Of course I'm seeing you home. If that last crack of mine was a bit ill-tempered, forget it. But I've had a long day and it wouldn't have been such a good end to it to have you flattened out under my tires! Next time you want to stop me for some hare-brained reason, please try to do it a little less dangerously."

He was edging the car round, and even as he spoke accelerated and they shot off with a roar of supercharged engines. It wasn't the kind of driving that encouraged conversation, which was, Gail felt bleakly, just as well. There wasn't really very much left for them to say to each other now, or indeed at any other time. Rod's opinion of her seemed to sink a little lower at each unfortunate encounter, and tonight's incident closed a final door between them. He heartily disliked her—and that was the end of it. There was nothing she could do but keep out of his way as much as possible during the weeks remaining to her at Kildoona Lodge. Thinking these things as they raced through the moist, warm darkness she sat mute by his side, her eyes burning with the tears she was too proud to shed.

CHAPTER THIRTEEN

MISS ROSS came back from the Dublin nursing home a changed woman. It wasn't that she could walk any more easily than before, but for the first time in thirty years she was free from pain. Her nights were no longer vigils of tormented wakefulness; she slept deeply, dreamlessly. As her frayed nerves healed, faint echoes of her lost youth came back to her. Her dark blue eyes under their misty Irish lashes lost the look of strained endurance; held laughter at times. The energy which had been spent resisting pain turned to a fresh enthusiasm for the ordinary demands of day-to-day living. With a new zest she threw herself into the preparations for the forthcoming wedding, driving Gail, Miss Quinn, the entire household before her. Rooms which had already been spring-cleaned must be turned inside out again, carpets taken up and beaten, the big gilt picture frames cleaned with special spirit. Decorators were summoned to refurbish the exterior of the old house. Flower beds, under the personal supervision of the invalid, were replanned, filled with exotic offerings from the Castle greenhouses.

There were gay little dinner-parties, with Sir Charles a constant visitor, and of course Rod . . . and the young local doctor, daily in attendance now, working with the grave young woman physiotherapist who had been sent down by Darnow: Jane Drewitt. It became the accepted thing that Jane and Gail and Miss Quinn should dine together in the little study on the evenings Miss Ross was entertaining. An arrangement Gail welcomed. The days, the weeks, raced by and for all she saw of him Rod might have been living in another country. Odd . . . and hurtful . . . what a relief that could be! There were fleeting glimpses of him as he came and went with Shelagh, the afternoon when from her bedroom window she watched him on his great black horse in the paddock jumping the brushwood fences Pat had erected for Shelagh and her Finnmacool. But since the night he had found her in terror on the lake road she had exchanged barely a word with him.

Then Sonia arrived at Laheen, bringing a batch of guests with her, the nucleus of the house-party that was to include the famous French dress designer; and the social tempo quickened. Somehow it resulted in Gail being thrust more and more into the background, her duties multiplying.

But if it was a relief to be able to avoid Rod, it was even more of a relief not to have to encounter Sonia. On the one occasion they did come face to face on the Castle steps— one morning when Gail made a hurried trip over to Laheen to talk to the head gardener about the wedding flowers— Sonia stared blankly at her and through her with no sign of recognition. Perhaps she had genuinely forgotten who she was, Gail decided humbly, though it wasn't altogether

148

likely. But Sonia's life, she imagined, would be a very full and varied one. She would meet so many people, see so many faces. Her brief encounters with Gail had been always on more or less dressed-up occasions . . . parties in London last year, the night of the Castle ball in June, and on this grey blustering July day she was wearing her old mackintosh and had her head bundled up in a handkerchief scarf.

Shrinking back against the terrace wall, waiting for the gardener to come to her, Gail watched the slim figure in its beautiful *haute couture* tweeds getting into the car that stood at the foot of the steps. "To Ardrossa Station, Foley," she heard Sonia say to the chauffeur who held the door for her.

She'd be on her way to meet Chardin, Gail guessed. He was due to arrive that morning. Tomorrow he would be coming over to Kildoona to superintend the final fitting of the wedding gown, which already hung in the little sewing room on the attic floor, veiled in shrouds of protective sateen. Little more than a week from today Shelagh would be wearing it. Gail closed her eyes and saw the chapel the way she was planning it, the banked Madonna lilies and the shell-pink carnations, and the tall, richly colored delphiniums, as blue as the eyes of the bride . . . Shelagh grave and lovely, with her hand on the arm of her new husband, walking down the little aisle while the organ stormed its way through Mendelssohn's honeyed phrases, and the joy bells rang.

"Mr. O'Toole is over at Creek Cottage, Miss," she heard a voice at her elbow. It was Tim, the youngest of the under-gardeners. "He's making a lay-out of the ground over there with Major Sterne. 'Tis a fine pleasure-garden they will have in it, I'm thinking . . . geraniums he took over with him, and a hundred of them scarlet begonias. He said if 'twas in the car you came, would you go over by the lake road and have a word with him. The Major thinks maybe there should be a few potted palms to make a kind of screen for the organ in the Chapel. He wants you to phone up some place in Dublin and order them right away."

149

Gail's heart sank at the thought of having to talk to Rod—even briefly, and about something as impersonal as potted palms. But if he had more or less sent for her there was no help for it. She would have to face him and get it over. As she drove along the lake road she grew more and more nervous. Potted palms would be all wrong for the Chapel, she decided, but the easiest thing would be to let Rod have them if he wanted them.

The clouds which had darkened the morning, hinting at rain, were beginning to clear now and by the time she reached Creek Cottage the sun was shining. She left her raincoat and head-scarf in the car and went in her trim slacks and crisp white blouse up the narrow pathway that climbed the terraced land—all groomed and dug now, laid out in richy loamy beds, between the strips of very green grass. O'Toole and his helpers had worked hard this morning, and already the well-matured plants he had brought from the Castle greenhouses made a brave show.

"It's wonderful, O'Toole, an absolute miracle! Last time I saw this garden it was a wilderness of grass and weeds," Gail couldn't help exclaiming.

The old gardener, leaning on his spade, beamed at her praise. "Anyone would think 'twas Mr. Rod himself that was going to live here, the interest he takes in the place!"

Gail gave a rather hunted glance around. "He wanted to see me, Tim said. . . ."

"Aye. He'll be along in a minit, Miss. And then when you've had your word with him maybe you'd give me a lift back to the Castle. I want you to pick out the delphiniums I'm to keep back for the Chapel on the twenty-eighth. I was thinking it might be best if we didn't cut the Madonna lilies . . . but left them in the pots the way they'd keep fresh."

"We could mask the pots with moss and ferns . . ." Gail mused. She looked up at the pleasant old house dreaming in the sunlight. Gail's House. Ah, if it really were! To live a lifetime here in peace and beauty beside these wide still waters. To live here loved . . . and loving. With a stab of pain she switched her mind away from the

150

fruitless thought. But it was a heavenly spot. No wonder Rod was throwing himself heart and soul into its restoration . . . even if in the end it was a stranger who would come to it.

She heard the hall door bang—an angry sound in the sunny silence—and saw Rod emerge from the house, his face set and grim, his tawny eyes ablaze. Rod in a towering temper! She felt O'Toole at her side stir and stiffen. " 'Tis that Leahy fellow," he murmured, warning her. " 'Tis a bad moment after all that you walked in on us. I never seen the Major so mad."

"Leahy!" Gail echoed . . . whispering, though Rod was well out of earshot, halting in the rose-covered porch to light a cigarette.

" 'Tis how the Major came across a potheen still he left in one of the cellars, where he used to keep his turf. Distilling the stuff, he must have been, illicit whiskey, ye know. A lot of people do be making it in these parts, but if they are caught by the police they get a terrible fine. They are always on the hunt for a potheen hide-out, the lads in the Garda. A nice disgrace it would be for the Major if they'd taken it into their heads to search Creek Cottage! No wonder he was lepping mad." The old man laughed mirthlessly. "Sent for Leahy, he did, and told him he'd a good mind to give him in charge . . . and Leahy shouting back at him, as brazen as you please, threatening blue murder. You never heard such a shindy as there was . . . the Major isn't the better of it yet, God help him!"

Her hands thrust deep into the pockets of her slacks, Gail watched Rod come towards her, his dark face grim. Leahy and illicit whiskey and police and threats. But she must not again jump to panic-stricken conclusions. This country which, once more she reminded herself, she did not wholly understand, had a way of sorting out its affairs without her aid.

A tremor shook her nerves as Rod nodded to her carelessly. "Ah, Miss Darnley. . . ." So it wasn't even to be Gail any more. "I've been looking at your neatly drawn-up

151

little plan for the flowers on the twenty-eighth, and it struck me you hadn't done anything about the organ . . . an ugly Victorian instrument with all that shiny pitch-pine around it; can't think why my uncle hasn't had it replaced by something more suitable long ago. I'd like you to order half a dozen large potted palms. Three on each side of the keyboard ought to mask its worst features."

Gail clenched her hands inside her pockets. Really, Rod's manner was insufferable. That lofty, autocratic tone! For the first time since she had known him she had a feeling of wanting to quarrel with him . . . a heady, intoxicating feeling that brought the rich color to her cheeks. Straightening her slim shoulders she stood before him, very slight and boyish in the neat dark slacks, which made her seem taller than usual. She said: "I don't think hired potted palms would go with the scheme I've thought out, Major Sterne. After all, it's a small country chapel in a very wild and lovely setting here by the lake and . . . potted palms always seem to be cheaply theatrical."

"Indeed! So my taste, you consider, is cheaply theatrical?"

"In this instance . . . yes."

His eyes flashed, and she saw his jaw tighten. Perhaps it was unwise to goad him like this when he was already in a bad temper . . . but she didn't care. She was right about the palms; they would be absolutely hideous. It would be cowardly, she thought now, to let him shout her down.

He said: "Well, interesting as it is to discover your opinion of me, I'm afraid I must ignore it. Please be good enough to carry out my order."

Gail caught her breath sharply, so angry suddenly that it was impossible to be objective about it any more. Carried away on a hot tide of recklessness, she only wanted to hurt him now. Somehow it wasn't potted palms that were the issue any longer, but the whole miserable tangle of misunderstanding that lay between them. He had no right to treat her so scornfully; it was unfair, unjust. That week last year in London they had been such good friends . . . if nothing more, and in her heart she knew it had

152

been a good deal more. Until Sonia had ruined it all. And she couldn't tell Rod this, could only stand by now watching his dislike for her grow more and more obvious. That night by the lake when he had kissed her in that hideous, humiliating fashion! Treating her like a cheap little flirt. How could he think that of her! "*You're not unique, Gail; there's a good many of your sort in a man's lifetime!*" As the cutting words came back to her tears ached in her throat. But she would not weaken now, would not lose her fine, brave anger. Anger was best. She had grieved enough over this proud, intolerant man!

She said with a deadly quietness, giving him scorn for scorn: "It is a little difficult to take orders from two people at the same time, Major Sterne. Miss Ross has asked me to be responsible for the decoration of the chapel, and has sufficient confidence in me to have given me a free hand. I have worked out a scheme which I find simple and . . . suitable, and I cannot introduce an entirely different element. . . ." Oh, it was dreadful, she thought, fighting over flowers for a chapel . . . flowers for a wedding. Rod's wedding.

"So you refuse to order the potted palms?" he thundered.

"Yes."

"There could be some other kind of a screen for the organ maybe," the hovering O'Toole put in reasonably. Which was exactly what she had had in mind; a trellis of little white roses perhaps, or sheaves of big pale daisies . . . but she wasn't going to placate Rod with any alternative suggestions at the moment. She didn't want to placate him.

"I'll speak to Miss Ross about this," she heard him say.

"By all means, do." With an icy little smile she turned and left him, knowing she had been disrespectful, impolite; all the things a good employee should never be. But she was not Rod's employee, nor did he treat her with as much consideration as he would have offered to a . . . servant. Sending for her high-handedly, *ordering* her to include those wretched palms, not even discussing the idea with her, or condescending to consider with her just what their effect might be. It served him right if she had been rude.

Still carried high on the fine wave of her defiance, she got into the car and the old gardener was there beside her as she drove back along the lake road, talking of the screen for the organ, all out for peace-making on this morning that had held too many storms. "A bit of a hot-head, the young master, but he's all right if you know how to take him...."

"But potted palms!" said Gail.

Back at Kildoona she found Shelagh in tears. It seemed as if there was to be no end to this day's disturbances. Miss Ross had found out about the entry for the Races and was adamant. Shelagh was *not* to ride in this rough-and-tumble country hazard on the day before her wedding. "She was so angry," Shelagh recounted. "Usually I can wheedle her into agreeing to anything I badly want, but this time she's being just horrible; because I arranged it all behind her back, she says. She stormed at me and I stormed back and I've said I'll ride in the race whatever she feels about it . . . and so I will. Rod doesn't mind and after all Rod is the person I've got to obey now . . . the way all good wives obey their husbands."

"Only that you're not his wife yet," chimed in Miss Quinn who was a shocked thirty party in the conversation, "and never will be if your break your neck flying over a lot of stone walls with all the wild men of the county riding before and behind you. It's a death trap for any woman to be competing with them. Major Sterne ought to have more sense than to tell you you could enter for that race."

"He didn't tell me. I entered without asking him. But when he found out about it he didn't mind, and we thought it would be fun for the three of us to be in the race, Rod and Pat and me." Shelagh dried her wet eyes with a screwed-up, dirty handkerchief taken from the pocket of her worn old jodhpurs.

"God give you sense, the whole lot of you!" groaned Miss Quinn. "And as for you, Shelagh, my child, it's high time you stopped playing the madcap and began to show a little more rightful pride. Haring about the countryside

154

with stable boys and jockeys and trainers! Maybe th^e Major thinks it a joke at the moment, but the time will come when it won't seem so funny to him. A man likes a certain amount of dignity in the behavior of the woman he marries. Amn't I right, Gail?"

Gail hesitated, hating to side with authority against Shelagh who was looking at her appealingly. But she remembered that she was supposed to exercise a restraining influence on the younger girl . . . that it was partly for this Miss Ross had brought her to Kildoona Lodge. Besides, there was something reckless and a little disturbing about this notion of racing on the wedding eve. It made it seem as if neither Rod nor Shelagh was taking their great day in quite the right spirit. Almost as though they were facing it with a kind of desperation.

She said with her most reasonable air: "I do think, Shelagh, that it would be frightfully tiring for you to enter for the village races; if it were on any other day it might be different, but you'll have a great many things to see to on the twenty-seventh and it would spoil your wedding completely if you had to go through with it in a state of exhaustion."

"Go on back to Miss Ross' boudoir now," coaxed Miss Quinn, "and tell her you're sorry and that you'll cancel your entry."

"I can't," Shelagh murmured unhappily. "Pat would be so disappointed."

"Pat!" Miss Quinn flung her hands up in despair. "And would the world come to an end if he was? Honestly . . . !" She shook her head in bewilderment. "There's times when I don't know what to make of you. Anyone would think it was Pat Crampton you were in love with the way you are always considering him, fussing around him, spending every hour of the day out there in the stables and paddocks with him, when any right-minded girl would have no other thought in her mind but to be getting her things ready for her marriage and her new home."

Shelagh gave her a tearful, puzzled glance. "It is a bit queer, I suppose," she agreed dispassionately. "But Pat . . . he seems to be a part of me; we've been together

155

all our lives. I'm not in love with him ... but I ... love him; it's quite different. . . ."

"Well, I hope to goodness it *is*!" Miss Quinn interrupted vigorously.

For the rest of the day the discussion raged, a domestic storm that threatened to blow up into a first-class family row. In the afternoon Rod turned up to take part in it, and Sir Charles, summoned by Miss Ross, was enlisted on the side of convention and good sense. The wedding-eve escapade was unthinkable, he declared. It would be the talk of the county.

"They're at it hammer and tongs, the four of them," Jane Drewitt relayed when she joined Gail and Miss Quinn in the study for tea. "The Major siding with Shelagh and Sir Charles with Miss Ross. And a lot more than the village races is coming into it—with arguments about the kind of life the Major wants at Laheen when he takes over there. Some house-party Miss Ross has set her heart on for the autumn, and the Major telling her he will have no time for entertaining on a big scale and only wants to be left in peace to get on with his horse-breeding. She's working herself up in such a state over it all that I was afraid she would take some harm until I saw her—in her indignation—walk right across the drawing-room just now without the support of her canes. I don't think she even knew she was doing it!"

"Glory be to God!" gasped Miss Quinn.

"It's wonderful," said Miss Drewitt calmly, "what a little healthy anger will do for an invalid sometimes; any strong emotion indeed that will take them out of themselves. It doesn't mean, of course, that she'll always be able to walk that way . . . yet. She'll be dependent on the sticks again when she remembers them. But it does show we're on the right track with her."

"And the village 'free-for-all'?" Gail put in.

"Oh, I believe the Major and Shelagh will ride in it," Miss Drewitt declared. "The stand they've taken over it they'll *have* to. Unless some miracle intervenes."

Miss Quinn picked up the teapot absently and holding it poised in the air gazed into space, her round blue eyes

156

wide and troubled. "I'll be glad when this wedding is safely over," she said oddly. "Sometimes I get the queerest feeling about it . . . as though a shadow of ill-luck was there ahead of us all, instead of the clear sunlight it ought to be. A terrible darkness threatening. Maybe it's just this quarrel breaking out over the Races that is upsetting me . . . *but I wish the Major hadn't cut down that fairy tree!*"

CHAPTER FOURTEEN

THE next day Chardin came to lunch, a quicksilvery little Frenchman with an ugly attractive face and a smile that would charm the birds off the branches. Shelagh, pale and defiant, wan with the strain of the unresolved argument over the Ardrossa Races, met him in her old jodhpurs and washed-out shirt. But when the meal was over she stood patiently in the sewing room while Gail fastened petticoat after petticoat about her slim waist. Then the frock . . . a shimmer of snowy French lace patterned with silver flowers, the whole thing fine as a cobweb, ethereal, breath-takingly lovely. Kneeling before her, absorbed as an artist should be, the great dress designer straightened a fold here, pinned a seam there, talking meanwhile in rapid French to the seamstress he had brought along with him to help with these last-minute touches. But there were few alterations needed. The initial fittings given during a visit earlier in the year—before Gail's arrival—had in the skilful hands of the master brought the creation close to perfection.

Surveying herself in the long mirror, Shelagh's blue eyes darkened and the color came back to her cheeks. Gail saw her draw herself up, holding herself with a new pride. She was no longer Shelagh the madcap, the rough-rider. It was as though the beauty of the frock had laid its spell on her. With a touch of instinctive grace she folded her hands before her, a small eloquently feminine gesture. "I feel like . . . a princess!" she said.

"And look like a queen!" murmured the Frenchman gallantly.

From the doorway, where the women of the household had gathered, came gasps of admiration. Miss Drewitt in her white surgical overall, Mrs. Murphy in her kitchen apron, Bridget, her grey eyes full of dreams, Miss Quinn; they were all there to see the bridal frock and envy and marvel.

"And now the veil." With nimble fingers Chardin fastened the softly flowing folds about the dark curls, binding them with a wreath of orange blossom. "*Ravissante!*" he sighed ecstatically.

Turning herself about before the mirror Shelagh innocently admired the effect. "It does make me look nice," she agreed mildly. And then, with a sparkle of her old mischief: "Seems an awful waste to take it all off straight away, after the trouble we've had dressing me up so beautifully. I think I'll go downstairs and show off a bit. Rod is just about due. He's riding with me this afternoon. . . ."

She went slowly towards the doorway, train and long skirts and numerous petticoats impeding her. The women moved aside to make way for her, only Miss Quinn blocking her path. "You can't show yourself to the Major . . ." she was saying in a tone of sheer horror. "It's the height of ill-luck for a bride to go to her groom in her wedding-dress before the ceremony!"

"Indeed then, it is, Miss," Mrs. Murphy chimed in, while Bridget hurriedly crossed herself.

Shelagh laughed . . . and calmly continued on her way. "Gail, do be an angel and hold up my train!" she begged. "It's dragging like a ton weight behind me."

Gail glanced a little apprehensively at Chardin. "Is it all right for us to take this exquisite frock downstairs?" she asked.

The little Frenchman shrugged and smiled. "The princess has spoken! *Que voulez-vous?* As for the so-charming superstitions of Madame"—he bowed to Miss Quinn—"I pray you not to distress yourself. The Chardin wedding-gown, eet ees always lucky."

"Well, I'm sure I hope you're right," Miss Quinn grumbled doubtfully as the little procession left the room, Chardin bringing up the rear, gazing in delight at his handiwork.

Rod was in the hall and as they descended the wide shallow staircase Gail saw him look up, startled, arrested. Was it wonder that brought the strange, almost terrified look into his eyes?

"Shelagh!" There was awe, adoration, in his tone.

Halting, she stood on the lowest step. "I had to show you, darling! It's so . . . unlike me; I wanted you to see the way I'm going to look for you on the twenty-eight. . . ."

He held out his arms to her.

"And thees is where we leave them," murmured Chardin tactfully in Gail's ear.

Discreetly they slipped away, Chardin to the drawing-room where Miss Ross awaited him, while Gail, moving with a curious blind haste, went through the baize door that led to the servants' quarters. It was dreadful how much Rod could still hurt her. All her efforts to school her heart seemed in vain. She had thought she had almost succeeded in disliking him since the rather silly little row over the potted palms. But the sight of him just now, holding his arms out to Shelagh—lovely as a dream in her wedding-gown—had been almost more than she could bear. What was the matter with her? Why was it that somewhere deep in her heart, no matter what she did about it, there persisted this feeling of unity with Rodwell Sterne? So that every unhappy contact with him, every glimpse of his affection for Shelagh, was a deep outrage.

Drifting into the kitchen, littered with luncheon dishes, she stood by the big central table, still holding the remains of the servants' midday meal. She was thankful that Mrs. Murphy and Bridget were upstairs in the sewing room and that in this odd sanctuary she could, for a few moments, be alone. Her mind went back to that brief interlude last summer when for a few halcyon days her whole life had seemed to centre on Rod. Had she dreamed the growth of that quick strange harmony between them? And of what

159

had it consisted? Vividly she remembered the look on his lean, dark face as they talked during those snatched lunch hours . . . that evening they had dined in Soho . . . the night of the riverside dance; the eager look of a man newly alive, questing, sensitive, vulnerable. How cleverly he had drawn her out to talk about herself, her background, her likes and dislikes; books they had talked about, pictures, her longing to travel and see the colorful countries of the great world. He had seemed to revel in her curiosity, her hunger for knowledge; telling her about Madrid, South America, Greece, Paris; all the places he had visited as a show rider; a horseman with a capacity for so much more than the somewhat narrow equestrian circle in which he inevitably moved. Wherever he went he had broken through that narrow circle, sight-seeing, exploring, absorbing all that his quick intelligence uncovered of the country in which he found himself. And he had enjoyed recounting his impressions; enjoyed too the discussions about books and plays. It was as though for most of his life he had been with sporting, riding people who were not interested in these things and it had been good at last to find someone with whom he could share them, even someone as young and naive as herself.

But was that a sufficient reason for the enchantment which they had seemed to share that heavenly week? Gail asked herself as, absently, she removed the kitchen cat, who sensing her preoccupation had jumped on to the table to investigate the tempting array of scraps left on the servants' plates. Would the rather curiously assorted friendship have blossomed into something warmer and— more lasting . . . if Sonia had not intervened? It was a question which would for ever remain unanswered. Rod was in love with Shelagh now. In a few days' time she would be his wife. Foolish how sharply, how consistently, that thought could hurt!

Hearing the banging of the baize door Gail made a small hunted movement, running out of the kitchen into the cobbled, sunlit yard beyond. She was in no mood to listen to Mrs. Murphy and Bridget exulting over their visit to the sewing room and their glimpse of Miss Shelagh's

160

bridal loveliness. Neither did she feel like returning to the study where a batch of letters awaited her.

Crossing the yard she went through a wicket gate in the high wall that bounded it and found herself in the weed-grown lane that led to the stables. She could hear Finnmacool fidgeting and nickering in his stall, and someone remonstrating with him. Pat. Not caring very much what she did as long as she kept away from the house until Shelagh had changed out of her frock and gone off with Rod for their afternoon ride, Gail decided to go and talk to Pat. She found him busy with brushes and curry comb, grooming the horse after its morning exercise.

"Stable boy's work," he grumbled when he saw Gail, "but Lanty has been roped in to help mow the lawn for that damned marquee they're putting up next week. And Finn was in a bit of a lather. Shelagh didn't give herself time to rub him down after her ride this morning . . . had to rush off to meet that dressmaking fellow. . . ."

Leaning against the loose-box door, Gail watched him brushing the great shining flanks. He looked tired, she thought; tense and strained, and his eyes were unnaturally bright and restless.

"She ought not to take Finn out again this afternoon," he was saying, "but Rod wants to go over to Darcy's." The words trailed away, and the brush went slack in his hands, his head raised sharply, listening to the sound of the yard gate banging. Finnmacool gave a soft, excited whinny, pricking his long velvety ears, and suddenly Shelagh was there, crossing the stable yard in her lacy wedding gown, her train looped expertly over one arm, the other arm linked in Rod's.

"Here comes the bride! Here co . . . omes the bride!" she sang to the tune of the famous wedding-march. "Pat!" she called, even as she had called a little earlier to Rod, "I had to show you! Did ye ever see such grandeur?" Abandoning Rod, she made a little pirouette, and Gail heard Pat catch his breath sharply.

"Mad," said Rod with happy resignation. "Mad as a coot! Chardin would be apoplectic if he knew she was trailing all this glory around the stable yard mud!" He met Gail's glance and twinkled affably.

"Do you like me this way, darling?" crooned Shelagh to Finn, leaning against his massive shoulder. The big horse arched his neck, nuzzling his head against her lovingly. There were fiery centres in Pat's grey eyes as he watched them . . . girl and horse. His lips had gone very white.

"Do *you* like me?" she urged him, turning on him her dazzling look. So happy in her beautiful frock, so carried away by it, so . . . young.

"*Like* you!" Pat echoed in a strained dry whisper.

"I never saw such vanity," teased Rod. "If we're not careful she'll be off to Darcy's with me just as she is!"

Shelagh giggled. "And why not? In the Middle Ages women always went about on horseback dressed like this . . . there's a picture of one of them in that fourteenth-century French tapestry in the salon at the Castle. . . ."

"Come along," Rod broke in a little nervously, for in this mischievous mood she was quite capable of mounting Finn as she was in sheer bravado. "You get back to the house and change into your jodhpurs." Seizing her arm, he led her firmly away. She went reluctantly, looking back over her shoulder, crying out: "But you haven't wished me well, Pat . . . you haven't said a thing!"

He waved a hand with attempted airiness. "You know what I wish you!" he called out, and flung after her then a phrase in Gaelic which caused her to turn quickly away.

"What was it you said?" Gail demanded unthinkingly.

Pat laughed mirthlessly. "Well-wear to the new dress and take care she didn't stand up and marry the wrong man in it."

"A good thing you said it in Irish!" Gail couldn't help sounding a little shocked and disapproving, though it hadn't been very sensible of Shelagh, knowing quite well how Pat felt about her, to come flaunting her wedding-gown before him.

With a hand that wasn't quite steady he flicked open his cigarette case and offered it to Gail. As he held the lighter for her he asked softly and with a desperate attempt

162

at casualness: "Do you think, by any chance, that she *is* marrying the wrong man?"

Gail inhaled swiftly, flung back her head and regarded him sternly. "I'm quite certain she isn't. She adores Rod . . . you know she does!"

Pat nodded. There were sudden deep lines about his mouth. "It would break her heart if anything were to happen to him, wouldn't it? If anything were to take him from her?" he demanded with odd intensity.

Gail stared at him, uneasiness assailing her. "What on earth are you getting at, Pat?" she asked a little crossly. She was sorry for the boy, but after all she too knew something about heartache and frustration. It had been a nerve-racking half-hour for both of them, if Pat only knew!

"Ah, nothing. Don't mind me. I'm just blethering." With a sudden furious energy he returned to the grooming of Finn. "Shelagh will be wanting him in a few minutes and I have to get him saddled. . . ."

But it would take more than a few minutes to get out of all those petticoats, Gail thought. With a vision of the hurried changing, exquisite petticoats as likely as not flung all over the floor of the sewing room, she murmured vaguely to Pat of work awaiting her and ran back to the house.

There was nothing to warn her that she would later look back on this hasty exit with bitter remorse, or that in the dark hour so rapidly approaching she would blame herself for not sensing in Pat's queer mood the strain under which he labored. Would tragedy have been averted if she had been more sympathetic, encouraged him to talk more freely? It was unlikely—but the thought was to haunt her nevertheless.

* * *

There was a dinner-party for Chardin at the Castle that evening. Having helped Miss Ross and Shelagh to dress for this glittering event—at which every woman present would do her best to appear smart—Gail settled down to arrears of work. It was a heavy thundery evening and she felt tired and depressed. But the threat of an electric

163

storm often affected her in this way, she reminded herself' and tried to throw the feeling off.

Sir Charles brought Miss Ross home soon after ten. "She says you'd better not wait up for Shelagh," Miss Quinn told Gail, coming into the study with their nightly cocoa a little later. "The young people at the Castle have started dancing, it seems, and the Major will be bringing Shelagh home any old hour, I suppose. Anyway," she finished with comfortable informality, "you're to go to bed."

An order Gail was only too pleased to obey! She slept long and deeply that night, vaguely aware through the mists of sleep of the sound of car doors banging somewhere. Rod and Shelagh, she just had time to decide before she drifted off again.

When she woke again the sun was shining and she got out of bed and padded barefoot to the open window. The threatening storm had cleared away harmlessly and it was a perfect morning. A silvery carpet of dew spread over the grass in the paddock. The hills beyond the lake were almost the same color as the sky and had the insubstantial look they always wore in fine weather. It was very early—barely six o'clock. On a sudden impulse Gail decided to have a quick swim in the lake before breakfast. She sometimes did this when she managed to wake up in time, enjoying the brief interlude of peace and leisure before the rush of the day's work began.

Slipping out of the sleeping house presently, running down the rough boreen that was a short cut to the lake road, she was happier than she had been for some time—with an odd almost impersonal happiness that seemed to lift her above all heartache and worry. The queer oppression that had filled last night with indefinable apprehension had quite vanished. It was enough now to be young and strong and vividly alive—with an hour of freedom to spend in the early sunlight. It was all hers at that moment, the song of the larks, the silken sheen of the blue water before her, the perfume of the dew-wet meadow-sweet and grasses crushed beneath her feet, the majesty of pine-woods and mountains that encircled this, her own, her secret paradise. A magic morning! Oh, a hopeful new and shining morning in which anything could happen!

Standing on a flat slab of granite by the water's edge— the freckled rosy stone already warm with the sun's first rays—she slipped off the creamy woollen tennis coat (brought for its cosiness after the icy water), unfastened the skirt of her cotton sun-frock and stood a moment hesitant in her brief white swim suit. She could see the two swans who seemed to haunt this end of the lake near Kildoona . . . always the same two, she thought. Obviously they had a nest somewhere and would presently appear with a little flotilla of cygnets in tow. But this morning they were alone and she could pretend they were Caer and Aengus linked by the silver chain of their love, waiting to sing their song of enchantment.

Lifting her arms above her head she dived bravely then, cutting through the clear amber-colored water, letting herself go down . . . down into the cold depths, until, flattening out and raising her arms a little, she found herself rising again. The upper layer of the water seemed quite warm in comparison as she surfaced, shaking the moisture out of her eyes, out of her short thick hair.

Glowing all over, filled with a sense of exhilaration, she struck out and swam vigorously away from the shore. When she turned over on her back to rest a while it was as though she floated between earth and heaven . . . the blue sky seemed so near, now touched with its little rosy morning clouds. Diving again with the abandon of a water nymph she swam for a few yards, coming up breathless but triumphant . . . to see Rod sitting on the slab of granite watching her gravely.

For a moment she felt no surprise—she was too much a part of the lake and sunlight to be touched by any outside sensation. Cool, insulated, she moved through the rainbow spray of her own going. With deft, overhand strokes she drew nearer and nearer to the shore, and it was only when she noticed that Rod was still wearing his evening clothes that it all began to be a little peculiar . . . and vaguely frightening. He looked so grim, so motionless, sitting there waiting for her!

Quickening her pace she reached the granite slab and, gripping its edge, hung in the water, her eyes wide with enquiry. But he did not speak, merely holding out a hand to help her up on to the rock. She shook her head. "I'll only wet you, Rod; you'd better move away and let me scramble out on my own."

With a lithe upward spring she was on the big warm stone beside him. And even then he did not speak, standing by in that curious stony silence watching her while she reached for her towel and began to scrub vaguely at her face, her hair, which clung about her head now, a mass of wet, bronze-tipped curls.

"Rod, what is it?" she found herself whispering presently, her heart halting with the sudden sure knowledge that something was very wrong indeed.

She saw him moisten his lips with the tip of his tongue—nervously. Rod who had nerves of iron! "I was driving past and saw you swimming," he said, and stopped helplessly. "Look . . ." he began again, all but choking over the simple word, "you get out of that wet swim suit and into something warm and dry. I'll go back to the car and wait for you. It's there on the verge of the road." He turned away, paused, looked back at her. "Something pretty grim happened last night. I was on my way to Kildoona to tell Shelagh . . . Miss Ross . . . but it's too early to waken them. . . ."

He left it at that for the moment, abandoning her. With trembling hands she towelled, changed into the sun frock and woolly coat, knelt groping over sandals that refused to be fastened! But at last she was running to him over the narrow strip of marshy verge which separated lake from road. He was leaning against the long rakish bonnet of his car, smoking; an incongruous figure in his tailed coat and impeccable white waist-coat. Sunshine caught the gold links in his cuff as he offered her a cigarette. But she shook her head. Her eyes were wide, mystified, fixed on him, imploring him to end her suspense.

"It's Pat," he said, as though in answer to a spoken question. "He was found last night not fifty yards from

the entrance to Kildoona Lodge . . . shot through the
chest. There was a card pinned to his shirt with the one
word printed on it: 'Informer'!"

CHAPTER FIFTEEN

GAIL's knees seemed to turn to water beneath her. With a
small strangled sound she sank down on to the running-
board of the car. "Pat!" she said stupidly. The uneasy
suspicions of the last few weeks churned in her brain—like a
chorus of mad inner voices. There was no rhyme or reason
anywhere any more. Pat was the last person she had
imagined to be in danger. "I don't understand . . ." she
murmured. A sudden wave of horror overwhelmed her and
she buried her face in her hands. "It can't be true," she
whispered through her fingers. "He was so young . . .
so alive . . ."

She felt Rod's hand on her shoulder. "I'm doing this
very badly, Gail. I'm sorry I blurted it out to you so
abruptly. Pat is still alive, but very seriously hurt." He
sat down on the long running-board beside her. "It must
have happened some time during the late hours of last
evening," he went on. "I brought Shelagh home about
one-thirty and saw Sergeant O'Grady with a couple of men
standing at the corner of the road just before we reached
the gate. I thought they were out on some kind of patrol—
but it seems now they were searching the spot where Pat
had been found an hour earlier by a home-going farmer
named Donlan. O'Grady let us pass, not wanting to break
the news before Shelagh, but he was waiting for me when
I came back after leaving her at the house. I've been with
him all night . . . at the hospital where Pat is lying. . . ."

Gail lifted her shocked young face and turned to him,
her eyes wide and dazed. "Is he going to b· all right, Rod?"
In the welter of the questions that waited to be asked, that
was the only one that somehow really mattered at that
moment.

She saw Rod shake his head. "It's early to say, Gail;
the bullet rested dangerously near to his heart. He had lost

167

a good deal of blood by the time Donlan found him. They don't dare to operate for the extraction of the bullet until he is a bit stronger, but they gave him a blood transfusion while O'Grady and I were waiting at the hospital, and afterwards they let O'Grady see him for a few minutes. He was able to give a whispered brief account of what had happened to him." Rod passed a hand across his brow; a small gesture of weariness that caught at Gail's heart. In the clear level sunlight his strong dark face showed lines of strain and fatigue. For a moment he seemed reluctant to go on.

"Did he know who it was that attacked him?" Gail prompted.

Rod gave her a hollow look. "It was Leahy. But actually I . . . feel myself very much to blame for the whole thing. You see I'm the person Leahy was really after."

"Oh no, Rod!" Gail cried out in shocked, sharp protest. Her hand shot out, clutching at his arm—an instinctive, involuntary gesture of which she was instantly ashamed. But Rod seemed quite unaware of the brief touch. Looking out over smooth pale water he went on in a wooden tone:

"It seems I'd committed the unforgivable sin in threatening to report Leahy to the police the other day. He'd been using the cellars of Creek Cottage as a hiding-place for the illicit whiskey he has been distilling. I came across part of his distilling equipment and went for him bald-headed. I *didn't* report him to the police . . . I didn't even mention the matter to my uncle, who is a magistrate and might have felt he ought to do something about it. All I intended was to give Leahy a fright . . . but what I'd overlooked is that the chap is three-parts mad from years of brooding on his imagined wrongs, and my more or less innocent threat tipped the scales." Rod gave a brief, mirthless laugh. "He seems to have decided to take a pot-shot at me and be damned to the consequences, and he had worked out an elaborate plan to ambush me at some unspecified date and place, had even enlisted a couple of silly youths to help him . . . lads who work with him at the turf cutting. One of the boys, however, was a decoy . . . sent to work with Leahy by Pat. The whole thing gets frightfully complicated at this stage . . ." Rod broke off with an impatient shrug and standing up began to pace the grass verge nervously, startling a water-hen which went skimming out of the reeds with a shrill cry.

His hands thrust into his pockets, Rod looked after it in an exasperated way, very tall and tense in his immaculately creased evening black, one Byronesque lock tumbling across his corrugated brow. "Why Pat didn't *tell* me!" he cried out. "It seems he has been uneasy about Leahy's carryings-on for some time, suspecting the chap was cracking up. Joe Lattery, the boy he used to watch Leahy, was brother of one of his stable lads. He'd been helping Leahy with some kind of smuggling racket he has been carrying on, and wasn't very easy in his mind when he discovered Pat knew of these activities. Anyway, he seems to have been glad enough to put himself on the side of law and order as represented by Pat. He was scared of Leahy—blackmailed by him practically. Pat promised to protect him and the boy was only too relieved to be saved from complicity in the attempt to murder me." Rod shuddered visibly.

"If only Pat had come straight to me about the whole grim business!" he said again. "But gallantly he tackled it alone. He must have known he was risking his life when he faced Leahy yesterday afternoon, confronted him with the evidence of the proposed ambush and told him he was taking the whole story to Sergeant O'Grady."

"Yesterday afternoon," Gail broke in, her voice shaken with horror. With awful clarity she was remembering the rather odd conversation in Finnmacool's loose-box the day before . . the look of strain on Pat's young face, the barely concealed fear in his grey eyes.

"Leahy didn't waste much time," Rod said.

"How did he know Pat was going to be there . . . near Kildoona gates last night?" Gail whispered.

"Oh, he worked that very cleverly. He phoned Pat about eleven o'clock at his home, disguising his voice, pretending to be O'Toole, my own head gardener. This

Leahy-O'Toole disembodied voice asked Pat to come to Kildoona gates right away on a matter of gravest urgency. 'It concerns the safety of a mutual friend of ours, and it cannot be discussed on the phone,' the supposed O'Toole said. Pat fell into the trap, imagined O'Toole had stumbled upon some evidence concerning Leahy's vicious intentions towards myself, and out he rushed in his car. Found not O'Toole, but Leahy waiting for him . . . with a revolver. That's about all the poor boy knows, but it's obvious Leahy left Pat for dead—and if he'd known a bit more about anatomy he'd have been right. Then he apparently made off in Pat's car; he's probably the other end of Ireland by this time."

Gail stood up. She felt curiously weak and limp. The morning sun seemed to have lost all its power to warm her. With a shiver she wrapped her creamy coat more closely about her.

"You're cold!" Rod said in a tone both anxious and faintly surprised. For the first time he seemed to be really aware of her—as herself; not just a convenient listener to whom he could pour out his overcharged heart. The dead look went out of his eyes. They were vital, alight, fixed on her with an intensity that sent a queer little electrical thrill through her veins. And yet she couldn't stop her teeth chattering.

"I suppose it's shock making me shake so stupidly," she offered apologetically. "Oh, Rod, it so easily might have been you instead of Pat!" Suddenly she felt so sick and giddy that she closed her eyes, waiting for the wave of nausea to pass. Rod put a steadying arm about her shoulder. "That night when Leahy was crouching by the lake road with a gun . . . it *was* you he was waiting for. I knew it . . . I felt the awful danger in the air . . . although I couldn't explain it to you," she whispered shakenly.

"I wasn't very nice to you that evening, Gail," Rod said gently. His arm tightened about her shaking shoulder. It was all quite crazy, of course, a momentary tenderness born of this hour's grim tidings, but all at once it seemed the most natural thing in the world that she should give herself up to the comfort of his embrace, resting her head against his shoulder.

"You thought I was being silly and nervous on my own account," she said, "but I wasn't. I was . . . so terribly afraid for you! I knew how angry Leahy was with you over Creek Cottage . . . and there was the day Tara Lad bolted; I remembered how bitterly he cursed you. . . ."

"So you came rushing forward to warn me," Rod went on for her, "not giving a thought for your own safety. Didn't it occur to you that Leahy might have been mad enough to send a bullet after you that night?"

"I suppose I did realize it in a vague way . . . but I could only think that I'd got to keep you from bringing the car round that corner into range of his gun." She could feel his hand closing convulsively about her shoulder; even through the folds of her coat the grip of his steel-hard fingers was painful . . . and very disturbing.

With a quick convulsive sigh she moved away from him and stooped to pick up the wet swim suit she had left on the grass. For a moment she busied herself folding it away inside the towel, not daring to meet Rod's eyes. It was disconcerting the way he just stood there in that throbbing silence . . . watching her. Her heart thudded as she knelt on the grass, folding and refolding the towel.

"Why didn't you tell me all that at the time . . . instead of putting up with my ill-temper . . . letting me bully you?" he asked.

"It wasn't easy," she said, adding recklessly after an instant: "I guessed what you were thinking about me, you see; that I was stopping you for some . . . silly reason of my own." The shamed color ran up into her cheeks. But suddenly she knew that now, in this moment when they were both lifted out of themselves by their shared horror over Pat's accident, she might speak freely. It was intolerable that he should go on misunderstanding everything she did or said. Moving towards him over the moist marshy grass, her bathing bundle tucked in the crook of her arm, she regarded him squarely. "You haven't made much of a secret of your poor opinion of me this summer, have you, Rod? I don't quite know what I've done to deserve it . . . we were such good friends in London last year."

"Perhaps I imagined we were rather . . . more than friends," Rod said with a quiet purposefulness that sent the blood racing back to her heart. She stood halted before him, her courage faltering; for she had not foreseen that the conversation could take so definitely challenging a turn.

"I thought of you last year, Gail," he went on, "as someone pretty wonderful; refreshingly different to the usual run of girls . . . and utterly honest. It hadn't occurred to me that you were just amusing yourself . . . going about with me merely because it was rather fun to be seen with the star rider of the season's most important Horse Show. I expect I was a fool and got it all wrong from the start . . . but it was a bit of a jolt that last evening of the Show when you said goodbye to me with such jaunty finality and announced that you were shortly to be married. Probably it was ridiculously old-world of me to find it a little odd that an engaged girl should have had the wish to spend every moment of her spare time for nearly a fortnight with a chap who could mean nothing to her . . . without even mentioning that she was engaged."

"But I wasn't engaged, Rod!" For the life of her Gail couldn't keep the sharp denial back. The truth bubbled up to her lips and somehow poured itself out of its own accord. She was past all thoughts of discretion now. "I wasn't going to be married . . . there was no one in my life but a boy who lives in the same road as my family and was a childhood sweetheart. But I wasn't the least bit in love with him. . . ."

"Then why on earth did you say you *were* going to be married?" Rod demanded with justifiable exasperation.

Just for an instant Gail hesitated—then once more she let herself go on the incautious flood-tide of candor. It was seven o'clock in the morning; she was stunned with the shock of hearing about Pat . . . a little dizzy after her early swim, and somehow the sight of Rod standing there in the bright morning sunlight in his evening tails and

172

white tie added the last touch of improbability to the moment. "I had to say something to save my pride," she heard herself declare with utter recklessness. "You see, it had meant rather a lot to me, too, that fortnight of friendship with you, and then when I heard you were going to marry Glenda Grayson . . ." She broke off, halted by the sheer blazing astonishment in his eyes.

"Who told you such an outrageous and malicious lie?" he demanded with a terrible directness that made it difficult to reply truthfully without reducing Sonia to the level of the most unpleasant kind of liar. And yet she had to go on with it, now that she had begun. Rod would insist on the whole story now.

Softening it down a little, Gail murmured uneasily: "Sonia seemed to be very certain that was what was going to happen . . . and perhaps felt it was kind to warn me. . . ."

"So it was Sonia!" Rod's face was so thunderous that Gail said quickly and not very convincingly: "I'm sure she meant well . . . and anyhow it's all in the past, isn't it? It can't possibly make any difference. I mean . . . if it wasn't Glenda it was Shelagh . . . and that's so wonderful . . . so right . . . she's such a darling!" The words trailed away into an awful hollow silence.

Thrusting his hands savagely into his pockets, hunching his shoulders, Rod began to pace up and down once more, his face still wearing its thundercloud look. Had she said too much? Gail wondered unhappily. Had it been wrong of her to try to vindicate herself, making Rod realize she wasn't the cheap, horrible flirt he had thought her? At the bottom of her heart lurked the conviction that—at this particular juncture in their lives, with the wedding barely a week away—it might have been wiser to say nothing. But the unnerving news about Pat—with its implications of Rod's own narrowly escaped danger—had thrown her off her guard. His mood of unusual gentleness with her too had made her feel it would be a unique opportunity of clearing away some of the bitterness that had lain between them. She had not meant to do more than assure him of her innocent good faith last summer, but somehow the conversation had got out of hand.

173

She said in a small uncertain voice: "I think perhaps I ought to be getting back to the house now. . . ."

Halting in his pacing, Rod swung round. "I'll run you up in the car," he offered brusquely. Gail felt she ought to point out that it would only take her a few moments to go on foot if she took the short cut through the boreen, but already Rod was holding the car door open for her with such a fiercely determined air that she was afraid to argue with him. He looked so angry and forbidding that she kept silent as they set off. Men hated emotional scenes, she reflected bleakly, and if she hadn't exactly made an emotional scene she had launched them both on a pretty disturbing kind of inquest on their past friendship.

It was a short drive along the lake road and then up the hill to the gates of the Lodge. When they were half-way down the long avenue with its dense border of shrubs and beech trees Rod stopped and switched off the engine. "I'm glad we've had this talk, Gail," he said in a gruff hard tone. "And I want to tell you now that I'm more sorry than I can say for the way I've misjudged you. Will you forgive me?"

"There's nothing to forgive, Rod," she tried to answer in a bright matter-of-fact way. To her horror she felt her eyes filling with tears. If Rod were going to be nice to her about everything, it was almost more than she could bear. She turned her head away quickly, but not before he had caught the glitter of tears on her lashes.

"Gail . . . darling . . . don't cry!"

Somehow she was in his arms then, her damp curly head on his shoulder. She couldn't think clearly any more, clinging to him on a blind surge of feeling that was too intense to have anything to do with ordinary happiness. This was rapture and pain . . . and bewilderment; a tornado of half-terrifying emotion sweeping her along. And it was all wrong. She had no right to be here with Rod holding her against his heart as though he would never let her go.

"What a muddle! What an all-time, incredible mix-up!" His voice floated away despairingly above her head— still angry. Not with her any more . . . but with Sonia.

174

The things he was saying about his sister then were justifiable rather than polite, and if his language became a little lurid occasionally it was understandable. No man enjoys being made a fool of by an interfering female relative. "She knew perfectly well I had no intention of marrying my cousin Glenda," he stormed. "Such a thing had never entered my mind. I'd even talked it over with her . . . with Sonia. . . . I made it quite clear to her I wanted to marry *you*!"

Gail caught her breath sharply. Triumph flooded her heart . . . warm, healing, intoxicating. Whatever happened now she could go through the rest of her long lonely life with her head held high. Rod had wanted to marry her . . . he had loved her as much as that!

"When was it she told you this fiendish lie about my matrimonial plans?" he was asking her.

She drew away from him a little, looking up at him through her wet lashes. "It was after that cocktail party at Regency Gardens the last day of the Show. Glenda had just arrived. . . ."

"Why didn't you tell me right away?"

"Rod, how *could* I have told you? I was so unsure of myself . . . feeling that I was such a little nobody compared with all the dazzling people who were your friends. It seemed to me . . . well, absolutely inevitable that it should be someone smart and clever and sophisticated like Glenda you would want to marry. It had been such a wonderful few days . . . knowing you, being with you; but I'd never really dared to hope it meant very much to you. It didn't occur to me for an instant to doubt Sonia's word."

In bleak silence he regarded her until at last he exploded forcefully: "Lord! What a ghastly mess the whole thing is!"

The raw misery in his voice tore at her heart. She said bitterly: "Oh, Rod, I wish we'd never started on this conversation! It's all so useless. What happened last year is over and done with. You've got Shelagh now. She's so . . . right for you, and . . . she loves you terribly."

Somehow she made herself say it brightly, courageously, with an air of utter conviction. It was the right thing to say. It was *true*.

Rod's face went rigid; his eyes had a burning, tortured look. "Gail," he whispered brokenly, "you're . . . superb! All that I thought you were—and more. You'd do the honest thing every time if it killed you . . . wouldn't you?" He turned away from her and when he spoke again it was in an altered tone, dead now and wooden as though he repeated a lesson unwillingly learned. "You're so right, of course! I've got Shelagh, and she is, as you say . . . adoring and adorable. Too sweet, too young and trusting to be hurt. So . . . that seems to be very much that!" With a goaded movement he flicked at the ignition switch, bringing the engine to life. In a moment or two they would reach the house and this strange interlude with its mixture of pain and forbidden rapture would be over. And afterwards? For one clear, blinding instant, as they drove under the dark trees, Gail looked into the abyss of emptiness that stretched ahead of her, and her courage faltered. To have learned of the happiness that might have been; to have learned . . . too late. It was almost more than she could bear.

And then Rod was stopping the car again where a bend in the avenue still hid them from the house. But it was only to say in a hard tired voice that he thought perhaps he had better go home and change before he disturbed Shelagh. "I can't go round in tails and a white tie all day," he pointed out with dreary resignation. "And I expect Shelagh will want me to take her over to the hospital." But there wasn't all that immediate hurry, he went on. "Pat was sleeping when we left him, heavily doped. I may as well let Shelagh have her sleep too. Poor little Lalagh," he added gently, "she'll need all the rest she can get before she faces what the day may bring to her. She's going to feel this a lot—she's very fond of Pat."

They were talking about Pat again then, in quick hushed sentences, their faces grave with concern, their own tangled affairs for the moment forgotten. "He's young and strong and terrifically healthy," Rod summed it up. "If

176

there's as much as one chance in a hundred for him he'll be able to cash in on it with his magnificent constitution. But we'll know more about that when the bullet has been extracted."

They sat silently, thinking of Pat, and then Gail leaned over and pressed the catch of the car door. "Don't come any farther with me, Rod," she said, meaning only that it was but a few steps to the house, but suddenly the words seemed to echo hollowly, with a profounder and infinitely more tragic meaning. All her heart in her eyes, she turned to look at him in farewell and with a muffled exclamation he took her in his arms and kissed her full on the mouth.

"What are we going to do, Gail?" he cried out. "What are we going to do? I can't lose you now that I've found you again . . . I can't let you go!"

Blindly she tore herself away from him and went running down the curving avenue, into the house.

CHAPTER SIXTEEN

THE days that followed had a nightmare quality for Gail. She felt as if she were living through one of those endless and confusing dreams that have no clear meaning, but are haunted by an unutterable sadness. Her early morning meeting with Rod by the lake and the tragedy of Leahy and Pat seemed inextricably mixed up. Rod's dear, forbidden love had come to her in an aura of death . . . and was as hopeless as death. But she wouldn't let herself think about it. She didn't dare to think. Time enough for that in the bleak and lonely years that stretched ahead of her. Heartache would keep. The clear terrible knowledge of all she had lost awaited her, a cup she must drink drop by slow bitter drop as long as she lived. For the moment she occupied herself feverishly, evading it. And there was plenty to do at Kildoona Lodge.

The preparations for the wedding had to go on, though no one had much heart for them now. Presents were pouring in; car loads by every post, a constant stream of messengers bringing the local offerings to the door where they were taken in by Bridget who was as excited over each fresh gift as if it had been brought for herself.

Gail, with Miss Quinn to help her, unpacked the endless parcels, setting them out on a long trestle table in the little-used library that had once been Shelagh's school room. Cake-stands and silver cruet sets and canteens of cutlery and crystal-ware; porcelain ornaments from Copenhagen, pewter from Sweden, a Limoges dinner service from Glenda Grayson and her Embassy brother in Paris.

It was the third day after the shooting, the day of Pat's operation, that Gail knelt on the floor, waist-deep in straw and tissue paper, taking the exquisite dishes and plates from the immense wooden crate. Seated in a shabby leather armchair by the fireless hearth, Miss Ross watched her with lack-lustre eyes. All morning they had been waiting for the telephone message which was to tell them of Pat's condition. Shelagh was at the hospital, with Sir Charles and Rod.

"Anyone would think young Crampton was a member of the family," Miss Drewitt had remarked rather acidly at breakfast time after Shelagh, refusing to eat anything, had swallowed a cup of coffee and rushed out to join Rod and Sir Charles who had called for her with the car.

"Indeed then, he might well be," Miss Quinn returned equably; "wasn't he practically brought up alongside of Shelagh? The only young companion she had from the time she arrived in this house, a lost little girl of five after her parents being killed in a plane smash-up. I remember well the way she fretted the first few days and how Pat was the only one who could do anything with her. A fine little boy of nine he was at the time, with yellow curls like an angel. He brought a weeshy Shetland pony over for her and taught her to ride it . . . and from that day to this the two of them have been as inseparable as a brother and sister. It will be the death of her," Miss Quinn had ended tragically, "if anything were to happen to him!"

"She'd still have the Major left," Miss Drewitt had suggested dryly.

At which Miss Quinn lost her temper and said: "Of course she would have the Major left—but if you can't see that if things go wrong with Pat today it's going to ruin the wedding for the whole of us . . . the Major included, he being a man with a warm heart in his body . . . then there is no more to be said!"

The trouble with Jane Drewitt, Gail thought now, as she went on shaking the dusty straw out of the packing case, was that she had a precise clinical mind that liked everything to be clearly defined. Pat wasn't really Shelagh's brother and yet he was obviously something more than a friend. It was difficult to tie a neat label on his relationship to the folk at the Castle and Kildoona Lodge. And that annoyed Jane, who had spent a great deal of time learning to apportion labels to the bones and organs of the human body and thought you could specify the emotions in the same precise fashion. Even Miss Quinn, who was jealous for Rod's rights, and had more than once appeared suspicious of Shelagh's affection for Pat, could find it natural now that she should put everything aside but her anxiety for him. He was her childhood's friend and it was right that she should spend most of her time these difficult days in the small private ward at the Convent Hospital where he lay fighting for his life. The fact that Rod sometimes joined her in her vigil made the situation even more safely conventional. And there was Sir Charles—as deeply involved in neighborly pity as the rest of them—putting himself and his car at the disposal of poor distracted Mrs. Crampton any hour of the day or night. Miss Ross, too, disrupted her invalidish routine to join Sir Charles on these errands of mercy. The two of them would sit up half the night, closeted in the drawing-room with a spirit lamp ready for the brewing of fresh coffee, waiting for Rod and Shelagh to come home with the latest news of the invalid. Disquieting enough news it had been . . . and today when it came it would be decisive. On tenterhooks they awaited it.

179

"Twenty-four of everything and not a single crack in the lot," Gail pronounced, sitting back on her heels to survey the stacked china.

"How splendid!" Miss Ross murmured with forced enthusiasm, breaking off sharply at the sound of a light footstep in the hall.

The door opened and Shelagh came in; white-lipped, subdued. In the short interval since Pat's accident she had altered perceptibly, losing all her gaiety and young inconsequence. Perhaps it was that she had at last, and rather tragically, been forced to grow up.

With an exhausted sigh she sank down into the nearest chair. Her face wore an unnaturally blank expression, as though she was determined not to let the smallest sign of feeling show through the rigidly controlled mask.

"Pat's operation is over," she said.

Unseeingly she gazed at the array of presents on the library table. "They've got the bullet out and done something very clever and complicated about a small wound they found on the heart . . . a laceration of the left ventricle I think is what the surgeon called it . . . and now . . ." She broke off, her blue eyes black-centered and hollow. "Now it's a matter of waiting. Pat has gone pretty far away . . . they're . . . not sure if he'll be able to come back." Suddenly the facade of unnatural composure crumpled. With a sob she buried her face in her hands.

Miss Ross got up and hurried over to her. Gail thought in a quick, astonished aside that she had never known her move so nimbly.

Standing with her arm about Shelagh's shaking shoulders, she looked straight and alert, her eyes bright with concern, her fine-boned face that was usually stern with endurance, soft now with sympathy. But she didn't, Gail observed, offer any fatuous words of comfort, merely saying gently: "You're tired out, poor child; you ought to go and lie down on your bed and get some rest. All this has been such a strain for you. . . ."

Shelagh lifted her tear-stained face and, producing a screwed-up, characteristically grubby handkerchief, blew

180

her nose vigorously. "I'm not tired," she protested. "It's just . . . everything. I met Mrs. Leahy on the road as I was driving back from the hospital. She had the whole of the Leahy tribe with her and they were all wailing and keening. . . ."

"And so they should be!" Miss Quinn interposed in a tone of vicious satisfaction.

"I stopped and spoke to them," Shelagh went on. "Leahy has been found. Dead. He wasn't much of a driver, it seems, didn't understand Pat's car, and a few miles from the Border, for which he was apparently making, he drove smack into the side of a house on a blind turning, and the steering wheel pole-axed him."

A gasp of horror went through the room. Gail's feeling, however, changed almost at once to a sense of relief. As long as Leahy lived she would never have felt altogether assured of Rod's safety. But now . . .

"Good riddance to bad rubbish!" Miss Quinn declared stoutly, adding a little guiltily: "The Lord have mercy on the poor man, all the same!"

"He has probably saved himself and everyone concerned a good deal of trouble, by fading out of the picture at this juncture," Miss Ross put in mildly.

Miss Quinn crossed herself. "That makes two of them. . . . God send there isn't a third! I knew we wouldn't have a day's luck after Mr. Rod cut that tree."

"Quinney, for heaven's sake!" Shelagh jumped up impatiently, her face ashen grey. "The nonsense you talk! It doesn't make two . . . Pat isn't going to die!" Her voice rose hysterically.

"Of course he isn't," Miss Quinn agreed a little too hurriedly. "All I meant was that we've had two misfortunes now and I hope to goodness there isn't going to be a third . . . for that's the way ill-luck runs as a rule."

On Shelagh's wan face the ghost of a smile wavered. "Quinney, darling, you're hopeless!" And then, under her breath: "If Pat gets better, nothing will ever again seem like a misfortune to me as long as I live!" Picking up one of the cream and gold dinner plates she gazed at it absently.

181

"From Glenda and Trevor Grayson," Miss Ross said in a conscientiously bright tone.

Shelagh put the plate down again. "What happens about wedding presents when the wedding is postponed?" she asked stonily.

Miss Ross made a small startled sound. "Postponed, Lalagh!"

Shelagh gave her a bleak, wild look. "It will be at least ten days before Pat is out of danger. I couldn't be married thinking of him lying alone in that dark little room at the hospital. How could I possibly go away on a honeymoon—not knowing what was happening to him?" Her voice quivered ominously. "I've talked to Rod about it, and he quite understands. After all, this terrible thing would never have happened to Pat if he hadn't been trying to save Rod's life. It would be pretty callous of both of us to forget that."

Gail bent over the piece of packing rope she was folding and refolding nervously, her heart racing with a crazy sense of sheer reprieve. The wedding postponed! How ridiculous it was to seize on the possibility as if it were in some way a promise of fresh life! But illogical as it was, she couldn't help the quick surge of joy.

"But what about all the arrangements . . . the invitations . . . the guests? It would be a terrific task altering everything at this stage," Miss Ross was saying, aghast. "Think of the work it would make . . . specially for Gail, who would have to write to all the guests. . . ."

"Oh, please don't bother about that," Gail put in quickly, and then, wondering if she hadn't sounded altogether too enthusiastic, blushed painfully.

Since that morning by the lake she had been careful to avoid any contact with Rod, keeping rigidly out of the way when he came to the house. She had refused to let her mind dwell on the agonizing scene played out between them, steeling her heart, telling herself that the few days that must intervene before the wedding were nothing. For that short space of time she could behave honorably, blotting out the memory of his anguished: "What are we going to do about it, Gail? I can't let you go!"

182

But now . . . if the interval were to be stretched out indefinitely, would her strength continue? Her first instinctive glow of relief at the postponement of the wedding faded into cold apprehension. She felt as if the ground were slipping from under her feet.

"We could put a notice in the papers," she heard Shelagh suggesting helpfully, if a little ambiguously.

"Announcing the wedding . . . say, a month from the original date?" Miss Ross said.

But Shelagh was already leaving the room, with an impatient: "Oh, we can decide about dates later. Just now I've got to get back to the hospital. I only came home to fetch some night things. I'm going to sleep there to-night. I've promised Mrs. Crampton I would . . . she has gone home in a state of collapse. And Pat needs me. I told him I'd be by his side when he came out of the anaesthetic."

For the next few hours Miss Ross was as nearly rattled as Gail had ever known her. Her thin face flushed, her usually immaculate hair coming adrift from its pins, she limped about the house, mislaying her canes, losing her spectacles, issuing orders and cancelling them, and then issuing them all over again.

If only Shelagh had given them a fresh date for the wedding the postponement would not look so bad. And there was no time to be lost. The notice for the newspapers ought to be sent off right away—but it was so difficult to know how to word it. They must find Rod, Miss Ross decided. "See if he is at the Castle," she ordered, coming into the study where Gail was wrestling with the list of gifts to be acknowledged.

"You could hold those acknowledgments back until we are able to include something definite about the new date for the wedding day," she went on. "Ask Major Stern to come over here at once: explain to him that I can't possibly act until I have something more precise than Shelagh's vague postponement to go on. Tell him they *must* give me an alternative date. It is ridiculous, even if Pat is dangerously ill, to leave the whole thing in the air in this hapless fashion!"

Gail picked up the telephone, her heart thudding against her ribs. How could she possibly embark on a discussion of wedding dates with Rod . . . with Miss Ross at her elbow! The thought of hearing his voice on the other end of the line made her feel sick with apprehension. It was an almost unbearable relief to learn, after all, that he was not available.

"He might be at Creek Cottage, Miss," the footman who spoke to her suggested, "or away at Ardrossa, for I heard him saying this morning that he had to see the Race Steward to cancel the entries himself and Miss Shelagh and poor Mr. Crampton were making for the open event on Wednesday. . . ."

Gail relayed this to Miss Ross and saw that her tired blue eyes held the shadow of a twinkle. "Well, that piece of foolishness has taken care of itself!" she said dryly. "I'd almost forgotten that stupid race . . . and now our ill winds have blown it right out of the picture."

With an exclamation of relief she turned to the window, beyond which Sir Charles' car could be seen coming up the drive, and with what in any less stately woman would have been a flutter of helplessness she went out to greet him.

After that things went a little more smoothly. Sir Charles with his business acumen made short work of the surface difficulties of the postponement. What he thought of it privately Gail could not guess, for his kind pink face was as blandly unperturbed as ever as he helped her to draft the newspaper notice and make lists of the most urgent contacts to be notified . . . clerics, caterers, florists, guests, in the order of their importance. By bedtime the whole plan of campaign was organized and Gail got up at cock-crow the next morning to start on the heavy day's work that lay before her.

Dull work, but exacting; the very insistence and volume of it had a numbing effect. For three days it went on incessantly. In a sort of vaccum in which all her personal life was suspended, Gail typed and wrote and telephoned and answered the inevitable incoming calls from the more fidgety and self-important guests who didn't like being put off by the brief little notices they had received.

184

On the afternoon of the third day she took a final batch of letters to Miss Ross for signing. She was in the drawing-room seated on the chintz-covered couch with the big silver tea tray before her. Sir Charles, who seemed to be a fixture at Kildoona these troubled days, was sitting beside her. There was a lost, curiously young look in her speedwell blue eyes as she glanced up, and Gail saw that they were wet, as though she had recently been weeping.

With her usual air of composure, however, she signed the letters and told Gail to give them to Thady for posting. "And then," she added kindly, "you had better come and have some tea with us. You look tired; it has been a very strenuous time for you."

Tea in the drawing-room. A reward for a hard-working secretary who had, by force of circumstances, been more than a little put upon. Gail would much rather have had tea alone in the study, or with Miss Quinn and Jane Drewitt who were already installed with their cups and saucers in the arbor at the end of the lawn. But an invitation from Miss Ross was in the nature of a Royal command. With listless resignation, having given the letters to Bridget for Thady, she returned to the bright chintzy room where the hot July sun made patterns on the carpet, the breeze that perpetually flowed cool across the lake lifting the curtains gently from the open windows. There were poppies in a big bronze vase on the fireless hearth, their petals glowing like vermilion flames, giving out an almost palpable warmth.

Sir Charles stood up politely as she entered, drawing a chair forward for her, bringing her a cup of tea which he set on a low table at her side, hovering then to offer wafer-thin sandwiches. Even as she thanked him for these small attentions she heard the deep familiar voice in the hall outside and her heart plunged. *Rod!* But she would have had to face him sooner or later. To meet him here with Miss Ross and Sir Charles would be less difficult than if she had come across him when she was alone.

I will go home next week, she found herself resolving in sheer panic. This hanging about in a place where she must constantly risk running into Rod was more than she could endure. Her only safety lay in flight. She would have to invent some reasonable excuse for a hurried departure. After all, Miss Ross had engaged her to help with a wedding arranged for the end of July . . . and now that the wedding had been more or less indefinitely postponed she could say it was impossible for her to stay on.

Wildly her thoughts revolved as the drawing-room door opened slowly and Rod came in—not alone as she had pictured him, but with Shelagh by his side. The strained grim look on their faces frightened her. Had something terrible happened to Pat? Had he failed to make that long journey back through the shadows so ready to engulf him? Her hand shook as she put her tea-cup down on the little table at her side.

Miss Ross was talking brightly of more tea, more cups, ringing for Bridget. Couldn't she feel the hint of menace that hung palpable as a dark cloud in the bright, sunlit room?

In ominous silence Shelagh sank down on to a pouffe set before the hearth with its blazing poppies. Rod remained standing, leaning one elbow on the marble mantelpiece. With a herculean effort of will Gail forced herself to meet his glance. His agate-colored eyes were waiting for her, the pupils wide and dark, their deliberate intensity signalling to her some message she could not decipher. But the brief encounter left her breathless, and feeling the color fluctuate in her cheeks she turned sharply away, hearing Miss Ross pursue, in a tone that continued to ignore all disturbing undercurrents: "And how is the invalid today?"

"He's . . . better," Shelagh answered with a curious touch of reluctance. Her pale lovely little face went suddenly crimson and she drew herself up, visibly trembling now against her background of bright poppies. Her hair, Gail noticed irrelevantly, had the same blue-black density as the dusky centres of the big, flaming flowers.

"He's going to get well, Aunt Dodie. Until today we couldn't be certain. Ever since his operation he has been lying there . . . inert, not making any effort. It was as if he didn't care whether he died or not . . . as though he

has nothing to live for. I . . . couldn't bear it. But now
. . ." She stopped abruptly and threw at Rod a glance of
wild appeal. Gail saw him square his shoulders.

"Keep your pecker up, Lalagh," he murmured en-
couragingly. "Remember this is just a . . . bad moment
we've all got to get through."

Shelagh gulped, swallowed. "Aunt Dodie," she began
again desperately, "I've been making a pretty big decision
these last few days. Seeing Pat so ill has made me realize
the way I really feel about him. Until I thought he might
be going to die I didn't discover how much more important
he is to me than the romantic infatuation I've had for Rod.
I've . . . talked to Rod about it and he is being very
kind. He wouldn't want me to marry him when all the
time it is . . . to Pat my heart belongs. . . ."

In the breathless hush that followed this startling
declaration Gail found herself on her feet, murmuring in a
stupefied way to no one in particular: "I ought not to be
here . . . wouldn't you rather I went? I feel I am . . .
intruding on what is very much a family discussion."

"Sit down, Gail!" It was Rod who had taken it upon
himself to answer for the rest of them, speaking quite
sharply. Automatically Gail subsided into her chair, and
saw Miss Ross' bewildered glance go from one young face
to another. Then without looking at him she put her hand
out blindly to Sir Charles at her side, as if seeking his
support.

"Pat and I were married this morning in the little room
at the hospital," Shelagh said.

It was so quiet in the sunny room now that when a
poppy petal dropped on the tiled hearth it could be heard,
like a small rustling sigh. And then Shelagh was speaking
once more, her words rushing out in a torrent. It was all
so inevitable if only they could see it. She and Pat loved
each other with the only sort of love that mattered. "The
morning Rod came and told me he had been shot I knew
how it was with me . . . that there would be no real life
for me ever again if he died. And then these last days as
I've sat with him . . ."

"With Mrs. Crampton fading out of the picture just at
the psychological moment, leaving you romantically

187

alone." Miss Ross interjected. "Oh, she has worked on your feelings very cleverly! But she always meant you to have Pat. She needn't think I haven't seen the way she has schemed for this for many a long year. . . ."

Somehow, it was not quite the reaction Gail would have expected, and there was something curiously forced about the indignation in Miss Ross' tone. It was as though she were playing for time, bringing Mrs. Crampton into the picture when surely there were more vital factors that ought to have been mentioned first. However much Pat's mother might have tried to influence Shelagh it was quite clear that she had had nothing to do with the tragic sequence of events which had today settled matters so decisively.

"Maybe she has schemed a bit," Shelagh agreed, adding with a touch of her old light-hearted pertness, "I can only say I wish her schemes had had an earlier success! It was a terrible mistake . . . getting engaged to Rod."

"Does Rod think so, too?" Miss Ross demanded sharply. She was very pale suddenly, her blue eyes blazing. With a quick, perceptive glance, Sir Charles slipped a supporting arm about her.

Rod said quietly: "Of course it was a mistake, if Shelagh feels it was. There doesn't seem to be any more to be said."

"I don't know how it all happened!" Shelagh cried in a lost voice. "Rod . . . dazzled me. He still does in a certain way. But it wasn't ever right somehow. Not absolutely happy for either of us. I don't quite know why. It's as if after that heavenly time of the Horse Show we had got caught on a tide of circumstance that swept us along. There were so many other things in it besides what we felt about each other. The need for us to live at La'heen, for instance. We knew you wanted that, Aunt Dodie, and Charles wanted it, too. You hoped so much that we would be able to bring the Castle to life again . . . make everything the way it used to be for you in the old days."

"We expected you to live our lost lives for us," Sir Charles put in softly. "Perhaps that was a mistake, too

. . . *our* mistake. I've been uneasily aware for some time that we were forcing you two into a situation that wasn't altogether to your liking. But I thought it concerned only the fact that you didn't really want to share your first home together with an old man; even if it was a home as large as Laheen Castle." He laughed, and there was an unexpected joyousness in the sound, almost as though he had heard with relief rather than dismay Shelagh's bombshell announcement. "As a matter of fact we were going to talk to you about it today . . . Dodie and I. Shelagh's astonishing announcement makes what we had to say to you very much easier. For one thing we were going to offer you Creek Cottage as alternative accommodation— if, as seems highly probable, the Castle should not lack a chatelaine after all. . . ."

"Miss Darnley!" From the circle of Sir Charles' protective arm Miss Ross stirred, leaning forward, the returning animated color in her thin cheeks giving her a curiously youthful look. "I think perhaps you were right . . . this is very much a family discussion; I should be glad if you would leave us."

Gail stumbled to her feet, feeling vaguely snubbed and at the same time relieved. Sir Charles' last remark about the Castle and its chatelaine had hardly penetrated her bemused senses, but she was aware of the almost unbearable tension in the air. Aware, too, most painfully, of Rod holding the door open for her. As she went out he took a step after her into the hall, saying in urgent undertone: "Will you meet me by the lake after supper? About eight-thirty! I'll be waiting at that spot where you go in for your swimming."

Hardly knowing what she answered, she fled into the study, where she began sorting the litter of papers on her desk in a blind and mechanical fashion. Shelagh was married to Pat. A runaway marriage, but not quite as Pat must have dreamed it time and time again. "I'd put you up on the saddle before me and away with us to the nearest priest," he had threatened that day at Laheen Chapel. But Shelagh had sat on the edge of a hospital bed, instead of on the pommel of a saddle . . . and the

189

priest had come to them, the nursing nuns around him, their faces innocent beneath their pure white coifs. A sick-bed wedding.

And Rod was free! She tried to think about that calmly, but every conceivable human emotion seemed to be whirling through her quivering heart.

Afterwards, when she looked back at that evening, she could never remember just how she got through the interval that followed. It was, in retrospect, a chaotic vacuum, leaving only the dim recollection of herself running down the boreen to the lake. She had changed from her working blouse and skirt into a summery frock of light flowery silk. Her face in the mirror had seemed strangely unfamiliar—like a face seen in a dream, the gold-flecked eyes too brilliant, the red lips parted. It was as though a light had been lit within her, giving to everything about her an odd transparent radiance. And though she noticed these things they seemed curiously remote, utterly unconnected with herself.

Rod was waiting for her just where he had said he would be, only that he was in a rowing boat drawn up by the flat slab of granite, and somehow she had not expected him to be in a boat. He held out his hands to her in silence, and she went to him without a word, stepping down into the boat, which rocked under her light weight so that she had to concentrate on getting to the stern seat to which he was guiding her.

He was pushing off then, sitting opposite her, the sun which was low in the sky shining full into his face and making it look even more richly bronzed than usual. His eyes, very clear and quiet, regarded her unwaveringly, quite undazzled by the powerful light. That knack he had of being able to face the sun, unblinking; Gail found herself remembering how startling it had seemed to her the first time she had met him in the August glare of a London noon. In a trance-like way she gazed at him, every thought and impulse halted within her. There was no need for thoughts now, no need for words. She felt as if she were melting away, dissolving into the sunset glory that lay about them, bathing lake and hills and sky. There was nothing in the whole world any more but the level flood of evening gold . . . and Rod's strong, resolute look, absorbing her, drawing her into him. Resting her head against the cushioned back-rest she felt a deep peace possess her. All at once everything seemed very simple and right. There were no more problems. Chaos was resolved.

She saw his teeth flash, very white in his dark face, as suddenly he smiled at her. "Darling," he said, "I'm sorry if I'm staring at you . . . I can't help it. It's so wonderful, so utterly incredible to have you here! And your eyes are so beautiful this evening—all freckled and shining, like a trout in a sunny stream."

"Oh, Rod!" She tried to think of something more eloquent, but words still eluded her and a foolish knot of tears ached in her throat. Turning her head she saw the two swans, circling the clump of rushes that was their home, advancing slowly to survey the oncoming boat; too regal to be vulgarly curious, but a little disturbed all the same by the intrusion into their quiet waters.

"Do you remember the story you told me about the singing swans . . . that day at Carna House?" she asked softly, daring once more to meet his intent, impelling, unwavering look.

"I remember," Rod said. "I don't know what made me tell you about the bewitched Caer who had been turned into a swan, except that you looked so young and lost when I came upon you sleeping on the big sunny stone by the edge of the lake, and the old tale of unhappy love came into my mind. You listened so quietly, and there were tears in your eyes afterwards. Why did you cry, darling? Was it because you loved me?" Leaning towards her, he rested on his oars.

"You know that I loved you then . . . and always," she whispered.

He drew in a long steadying breath. "I wanted to hear you say it, Gail."

"They were rather like us, Caer and Aengus, weren't they?" Gail offered presently a little tremulously, breaking the throbbing silence that hung between them.

"With Sonia as the wicked spell-binder," Rod said grimly.

191

"But it's all gone now . . . the dark spell is broken."

"It *had* to be broken," Rod said. "I knew it the other morning when I held you in my arms and felt your quick response. Just how I was going to manage it, with my marriage to Shelagh so near, I couldn't quite see, but I knew, once I had found you again, I couldn't let you go."

"I was going to . . . disappear, Rod . . . run away. . . ."

"If you had done that, I would have followed you—to the ends of the earth. But in the meantime I was . . . waiting, with the queerest assurance that things were working out. It was the same feeling I had that week last year in London; the absolute certainty that we belonged to each other. Only this time it was much stronger, and so right and inevitable that all lesser things would have had to give away before it. Perhaps I sensed, too, Shelagh's odd uneasiness as our wedding day drew near, though naturally I had no idea how simply she would resolve all our difficulties! I only knew there could be no compromise, no half-measures." His jaw took on its most dogged line as he looked out over the wide waters. "If poor mad Leahy only knew how strangely he played into our hands!" he mused.

With a sudden movement then he picked up the oars and began to row purposefully. Trailing her fingers in the warm limpid water, Gail turned her thoughts backward, and shivered. "What an impossible tangle it all was, Rod!" she said, her voice full of wonder that it was a tangle no more.

"And now here I am rowing you . . . home." His smile flashed out, assured, triumphant, and she saw that they were turning into the narrowing waters that led to Creek Cottage. "We are going to look at it together," he said. " 'The House of Gail.' Its name has rung in my heart so long with a promise that seemed a mockery. But now . . . this evening, my uncle has made me a present of it; though he doesn't know yet how timely a present it is, in fact a wedding gift!"

"Rod . . . don't tell them, Miss Ross and Shelagh and everyone, about us, I mean." Gail's voice was breathless. "let me go back to my own family first. Let me get away."

"Only that if you do go I shall come with you!"

"Then tell them from London; write to them. I couldn't bear all the comments and excitement, and perhaps opposition, there would be if we were to blurt it out now. Miss Ross especially; I feel so sure she would disapprove . . . thinking, quite rightly, that I am not nearly . . . important enough to . . . to be your . . . wife." The rich color rushed up into her face as she brought out the incredible word.

Watching her, Rod's eyes twinkled. "I should hate to marry an important woman," he laughed. "And in any case Miss Ross will be far too busy with her own affairs to have time to oppose anything. You left the drawing-room too soon this afternoon and missed the most startling revelation of all. My uncle and Miss Ross have decided to announce their wedding!"

Gail stared at him in such utter blankness that he threw back his head and laughed again. "Apparently they have been worrying themselves ill over it for the past fortnight, wondering how they were going to break it to us that Aunt Dodie had at last succumbed to a life-long courtship and come to the conclusion that she is sufficiently restored in health to make my uncle a happy man. The most awkward part of it all was that they would want Laheen Castle for themselves now and they weren't quite sure how we would feel about that. Shelagh's elopement has been an absolute godsend to them, actually."

Gail shook her head. "I . . . just can't take it in, Rod. There have been too many miracles already today."

His happiness seemed to flow all about her, his eyes brimming over with it, as on one last strong stroke he drove the boat in under the willows and jumping out, tied up.

"But the miracles have only begun," he said.

She was out of the boat now and his arm was about her. Together they turned to look at the long, low white house that waited for them beyond the sweep of terraced lawn. Untenanted as yet but already cared for, the woodwork of doors and windows freshly painted, the fragrant climbing roses trimmed back, paths weeded, flower-beds gay with color. Seeing all this, Gail turned to the man at her side, her heart in her eyes. "You've worked so hard on it, Rod;

made it so beautiful . . . it's almost as though you somehow *knew* why you were doing it."

"I think perhaps I *did* know, my darling, in some curious way. I was oddly attracted by this old house, seeing it as a place of peace and fulfilment, in which, if I had the chance, I could be very happy. And now . . ."—his strong voice faltered—"it seems as if I am to have the chance, though it is almost too much to believe. Tell me it's true, Gail, darling; tell me again and again!"

She lifted her face to him, her answer in her eyes, and as he kissed her there were no questions left between them, no doubts, no shadows of misunderstanding. Certainty flowed into their hearts, golden and clear as the evening sunlight that touched their heads in benediction as they stood by the lapping water locked in each other's arms.

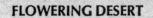
FLOWERING DESERT

Flowering
Desert

Tim Gregson had a peculiar knack for finding Lorraine in compromising situations. He evidently thought she was a cheap little flirt, addicted to promiscuous kissing with any man who happened to be around.

He annoyed Lorraine intensely. How dared this prig of a Scotsman set himself up as judge of her character! And suppose he did think she was only a featherbrained manhunter? It couldn't matter less.

Yet, deep inside, she had to admit it did!

"WHAT
Comtess
down th
was lost

"Pairii
I hoped n
very asha
provincial
types, mal
my heart
cheeks. Bu
African sun
muscular, sl
my own. In

She was proud, she said, to be the
blue-stocking who had taken an
English at the age of twenty
was the sort of nineteenth-c
use! But she was a dear
an exotic blossom on o
because away back
into the realms
was what is
financier, o
was one
in an

posed, and t ... an odd ache in my throat.
The day was suddenly too beautiful.

"Come on!" I said, tugging at Del's hand.

We ran down the tiled path between the ranks of exotic shrubs, slowing up when we came to the steep descent to the beach. A moment or two later we were in the warm, incredibly blue sea. I struck out, putting all my energy into it, swimming away from Del, who was rollong around, making porpoise noises. Del could swim like a fish and was as happy under the water as above it. I wasn't in love with him, I told myself as I cut through the silken water. His attraction for me was mainly physical. It must be so. He was so different from the university characters I'd had crushes on before. In fact, I had never met anyone quite like him, and he fascinated me. He was part of this exciting Tunisian holiday.

Aunt Vinnie, or Lavinia to give her her full name, had offered it to me as a graduating present.

199

great-aunt of a
honours degree in
-one. Blue-stocking
entury word she would
, and I loved her. She was
ur very ordinary family tree,
n the dim past she had married
f high finance. Her late husband
nown, somewhat mysteriously, as a
r, alternatively, a financial wizard. That
of the things which was said about him
mpressive obituary notice in *The Times*.
nyway he had left a whale of a lot of money
ehind him and Aunt Vinnie seemed to spend as
lavishly as she wanted to, mostly on good works.
But she didn't stint herself when she went on
holiday, and very often she invited me to go with
her. I was her goddaughter, her favourite. She
had taken me to Spain, to Italy, to the French
Riviera. And this spring, tired of the tourist-
trampled resorts of Europe, we had come to
Tunisia, to an exquisite little seaside resort, called
Sidi Akbar, not far from Tunis. Here Aunt Vinnie
had found sunshine, plus novelty, plus the peace
and quiet which are becoming more and more rare
in a world of cut-rate packaged tours. Also she
had found Natalie, Comtesse de la Fontaine, a
jaded elderly American socialite who at some time
in her many attempts at matrimony had married
into the French aristocracy. She wasn't at all
Aunt Vinnie's type, I should have thought, but
she was gay and gallant in her battered way, and
they got on famously. An attraction of opposites
perhaps. And Del—Delmer Lloyd to give him his
full name—was, improbably, her secretary.

"Hi-ya!" he called out to me now. He had
reached the anchored raft with the name of our
hotel painted in white on its side. When I swam

over to him he pulled me up beside him and we lay face downward on the hot, damp drugget that covered the boards of the raft. The hot April sunshine beat down on us, the sea and the sky were a sapphire blue, and Del's sherry-coloured eyes regarded me with a frank adoration that sent little shivers down my spine. It was all too good to be true. He couldn't really be all that crazy about me. I wasn't going to be taken in by the way he was looking at me.

He touched my bare shoulder lightly, caressingly. "The less you wear the more beautiful you are," he said.

I buried my face in the curve of my arm. "Picture me a few weeks from now in a stuffy classroom, teaching a bunch of bored schoolgirls how to study Shakespeare for O level English without growing to hate him."

It wasn't only Del I was trying to bring back to reality.

"I refuse to picture anything of the sort," he declared emphatically. "Why spoil this perfect moment? You don't have to go back to England and become a schoolmarm. There are far more exciting possibilities ahead of you."

"Such as?"

"Remind me to tell you some other time." He threw me another spine-tingling sherry-coloured glance. "We've been long enough baking on this raft."

He was right, of course. Even as early as April it can be dangerous in Tunisia to lie in the full glare of the midday sun.

We slid off the raft into the beautiful warm water, Del diving, rolling, showing off. I followed him slowly, admiring his skill. There was no doubt he had 'made' my holiday. Fond as I am of Aunt Vinnie it might have been a little dull, even in

Tunisia, gearing myself to her routine. Little walks, little talks, afternoon naps, endless hours spent sitting about on the *terrasse* of the Hotel Alzara watching the livelier residents come and go. Aunt Vinnie, after all, is seventy-five, and though young in mind for her age, hardly to be treated as my contemporary. So I had been glad of Del's company, enjoying his easy charm and his good looks. It was amusing to feel the envious glances of other women when he escorted me to the cocktail bar, or kissed my hand when we meet in the foyer. That was the sort of thing he did superbly. The elegant Continental bow, the worshipping glance as he pressed a woman's hand to his lips. Any woman—Aunt Vinnie, the Comtesse —he never missed an opportunity of showing how well he could do it. And if it was all a bit theatrical that wasn't to be wondered at. For Del's career was acting. When he could land a suitable part, in a film or on television.

Like the Comtesse he came from a French-American family. There was a widowed mother and sister who lived in a remote Provençal village. Del's headquarters were, of course, in Paris, where he rented a humble room on the Left Bank. He was perennially hard up, he told me, though he drove one of those enormous shining American cars, and seemed to have an endless supply of clothes in the latest fashion, all of superb cut and quality. When he wasn't acting he scraped a living editing scripts, dubbing French films into English, or posing for commercials. Occasionally he did a little freelance journalism. At the moment he was helping the Comtesse to write her memoirs.

"I can't afford to be fussy," he had said to me one day when he was explaining how he had come to undertake this task. There were times, he admitted, when the Comtesse almost drove him up the wall, ordering him about, expecting him to fetch and carry for her like any humble paid companion. "But one has to live," he said, "and the theatre or television jobs that are really up my street are few and far between." When he talked like that I felt he was an idealist, refusing to lower his standards, or prostitute his talents. His real ambition was to write a play, act in it and direct it . . . and set the Seine on fire.

Now he surfaced in a flurry beside me, spouting like a whale. "Come on, lazybones!" he challenged me. "I'll race you to the shore."

Walking across the hot sands I whipped off my bathing cap and shook my hair free.

"Goldilocks!" Del murmured fatuously. "I'm glad you wear a cap and aren't one of those girls who come out of the sea all rats' tails."

"I hate salt water in my hair," I said. "And, incidentally, it isn't golden—just plain mousey. You must have the sun in your eyes."

"Maybe it was a bit on the mousey side when you first came here," Del conceded. "But it isn't mousey now." He studied it critically. "It's a gorgeous sort of honey colour; just right with those dark blue eyes of yours and your sun-tan."

It was true that my weeks in the North African sunshine had burnished me up a bit, but I was still a long way from being a true blonde.

"Has anyone ever told you your eyes are the colour of wet violets?" Del enquired.

"Oh, lots of people." I made a grimace at him. "My professors at Trent University used to tell me every day."

Under their striped umbrella Aunt Vinnie and the Comtesse were sipping their before-lunch aperitifs. We stopped to talk to them for a moment, and I collected my beach-wrap, a smart little coolie

203

coat I'd made myself out of a bargain remnant and was rather proud of.

In the cocktail lounge it was cool and dim. Del ordered Martinis and we took them over to a small table in one of the arched Moorish alcoves, overlooking a garden full of lemon trees and roses and big red lilies with thick fleshy stems. Beyond the lemon trees was a superb view of the coastline—Carthage and Cap Bon; the mountains behind Carthage all misty purple against a swooning sky. The whole world swam in the noontide heat haze. And after a couple of Martinis my head began to swim too. Mid-morning drinks on an empty tummy always make me feel cheerfully disembodied. Not that I'm in the habit of having mid-morning drinks—alcoholic ones. Hot cocoa in the University canteen was more my mark. A fact I pointed out to Del, still, I suppose, with a faint hope of keeping my feet on terra firma.

"Cocoa!" he shuddered.

"Hot," I said, "and sustaining. Also very cheap. Students are invariably penniless."

"But you're no penniless student," Del said.

"No, I'm a penniless graduate looking for a job as schoolmarm."

He laughed. "Anyone less like a schoolmarm I've yet to see! You know you'd hate it, and after all, what need is there for you to earn your living in such a dull way? You'd be much better off sticking around with your godmother. She'd adore having you to live with her." The laughter in his eyes had been replaced by an oddly shrewd look which vaguely troubled me.

"Who told you Aunt Vinnie was my godmother?" I asked rather sharply. His idea of me tagging after my aunt as a sort of rich relative's parasite annoyed me.

204

"The Comtesse," Del said. "And it's quite obvious that your aunt, with no children of her own, is very fond of you." His handsome features creased in a whimsical smile. "Any day now she'll be waving her wand and whisking you away in a golden coach to meet your fairy prince."

"Honestly, Del!" I gave a loud unmusical hoot. "How can you talk such rubbish?" I'm no Cinderella, let me tell you, and I don't believe in golden coaches or fairy godmothers."

"No?" Del queried softly. Over the rim of his glass he gave me one of his most melting glances, but all it did to me was increase the small nagging doubt.

This isn't real, I told myself, looking out at the travel folder scenery. Del isn't real. The pretty speeches he makes could have come out of the parts he plays on films and television, or from the scripts he edits. Being in North Africa has turned my head. It is all so exotic . . . including Del. And what business has a plain straightforward girl like me with the exotic?

I turned my mind firmly to the small country town in Sussex that is my home. We live in a mock Tudor villa that has seen its best days. It is a roomy villa, since we are a large family. My father is a bank manager. One of my sisters is training as a nurse, the other is a secretary, my two brothers are still at school. My mother slaves away, looking after us all with a cheerful good will, cooking, shopping, house-cleaning, with no more than the help of an indifferent char who comes in twice a week. *That* was my environment. The fact that I was sitting in the cocktail bar of a Tunisian luxury hotel sipping Martinis with a dream-boat like Delmer Lloyd had nothing to do with my real life. It would be as well if I kept that fact firmly in mind.

Refusing a second Martini, I went to my room to change for lunch. Crossing the foyer on the way I exchanged brief greetings with Elaine Ben Akhtal—a Frenchwoman married to a young Arab who was a member of the Bourgiba Government. I had struck up one of those casual hotel friendships with her and longed to know her better. Her life with its Oriental background intrigued me. They lived in Tunis, she had told me, but during the spring and summer she spent a good deal of time at the Hotel Alzara with her two children, so that they could have the benefit of the sea air. Raschid, her husband, joined them at weekends. I had met him briefly and found him interesting.

After lunch Del disappeared to work on the memoirs. Aunt Vinnie retired to her room for a nap and advised me to do the same. But I decided to go into Tunis and look at the shops. I couldn't waste a gorgeous afternoon sleeping. The constant sunshine at Sidi Akbar still seemed to me a miracle. It seemed impossible that it wasn't going to change overnight into the cool rainy weather that so often succeeds an English heatwave in April.

How far I was from an English April! I thought, as I sat in the local bus, driving along the beautiful coastroad towards Tunis. If we had been going south instead of north we would have been heading for the burning sands of the Sahara, where Sheikhs ride in splendour on their pure-bred Arab mounts, and caravans of camels go their proud, soft-footed way, laden with silks and spices. After which flight of fancy I found the city of Tunis rather disappointing. With its wide tree-lined boulevards and tall modern buildings, its plate glass department store windows and pavement cafés, it might have been Marseilles or Nice. And there were tourists everywhere, shaven-headed Germans, pale eyed Scandinavians, Englishwomen in summer frocks. Amid the babel of tongues French seemed to be predominant. In the main thoroughfare where I found myself there was scarcely an Arab to be seen—not a fez or a djellabah or a veil in sight. Only the little shoe-shine boys, with their skull-caps and picturesque rags, provided a touch of local colour.

I sat down at one of the café tables to watch them at work. They had bold darting black eyes and beautiful profiles. Selecting a customer, invariably a man, I noticed, they would kneel in front of him and fall upon his smartly or shabbily shod feet without a by-your-leave, and set to work; the customer continuing to read his newspaper, sip his coffee, or chat to his friends as if unaware of the boy's existence. When the boots or shoes had been dealt with a coin would change hands—still without a word being spoken—and the boy would move on looking for a fresh victim. It all seemed completely impersonal, as if the shoe-shine boys were some kind of automation. I felt sorry for them, they were so thin and anxious-looking. I was sure they didn't get enough to eat.

As I drank the tea I had ordered I became aware that the man sitting at the table next to mine was reading a copy of a London daily newspaper. Just another English tourist, I assumed—yet he didn't look like one, in his rough khaki bush shirt and nondescript slacks. The hands holding the paper were rough and discoloured. He might have been a farm worker, or a garage mechanic, only that he looked far too intellectual. If he worked with his hands he worked with his head as well. There was something in his cast of countenance that reminded me of the dons and professors of my university days. Perhaps he was an archaeologist, exploring the ruins of Carthage, or an engineer prospecting for oil in the desert. Whatever he did, it was obvious he did it out of doors. He was tanned to the same hue as his khaki shirt. Even his close-cropped light brown hair seemed sunburned. A tough, tawny, lion-coloured young man with an arrogant tilt to his head and a grim jawline. I don't know why I was so interested in him. Perhaps it was the English newspaper. One of the little shoeblacks approached him. *"Imsha!"* he snapped, waving an imperiously dismissive hand.

The boy, svelte as a cat, slid away from him, and before I quite realised what had happened he was kneeling in front of me, setting up his footrest. A skinny brown hand reached out for one of my white sandals.

"No, thank you," I said firmly, and then remembering the prevailing tongue added hastily, *"Je ne le veux pas!"*

But the boy took no notice, taking my foot in a vice-like grip and placing it on the foot rest.

"Laissez moi!" I cried in agitation.

There was a rush of air at my elbows and the folded copy of the London newspaper came down on the velvet skull cap with a crash. *"Imsha!"* shouted the voice of the man at the next table. "Scram!" There followed an unintelligible flood, probably of Arabic, unmistakably abusive.

The boot-black fled.

"Thank you," I murmured a little uncertainly to my rescuer. "But I wish you hadn't sent him away before I'd given him some money. He looked so poor."

"Oh, he's all right," my neighbour returned roughly. "These urchins make quite a good living with their shoe-shine racket, and they know very well they have no business pestering a woman.

It's not usual for a woman to have her shoes shined in the streets in Arab countries."

"I suppose not," I murmured, thinking of harems and purdah and veils and all the other ways in which Moslem women are, or used to be, segregated. I said, "The only reason I didn't want the little boy to clean my shoes was because I was afraid he would put some peculiar cleaning substance on them. They're white kid and rather precious."

"Quite," the young man returned absently. He gave me a long appraising glance. He had rather nice eyes, I noticed, a warm grey with thick smudgy lashes. Irish lashes. Celtic, anyway. Eyes put in with a sooty finger. They redeemed his face from its hint of hardness. "Is this your first visit to Tunis?" he asked.

"My first visit to any part of North Africa." I looked out over the neat, placid boulevard. "I'd expected a bit more native colour, but I suppose there isn't very much left."

"Not in Tunis itself, at least not in the central part of the city. Our enlightened President favours westernising influences, and I'm sure he's right. But we still have the Souks tucked away behind the glass and concrete office blocks. The native market, that is. You ought to explore it some time."

"Is it safe?" I ventured.

"Good lord, yes!" The young man threw back his head and laughed. "Though I wouldn't perhaps wander alone there after dark, if I were you. During the day you'll find yourself in an endless stream of tourists with cameras, so you'll be perfectly all right." He picked up his newspaper, ending the conversation.

I stood up. "Thank you for rescuing me from the shoe-shine boy," I said, and went into the café to pay my bill. When I came out again the tawny young man had vanished.

As I crossed the square to the bus stop a car pulled up beside me, and Elaine Ben Akhtal in the driving seat called out, "Hullo, Miss Marlow! Would you like a lift back to the hotel?"

Gratefully I got in beside her. Her children in the back seat gave me shy, dark-eyed smiles: Jules aged seven, and Denise aged five. The boy in a white sailor suit, the girl in organdie frills, had the band-box freshness that only French infants *en fête* seem able to achieve. They had all been to lunch with Papa, Elaine explained. Then the children had gone to a dancing class while she went to the hairdressers. I shot an envious glance at her shining helmet of skilfully bleached blonde hair, and put a hand to my own rather sticky locks.

"That's were I ought to have been," I confessed. "My hair is a mess. I wish someone would invent a bathing cap that doesn't let in even a teaspoonful of salt water."

Elaine said somebody had, and began telling me about it. I listened in fascination to her beautiful throaty Parisien French. Elaine Ben Akhtal was one of the most romantic contacts I'd made since coming to Tunisia, I decided. Romantic in a different way from Delmer Lloyd, of course. Elaine with her Arab marriage moved in a world that seemed to me mysterious. And she was so smooth, so sophisticated; Parisian to her elegant fingertips. Was she happy with her husband? I wondered. In the glimpse I had had of him Raschid Ben Akhtal had rather overawed me. He was devastatingly handsome—most high-born Arabs are. Was there a hint of cruelty in the slightly hooked nose and beautifully cut mouth? Probably not. From what I'd gleaned in listening to the gossip of the Comtesse de la Fontaine, Raschid Ben Akhtal was one of the most liberal young Ministers in a liberal and progressive Cabinet. Nor was there anything very extraordinary about his marriage to Elaine. Many upper-class Arabs in modern Tunisia had French wives. It was part, perhaps, of the tendency towards westernisation, or even a relic of the old Colonial days. At all events Elaine Ben Akhtal seemed to be happy enough—and indeed, on the face of it, why shouldn't she be happy? With an adoring husband, two lovely children, plus an apartment in one of the most luxurious blocks in the city, with the Hotel Alzara for a holiday home.

As we drove along the coast road she told me her special hair-do was in honour of an official banquet she and her husband were attending in Tunis that evening.

"What time will you come home?" Denise enquired in a quavery voice.

"Oh, long after you've gone to sleep," Elaine returned lightly. "Samia will put you to bed."

Samia was the young Arab maidservant who helped Elaine with the children.

"But she won't stay with us all the time," Denise complained, "and a lion might come along the *terrasse* outside our room."

"*Imbécile*!" Jules laughed. "There aren't any lions in this part of Africa."

"How do you know?" Denise argued.

"Denise, you mustn't be silly," Elaine put in sternly. "You're just going on this way because you hate me to go out."

"Would it be any help if I came and read you a story after you're in bed, Denise?" I offered.

"Oh, would you?" Elaine breathed gratefully. "That is kind of you."

211

Denise leaned over the back of my seat, breathing down my neck gustily. "Will you stay with me until Maman comes home?" she bargained.

"Of course she won't," Elaine broke in before I could answer. "Miss Marlow will have her own plans for the evening. She'll have to go to dinner for one thing, then she'll be dancing or talking to her friends."

"But I won't forget you, Denise," I promise. "I'll come along the *terrasse* every now and then and peep in at you to make sure you're safely asleep."

Elaine threw me a troubled glance. "You mustn't let Denise be a nuisance to you . . ."

"She won't be," I said.

Denise put two hot little arms round my neck, all but strangling me. "I love you!" she said. "You're pretty and nice and kind . . ."

"Also she is English," Jules piped up. "And she can read to us in English."

"Really, Jules!" Elaine turned to me with a despairing shrug. "My children's manners! What will you think of them? But Jules is weak in English and he's studying for an entrance exam to an English preparatory school, to which we're hoping to send him in a few weeks' time. The summer term begins in May."

"Isn't he very young to be taking an exam?" I said.

"Oh, it's a very simple examination. If Jules had been brought up in England it would present no difficulties at all. But as he has always spoken French it's a little harder for him. And we're very anxious for him to get into this school. Then he can go on to his father's old public school, and finally to Oxford."

I digested this educational programme in silence. So Raschid Ben Akhtal was the product of an English public school and university. There was nothing unusual in this. Boys of every Oriental nationality have been coming to English schools and colleges for generations. But it seemed to make my Tunisian contacts just that little bit more mundane. If only I could have seen Raschid Ben Akhtal in his native setting, riding on a thoroughbred Arab across the desert sands, at the head of a column of troops in full regalia! How impressive he would have looked! Putting him into an English morning suit and tucking a brief case under his arm was a complete waste of his natural glamour.

Del was sitting on the *terrasse* with the two old ladies when we got back to the hotel. He looked sultry and bored, but at the sight of me his face lit up.

"You're just in time for tea," Aunt Vinnie hailed me.

Del did his bowing and handkissing act with his customary grace, but, strangely, it failed to impress me, my thoughts shooting off at a tangent to the tawny-haired oil prospector I had met in the café in Tunis. (I had quite made up my mind than he was an oil prospector.) You wouldn't catch him bowing over a girl's hand, I reflected. Such namby-pamby courtesies were not for tough characters like him. It made Del seem very 'foreign' all of a sudden, and though he held out a chair for me next to himself I pretended not to see it and sat down beside Aunt Vinnie.

The Comtesse was talking to Elaine and the children who had taken the adjoining table.

"Let's keep to English, for Jules' sake," Elaine suggested. Once more she explained about the preparatory school to which he was going, and how backward he was wiht his English. "We had

213

engaged a tutor for him for the next few weeks, a young undergraduate from London who was going to spend his Easter vacation with us. But some family crisis prevented his coming, so we're struggling along without him. Every morning Jules and I pore over an English grammar together. But I'm afraid it's a case of the blind leading the blind," she ended ruefully.

"Would it be any help if I gave Jules a few lessons?" I asked impulsively. "I could easily spare an hour or two each day."

Elaine's face glowed with gratitude, but she said she couldn't possibly expect me to give up time during my holiday in order to teach a little boy.

"But she's going to be a teacher," Aunt Vinnie put in. "It will be excellent practice for her."

"Of course it will," I agreed, a little amused at Aunt Vinnie's intervention. Given to good works herself, she was all in favour of my doing something useful even if I was on holiday.

"I really don't know what to say . . ." Elaine wavered.

"But if Miss Marlow *wants* to help, Maman," Jules cut in, obviously tired of all this grown-up palaver over something so simple. Children are so much more direct than their elders.

"Let's have a trial lesson tomorrow morning," I settled it.

When the group around the tea tables broke up and scattered Del drew me aside. "How could you have made that arrangement to give Jules a lesson?" he reproached me. "What about our morning on the beach?"

"Oh, we'll have time for a swim," I promised him.

He made a wry, very French grimace. "I want *all* your time," he said. "I'm more and more jealous of everyone and everything that takes you away from me. What are you going to do now until dinner?"

"Have a walk with Aunt Vinnie. This is the hour she likes her little stroll along the path above the beach."

"All these old ladies!" His eyes were angry. "If only you and I were here in Sidi Akbar on our own!" The passion in his voice startled me. But his next words were banal. He had had a difficult afternoon with the Comtesse. "Natalie and her piffling little memoirs," he fumed. "Page after page of name-dropping! She's such a snob."

He caught my hand as I turned to leave him. "Don't go for a moment. Let me go on grumbling to you. It does me good. You don't know how frustrated I feel at times, dancing attendance on a silly old woman, when I know I have it in me to write . . . to act . . ."

"Can't you make something of literary value of the memoirs?" I asked.

He shook his head. "The outpourings of a trivial egotist, who's led a trivial, pleasure-seeking life? They'll be published, of course, because of her name. But they don't amount to anything worth while."

"And you think you, on your own, could write something worth while?"

"I know I could?"

I joined Aunt Vinnie for her walk feeling oddly disturbed by Del's confidences. It hadn't occurred to me that he found his job with the Comtesse so galling. I wished I could do something to help him. I was flattered that he had turned to me. I want all your time, he had said. I'm jealous of everyone and everything that takes you away from me. How deeply involved was I becoming with Delmer Lloyd? How involved did I want

215

to be? I admired his poise and good looks, found his company entertaining, was physically attracted by him. And yet the indefinable doubts lurked, making it impossible for me to take him altogether seriously. Was it simply my Englishness? Del was an out-and-out cosmopolitan; a type I had never met before.

When the walk was over I went along to the Ben Akhtals' suite, three large rooms that opened on to the far end of the *terrasse*, well away from the central part of the hotel. Samia had just finished putting the children to bed, and Elaine, ready to leave for Tunis, looked beautiful in black lace and diamonds. I watched her fussing over last-minute touches, grumbling a little that Raschid hadn't been able to drive out to fetch her. She was meeting him at the hotel where the banquet was to be held. Meanwhile Cabinet duties chained him. "Politics," Elaine mourned, "take up so much time!"

An opulent, chauffeur-driven car awaited her, the sort of darkly glossy mammoth one sees lurking outside embassies and legations the world over. It had come up a side driveway, and stood at the foot of a flight of steps close to the Ben Akhtals' suite. Denise insisted on getting out of bed and running on to the *terrasse* in her nightdress to wave her mother goodbye.

Then we settled down to our reading, a French story first for Denise, then an English one for Jules. I found that the book he and Elaine were struggling with was Lamb's *Tales from Shakespeare*.

"I don't understand it very well," Jules complained. "I thought Shakespeare was a great poet, and I like poetry. Do you think we could buy a real Shakespeare book in Tunis and read that instead?"

"It might be a bit complicated for you," I told him. "But I have a book of verse with me, an anthology; there might be something in it that you would like. I'll bring it along for our first lesson tomorrow."

After dinner Del wanted me to go off with him in his gorgeous feather bed of a car. But, remembering my promise to keep an eye on Denise and Jules, I persuaded him that the hotel was the best place in which to spend the evening. It wasn't very difficult to prove my point. Tunisia isn't very strong on night-life attractions. Modern dancing has little connection with the local culture and night clubs are few and far between. There are official amusement centres where you can see native folk dancing and listen to the strange Hispano-music known as Malouf. But if you want ballroom dancing the large tourist hotels are the best bet, and the Alzara had one of the finest dance bands in the locality.

I had put on my favourite, rather daring, frock that evening, a backless rose chiffon. But if you can't go bare-backed on a near-tropical night in Tunisia, where can you go bare-backed? And I've got the right sort of back. Anyway, Del liked the frock, what there was of it, and lost no time in telling me so.

The dancing soon spilled over from the ballroom to the curving sweep of *terrasse* outside. Fairy lamps twinkled in the branches of the trees. Beyond the balustrade the sea was a gently breathing presence, its darkness touched here and there by gleams of phosphorescence. The sky sparkled with stars, so bright and large and near that they seemed to be caught in the tree tops of the sleeping garden. There was a scent of lemon flowers and jasmine on the warm languorous air.

217

In such an atmosphere beat rhythms would have had no place. We danced to old-fashioned waltz tunes, and there were leisurely tangos and rhumbas. Del and I strolled through it all, making up our own steps. I found I could follow him perfectly. A good sign, he said. Of what? I asked. He laid his cheek against mine. "It shows that we suit each other."

"I wonder?" I murmured.

"Don't wonder," Del said. "Just let yourself go."

A good moment I thought cautiously to call a halt and remember my promise to Denise. I began to edge along the *terrasse* in the direction of their room.

"What's all this in aid of?" Del asked, as we left the music behind us.

"I want to go and have a look at the Ben Akhtal children," I said. "I promised Elaine I would."

"What on earth possessed you to do that?" Del demanded crossly. But before I had time to answer him Denise had heard us approaching and a nervous little voice called out, "Is that you, Miss Marlow?"

Leaving Del to his indignation, I tiptoed into the shadowy room. A night light burned on the dressing table. Denise was sitting up in bed, her pillows tossed and tumbled. "I want Maman," she began plaintively. "I can't ever sleep when she's out . . . I have bad dreams."

Smoothing the pillows, I pointed out to Denise that she must have been asleep if she had been dreaming.

"It was about Grandpère," Denise went on, ignoring my logic. "I thought he came rushing in from the *terrasse*, all big and scary in his Arab robes. I was afraid he was going to take me away." She rolled her eyes dramatically. "My

218

grandpère is an Arab Caïd," she explained with a touch of pride. "He lives in a big white house in the desert and has camels hung with silver bells, and he rides a great black horse and all the people in the villages he owns bow down to him. He has soldiers too, and guns and a dungeon. Samia says he'll shut me up in the dungeon if I'm not a good girl."

"That's nonsense," I assured her. "Samia was only teasing you. It's very naughty of her to talk like that."

"But it might be true," Denise argued. "Arab noblemen do have soldiers and dungeons."

"But not to shut little girls up in. You know perfectly well your grandfather loves you very much."

A musing look came into her drowsy eyes. It was clear she didn't altogether believe Samia's horror stories, but at this hour of the night with her mother out of sight it was easy to work up terrifying phantasies.

"Don't go away," she begged, throwing her arms around my neck.

I disentangled myself gently. "I'll be just outside on the *terrasse*," I promised. "I'll stay there until you fall asleep." Tucking the covers about her, I dropped a light kiss on her forehead and went firmly from the room.

Del, hovering by the french window, greeted me impatiently. "I thought you were never coming! Lets get back to the dance band . . ."

"I'd rather stay here a while." I indicated a seat in the shadow of a palm tree close to the top of the *terrasse* steps. "I told Denise I'd stay within call until I was sure she had got off to sleep."

"What *is* this nursemaid act?" Del's spurt of laughter didn't sound amused. "Not that this shady nook interval is such a bad idea," he added, somewhat mollified. He put a purposeful arm about me as we sat down. I moved away from him a little, just to show that the shady nook angle of the situation hadn't been uppermost in my mind.

"Denise is scared because her mother isn't here," I explained. "Really scared. The fool of a maid has been filling her head with nonsense about Sheikhs and dungeons. It seems her grandfather is an Arab Caid who lives somewhere in the desert. And Denise is having nightmares about him—she thinks he's going to creep up in the darkness and carry her away."

"Perhaps he will!" Del said jokingly. "At all events, he's a Sheikh of the old school, it seems. Raschid was telling me about him the other day. He lives in the oasis of El Garza about two hundred miles from here, and owns quite a slice of territory. It's a very pro-Arab set-up and the old man, I gather, doesn't altogether approve of Raschid's political activities. He's all against Jules being educated in England."

"Although Raschid himself went to Oxford," I put in.

"That's something the older Akhtal now regrets. He doesn't subscribe to the present westernising influence in Tunisia, and if he had his way his grandson would be brought up as a strict little Moslem." His voice faded away, and his arm tightened about my shoulder.

"To hell with the Ben Akhtals and their family quarrels," he whispered, as his mouth came down on my own. It was the sort of kiss that leaves no room for reflection. The stars whirled in the sky, the dark fronds of the palm tree curved over us. I shut my eyes and let the magic moment engulf me.

"Oh, Del!" I murmured brokenly at last, breaking it up.

"I love you!" Del said. "Oh, Lorraine, I adore you!"

We kissed again. Just how long that embrace went on before I realised we were not alone, I don't know. Nor was the shady nook as secluded as I could have wished. In the light from the *terrasse* lamps we must have been clearly visible to the young man approaching from the drive. As he came up the *terrasse* steps I recognized him with a start—the oil prospector who had rescued me from the shoe-shine boy in Tunis that afternoon. He was still wearing his shabby bush shirt and nondescript pants. In the lamplight his grey eyes had a yellowish tinge, that made me think of some night prowling animal. Coolly they surveyed me as I disentangled myself from Del's arms with what dignity I could muster.

"I beg your pardon," he said in sardonic tone. "But I seem to have the wrong way. I was looking for the main entrance to the Hotel Alzara."

CHAPTER TWO

"IF you go along the *terrasse* you'll find yourself just outside the bar," Del told the stranger, adding a trifle acidly, "if that's what you want."

"Actually I'm looking for Madame Ben Akhtal," the young man returned.

"Then you're unlucky," Del snapped. "She's in Tunis."

"But she is staying here, isn't she?" The young man sounded distinctly rattled.

221

"Yes, she is staying here," Del confirmed. "But I'm not the reception clerk, you know. If you want any more information I wish you'd push along to the office and get it."

"My apologies!" The oil man's tone was sardonic. Giving me a withering glance, he walked away. Was he taking it upon himself to disapprove of my love-making with Del? If so, how dare he? It had nothing to do with him. Yet I felt my cheeks grow hot, and when Del started kissing me again I couldn't respond. He was calling on Madame Ben Akhtal, the oil man had said. What did he want with Elaine at this time of night? It was late for a casual call. And in those scruffy garments . . .

I stood up. "I expect Denise is asleep by now," I said. "I'll just look in on her to make sure."

"All right, *Nanny!*" Del grumbled.

I tiptoed over to the french window. Denise's arms were flung out across the coverlet in that lovely abandonment to sleep which only small children achieve.

I went back to Del. "You weren't very polite to that man just now," I said.

"Why the heck should I be?" Del answered without much interest. "Creeping up on us out of the shrubbery . . . Like some darned peeping Tom. Why didn't he go round to the servants' entrance?"

"Perhaps he isn't a servant. He said he was looking for Elaine."

"He could still be a servant, a garage mechanic or something. Anyhow, what does it matter?" He caught at my hand, trying to pull me down on the seat beside him again.

"Let's go back to the dancing," I suggested.

"I'd much rather go on kissing you."

"Come on!" I gave his hand a purposeful tug. He stood up. "What's the matter?" he demanded.

"Nothing is the matter."

"But you don't want to kiss me any more?"

"Not just now."

"And a few minutes ago you were . . ." He broke off, leaving the sentence unfinished. "Oh, hell! Women!"

I walked beside him along the *terrasse* wondering what had happened to me. Why had the arrival of the tawny-haired oil man made me feel so . . . cheap? Was I ashamed of kissing Del, who had just said he loved me? Del with his charm, his good looks, his Continental polish . . . I ought to be proud of him. But somehow I wasn't. Something critical inside me was always tearing him to pieces. Poor Del! And tonight for a little while I had forgotten to be critical and succumbed to the magic of the tropical night. Then Tawny Hair had appeared. And, hey presto! the magic had vanished.

We had to pass through the bar on our way back to the ballroom, and there he was, seated at the counter drinking what looked loke a modest glass of beer. He treated me to another of those withering glances, and there was just enough recognition in it to suggest that he might have remembered our encounter of the afternoon. But he wasn't going to claim acquaintance.

The band was still playing the rather treacly music that seemed to be the fashion in Tunisia, all violins and sweetness and Old Vienna. It had a certain magic, specially when the lights were dimmed and Del held me close. And he danced superbly. I put the oil man out of my head and let the music carry me away.

It was not, however, to be our lucky evening. Before very long a page-boy brought Del a note from the Comtesse. He read it, his face clouding. "She wants to see me in her suite. At this hour! I ask you! Am I supposed to be on duty twenty-four hours a day?"

"Perhaps she feels you've rather neglected her this evening," I suggested as we left the dance floor.

"I'm not her paid companion," Del grumbled.

But you *are* paid, I thought, and if appearances were anything to go by (that magnificent car, for instance) paid pretty well.

"Why hasn't she gone to bed long ago?" Del was asking me angrily—as if I had anything to do with it! "She's a miserable, egotistical old woman, determined to get her pound of flesh . . ."

Suddenly I was a bit tired of it. After all, Del must have known the kind of thing he was letting himself in for when he took on the job. And as far as I could see it was a fairly easy job. No one could call Del overworked. His usual stint at the memoirs was two or three hours in the afternoon. The rest of the time he seemed to be able to roam about at will, swimming and sunbathing with me, taking me for drives.

We were walking along the mosaic-tiled corridor towards the lift. "Will you wait in the foyer for me?" Del asked, as the lift gates opened.

"No, I don't think so. It's getting rather late. If you don't mind I'll be off to bed."

"I *knew* you'd say that," Del exploded. "Natalie has ruined our evening." He was borne upwards, still muttering.

My room was along the *terrasse* not far from the Ben Akhtal's suite. I could look in on Denise once more before turning in. The oil man was still in the bar when I passed through. This time he didn't even bother to glance at me. Leaning against the bar rail, he chatted with the barman his tawny head at an arrogant angle. He didn't seem to realise how out of place he was in those awful clothes. Dinner jackets are the rule in the Hotel Alzara. The wonder is that he hadn't been thrown out. Perhaps it was his connection with Elaine Ben Akhtal that saved him. He must be very anxious indeed to see her, I thought, if he was prepared to sit around until she came back in the small hours of the morning. Once more I wondered what his business with her could be.

Denise was still fast asleep, and it wasn't long before I was in bed, following her example.

I woke early to find the sun pouring in at my window, and lay still a while contemplating the miracle of yet another day of perfect weather. The hands on the travelling clock on my bedside table pointed to seven-thirty. At this hour it would be deliciously cool and fresh on the beach. I jumped out of bed, slipped on by bikini and coolie coat and went out on to the *terrasse*. There wasn't a soul in sight. I looked pityingly at the rows of closely fastened french windows and ran down the steps to the cliff path. Below me the beach was a stretch of golden sand tucked into the curve of the rising land, its terraced slopes planted with fruit and olive orchards. Peach trees, lemon trees and orange trees were all in bloom. It was springtime in Tunisia, and I had to stand for a moment at the top of the cliff path drinking in the beauty of the scene. The sea was smooth as silk, a deep blue shading to lavender and green. Fishing boats, becalmed, lay at the mouth of a small harbour to the south, their coloured sails reflected in the still water.

When I got down to the beach I took off my sandals. The sand was already warm and I walked over it, curling my toes luxuriously, stretching my arms out to the lovely morning, glorying in my solitude. I seemed to be the only person at the Alzara who bothered to get up early. Del never appeared in public before ten o'clock, and Aunt Vinnie and the Comtesse a couple of hours later. So my early morning swim had a special value for me—a rendezvous with myself before the bustle and excitement of the long hot day. Much as I enjoyed those days, this lonely hour was very precious to me, and it was with a pang of annoyance that I saw a towel lying on my favourite platform of rock, the place where I usually sunbathed. Then I glimpsed the head of a swimmer about twenty yards from the beach. A tawny head!

"Oh, no!" I muttered aloud. This was altogether too much! My feelings of outrage was out of all proportion. What was it about this young man that annoyed me so intensely?

He was making for the shore, swimming strongly, arm over arm. My only way to avoid him was to turn and go back to the hotel. But I wasn't going to be guilty of such cowardice. Besides, I wanted my swim. So running a little way along the beach I found an alternative rock for a dressing room, discarded my coolie coat and walked into the sea just as Tawny Head was walking out.

"Good morning," I offered brightly.

He gave a sort of grunt and turned his back— a smooth muscular back, brown as a hickory nut. Enraged at this snub direct, I splashed on through the shallows. What a boor the man was! Why had I bothered to speak to him? I hadn't really wanted to, but as we seemed fated to bump into one another it was stupid not to pass the time of day. And it seemed now that he was staying at the hotel. A friend of Elaine Ben Akhtal's. How much of a friend? Was I going to find him included in

226

our comfortable little circle? Thrusting this awkward possibility aside—it was really too gruesome to be taken seriously—I swam out towards the raft. The water was just cold enough to be stimulating, the sun on my face deliciously warm. Rolling over on my back, I floated, gazing up into the fathomless blue sky. Then I turned and dived and swam under the surface. The sea was beautifully clear. I could see the white sandy sea bed with its trails of delicately coloured weed, and darting many-hued fish. I wished I had a snorkel and flippers—this under-water world was full of fascination. I stayed down as long as I dared, then came up, my lungs bursting. What happened next isn't very clear. Perhaps I'd swum under water for too long and I was suffering from oxygen hunger, but suddenly I felt utterly exhausted and began to black out. Thank goodness I was within an arm's length of the raft. I reached out for it desperately, and heaving myself up on it, twisted my shoulder. The pain for a moment or two was excruciating. I lay face down on the wet drugget, panting, fighting off the faintness. After a little while the pain eased up and I felt better. The sun was reviving, warming me through. But it was some time before I was able to sit up and take stock of the situation.

Tawny Head was stretched out on my favourite rock, smoking a cigarette. I wished he would clear off. Then I could go back to the beach and pick up my wrap without the embarrassment of another encounter. I was beginning to want my breakfast. After that frightening near-blackout a cup of coffee would be very welcome. I moved my strained shoulder tentatively, and the pain came back again. How on earth was I going to swim to the shore? I looked at the stretch of blue silken water despairingly. In so short a time it had become my enemy. Once more I lifted my arm, and gave a loud 'Ouch!' of protest at the stab of agony which resulted.

There was nothing for it. I'd have to stay where I was until the mid-morning bathers appeared— with the strengthening sun scorching the skin off me—or throw myself upon the mercy of the one human being within hailing distance.

Wretchedly I contemplated the figure lolling on the distant rock. If only it could have been anyone but Tawny Head! For what seemed an endless time I waited. Then Tawny Head rolled off the rock, disappearing behind it. In a moment or two he emerged in bush shirt and shorts. In another moment or two he would have gone.

"Hi!" I called experimentally.

He turned briefly in my direction.

"Help!" I yelled dramatically. "I've hurt myself and can't swim back to shore."

He waded into the water knee-deep, and making a trumpet of his hands bellowed, "What's the trouble?" It wasn't a friendly bellow by any means!

"I've wrenched my shoulder," I yelled back. "Will you please find out at the hotel if there's someone who can row out and pick me up?"

How much of this plaintive appeal got across the considerable stretch of water I don't know, but the man on the beach must have gleaned the general idea. I was marooned on the raft, and asking to be rescued. I saw him turn and wade back to the shore, where he walked firmly away from the path that led to the hotel, disappearing behind a promontory in the opposite direction. He disliked me so much that he was prepared to leave me on a sun-drenched raft to perish! Hungry, scared and in pain, I could have wept.

Then I saw the dinghy coming out from behind the promontory, and Tawny Head seated in it, rowing steadily in my direction. So he wasn't the monster of indifference I had thought.

The dinghy drew nearer, Tawny Head gentling it expertly alongside the raft. In the strong light I saw that his short hair was tinged with red, and there were freckles on his blunt, shapely nose. With this pigmentation his dark lashes were striking. His grey eyes had new colour in them this morning, green flecks and gold flecks. They were like pebbles seen beneath clear running water. The look he gave me was hard and suspicious. "I gather you're in some sort of fix," he said.

"I've hurt my shoulder," I explained once more, gingerly fingering the injured member. "I think I must have wrenched it reaching for the raft just now."

He watched me move it cautiously. "There doesn't seem to be much wrong with it," he growled. "I expect it is just a touch of cramp. However . . ." he jerked his head grudgingly towards the empty seat in the dinghy, "get in! As I'm here I may as well row you ashore."

I clambered into the dinghy. It wasn't an easy transition, and Tawny Head did nothing to help me. Quite clearly he thought I was making a fuss about nothing.

"I was swimming under water," I explained as we moved towards the shore, "and I must have stayed down a little too long. When I surfaced I was quite dopey, and it scared me. I made a lunge for the raft and that was how I twisted my shoulder . . ."

"Indeed!" Tawny Head murmured sceptically.

My temper flared. "If you think I'm making the whole thing up," I exploded, "just to attract your

229

attention, you're the most conceited man I've ever met!"

He burst out laughing—superior male laughter. "I wouldn't dream of doubting your word," he said in a tone that conveyed the opposite. "But you do have a knack of getting yourself into awkward situations when I'm around."

She did remember the shoe-shine incident.

I retreated into offended silence, and gazed longingly at the shore. How soon could we get there? The sooner the better. And by the vigorous way he was pulling on the oars Tawny Head seemed to agree with me. In a few moments we were running into shallow water. Tawny Head jumped out and pulled the boat up on to the sand, stretching out a hand to help me alight. At first I tried to ignore the hand, but the boat lurched over on its keel and I lurched with it. It is impossible to be haughty getting in out of small boats, I reflected bitterly, clutching gratefully at the strong brown hand. It took my whole weight as I jumped out on to the beach.

"Thank you," I said shortly, and then because he had, after all, come to the rescue, warmed it up a bit with a, "Thank you very much indeed."

"Your welcome. Glad I happened to be around. And if I might make a suggestion, I don't think it's very wise for you to have an early morning dip all on your own. Next time bring that good-looking boy-friend of yours along with you."

"He's not my boy-friend," I blurted.

"Your fiancé, then."

"Not that either."

"I see." Tawny Head shrugged as if it were of little account to him either way. But the look he gave me was full of scorn . . . and something else I didn't like one bit. Slowly the grey eyes raked me from head to foot as I stood there in my

230

bikini. A look I suddenly realised he felt I merited —the sort of look to be given to a cheap little hotel flirt, addicted to promiscuous kissing in the dark with any fellow guest she happens to have picked up. I felt my cheeks blazing. "Well, thanks again," I muttered, and went over to the rock where I had parked my coolie coat. Tawny Head returned to the dinghy, apparently taking it back to wherever he had got it from.

I climbed the cliff path slowly, my thoughts confused and unhappy. Why had I denied my friendship with Del? We were scarcely ever out of one another's company, and I was more than half in love with him. Or had thought so . . . until yesterday, when everything seemed to have gone wrong, and I had done nothing but criticise him mentally, finding him unreal, seeing his charm as hollow. Yet I had let him kiss me last night under the palm trees, and had kissed him back, because the night and the music were beautiful. Was that a valid reason for kissing a man? It was, at least, a very human one. Then why was I regretting it now? Because Tawny Head had seen us embracing?

Bother take the man! Supposing he does think I'm a feather brained man-hunter, I argued with myself—it couldn't matter less.

What did matter was the ache in my shoulder. But by the time I had soaked it in a hot bath it felt better, and the luxury of having my own bathroom soothed my ruffled ego. The Alzara was, on the whole, a very soothing hotel, if sheer luxury counts for anything. And it was sufficiently a novelty to me to count quite a lot. Considerably cheered, I dressed, putting on a sleeveless cotton frock of sunshine yellow with a slim white kid belt—to match the white kid shoes which had caused my difference of opinion yesterday with the shoeshine boy.

My intention was to have breakfast with Aunt Vinnie in her room, but as soon as I stepped out on to the *terrasse* I saw the Ben Akhtal family ranged around a table outside their suite—Tawny Head in their midst.

I caught my breath sharply and would have dived back into my room, but Denise, who had caught sight of me, greeted me with glad cries. Elaine waved a welcoming hand.

"Lorraine, my dear, do come and join us!

"Raschid," she turned to her husband, "ring for the waiter and order another cover for Miss Marlow."

Nobody seemed to hear my murmured protests, and before I could really assert myself a chair had been produced and Denise had dragged me over to it, while Elaine set about introducing me and the young man at her side.

"Lorraine Marlow, Tim Gregson." She waved an airy hand over us as if weaving some occult spell. "Lorraine—Greg. Greg—Lorraine."

Tawny Head, or to give him his correct name, Mr. Tim Gregson, stood up formally and gave me a stiff bow. "Hullo again," he said. "How is the shoulder?"

"Oh, you've already met?" Elaine's fine black brows shot up.

"We shared the beach this morning," Gregson explained as we sat down.

"And I ricked my shoulder swimming out to the raft," I took up the story. "It was so bad for a bit that I couldn't get back to the beach, and Mr. Gregson came to my rescue with a dinghy."

"How dramatic!" Raschid gave me a rather wicked grin. "I hope the ricked shoulder isn't serious."

232

"Not really." I avoided Tim Gregson's eyes. Though the hot bath had helped it, it still ached. I wouldn't be able to swim with Del this morning, I decided—with an odd sense of relief.

"Lorraine is staying here with her aunt," Elaine told Tim Gregson as she passed me a cup of coffee.

"She's going to give me English lessons," Jules added importantly. "She knows a lot of English poetry."

"Does she, indeed!" Tim Gregson managed to make it sound like a sneer.

The waiter appeared and put an iced grapefruit in front of me. A cup of coffee was one thing, but embarking upon a full-sized meal was another. I pushed the grapefruit aside and turned to Elaine appealingly. "I really mustn't stay, Elaine. Aunt Vinnie will be expecting me. I always have breakfast in her room, and," I added a little guiltily, "it's little enough she sees of me . . ."

"Thanks to the handsome Del!" Elaine laughed.

I could have thrown the unwanted grapefruit at her! Tim Gregson, helping himself to a hot croissant, flicked a bored glance at me. "Will you pass the honey, please, Elaine?" he asked, sounding very much one of the family. I wished someone would explain him to me. Just what was his connection with the Ben Akhtals? And why had he arrived so late last night . . . without luggage, clad scantily for the desert rather than for a smart hotel?

I finished my coffee and stood up. "I'm sorry, but I really must be off. Do please excuse me."

The two men rose, disturbing their meal. And Elaine made it worse by putting out a detaining hand as I moved away. "Thank you a million times, Lorraine dear, for taking such good care of my babes while I was away last night."

233

I murmured some embarrassed disclaimer.

"She read stories to me in the middle of the night," Denise announced triumphantly.

"Fibber!" Elaine laughed. "I was home soon after midnight and you were fast asleep then."

"When are you going to give me my lesson?" Jules chimed in, in his practical fashion.

"As soon as I've had my breakfast," I promised. "Will that suit you, Elaine?"

"Indeed yes, if it suits you. It is so kind of you to bother . . ."

"It isn't a bother. I shall enjoy it."

Somehow I extricated myself at last and went on my way.

CHAPTER THREE

AUNT Lavinia Vardon is a plump cosy little person, with a fund of good nature and an air of inner contentment which, I imagine, has nothing to do with the cushioned ease of her moneyed existence. No doubt she enjoys being wealthy, but she doesn't depend on her wealth for satisfaction. Apart from her holidays abroad she lives quietly, dresses quietly and devotes an immense amount of time and energy to her pet good causes: child care and animal welfare.

Breakfast had already been brought in when I reached her room. Seated by the daintily appointed table in the sunny window, she greeted me affectionately.

"How did the swimming go this morning?" she enquired.

I told her of my mishap at the raft, and of the young man who had come to my rescue. "His name, it appears, is Tim Gregson," I ended. "And he seems to be a friend of the Ben Akhtals. At all events he stayed here last night and is having breakfast with them this morning."

"Tim Gregson," Aunt Vinnie mused. "That must be the young man Elaine was telling Natalie and me about the other day. He works for the Caid, Raschid's father, who owns one of the largest date-growing concerns in Tunis. This man Gregson is an agricultural expert of some kind, and has done a lot to improve the Caid's land, with clever irrigation schemes, and so on. He's a Scotsman, I believe. Raschid and he met at Oxford, where they were at the same college."

So Gregson was a Scot. That accounted for the hint of red in his hair—and the hint of fire in his temper! I helped myself to scrambled eggs—Aunt Vinnie doesn't hold with Continental breakfasts—pondering on what I had just heard. Tawny Head wasn't an oil man, after all, then, but a type of farmer, even if a scientific one, and he was very much a part of the Ben Raschid family. But that didn't quite explain his late arrival last night, grubby and tired-looking and without luggage.

"Don't you think you ought to see a doctor about your shoulder?" Aunt Vinnie suggested presently.

"Oh, no," I protested, "it's only a slight strain. If I rest it for a day or two it'll be all right. I won't be able to go swimming with Del, I'm afraid . . ."

"Just as well, perhaps!" Aunt Vinnie said drily. "Natalie is beginning to be very jealous of the amount of time he spends with you."

"Is that why she sent for him last night when he was dancing with me?" I asked, feeling faintly disgusted. The idea of the elderly Comtesse indulging in anything so emotional as jealousy over her good-looking secretary seemed to me obscurely

235

distasteful. "Surely she wasn't going to work on her memoirs at that late hour!"

"I wouldn't be surprised," Aunt Vinnie laughed. "But more likely it was simply that she was lonely. She was in her sitting-room playing patience when I left her about eleven-thirty. She sleeps very badly and goes to bed late. Perhaps she wanted Del to give her a game of chess, which she loves."

"In the middle of the night?" I expostulated.

"Why not?" Aunt Vinnie returned placidly. "Del is a strong, healthy young man—not, as far as I've noticed, given to keeping early hours when he's bent on his own amusement, and he certainly doesn't hurry to get up in the mornings. If Natalie kept him chess-playing until the small hours I wouldn't be sorry for him. After all, he owes her a great deal, and he ought to show her some consideration. The new car she's just given him, for instance . . ."

"You mean she *gave* him that gorgeous Packard!" I exclaimed with a revulsion I couldn't quite have explained. "I thought perhaps he was buying it out of his salary—on the never-never."

"Oh, no, it was an outright gift." Aunt Vinnie threw me an odd look and then busied herself with toast and marmalade.

"What do you think of Del?" I asked her bluntly.

She popped a piece of toast into her mouth and crunched it noisily. "You're rather attracted to him, aren't you?" she said, when the toast had been disposed of.

"I don't know," I hedged. "I don't think I un-stand him. His high-powered charm rather puts me off. And he's so good-looking, always so perfectly turned out—the right costume for every occasion. Sometimes I just don't feel he's real."

"The typical expatriate," Aunt Vinne mur-mured. "Born and brought up in France by an

236

expatriate American father and a French mother. I've met so many of his kind in Paris, haunting the salons, the left bank cafés, talented, but rootless, and seemingly unable to put down any roots. Like Del, they work at many jobs, all on the fringe of the arts—journalism, ghosting, scriptwriting, the odd spot of acting."

"Del wants to write a serious play," I said. "If he could take time off from the grind of having to earn a living."

"Many a serious play or novel has been written by a man with a full-time job," Aunt Vinnie reminded me. "James Joyce took seven years over his *magnum opus Ulysses*, writing at night after a hard day in the schoolroom."

I made a dubious grimace. Somehow I couldn't see Del burning the midnight oil.

"Talking of schoolrooms," I said, glad to change the subject, "I've promised to help little Jules with his English, and I have a date with him right after breakfast. I thought I'd start him off with some simple poetry. I've got an anthology with me . . ."

"I'll lend you my William Blake," Aunt Vinnie interrupted. A fiery light came into her eyes and she began to quote:

"A robin redbreast in a cage
Puts all Heaven in a rage . . .

"Each outcry from the hunted have
A fibre of the brain doth tear . . ."

She broke off to gaze at me earnestly. "Not only will you be teaching Jules English if you nuture him on that sort of thing, but you'll be making him aware of the sufferings of dumb animals. When I see the thin little donkeys out here, driven along in the noonday heat, so cruelly overloaded,

I don't know how to contain myself. And the sad faces of the camels . . ." She sighed profoundly.

"I think the camels are all right," I tried to comfort her. "They're evil-tempered beasts and quite able to look after themselves."

"But the donkeys are not." Aunt Vinnie fanned herself agitatedly with her table napkin. "I know our international animal welfare societies are doing what they can in the big towns out here, but in the country villages the people still seem to think animals have no feelings." A musing look came over her face, a look I have come to dread. It means some fierce campaign is being hatched. "I think," she said, "I'll try to see that nice President Bourgiba before I go home, and enlist his sympathies. Raschid Ben Akhtal would probably be able to arrange it for me."

Jules was waiting for me on the seat beneath the palm trees. The seat I had shared with Del last night. The rest of the family had disappeared. There was no sign of Tim Gregson. Jules, looking pathetically small and earnest, gave me a welcoming smile. His thin pointed face seemed all eyes. He had that appealing air of fragility that is so misleading in small boys.

"Have you brought the English poetry book? Maman says I'm not to be a nuisance to you," he greeted me, all in one breath.

I sat down beside him and opened the William Blake collected poems. Some of them were wildly abstruse and unsuitable. I found "Little lamb, who made thee?" and thought that would do for a start.

Jules listened respectfully while I read it. "Do you understand it?" I asked, to find out if he had been able to follow the simple words in English. But Jules, it appeared, was delving deeper.

"It's a bit childish, don't you think? How could the lamb know who made him? And anyhow, who did? Wasn't he just born like any other lamb?"

I was, I realised, up against that analytical French intelligence that can be so disconcerting.

"That's fazed you a bit, hasn't it?" a deep voice laughed.

I turned to find Tim Gregson sitting on the flat top of the *terrasse* balustrade, a couple of feet away from us. Evidently he had crept up on us, unheard in his rope-soled sandals, while I trotted out those unfortunate verses of Blake's. He certainly had a knack of turning up at the wrong moment, this Gregson character.

> "To see a world in a grain of sand
> And all Heaven in a wild flower ..." he qouted.

"I didn't know anyone read Blake nowadays."

"My Aunt Lavinia does," I supplied with dignity. "But I shouldn't have thought Blake would appeal to you."

"Do I seem to you, then, so rough and unlettered?" The grey eyes surveyed me coldly. What warmth and amusement there had been in them died out.

"Of course you're not unlettered. I didn't mean that," I began, but before I could go any further with my stumbling apology, Jules, who had picked up the book of poems, began to read in a puzzled, halting way:

> "There is a smile of love
> And a smile of deceit
> There is a smile of smiles
> In which these two smiles meet ..."

He looked up. "What does that mean, Uncle Greg?"

Greg swung his long legs to the ground, and was sauntering off as he answered, "Ask your charming teacher! I imagine she's an expert on smiles of the kind poor Mr. Blake had in mind."

He was away down the steps and along the shrubbery path before I could think of a suitably crushing reply. That slow, seemingly unhurried gait that yet covered the ground so rapidly. He walked beautifully, arrogantly, as if at the head of some unseen procession. A conceited and impossible young man, bad-mannered into the bargain—breaking into my lesson with Jules. And that low crack of his, as he strolled away! So I knew all about smiles of deceit, did I? How dared the man! How dared he?

Trembling with anger, I picked up the poetry book and turned over the pages, hardly knowing what I did.

Jules, watching the retreating form, said "Uncle Greg is going into Tunis this morning, down to the wharf to meet a ship that's bringing some machinery from England for my grandfather's lands at El Garza. It should have come yesterday. He drove all the way from El Garza to collect it, but the ship was delayed. It's a long way to El Garza, so instead of going back there he came here and stayed with Maman and Papa for the night. Papa had to lend him some pyjamas and a toothbrush."

Odd the way information about Tim Gregson was coming to me piecemeal, filling in the picture. And odder still the way I seized on it. What possible interest could I have in his doings? None at all, I told myself firmly. He was the aggressive type that forced himself on one's notice. The reason

I kept on thinking about him was because he annoyed me intensely. That was all.

"Let's get on with Blake," I said firmly.

A shabby Land Rover went clattering down the side avenue. Mr. Tim Gregson on his way to Tunis, in search of his machinery. Well, good luck to him! I hoped he would find it this time—and take himself out of my orbit, back to the wilds where he belonged.

Del, when we met after the English lesson, was all solicitude about my strained shoulder. "You'll have to have your swim alone today," I told him. But he wouldn't go down to the beach without me.

"Couldn't you come and sunbathe while I swim?" he suggested.

I shook my head. "I would be too hot, lying there on the rocks, without the chance of cooling off in the sea now and then."

All I wanted, I realised, was a morning freed from his company. His assumption that he must spend all his free time with me now seemed to me an imposition. But I was being illogical. For the whole fortnight I had encouraged him; I couldn't just cast him off now without any apparent reason. And why should I want to cast him off? Surely we could be good friends for the remainder of the holiday. I knew now, quite clearly, it was friendship and nothing more that I wanted from him. But that shouldn't make me turn against him. Surely I wasn't letting myself be influenced by Tim Gregson's cracks about 'smiles of deceit.' Who was he to set himself up as a judge of my conduct? A prig of a Scotsman who, apparently, had never heard of kissing at dances, or mild holiday flirtations!

"I could drive you into Tunis," Del said. "You wanted to see round the Souks. We could have lunch afterwards at a restaurant on the Cap Bon road where they serve very good native dishes."

"Won't the Comtesse be annoyed if you aren't back for lunch?" I asked.

Del's face darkened. "Since she kept me up half the night listening to her twaddle and letting her beat me at chess I'm entitled to a bit of peace today."

I wasn't altogether convinced, but driving along the coast road my scruples vanished. It was such a glorious morning; the sea was so blue, the sunshine so golden. Del had opened the roof of the car and the soft wind blew through my hair. There were flowers everywhere, cascading over the tall white garden walls; bougainvillea, purple wisteria, climbing geraniums, their blossoms in great clusters, from white to pale pink, on to deepest scarlet. It was impossible to go on worrying about the Comtesse, my relationship to Del, or the irritating Tim Gregson.

When we got to Tunis and had parked the car Del led the way to the Souks—the Tunisian market-place, a network of dim vaulted passageways, and narrow streets. The tiny dark shops are filled to overflowing with beautiful carpets, leatherwork, pottery, and in the food shops the proprietor sits on the floor surrounded by heaps of dried fruits, spiced cakes and other delectable oddments. There were silversmiths and goldsmiths working away at their ancient crafts, squatting on priceless prayer rugs in the unglazed windows.

We walked on and on, fascinated by the sights and sounds and smells, jostled by Arabs in voluminous robes, Bedouin tribesmen in ragged black, young men in tight jeans and pullovers, European save for the inevitable scarlet fez. Through the sunshine and shadow of the latticed walks came a woman carrying a water pot on her shoulder, her uplifted arm rounded and beautiful in the immemorial gesture.

We turned down labyrinth after labyrinth. It seemed never-ending. A camel padded past softly, its small head lifted in proud disdain. And there were lots of Aunt Vinnie's poor little overladen donkeys.

"At last I've met a camel face to face," I said with satisfaction. "A real camel, not one in a zoo. I love their scornful air. They don't seem to have any idea, poor things, how ugly they are."

"The Arabs have a legend about that," Del said. "It seems Allah has one hundred names. Ninety-nine of these names are known to men, but only the camel knows the hundredth. Hence its look of superiority."

"What a lovely story," I laughed, and rounding yet another bend in the tortuous way saw Gregson, with Denise and Jules, advancing towards us. It would have been impossible to avoid them in the narrow space.

"Lorraine!" Jules hailed me shrilly. He ran to me with hands outstretched. "Uncle Greg doesn't have to return to El Garza until this evening, so he came back to the hotel and invited us out to lunch."

"How nice," I said flatly, as Greg drew level with us, Denise swinging from his hand.

It was just at that moment a whole string of camels bore down on us, taking up almost the whole of the narrow lane. In the scatter to avoid the great beasts I found myself thrust practically into Tim Gregson's arms. "Here!" He grasped me firmly by the elbow and pulled me into a small dark shop where, by the light of the filigree lamp, a very old man was hammering at a metal that looked like gold, fashioning—as I was to discover later—small attractive charms. At the moment

I was looking round distractedly for Jules, and saw with relief that he was safely behind Gregson. Del was the other side of the street, somewhere behind the slow procession of camels.

"He'll be all right, the boy-friend that isn't your boy-friend," Greg remarked drily, misreading my anxious glance.

"It was Jules I was looking for," I snapped. "Del is big enough to take care of himself."

"He'd need to be!" I thought I heard Greg mutter.

Denise and Jules were by this time hanging over the charms spread out on a brass tray at the old man's side, tiny golden slippers, little holy lamps, cabbalistic signs and crescent moons.

"Oh, Greg, will you lend me some money?" Jules begged. "I'll pay you back out of my pocket money when we get back to the hotel."

Greg produced a handful of coins.

"I want to buy a present for my special friend, Lorraine," Jules explained as he took the money.

"You catch them young, don't you?" Greg grinned at me.

I glared at him. "Just how revolting can you be?" I wanted to shout at him. But it wouldn't have been the slightest good. Nothing I could say would penetrate that glacial self-possession.

I turned to Jules, busy bargaining with the old man in a way that made me remember he had Arab blood in his veins. Similar bargaining was going on all over the market. Presently a few of the coins were exchanged for a pair of the little golden slippers. Then Denise had to buy something for me, too, and chose a miniature lamp.

"You ought to have a bangle to hang those charms on," I heard Greg say, and before I could stop him he was fastening the slippers and lamp on to a thin silver bangle. With an almost sleight-of-hand movement he snapped it on my wrist. Like an ornate fetter, I thought. A slave bangle, binding me in his service. Of all the crazy notions! The oriental atmosphere of the Souks must have gone to my head.

"You mustn't . . . I can't really accept . . ." I began, fruitlessly tugging at the bangle.

"Oh, but it's lovely!" Denise cried in her pure quick French. "It will bring you good luck."

It was then I noticed the extra charm hanging with the slippers and lamp; a twist of golden wire fashioned in the shape of a heart.

"My humble contribution," Greg whispered in my ear. "A love charm . . . though you'll hardly need it, I imagine." His thin brown face was alight with mischief. Why did he take such a delight in ribbing me? I gave a final tug at the unwanted bracelet, failed to remove it, and had to content myself with a helpless and I hoped baleful glance into the amused grey eyes watching me.

I turned to find Del at my side. In the excitement over the bracelet I hadn't noticed that the camel train had come to an end.

"Pooh!" breathed Del, holding his nose. "Those camels! What a pong! Let's get out of this, Lorraine. I've had enough of camels and Souks for one morning."

Greg was already moving away—much to my relief—saving me the embarrassment of having to introduce him to Del.

"Au 'voir, Lorraine. Au 'voir!" the children called over their shoulders as they vanished down a shadowy alleyway in Greg's wake.

Del took my hand. "There's a turning just here that leads back to civilisation, I think." He made no comment on our encounter with the young man and the Ben Akhtal children. And in a few moments we were walking down one of the wide

245

tree-lined boulevards to where we had parked the car. The hotel to which we went, on the outskirts of the city, had once been an Arab palace, a long low building bounded by a high white wall. Crossing the outer courtyard, we came to a great carved doorway. Beyond this was the vast circular space now used incongruously as a foyer. Beautiful leopardskin rugs were scattered about on the cool paved floor. There was a low divan or two piled with cushions, otherwise the only furniture was the reception desk with its out-of-key modern equipment. The light was dim in here, coming chiefly through the low Moorish arches which led to an inner courtyard, where a fountain rose out of a small clear pool inhabited by a fat goldfish. On the far side of this courtyard we found the dining-room, where we ate in a secluded corner, overlooking an Arabian Nights garden.

The waiters, in elaborately embroidered short jackets, voluminous silk trousers and tall tarbooshes, brought the unfamiliar dishes. Del talked knowledgeably about wine. Though Moslems are strictly non-drinkers, some very good wine, he said, was made in the Cap Bon district—for the benefit of tourists. He ordered a red wine something like a Burgundy, which went well with the main course—spiced roast lamb served with baby marrows fried in butter. There were platters of delicious fresh vegetables of every sort to go with it, and the inevitable *cous-cous*. We had started with *brik*, the local delicacy, made of eggs cooked in wafer-thin pastry, flavoured with aromatic herbs. For dessert there were various sticky sweetmeats, concoctions of honey and nuts, and bowls of fresh fruit. The dates were juicy and large, wholly unlike the rather rubbery mouthfuls one eats in England round about Christmas time. We finished off with coffee and liqueurs.

"You'll never be able to work on those memoirs this afternoon!" I warned Del, as he ordered a second liqueur.

"I'm not going to work on them," he answered defiantly. Leaning across the table, he covered my hand with his own. "Oh, Lorraine, it's so good to be here with you . . . just the two of us alone. Why can't it always be like this?"

A rhetorical question I didn't attempt to answer.

"Let's take the car and just drive into the blue," he went on recklessly. "I'll square it with Natalie when we get back. After all, she did keep me up the best part of the night, which means she didn't get much sleep herself. I bet you anything she's deep in her afternoon siesta by now and won't waken for hours if I don't disturb her.

"Let sleeping Comtesses lie," he laughed as he stood up from the table.

In a haze of well-being after my exotic meal, the thought of the drive appealed to me. If the Comtesse was sleeping she wouldn't miss Del, nor would my own absence matter. Aunt Vinnie always rested between lunch and tea-time. I felt a stab if pity. How awful to be old, I thought, to have nothing better to do on this golden afternoon but sleep.

The road we took by-passed Tunis and our own little seaside town of Sidi Akbar and, running southward, found the coastline again. Del was driving superbly, at about ninety miles an hour, with that perfect co-ordination which comes to the slightly intoxicated. The speed, the rush of deliciously cool wind in my face intoxicated me too. At that moment I shared in Del's recklessness. It was all so perfect, the sun warm without being too hot, the breeze fresh without being cold and blustery like an English breeze would have been. And the scenery was breathtaking—the flowers, the wild olive groves, the great jagged rocks towering up into the tranquil sky. We passed the ruins of a temple on a hillside, a temple of Baal, Del said. It sounded like something out of the Old Testament, and probably was. This land looked ancient and wise.

Presently we were surrounded by gardens, low hills rising up from the coastline covered with geraniums, jasmine, roses. There were orange orchards white with blossom, and lemon groves perfuming the air. We came to the town where the essence of these flowers was distilled. The Grasse of Tunisia, Del said, reminding me of the hillside town in Provence where French perfumes are made. We stopped at a picturesque Souk nearby to buy small flasks of the various exquisite perfumes.

Now and again, as we drove on, my conscience stirred. Firmly I stifled it. Hours like this came once in a lifetime—the perfect weather and a car that went on magic wings; the whole novel panorama of this fabulous North African countryside unrolling before me. If only it had been someone else driving me! Or if Del had been different— more solid, less of the typical playboy, someone with whom I could really talk, share ideas. I fingered the bangle on my wrist, turning the little heart-shaped charm about. What had possessed Tim Gregson to buy it for me? A small sardonic gift to mock me. For an instant I was seeing much too clearly his thin brown face with its level grey glance. I glanced at Del's far more distinguished profile. More classically distinguished, that is. Yet it somehow lacked the dignity of that other face.

"It's four o'clock, Del," I said. "Oughtn't we to be turning round now? It'll take us all of two hours to get back to the hotel."

"We're not going back," Del announced calmly.

At my shocked exclamation, he burst out laughing and swung the car into a grassy lay-by hundreds of feet above the jade green sea. Switching off the engine, he slid an arm about me.

"No, Del!" I protested.

"Yes, Del!" he mocked. His lips came down hard on my own. I struggled to free myself, but he held me close.

"We're running away," he whispered into my windblown hair.

"Del, are you mad? Turn the car for home at once!"

"We could drive away into the desert," he tempted me. "You said you wanted to see the Sahara. There are little oasis towns with comfortable inns . . . where we could put up tonight. We could tell them at Sidi Akbar tomorrow that we drove further than we meant to and the car broke down in the wilds."

"What is this?" I asked coldly. "An illicit honeymoon?"

"We could soon legalise it, if you'd like that better."

I moved away from him. "Please drive me home, Del."

He started the car, his handsome face sulky. Nosing out on to the highway, he hesitated. "We're only a few miles from Djerba. There's a ferry boat across to the Island of Djerba. We could have dinner there."

"If you don't start back towards Sidi Akbar this very minute," I declared hotly, "I'll never speak to you again."

"Oh, very well, then!" With an angry crashing of gears he headed the car for home.

"What's the matter with you the last couple of days?" he asked presently. "You've changed towards me. It's as if you'd suddenly decided to put on the brakes."

"Perhaps I have," I agreed.

We drove on for a while in silence. Lying back in my superbly sprung seat, I closed my eyes. Lightly the great car floated over the road, eating up the miles. Was Del mortally offended? I wondered—and half hoped he was. It would simplify things if he got really angry with me and decided I was a dead loss. Wanting to take me off into the desert for the night—sweetly and charmingly planning my seduction!

"Darling!" his voice crooned in my ear. "You look so adorable with your eyes closed." His lips touched mine briefly—a butterfly kiss, but it might have cost us our lives. I sat up abruptly.

"Are you stark crazy?" I flung at him. "Driving at nearly ninety miles and hour and . . . kissing people!"

"Not people," Del laughed. "Only my girl. You are, you know, whether you realise it yet or not. I'm not giving you up so easily. One day we'll be off on that honeymoon. I'll take you to Paris . . ."

"Where we'll live on fresh air?"

Del flashed me a reproachful glance. "All right, I dont earn enough to keep a wife. You don't have to rub it in. But that doesn't stop me from loving you, and sooner or later my luck will turn. Meanwhile I could continue to scrape a living, and maybe for a time you could work too. Lots of wives do nowadays. You could do scripting, dubbing, even the odd spot of acting, walk-on parts and crowd scenes and so on . . ."

"Thanks a lot," I put in drily, "but I'm not particularly drawn to being an anonymous face in a crowd scene. I've got qualifications for something much better."

"Sweetie, I *know*! You are the *cleverest*! All these terrifying degrees and so on. I hate to think of them. But what sort of career can you get out of them? Just a dull job of teaching. You would find life in Paris far more amusing."

Secretly I agreed with him. Life in Paris . . . but not life in Paris with Delmer Lloyd. Ever since I had graduated I had felt more or less let down. Teaching was all very well, but there were so many things I would rather have done. However, they all meant additional training, and I'd already cost my parents more than enough. So I had applied for a job at a large school in London just before coming away.

"Not that you really need to worry about jobs at all," Del was saying. "Your aunt and godmother is a rich and ageing woman. In the nature of things she can't go on for ever, and . . ." he paused to look at me significantly, "she has no children."

"Just what are you getting at?" I asked, in a tone that ought to have warned him off.

"Work it out for yourself," he said lightly. "Your aunt adores you, she has no heirs. Isn't it obvious that you'll benefit?" He gazed into space musingly. "It will all work out. You'll see! One day youll be rolling in money." He turned to me with an impudent grin. "Quite able to keep me in the style to which I'm accustomed!"

I was so taken aback by this blatant forecast that I was completely silenced.

A flock of sheep ahead of us took Del's attention. When he spoke again it was more seriously —for surely his earlier tasteless remarks had been a sickly joke!

"I'm not mercenary, Lorraine—just realistic. It's the French streak in me, I suppose. Though the French can be the most romantic people on earth, they're pretty shrewd when it comes to marriage settlements and so on. Not that I approve of marriage settlements, nor have I anything to settle on you, my love, but my brain potential. I'm not being conceited when I say that's something worth offering you. If, through your help, I was freed from financial worries for a year or two, I know I could write that play."

You can't dress it up, I thought. No matter how you put it, you can't make it less ugly than it is. Loving me—with an eye on Aunt Vinnie's moneybags!

"It's no use, Del," I said. "I'm sorry—but if this is your idea of a proposal of marriage I've never thought of you in that way. So please let's forget about it."

"Never!" Del returned fervently. His sherry brown eyes regarded me reproachfully. "It's just that I've spoken too soon. I could make you love me if I had the chance. I know that. And I *will* make you love me. I'm not giving up."

I saw with relief that we were nearly back at the hotel.

An explosive welcome awaited us. The Comtesse, sitting on the *terrasse* with Aunt Vinnie, was furious, her ravaged old face crimson. "Where have you been all these hours?" she shrilled at Del. "I was beginning to think you had had an accident!"

"And now you're mad with me because I haven't," he teased her. "All right, Natty, hold it!" He raised a silencing hand as the Comtesse went off into another tirade.

"Don't nag, darling. Let me explain. I took Lorrraine out to lunch and afterwards we went for a drive along the coast road, going rather further than we'd intended. You know how it is, the weather was so lovely, and the Packard so gorgeous. This country gets you!" He waved an airy hand towards the evening sky where the setting sun poured its molten gold on to mountain and sea.

"I'm sorry, Natalie darling." He stooped to kiss her lightly. "I'll make up for my truancy. I'll sit up and do memoirs all night."

"It won't be necessary," Natalie told him coldly. I could see she was trying not to be mollified by that kiss. "There'll be no time for memoirs this evening. You will be driving. We're going to Biskra. I've had a telephone call from some friends who have just arrived there and want me to join them."

"But, Natalie!" Del flung me a despairing glance. "You can't surely want to leave Sidi Akbar . . . and this very comfortable hotel. Biskra is inland, right in the desert, hot and dusty . . ."

"And the gayest town in the whole of North Africa," Natalie said. "You'll love it. We'll leave right after dinner and drive through the night. I like driving at night. It's so cool and quiet, and tonight there will be a moon. Think of it, Del, moonlight over the desert!"

Murmuring something about packing to be done, she left the *terrasse*, followed by Del, still arguing fruitlessly.

Aunt Vinnie gave me a wicked little grin. "Now see what you've done!"

"I really couldn't help it, Aunt Vinnie," I pleaded. "I didn't mean to keep Del out so long —it was his idea to go off down the coast road and drive on and on. I did protest once or twice— but you know how it is. The hours just slipped away like magic . . ."

She gave me a startled glance.

"Oh, not that sort of magic," I assured her. "I'm not in love with Del. Don't worry."

253

"I'm glad. Once or twice during the last few days I've wondered. It's been so obvious that he is—or fancies himself—in love with you. You've been making Natalie frightfully jealous."

"I'm sorry."

"Poor old Natalie and her moon over the desert. It's rather pathetic, isn't it? And I'm sure she invented those friends who are supposed to have telephoned her from Biskra. She's just whisking her precious boy away from your feline clutches."

"You surely don't mean she's *romantic* about Del!" I burst out, horrified. "Not at her age!"

Aunt Vinnie shrugged. "Age hasn't a great deal to do with it. She's a lonely old woman and she warms her heart with his youth and good looks. It's all quite harmless, and rather sad. There are so many like her drifting about the world's playgrounds, rich, ageing and desperately alone. Natalie is a widow, her family grown up and scattered."

"You're a widow, Aunt Vinnie," I pointed out. "But you don't have to hire young men to keep you company."

"Maybe I haven't time to be lonely," Aunt Vinnie answered. "Running from this committee meeting to that, opening bazaars, organising fêtes to coax the money out of people's pockets for my children and animals. And when I get tired of it all and need a change I send for my favourite great-niece and take her off into the sunshine for a holiday."

I lifted her worn, frail hand and held it to my cheek. "I'm a very lucky great-niece."

She stood up, and taking my arm, gave it an affectionate squeeze. "I suppose we'd better go up and dress for dinner."

We dined alone. (So, I noticed, did Elaine Ben Akhtal. Raschid had evidently returned to his

254

politics and Tim Gregson would have collected his machinery and vanished into his fastness in the wilderness.) The Comtesse and Del, Aunt Vinnie said, were dining upstairs in the Comtesse's suite. "She's taking good care to keep him out of your clutches during his last hour in the hotel," she laughed.

"If only she knew how grateful I am to her!" I said.

I saw Del again briefly—just before he left. Aunt Vinnie couldn't let her friend the Comtesse depart without due ceremony, so we hung about in the foyer until they appeared, followed by servants carrying an amazing assortment of luggage. Del grasped my hand and held it tight, while the two old ladies kissed.

"This isn't the end, Lorraine," he whispered desperately. "I'll be back . . . I'll write to you . . ."

"Delmer!" the Comtesse called to him curtly. She gave me a frigid nod. "Goodbye, Miss Marlow!" If looks could have killed!

"Goodbye, Comtesse!"

She swept out to the waiting car, Del looking tragically handsome in her wake. Just how much did he really feel at leaving me? I thought uneasily of his passionate declarations this afternoon, and deep in my heart I knew it wasn't quite all an act. Perhaps he was, in his own fashion, in love with me—in spite of the way he had talked of Aunt Vinnie's money, in spite of his odd relationship with the Comtesse who had given him that expensive car.

Just for an instant I envied Natalie—not because she had poor weak Del so blantantly in tow. But because of the moonlit night that awaited her on her journey through the desert. Would I ever see the Sahara? Having come so far it seemed tragic to have to go back to England without

255

having touched even the fringe of that fabulous terrain. But following Aunt Vinnie into the luxurious lounge, I reminded myself how lucky I was to be having this holiday at all.

CHAPTER FOUR

THE tempo of life at the Hotel Alzara changed after Del's departure. No rushing hither and thither in the luxurious Packard, no long evenings of dancing. I had more time to spend with Aunt Vinnie. She was so happy over this that I felt a little guilty, remembering how often during the past fortnight I had left her to go running off with Del. Now she would come and sit on the beach under her green-lined parasol while I had my morning swim, and if she found the climb back up the cliff path a bit of a pull she didn't complain. In the afternoons her rests were much shorter and we would hire a chauffeur-driven car and go for drives out to Cap Bon, or up into the hills to some picturesque village.

This was no doubt how she had visualised our holiday when she had planned it—a repetition of the pleasant times we had had in Brittany, or on the French Riviera in other years. Days of gentle enjoyment, with just enough of the foreign-land atmosphere to make us realise we were not in Torquay or Bournemouth. It was all very pleasant, and she was far from being a dull companion, but I couldn't help wishing I was seeing more of the native side of life in Tunisia. I don't mean the rather artificially produced 'Belly-dancing' in the night clubs (which would have shocked Aunt Vinnie to the core), or the Hispano-Moorish music in the culture centres, but the real day-to-day life of the people I had seen in the Souks.

What went on behind the blank windowless walls we passed on our drives? Walls concealing Arab homesteads of the more prosperous kind. The schools, too; I should have loved to follow the new Miss Arab in her smart Western gym-slip, hurrying along the Tunis boulevards to classrooms undreamed of by her mother and grandmother. And the mosques intrigued me with their graceful domes and towers, where the *muezzin* stood at certain hours of the day calling the faithful to prayer. I had read in a guide book of the beauty of the interiors, but infidel tourists, I imagined, would not be welcome in them, especially women tourists.

I asked about this, and she said it wasn't usual for tourists to be admitted to mosques, though in certain cities it could be arranged. As for women, even those who were Moslems had to sit hidden behind the screens during the hours of worship, not mixing with the men.

Elaine herself was not a Moslem, but a Catholic. So were her children. Raschid went to the mosque on Friday, keeping to the faith in which he had been brought up. But there seemed to be a lot of latitude in the Ben Akhtal family. The more I knew of them, the more I liked them.

The weekend after Del's departure Elaine invited Aunt Vinnie and me to join them in a picnic at Hammam-Lif, a beautiful beach sheltered by forests of eucalyptus and pine some way farther down the coast. It was a perfect day, the sea calm as a millpond, delicate in colour as the inside of a shell, its tones ranging from palest pink to lavender and lilac, shading away to deep blues and greens in the distance.

That was the weekend I really got to know Raschid, Elaine's Arab husband. Why I had expected him to be mysteriously 'different' I don't know. Apart from his Moorish good looks he was just the same as any other young husband, released from the cares of office, enjoying his wife and children in a long day by the sea. He talked to me about the Bourgiba reforms; the schools, the clinics, the improved status of women, and he promised to take me over one of the new schools before I went back to England, if he could spare the time from his political duties. As a junior Cabinet Minister, at the mercy of this crisis or that, he was, he explained, hardly his own master. But he would do his best to get away one day. He was grateful to me, I think, for the simple lessons I was giving Jules, amused by the little boy's growing devotion to me.

"My special friend," Jules called me. As we lazed on the sands that picnic day at Hamman-Lif he pointed to the golden slippers dangling from the bangle on my wrist.

"Lorraine is wearing my charm today," he told his father proudly.

"And she's wearing mine too," Denise broke in jealously. In her brief swimsuit she flung herself on top of me, egging me on for a romp. I tickled her, and she roared with delight. We rolled over and over, getting ourselves covered with sand, so that we had to run down to the sea to wash it off.

It wasn't until I was rubbing her down with a large rough towel that Denise remembered the charms again. What she really wanted to know, she said, was whether I thought as much of the little lamp she had given me as I did of Jules' slippers.

"I like the little lamp very much," I assured her. "Every time I look at it I think how sweet it was of you to give it to me."

"And do you think how sweet it was of Uncle Greg to give you the bangle to fasten it on?" She fingered the trinkets on my wrist with a thoughtful air. "He gave you his heart too, didn't he?" she demanded, bringing an amused glance from Elaine, and a hoot of laughter from Raschid.

"Just a little toy heart," I answered in a ridiculous flurry.

"Greg doesn't strike me as a chap who would give himself or his heart away very easily," Raschid said.

I pulled Denise back on to my lap, glad to hide my hot face in her cloud of dark hair. I blew softly into her neck. She giggled and squirmed and flung her arms around me. "Mr. Gregson," I said through a mouthful of hair, "hardly knows me . . . and the little he knows I don't think he very much likes."

"You're wrong," Elaine said quickly. "The impression I got was quite different. I should have said he's quite taken with you. And he thinks it's marvellous of you to give up some of your holiday time to teaching Jules."

It was idiotic the way one part of my mind seized on these casually made remarks, as if they contained rare compliments to be treasured and remembered. The sane part of me knew it was simply Elaine's kindly if not very penetrating summing up of a situation she really knew very little about.

"I wish Uncle Greg would come and see us again," Jules said.

"I don't think that's very likely, *mon vieux*," Raschid told his son. "Greg's visits to Tunis are few and far between. Now he has got that electrical harrow from England he'll hardly come to town again until it's time for the next shipment of

259

dates to go out. He'll be far too busy at El Garza."

"What exactly does he do there?" I asked.

"He's reorganising and improving the irrigation systems on my father's plantations, and generally seeing to the running of the estate. It's quite a sizeable district, including several small villages, where the agricultural workers live. I'm not sure how many Greg employs, more than a hundred. He has done wonders since he took over some years ago. They're growing oranges and lemons now as well as dates. There are wheat and oats and barley on what used to be scrub land, and recently he has started a large market garden."

"It sounds as if he's quite an enthusiast," I murmured inadequately.

"Oh, he is!" Elaine nodded vigorously. "You would think he would be lonely out there, away from his own kind, and it isn't even as if he lived in the household of Raschid's father. He has his own house some distance away."

"And he isn't married?" I blurted—much to my own surprise. I hadn't meant to ask such a personal question. However, Elaine seemed to think nothing of it.

"He's not married," she confirmed. "Poor old Greg is a bit of a mystery where women are concerned—in fact he's a mystery altogether. Why, having graduated as an ecologist, should he choose to isolate himself in a remote corner of the world like El Garza?"

"An ecologist?" I echoed, mystified.

"A scientist trained to conserve land and wild life, in a world where both are threatened with exploitation," Raschid explained. "And I don't think there's any mystery about Greg's choosing El Garza for a stamping ground. He and I were at Oxford together, and after we had graduated he came out here with me for a long holiday—

fell in love with El Garza, found that he was needed there and decided to stay on. I don't imagine he finds it lonely. He was brought up, after all, in a remote Highland village, so he's not unaccustomed to wide open spaces, and a certain amount of solitude."

"All the same, I wish he would get married," Elaine persisted. "He's such a dear. He would make some lucky girl such a good husband."

"He will, in his own time," Raschid predicted. "Probably there's a bonny lassie tucked away in the Highlands waiting for him."

"If there is, I'm sorry for her," Elaine said forcefully. "Greg isn't being particularly attentive. It's ages since he's been home."

"Oh, well," Raschid dismissed his own theories lightly. "I expect he's too busy . . . wedded, as they say, to his work. Greg is the good old Scottish Covenanter type—slow and conscientious, painfully conscientious. He takes everything almost too seriously—his work, his friendships, his loyalties. And it will be the same when he gets around to marriage. He won't embark on it lightly, and when he does it will be for keeps. He's not the sort of chap who goes in for having affairs—and he'll be careful to pick a girl with the same high standards."

I found this conversation oddly depressing, and to change the subject I said I thought El Garza sounded fascinating—a scatter of villages and fruit orchards, set in a beautiful oasis, ruled over by a Caid. Just the sort of place I would love to visit while I was in Tunisia.

"Why not come along with us when we go there next week?" Elaine suggested. "I shall be taking the children for a short holiday with their Grandpa Hassan, the Caid. He's anxious to have Jules with him for a while before he goes off to his English school."

My heart leaped at this unexpected invitation, then sank again like a stone. It was no good; we were leaving Sidi Akbar at the end of the week, and I knew there could be no question of our postponing our departure. Aunt Viniie had engagements in London and Paris and I ought to be at home in case I had to go and be interviewed by the school board to which I had applied for a job.

So I had to refuse Elaine's kind offer. "It's maddening," I said. "I'd have given anything to see this beautiful oasis set in the desert country, and it would have been so romantic to meet a Caid."

"Perhaps some other time," Elaine consoled me, and added with a laugh that I'd got quite the wrong idea of Grandpa Hassan. "He's the dearest old soul, but with his rheumatism and spectacles hardly a figure of romance. Khalid would probably be more satisfactory. He's beautiful enough!" Elaine gave an odd little shrug, and I got the idea she didn't like this Khalid character very much.

"My brother," Raschid supplied in a dry tone, and changed the subject.

Brooding over my disappointment, I let the conversation go over my head. Here I was in Tunisia, getting to know an important Tunisian family, who would, given time, have taken me into their excitingly different Oriental world. And I had to turn my back on it all and go back to my small town home in Surrey. It was infuriating. Not, I assured myself, because I was to be deprived of any further contact with that rather unpleasant Scot, Mr. Tim Gregson, but because I had longed to know more of this interesting country, in which, it seemed, I was fated to be only a fleeting tourist, content with a tourist's eye view.

Two days before we were due to depart, the weather broke. That helped, in a way; made it easier to contemplate saying goodbye to this land that had seemed all sunshine and golden beaches. Now the rain pelted down from a leaden sky, and it was chill and drear. Freak weather, the locals said, the sort that belonged strictly to the brief winter. But that is the kind of shamefaced explanation offered by all residents at seaside resorts when the weather lets them down. I'd heard it in Bournemouth and Torquay.

On the second morning of rain I paddled about the dripping boulevards in Tunis, buying presents to take home—small pieces of pottery from Hammamet, perfume from Nabeul, tooled leather handbags and belts and a beautifully embroidered goatskin pouffe cover for my mother.

In the afternoon I sat in the lounge of the hotel with Aunt Vinnie, thinking regretfully of the trip we had planned to the museum at Carthage. But it was too wet and cold for Aunt Vinnie to venture out. Elaine had taken the children to a party at the French Embassy, so we had not even their cheerful comings and goings to enliven the long hours. Listening to the rain dripping on to the flagged terrace, we drank our afternoon tea, and out of sheer boredom ate more than we wanted of the little cakes and dainty sandwiches provided. After a more than adequate luncheon neither of us was hungry.

Aunt Vinnie said it was the kind of weather that made her long for a nice English coal fire. Mosaic-paved patios and date palms were all very well in the sunshine, but there was something terribly depressing about them on a grey and rainy day.

When a page-boy approached us with the afternoon mail on a silver salver we both perked up.

One official-looking envelope was addressed to me, the remaining handful of letters was for Aunt Vinnie, including, I heard her exclaim, one from the Comtesse at Biskra. I tore my official communcation open. It was from the school board in London informing me that my application for a post had been turned down. Just what I needed to put the finishing touch of gloom to the desolate afternoon! Now I didn't even have a job to go back to. Just for one wild moment I considered the possibility of accepting Elaine's invitation to El Garza, but firmly put the temptation behind me. Now more than ever it was important for me to be in England if I was to apply for a teaching post before all the new term arrangements had been made. Hanging about at home for months, out of work, was unthinkable.

"Is something wrong?" Aunt Vinnie asked, sensing my gloom.

I told her the school I had applied to had turned me down.

She said, "There are other schools, Lorry dear. With your brilliant qualifications you'll have no trouble in finding a suitable billet."

Kind of her, but my qualifications weren't all that brilliant, and anyway, I didn't really want to be a teacher. What did I want? A job that entailed travel, seeing the world and finding out how the people lived in remote places, perhaps doing something to help in primitive places— social work of some kind. There were all sorts of exciting organisations now for overseas work, but to be employable by any of them I'd have to take extra courses—in sociology, psychology . . . And I just couldn't afford extra courses.

"What's the news from Biskra?" I asked, half relieved, half annoyed (so vain is the human heart!) that Del hadn't written to me. After all his protestations of undying devotion he seemed to have forgotten me very quickly. This, added to the snub from the school board, made me feel drab and unwanted.

"Biskra," Aunt Vinnie was saying brightly, "seems to be all sunshine and gaiety, and Natalie has found a number of her lotus-eating pals there, people she usually meets in Monte Carlo or St. Tropez or Rome—the international set in which she moves. Biskra, it appears, is all the fashion at the moment. Another season it could be Teheran, or even Delhi. They get around, these smart set wanderers!"

"Does she mention Del?"

"Not a word about him. If he sent you a message she's been careful not to pass it on."

We both laughed. Then Aunt Vinnie gave me one of her shrewdest glances. "Not missing him, are you?"

"Of course not, Aunt Vinnie! He's not at all my cup of tea, poor old Del. You know that."

Aunt Vinnie nodded. "Yes, I think I do, and I'm glad. At first I was afraid you were going to be taken in by his charm. It's an immense relief that you . . . were not!"

"Why? Don't you like him?" I probed.

"Not really," Aunt Vinnie looked embarrassed. "It's probably very wrong of me, but I couldn't help wondering if he was something of a fortune-hunter. I felt he was exploiting Natalie, getting her to buy him that very expensive car. A young man with the right sort of independent spirit would never have accepted such a gift."

Unfortunately I remembered how Del had tried to find out if I were Aunt Vinnie's heiress. But I stifled the recollection and said stoutly, "He couldn't have hoped to get many luxury cars out

265

of me—poor schoolmarm, without even a job to go to!"

"But he will hardly have overlooked the fact that you are the niece and goddaughter of a childless, wealthy old woman."

I felt my cheeks grow hot, with shame for Delmer, and embarrassment for myself. "If you think that aspect of our relationship ever enters my head . . ." I began heatedly.

"Dear, I'm sure it doesn't." Aunt Vinnie put a soothing hand on my arm. "But perhaps it ought to. After all, I am rich, and it would be natural for you to have what they call 'expectations'."

"Aunt Vinnie, please don't talk like this!" I was really upset now. "I hate it. I've never for one moment thought of having 'expectations'! Of all the revolting words! The only thing I want is for you to go on being the way you are now for ever and ever."

"That's sweet of you, darling," Aunt Vinnie laughed. "But you aren't being very realistic. I've got to die some time and in the natural course of events it will be before you do. So I think you ought to know how you stand."

We were in a secluded corner of the lounge. In the distance a newly arrived Scandinavian family waded earnestly through afternoon tea, calling for fresh relays of little sandwiches and cake—which they probably took for an emasculated kind of *smorgësbrod*. Somewhere a radio transmitter poured out soft music. On the terrace the rain continued to fall and the palm trees drooped their dismal fronds while Aunt Vinnie embarked on a long boring dissertation about company funds and dividends and shareholders. Most of her late husband's fortune (tied up in these mysterious bodies) would, at her death, revert to a distant male cousin of her husband's. She herself had control of only a small part of the vast amount he had left. Of the money at her disposal she was bequeathing some to her favourite charities, a small sum to my mother and five thousand pounds to me.

"On my lawyer's advice," she went on, "I'm making the gift to you very soon, since if I live on for a few years it will mean you can have the money free from death duties."

I kissed her warmly, conscious of a vast relief. Five thousand pounds in the not so distant future was a nice round sum, but not in present-day terms a fortune, not sufficient to tempt the Delmer Lloyds of this greedy world. I think I was glad, too, that the money was to come to me in a way quite unconnected with Aunt Vinnie's death. I couldn't bear to think I might profit by that, even though I realise wills and bequests are an inevitable part of family life.

She talked on for a while, giving me advice about investments and so on . . . to which, I am afraid, I only half listened.

Later I went for a walk in the dusk. The rain had eased off a little, but the wind still shook drops from the palm fronds and the bougainvillea on the terrace was a sodden mass of washed-out blossom. Buttoned into a raincoat, I strode briskly along the beach, glad of the exercise. The sea was a muddy brown, the small flattened waves topped with grey foam. Far away the mountains were sullen, black clouds pressing down on them out of a bilious-looking sky.

"Where have all the flowers gone?" I hummed to myself nostalgically. Three days from now I would be arriving at home—precisely at this evening hour. Already I was beginning to feel detached from my surroundings. Earlier, for a few mad moments, I had wondered if Aunt Vinnie's five thousand pounds would make it possible for me to stay on at Sidi Akbal long enough to go to El Garza with the Ben Akhtals. But of course it was out of the question. The money was not mine yet, and if I knew anything of the ways of solicitors it might be some weeks before I had access to it. Meanwhile I couldn't afford to remain at the expensive hotel for even a few days on my own. So there was nothing for it but to go home.

Perhaps when I got my five thousand pounds I could see about taking one of those extra courses instead of looking round for a school. But whatever my future held, Tunisia had no part in it. Soon this holiday would fade into the limbo where all pleasant holiday memories go. Even now it was taking on an air of unreality that made me feel sad and lost . . . a little ghost-like in the twilight.

So that it was with almost a sense of shock I saw the light streaming from the Ben Akhtal's suite as I came up the *terrasse* steps. The door was open to the damp sultry evening and I paused at the threshold, my gloomy mood vanishing as I watched Elaine trying to catch Denise, who, clad only in a brief vest, ran, laughing, away from her mother, jumping over the beds.

"The children have gone completely mad after their party," Elaine called out to me.

"Come and catch me, Lorraine!" Denise challenged me.

After that it degenerated into the wildest of romps, in which even solemn little Jules joined. By the time we had both the children safely in bed, it was the aperitif hour.

I hurried away to change, and then found Auntie Vinnie in the lounge ordering her usual sherry. Presently Elaine joined us. I drank a mild vermouth Cassis, pleasantly relaxed after my walk and the tussle with the children. Elaine had a straight Scotch, saying she needed it.

"A maddening thing happened today," she confided. "Raschid has unexpectedly been briefed to go to New York and Washington on a diplomatic mission of some kind. The senior Minister who was to have covered the assignment has suddenly become ill and Raschid has been asked to take his place. The tantalising thing is that I could have gone with him. It's the sort of trip on which wives are not only permitted, but actually welcomed, since there will be many social engagements in which they would be a help. But it's no use." She shook her head mournfully. "I'm booked to take the children to their grandfather's, and I can't possibly disappoint him."

"Couldn't that visit to the grandfather be postponed?" Aunt Vinnie asked.

"I'm afraid not," Elaine answered. "Jules will be going off to his English school so soon, and the Caid has set his heart upon having him at El Garza for a while before he leaves. Probably he wants to give him a good wholesome dose of Arab life before he's delivered to the English infidels!" Her smile took the edge off the words, but it was clear that she was troubled.

"Raschid needs me," I heard her murmur, as if to herself. With sudden purpose she fixed her great dark eyes on me. "I hate letting him go off all that way alone. But what can I do?"

I felt a throb of excitement, sensing dimly what was in her mind.

"Isn't there some nurse or governess, some trustworthy servant who could take the children to their grandfather's?" Aunt Vinnie was asking.

Elaine said, "There is absolutely no one I can turn to. My only servant at the moment is that silly little girl Samia, who amuses herself telling

Denise frightening stories. So there's nothing for it; I shall just have to give up this wonderful trip to America and take the children to El Garza myself." But once more the great luminous eyes fixed themselves on me. It was almost as if their appeal hypnotised me.

"Could I be of any help?" I found myself asking.

Elaine's expressive face lit up. "My dear, what a marvellous suggestion! But no . . . it's too much to ask of you, and you said you had to return to England . . ."

"It's not so urgent now as I thought it was. I could easily spare the time."

"Just two weeks," Elaine put in breathlessly, "and you did say you wished you could have penetrated further into the country, seen more of Arab life. This might be your opportunity."

I caught my breath, seeing myself crossing a desert of golden sand, coming to a place of fertile loveliness. Fruit, flowers, lush green grass. The Oasis of El Garza. I had only the haziest notion what an oasis might really be like, only that at that moment it seemed to me a place of fabulous beauty. A paradise on earth . . . with a dour young Scotsman as its custodian.

I glanced enquiringly at Aunt Vinnie. She peered at me over the rim of her sherry glass. "It's worth thinking about," she murmured cautiously. "An extension of your holiday, and a chance, as Elaine says, to live for a time in an Arab household. It would be a unique experience. Also," she added practically, "you would be helping Elaine out of a difficult situation. . ."

"She certainly would!" Elaine agreed heartily. "And the children would adore having her." She turned to me, looking slightly guilty. "But don't let me talk you into it, Lorraine."

"What would it be like at El Garza?" I asked. "Would I, for instance, have to live in a harem?"

"But of course!" Elaine burst out laughing at my exclamation of horror. "Don't look so scared, Lorraine. A harem isn't a prison nowadays, but merely the part of the very large house in which the womenfolk of the family spend a good deal of their time."

"Womenfolk? Do you mean the Caid's wives?"

"Good heavens, no! Moslems in Tunisia aren't polygamous any more, and anyway, Grandpa Hassan never was. He was devoted to his one and only wife and has been an inconsolable widower since her death some eight years ago. He's really rather a dear, in his solemn, important way. I'm sure you would like him."

She turned to Aunt Vinnie. "Your niece would be in good hands with Grandpa Hassan, Mrs. Vardon. He is kind, honourable, a truly gentle man. Then there's Mairik, Raschid's widowed aunt who lives at the Palace, with her two daughters, Jamila and Alya, besides a whole host of cousins and other indefinable kinswomen. The Ben Akhtal family has many ramifications. It is, in fact, a large tribe. Many of the men work on the estate, some of them living in the surrounding villages, while the more immediate members of the family live at the Casa, as the big house is known."

"So I should have plenty of company," I put in, adding with an excited laugh, "When do we start?"

"Think it over," Elaine advised. "Talk about it with your aunt. I don't want you to make up your mind on impulse. Let me know in the morning what you decide, and whatever it is I shall be grateful to you."

She put a slim brown hand over mine. "I'm already deeply indebted to you. You mustn't let

271

me be a nuisance to you with my family problems. Promise me you'll make your decision about this trip more in your own interests than in mine."

"I promise," I agreed. And I don't need all night to think it over, I could have added. I knew as I sat there in the softly lit hotel lounge that I wanted to go to El Garza, more than I had ever wanted anything in my life.

CHAPTER FIVE

IT was with mixed feelings that I learned that Tim Gregson was coming to take us to El Garza. Elaine fixed it by telephone before her departure for Paris—the first stage of her husband's diplomatic mission. How the Caid—or Greg, for that matter—had taken the news that I was to accompany the children to El Garza I would never know. Elaine, in a flurry of last-minute preparations, merely told me she had arranged everything, explained everything, and that Greg would be driving over to fetch us a few hours after she herself had left the hotel.

It was soon after breakfast that she had left, and now I was pottering about her rooms with the children, waiting for Tim Gregson to appear. He was due about noon, leaving an interval of two hours during which I had to try to keep the children happy. Upset by their mother's departure, they were not easy to handle. Had I, I began to wonder, taken on more than I could manage? Here I was going off into the blue, to live in an improbable Arab household, with the responsibility of two small children on my shoulders. And my only contact with the sort of world I understood would be an antagonistic Scotsman. To be truthful, ever since I had seen Aunt Vinnie off on the Tunis-

London plane the night before I had been feeling decidedly jittery.

"I want Maman!" Denise wailed. "I don't want to go and stay with Grandpère Hassan. I'm frightened of him. Samia says he carries a big dagger in his belt and that he has a dungeon where he'll shut me up if I'm not good."

"Samia doesn't tell the truth," I reminded Denise. "That's why you *maman* sent her away. She was a very naughty girl, making up those stories about your dear kind *grandpère* just to frighten you."

I took her in my arms, and she clung to me. "When will Maman be coming back?" she demanded.

"Just as soon as ever we've had our lovely holiday with Grandpère Hassan," I promised.

She twisted round on my lap to give me a long searching glance. "How do you know it will be lovely?"

"You will have all your little cousins to play with . . ."I racked my brains for further inducements.

"I don't like my little cousins," Denise remarked coldly. And then, "Will Uncle Greg be at El Garza?"

I nodded, and felt Denise relax. "That's all right, then. Uncle Greg won't let anything bad happen to us. I love Uncle Greg . . . don't you?"

I murmured something noncommittal and called to Jules to come in from the *terrasse*, where he was running up and down trying to launch paper darts into the windless air. It was a day of blazing sunshine again, the recent rains forgotten. And Jules had no hat on. He would get heatstroke, I decided nervously, once more feeling the weight of my responsibilities. He came at once to my call, looking impossibly cool and pale in his neat white sailor suit.

"Darling, you'll be worn out before we start for El Garza," I admonished him. "Come and sit down quietly beside me and we'll read some more of *The Water Babies.*"

"Read it to me, too," Denise put in jealously. "Make it in French, and tell me about the little boy called Tom who fell into the stream."

I had to put her down while I searched for the book in my haversack. It was with the children's modest luggage and my own, piled up by the *terrasse* door. As soon as I sat down Denise clambered on to my lap again, and in spite of the heat Jules pressed as close as he could to my side. Poor kids, they were missing their mother and really being very good about it. But I could see I was going to have to do a lot of comforting during the next few hours.

Engrossed in our story, we didn't hear Tim Gregson's car drive up, and suddenly he was there, crossing the *terrasse* towards us.

"Well!" he drawled, as I started up, "you do look a forlorn little lot, clinging together, like a bunch of refugees, surrounded by your bags and baggage." He held out his arms and both children ran to him. Over their heads, he looked at me impassively. "So Elaine has gone off and left you in charge of the children?" There was the slightest sardonic emphasis on that 'you', but it brought the quick colour to my cheeks.

"Don't you think I'm fit to be left?" I asked.

Greg shrugged. "That's up to Elaine."

He lifted Denise and she flung her arms round his neck. "Maman has gone a long way away and we're coming to live with you until she gets back," she told him. "We *will* live with you, won't we?" she went on a little doubtfully.

"I won't be far off," he promised ner.

"Because I love you." She kissed him vigorously. "We all love you, Jules and Lorraine. Lorraine said so. She always wears your bangle on her wrist, the one you gave her with your heart."

"How nice!" Greg laughed, flashing me a wicked glance. He was looking very spruce today, in a white linen suit and dark silk shirt, his thick hair with its tendency to curl severely slicked back from his brow.

"I ordered an early lunch," I told him. "Elaine said you would want to start back to El Garza without too much delay."

"I do," he agreed, as we started down the *terrasse* towards the dining room with the children. "But I've got to have a bit of a let-up first. I've been on the road since the crack of dawn. El Garza, you know, is all of two hundred and fifty miles away."

"Of course you must have a rest," I murmured, feeling like a slave-driver.

"We'll all rest," Greg declared autocratically. "The kids ought to have some kind of siesta during the hot hours of the afternoon, and I'll go down to the beach and cool off in the sea."

I could only agree to this arrangement, though I couldn't see the children, in their excited state, settling down to an afternoon nap. And of course they didn't. What it came down to was a rather wearying session in a hot bedroom, where I read *The Water Babies* endlessly, while Greg presumably dozed on the beach until his lunch was digested and then had his swim.

It was nearly four o'clock when we finally set off in a large rather shabby van. Greg made no apology for it as he bundled us in. I thought of Del's feather-bed tourer as I climbed over the various bundles and bales in the back of the vehicle—a sack of some grain or other, the handle of a hoe, a roll of wire netting.

"I'm afraid it's not very tidy," Greg remarked cheerfully. "We'll let the kids sit in the back amongst the clobber. You come in front with me." A concession to my more mature years, I imagined. There was no particular warmth in the invitation.

When we had contrived seats for the children and I was settled on the bench in front, Greg took the wheel. It was still very hot, but the slight breeze induced by the movement of the van gave an illusion of fresh air.

At intervals I cast anxious glances over my shoulder, but Jules and Denise seemed quite content amongst the bundles and bales. When I asked them if they were comfortable, they answered in chorus that they were. "I like this funny car," Denise declared. "It's much nicer than our Citröen. There's more room in the back. It's like a little house where we can play," she ended ecstatically.

"You see!" Greg gave me an admonitory sidelong glance. "Children aren't car snobs."

"If you mean I'm a car snob . . ." I began indignantly.

Greg laughed. "I wish you could have seen the look of dismay on your face when I drove this van round to the *terrasse* steps! Don't tell me you didn't expect something more glamorous from the Caid in the way of transport."

"Does *he* drive round in this?" I countered.

"He has a small Volkswagen which wouldn't have been roomy enough for you and the children and your luggage. He's not car-minded, and doesn't drive anywhere very much. Mostly he travels on horseback. Like all Arabs he's a superb horseman—which is just as well, for he could hardly afford the Rolls-Royce luxury of his neighbours, the oil king Sheikhs. There's no oil

276

on the land of the Caid Hassan—which makes him a comparatively poor man."

"Dates," I said, "are more picturesque than oil."

"But not so profitable, even though we grow some of the best dates in the world, the famous Deglet Nour variety."

We had left civilisation behind by this time, and turning aside from the coast road entered a land of scrub and sand.

"Is this the beginning of the Sahara Desert?" I asked hopefully.

"I suppose you might call it that," Greg conceded. "Though the Sahara proper is a much more imposing sight; even nowadays, when one meets a five-ton lorry more often than a camel."

I looked at the road ahead; dark-surfaced, well made, it wound through groves of tamarisk and cactus. Young Arabs in tight jeans and berets lounged outside a roadside café advertising Coca-Cola. A lorry bore down on us, roared past and streamed off into the distance trailing clouds of diesel oil.

"Can you imagine any self-respecting camel putting up with this?" Greg asked. "Their feet, for one thing, are constructed for walking over soft sand. This metallic surface would be torment for them. But one doesn't very often see them on these main roads. The day of the camel as a means of transport is almost over."

"What about those camels we saw in the Souks the other day?" I asked.

"Probably on their way to the knacker's yard," Greg said with a shrug. "Camel meat is, I believe, as much in demand as horseflesh in these parts."

"What a shame!" I burst out.

"Progress!" Greg said tersely, as another great stinking lorry roared past us. "Speed means money, and camels don't move fast enough."

"I hope that doesn't mean they're going to disappear altogether," I said. "They're such appealing animals, with their ridiculous air of dignity and film-star eyelashes."

"I don't think they'll disappear as long as the nomads use them," Greg said. "Indeed they're part of the nomad family life, sharing the small encampments with the air of a tolerant grandmother, baring their teeth when pushed beyond endurance, but seldom using them, so docile at heart that even the smallest child can lead one of them, and a delightful sight it is to see."

"There ought to be a society for the preservation of camels," I said. "Why don't you start one? After all that, I understand, is your job as an ecologist; the conservation of land, wild life, and so on."

Greg laughed. "I can see Elaine has been talking to you! But I don't think I'll start conserving camels just yet. Not while the great salt caravans still exist, with their thousands of camels trekking across the desert taking loads of salt to the ports."

"Grandpa Hassan has camels," Jules contributed from the back of the van. "His bodyguard rides on them. One day one of the soldiers let me ride on a camel."

"He let me too," Denise put in, more hurriedly than truthfully, I suspected. "It was a dear little baby camel named Violetta, and its nose was made of velvet."

"That's a toy she has at home in our house in Tunis," Jules explained.

"I'm thirsty!" Denise complained. "And hot."

We were driving through one of those sandy valleys called a *gadi*. In the enclosed space the heat was merciless.

"Couldn't we open the back door of the van to let a current of air blow through?" I suggested.

"As long as the children don't fall out," Greg said doubtfully.

"I'll go in the back with them," I opted. "Or better still, I'll change places with them and let them come on to the front seat."

And so, making a brief halt by the way, we arranged it. But after a while Denise got tired of the rather hard front seat and crawled over the barrier to me. I took her on my lap, and crouching among the bundles made her as comfortable as I could. Soon she was fast asleep. I think I must have nodded off too. The journey seemed to go on interminably. Every now and then one of the great lorries raced past us. Sometimes it was an oil truck. It occurred to me that whatever merits our sturdy little van possessed, speed wasn't one of them.

It must have been around six o'clock that we stopped, in a street of those windowless white houses that always seemed to me faintly sinister.

"I thought you and the kids might like a bite to eat and a rest," Greg said. "We still have some way to go."

He came to the back of the van where I was disentangling myself from the heavily sleeping Denise. She didn't like being roused and wailed dismally when I passed her out to Greg. He put her down and turned to give me a hand. I was, I found, ridiculously stiff after my spell of sitting cramped on the ill-sprung floor of the van.

"Have you seized up?" Greg enquired mildly. He held out his arms to me and I put my hands on his shoulders, meaning to spring lightly to the ground. But somehow the spring didn't come off. Instead I collapsed against Greg's broad chest, and for an instant, as he took my whole weight, I was held close in his arms. It was over so quickly, but I had time to feel the hardness of his

279

muscles, his sinewy strength, feel too my own unexpected, instinctive response. Hurried pulses, a blurring of the vision, an odd breathless happiness —an idiotic female reaction of which I was thoroughly ashamed. Big strong man and clinging little woman act. Looking up from under my lashes, I met Greg's glance. His grey eyes were angry and defensive. It was a "Don't-you-try-that-sort-of-thing-on-me" look. My cheeks burned and I was glad to turn my attention to the crumpled, forlorn Denise.

Coaxing her along, we followed Greg through a door in one of the blank walls into a small courtyard, where elderly Arabs were sitting round wooden tables drinking mint tea. We went on into an inner room, stone-flagged and cool, where we sat on rough benches at oilcloth-covered tables. But the food when it came was appetising; a dish of rice flavoured with green peppers and little bits of savoury meat. Fresh fruit followed, oranges and dates and bananas, all locally grown, Greg said. I hadn't known bananas could be so luscious and juicy, bearing no resemblance whatever to the rather woolly fruit to be found in greengrocer's shops at home.

Denise, who had sat on my lap throughout the meal, watched me peel a banana for her and cut it into sections.

"Why are you babying her?" Greg asked.

"Because she's dead tired," I explained, rather obviously.

Across the oilcloth cover Greg eyed me musingly. "A bit of a puzzle, aren't you?" he said presently. "All this mother love and so on; making a martyr of yourself sitting on the floor of the van with that heavy child on your lap. Taking them on, for that matter, embarking on this trip

with them, shouldering the inevitable responsibility . . . it just doesn't fit in."

"Fit in with what?" I asked, uneasily.

"Into the picture I'd formed of you on the
evidence available . . . the good-time girl, all
glamour and sophistication."

"Glamour . . . sophistication . . . me?" I burst
out with more indignation than grammar.

"Yes, glamour; studied, experienced. The dark
glasses and bikini type. Natural habitat, the luxury beaches of the South of France and the North
of Africa." There was more than the hint of a
sneer in his tone. "That boy-friend of yours with
the twenty-foot-long Packard," he went on, "what,
by the way, does he think of your departure for
the desert in the role of nursemaid?"

"If you mean Delmer Lloyd I haven't a clue,"
I answered coolly. "He left the hotel some days
ago and can have no more interest in my whereabouts than I have in his. So I wish you would
stop referring to him as my 'boy-friend'. He was
nothing of the sort."

"Just a ship that passed in the night," Greg
mocked.

"I don't see that it's any concern of yours what
he was," I exploded, my temper slipping.

"*Je veux faire pi-pi!*" Denise whispered urgently in my ear. Never had an interruption been
more welcome!

I stood up with a murmured, "Excuse us", and
went over to the Arab girl who had waited on us.

"*Par ici, madame,*" she murmured, sensing our
urgency, and led the way through tortuous passages to a strange, dark, odorous cavern, where I
somehow contrived to deal with Denise's needs
and my own. When I had escorted Jules to the
same place of dubious comfort we boarded the van
again, and this time Greg insisted on my sitting

281

on the front seat at his side. He had succeeded in finding two large sacks of hay while we were making our journeys to the toilet, and with these we were able to make comfortable beds for the children.

It was now the hour of sunset, the coolness of evening already stirring in the streets of the little town. From the tower of some near-by mosque came the haunting, sing-song call to prayer. Moving into open country the sky unfolded before us, a panorama of rose and gold. The dun flat country around us was touched with its glory. On and on we went, passing the outcrops of camel scrub, the occasional whitewalled village, a shepherd driving a flock of goats.

The twilight deepened, and there was a moon— the moon that had been new when Del and the Comtesse drove through the night to Biskra. Now it was waning. Curved like a scimitar, thin and sharp, it hung in the eastern sky, a brilliant satellite in attendance, Venus perhaps, or Jupiter. But I wasn't sure how the planets were oriented in North Africa and didn't feel inclined to consult my companion. Since his oddly bitter attack on me in the café I hadn't encouraged conversation, and finally he had given up and now sat hunched over the wheel looking remote and self-sufficient. He drove with the ease of a man to whom the way is familiar, even managing to get a little more speed out of the rickety van. In the back the children slept peacefully. The stars grew bright in the vast velvety sky. In their faint light I could see the shadowy hummocks of sand stretching away into the distance. Surely this was the real desert country at last, wide, mysterious, utterly empty and silent, save for the clamour of our little van.

I must have dozed again for a while. The slowing up of the van roused me and I saw that we were entering a brightly lit town. There was a tree-lined boulevard with gaily lit cafés and shops. It couldn't be El Garza! If so my dream of a pastoral existence was to be rudely shattered.

"Where are we?" I asked Greg.

"Passing through the oasis town of El Mersa," he replied. "El Garza is about ten miles further."

An oasis town. I had had no idea an oasis could be large enough to contain a town! Perhaps not a very large town; the end of the tree-lined boulevard saw us in the sand and scrub country again.

Those last ten miles seemed interminable—sand, sand and more sand. Then suddenly we were driving into a thicket of trees. There were date palms, tall against the starry sky. We passed cultivated fields, gardens. The air was filled with the fragrance of jasmine and roses, gentle air, moist and cool. The twinkling lights of a village showed not far ahead. We turned down a rough road that brought us to the inevitable blank wall—a towering wall this time, its line broken by a great arched doorway, elaborately carved.

"The Casa El Garza," Greg announced, and hooted loudly on his horn, until the imposing door swung open.

We had arrived.

CHAPTER SIX

GREG called a greeting to the man who had opened the gate to us, a tall, dimly seen figure in burnous and flowing headdress, the glint of a cartridge belt across his chest. We drove slowly across a large courtyard where more robed figures could be seen squatting around open wood fires. Ruminating camels lurked in corners.

Another entrance loomed before us; this time an ornately carved latticed doorway. I didn't see who opened it, but now we found ourselves in a second smaller courtyard, obviously the centre of the two-storied balconied house built around it. Moorish lamps hung in the verandah beneath the balcony, lighting up the mosaic paving of the courtyard and the fountain, which stood surrounded by tubs of exotic, vivid flowers. Everything seemed theatrical and unreal. Drugged with the fatigue of the long journey, I felt I was in a dream.

Somehow we were all out of the van. With Denise in my arms I followed Greg into a long room, illuminated by more of the Moorish lamps. Its furniture was mainly cushions and gorgeously coloured rugs, dotted about with low brass-topped coffee tables and an occasional embroidered skin pouffe.

At the far end of the room—it seemed an immense distance away—was a raised dais with a low divan on it, covered with velvet draperies and a magnificent leopard-skin rug. An elderly Arab reclined upon the couch, looking like an illustration out of the Bible. Behind the dais, half hidden in shadow, one immense Persian rug hung from ceiling to floor. The whole effect was like a stage set. If I had wanted Oriental atmosphere, here it was in good measure.

The old man rose from the divan and came forward to greet us. The Caid Hassan Ben Akhtal— there was no mistaking his identity. Tall and stately, in the light from the overhead lamps he was a regal figure. A gold-embroidered skull-cap covered his closely shaven head, his robes were of the finest linen, pure white save for the multi-coloured woven belt about his waist. Dark eyes

284

burned under beetling brows, but his smile, as he turned to me, was of singular sweetness.

"Miss Marlow?" he said. "You are welcome to El Garza. My house is your house."

Stooping, he lifted the sleepy Denise from my arms. I thought she would have protested, but after one searching look into his gentle face, she put her arms around his neck. "Grandpa Hassan!" she whispered contentedly, and let her head drop on his shoulder. So much for the effect of Samia's silly stories. I was glad to see they were completely forgotten. Grandpa Hassan in the flesh had, apparently, little to do with the ogre conjured up by the Arab maid's spiteful fantasies.

Over the child's head the old man then spoke to Greg. For a few moments they conversed in Arabic —Greg obviously giving an account of our journey from Sidi Akbar. The Caid nodded, as if satisfied, then, calling to Jules who had been hiding behind me, he took the little boy by the hand, and looked down at him rather sadly. "So they are sending you away to a foreign land to school!" he said. "You must never forget you are an Arab."

"No, sir," Jules murmured, none too happily. He looked very small and tired standing there beside the imposing old man. But they made an impressive group, the two children with their picturesque grandfather.

"Jamilia!" he called out.

A girl came from the shadows behind the couch. She was small and slight, dressed native fashion, her bare arms covered with bangles. She might have been eighteen—more or less, it was difficult to tell in the half light. Her pale oval face was impassive, but in her sombre eyes there lurked a vague discontent.

"Take Miss Marlow and the children to your mother," the Caid ordered her. He handed Denise back to me.

"*Par ici*," Jamilia murmured unsmilingly.

So we were being banished to the women's quarters. I turned, a little desperately, to say good-night to Greg. "Will you be here tomorrow?" I asked, clinging to him in this strange household.

"I'll be around," he answered casually.

Jamilia led the way towards the dais. There was a door, it seemed, behind the hanging Persian rug, which moved aside as we approached it. The young man who appeared stood for a moment on the threshold, holding the curtain back, making a studied entrance. He was strikingly handsome, with delicately cut features and large flashing dark eyes. I saw to my astonishment that they were heavily made up with kohl. Yet there was nothing effeminate about the young man. He had an air of command, and even ruthlessness, that was all male. Taller than the usual Arab, he wore a flowing scarlet cloak, embroidered in silver and gold. There was a cartridge belt across his chest, and an unsheathed knife gleamed at his side.

A shiver ran down my spine as I looked into his kohl-darkened eyes. If ever I had encountered pure malevolence it was in that brief exchange of glances.

"My son, Khalid," the Caid announced as the young man advanced into the room.

He lifted his hands to me in the Moslem salute. "How do you do?" I responded in French. It sounded foolish, and went unanswered. Should I have said, "*C'est un plaisir de faire votre connaissance*"? Only it wasn't a pleasure!

"So you have brought the children." He touched Denise lightly on the head. She shrank away from him, burying her face in my neck. He put a hand on Jules' shoulder. "You are small, *mon-vieux!*" he said. "But if you are a Ben Akhtal you are tough. Tonight you go with the women. But tomorrow you will come with me. I will teach you to ride, to shoot, to hunt with the falcon."

Jules looked up into the cold, sculptured face, and moved a little closer to my side.

"Have you no tongue, my nephew?" Khalid demanded.

"Yes, Uncle Khalid. Thank you, Uncle Khalid," Jules murmured shakenly.

"Bien." Khalid waved the imperious hand. *"Va t'en, alors!"*

Jamilia, who had been standing in a frozen attitude, came to life. As we left the room, Khalid lifted the Persian rug portière for us to pass through, and once more I encountered the glitter of hatred in his eyes.

The other side of the door we were in the courtyard again. It had suddenly turned bitterly cold— the quiet penetrating cold of the desert. Passing the fountain, I shivered, my thin summer clothing all at once inadequate. And Denise was increasingly heavy. Jules, tugging at my skirt, began to whimper, "I don't want to hunt with falcons. Lorraine!"

"It's all right, darling," I assured him. "You don't have to. And you'll soon be in a nice cosy bed." I hoped this was true. What sort of beds did they have in oriental households? I had no idea.

"That Khalid!" said Jamilia, taking Jules' hand. "He thinks he rules the world." Her voice trembled with passion.

"I don't think I like falcons," Jules said, feeling he had found an ally. "I don't know what they are."

"They are big birds," Jamilia told him. "Big birds with claws, that catch rabbits.

287

"Par ici," she murmured once more, and opened a door leading into a long low room, that seemed at a first glance to be milling with women and children in colourful Arab garments. The noise and heat were terrific. I was thankful for the heat —which came, I saw, from a central stove filled with burning wood. I had a confused impression of stretches of rough white wall, covered with an amazing assortment of mirrors. Oval mirrors and oblong mirrors, some of them in frames of elaborately wrought gilt. They gave back the light from the naked electric bulbs hanging from the ceiling. There were the usual Persian rugs on the floor, and round three sides of the room ran a low velvet-covered banquette. The rest of the furniture was made up of Moroccan wickerwork lounge chairs and tables.

As we entered, the hum of chatter ceased.

"Maman," said Jamilia to the plump matronly woman advancing to meet us, "this is Miss Marlow, whom Tante Elaine sent with the children."

"Ah, the children!" said the plump woman, holding out her arms so widely it was as though she would embrace all three of us. She had the loveliest smile. Her pink silken robe flapped about her outstretched arms looked like rose-coloured wings, and she smelled deliciously—of jasmine perfume.

"Miss Marlow, how kind of you to come . . . to honour our house . . . and to bring my my little ones. Denise, Jules! You remember your Tante Mairik?" She scooped Denise out of my aching arms, embracing Jules almost in the same movement.

"I want my *maman*," Denise whimpered.

Tante Mairik rocked her expertly. "Poor little one. You are tired, but your Tante Mairik will take care of you. And soon, soon your *maman* will come back to you."

"Have they eaten, *mem'selle?*" she asked me.

I told her we had all had an excellent supper on the way.

She nodded. "Mr. Gregson would see to that ... he is so kind, so thoughtful, so devoted to the little ones, our dear Mr. Gregson."

Was the prickly side of that young man's nature a closed book to her?

"You would like to put the children straight to bed, I expect," she said. As she led us across the congested room, I was conscious of the many pairs of dark, bright eyes watching us. We went through a doorway into a smaller adjoining room. Here too there were roughly plastered white-washed walls, and naked glaring lights. In the centre of the floor was a vast brass bedstead, covered with gay handwoven rugs. A sheepskin rug lay on the floor beside it. To the right of the bed, in an alcove scooped out of the wall, a porcelain basin had been installed with a single tap, which I later discovered provided only cold water.

"There is a bathroom across the courtyard," Tante Mairik told me with some pride. "Mr. Gregson put it in for us. He arranged the running water, and the electric water heater. It is thanks to him that we have electricity out here in the wilds. He runs a small plant which produces the current.

"I'll show you the bathroom tomorrow," she promised. "The children will be too tired for baths tonight. Jamilia will bring you some hot water. We only have cold water in here, as yet, but I expect Mr. Gregson will extend the plumbing one of these days—there does not seem to be anything he cannot do."

I looked round for the children's beds. There was a stretcher in a far corner behind a latticed screen. That was for Jules, Tante Mairik explained. Denise was to sleep with me in the big brass bed. There was certainly room enough for both of us.

I showed the rather doubtful Jules his sleeping place, while Tante Mairik undressed the quietly whimpering Denise. Jamilia came in with a tall brass pitcher filled with boiling water, and a slim girl of about fourteen came staggering behind her with our suitcases. I took them from her, horrified that she should have carried such a weight. But it would have been unthinkable, I suppose, for a man servant to enter the harem quarters.

"This is Zoubeida, the daughter of Khadija," Tante Mairik introduced the girl. "Khadija is the widow of Mahmoud, a second cousin of the Caid's. Zoubeida and Alya, my second daughter, went to school in Tunis together."

Was I going to be introduced to all the women in the living room, I wondered, and if so would I ever be able to catch up on their varied histories? Cousins and second cousins, and kinswomen of every kind.

"Shall I stay and help you to unpack?" Zoubeida offered.

I thanked her, guessing she really wanted to remain to find out what the European stranger was made of. She watched with interest while I produced Denise's dainty little nightgown and Jules' pyjamas. Then I remembered the gifts Elaine had thoughtfully tucked away at the bottom of the largest case—presents for her husband's relations. Unearthing them, I handed them to Tante Mairik for distribution; flasks of perfume, boxes of crystallised fruits, at least a dozen pairs of nylon stockings, some chocolates and bon-bons.

They were all beautifully done up, in the French fashion, in coloured paper, tied with lavish satin bows, and there were little cards with Elaine's personal messages on them.

Childishly delighted, laden with their spoils, Tante Mairik and Zoubeida went off into the living room. Jamilia appeared once more, this time carrying a bowl of rather odd-smelling warm milk. "It is camel milk," she explained. "For the children. They liked it last time they were here. I have put honey into it so that it tastes fragrant and good."

I put the bowl to my lips and found that the milk was not unpleasant. But the children didn't think much of it. Probably they were too tired for it. I tucked them up in their beds, promised Denise I would leave one of the lights burning, and went with Jamilia back to the living room, where for an hour I was the centre of interest. Small friendly women flocked about me, chatting and laughing with the natural abandon of children. Though they were curious about my background, my clothes, my travels, my relationship to Elaine Ben Akhtal, their questions were put tactfully and with the utmost politeness.

After a while I began to sort out who was in this cheerful gathering. None of the women were veiled, and they did not strike me in the least as the subservient down-trodden Oriental females of tradition. Zoubeida's mother, Khadija, was extraordinarily young and beautiful, I thought, to be the parent of a teenage child. I found myself watching her with interest. Restlessness, and the same air of discontent I had seen on Jamilia's face, looked out of her great dark eyes. She surprised me by speaking to me in halting English. She had learned it during her schooldays, she told me, and had never forgotten it.

"Khadija was always the clever one," Tante Mairik put in, while Khadija shook her head disclaimingly. But she had won all the prizes at her school, it seemed. "I could have gone on to the university," she said, "only that in those days it was not the custom for Moslem women to remain in the outside world once they had passed the age of puberty."

"Does Zoubeida take after you?" I asked—at which Zoubeida, busy trying on her nylon stockings, giggled and blushed.

"Alas, no," Khadija said. "Zoubeida was only too pleased to be done with school and come home to the harem. She is not a career girl, which is just as well perhaps, for the women of the Ben Akhtal family are not encouraged to adopt modern ways. The Caid is all against it."

"It is not so much the Caid," Tante Mairik corrected. "He is old and gentle and lazy and does not really care what we do. It is Khalid who hates all Western ways and culture. He is fanatical for the Arab life, that one, a nationalist to his fingertips, and in too many ways he overrules his father, the Caid."

So the handsome piercing-eyed Khalid was a factor to be reckoned with in this diverse household! I was not surprised—having encountered him. He had the air of a natural ruler—rather a cruel ruler. For a moment the thought of him disturbed me. But just then coffee was brought in. There were sweetmeats too and an assortment of rich little cakes. I ate sparingly of this unsuitable night-time fare, and as soon as the repast was finished, I succeeded in saying my last goodnights and going off to bed, half asleep on my feet after the long eventful day.

CHAPTER SEVEN

I SLEPT well in the big bed, sunk deep in a feather mattress, Denise cuddled beside me. When I woke light was filtering through a curtained french window I hadn't noticed the night before. Where did it lead? I wondered. An overwhelming desire to explore my novel surroundings got me out of bed, though it was barely half past six. Denise and Jules were still fast asleep, so it would be all right to leave them for a little while. I dressed in dark linen jeans and a brightly coloured sports shirt, washed my face in the stingingly cold water which came from the single tap in the wash basin and cautiously opened the french window. It led to the inevitable courtyard—not the main one with the central fountain and formal flowers, but an obviously lesser enclosure, bordering, I suspected, on the domestic quarters; kitchen, bakehouse, wash-house, and such like. An odour of freshly baked bread floated on the air, mingled with the aromatic invitation of freshly ground coffee.

Turning my back on these appetising intimations of breakfast in preparation, I made for a small door on the far side of the courtyard, and, opening it, found myself in an enchanting garden. It sloped in terraces from the house to a great expanse of date palms and orchards. A marble-paved pathway led me on, past the flower-laden terraces, where roses and jasmine, lilies and gardenias all flourished together. The perfume of the flowers in the clear morning sunlight was light and delicious, jasmine predominating. Beyond the garden was a rough plot of ground in the centre of which lay a stone-enclosed pool of dark stagnant water. A watering cart and an array of curled rubber hoses ranged to one side of the pool proclaimed its purpose. Somebody worked hard to keep all those flowers fresh and blooming!

The path, deteriorating into a beaten sandy track, took me into the shade of the groves and orchards. Now there were fig trees with dark shining leaves to hide the purple fruit, orange and lemon trees bowed with their golden burdens, rosy pomegranates, peaches, apricots, and over them all the soaring feathery tops of the date palms. The air was pleasantly moist, and I saw that there were many narrow irrigation ditches making their symmetrical way beneath the trees.

Then I came to a natural stream with curving banks and clear running water, its banks edged with lacy ferns and tall yellow irises. Here in a clearing the grass was brilliantly green and soft as silk. The sun was already making itself felt, the chill of the night disappearing. So this was the oasis of El Garza! Entranced, I stood still, looking about me. Ought I to go back to the children now? I wondered. Turning on the path, I found myself face to face with Tim Gregson. He stood arrested, seeming to be almost as foolishly astonished as I was myself. That silly flutter of my pulses! Why was I so nervously aware of this man?

"Hullo, early bird!" he drawled. "Fancy meeting you here at this hour. What hapless worm were you hoping to catch this time of day?"

A feeble joke, spiked with a sneer. I ignored it. "I'm just having a look round," I said. "It's so beautiful."

"So you like my domain?"

"Your domain? Do you mean you're responsible for all this?" I waved a comprehensive hand. "The flowers, the fruit, the gardens . . .?"

"In a sense, yes. I think I can fairly lay claim to it as all my own work." He was strolling along beside me now, leading me away from the Casa in the direction of the village.

"When I took this place over a few years ago it was in pretty bad shape. There were just the date palms and a few oranges, with very little irrigation to help them. Everything depended on the intermittent rains, and a couple of dry seasons with the rains overdue could work havoc. I was just down from Varsity, wondering what to do with my agricultural and horticultural know-how, not terribly keen on the land and plant conservation for which I had been trained. At least the conservation of land in Britain didn't appeal to me. It seemed to me dull, and there was too much red tape about it for my liking. I wanted to move around . . . see the world." (Just like me, I thought; trained to be a schoolmarm and longing to travel.)

"I was spending a holiday here with Raschid," Greg went on, "and somehow quite naturally, almost inevitably, I decided to stay on and give the Caid the benefit of my up-to-date knowledge. I intended to remain only a few months, a year at most. But . . ." he laughed, "here I still am!"

"Don't you ever go home?" I asked.

"To Scotland?" He shrugged. "Very occasionally. There doesn't seem much point in it now both my parents have died."

"I'm sorry," I murmured, rather awkwardly.

"My home seems to be here," he said.

"But don't you sometimes find it lonely?" I blurted, and got a baleful glance from the smoky grey eyes. "Now don't you start anything like that, my girl!" I could almost hear him saying. But what he actually did snap out was, "Yes, it is lonely. And that's how I like it." It sounded like a

295

snub. I decided it was intended to be one, and said no more.

We had come through the date grove and orchards now to a wide sandy clearing, dotted with small white square houses, like giant cubes of sugar set down under the deep blue sky, roughly planned to form a village. There was a main thoroughfare leading to a central square dominated by a stone-enclosed well. One solitary date palm cast its shade over the water, and on the coping stones a group of women had gathered to fill the red earthen jars which they carried on their shoulders. Once more I was seeing an illustration straight out of my old Sunday-school Bible!

As we passed the women they turned their backs shyly, not offering any greeting. One or two of them, I noticed, pulled veils up to cover the lower part of their faces. Greg, ignoring them, walked me on through the village to a house larger than the sugar cube cottages, standing apart from them.

"My bachelor fastness," he said. "Come in and rest a while, if you like."

A carefully careless invitation. But I felt a thrill of expectation as I followed him over the threshold into a sparsely furnished room which seemed to be half living room, half kitchen. The rough white walls were bare, save for an assortment of hanging saucepans and culinary tools, but there were the usual gorgeous Persian and Turkish rugs on the beaten mud floor. Through an archway in the wall facing me I could see a bed piled with tumbled blankets, and a sheepskin rug. An alcove housed a modern electric cooking stove.

"Electricity," Greg said, "is easier to come by than water in these parts." He told me about the small power-house he had contrived, run on oil fuel which came from an neighbouring oil field.

"I'll make you some coffee." He was busy with

kettle and pot as he spoke. "You've had quite a long walk, and I don't suppose you had anything to eat before you set out."

"No, I didn't," I admitted. "But I really ought to get back to the children. They were asleep when I left them, but they may be awake by now, frightened to find themselves in strange surroundings."

"Not they!" Greg dismissed the matter carelessly. "It isn't their first time at the Casa El Garza, and Tante Mairik adores them—to say nothing of Khadija and Fatmah, and Meyriem and Sato, and the whole horde of women up there. They'll be well looked after—spoiled to death, in fact. So you forget all about them and tell me what you think of my coffee. I grind it freshly for every brew . . . and this is the latest idea in percolators . . ."

It struck me as a little pathetic—this preoccupation with coffee mills and percolators; the playthings of a lonely man. Small things would take on a disproportionate significance in this silent house.

But the coffee was excellent, and so was the freshly baked bread and honey that accompanied it. He apologised for the absence of butter. "Milk and butter," he said, "are quite a problem round here, where we have so little grazing land for cattle. So the milk come out of tins, and the butter from abroad. We buy it in Tunis, and I happen to have run out of stock."

The honey, he explained, was made by bees he had introduced into the oasis.

"It tastes of jasmine," I told him. "And roses and lilies . . . all the flowers I saw in that beautiful terraced garden close to the house. Did you make that, too?" I asked him. And he told me how he had formed it out of what was once a pile of stones and blown sand.

When we had finished our light delicious breakfast I said once more that I ought to be on my way. "Can I help you wash the cups before I go?" I offered, standing up from the table and beginning to collect the used crockery.

"Leave it!" Greg's voice was oddly harsh. "The ancient crone who looks after me will be here presently, and she'll see to them." He had come to my side as he spoke, and took the small pile of dishes from my hands.

Then, quite suddenly, without any warning whatsoever, I was in his arms. Just what went through my mind at that moment, I don't know. I was so taken unawares I was incapable of coherent thought. I must have turned my face towards him, perhaps with some notion of protesting. But no protest came. His lips were hard and purposeful, kissing me full on the mouth. It was a rough kiss, hurtful, completely without tenderness, and his arms were to tightly around me I could hardly breathe. Rage, resentment, mixed contradictorily with something else I wouldn't admit was answering passion, swept over me. I wrenched myself free from his grasp and stood glaring at him, my heart racing.

"I've been wanting to do that for a long time," he said coolly.

"How dare you!" I gasped. "You ask me in here for coffee and then—without the least suspicion of anything leading up to it—turn on me and attack me like some sort of wild animal. I thought you were supposed to be a gentleman!"

He shook his head, and smiled his slow conceited smile. "Not a gentleman, honey. Just a man. One more of your ships that pass in the night, if you like."

It was too much, that mean innuendo recalling my perhaps foolish but harmless involvement

298

with Del Lloyd. Before I realised what I was doing I had lifted my hand and dealt Greg a swinging blow across the face. He staggered back a pace, looking utterly astonished.

"Well!" he breathed. "You pack quite a punch!" His hand went up to his cheek, already turning crimson from the blow I had given him.

"I'm sorry," I muttered unwillingly. "But maybe we're quits now."

Greg nodded and grinned. "Non-lady sets about non-gentleman, leaving the game at love-all!"

I turned and ran out of the house, my temper still boiling, my thoughts in chaos—quite needlessly. It wasn't, I told myself, a situation that warranted this panicky reaction. All that had happened was that I'd walked into the kind of trap that can await any girl, at any time, if she is too trustful and off her guard. And I suppose I had been both. Greg, living alone, woman-starved, lonely, had felt like pouncing on me . . . and pounced. That's all there was to it. Why then was I in such a dither? Because once more he had made it plain that he thought of me as a cheap little flirt. And that kiss had meant nothing to him. Ye gods! Did I want it to mean anything? Tim Gregson couldn't possibly matter to me! I scurried along down the village street and up through the orchards as though the furies were after me—running from I knew not what—some demon in my inmost secret heart, something I could not, would not face. But all peace was gone from the terraced garden now; I hardly saw the roses and lilies as I passed them by, my throat hot and tight, my eyes burning.

At least Greg had been right about the children. I found them, as he had foretold, surrounded by adoring aunts and cousins. Jules was in the courtyard with a gang of small boys, and Denise in the living room fraternised with a bunch of little girls, with whom she was sharing a favourite doll she had brought with her. They hardly noticed my entry.

It was Tante Mairik who greeted me. "You have had an early promenade, *mademoiselle*. Now you must drink the coffee . . . if it has not been standing too long." She peered into the pot on the wicker table in front of her—set with the litter of used breakfast dishes.

"Jamilia!" she called. "Tell Fatmah to bring some fresh coffee for Miss Marlow."

For some idiotic reason I was quite unable to say I had already breakfasted with Tim Gregson. So I had to make a pretence of eating and drinking again. Struggling with the very black, thick coffee and a slice of unleavened bread, I looked round the congested room trying to work out relationships. Were all these women and children directly connected with the Ben Akhtal family, or were many of them dependents, in a feudal sense, wives and offspring of the men who worked on the large estate? Sato, a young woman breast-feeding a very young infant, was I discovered the daughter of Fatmah, who seemed to be in charge of the kitchen arrangements. Was she some sort of servant?

Children came and went noisily. The women sat about. There was no sign of any domestic routine. Some of the younger women sat in front of the mirror braiding their long black hair. It was all very friendly and easy-going in the bright early sunshine. But too much of this way of life would be very boring. What was I supposed to do for the rest of the day? I felt suddenly suffocated, imprisoned.

"Jules!" I called to him, "let's have an hour's English lesson, shall we?"

He came running to me at once good little boy that he was! I looked round in despair for a quiet corner.

"Take him into the central courtyard," Khadija suggested. "It is always fairly quiet there, because it is outside the Caid's apartments. I will bring some chairs and a table for you."

We carried the wicker chairs to a shady corner of the big cool courtyard, the door that led to the harem closed firmly behind us.

"Do you mind if I stay?" Khadija asked shyly as we settled down. I told her she was welcome. She had spoken in French as usual.

"You must speak only in English when we are having an English lesson," Jules informed her severely.

"I will try," she said—in English—"but I have forgotten most of what I knew." She laughed nervously, her fine dark eyes alight with intelligence.

How wasted she was, I thought, in this pleasant but enervating harem atmosphere! Poor Khadija; it was obvious she was starved for mental stimulation.

I opened my anthology at random, and decided to read Tennyson's *Song of the Owl*.

"When cats run home and light is come
   And the dew is cold upon the ground . . ."

It was amazing how much explaining there was to be done in answer to Khadija's eager questions. The whirring sail of the windmill, and just what its purpose was, the belfry in which the white owl sat, the merry milkmaids of Tennyson's early nineteenth-century England . . . even the cock in the thatch. Neither Jules nor Khadija could easily visualise an English village of thatched cottages, and I was deeply involved in making word pictures

301

of it all when a shadow fell across the book in my hand, and I looked up to see Khalid standing over us.

"We are having a poetry lesson," Khadija told him.

Khalid made a noise like a soft snarl. "Poetry! In English!"

"It is to help me to pass the entrance exam to my new school," Jules offered nervously.

"So! They make you pass an examination. Is it not enough for these infidels that you are the son of a distinguished Tunisian politician, the grandson of a Caid?"

"It's not a difficult examination," I put in hastily, seeing the temper flash in Khalid's eyes. "But the more English Jules knows before he goes to Stokeley, the easier it will be for him to cope with his studies."

"Nonsense!" shouted Khalid. "The whole idea is nonsense. We have schools in Tunis, in Baghdad, in Teheran—colleges, universities. But Jules must go to this English Stokeley because his father went there before him. And shall I tell you why Raschid went to Stokeley?" He moved towards me threateningly; instinctively I shrank back. "Simply because he was the victim of my mother's ambition. Allah forbid that I should speak ill of the dead, but she was a foolish woman. Her only reason for wanting Raschid to go to England was that the sons of the princes and the oil kings were there. Pure snobbery, that's all it was. Arab education was not good enough for them, these great ones; they must go to English public schools and learn to dress and speak like Englishmen. But now things are different. Times have changed. The Arab is proud of his heritage . . ."

He was shouting now, as if he addressed a public meeting. Dramatically he gesticulated. It might have gone on indefinitely if Jules had not interrupted the outpouring, to say in a tearful voice, "I don't want to go to England. I want to stay in Tunis with Papa and Maman . . . and Lorraine," he added, politely including me.

Cut off in the midst of his eloquence, Khalid glared at him. A stupid, humourless young man, I decided. But that didn't make him, any the less dangerous!

"Come here!" he ordered Jules. He held out his hand, and as if mesmerised, Jules went to him.

"Now stop that crying. Only women shed tears. You have had your English lesson, now you will come with me and have a lesson in horsemanship."

I didn't know quite what to say to this. I glanced at Khadija despairingly. "It's all right," she said. "Jules has ridden here before. His mother allows it."

"Of course she allows it," Khalid snapped. "She does not want her only son to grow up a timorous weakling. All the Ben Akhtals ride."

"May I have the pony I had when I was here last time?" I heard Jules ask as they moved away. "The little black pony called Shabo."

"Will he be all right?" I murmured doubtfully to Khadija.

She shrugged. "I expect so. They will ride in the open country beyond the stables, which are about a qaurter of a mile along the main road. Khalid is an excellent horseman . . ."

"But I shouldn't think he would have much patience with children," I put in.

Khadija fingered the heavy gold bracelet on her wrist. "I hate him!" she burst out suddenly. "He is proud and tyrannical. If it were not for him life here would be so much better. Jamilia could go to university, as she wants to, and Alya could train as a nurse. But Khalid will not hear of it, and the

303

Caïd gives in to him. He is old and lazy, as Tante Mairik says. So Khalid has it all his own way, and if anyone crosses him they had better look out!" I saw her shiver in the warm sunlight. "He can be cruel, that one!" I heard her whisper to herself.

"I wish now I hadn't let Jules go off riding with him," I said uneasily. "I think I'll go along presently and see how they're getting on.'

CHAPTER EIGHT

I DIDN'T like to set off too soon. Khalid would not relish my interference. I could only hope there would be no need for it. But I wasn't very optimistic, as I pottered about my room, putting away the books I had used for our English lesson. It was well on into the morning and the sun was strong when I set out, hurrying through the terraced garden until I came to the main road. The stables, according to Khadija's directions, were on the El Mersa Road, well away from the village and Greg's house. Which was just as well. I didn't want to run into Greg! The memory of our morning encounter still rankled, if that isn't too mild a word for the hot angry pain that shot through me every time I thought of his scornful kiss. Once I caught myself putting my hand to my mouth as if to wipe away the remembered pressure on my lips.

I jerked my mind back to Jules, trying to assure myself that he would be all right. After all, he went to a riding school in Tunis and had told me about Pandy, the pony he rode there. Probably he was quite proficient and I was worrying about him unnecessarily.

It was blindingly hot on the open road and I was glad to see the group of barnlike buildings ahead of me. They would be the stables. Passing them, I heard the distant thudding of hooves. Lots of hooves. It sounded like a cavalry charge!

I had come to a wide stretch of rough sandy ground, dotted with camel scrub, and rounding a clump of bushes saw the cavalcade racing towards me. I shrank out of the way, into the bushes. I could see Khalid, leading the cohort on a great black stallion, his bright robe flying behind him, his head flung back. When he was almost on top of me he shouted some kind of order and the procession wheeled about, to race back the way it had come. First Khalid, then a string of about a dozen horsemen, all on spirited Arab mounts. Surely Jules wasn't with this wild-looking gang! But as they passed me I caught sight of him at the tail end of the string of riders, clinging to the neck of a huge chestnut mare, his face white with terror. In the brief glimpse I had of him it seemed as if he was clutching on to the mane of his mount, rather than the reins. And he was bumping about in the saddle, periously out of control.

Sick with fear for him, I raced over the sand in the wake of the galloping horses. Not that I could hope to overtake them, but I couldn't just stand there waiting for Jules to come to grief.

"Khalid!" I called, cupping my hands. "Khalid! come back! Jules is in difficulties."

It was quite hopeless, of course. He couldn't possibly hear me. It wasn't my cry that brought him wheeling round again on his ebony stallion. This racing back and forth across the same strip of sand was apparently all part of the morning's exercise. In a few seconds he was level with me again, and this time I didn't hide in the bushes, but rushed forward, right in his track. He reined sharply, his horse rearing up, pawing the air.

Somehow I avoided those iron-shod hooves as they crashed down, inches away from me.

"What the devil do you think you're doing?" Khalid called out furiously.

"It's Jules!" I shouted, and ignoring Khalid ran along the now disordered cavalcade to find the child. It seemed to me that horses were rearing and pawing the ground and whinnying all round me as they were brought up to an abrupt halt. Jules' mount was sidestepping dangerously, its teeth bared in an ill-tempered grin. It looked horribly vicious, but bracing myself, I caught hold of its bridle. Jules, giving me one wild-eyed, despairing look, went limp and slid to the ground. I had to let him lie—my one preoccupation was to keep the dancing hooves of the big mare away from him. Then Khalid, on foot, was beside me.

"How dare you break us up like this?"

"Here!" I thrust the reins of the chestnut into his hands and turned to pick up Jules. But he was already on his feet. With a cry he threw himself at me. I put my arms protectively around him, and turned on Khalid in cold rage. "You had no business to give Jules such an enormous mount. You must know perfectly well that this is not the sort of riding to which he is accustomed."

"But it's the sort he is going to get from now on!" Khalid seized hold of Jules' arm and dragged him away from me. "What made you come off old Sheba?" he asked the little boy. "Come along! Jump up again."

"He can't," I broke in. "I won't allow it."

Khalid glared at me. "You won't *allow* it! Are you out of your mind?"

"I'm responsible for Jules' safety."

"My dear Miss Marlow, you certainly have an inflated idea of your position. You are here in the role of nurse, or governess, to help with my

306

brother's children in a general domestic sense. For their safety and well-being it is the Caid and myself who are responsible. Come, Jules!" With one swift movement he scooped up the child and placed him on the mare's back.

"I don't want to ride any more!" Jules wailed, holding his arms out to me. I moved towards him, but Khalid stepped in front of me.

"Leave him alone!" he ordered. "You have done quite enough harm already with your poetry and coddling, turning my nephew into a whimpering little coward! Sit up, Jules! Get hold of the reins." With the flat of his hand he struck the mare on the rump. It was too much for her. Infected perhaps by the shivering, terrified little bundle on her back, she took to her heels and bolted.

I stood frozen to the ground, waiting for the inevitable catastrophe. It seemed impossible that Jules could survive that wild gallop. Then Khalid on his stallion was racing alongside him. I saw him lean forward, while they were both still going at full speed, and lift Jules out of the saddle on to his own mount. The chestnut sped on her frenzied way, pursued by one of Khalid's outriders. Khalid with Jules in his arms turning and riding slowly back to where I stood, looking smugly pleased with himself. He had performed a superb piece of horsemanship, but I was in no mood to be impressed. My whole concern was for the limp form lying across the saddle.

"Is Jules hurt?" I cried out, as they reached me.

"Of course he isn't! He's just a trifle winded. He will be all right. I'll take him home. He has done very well for today." The beautiful cruel face smiled down at me. "I'll make an Arab horseman out of him yet! He has the seat, the hands; he is good, this boy . . ."

He gathered up his reins, preparing to move off. "And tomorrow when we ride," he called over his shoulder, "I trust you will keep where you belong . . . in the women's quarters."

It was the last straw. Rage choked me. "There'll be no tomorrow!" I shrieked after him as he rode away. "I'll speak to the Caid. I'll telegraph to Raschid . . . I'll take Jules away . . ." Empty threats blown away on the desert air. Tears of frustration poured down my cheeks.

It seemed an endless way back to the house. The sun was merciless. I felt sick and shaken. How was I going to stop these dangerous riding lessons? Khalid had the upper hand in the Casa El Garza. Khadija had said so—and indeed it was fairly obvious. I had spoken of sending a wire to Raschid, but he was on the move, four thousand miles away, the other side of the world. I had no idea where to reach him. Meanwhile Jules' neck could be broken half a dozen times over. Poor little Jules! When I thought of all he had been through that morning, my blood ran cold.

So that it was something of a surprise when I got to the house to find him seated at one of the wicker tables with Denise and an assortment of cousins, calmly eating a midday meal of *cous-cous* —that popular Arab dish made of boiled semolina flavoured with titbits of chicken and meat and vegetables.

"*Moi,*" he declared to the admiring group. "I have galloped across the desert on an enormous horse today. I have fallen off and got up again. I have hurt myself and not cried. *Mon oncle* says I am brave and strong."

I kneeled beside him, putting an arm around his thin little shoulders. "Are you all right, darling?" I asked.

He gave me a dazed, drunken sort of look, and I saw that there was a bruise on his forehead. "You knocked your head when you fell," I said.

He put a finger to the bruise. *"C'est pas grave,"* he pronounced solemnly. "It is not serious. Uncle Khalid says I am a man now, and a man does not count his wounds." He spoke mechanically, as if repeating a lesson. Perhaps he was still a little stunned from his fall. When he had finished his lunch I made him lie down on the bed behind the filigree screen.

Lunch for the adults, served in the living-room, was also *cous-cous*. There were not nearly so many women with us today. Many of them last night and this morning, had, I guessed, come from the village to have a look at the strangers. Now we seemed to have been reduced to close members of the family; Tante Mairik with her two daughters, Jamilia and Alya; Fatmah and Sato with her baby, and two women I hadn't yet placed, but who seemed to be the mothers of most of the children still with us. And of course there was Khadija. Dear Khadija, she was rapidly becoming my most valued friend at court. I told her of Jules' disastrous riding lesson. She was full of sympathy, racking her brains for helpful advice. How was I to stop these lessons? "You must approach the Caid," she urged. "It will be easy for you. He gives a feast for you tonight. Always when Elaine and Raschid visit us, he makes them the banquet, and tonight, even though you are not of the family of Ben Akhtal, he wishes to do you this honour."

"It's very good of him," I murmured, a little doubtfully. "Will I be the only woman at the party?"

"Oh, no. I shall be eating with you," Khadija promised. "And Tante Mairik, and Jamilia and Alya."

I spent the afternoon resting in a shady corner of the harem courtyard, and making visits to Jules, still heavily sleeping. He felt very hot, but I didn't like to disturb him, taking his temperature, and in any case I had no thermometer with me. This long sleep was probably the best thing for him after the shock of the morning's events. He woke about tea-time, subdued and tearful, the bombastic mood of lunch-time all gone.

"I don't want to ride with Uncle Khalid any more," he told me, when later I bathed him and put him to bed.

"You aren't going to," I promised him rashly, and wondered with a sinking heart how I was going to make the words come true. By the time I was ready to leave for the Caids apartments he was asleep again, his skin cool, his appearance much more reassuring. In the morning he would be quite himself once more . . . until Khalid appeared to take him away for another riding lesson. A lesson I'd got to stop at all costs. But how? Was it true that the Caid would help me? Had he any real power over his headstrong son?

Abstractedly, I dressed, putting on a frock I was particularly fond of, though it wasn't new. It was a cream jersey silk, with a narrow gold belt. Aunt Vinnie had bought it for me at a choice little boutique in Cannes two summers ago. At the last moment I slipped Greg's charm bracelet on to my wrist. Perhaps it would bring me luck. Goodness knows I needed it! In the living-room mirrors I saw myself, white and gold and startlingly blonde compared with the sloe-eyed beauties around me.

310

Even Tante Mairik contrived to appear seductive as we set out to present ourselves to the lord of the household. I looked with awe at the silks and satins of my companions, the heavy gold ornaments, the flashing jewels. Khadija, obviously a little shocked at my plain unadorned frock, had offered to lend me a gold necklace, studded with turquoises. Tactfully I had refused it, telling her that it was the fashion in my country at the moment to wear very little jewellery—unless one were old, or important, or going to the Queen's court, an explanation that seemed to make sense to her. "Anyway, you look very nice the way you are," she said kindly.

The long sparsely furnished room we entered, struck me tonight at a second glance, not so much bare as graciously spacious. No furniture in this room could be as beautiful as the absence of furniture. The one concession that had been made to the evening's hospitality did little to mar the effect; it was a narrow modernistic dining table, flanked by matching spindly chairs, specially hired from El Mersa in my honour, Khadija whispered to me. "We usually eat sitting on cushions round one of the low coffee tables."

From his dais at the end of the room the Caid rose to greet us, Khalid at his side resplendent in cloth of gold. And behind him, in the shadows, I saw a tall figure in a European lounge suit; Tim Gregson. My heart did one of its silly somersaults. I don't know why I hadn't expected Greg to be present—but somehow it just hadn't occurred to me. He bowed to me stiffly.

When the preliminaries were over and I was seated at the dining table I found him beside me. On my other side was a fierce-looking Arab with an enormous black beard. His kinship had been hastily explained to me by Tante Mairik before

311

she took her place by the Caid's side. Water was brought in small silver bowls and I saw that we were supposed to dip our hands in them and wipe them on the small linen towels provided—which I had mistaken at first for table napkins.

There was *brik* to start with, the egg and pastry delicacy I had eaten on that fatuous occasion Del had tried to persuade me to run away with him. I wondered where he had got to by this time ... was he still at Biskra, about a hundred miles away? How shadowy and unreal he seemed in retrospect! How could I ever have been even mildly interested in him? I glanced at the stern profile on my left. When we sat down Greg had held my chair back for me, but since then had in no way acknowledged my existence. My Arab neighbour, I had discovered, couldn't speak a word of English or French, so it looked like being a gay evening!

The main course was now brought in—a goat's carcase on a huge silver platter. One of the servants carved it into sizeable portions, having first poured ceremonial water over his hands. I was given a lump of this unappetising-looking but savoury-smelling meat, and saw with relief that a knife and fork had been provided for dealing with it. My Arab neighbour manoeuvred his into his mouth, by scooping it from his plate between lumps of bread.

I stole another look at Greg to see how he was faring, and caught him doing the same thing to me. Simultaneously we both laughed. It was so silly.

"Hell!" Greg exclaimed forcibly. "We can't sit here glaring at one another all the evening ... and anyhow, I owe you an apology for the way I acted this morning."

I could hardly believe my ears. An apology? From the conceited, impossible Mr. Tim Gregson?

"It was unforgivable," he went on, doing the thing thoroughly. "I don't know what came over me, only that you were standing there, looking so kissable. It wasn't exactly fair, so early in the morning." He lifted quizzical eyebrows, his grey eyes watching me closely to see how all this was being received.

"It's all right," I murmured inadequately. "Please don't say any more about it."

"Does that mean we're friends?"

"I hope so."

"Good!" Greg returned to his plate of goat's meat, attacking it hungrily. Did he get enough to eat in a general way? I found myself wondering. He was thinner than he ought to have been, I decided. Those gaunt Scots cheekbones, too sharply defined. What sort of a cook was the old crone who kept house for him? I thought of the stark, whitewashed cottage in which he lived, with its minimal comforts. Why had he chosen such a life? It was all rather an enigma—an enigma that would have to go unsolved—at least for the moment. Our relationship, only just rescued from the blasts of open enmity, had not reached the stage where I could put personal questions.

"How are you finding life in the harem?" he asked, his grey eyes twinkling.

"It's all very leisurely and relaxed," I told him. "Though too much of it would, I imagine, become very boring. Everyone in the Casa is very kind to me . . . the females of the family, that is. I'm not so struck on the males. That Khalid!" I glared down the table at the handsome young man, eating roast goat with a savage concentration.

"You've been having a spot of bother over Jules' riding lessons," Greg said.

313

"How did you know?"

"Things get around in this small community. I gather it was all a bit grim out on the tan this morning."

"It was horrible!" I told him exactly what had happened. "What am I going to do about it?" I ended despairingly.

Greg shook his head. "It's not going to be easy, but Jules must obviously be protected."

"Khalid is unspeakable!" I burst out.

"He's just a virile young Arab," Greg said, "with the traditional Arab outlook. Jules has to be indoctrinated, and there isn't much time—as Khalid sees it. A brief two weeks against a possible ten years of English schools and colleges."

"If he lives to go to England," I put in. "That mare he rode this morning was a killer, if ever I saw one."

"Sheba?" Greg said. "Actually she's a pretty safe old thing, but she gets excited when she's out with the stallions. And obviously Jules can't control her. What he wants is a smaller animal on which he can potter about; not with a whole host of horsemen, but with one or two quiet companions. What about yourself? Do you ride?"

"In an amateur fashion. I'm hardly up to Khalid's circus standards."

Greg ignored the quip. "That's your best bet, then. When the Caid summons you to sit by him, as he will after the meal, he will probably ask you if there's anything he can do to make your visit more pleasureable. That will be your chance. You must tell him how worried you are about Jules' riding lessons and ask permission to ride with him."

"And if the Caid agrees will Khalid give in?"

"He won't like it, but he'll have to. Though he often overrules the Caid in matters of policy, he'll

314

be powerless in this case, since it entails the laws of hospitality, which are sacred. Your wish, as a guest, will have to be granted."

"Well, that sounds marvellous!" I gave a sigh of relief.

We were at the dessert stage now, the usual sticky little cakes made of nuts and honey, and great platters of fresh fruit. When the coffee was brought in the Caid moved back to the raised dais, the assembled company distributing themselves on cushions and banquettes around the room.

As Greg had predicted, the Caid sent for me. "Come with me!" I whispered urgently to Greg. He followed me across the mosaic floor. The Caid motioned me to sit on the divan beside him. Greg folded his long legs on to a cushion on the dais at our feet. I was aware of Khalid, standing in the shadows by the portiére watching us narrowly, like a soldier on guard, one hand resting on the hilt of the knife tucked into his waist belt.

The conversation went very much as Greg had predicted. The Caid's French wasn't easy to understand, which made things a little difficult, but I told him of my anxiety over Jules' riding lesson that morning, with Greg's help getting my points across.

"If Jules could have a smaller mount," I ended. "He is too small to control that big mare, Sheba. And I should like to ride with him. I feel so responsible for him . . . after all, he has been left by his parents in my care . . ."

"And in mine," the Caid reminded me gravely. "It shall be as you wish, *mademoiselle*. I will command Khalid . . ."

From the shadows Khalid, having overheard every word, gave me a murderous glance. But he made no move to question his father's decision.

315

Greg had been right about that too, it seemed. Thank God for Arabic hospitality laws! I thought.

"And now, *mademoiselle*, tell me what you think of my house, my lands, my gardens," the Caid invited, with an old man's egotism. "Has Mr. Gregson shown you his wonderful irrigation system, by which he has increased a hundredfold the yield of my fruit trees?"

"Not yet," Greg put in, "but any time Miss Marlow likes I'll be pleased to take her for a tour of the estate." He gave me a mischievous grin as he spoke.

Somewhere in the courtyard an unseen orchestra began to play the wistful tinkling music of the Orient. The Caid after another sleepy remark or two gave up trying to converse with me, and closed his eyes—listening to the music, perhaps. Or it may have been that he found me too tiring to talk to. He was old, he had eaten a heavy meal, and did not feel like coping with the difficulties of our language barrier. So we all sat there in respectful silence.

"This is terribly boring," Greg whispered to me presently. "I wish we could escape."

"Couldn't we?" I asked rashly.

He shook his head. "It's absolutely unthinkable." The hospitality laws, it seemed, worked both ways!

"But we'll make up for it another evening," he went on. "That is, if you'll let me take you out to dinner. We could run into El Mersa. There are some quite amusing places where we can eat."

"That would be lovely!" I hoped I was managing not to sound too eager.

"That's settled, then."

I looked into the warmly lashed grey eyes, and something in their expression sent my heart somersaulting. It wasn't really anything more than a friendly and interested scrutiny. But suddenly, without any doubt, I knew that I was in love with Tim Gregson. Fool that I was! In love with a hardbitten exiled Scotsman, who had apparently managed to survive well into the thirties without getting himself romantically entangled. A desert hermit, wrapped up in his date palms and irrigation schemes. Furthermore, I reminded myself bitterly, this was the first time I had been in his company without being made to feel that he despised me heartily. If he ever did anything so weak-minded as to fall in love, it wouldn't be with a frivolous type like me. He would choose somebody older, and more important. Some famous woman traveller perhaps; one of those formidable ladies one hears of penetrating the wilds of the Sahara to study anthropology, or ethnology. Or, while we were on the 'ologies,' what about a woman in the same line of business as himself—a female ecologist? If such creatures exist!

Sweetness and despair filled my heart as I looked down at him, sitting cross-legged at my feet, his head turned away from me—a proud and shapely head. I longed to put out my hand and touch the short crisp hair with its unruly hint of a curl.

Someone out on the patio was singing now, to the accompaniment of throbbing strings. It was a man's tenor voice, high and pure.

Greg turned to look up at me. "You're being serenaded, with an old Arab love song," he said. "How does it feel?"

"I'd know more about that," I told him, "if I could understand the words of the song."

There was that disturbing look once more in the level grey eyes. "You're being offered honey and spikenard and the roses of Sharon," he said.

Softly he quoted:

317

"A bed of spices, a fountain of waters
Or the wild white wings of a dove,
Now when the winter is over and gone,
Is it these that should please my love?"

In the silence that followed the song, our glances held. I turned away, my thoughts in a turmoil. If it had been anyone else but Greg I would have recognised the moves in the game. A good dinner, soft lights and sweet music, and a touch of subtle flirtation to round off the evening. But Greg wasn't like that. For one thing, I couldn't imagine him being subtle. That savage kiss this morning!

But the moment, whatever it boded, was over. With the ending of music the Caid came to life, making some rumbling remark to Tante Mairik on her cushion on the far side of his divan. She stood up, gathering her robes about her. "It is time we retired to our own quarters," she said, taking me by the hand.

CHAPTER NINE

THE week that followed was peaceful and happy. The calm before the storm. How could I have imgined everything would sort itself out so simply? The truth was I was living in a golden dream, in which the sun for ever shone and the world grew more and more beautiful.

Each morning I rode with Jules, accompanied by an Arab groom. I was given the chestnut mare and Jules had the little black pony, named Shabo. Khalid, with whom I had been dreading some sort of scene, had kept out of the way, having informed me coldly that since I was to supervise Jules' riding, his presence would be unnecessary. "I do not go riding with nursery governesses," he added insultingly. "So if you will excuse me, Miss Marlow, Ahmad, my groom, will take care of you."

I was only too pleased to be taken care of by Ahmad, an ageing, kindly Arab with the wizened face and bowed legs of an old jockey. On the ground he was rather pathetic to look at, but once in the saddle he and his mount were one. Jules liked Ahmad, and soon forgot his unfortunate experiences with Khalid. Comfortable on the smaller pony, he cantered by my side, sometimes galloping off over the sandy wastes with an abandon Ahmad had to curb. Khalid had been right about that at least—Jules had the makings of a good horseman.

On the second morning we went riding, Greg joined us, mounted on a mettlesome bay. Sheba, who had so scared me when I saw her being ridden by Jules, turned out to be a gentle old thing, though she did try a skittish trick or two when Greg appeared on the bay. However, she soon settled down and we spent a pleasant hour riding over the rough tussocky land and through a shady plantation of pine trees and eucalyptus.

"When are you going to let me show you over the estate properly?" Greg asked me, just before we started home for lunch. "Why not bring the children over to tea this afternoon? I'll make you some Scotch pancakes."

"We'd love to come to tea," I told him.

It was the hottest hour of the day when we set out for Greg's house. Tante Mairik thought we were mad. Going out to tea wasn't an Arab custom. We could have all the tea we wanted at the Casa, she pointed out—those endless glasses of infused mint that had nothing to do with the good cup of Scotch brew I was expecting to go with the pancakes!

I had put on the coolest cotton frock I possessed, low-cut and sleeveless, and dressed the children suitably; Jules in a thin T-shirt and brief pants, Denise is a very French little-girl's muslin. And we all wore big shady hats.

The village when we passed through it swooned in the heat. A few scrawny hens scratching in the dust were the only signs of life, all the doors were closely fastened, the blank windowless white-washed walls reflecting the light.

It was a relief to reach Greg's big cool kitchen-cum-living-room.

"Maybe those Scotch pancakes weren't such a good idea," he said as he greeted us. "The heat is terrific this afternoon, in fact I felt guilty at bringing you out in it." He wiped his brow with an enormous handkerchief, and there was a dark patch of moisture, I noticed, on the back of his thin khaki shirt. He was wearing the briefest of shorts, but he didn't look unclothed, his long, muscular, rather hirsute legs were so deeply tanned.

Opening a refrigerator with a flourish, he announced triumphantly that he had succeeded in making some ice-cream for the children.

"Ice-cream! Oh, good!" Jules exclaimed, jumping up and down with delight. "Tante Mairik never gives us ice-cream."

"It's made with tinned cream," Greg apologised, "but I've put some strawberry flavouring in it which ought to help."

There was a pitcher of lemonade to go with it, I saw, as we sat down to the table. "And I was looking forward to a cup of real English tea," I couldn't help saying. "Even on the hottest days I like my cuppa."

"So do I," Greg agreed. "You didn't really think I was going to fob you off with lemonade, did you? That's for the kids. I've got some very special Earl Grey here, I keep for special occasions." He was busy with the kettle on the stove as he spoke.

It was bliss, that tea, after more than a week with nothing to drink but crushed mint floating about in sweet tepid water.

"How is the ice-cream?" Greg asked the children.

"*C'est formidable!*" Denise told him, producing that improbable French adjective which is the highest of praise. She held out her spoon to him. "Taste it and see!"

He lifted her on to his knee. She spooned ice-cream into his mouth. He made appreciative, smacking noises with his lips and rolled his eyes.

"Have some more!" Further spoonfuls were shovelled into his mouth on a more or less hit-and-miss basis, Denise chuckling with delight. "You'll have to wear a bib," she told him, as ice-cream spilled down on to his shirt.

Producing his handkerchief, he tied it round his neck. Denise thought this was exquisitely funny, and laughed until she subsided exhausted, her head on his shoulder.

He gave me a quizzical glance across her curly head.

"You're so sweet with children!" I blurted, a spontaneous tribute that somehow left me feeling a bit embarrassed.

"So are you," Greg answered. "And a good deal more than just sweet. The way you fought for Jules the other day was nothing short of heroic. Flinging yourself in the path of a bunch of ferocious stallions, standing up to that young thug, Khalid. Oh, yes, I heard all about it! Not many girls would have had the pluck."

"It wasn't anything," I murmured, overcome by this praise.

"Oh yes, it was. It was Ahmad who told me just how bravely you behaved. It gave me quite a new angle on you."

"Do you mean," I asked demurely, "you decided I wasn't quite so bird-brained as you'd thought?"

"I never thought you were bird-brained."

"Lightheaded, then. A good-time girl."

He nodded. "Something like that. I misjudged you, Lorraine. I'm sorry . . . as I've already tried to tell you in my rather clumsy way."

"Why are you sorry?" Denise piped up, lifting her pert little face, smeared with strawberry ice-cream. "Were you mean to Lorraine?"

"Yes, very mean."

"But now you love her again?"

"That's it," Greg agreed, throwing me one of his most mischievous glances. "Now I love her."

"And do you love Uncle Greg, too?" the frightful child demanded of me.

"Of course I do," I said, not looking at him; hoping I was making it sound casual enough to mean nothing. But I could feel myself blushing furiously.

"That's fine!" Greg said softly. Then he laughed, and gave me another of those devastating looks. "Let's have another cup of tea on it!"

It was beginning to grow cooler when we set off to make our tour of the estate; the four of us packed into the roomy front seat of an old army jeep. I was amazed at the extent of the Caïd's territory, and its sheer beauty. Down sandy tracks we drove, through avenues of fruit trees and olives. There were date groves and orchards, peaches and oranges, lemons and figs. Beneath the neatly ranked trees the green grass was studded with flowers, the whole thing a dazzling tapestry of colour. At one point a field of violets made me exclaim. Greg stopped the jeep and told me to gather as many as I liked. I have never seen such large, richly coloured violets, and their scent was delicious. The children and I filled our hands with them and Greg found us some damp moss to keep them fresh until we could get them home. The moss came from a little stream which ran through the field. But there were streams everywhere, and wells, and irrigation ditches, and reservoirs made of huge cement-lined tanks, all contrived or utilised by Greg to conserve the rainfall.

Here and there we came to small colonies of white houses, where the workers lived. In one place we saw a camel being used to turn the capstan of an old water-mill. Round and round it went with its stately tread, its strange inscrutable face turned patiently to the sky.

"We employ everything that comes to hand, ancient and modern," Greg told me, stopping to show me an electric pump he had ingeniously installed over a deep well in what had once been a sandy waste, and was now a fertile garden.

"And I've done it all in five years," he boasted. "You should have seen this place when I took it over!" He spoke of some of the difficulties he had overcome.

"Now it's got me," he ended. "I feel that in my small way I've created all that we see here." He made a sweeping gesture. "So that it is, in a sense, a part of me. I don't see how I can ever leave it." His tone was troubled.

"It isn't only the plantations and gardens," he went on, "but the people I work with. They've become my friends. And—perhaps this sounds conceited—but I feel they need me."

He gave me a quick embarrassed glance. "I'm no do-gooder or missionary, but when I see things that want doing I just have to rally round. When I first came here so many of the kids had sore eyes—because of the flies crawling everywhere. There wasn't a glimmer of an idea about simple hygiene. I talked to the Caid about it. He's a good old boy and gave me *carte blanche* to do whatever I thought best to remedy matters. So I started a sort of clinic, using what elementary medical knowledge I possess. It's held in the village, in a hall next to the village school. Every morning I have an hour's surgery there. You ought to come along one day and see it."

"I'd love to," I told him, more impressed than I cared to show by this glimpse of him as an altruistic character.

"It's surprising the number of small ailments I've learned to deal with," he went on. "Even the women come to me sometimes, for themselves as well as for their babies. At first there was a spot of difficulty about this, as Arab women don't usually consult male infidel doctors. But now Alya is my assistant and it's all much easier. She longs to train as a nurse, and has picked up a good deal of nursing knowledge in a course she took at school. So she's very useful."

So that was why I had seen so little of Alya about the harem. A pang of jealousy pierced through me. Lucky Alya, working every day with Greg, seeing him at his best. "It all sounds marvellous," I murmured inadequately.

"There's the social side to our communal life too," he enthused. "We have a club where the boys and men come to play darts and dominoes and listen to lantern lectures during the winter evenings. I've even managed to rustle up an old billiard table; I found it at an auction sale in Tunis, going cheap. I play western music to them on my much-worn record-player, and they teach me to understand Arab music in return. Quite a cultural exchange, in fact. I enjoy it. I should miss it all very much if I went back to Britain.

"So here I am!" He gave me one of his swift, enigmatic glances. "Doomed to a bachelor existence, for it isn't the sort of life one could very well invite a girl from home to share."

"I don't see why not," I burst out impulsively, and at once began to grow hot-cheeked again. But having committed myself I went bravely on. "It would just be a question of finding the right person."

"Miss Right." Greg grinned. "You really believe such a person exists?"

"Of course she does," I declared, in a casual tone, which I hoped made it sound convincingly impersonal.

"You must tell me more about her," Greg said. The grin was gone now, the deep grey eyes disturbingly serious. "Come out to dinner with me in El Mersa on Saturday evening?"

"I'd like to," I agreed.

"El Mersa!" Jules piped up. I had almost forgotten the presence of the children. "That's the town we came to one day in a train, when we were visiting Grandpère and the car broke down. There's a railway there that runs all the way to Tunis, and you can have lunch on the train. I liked that train and I liked El Mersa. We slept in a hotel there one night, and in the morning Papa took me to the shops and bought me a model aeroplane. Will you take me to El Mersa some time, Uncle Greg?"

"Sure I will," Greg agreed easily. "But not on Saturday. When Lorraine and I go there on Saturday evening you'll be asleep in bed." He looked at me over the little boy's head. "It's a firm date, then? Saturday about eight?"

I nodded. "I shall look forward to seeing something of night life in the desert."

"I hope you won't be disappointed. There aren't any night clubs, and not a restaurant that I know of with a floor show. But the town is beginning to be opened up as a tourist centre. More's the pity," he added in parenthesis. "There's one resplendent newly built hotel called the Palazzo, where there's a good dance floor and a passable band. But if it's cabaret you want . . ."

"It isn't," I broke in emphatically. "It isn't for cabaret shows I'm coming out with you."

"I hoped it wasn't," he said softly.

It was dusk by the time we got back to the harem. "An odd place to picture you!" Greg said when we parted at the strongly latched gateway which guarded the harem courtyard.

"It's really very comfortable," I assured him, "and Tante Mairik couldn't be more kind."

"You're extraordinarily adaptable," he said, and there was a ring of satisfaction in his tone.

Putting the children to bed I was so happy I couldn't stop singing little snatches of song. The evening light filled the room with an almost unbearable radiance, and there were bowls of violets everywhere. Was Greg in love with me? I didn't know. But the feeling I had for him altered the whole face of the world. Everything seemed touched with an unearthly beauty—this sunset hour, the perfumed violets, the children, laughing and romping, with the evening skittishness of all young animals. If this was what was meant by being in love it was pretty marvellous. Where was it leading me? But I wouldn't allow myself to think about that. I just let the waves of bliss and well-being sweep over me, and even in my sleep that night my heart was singing.

Greg didn't ride with us the following morning. I hadn't expected him; he had told me he would be too busy to come. Everything was still wonderful. There was nothing to ruffle my golden mood.

As we were walking back to the house for lunch, Jules slipped his hand into mine and said, "I like riding with you, Lorraine. I'm so glad I don't have to ride with Uncle Khalid any more. Thank you for fixing it for me." He lifted a small crumpled face, his dark eyes troubled. "You didn't do it because you think I'm a weak, silly baby, like Uncle Khalid said?"

"Of course not, darling," I assured him. "Uncle Khalid is an extremely expert horseman, and he gets impatient when he has to ride with beginners like you or me. When you're older he will take you out and you will enjoy all the wonderful things he can teach you. In the meantime you're getting on famously with Shabo—the way you handled him this morning was terrific."

"Do you really think so?" The crumpled little face smoothed out. "I love you, Lorraine," he said presently. "Next to Mama and Papa you're the nicest person in the whole world."

After lunch all life ceased in the Ben Akhtal household. Everyone rested. Lying on the big bed with Denise asleep beside me, I wondered if Greg would be able to ride with us tomorrow. Or would I have to wait until Saturday before seeing him again? Not that Saturday was very far off. Today was Thursday. I began planning what I would wear. The cream jersey silk again, or a little black number that was a little more formal? I had a hunch that this dinner date was going to be a rather important landmark in my life. Either Greg was having the sort of thoughts about me I hoped he was, or he wasn't. On Saturday evening

I would find out. So that dinner date loomed ahead of me like a great full stop, or more truly, a question mark. After Saturday my life would never be quite the same again.

When the siesta hour was over Khadija gave me a lesson in tooling leather. She was helping me to make one of those beautiful goatskin handbags one sees in North African tourist shops. In exchange for the English lessons, she said. She was still joining us at our reading sessions every morning, and making rapid progress. She had, I think, a first-class brain, and it was a shame she couldn't have the opportunity of using it, studying at a university for some kind of degree. She would have loved when she was younger to go to Paris, to the Sorbonne, she told me. Then when she was qualified she could have come back and taught in the big school for girls in Tunis, living in a hostel for teachers, or in an apartment on her own.

We talked about her dreams and ambitions that afternoon as we worked. Hopeless ambitions. Khalid with his old-fashioned notions of women's status baulked her at every turn. "He has a fanatical hatred of Western education and Western ideas," she said.

"And Western people," I added. "I'm surprised I haven't had more trouble with him over my interference with Jules' riding lessons. He seems to have taken it all very quietly."

"He hasn't really," Khadija told me. "He was in such a rage he went off to stay with some distant relatives of ours over the Algerian border, men with the same Pan-Arab tendencies as himself. We don't know what he gets up to over there, and it worries the Caid—it may be he is mixed up in subversive activities of some kind. But don't say a word of this to Tante Mairik, or Greg, or anyone. It's a sore point with the family."

"Of course I won't," I promised, feeling vaguely uneasy that I had driven Khalid away.

It was while I was giving the children their supper that Fatmah came to tell me Mr. Gregson was at the door of the courtyard and wanted to speak with me.

He had come to make the final arrangements for Saturday, I supposed, or perhaps to arrange where we should meet when we went riding tomorrow. Happiness welled up inside me as I hurried out to the courtyard. It was as if a whole orchestra of violins was playing in my heart. I went through the gate into the outer courtyard, where he would be waiting for me. The courtyard with the flowers and the fountain and the Moorish lamps, already alight as the brief twilight faded. At first I could see nobody in the dim light, then from the cloisters beneath the balcony he came towards me. He was not alone. There was a tall elegant figure beside him. Delmer Lloyd!

The shock was so great that for a moment I was beyond all thought. It did not occur to me that the way I stood there transfixed could mean intense delight, as well as horror.

"Del!" I gasped.

He caught my two hands and drew me towards him.

"Darling!" he cried. "It's so wonderful to see you after all this time! Why didn't you let me have your address sooner? The moment I got your letter this morning I came . . ."

"My letter?" I echoed in bewilderment.

I saw Greg turn on his heel and stride away, muttering something as he went. It sounded like a sullen, "Well, I'll leave you to get on with it." The gate of the outer courtyard slammed and he was gone. I stared after him, trying to sort it out. But it was all very confused. I only knew that Greg had walked out on me and Del was beside me, handsome and debonair as ever in an immaculate tussore suit. He was still holding my hands.

"What do you mean . . . my letter?" I repeated. "I didn't write to you."

"Did I say *your* letter?" Del enquired, with an exaggerated air of innocence. "I meant your aunt's letter. You'll have to forgive me, darling; I'm so thrilled to be with you again that I hardly know what I'm saying. Aren't you just a little bit pleased to see me too?" He tried to draw me closer to him, but I snatched my hands away from him.

"Lorraine!" he protested. The misery in his voice penetrated my confusion.

"I'm sorry, Del," I offered. "But I wasn't expecting you."

I was still trying to assess in my mind the amount of damage he had done, presenting himself to Greg when he was in search of me, and then making that unfortunate slip about the letter.

"Come and sit down." I indicated a stone bench under one of the lamps. "Tell me about this letter from my aunt." I hadn't heard from Aunt Vinnie since my arrival at the Casa, and was anxious for news of her. It seemed odd that she had written to Del.

But she hadn't, as it happened. Stupidly, or on purpose, he had got that detail wrong too just now in front of Greg. It was to the Comtesse Aunt Vinnie had written, to the hotel at Biskra.

"She told us you had gone off into the wilds with the Ben Akhtal children," Del explained, "and suggested we should look you up if we happened to be motoring in the district. As a matter

330

of fact we were planning a few days at El Mersa, so we drove over straight away. We're staying at the Palazzo. Natalie hopes you'll come back with me this evening and dine with us."

"I'm not sure if I can," I mumbled, feeling I was sinking deeper and deeper into a morass. "What else did Aunt Vinnie say in her letter?" I urged, playing for time.

"I can't quite remember," Del hedged. "Come on back to the Palazzo and you shall read the letter for yourself. There are all sorts of messages in it for you."

Were there? Or was Del just being fiendishly cunning? What would Greg think if I went off with Del this evening? Surely I would be able to make him understand how it had come about!

"Don't tell me you can't leave the children," Del was saying. "This harem, or whatever it is, must be overrun with females who'll look after them. So just pop along like a good girl and put on your pretties. We'll be back with Natalie in time for cocktails. She'll be so disappointed if I turn up without you."

"Since when has the Comtesse been so anxious for my company?" I asked dryly.

Del laughed. "Oh, I know she got a bit peeved at the amount of time I spent with you at Sidi Akbar. But all that's forgotten now, and she'll specially want to see you tonight, since she's already written to your aunt saying we were on our way to El Mersa and would be taking you out to dinner."

It was all so plausible. What could I do? I was trapped in what seemed almost like a family obligation. A link with Aunt Vinnie. I hadn't written to her since coming to El Garza, because she was on the move and I hadn't got her address. If I went into El Mersa and read her letter, presumably telling of her whereabouts, I could write to her tomorrow.

"If you wait here," I told Del, "I'll go and get changed."

"Good girl!"

But as I rose to leave him he pulled me down on the seat again beside him. "Havent you forgotten something?" he whispered. His arms were tightly around me and he was kissing me expertly.

"No, Del, no!" I pushed him away from me and stood up.

"What's wrong, Lorry?" (That family diminutive I hated him to use!) "Aren't you glad to see me? This isn't how it was between us at Sidi Akbar."

No indeed, this wasn't how it had been those mindless, sunny days. I'd played with love . . . and with Del . . . and now I was paying for it.

"Look, Del," I said urgently, "things change, people change. We had fun at Sidi Akbar, but it was just . . . holiday fun. No one was being serious."

"I was," Del put in quickly. "I still am. I've missed you every moment of the time since we went to Biskra. I wrote to you at the Hotel Alzara, but there was no reply. I was desperate. You hadn't given me your address in England and I couldn't see how I was ever going to find you again. Then this morning your aunt's letter arrived . . . But more of this anon." He gave me a gentle push. "Go along and get dressed and we'll be on our way. We'll have plenty of time to talk about ourselves later on."

As I left him a tall figure came out of the shadowy cloisters and went into the Caid's apartment. Khalid! So he had returned from his flight to Algeria! How much had he seen and heard of my session with Del? I wondered uneasily as I hurried away to my room to change into the little black frock I had been keeping for my evening with Greg.

The great lush car was waiting for me. If only it had been Greg's rickety old jeep! I thought, as we raced smoothly along the El Garza road.

There hadn't been any difficulty about leaving the children. Tante Mairik would enjoy putting them to bed. I was going to have dinner with the Comtesse de la Fontaine, an old friend of my aunt's who was staying in El Mersa, I explained. She had sent her secretary to fetch me. Perhaps I was nursing the forlorn hope that this version of my trip to El Mersa would be relayed to Greg. Harems operate a pretty active grapevine!

Consoling myself with this thought, I prepared to enjoy what I could of the evening ahead of me. The air was warm and balmy. As we sped across the sandy wastes that separate El Mersa from El Garza the first stars came out in a dark blue velvet sky.

And Del at my side was at his most gallant and handsome, far better-looking than Greg, far more anxious to flatter me, yet my heart lay dead in my breast. I was more beautiful than ever, he told me. He was crazy about me, and had been utterly wretched, cut off from me in Biskra. But it was all quite unreal. When he handed me out of the luxurious car at the glittering doorway of the Palazzo I felt as if I were acting in one of his plays. Del with his airs and graces had no more substance for me than a shadowy figure seen on a television screen.

The Comtesse greeted me kindly. In spite of her expertly applied make-up she looked tired and old. The heat was trying her, she said. Soon she would return to the cooler climate of Paris, and she hoped to see Aunt Vinnie there. From her letter, which the Comtesse allowed me to read, Aunt Vinnie said she had been briefly in London, but was now going to be at the Hotel Royale in Paris where she had a series of engagements connected with her various charities. So I now had an address at which I could write to her. She sent me loving messages and longed to hear from me. She would write to me as soon as she got to Paris. All this was in itself enough to make this rather worrying evening endurable.

Over the elaborate dinner, for which I had little appetite, the Comtesse questioned me about my life at El Garza. When would I be leaving there? she asked me.

"I don't quite know," I told her. "The date of Elaine's return from America is a little uncertain." But the question had startled me. The thought of going back to England, away from Greg and the paradise he had created in his flowering wilderness, made me feel cold and lost. In so short a time I seemed to have taken root there. But this was madness. I must pull myself together, control these romantic maunderings. Just because Greg had been tardily kind . . . said a few mildly sentimental things to me . . .

"Would you like to dance?" Del's voice broke into my thoughts.

We went into the adjacent ballroom, the Comtesse following us to sit at one of the small tables on the sidelines where after-dinner coffee was being served. "She's watching us like a hawk," Del grumbled, as we drifted off into a waltz. "Why doesn't she go to bed? God knows, she could do with a spot of beauty sleep." The way Del spoke of Natalie always jarred on me. She was so kind to him, and if she was possessive as well, he ought to suffer it with good grace—so long as he stayed with her, accepting the benefits she heaped on him.

Presently he swung me off the floor into an alcove contrived with potted palms and a Moorish screen of latticed wood. There was a red plush couch, on which we sat, my heart sinking as I waited for the inevitable declarations of devotion. They were not long in coming.

"I was a fool when we were in Sidi Akbar," Del burst out. "Messing up all my chances with you, handling everything the wrong way. That idiotic day I tried to rush you into a runaway honeymoon! What you must have thought of me! I can only suppose I'd had too much of that heady Tunisian wine."

"Really, Del, it doesn't matter," I told him. "I'd forgotten all about it."

He looked hurt. "There isn't one single moment I've had with you that I can ever forget," he declared romantically. "When are we going to get married, Lorraine? You're the only girl in the world for me. I can't live without you."

"Please, Del!" I begged. "It's quite impossible. I could never marry you. We're poles apart. We come from such different backgrounds, have different ideas . . ."

"Darling, I know I'm rushing you." He assumed an air of sweet reasonableness. "But if I don't speak out now, heaven knows when I'll have another chance. Natalie will be whisking me off to Paris. I want to feel you'll soon be joining me there . . . I can be looking out for a cute little apartment on the Left Bank . . ."

"And who's going to pay the rent?" I put in. "Have you any idea of the astronomical cost of cute little apartments in Paris nowadays?"

"I could be getting on with my play," Del offered feebly. "Perhaps you could teach for a little while, until we get on our feet. But I'm sure your aunt would give you a generous allowance to see us through . . . and in the end you will have the bulk of her money . . ."

Here it was again! The blatant fortune-hunting! I gave him a long steady look. From his beautiful sherry-coloured eyes his false and shallow soul looked back at me.

"Oh, Del!" I sighed. "Why do you bother to talk to me about love? It's Aunt Vinnie's money that really interests you, isn't it?"

Del made a shocked exclamation. "Lorraine! How can you say such cruel things to me? If you hadn't a penny beyond what you earn by your teaching I'd love you just the same."

"I haven't," I said.

Del sat up abruptly. "What did you say?"

"I'm not Aunt Vinnie's heiress. There's nothing to inherit. Most of the money she has belonged to her husband, and will revert to distant members of his family when she dies."

That was the truth, if not quite the whole truth, but I had no intention of telling Del about the gift Aunt Vinnie was making to me out of her own resources. He looked at me in blank dismay. Beneath his beautiful sun-tan he went a sickly yellow.

"Let's go on with our dance," he said. He was giving himself time to think, time to absorb the shock. We circled the floor a couple of times in a desultory fashion and then rejoined the Comtesse. It was time I was getting back to El Garza, I said. Neither the Comtesse nor Del tried to persuade me to prolong the evening.

I went to the cloakroom and picked up my coat. Del was waiting for me at the florid portico with its dazzling neon lights. The ten-mile drive would not take long, I consoled myself. My hours, my moments with Delmer Lloyd were numbered. After tonight he would never trouble me again.

For the first few miles he drove in silence, then he turned to me and said, "What you told me this evening has been a shock, Lorraine. There's no use in pretending it hasn't. Not because your aunt's money interests me in itself. I'm the least avaricious of mortals. But one has to live. Earlier we talked of marriage . . ."

"*You* talked of it," I corrected.

He ignored the interruption. "Now," he went on, "I have to face the unpleasant fact that I'm in no position to make you my wife. I couldn't keep you in any degree of comfort. At the moment, unless I stay with Natalie, I could hardly succeed in keeping myself."

"I know, Del," I assured him. "Don't worry about it. I don't want to marry you. Can't you get that into your handsome head? I'm not in love with you. I never have been. If I led you to think differently at Sidi Akbar, I'm sorry."

Del hunched his shoulders over the wheel and drove on in silence. "You don't know what a blow this has been to me," he groaned presently.

But I did know, only too well. False gallantry, false romance had collapsed, like a cardboard façade, leaving nothing but emptiness.

"Cheer up," I rallied him. "We all make mistakes. You ought to have done a little more tactful investigating before jumping to the conclusion that I was a gilded heiress."

He shot me a reproachful look. "I don't understand you, Lorraine. You can't be as heartless as you seem."

Heartless! If only I were! We were approaching the Casa El Garza now. I could see the high white walls, caught in our headlights. Del stopped the car, and as I was moving to get out drew me back

337

into his arms. "Goodbye, Lorraine!" His voice choked over the words. "Think of me sometimes. I'm not altogether the gold-digging heel you imagine I am. I love you. If things had been different I could have made you believe that."

His mouth came down on my own with purpose and passion. I was powerless to resist. Perhaps I didn't try very hard. Suddenly I was sorry for him. There had been a note of genuine suffering in his voice, and for once, I felt, he was not acting a part.

"Goodbye, Lorraine. My lovely lost Lorraine!"

"Goodbye, Del."

As I got out of the car I saw a tall figure coming from the shadow of the arched gateway, moving down the road to the village. Greg! Had he seen us making our lingering farewells? It seemed more than likely. I put my hand to my breast. The pain in my heart was actual . . . physical, catching my breath.

"Goodbye, Del," I said again mechanically. "And thanks for the festive evening."

Slowly, without looking back, I went through the gateway, and across the courtyard to my room.

CHAPTER TEN

I DIDN'T sleep very much that night, and it wasn't pity for Delmer Lloyd that kept me awake. (Poor shallow Del, who had perhaps been in love with me a little.) It was the vision of Greg's back as he walked away under the high white wall that haunted me. What would he think of that farewell kiss I had given to Del? The fact that I had gone off to El Mersa for the evening with Del must look black enough, giving the lie to everything I had said about my relationship with him.

That it was quite over. That I had no idea where he was. And there was that madly unfortunate slip Del had made when he said he had had a letter from me. 'This morning', he had said. Which made it look as if I had rushed straight home from my wonderful afternoon with Greg to write to Del, inviting him to come out and see me!

The more I thought about it the more I was convinced that mistake had been no slip of the tongue. Del had probably said it to impress Greg, give himself some standing as my friend. Perhaps Greg had been making him feel like the intruder he was.

Miserably I mulled it over, trying to persuade myself that I would be able to make Greg understand what a silly muddle it had all been. Surely he would believe me when I told him the whole story.

I must have been mad! He didn't give me the chance even to begin those explanations. There was no sign of him when we went riding. All the morning I watched out for the big bay, taking the bridle paths that lay nearest to where I thought Greg might be working. But the fields and gardens were oddly deserted. I remembered it was Friday, the moslem holy day. All the workers would be at the mosque. Presently I saw the Caid riding off in state, to the morning ceremony, accompanied by an escort of soldiers. The resplendent figure on a great white horse at his side was, I realised with a sense of shock, Khalid. So he had returned from his Algerian visit.

As the procession drew level with Jules and myself on our humble mounts Khalid gave me a long look, charged with hatred. It left me with the uneasy feeling that I hadn't yet finished with him. My interference with the riding lessons wasn't going to be so easily forgotten.

But at the moment I couldn't really worry about Khalid and his possible revengefulness. I was too preoccupied with Greg. Tomorrow was Saturday, the day he had promised to take me to El Mersa. Would he keep that promise?

I spent another restless night. It was unseasonably hot and sultry, more like high summer than early spring, and Denise at my side moaned restlessly and tossed in her sleep. It was almost dawn when I dozed off at last and had a terrible dream about Khalid. I was in Del's fabulous car, but it was Khalid who was driving. He was taking me away into a dark nightmare country and I knew I would never see Greg again. There was a shadowy desert road ahead of us, and Khalid was driving at a reckless speed. Suddenly a small form ran out in front of us. It was Jules in his white sailor suit. His terror-stricken face looked up at me as he fell under the wheels of the car, and Khalid, laughing, drove on. I woke hearing Jules' screams in my ears, and found my face was wet with tears. After that I gave up trying to sleep any more and lay watching the daylight filter through the curtained french window.

Soon after seven I got up and had a bath and dressed, by which time the children were awake. Denise was crotchety and fretful, and when I felt her forehead it seemed rather hot. I wished I had a thermometer, but Elaine hadn't thought of supplying one and it wasn't a thing I carried about with me as a rule.

"Would you like to stay in bed?" I asked Denise. But she shook her head vigorously. She wanted to go out and play with the other children, she said, and in answer to my questions declared she had no pain in her head, or in her tummy. The good breakfast she ate reassured me, and the day was launched on its normal course. First the read-

340

ing lesson with Jules and Khadija. We were reading Kipling's 'Just So' stories now. Both my pupils liked them and made rapid strides in proficiency. In any other mood I would have been elated about this, but today I could only think of Greg. It was Saturday—he was to take me into El Mersa. At last I would have the opportunity of explaining Del's visit to him.

It was as I was getting ready to go out riding that Fatmah appeared, with an envelope in her hand. "A boy from the village has just brought this for you, *mam'selle*," she said.

I think I guessed what was in that note, even before I tore open the envelope. It was from Greg, short and cruelly to the point:

"Dear Lorraine:
    I'm sorry, but I will not be able to keep our dinner date. I don't imagine you will be altogether surprised when I say that certain circumstances which have arisen make it impossible, and in fact quite pointless. However, as you have already sampled the delights of El Mersa, on a much more lavish scale than I could manage to provide, I don't suppose you will be disappointed.
                    Sincerely,
                    T. Gregson."

I let the single sheet of notepaper flutter to the ground. From the small mirror over the wash basin my face looked back at me, rigid and pale. Mechanically I brushed my hair into a ponytail, dabbed a little powder on my nose, and picked up my hat. When I reached the door I turned back to retrieve Greg's letter from the floor. Folding it carefully, I tucked it into the belt of my jeans. "Dear Lorraine, I'm sorry, but I will not be able

341

to keep our dinner date." So that was the line he was taking . . . just dropping me cold! I wasn't even to have the chance to defend myself.

Jules was waiting for me in the courtyard. We went along to the stables and Ahmad appeared with the horses. "We will ride out in the open country today," I told him. The further away from the estate, the better. There must be no risk of running into Greg. Now and then my hand went to the fold of paper tucked into my belt. There was no need to take it out and read it again, its few words were burned into my brain. Greg was hurt because I had gone out with Delmer Lloyd, and didn't mind showing it. Which meant, I tried to console myself, that he felt in some way involved with me. Or *had* felt involved. It was all over now. I was a liar, a cheat, an incurable flirt. I could just imagine all the things his rigid Scots mind was thinking about me. Deplorably square, perhaps, but that was Greg. Greg whom I loved and had, it would seem, hopelessly lost.

Somehow the day dragged on. It was airless and hot and all the children in the compound, including my own two, were naughty and fractious. I got Denise and Jules to bed early, and settled down to a long dull evening of getting on with my leather work, trying not to thing of how differently I might have been spending these hours. It was a relief when it was time to go to bed, and after two rather broken nights I surprised myself by sleeping the clock round.

Jules was already up when I awoke, manfully dressing himself behind his latticed screen, but Denise at my side slept on heavily, her small face crimson, her breathing shallow and quick. I felt her brow; she was burning hot. This time there was no mistaking the soaring temperature. I ran to find Tante Mairik. Plump and kindly, she trotted back into the bedroom in my wake, and after feeling Denise's hot hands said that what the child needed was some cooling medicine.

"If she were one of my own I would give her some of my special herb mixture, but perhaps you would rather have one of the more modern remedies Mr. Gregson keeps in his clinic. You'd better go down and see him."

"Couldn't Alya go?" I countered. "I don't like to leave Denise."

"I'll stay with her," Tante Mairik declared. "Alya is already down at the clinic, and anyhow you are the best person to explain to Mr. Gregson just how it is with Denise. You'd better get off at once. The clinic closes about nine, and it's nearly that now."

I was still in my dressing gown, but it didn't take me long to slip on a frock and splash my face with cold water. As I drew near to the village I felt sick with nervousness. There was the school with its open door, through which I could see the rows of shaven-headed little boys sitting on the floor reciting the Koran, which, Greg had told me, seemed to be their main source of study.

The clinic, in the adjoining building, had perhaps at one time been part of the school, for the door through which I passed led into a wide hall, which served as a waiting room. Here on benches ranged round the walls sat a collection of white-robed figures, mostly old and middle-aged men. A curtain had been fitted up to hide the women who waited with their babies. Should I go and join them and await my turn? As I stood there wondering what to do, a door which presumably led into the surgery opened and Greg appeared.

At the sight of me he stood arrested, his expression grim. "Miss Marlow!" he said stiffly.

"Denise is ill," I began hurriedly. "Tante Mairik said you might be able to give me some medicine for her."

"What are her symptoms?" he asked.

"She seems to have a very high temperature, but I have no thermometer with me, so I couldn't take it. She's restless and fretful and doesn't want any breakfast."

"I'd better come along and have a look at her." Greg closed the door behind him, said something in Arabic to the people who were sitting on the bench, waiting, and walked with me out into the sunshine.

"It's very good of you to leave everything . . . your patients . . ." I began in a rather confused way.

"Oh, they won't mind. Patience is an Oriental virtue. They would sit there all day without turning a hair."

It was a ten-minute walk to the Casa. With a sudden desperate courage I resolved not to waste it. I said, taking the bull by the horns, "I'm glad to have this opportunity of speaking to you, Greg. I think you owe me an apology or at least an explanation for that very peculiar note you sent me on Saturday."

"I owe *you* an apology!" He stood still to glare at me. "If there's any explaining to be done it should surely come from you."

"Just because an old friend of my aunt's invites me out to dinner . . ."

"So Mr. Lloyd is an old friend of your aunt's," he echoed with a dry laugh. "Isn't he rather young for such a role?"

"I wasn't talking about Del Lloyd," I returned indignantly, "but about the Comtesse de la Fontaine. She is staying at the Palazzo in El Mersa and decided to look me up. My aunt had written

344

to her, asking her to do so. She sent Del to fetch me."

"Your aunt wrote to this Comtesse?" Greg repeated doubtfully. "What about your own letter? The one you wrote to the chap? Surely it was that which brought him here."

"I didn't write to him. When he spoke of a letter, he meant the one my aunt had written to the Comtesse. It was a slip of the tongue."

We were walking on again, but I could feel Greg's glare intensifying. "You must have a pretty poor opinion of my intelligence if you expect me to believe that!"

"You can believe it or not, as you please," I retorted angrily.

He made an exasperated gesture. "How *can* I believe you, Lorraine? You've told me so many lies already. You gave me to understand, when you came here, that this Del Lloyd was the merest acquaintance, in spite of the fact that he would seem to the casual observer to be a good deal more when you were both staying at the Hotel Alzara. However, all that was over. You assured me that you didn't know where he was, nor, by implication, did you want to know. Then suddenly he turns up, with all the assurance of an accepted lover, behaving like an accepted lover if embraces are any criterion, and he announces that he has come in answer to your letter. Off you go with him for the evening without the slightest hesitation, and don't tell me it was for some mythical Comtesse you made yourself look so glamorous . . . setting off in your boy-friend's superlative car . . ."

"The Comtesse is *not* mythical," I cried, when I could get a word in. "You can ring up the Palazzo if you like and verify her existence. Del

345

is staying with her at the moment, helping her to write her memoirs. He's a sort of secretary."

"Who owns the glossy car?"

"Del does."

Greg shrugged. "Secretaries don't usually have cars of such magnificence. Your story, my dear Lorraine, is full of holes."

"Meaning," I choked, "you don't believe a word of it."

"I'm afraid not. There's the evidence of my own eyes, you see. Your kisses were pretty openly indulged."

"So you were spying on me!" I was so angry I could hardly go on. "Watching me, no doubt, when I left the Casa with Delmer, taking care to be on hand when he brought me back again."

"I had been playing a prolonged game of chess with the Caid," Greg condescended to explain. "You surely don't imagine I spent the entire evening hanging about the main gateway on the chance of witnessing your touching good-night embraces? By that time I had ceaseed to care whom you kissed, or how you came and went." His lean jaw tightened. "The implication being that there was a time when I *did* care . . . deeply. Funny, isn't it? Something for you to laugh over when you're counting scalps."

"Greg, *please*!" I cried. "You've got everything wrong. How can I make you understand?"

"You *have* made me understand," he answered coldly. "Only too well. And now . . ." his tone changed, "tell me some more about Denise. Has she been sick, does she cough, are there any spots on her face or chest?"

These down-to-earth questions were like a door slammed in my face. Somehow I answered them. We had reached the Casa by this time. Tante Mairik came to the sickroom with us, where we found Denise propped up against a pile of pillows looking a little less flushed.

"Oh, Greg!" She held out her arms to him dramatically. "I have a sore throat. I want my *maman.*" Tears rolled down her cheeks. Sitting on the bed, he gathered her into his arms, comforting her. Greg's way with children was very appealing. I watched him with an ache in my heart. I could imagine him in his clinic with the little Arab boys and girls, binding up wounds, doling out simple medicines. An unprofessional healer, working by the light of inspiration and love. He would care for plants and trees and animals, all in the same way. An unconventional character; pig-headed, independent and maddeningly self-opinionated but warm-hearted and straight as a die. Dishonestly was the one thing he would find it hard to forgive. And he believed I was dishonest. I thought of the scornful things he had said to me on the way up from the village. In an oblique way it had been a confession of love . . . the love that might have been. Sick with the sense of loss, I watched him gently examining Denise, his thin brown face alight with tenderness.

He didn't think there was very much wrong with her, he told us, when he had taken her temperature and felt her pulse. It was probably a touch of the sun. He would send some medicine for her, and some throat tablets. "We've got to watch that throat," he said after we had left the room. "If it doesn't clear up in a few hours we must get a doctor out from El Mersa to take a swab."

Diptheria was not unknown in El Mersa, Tante Mairik told me when he had gone. "But it is far less frequent since Mr. Gregson came to live

347

with us and insisted on the babies being in-oculated."

I spent the rest of the day with Denise, spong-ing her down, reading to her, keeping her happy. Jules, missing his ride on Shabo, drifted in and out restlessly. Towards evening Greg looked in again, and pronounced Denise's sore throat to be much better.

"I'll come again in the morning," he promised as he went away. It had been the briefest of visits, and he had been careful to come into the room accompanied by Tante Mairik . . . so that there could be no danger of any intimate con-versation between us. He had, I guessed, said all he had to say to me. Whatever had been between us was finished, completely, irrevocably. I had no hope now of clearing up the misunder-standing between us. He had made up his obstin-ate mind about me — not unreasonably. The evidence against me was pretty black on the face of it, beginning, as it did, way back that first night he had walked on to the *terrasse* of the Hotel Alzara and found me locked in Del's arms. A lighthearted holiday flirtation I was to pay for for the rest of my life.

I would get over it, I told myself bracingly as I lay in bed that night. I'd have to. Life went on, sweeping you along on its relentness tides. I'd go back to England and find a job. Gradually I would forget the pain of a heaven glimpsed . . . and lost. The pictures would grow more dim. I'd think less and less of Greg working in the date and olive groves, going back to his lonely house at night. Maybe in dreams I would see it some-times, this oasis in the desert brought to life by the patience and skill of one man. A flowering paradise I might have shared! Tears stung my eyelids. I buried my face in the pillows and let the

348

tide of misery and self-pity wash over me. In the morning I would find courage again, but here in the darkness for a little while I could give way.

It was almost noon the following day when I missed Jules. He hadn't, I realised, made any of his rather restless visits to the sickroom for the best part of two hours. What was he up to? I hurried out to the living room, but none of the women there had seen anything of the little boy. Increasingly uneasy, I went into the courtyard where a handful of children were playing. Had they seen Jules? I asked them. "He had gone with Khalid," a small girl told me. "Very early, soon after breakfast Uncle Khalid came for him."

I ran back to the living room. "Khalid has taken Jules riding again," I told Tante Mairik indignantly. "I'm going right after them to bring him back. Will you keep an eye on Denise while I'm away?"

Fortunately Denise was much better, so that I had no qualms at leaving her. Greg had popped in for a few minutes earlier in the morning and said her throat was clearing nicely, but that she must stay in bed until her temperature had quite settled. I'd managed to face him with apparent equanimity, but it was a relief when he said there would be no need for him to come and see Denise again unless I sent for him. The few formal words we had exchanged had been agony.

But it wasn't of Greg I was thinking as I scurried along the dusty road to the stables. I was filled with anger against Khalid. No doubt he had heard Denise was ill, and realising I would be occupied with her he had lured Jules away. What threats or promises had he used? The

349

sky was overcast, the sun shining through a strange metallic haze. But it was very hot — the same strangely airless heat I had noticed a day or two before. There was something menacing about it. Everything seemed distorted, as though seen through a film of dirty yellow gauze.

Sheba was in her stall. So at least Khalid had permitted Jules to ride on the smaller pony, Shabo. I called to Ahmed to saddle Sheba for me, and asked him if he knew in which direction Khalid was riding this morning.

"They have taken the falcons into the pine wood," the man told me.

The falcons! I remembered now how Khalid, on that evening we arrived, had spoken of teaching Jules the art of falconry. What that entailed I hadn't a clue—but at least, I supposed, it would be safer for the child than galloping over the desert with a herd of half-wild Arab horses.

The pine wood was one of the places I had driven through with Greg—that halcyon afternoon he had shown us over the estate. It seemed an eternity ago!

After losing my way once or twice in the maze of sandy tracks I came to the place at last. There was no sign of Khalid and his falcons. I rode on. The pine trees gave way to a deep thicket of scrub and camelthorn, and here in a wide clearing about a dozen men on horseback formed a ring. Jules, on his pony, was beside Khalid, his small face paper white, his dark eyes enormous. As I approached the men turned to stare at me, their dark faces scowling. Khalid called to me sharply to stay where I was and remain motionless. I realised I was interrupting a ritual of some kind connected with the hunting, and reined in my mount. Jules seemed unaware of my presence, his gaze fixed on the great hooded falcon perched on Khalid's gauntlet-covered wrist. Most of the other men had similar birds, all of them with their heads hidden in richly tooled leather hoods. Sitting there under the hot lowering sky the men and their falcons seemed like figures in a sinister dream. Sensing the tension, Sheba began to tremble beneath me. I whispered to her soothingly, not daring to stroke her neck for fear that my movement might break the spell which seemed to hold the scene in thrall.

Suddenly a beater ran out of the scrub, waving his arms, his voice raised in a high thin cry. The hood was slipped off Khalid's falcon; it soared into the sky, where it hovered, like a hawk, spying out the quarry. A hare, driven by the beaters, came scuttling out of the bushes, to lope uncertainly across the clearing. The falcon dropped, straight as a stone, to sink its talons into the back of the crouching hare. A brief struggle followed, the hare screaming. There was an almost human quality about that urgent terrible cry. The hare hadn't a chance. A second falcon had now joined in the fray and between them the two birds tore the warm, living animal to pieces, gorging themselves on its flesh. Blood dripping from their beaks and claws, they were recovered by their masters, the hoods slipped once more over their eyes rendering them powerless. The beaters melted back into the bush. The terrible game of waiting began again.

My heart hammered against my ribs. I'd got to get Jules away from this horrible business. He looked dazed with horror, and I saw Khalid had looped Shabo's reins across his arm, so that the little boy could not ride away if the hideous sport became too much for him.

Two little birds like sand grouse were now flushed by the beaters. The falcons swooped. Death came once more, violent and cruel. Something snapped inside my head . . . I could stand no more of this. It wasn't courage but desperation that sent me hurtling across the clearing to where Jules and Khalid sat on their mounts. I reached for Shabo's reins. "Jules is coming home with me!" I shouted hysterically. "This is no fit spectacle for him. It's cruel, revolting . . ."

Khalid bared his teeth. With the bloodstained bird on his shoulder he seemed monstrous, inhuman. "How dare you break in on us like this?" If looks could have killed me I would have fallen dead there and then. "Get out of the way, you stupid Englishwoman!" I saw his hand go instinctively to the unsheathed knife at his belt. "You are ruining our sport, disturbing the birds . . ."

"Let go of Shabo's reins!" I heard myself cry.

The falcon began to dance menacingly on its blood-stained feet. Perhaps Khalid would release it to have a go at me!

"Miss Marlow, I beg you!" He seemed to be trying to introduce a little more courtesy into the exchange. "Will you not see reason? Why do you come here interfering with my effort to teach my young kinsman the manly arts? First you get round the Caid to stop his riding lessons, now you declare falconry to be cruel. So it is. But a man must learn cruelty. Women can only teach cowardliness, softness. You make a milk-fed baby of this boy . . ."

"In England we don't consider cruelty to be manly," I burst out.

"In England!" Khalid spat out the words with venom. "You speak with the tongue of the West, where dwell the effete, the weak, with their so-called civilisation. What is your civilisaton but a rottenness that eats into the heart of free and natural man? You are finished, you English;

352

finished, and you do not yet realise it. It is we of the East who are rising into the ascendancy, because we are strong and proud, untainted by what you call progress but we recognise as decadence." He seemed besde himself, his eyes dilated, his lips flecked with spittle, his head flung back.

"Now leave us!" He flung out his arm dramatically, an unguarded gesture that enabled me to get hold of Shabo's reins.

I looked at Jules. He was green, biting his under-lip. "I'm going to be sick!" he mumbled. And was—violently and heartily. Disgusted, Khalid edged away from us.

"I want to go home!" Jules wailed as soon as he could catch his breath.

"You are going home, darling," I assured him. I turned Sheba about and tugging Shabo along with me, trotted across the clearing. Presenting my back to Khalid was an uncomfortable sensation. I half expected to feel that knife of his whistling after me. But nothing happened. Not a word was spoken as I led poor shattered Jules away. His attack of retching had, I guess, accomplished far more than my impassioned pleas. As we reached the pine woods I heard once more the savage cries of the beaters, the shouts of the huntsman as the falcons were released.

"I didn't like those big birds," Jules whimpered. "I wouldn't have gone with Khalid if I'd known how it would be. He told me he was going to teach me something my father would like me to know about. Something my father had learned himself as a boy. He said the falcons were beautiful, and he wanted me to let one perch on my shoulder, but I was afraid. Then he was cross with me." A sob caught in his throat. "I'm sorry I was sick, Lorraine!"

"It's all right, darling. We'll soon put that right." We had come to one of the flowing streams that criss-crossed the estate. Tethering the horses, I lifted Jules down from his saddle and we knelt by the water, where I helped him to clean his hands and face and poor little stained shirt. I saw that his legs were blistered and red from contact with the saddle. He was wearing his almost non-existent summer shorts—and was quite unsuitably dressed for riding. But Khalid had rushed him off—not caring. I was so angry that for a moment or two I felt as if I were suffocating. But that sort of anger gets one nowhere. It was Jules' safety that was my concern. How was I going to guard him from Khalid's brutality? If only I could feel Greg was still my ally!

"I don't like it here," Jules said, as we rode on. "When can we go home, Lorraine? Back to Tunis."

"In about a week," I hazarded, my heart sinking as I thought of the days stretching ahead.

"Can't we go at once?" Jules gave a long quivering sigh. "Today, Lorraine. I'm afraid of Khalid." The last words were a shamed whisper.

We had reached the stables now. I lifted him down from the pony's back and held him close. "Don't be afraid, darling. I'll take care of you," I promised.

He looked up at me, his small white face full of doubt. Was I any match for Khalid? he seemed to be asking. It was a question I had, with some misgiving, already asked myself.

If only I had turned to Greg for help in this difficult situation! But I shrank from seeking him out, asking favours of him. Every contact with him now was so sharp a pain. So I did nothing, apart from having a good grumble to Tante Mairik. "It needn't happen again," she

354

consoled me. "All you have to do is to keep a stricter eye on Jules' coming and goings. Meanwhile, I'll have a word with the Caid, and ask him to tell Khalid you don't wish to see any more falconry.

"Most boys enjoy it," she added after a moment.

I got the impression that she thought I was being needlessly squeamish, and encouraging Jules to be the same, but I left it at that, hoping for the best. What Tante Mairik thought of my methods of bringing up a small boy I didn't care. If she spoke to the Caid as she had promised, all would be well. Once more I had invoked the sacred laws of hospitality—against which not even Khalid dared to offend.

If only I had guessed how bitterly I was to regret this mood of easy optimism!

CHAPTER ELEVEN

THE next two days passed uneventfully. Denise was well enough to be up playing with the other children—so there was no need for any more visits from Greg. Jules was unwilling to go riding any more, so we gave up our morning canters. I watched the little boy rather anxiously. His nerve seemed to have been broken by the cruelty of the hunting falcons. Looking smaller and paler than ever, he sat about in the courtyard, taking no part in the games in progress. Not even Denise could rouse him. I spoke to Khadija about him as we sat in a shady corner, stitching away at our leather work.

"Poor Jules!" Khadija sympathised. "Khalid has been too rough with him. He is so strong himself he does not understand weakness."

"He's just a big bully," I exploded. "And I don't see his sort of blustering as strength. He's insensitive . . . stupid, and downright sadistic. I believe he likes scaring Jules half out of his life." Perhaps it was not very tactful of me to talk to Khadija like this about her kinsman, but every time I thought of Jules surrounded by those bloodthirsty falcons my blood boiled.

Khadija picked up a skein of gold metal thread and selected a length. "It is not easy for Khalid," she said. "Because he is a second son. It is Raschid, the elder, who really matters in the family. It is Raschid who was sent to an English school and who now holds high rank in the Tunisian Government, while Khalid attends to the fields and orchards. And even here he is not supreme, for it is Mr. Gregson who introduces the clever irrigation schemes and the machinery, and has the last word on the cultivation of the fruit trees and crops."

"So Khalid asserts himself by scaring little boys," I put in, "and ranting against Western civilisation."

Khadija shrugged. "Unfortunately he isn't just ranting. He is a fanatic about Arab nationalism, and sincerely hates European culture, believing it to be harmful." She shook her smooth dark head. "I don't know what will happen to him when the Caid dies. Perhaps he will take his patrimony and live permanently in Algeria, where the political set-up is more to his liking. That would be best for Raschid too. I cannot see the two of them working together."

"You mean Raschid will take over here when his father dies?" I asked.

"He will be responsible, as heir, for the estate. But I can't imagine him giving up his position in the Government to live out here in the wilds."

356

"I expect he will leave it mostly to Mr. Gregson. Elaine said Raschid might form a company to run our affairs, and appoint Mr. Gregson as director-in-chief. I know they have progressive plans, Raschid and Mr. Gregson. They would like to start a small canning and packing factory, for one thing. And of course, Mr. Gregson would have a share in the profits."

She gave me a speculative glance. "He is a very good person, don't you think? And very attractive; one day he will be rich." Her brown eyes widened earnestly. "It is sad to think of him spending his life alone in that little house in the village. Why don't you marry him? Then you could stay here with us all and we could go on with our English lessons."

I laughed, bending over my stitching to hide my heightened colour. "It wouldn't be much use my wanting to marry Mr. Gregson," I pointed out, "unless he fell in love with me."

"But he has done that already," Khadija returned decisively. "I have seen the way he looks at you. That night of the Caid's banquet he could scarcely take his eyes off you. If you ask me, he adores you!"

I shook my head. "No, he doesn't. He thinks I'm a silly frivolous girl—the kind that flirts with every possible presentable male she comes across."

"Because you went out to dinner with the young man who came in the big American car?" Khadija suggested shrewdly.

I nodded.

Khadija gave a gusty sigh. "It is not easy to be a woman when one is European. You go everywhere, unprotected. You are allowed to mix with men before marriage. For us it is all so much simpler. If a marriage seems good it is arranged by the parents. And I think," she added, after a

357

moment's consideration, "this marriage between you and Mr. Gregson would be good. I wish there was someone here who could speak for you in your parents' absence." She peered at me, her needle halted in her hand. "Have you a sufficient dowry?" she enquired.

"Yes," I said, playing her game, and remembering Aunt Vinnie's promised gift. "I have quite a good dowry."

"And you like Mr. Gregson?"

"Of course I do," I laughed.

"Then why do you laugh?" Khadija asked, looking hurt.

"Because you are talking to me as if I were an Arab girl, and dowries and matchmaking was all that is needed. It would take a lot more than that to overcome Mr. Gregson's prejudice against me."

"If it is simply that he is jealous of the handsome boy with the magnificent car that is all to the good. Where there is jealousy there is passion."

"There is also a complete unreasonableness." I tugged viciously at my embroidery thread. "Mr. Gregson, if you want to know, is a typical Scotsman—obstinate, pigheaded, puritanical . . ."

"You could help him with his clinic," Khadija mused, ignoring this outburst. And then, letting her imagination run away with her, "You could have English classes, and other classes as well, where you taught history and mathematics. Jamilia and even my lazy Zoubeida might go to them. And Alya too, for there is an entrance exam to be passed before one can start hospital training. It might be that I would reach matriculation standard at last . . . even go to a university as a late student. If only Khalid were out of the way!"

We were back on safe ground, discussing the tyrannies and tantrums of Khalid. It was amazing and rather frightening how much power he had in the small community, and how undesirably he used it. I wondered if Raschid knew about it. Perhaps when I saw him again I could open his eyes to the true state of affairs in the Caïd's household, where Alya and Khadija were virtually imprisoned by the fanaticism of this too powerful second son.

The next afternoon I put the children to bed as usual for their siesta. It was hotter than ever; the sky was overcast and a strange wailing wind had sprung up, bringing stinging grains of sand into the courtyard. This, Khadija had told me at lunch, was the beginning of a sandstorm. "It is a bad wind that blows with the sand," she said. "It makes everyone restless and ill-tempered, and it goes on and on, sometimes for three days. Like the Mistral in France, it can make people do strange things. Even commit murders!"

A picturesque exaggeration, no doubt, but there was no denying that being bombarded by sharp grains of sand and slowly cooked by the oven-hot wind was trying to the nerves. Unable to settle down with the children, I went back into the living room, where Tante Mairik was dozing on a low divan. Other female members of the family dozed around her. The air was heavy with the scent of the jasmine the women of the harem loved. Stretching myself on the velvet-covered banquette that ran round the room, I tried to join in the communal slumbers, but sleep evaded me.

Here I am, I thought, lying on a velvet cushion in an Oriental harem, and there is nothing glamorous about it, nothing mysterious, it is just deadly dull. Once again I pitied the brilliant and intelligent Khadija for the cramped existence to which she appeared to be doomed. How could she stand it; day after day, year after year, sitting in the courtyard making endless goatskin bags, listening to the trivial chatter of her companions! My thoughts flew to Greg, and to Khadija's flight of fancy yesterday when she had planned my life as his wife. Helping him with a clinic, a school, whole vistas of enlightenment opening up for poor Khadija and her kinswomen. But it would never be. Considering our brief friendship dispassionately, I knew that Greg had never been quite sure of me, never trusted me. I would always be to him the girl he had seen indulging in promiscuous kisses on the *terrasse* of a luxury hotel.

Drearily I went over and over it in my mind. From the beginning I had had bad luck with Greg. Given the slightest shift in circumstances it might have all been so different! It is terrifying to think how easily the whole course of one's life can be altered by small accidents in timing.

If I had never met Del . . . or having met him had not been discovered in his arms by Greg that fateful evening. If the shipment of machinery for El Garza had arrived in Tunis on schedule, so that Greg had not been forced to spend a night at Sidi Akbar waiting for it . . . I would have met him then, for the first time, when I came to El Garza with the children, and there would have been nothing to mar the mutual attraction we felt for each other. Tears forced themselves through my closed eyelids. I got up, goaded by the hopelessness of my thoughts. Sleep would not come to me. Looking enviously at the recumbent forms around me, I stole off into my room to find my embroidery.

Jules' bed was empty.

From beneath the light quilt that covered her, Denise peered at me owlishly. "Where is Jules?" I asked her sharply.

"He has gone away," she said. "He went out through the courtyard door, and told me not to tell anyone. He is going back to Maman."

My heart gave a sickening lurch. "What are you saying, Denise?" I seized hold of the child by the shoulders and had to restrain myself from shaking her. "How can Jules have gone back to Maman? She is away in another country far over the sea."

"I know." Shrugging me off, Denise sat up, pushing the tousled hair out of her eyes. "But Jules is going to wait for her in our flat in Tunis. He's going there in a big train," she ended importantly. "Because he's afraid of Uncle Khalid."

In a terrified flash I remembered how Jules had spoken of the railway between Tunis and El Mersa—that day we had driven with Greg through the orchards and gardens of the Oasis.

"But it's a long way to the train," I said. "How was he going to get there?"

"Along the road," Denise replied literally. "He knows the way to El Mersa, we have often driven there."

"He has no money for the train," I cried, almost as if I was begging her to assure me this terrible story was not true, that Jules was no further away than the toilet across the courtyard.

"He'll tell the man at the station that he is the son of Raschid Ben Akhtal, the ruler, and then the man will let him go on the train without paying. That's what Jules told me." Denise nodded her head impressively.

My heart banged against my ribs. It was all so carefully planned, so convincing. Jules setting off on foot for El Mersa. Poor little boy! Running away . . . and in this terrible weather.

"How long is it since he left?" I asked Denise, but she looked blank, having no idea of time.

361

"Everybody was asleep," was all I could get out of her.

I ran back into the living room. Nobody stirred, soft snores filled the air. If I waited to rouse Tante Mairik and raise the alarm precious moments would be lost. Jules couldn't have got far. If I hurried off down the El Mersa road now I might overtake him.

The gateway of the courtyard was locked, but there was a side door that opened on to the lane that led to the village. This was the way Jules would have got out of the Casa. Following in his steps, I turned right, up the El Mersa road. The sand was already blowing over it, piling up in drifts, blotting out the contours of the countryside. I bent my head before the wind, wishing I had brought a scarf to protect my face. When I got to the stables there was still no sign of Jules. It occurred to me that if I were riding Sheba I would make faster progress. I turned in at the stable yard, thinking that at least I might find Ahmad, who would advise me. It might be impossible to take a horse out in a sandstorm. But Ahmad himself would come with me as soon as he knew the little master was lost. I passed the shabby Land Rover which was one of the estate cars, and came to the harness room, its door shut tightly against the wind and sand. This was where Ahmad spent his time when he was not grooming the horses. I tapped hopefully and heard someone moving about inside.

The door opened, and I found myself face to face with Khalid.

"You!" he exclaimed, looking taken aback. "What in the name of Allah are you doing abroad in this weather?"

I stumbled across the threshold out of the stinging sand and wind and heard the door slam behind me. The room with its array of guns and saddles and harness was in semi-darkness, the light from one oil lamp picking out the highlights on gun-barrels and horse brasses. Khalid in the shadows was a dark robed figure towering over me, his flowing headdress framing his narrow, fine-boned face. Somberly he looked down at me. "What do you want with me?" he asked.

"Nothing," I blurted. "I was looking for Ahmad. Jules has run away." I turned back towards the closed door urgently. "I wondered if I could have Sheba so that I can go after him. But it would be better," I hurried on breathlessly, "if we could go by car." I was crazy enough at that moment to imagine Khalid might take me along the El Mersa road in the Land Rover.

"Jules has run away!" he thundered. "Are you telling me you have permitted that child to go off by himself in this storm? Is this the way you look after my brother's children?"

Stung by this unfair taunt, I shouted at him, "It's your fault he's run away! You've bullied him ever since he arrived here. He's terrified of you, and that falconry business just about finished him. So he's gone to El Mersa."

"A likely story," Khalid sneered. "Why in heaven's name should Jules want to go to El Mersa?"

"To catch a train for Tunis."

"What?" That childish seven-year-old sets off on foot in the middle of a sandstorm to take the train to Tunis? Really, Miss Marlow, what sort of a fool do you take me for?"

"Please!" I cried. "Every moment we delay he'll be further away, and the road is rapidly becoming impassable with heaped-up sand. Do you think we can get through in the Land Rover?"

Khalid's thin lips curled. "So that's it! You want transport to El Mersa. To meet your American fancy man, I suppose. This man with whom you enjoy in public the shameless embraces."

Was there anyone in El Garza who had not witnessed that unfortunate goodbye kiss Del had given me?

"You with your red lips and teasing ways!" Khalid took a step nearer to me, his face contorted with hatred. "I know your kind—the decadent woman of the West with her many lovers. We see you on the films, in the magazines, now you yourself come among us to corrupt our women. Why don't you go back to where you belong and leave us in peace?" His voice had risen hysterically and he had come uncomfortably near, his face thrust into mine. This, I remembered, was the attitude of Arabs when they quarrel. I had seen two workmen at it in one of the plantations, screaming at one another, nose to nose, like a couple of tomcats. I tried to move aside, but Khalid's dark face with its glittering eyes pursued me.

"English whore!" he shouted at me. "Liar! Infidel! Get out!" His hands came down like a vice on my shoulders and before I had time to realise what was happening he had picked me up and flung me against the closed door. So violent was the impact that the door burst open, and I went through it, landing on my face in the road. My head must have hit the bursting fabric of the door as I came through it. The pain was like an explosion of hot stars. Dazed, half blinded by the blood trickling from the wound in my scalp, I staggered to my feet and stumbled along the El Mersa road. Vaguely I wondered if Khalid in his murderous mood would follow me and finish me off. But I was too stunned to feel any fear. My dominant thought was still to find Jules.

I have no idea how far I trudged along that road with the wind whistling in my ears, and the said whirling about me. It was a timeless nightmare in which I moved through pain and darkness. There was no sign of Khalid. Either he had not believed my story about Jules, or he did not care what happened to the child. Certainly he wasn't going to worry about me. If I fell by the way and got buried in a sand drift, so much the better. Supposing that had already happened to Jules? I stood still, my heart failing with this new terror.

"Jules!" I called hopelessly. "Jules, where are you?"

I thought I was having illusions when the small voice answered me. "Lorraine . . . oh, Lorraine!"

In the fog of whirling sand I made out the small dark shape by the roadside, in the lee of a clump of bushes. Here Jules had taken shelter from the storm. The relief of finding him was almost too much. I pressed him to my breast, tears pouring down my cheeks.

His small troubled face looked up at me. "Don't cry, Lorraine. Come with me into the bushes. It's like a little house in here." He tugged at my hand, leading me through the opening into a leafy sanctuary. We crouched on the dry ground, close together. I felt weak and stupid from the wound in my scalp. The bleeding seemed to have stopped, my matted hair making a kind of pad to sop it up. A mess of sand had been added to the blood soaked hair. Jules peered at me anxiously. "You have hurt yourself, Lorraine?"

"I fell on the road," I told him. "I was in such a hurry to find you. Oh, darling, why did you run away? You gave me such a fright."

"I was afraid of Uncle Khalid," Jules said. "I thought I would go to our flat in Tunis and wait for Maman there. But it was bad on the road, I was scared of the sand beating against my face. I didn't know what to do. I was so glad when I heard your voice."

I hugged him tight to me. "You should have told me you were going, darling." It was no moment for reproaches, even if I had felt in a fit state to administer them.

"My hair is full of sand," Jules said. "And my ears."

Of course I had come without a handkerchief. With the corner of my cotton skirt I wiped his face and tried to clean out his ears. But even here inside the bush the sand was reaching us, drifting through the leaves and branches.

"Now we know why the Arabs wear those great enveloping robes and the flowing headdress," I said with an attempt at a laugh. "They are the only things that could keep this sand out."

It was dark inside our bush. I closed my eyes. My head ached abominably. Strange waking dreams flitted through my mind. I seemed to be losing touch with reality. What would Jules do if I became unconscious?

"Don't take me back to the Casa El Garza," I heard him pleading. "I don't like it there. Tante Mairik and Khajida are kind, but Khalid is cruel. I'm scared of him, Lorraine!"

With good reason, I thought grimly. The man was a thug! After what happened today how could we go on living at the Casa? It wasn't only Jules who was afraid of Khalid now. With his insane hatred of me there was nothing he would stop at! Or so it seemed to me, as I crouched in the sand-whipped bush.

366

"Couldn't you take me and Denise back to Tunis?" Jules suggested. "You could stay with us in the apartment there until Maman and Papa come back from America."

"Maybe we could do that," I hazarded. If we ever got out of this bush alive! Sandstorms, Khadija had said, could last as long as three days. Presently night would fall and the coldness of the desert would clamp down on us, adding to our misery. Should we try to make our way back to the Casa? I peered out of the bush, but the fog of sand was thicker than ever, and the whistling of the wind sounded like a lot of screaming Dervishes. I had no idea how far I had come in my search for Jules, nor if I would have the strength to retrace my steps. The loss of blood seemed to have weakened me. My head was hopelessly confused. Could I even find the road if we started out? It was rapidly disappearing beneath the drifts of sand.

"Is it soon going to stop raining sand?" Jules asked in a small scared voice, as I settled down beside him once more.

"I hope so!" I said weakly. "Meanwhile we're quite safe in here."

But were we? I could hear the interminable rustle and hiss of the sand piling up on the weather side of our shelter. In a matter of hours we might be buried beneath a sand-dune. How long would it be before somebody came to look for us? If Khalid found out my story was true and that Jules was missing, he would surely organise a search. Though he might not care what became of me, the safety of his small nephew would be a different matter. But would he return to the Casa? Wasn't it more likely he would remain in the shelter of the harness room, waiting for the storm to abate?

367

That left Tante Mairik. In due course she would miss us, and question Denise, who was scarcely to be relied on to tell the truth in an emergency. If she thought Jules had done wrong in running away she might try to cover up for him—say he had gone with Lorraine to Uncle Greg's house...

It was increasingly an effort to think it all out. Inertia took possession of me. My senses began to swim. As long as I could I resisted the oblivion that awaited me. But it was no good. I couldn't hold my head up any longer. There was a moment or two of frightening vertigo, then blackness engulfed me, and I knew no more.

CHAPTER TWELVE

I DON'T know how long it was before Jules forced me to rouse myself. Vaguely at first, then more clearly. I heard his frightened voice calling my name, and felt him tugging at my skirt. "What is it, darling?" I managed to whisper. My mouth was stiff and dry and full of sand. It was almost dark now, and bitterly cold.

"I was asleep," Jules whimpered. "Then I woke up and you were making funny snoring noises and I couldn't wake you up. There's blood on your face, and I thought you were dead."

"Oh, no," I mumbled stupidly. "I was only dozing." I put my hand to my cheek and felt the warm blood trickling down. The wound in my scalp must have opened again. The sand drifted right inside our bush now, and was up over my knees. We ought to get out of this, I realised. Keep moving, But I didn't know if I could stand up.

"I think we'd better go back to Tante Mairik, just for tonight," Jules said in a quavery tone.

"It's too far to walk to El Mersa. Why does the sand keep blowing in on us? I don't like it, Lorraine!"

"It's a sandstorm," I explained dully. "When the wind blows from the south it comes over the Sahara . . ." My voice trailed away. Despair threatened to engulf me. Every time I moved there was that deadly vertigo. I wanted to sink back into the bush and let the elements have their way with me. How long, I wondered, did it take to die in a sandstorm? Numbed with cold, we would lie there sleeping, until the sand piled over us, suffocating us. Then Jules pressed close to me and I could feel his thin little body trembling with fear. "Can't we go back to Tante Mairik?" he wailed.

"Of course we can, darling," I assured him, with a confidence I was far from feeling. But I must fight for Jules' life, if not for my own. A small spark of courage came back to me. Slowly, I struggled to my feet, pushing aside the hampering sand. As we came out of our shelter the wind hit us full force. Sand clogged our footsteps, blinded our eyes. I wasn't sure any longer in which direction El Garza lay. What with the dusk and the flying sand I couldn't see more than a few inches in front of me.

Bowing my aching head, I dragged Jules along, both of us silent with misery. It was useless, I thought; we would just stagger on like this until we dropped. It would have been better to die in the shelter of the bush. My head swam, the ground tilted under my feet. I was going to fall. I must not fall! The light flashing in my eyes seemed to be all part of the vertigo that I could no longer resist.

Then the noise of an engine reached me above the whine of the storm. It was a car. A jeep.

I ran forward, my arms outstretched, into the ray of the headlights. The jeep stopped. A man got out of it. Greg! I slumped against the radiator, my legs crumpling beneath me. "Jules," I gasped. "He's just behind me on the road. Get Jules!"

After that I didn't know any more.

The next thing I remember is finding myself lying on the big bed in the white walled room at El Garza. Tante Mairik and Khadija were bending over me, doing something to the wound on my head. Greg was there too, standing at the foot of the bed looking down at me. Tante Mairik had a blood-stained sponge in her hand, but I couldn't see her very clearly. Everything around me wavered and shifted as though I were seeing through water.

"Jules?" I forced myself to whisper. "Is Jules all right?"

"He is fine," Tante Mairik assured me. "Playing with the children in the other room. Don't you worry about Jules." She moved aside, and it was Greg bending over me now.

"How did you hurt your head, Lorraine? Try to remember." His grey eyes were full of compassion. Because I had been hurt. If I were well and on my feet those same eyes would be looking at me with cold disapproval, even dislike. Tears I couldn't hold back rolled down my cheeks.

"Everything is so horrible!" I sobbed. "Nobody in this place believes a word I say. You . . . Khalid. You think I'm cheap, empty-headed, and Khalid called me the most terrible names . . . he told me to leave El Garza, clear out . . ."

"When was this?" Greg's voice was fierce. I shrank back into the pillows.

"In the stables, during the storm. I was looking for Jules."

370

"Did he touch you . . . strike you? Is it Khalid who is responsible for this nasty gash on your scalp?"

I couldn't answer him. Hysterical sobs choked me. I only wished he would go away and leave me to die in peace. Tante Mairik put her arms around me, soothing me as if I were a child. "Husha, husha," she murmured comfortingly. And then sternly to Greg. "You shouldn't have questioned her, Mr. Gregson. She's not fit for it yet. You've upset her properly, and now the wound is bleeding again."

"It will have to be stiched," I heard Greg say. "It's no use our messing about with it. I'm going into El Mersa to fetch a doctor."

"What? In this storm?" Kradija protested. They went out of the room arguing about it. Tante Mairik took a cup from the bedside table and held it to my lips. It was filled with a liquid that tasted of honey and lemon. There must have been some native soporific in it as well, for I had hardly finished it when an irresistible drowsiness stole over me and I fell into a deep sleep. Even the coming of the doctor, I don't know how many hours later, didn't wholly rouse me. It must have been night-time, for the light over my bed was full on, dazzling my eyes. Dimly I knew that Greg was with the doctor. I could feel them both working over me, cutting chunks of matted hair away, swabbing the head wound; there was the rattle of forceps in a kidney tray, the pricking of the needle as the stitches were put in place. But it was all very far away. There was no pain, just the comfortable drowsiness. I don't remember the end of that session. I never saw Greg and the doctor go.

It must have been much later in the night that I was aware of Khadija sitting beside me. There

371

was only a small nightlight in the room now. Khadija's eyes were closed. I was glad she was having a nap and I wouldn't have disturbed her for the world, though my head was throbbing and my mouth was dry. When I fell asleep again I had terrifying nightmares, mostly about Khalid. Over and over again I was shut in that dark harness room with him, reliving the terrible moments when he had denounced me and flung me against the door.

After that there must have been some days and nights of fever. I don't remember very much about them, only that the doctor appeared at intervals, a spruce young Arab in European dress. Tante Mairik and Khadija nursed me, and the hours slid by in a timeless stream.

Then one morning I woke feeling cool and relaxed. The fever had gone. I was myself again. Early sunlight filled the room and there was a smell of newly kindled wood fires from the kitchen across the courtyard. Someone had put a pitcher filled with flowering jasmine on the bedside table. I thought I had never seen anything so beautiful as the pale waxen flowers.

I turned my head slowly on the pillow, conscious of the heavy bandage bound around my brow. Khadija was sitting in a wicker armchair beneath the window, her head lolling forward on her breast. The moment I spoke her name she was wide awake.

"What day is it?" I asked in a voice that came out rather weak and croaky.

"Friday," she answered. It had been Tuesday when I went in search of Jules.

Khadija came over and peered down at me anxiously. "Are you better, Lorraine?"

"I feel wonderful," I told her. "Poor Khadija, you look so tired." I studied the gentle oval face

372

under its sweep of dark hair. "How many nights have you been sitting up with me?"

"Tante Mairik and I took it in turns," she said. "And often Greg would join us, to watch over you for a while." Her brown eyes sought mine earnestly. "He has been terribly upset about you, Lorraine."

Pain twisted in my heart. "That was kind of him, but he is a humane person and would hate to see anybody suffering. I don't think I'm really very important to him."

Khadija sat down on the edge of the big bed. "Oh, but you are so wrong. If you could have seen the rage he flew into when I told him how Khalid had ill-treated you."

I put my hand to my bandaged head. "Khalid?" I echoed stupidly. "How did you know he had ill-treated me?"

"You told me about it one night when I awoke you out of a frightening dream, in which you kept calling his name. We had been wondering how you came by that gash on the head. Just being out in the sandstorm wouldn't have accounted for it."

"I came across him in the harness room when I was looking for Jules." I shuddered at the recollection. "He seemed to go out of his mind, when I asked him for help, picking me up and flinging me against the harness room door with such force that it flew open, splintering, and I was thrown through it on to the road."

Khadija nodded. "That's more or less what came out in your delirium. When Khalid was faced with it, he didn't deny it. In fact he seemed proud of what he had done and poured out his hatred of you, mixing it up with his dislike of all ideas and people from Western Europe." She gave a deep sigh. "We have had days of quarrelling over it all—Mr. Gregson and Khalid going for one another. There might well have been murder if the Caid had not intervened!"

"You mean that Greg stuck up for me?" I exclaimed.

"Stuck up?" Khadija queried, floored by my slang.

"Defended me."

"Oh, yes, he defended you all right. He wouldn't let Khalid say a word against you, and the more he praised you, the angrier Khalid became. They were making such a commotion over it in the outer courtyard one day that the Caid sent for them to find out what it was all about. And it was Greg's version of the story he accepted. He was furious with Khalid for the foul things he said about you."

"What sort of things?" I asked.

"Oh, you know . . ." Khadija looked embarrassed. "That you had been trying to get into El Mersa to meet some man, when the sandstorm overtook you, and that you had had the nerve to ask him to give you a lift in the Land Rover. He said he had been quite right in punishing you. According to Moslem law you ought to have been killed. But it was all pretty thin, and when the Caid asked Khalid if you had told him Jules was lost in the storm, Khalid couldn't deny it. He had to admit he just sat there in the harness room, making no attempt to find out if what you had said about being in search of Jules was true."

"But Greg came to look for us," I put in.

"That was because we missed you and Jules soon after the siesta hour and knew you wouldn't have gone out in the storm unless something was terribly wrong. Tante Mairik questioned Denise and she told us Jules had run away because of Uncle Khalid's cruelty and that you had gone to find him."

"I think it was that part of the story that most infuriated the Caid—that Khalid had bullied Jules and driven him away. He threatened to disinherit Khalid, but in the end it was arranged he should have his patrimony if he took himself off and went to live with his kinsfolk across the Algerian border, a country much more suited to his political beliefs. He went only yesterday, taking his servants, his camels and his share of the family fortune."

"What an upheaval!" I exclaimed. "And all on my account. I'm sorry to have brought so much trouble to this household."

"But it is much better so," Khadija returned cheerfully. "Khalid has been growing more and more troublesome lately, trying to thwart every improvement introduced by Mr. Gregson, of whom he has always been jealous. Perhaps now we shall have some peace . . . Jamilia may even go to a university, and Alya to her hospital training. Even I may be allowed to spread my wings a little, go into El Mersa occasionally and attend educational classes. There is a new Institute of Further Education there . . ." Her eyes shone. "But we have talked quite enough," she said guiltily. "I am forgetting what an invalid you are. I'll go and get you some breakfast."

Left alone, I lay listening to the morning sounds in the courtyard, thinking about Greg. Did his repudiation of Khalid's slurs on my character mean that he really believed in me? Or was it because I was a fellow Briton he had stood up for me? If he and Khalid had always been at loggerheads, as Khadija said, this final quarrel had no doubt included many old scores. I closed my eyes, feeling weak and forlorn and utterly depressed, just in the mood for a good cry. It was the inevitable depression of convalescence, I told myself. After I had

375

had something to eat I would feel better. But breakfast, when it came, consisted of the inevitable mint infusion and a bowl of savoury broth. All very nourishing, no doubt. But how I longed for a cup of heartening English tea, strong and brown, and laced with cream!

Khadija watching over me anxiously, persuaded me to finish the last drop of broth. "You've got to get some colour into your cheeks before Mr. Gregson sees you," she said. "After all, now that he is going to marry you . . ."

I sat up in bed with a start, forgetting all about my wounds and weakness. "What did you say?"

Khadija gazed at me, her earnest brown eyes enormous. "It is all arranged, Lorraine. I spoke to the Caid and he told him you were willing to marry Mr. Gregson and that you had a suitable dowry."

"You told him that?" I could hardly believe my ears.

Khadija gave a self-satisfied nod. "He was delighted. He has always been afraid Mr. Gregson would be lonely here, and go back to his own country. But now that you have come, and he is willing to marry you, he will not be alone any more."

I sank back on to my pillows, hardly knowing whether to laugh or to cry. Poor Greg, what on earth had the Caid been saying to him? I could imagine him humouring the old man along, even while tactfully evading his preposterous suggestion. "But, Khadija," I gasped, "that's not the way marriages come about in my country. It was very kind of you to try to arrange my affairs for me, but I'm afraid you misunderstand Mr. Gregson's attitude. He must have been terribly embarrassed when the Caid spoke to him about me. You see, he doesn't even like me very much;

376

he wouldn't dream of marrying me. He thinks I'm a silly, lightheaded girl . . ."

"Lightheaded?" Khadija queried, once more baffled by my colloquialisms.

"A flirt," I explained. "A coquette." Tears threatened. I choked down a lump in my throat.

"Oh, but you are wrong," Khadija assured me earnestly. "So wrong, Lorraine. You'll see!"

"How are the children?" I asked, firmly changing the subject.

"They are very well. Alya has been caring for them, and Zoubeida also. Yesterday there was a letter for Tante Mairik from their mother. She will be coming back to Tunis by the end of next week. She wrote to you, too, by the way. I was almost forgetting to give it to you!"

I read it while she went away to fetch a basin of hot water for my morning toilette.

Elaine wrote kindly. They were flying home on Thursday, and the following day she would drive out to El Mersa to collect me and the children. "I hope you will stay with us in Tunis for a few days before you return to England," she ended.

So that was it. My stay at El Mersa was almost over. A week in which to recover from my head injury and get on my feet. Another week perhaps with the Ben Akhtals in Tunis. Then the journey home. Why did I feel that *this* was my home— this flowering oasis set in the wilderness? In less than a fortnight I would be back in England, my holiday in Tunisia no more than a memory . . . and a heartache.

Khadija appeared with the hot water. It was a luxury to wash. I tried to make myself look a little less repulsive. In the mirror Khadija held for me my face was small and white beneath the turban-like bandage. Make-up only made matters worse, so I wiped it off and gave up the struggle.

It didn't really matter how I looked, I told myself. The visitors I was likely to have would not be critical. Tante Mairik, the children . . . I wouldn't let myself think about Greg. It was possible that now I was better he would not be permitted to enter the harem . . . nor would he want to, especially if he knew Khadija had told me all that nonsense about the Caid trying to arrange my marriage to him. On the whole, nis absence would be a relief, I persuaded myself.

It was quite a social morning. Tante Mairik and the children greeted me rapturously. Denise and Jules were a little shy at first because I had been ill and inaccessible, nor was the bloodstained bandage on my brow exactly reassuring. But they were soon chattering away, clambering over the big bed, telling me all they had been doing during the last few days. Jules, I was relieved to see, looked none the worse for his adventures in the sandstorm.

Jamilia and Alya and Zoubeida arrived, bringing bunches of roses and jasmine. Fatmah came and Sato, in fact the entire household, including the Caid, who appeared after the Holy Day ceremonies in his resplendent robes. But no Greg. Every time the door opened I looked up hopefully, then looked away again, disappointed, telling myself it didn't matter. I wasn't really expecting him.

It was late in the afternoon when the young Arab doctor called. Well pleased with my progress, he told me I could get up for an hour or two the following day. We bade one another a polite farewell. There would be no need for him to visit me again. He had taken out the stitches and removed the cumbersome bandage, replacing it with a neat adhesive dressing. Now my hair was revealed, dead and dull, and stiff with sand from the storm. The fact that it had been cut away on one side, from the temple, didn't improve matters. I could now earn my living as a scarecrow, I decided gloomily.

For a few minutes the passionate longing to have my hair washed and set swamped every other consideration. But I'd have to wait at least until I got into Tunis. Which meant I'd be forced to face Greg as I was. For presumably I would see him before I left, if only to say goodbye, and thank him for having come to my rescue when I was lost with Jules in the whirling sand.

When Khadija presently brought me a lemon drink, I asked her if she thought she could possibly get some of the sand out of my hair. She began to brush it, but she had to go so gently for fear of harming the scalp wound that it didn't do much good. "Perhaps we could contrive a dry shampoo," I said. We were discussing this suggestion earnestly when Greg walked in. Khadija, looking coy and conspiratorial, instantly vanished, leaving us alone. I was glad it was dusk so that Greg could not see what a battered object I had become.

"Would you like the light on?" he asked.

"Oh, no!" I answered quickly. "It would hurt my eyes." I covered them with my hands, longing to hide myself, my whole being shrinking from the pain of this contact with Greg. Had the Caid really talked to him of marrying me, repeating what Khadija had told him—that I was more than willing? Waves of hot shame washed over me.

I felt Greg seating himself on the edge of the bed. Gently he pulled my hands away from my eyes. "Look at me, Lorraine!" he said softly.

I lifted my eyes to his thin brown face, my heart melting within me. "Oh, Greg!" was all I could say. The weak tears threatened, and I tried to blink them away. If only I could think of some

379

jaunty remark that would cover my misery and confusion.

But to my astonishment I saw that there were tears in Greg's eyes, too, as he looked down at me, taking in the full horror of my appearance. "You poor little soul!" he exclaimed. "You *have* had a pasting! And it's all my fault."

"Your fault?" I echoed.

"If I hadn't been such a beast to you recently you would have turned to me for help when Jules disappeared in the sandstorm, wouldn't you? In fact, if I had kept in close touch, as I ought to have done, I might have been able to prevent that unfortunate session with the hunting falcons, and the kid wouldn't have run away at all."

"You mustn't reproach yourself, Greg," I murmured, hardly recognising him in this penitent frame of mind. I wished he would not keep holding my hands. The sense of his nearness was disturbing me.

"It isn't as if I didn't know what a brute Khalid can be," he went on. "Though I didn't quite realise how insanely he hated you. Anything might have happened to you that day in the harness room!" His grey eyes flashed. For a moment he looked quite murderous.

"Oh, well, it's all over now," I said lightly, giving my hands a little tug. But Greg only held on to them the more tightly.

"Can you ever forgive me, Lorraine?" he asked humbly. "I wish I could take back the cruel things I've said to you."

"Do you mean about my friendship with Del Lloyd?" I thought of the way he had gone for me the day Denise was ill, and he had walked with me from the clinic. For a moment I could not meet his glance. "I suppose you were right to be angry with me," I said dully, "since you thought I'd lied to you, pretending to be finished with Del, and then writing to him, asking him to come to El Garza and take me out. At least, that's how it must have seemed to you."

"I don't think I ever really believed you had been as dishonest as that," Greg put in quickly. "I knew in my inmost heart there must be some explanation for the rather odd way the fellow turned up. But I was so fiendishly jealous when he arrived at the Casa demanding to see you as if he had every right in the world to claim you that I couldn't think straight. Then when he said he had had a letter from you that very morning . . ."

"But he hadn't," I began hurriedly. "I never wrote to Del Lloyd in my entire life."

"I realise that now." Greg lifted my hands and pressed them against his heart. The smoky grey eyes smiled down at me very tenderly. "You were pretty talkative in your fever, Lorraine, did you know?"

I shook my head, once more covered with confusion. "Things people say in delirium are not to be taken seriously."

"Oh, yes, they are!" The smile turned into a mischievous grin. "If only you knew how many times you asked for me . . . and how touchingly you greeted me when I appeared."

"Oh, Greg, I'm so ashamed!" I mumbled. This time I managed to get my hands away and thankfully buried my hot face in them.

"Darling, I'm the one who ought to be ashamed," Greg was saying incredibly. "I've treated you so badly. But I love you, Lorraine. If only you knew how much!"

I dropped my hands to stare at him in amazement. He had called me 'darling,' said he loved me. For a moment I could not take it in.

"From the first I've felt you belonged to me," he went on. "It began way back that day I rescued you from the shoeshine boy in Tunis. Which was quite crazy, for I didn't imagine I had a hope of ever seeing you again—a tourist in a side-walk café filled with tourists. But there was something about you that went straight to my heart . . . the clear, no-nonsense way you looked up at me; and you were so concerned about the little Arab boys and their welfare. I liked that. There was a strength about you; you seemed very sure of yourself, and yet very feminine, very sweet. I went off about my business, wishing I could get to know you, telling myself I was a fool . . . that I had as much chance cultivating your acquaintance as a snowflake in hell. Then fate took a hand. The shipment of farm machinery I had come to Tunis to collect didn't arrive, and I decided to spend a night at Sidi Akbar, with the Ben Akhtals. Where I found you . . ."

"In the arms of another man," I added shamefacedly.

"Do you wonder I was a bit shaken?"

"It was all a mistake, Greg. I thought for a while that I was in love with Del, but I wasn't sure. Then suddenly, the day I met you in Tunis, I realised I could never marry Del."

"Because you knew I was your man!" Greg pronounced triumphantly. "That came out in the delirium, too. The whole shoe-shine episode and the way you felt about the rough-looking character sitting at the next table, reading a London newspaper."

"Was there anything I didn't give away?" I whispered in mortification.

Greg beamed down at me. "Very little. And what you left out Khadija and the Caid supplied." His grin widened. "You know, I suppose, that

382

according to Arab law we are already betrothed, you and I. The Caid, constituting himself your guardian, has arranged it all. Didn't Khadija tell you?"

I nodded, too overcome for speech.

The laughter went out of Greg's grey eyes. "Darling Lorraine, we didn't really need the Caid!" He slid an arm about me, gathering me close to him so that I was leaning against his breast, my scarecrow head on his shoulder. It felt very strong and comforting. He stroked my terrible hair and then with the utmost gentleness put his lips to the adhesive plaster on my brow. "You're such a plucky fighter, Lorraine! Made of the stuff of pioneers. Do you remember telling me once that you were sure I would find a girl who wouldn't mind sharing my rather odd life in the desert?"

"I remember, Greg."

"Do you think I've found her?" he asked softly.

"Yes, Greg, I'm sure you have!"

He tilted my face towards him and kissed me, gently at first, and then with increasing purpose. It was like the quenching of a great thirst, like dawn after darkness . . . peace after storm. For a while after that we did not speak. I rested in his arms, in a mindless haven, beyond thought, even beyond desire, gradually coming to terms with the miracle that had befallen me. It was amazing, after the first astounding impact, how natural it all seemed!

It was Greg who broke the silence. "I want to marry you, Lorraine. How soon can it be?"

I dragged myself back to a world where there were times, dates, family obligations. "I'd have to go home," I mused. "Tell my parents . . ."

"I'll come with you," Greg planned eagerly, "and ask for your hand in a way that would satisfy even the Caid.

"Oh, Lorraine, I cant believe it! It's all so wonderful!" We kissed again. Those first enchanted moments of our love . . . perhaps there would never again be anything quite like them.

It was almost dark now in the whitewashed room, lit only by the wavering lamps in the courtyard. Somewhere out there a voice was singing to the accompaniment of a lute. Plaintive Arab music, set to the words of a song that was faintly familiar.

"We're being serenaded," Greg said. "I bet this is Khadija's doing. She's very romantic about us."

Softly he began to sing the words of the old Arab love song that I had first heard the night of the Caid's banquet.

"Is it Lebanon cedars, or purpled fruits
    Of the honeyed southron air,
Spikenard, saffron, roses of Sharon,
    Cinnamon, calamus, myrrh?

"A bed of spices, a fountain of waters,
    Or the wild white wings of a dove,
Now when the winter is over and gone,
    Is it these that should please my love?"

384

HONEYMOON HOLIDAY

Honeymoon Holiday

"You like being disappointed in people," Marnie accused him. "It's easier to judge and despise than to love and understand. You'd do anything rather than submit to love. It's too risky for you!"

Very unwisely, Marnie had fallen in love with the disillusioned Conte di Valetta—a man prepared to enter a loveless marriage with a woman whose fortune would restore his ancestral estate.

Could she break through his wall of reserve before it was too late?

CHAPTER ONE

MARNIE wished her seat was nearer a window as they flew over the Alps. All she could see when the wing-tips tilted was an occasional snow-clad peak against a vivid blue sky. In the centre of a row of three, she had a fat businessman on her right, blocking most of the limited window space, and on her left, a younger man with his nose buried in a magazine called *Oggi*. That was Italian for "To-day". Marnie thought of the winter evenings she had spent at her local polytechnic attending an Italian class, hoping to pick up enough of the language to make this holiday a rewarding experience. It helped to be able to speak a little of the native tongue, even if you *were* on your honeymoon.

Her honeymoon! She flashed a wry glance at the young man sitting where Glenn might have been. But the sigh she gave was more of relief than regret. Because she was free of Glenn Wayland; free after three years of secret doubts alternating with periods of feverish happiness. The doubts had become more frequent, the spells of happiness more forced. The corrosive acid of their quarrels had bitten little by little into her love, until there was nothing left but the nagging suspicion that in marrying Glenn she would be making the most ghastly mistake of her life. An uncomfortable suspicion she had refused to face during her last busy days at St Margaret's Hospital, where she worked as a staff nurse. Things would sort themselves out once they were married, she told herself. Long engagements were notoriously difficult.

In the beginning of course it had all been wonderful. She had met Glenn at the local tennis club and had fallen in love with his crisp good looks and masterly air, which she had put down to strength of character, only to discover that it was compounded of self-conceit and a tendency towards bullying. If you didn't agree with him he lost his temper. And in the end they had disagreed over so many things: for instance, the sort of place they were going to live in after they were married; Marnie had plumped for buying a house, but Glenn would only consider a rented flat. He didn't want to be tied down to a mortgage, he said. But if she went on working they could afford a mortgage, Marnie pointed out. Glenn squared his shoulders and declared he would never permit his wife to go out to work, a point of view, Marnie had ventured, that was surely slightly out of date. But not nearly so out of date, Glenn retorted, as Marnie's insistence on a church wedding, complete with white veil and bridesmaids and all the frills. She and her family were so hopelessly "square", while he, the budding young scientist, was the great free soul, throwing church services and their superstitions overboard. Besides, he had added, a register office wedding was so much less costly.

Was he going to be mean about money? Marnie was a bit taken aback when he suggested she might like to pay her share of their honeymoon expenses. Yet he didn't want her to go on working so that she could contribute towards a mortgage on their home. It didn't quite fit in. But then nothing about Glenn quite fitted. A creature of contradictions. Split personality; the glib term, half understood, flashed through Marnie's mind as she gazed absently at the tilting wing-tip. Perhaps Glenn was just plain spoiled—the only son of a widowed mother, accustomed to getting his own way in every least little thing. Cosseted, adored, he had seen himself as the great big male, but encountering the demands of adult life, he couldn't quite stand up to them. Confronted with the signing of a large cheque at the travel agent's, he had drawn back in dismay. So Marnie had paid the half of it.

And having paid for her holiday she had decided to go ahead with it when their engagement came to grief on the very eve of the wedding. Maybe it was cold-blooded of her, but her mother had understood. It wasn't going to be easy at home with the presents to return to their senders, the wedding invitations to cancel, and Glenn's mother living only a quarter of a mile away.

"The change of scene will do you good," her mother had said. "You go, and get as much as you can out of your holiday in the rather unfortunate circumstances, and good luck to you!" There was a hint of defiance in her tone. She hadn't altogether liked Glenn.

"You're sure to meet young people you can chum up with at San Paolo," she had encouraged. "So many English folk go abroad these days." She would see to the presents and the cancelled invitations, she promised, and Francie and Sue, Marnie's sisters, would help. By the time she returned all the muddle would be cleared up, and Glenn would be the other side of the world. In Australia.

Marnie closed her eyes, and the handsome face she had fallen in love with floated before her, the small well-cut features, the deceptively melting blue eyes—that could go flint-hard when occasion demanded. The sort of good looks that had a boyish appeal. At twenty-six he could have been nineteen. The trouble with Glenn, Marnie mused, is that he has never grown up.

She shrugged the thought of him away impatiently. She wasn't going to spend her lone honeymoon holiday mooning about her lost bridegroom. That's for sure! she promised herself vigorously. She was paying her first visit to Italy and she was going to use every moment of her time profitably. Resolutely she opened the guide book lying on her lap. San Paolo : there were miles of silver sand, she read, bordering a deep blue sea. In the Old Town she would find Roman remains and Renaissance buildings. A short distance away was the Rubicon, the river made famous in history by Julius Caesar, who in crossing it achieved the most decisive victory of his career. The bridge that still spanned it had been built according to the guide book in 186 B.C. Marnie imagined herself standing on it with feelings of awe for its antiquity and associations. She would take a colour snap of it on her new camera, a wedding present from her father, which wouldn't have to be returned. I'm not going to be lonely, she told herself gallantly. I'll be too busy seeing and doing interesting things.

"Ladies and gentlemen," said a pleasant voice over the tannoy, "may I have your attention, please." They were approaching their destination, the voice continued, but owing to an accident on the runway of the airport they would not be able to land for some time and would be cruising around waiting for the all clear. The announcement was repeated in Italian and French, and an ominous silence ensued. Apprehension could be felt, like a current of cold air running through the cabin. The air hostesses, there were two of them, went up and down the aisle between the seats offering reassurances. As the first hostess drew near, the young man at Marnie's side spoke to her in Italian, obviously questioning her, but the words came so quickly Marnie couldn't follow them. Nor could she understand what the hostess said in reply. When she had gone on her way the young man turned to Marnie, as if sensing her uneasiness. "It is nothing to be alarmed about," he told her in his slightly accented English.

"What was the accident?" Marnie asked.

The plane going in ahead of them had had to land with its wheels out of action and it had torn up the surface of the runway, her neighbour explained. Nobody had been hurt, he added consolingly. He was good-looking in an austere way, not an English type, but not exactly Italian either ... that thick fairish hair and the hazel-grey eyes with the fine lines etched about them giving his age away. He could have been in his middle thirties. He wore countrified tweeds, well cut but shabby, and his tie was unquestionably old school and very English.

"Do we have to wait until the runway is repaired?" Marnie enquired ingenuously.

The young man smiled. "It's not quite so simple as that, I'm afraid. Repairing the runway would take too long. So we are going to have to land on an emergency strip which is a bit on the short side, and we are cruising around to use up our fuel in case there are ... difficulties." He hesitated over the last word.

Marnie went a trifle pale. "You mean we might crash-land?"

"It is a remote possibility."

And a crash landing could mean fire. Hence the using up of the fuel.

"How long shall we have to cruise around?" Marnie asked.

"About an hour, the stewardness has just told me."

Marnie subsided in her seat. She felt very small and lonely all of a sudden. A possible crash-landing ahead of them, and a whole hour in which to think about it. Her lively imagination got to work. She felt sick and cold. Why had she come on this trip? If only she had stayed at home and faced up to the dreary business of picking up the pieces of her cancelled wedding. But she hadn't. Half angry, half defiant, wholly humiliated, she had run away . . . and this was what had come of it!

"Not to worry!" her companion rallied her. Had he been watching her, reading her thoughts?

"We have a good British plane," he said, "and an excellent pilot. I've flown with him before."

"Do you often make this journey, then?" Marnie asked.

"I was at Oxford some years ago, and more recently I have been attending a short course in agriculture at one of your technical colleges, gleaning some knowledge about dairy herds and methods of breeding."

So he was in some kind of farming. That went with the tweeds.

"And you?" he was asking now. "Have you flown very much?"

"Quite a bit," Marnie said, thinking of the various holidays abroad with her sisters, or hospital friends. "But this is my first journey on my own," she admitted.

He appeared to lose interest, returning to his magazine. To keep her mind off her fears Marnie studied his profile. He had a good strong face, but there was an aloofness in his expression, as if he were accustomed to his own solitary thoughts; and there was something about his sensitive, tightly compressed mouth that suggested bitterness. Yet when he turned to her again presently his smile held a singular sweetness. "Would you care for a paper to read?" he asked, reaching for his briefcase. "I have some London dailies here and a magazine or two..."

She shook her head. "Thanks a lot, but I don't think I could concentrate."

· The hazel-grey eyes regarded her appraisingly. "You aren't feeling nervous, I hope? There is really no need." There was a note of warm concern in his voice.

"I can't help being a bit scared," Marnie confessed. "All this circling round and round... and an emergency landing at the end of it. Anyone with imagination..." She broke off to flash him a challenging glance.

He shrugged. "One is faintly uneasy, perhaps."

She liked him the better for the admission.

"But there is no real cause for alarm," he stressed again. "I'm certain our pilot can handle the situation."

But supposing he couldn't? Marnie had a swift, terrible vision of the great plane they were sitting in turning tail over nose on that treacherous runway, and bursting into flames.

The silence in the cabin became oppressive. You could sense the mounting tension. A child burst into loud sobbing and refused to be comforted. Marnie glanced at her wrist watch. Would this hour never end? The leaden moments crept on. She caught a glimpse of blue sea beneath the wing-tip and saw that the fat business man was callously asleep.

"We are flying above the Adriatic coastline," the young man told her. "Just about over San Paolo, at a rough guess."

"San Paolo? That's where I'm going to stay," Marnie volunteered. (If this nightmare flight came to a happy ending!) The young man received this snippet of information in silence. He wasn't, it seemed, interested in her destination.

The plane banked, turning inland again. A light flashed above the door leading to the flight deck. They were coming in to land, a disembodied voice announced. The stewardesses hurried up and down the aisle, making sure seat belts were securely fastened. Marnie closed her eyes. How much would one feel of that violent impact before the world ended in a roar of flame? She could feel the plane losing height. The nerves in her stomach tightened. She clenched her hands on her lap.

"Steady on!" her seat companion whispered in her ear. He took one of the clenched hands and held it firmly in his own. She could feel his palm, cool and dry. The strong, gentle fingers curled about her fingers conveyed a sense of assurance. It was quite clear he wasn't in the least nervous. His calmness communicated itself to her. She looked up at him, and met his glance. It was curiously whimsical, wholly tender. He was sorry for her and her feminine panic, enjoying "protecting" her. The look between them deepened, and for a moment there was something more than whimsical tenderness in the clear grey eyes, a flash of illumination, almost of recognition. Though how could that be? They had never seen one another before. Yet something in Marnie's heart acknowledged that look of recognition. She felt strangely at home sitting there with her hand confidingly in his. They stayed like that until the landing was safely accomplished, with only the merest of bumps. And suddenly life was ordinary again, safe and secure. The tense atmosphere vanished. Voices chattered in relief as the great machine taxied slowly to a halt.

"*Bene!*" the young man breathed. A blessing, or a thanksgiving? He turned to gather up his books and papers. When he stood up Marnie saw that he was tall. "Will you be all right?" he asked her casually. "Is somebody meeting you?"

"Oh, yes, thank you," Marnie said quickly.

He nodded, apparently relieved to be done with responsibility for her welfare. She thanked him for his moral support at a difficult moment. He murmured a preoccupied disclaimer. His mind fixed on the urgencies of arrival he had, she felt, already forgotten her. With a formal bow, he was gone, striding across the tarmac. She did not see him at the Customs barrier and a moment later she recognised the uniform of the travel agency official who would see her safely to the coach that was to take her to San Paolo.

It was a long drive. To her dismay, she dozed, missing her first glimpse of the Italian countryside. But it had been a tiring day; the early departure from her home at Hurstleigh in Sussex, then the excitement of the flight, the nervous strain of the emergency landing. The emotional strain of that last week at home was also taking its toll. Her dramatic break with Glenn, and the subsequent domestic upheavals. She was tired body, soul and spirit. It would be good to be alone for a while, she thought. Swimming, sunbathing, eating, sleeping. For the first few days she would leave sightseeing alone.

It was late afternoon when the coach swung into a long avenue of palm trees and came to a halt. "San Paolo!" shouted the driver, and the passengers began to disembark. Following in their wake, Marnie found herself on a paved promenade, bordering a wide strip of flower-filled garden. Beyond the garden was another promenade and beyond that again the stretches of silver sand and a vividly blue sea, all as breathtakingly beautiful as the guide book had promised. The flowers in the

397

garden were of every colour in the rainbow. At a swift glance Marnie recognised roses, clematis, bougainvillea, geraniums, oleanders and a tall fleshy scarlet lily she couldn't name. The air was heady with fragrance, the whole scene bathed in a rich golden light. It was gloriously hot; Marnie could feel the warmth soaking into her, easing her nerves. So this was Italy. She drew a deep ecstatic breath, and came back to earth at the sight of the driver dumping her two suitcases down beside her. Ought she to tip him? How did she get from here to the Pensione Primavera? This was a part of the journey the paternal travel agency hadn't provided for. It would have been all right if Glenn had been here ... Marnie thrust the thought indignantly aside. She would manage alone, if it killed her! Giving the driver a handful of coins which she hoped was enough, she picked up her suitcases and crossed the road to a row of white-canopied horse carriages. The cabby at the head of the row jumped down off his box and greeted her with a, "*Carozza, signorina?*"

"*Si!*" she murmured shyly, the monosyllable sounding foreign on her lips.

"*Prego!*" shouted the driver fiercely, and seizing hold of her suitcases, burst into a flood of Italian. No doubt he was merely asking her where she wanted to go. It was shattering to discover she didn't understand a word he said, but probably he was talking in some kind of rough dialect. At least it was consoling to think so. If only he were not so fierce and red-faced! He smiled, suddenly, disarmingly. "*Inglesa?*" he asked. "*Turista?*"

Marnie nodded.

The driver pointed down the avenue with his whip. "*Dove va lei?*" he asked slowly. Where are you going? Marnie translated, and glowed with success.

"Per favore," she ventured politely, *"vorrei andare a numero cinque, Via Veneto. La Pensione Primavera."*

"Bene!" shouted the driver triumphantly, and leaped on to the box, while Marnie took her seat in the open carriage. She was going, she had said, to number five, Via Veneto, and the driver seemed to have understood. *"Andiamo!"* he called to his sleepy old horse, and a moment later they were on their way. The avenue of palm trees came to an end and they turned into a small side road where the houses were detached with ornate porticos.

"Ecco!" announced the driver as they drew up opposite number five. *"La Pensione Primavera."*

The sisters Deladda, who must have been lying in wait before one of the large front windows, had opened the door almost before the carriage came to a halt. They were small dark-eyed women with severely dressed black hair, identically styled, and they wore identical white frilly blouses and tight black skirts.

"English spoken," they had boasted on their brochure. But their words of greeting were about as halting as Marnie's in Italian would have been. And they called her "Signora Wayland", looking over her shoulder for the Signor Wayland who ought to have been accompanying her. It was Marnie herself, not the travel agency, who had booked the accommodation at the *pensione*. She had written in her maiden name stating that she and her husband-to-be would be arriving in Italy after their wedding, to spend their honeymoon. Now, she realised with dismay, explanations were in order, a possibility she had overlooked in her somewhat flustered departure from Hurstleigh, after a week of chaos. A bride turning up without a bridegroom. Why hadn't she written and prepared the two women? But it was too late to think of that now. The driver had carried her suitcases into the hall and departed, and gesturing in unison, the sisters were showing her to her room.

It was large and lofty, on the ground floor. Gold pencils of light filtered through the louvres of the shuttered windows. The floor was tiled and cool, the walls washed white, and between the twin beds hung a silver and ebony crucifix. It was all rather austere, and the violet covers on the bed, together with the large crucifix, gave a slightly ecclesiastical air. But the absence of clutter was restful, Marnie decided, and she liked the crystal bowl of tuberoses someone had placed on the dressing table. The room was filled with their fragrance.

"*Il signore?* Where is he?" the sisters wailed in unison, no longer able to contain their curiosity. All day they had been looking forward to the romantic arrival of the honeymoon couple.

"There is no *signore*," Marnie blurted, and meeting the sisters' glances of blank non-comprehension, added in Italian, "*Niente marito.* I did not marry him after all."

The sisters gasped. "*Niente marito! Ma perchè?*" But why?

Marnie sank down on to one of the beds. This was going to take time, and the sisters would never understand it in English. She'd got to get it across somehow in her limited Italian.

For a moment the hopelessness of it defeated her. That last blazing row with Glenn, when he had told her he was going to Australia, where he had unexpectedly been offered a post in nuclear research. "There'll be no time for that white wedding you've been wasting your time over," he had told her brutally. "I've got a licence and we can be married tomorrow—sensibly—in a register office. We're flying to Brisbane on Friday next."

For a moment she had been speechless. "You mean you arranged all this without consulting me?" she managed at last.

"There wasn't much time. Anyway, I knew you would argue. So I decided to present you with the *fait accompli*.

"A wife goes where her husband goes," he had added with a self-satisfied air.

"Not a wife," Marnie spluttered. "A thing . . . a chattel!"

Then it had really started; shouting at one another, they had poured out all the bitterness and resentment in their hearts.

A wife's duty was to obey her husband, Glenn had stormed.

"You're half a century out of date," Marnie told him. "A wife nowadays is her man's companion, his equal, an individual with rights of her own. Did you stop for one moment to consider my feelings? Did you really imagine I would cancel my white wedding, dismiss my guests, walk out on my family and go with you to the other side of the world?

"You've never forgiven me, have you, for wanting my white wedding?" she had added in a stinging aside. "Well, now there isn't going to be any wedding, white or black." All the doubts she had felt about him over the years came tumbling out, her dismay at his selfishness and insensitivity. He was astounded, affronted, but not really touched. There was no heartbreak in the storm of invective with which he answered her accusations.

"If you loved me," he said at last, "you would go to Brisbane with me."

"I don't love you," she told him sadly. "Which is just

as well, for you wouldn't know what to do with me if I did."

Sitting on the violet-covered bed, rapidly reviewing all this in her mind, she decided that for the Deladda sisters this was the simplest explanation. "I found out in time that I did not love my fiancé," she said.

"Just before the wedding?" they asked in horror.

Marnie nodded. "Just before the wedding. He is going away to Australia . . . and I have come here, alone."

"Che tragedia!" moaned the sisters.

Marnie shrugged. "I wasn't going to give up my holiday. He had spoiled things enough without taking that from me."

"But to come to this place . . . to this room!" They looked meaningly at the empty twin bed. Then with bowed heads, their hands folded on their breasts, they crept away. At the doorway one of them turned to tell her that supper would be served in the *sala da pranzo* at eight o'clock. Her voice was cold, her glance stiff with disapproval. She had been a sore disappointment to the Misses Deladda, Marnie realised, arriving in a state of spinsterhood when they had expected a bride. No Mrs Glenn Wayland with a proud young husband in tow, but a mere Miss Hermione Gray, flippant and cynical, with a slab of flint where her heart ought to have been.

Left alone, Marnie lay on the violet bed, gazing at the gold slatted windows. Had she a heart of flint? What would she have felt like if Glenn had been lying on the other bed at this moment? Her colour deepened and her pulses stirred. So the strong physical attraction Glenn had sometimes had for her hadn't quite died! With an impatient gesture she got off the bed and began to unpack. Physical attraction wouldn't have been enough to carry them through. Their life together would have been

402

an endless bickering, soul-destroying, without real companionship or joy. If she had made a mistake it was in not having faced up to this earlier in their relationship —before the wedding arrangements had been made. Her lack of decisiveness had caused her family embarrassment and unhappiness, to Glenn's family and friends too. And perhaps in a small measure Glenn had suffered. But it wouldn't have gone deep. He was far too smug and well pleased with himself.

She took one of her trousseau frocks from its hanger, a peacock blue sheath of wild silk, that suited her admirably, making her, she decided, look a little less ordinary than usual. Not that she was lacking in looks, of a sort, but she had long ago resigned herself to the fact that there was nothing very outstanding about her. She had a neat little face; blue eyes that looked out at the world with candour and confidence, a small straight nose, a generous, humorous mouth and a mop of light brown hair with golden glints in it, which she wore cut fashionably short, so that it clung in loose gleaming waves to her shapely head.

She would wear the wild silk frock for supper, she decided. When she had washed and freshened up she slipped it on, and looking at herself in the mirror, approved the effect. The blue frock was certainly one of the most successful in her trousseau. A sharp pang caught her off guard. She spread out her ringless left hand that might have worn a gold band tonight, and was bereft now even of the simple sapphire engagement ring it had worn for the best part of three years.

The hand that the kindly stranger had held today during the moments of crisis in the plane. For one rather odd moment she was feeling again the pressure of his fingers, seeing vividly his lean sensitive face with its hint of bitterness. Who was he? Where had he vanished to? For a little while in the cabin of the circling plane she had felt so close to him. Which, of course, was ridiculous. She would never see him again. Yet the memory of the brief time she had spent in his company was enough to banish the momentary pang she had felt about her broken wedding.

Snapping a favourite silver bracelet about her wrist, she heard the brassy gong that summoned her to the evening meal. She would enter the *sala da pranzo* with her head held high. The lonely Miss Gray who ought to have been Mrs Glenn Wayland, and was glad, glad that she wasn't!

CHAPTER TWO

IT seemed to Marnie, lazing on the beach the first few days of her holiday, that she had never before known what sunshine could really be. Stretched on the silver sand in her bikini, she could feel the light and heat penetrating every pore of her body, a warm, golden drug that left her mindlessly inert. All through the long morning she would alternately sunbathe and swim, returning to the *pensione* round about noon, ready for the excellent lunch that awaited her. Some sort of pasta, usually, served with a delicious sauce, followed by veal or braised beef, cooked in a magical fashion with herbs and wine. The vegetables were outstanding, bearing little resemblance to the wet cabbage or soggy Brussels sprouts of an English seaside guest house; artichokes done in oil, fried aubergines, young green peas garnished with little pieces of ham, or stuffed baby marrows that melted in the mouth. The dessert was mostly fresh fruit, and of course there were the exciting Italian cheeses. After all that, the only thing to do was to lie on the bed during the hottest hours of the afternoon, and sleep it off.

Not exactly an energetic programme! It was all very well at first when she was nerve-racked and worn out and needed the rest. But now, five days after she had arrived, she was completely rested, and time and her own company were beginning to hang heavily on her hands. For one thing, she hadn't found any of those numerous English people her mother had visualised holidaymaking at San Paolo. Perhaps it was too early in the season for English tourists. The brown bodies stretched out on the patch of beach Marnie frequented belonged mostly to Italians, with a sprinkling of German and French. Marnie amused herself classifying them by the languages they spoke.

Her fellow boarders at the *pensione* were equally disappointing; an elderly Swiss couple, an Italian husband and wife with four small children, two plain fat middle-aged women who looked Dutch, and might, Marnie thought, be schoolteachers, and a small group of priests who read their breviaries all through meals. Though she exchanged polite *"Buon giornos"*, and *"Buona seras"*, with these people, conversation never got very much further. Nor did the Deladda sisters do anything to make themselves sociable, regarding her with cold withdrawn looks, if not with positive dislike. It was clear they had not forgiven her for arriving a spinster, instead of a bride.

So Marnie would sit at her lone table in the *sala da pranzo* in a succession of trousseau frocks, making the best of her solitary state. Twice she had gone out after the evening meal to walk on the promenade in the long warm twilight, visiting the gay little town with its brilliantly lighted shops and casino. The shops stayed open until well after midnight and the air was filled with the strains of Italian opera, or pop songs, relayed by loudspeakers hidden in the leafy trees—which were hung with little coloured lamps. Vespas and Lambrettas screamed up and down the long avenues, strollers thronged the sidewalks. Boys and their girls laughed and flirted and sang. Young men with beautifully oiled black hair, wearing foppish suits, wandered about in gangs, whistling after the girls, who, when they were not with escorts, kept together in closely knit groups. Marnie, walking by herself, was embarrassingly pestered by these foppish ones. Clustering behind her they would croon, *"Bella, bella!"* admiringly. *"Che bellezza!"*

When, hoping to shake them off, she sat down at one of the tables of a pavement café, a young man would materialise out of the dusk to take the chair opposite her with an elaborate bow and a murmured, *"Scusi, signorina. Mi permette?"* not in the least caring whether she permitted or not. There he would sit, while the rest of the gang melted discreetly away. She wondered how they arranged among themselves which was to be the one to claim a seat at her table.

The first time this happened she got up and walked away, taking refuge in a convenient gift shop. But the second evening she remained weakly with her pursuer, who looked harmless enough, and whose name, he disclosed, was Emilio. It was good practice for her Italian, she thought, as they struggled with the language barrier, over the ice-cream she had allowed him to buy for her. After that, of course, it was impossible to shake him off. The best she could do was to resist his efforts to entice her on to the deserted beach, where, he told her, he would show her how beautiful love could be. She preferred the music and lights of the promenade, she countered. They walked up and down under the lamplit trees until her feet ached, Emilio growing more and more amorous. But he was a good-tempered boy and showed no resentment, even when she steered him guilefully to the *pensione* and left him on the doorstep. He hadn't really expected to succeed in winning her favours, Marnie felt. But it had been worth a try!

Though it was almost midnight the Deladda sisters, who liked to know what was going on, were hovering in the hall. Peering over Marnie's shoulder as she entered, they could see the crestfallen Emilio retreating down the portico steps.

"You have made a friend?" sister number one shot at Marnie accusingly.

Marnie shrugged. "In Italy the young men are a pest... *cattivi*! Always they follow me."

"But of course, what do you expect?" sister number one demanded acidly. "For the young girl unattended men have little respect. How could it be otherwise?"

"Per una donna sola la vita è difficile," contributed sister number two more gently. For a woman alone life is difficult. But it was her own fault if she was alone, their manner implied as they bade her a chilly *"Buona notte, signorina."*

After that she did not go out in the evenings any more, but sat in the rather gloomy lounge watching television with the elderly Swiss couple, who invariably fell asleep, while the Italian news, dramas and commercials rattled on—too rapidly for Marnie to follow save in snatches.

Now the first week of her holiday was almost over. Two more weeks to go. Tomorrow she would start sightseeing in earnest. There was a coach trip to Ravenna, where, said the guide book, you could see the most wonderful mosaics in the world. Meanwhile here she was on the beach, writing postcards to her sisters, in the shade of a big coloured umbrella. Italy was fabulous, she enthused. She made no mention of her loneliness. Her pride would hardly allow her to admit it to herself, she certainly wasn't going to complain about it to her family. The letter she had just sealed up for her mother was full of descriptions of the scenery, and amusing comments on the *pensione* and her fellow guests.

"This is a view of the beach where I'm sitting at this moment," she wrote to Francie. "The sand stretches for miles on either side. The sea is cornflower blue. Have just had the most glorious swim."

She had bought a whole packet of gaily coloured post-cards at the beach kiosk this morning, meaning to send some to her nursing associates at St Margaret's Hospital. They would need cautious wording, for she hadn't told anyone at St Margaret's of her cancelled wedding. Her final row with Glenn had come some days after she had left the hospital for good. Or so she had thought. But now ... She sat with her pen poised wondering if she would have the courage to go back to her old job when this holiday was over. They would be glad to have her, she knew. Staff is notoriously hard to come by in the nursing world. But it wouldn't be easy, returning to the familiar routine, facing the kindly commiseration, the curiosity, the condemnation, perhaps. The girl who had jibbed at the starting post, throwing her young man over practically on the altar steps. She was twenty-four, they might remind her. Second chances didn't grow on trees.

"This is a view of the beach I am sitting on," she began again, too sleepy with sun and heat to think up any variation. But the postcard *was* a view of San Paolo beach, and to say so was safely non-committal. So was the bit about the glorious swim. She almost added, "wish you were here", but remembered in time that you didn't sit around longing for your friends and acquaintances to join you when you were on your honeymoon.

"Woe, Woe, Woe!" came a heart-rending wail, growing louder with each utterance. Looking in the direction from which this alarming sound came, Marnie saw a large Siamese cat trotting doggedly along the sands towards her. He had brilliant blue eyes in a brown velvet face. Glaring at Marnie, he gave once more his cry of distress. "Woe, oh, woe!" Or at least that was what it sounded like. His voice was harsh, yet musical, like somebody scraping a deep note on a cello.

Marnie held out her hand. "Puss, puss," she called. "Poor pussy!" Was that the correct way to address so exotic an animal? He stopped in his tracks and gazed at her enquiringly. Those wonderful blue eyes—more human than cat-like. As he looked at Marnie they seemed to fill with tears. But it must have been a trick of the light. Animals couldn't weep, any more than they could smile. But she could almost have sworn that the moisture in the extraordinary eyes was tear drops.

"Poor pussy!" She held out her hand. "What's the matter?"

No doubt he was an Italian cat and wouldn't understand a word she said. But the sympathy in her tone reached him. He moved towards her over the hot sand, giving a soft, pitiful miaow, so different from his earlier deep-toned bellowings that the effect was quite startling. A whole series of sounds followed; it was as if he were trying to tell her something of the utmost urgency. He sniffed at her outstretched hand as a dog might have done. She stroked his head. He was the most beautiful colour, his body a light beige, shading to cream, his ears, muzzle, tail and legs a rich brown, his long slender legs, elegantly shaped. Marnie could see he was an aristocrat to the tips of his dainty paws.

"Are you lost, darling?" she asked him, repeating it in Italian, *"Perduto, carissimo?"* It seemed odd that not one of the sun-worshippers had moved to claim him as he made his way along the beach, wailing his woe. But no one had shown the slightest interest in him, until he reached Marnie.

He sat down beside her, obviously glad of the shade of her beach umbrella, his sides heaving, his pink tongue protruding. Poor lamb, he was hot and thirty and exhausted. Marnie wondered how far he had walked.

"Pane, latte, gelati!" yelled the white-coated old man who wandered up and down the beach selling milk and rolls and ice-cream. His appearance at this moment couldn't have been more opportune. Marnie beckoned him over to her and bought one of the small cartons of milk. Opening it, she held it out to the cat, who lapped at the cool liquid ravenously. Once or twice he rested, then began lapping again. When finally he was satisfied he sat down once more, with a remark in Siamese cat language so eloquent of repletion and satisfaction that it might well have been, "Gosh, that was good! I certainly needed it!"

He proceeded to wash his face with one slender brown paw. Marnie watched him in fascination. Every movement he made was fluent and graceful. As if aware of her scrutiny, he turned to her with a conversational, "Mrrow!" more a purr than a cry. Obviously he approved of her.

"What am I going to do with you?" Marnie asked him, beginning to be faintly worried. What *did* one do with lost cats in Italy? Take them to the *polizia*? She couldn't imagine this beautiful creature languishing in a cell, or in the confined space of a cattery cage, while his owners were being sought. And if no owner materialised? A question she would rather not try to answer. The thought of this half-human animal being destroyed was something she could not face.

She stroked the brown velvet head absently, pondering her problem, and saw the cat yawn. With a purposeful look around, he spotted her large, soft bathing

411

towel, and pulling it towards him, he began to knead it, making himself a bed. This ritual was accompanied by loud purrs. In a few minutes he was curled up on the towel, fast asleep.

Marnie looked down at him with mixed feelings. It seemed she had got herself a cat! Tucking her letters and postcards into her beach bag, she decided to have a last swim before returning to the *pensione* for lunch. The cool water might clear her thoughts, bring her inspiration as to what to do with the cat. Barely acknowledged, there lurked within her the hope that during her absence he might, refreshed by milk and a nap, decide to go on his way. But she knew this was just a cowardly evasion on her part. If the cat moved on it would simply mean he had gone blundering along on his uncharted course, wailing and desolate. He was so obviously lost!

Hurrying out of the sea guiltily, she was relieved to see that he was still there, under the scarlet umbrella, sitting up and looking anxious. "Mrrow!" he scolded her. She had no business to run off, leaving him alone, his tone implied. It wasn't just fancifulness. This cat had a way of making his meaning clear, either by the varying intonations in his voice, or the expression in his intensely blue eyes. It was quite uncanny.

"I'm sorry, darling," Marnie apologised, sitting down on the beach mat beside him. He sniffed at her wet thighs with an air of distaste. "If I might have my towel..." she ventured, and drew it gently from under him. He watched her drying herself, and when she spread the towel across her knees he stood up, stretched himself, and stepped delicately on to her lap, where he curled up on the towel, once more settling himself for a nap. Marnie couldn't help feeling a little flattered. He had completely accepted her. Fondling him, she discovered

412

the collar under the thick fur of his neck. It had a brass disc hanging from it. She turned it about, reading the words engraved on it. On the one side was his name; "Chinky", and on the other his address: "Castello di Valetta, Monteviano." So this kingly cat came from a castle! She might have guessed it! She wondered if Monteviano was a town or a village, and where it might be. In a distant part of Italy perhaps. In that case he might have been brought to San Paolo by some visitor staying at one of the numerous hotels. Disturbed by his strange environment, he could have strayed. It seemed a possible solution, and if she was right, Marnie thought, her best course would be to go to the local police station and hand him over so that enquiries could be made. But she was strangely reluctant to do this. In any case it was almost lunch time, and she dared not be late at the *pensione*. The sisters Deladda made it very plain that they expected their guests to be on time for meals. They were perfectly right, of course, it would be a crime to have their beautiful dishes ruined by being kept waiting about.

Marnie slipped on her sleeveless beach coat and began packing the rest of her gear into her capacious beach bag, Chinky watching her suspiciously. She would have to take him with her, she supposed. Hide him in her room until after lunch and then work out what she was going to do with him. The police, she thought with a sigh, were the only answer.

"Will you walk, or do I have to carry you?" she asked him. "Mrrow!" he answered in an amiable tone. She began to move away from him. With a more urgent, "Mrrow!" he hurried after her. As she crossed the beach and the beach gardens he was close at her heels. She came to the wide avenue of palm trees where the

413

carrozza drivers and their sleepy old horses dozed in the shade. But it was a busy avenue at this lunch time hour, cars and motor bikes whizzing by in an endless stream. Chinky, not liking the look of it, took refuge underneath a clump of laurels nearby. Marnie dragged him out unceremoniously. She would have to carry him across the road. Clutching him in her arms, with her beach bag, she was surprised to find how solid and heavy he was. She stood on the kerb, waiting for a pause in the traffic. Chinky began to struggle. Low growls rumbled in his creamy throat. As she crossed the road the growls became loud screaming cat swears. He hissed, he spat, and finally turning on Marnie, gave her bare arm a sharp and purposeful nip with his pointed teeth. It didn't break the skin, but it shocked her, hurt her feelings. "Chinky!" she reproached him, "how could you bite the hand that's rescuing you?" Just in time to avoid another outburst of swearing, she reached the farther side of the road and flung the cat down on to the pavement with a sigh of relief. Quite unabashed by his own misbehaviour, with tail held high, he followed her into the Via Veneto, and up the steps of the *pensione* portico. She couldn't help being touched that he clung to her so closely, recognising her as his friend in a hostile world. Even his display of temper at being picked up endeared him to her. It showed a commendably independent spirit, and after all he could have clawed her savagely if he had wanted to. Whereas he had merely given her the gentlest of warning bites.

"Come on, Chinky, not a sound now!" she whispered to him, as she opened the *pensione* hall door. It was easy enough to slip in to her ground floor room, Chinky at her heels. The windows were closed against the midday heat, the green louvres drawn. Putting her bathing towel on one of the violet beds, she lifted Chinky on to it. "You've got to stay here while I go in to lunch," she told him firmly. Kneading the towel half-heartedly, he gave her a doubtful glance. "Stay!" she ordered, holding up an admonishing forefinger. "I'll be right back as soon as lunch is over." It was ridiculous the way she talked to him, as if he were a human being, and in English at that. But he seemed to understand. With an audible sigh . . . did ordinary cats sigh? . . . he sank down on the soft towel.

It didn't take Marnie a moment to slip out of her beach wear and into a crisp cotton frock. Maria, the little maid of all work, began to bang the gong in the hall just outside the door. Chinky took fright at the sound and dived beneath the bed. Perhaps that was as good a place for him as any. At least he would be invisible if one of the grim sisters happened to be snooping round bedrooms while the guests were busy eating. Marnie shuddered to think what the reaction of the Signorini Deladda would be if they discovered she had brought a strange cat into the house! She could imagine their white frilly blouses fairly bristling with indignation.

It was very quiet in the large airy dinng room, everyone engrossed in the delicious meal; a ham soufflé, followed by shrimp risotto. Whatever the shortcomings of the proprietresses, meanness about food wasn't one of them. For the sisters Deladda cooking was an art, and as Maria came and went, changing the plates, they appeared at intervals in the doorway, peering in to make certain that all was going smoothly. Occasionally they could be heard hissing warnings or admonitions to the downtrodden Maria as she passed them in her scurrying flights to and from the kitchen premises. A couple of old battleaxes! Marnie dismissed them. It couldn't be much fun working for them.

The salad course had just been served when a loud wail rent the air; Chinky, alarmed at being left alone so long in an unknown bedroom, was registering his protest. There was a pause in the clatter of cutlery. The diners stared at one another enquiringly. The strange rasping cry came again, this time more insistently.

"*Un gatto!*" exclaimed the sisters in unison. But where? They looked over their shoulders in bewilderment.

Marnie stood up. There was no help for it; she would have to speak out. In another moment the sisters would trace the cry and open the bedroom door across the hall. Chinky would bolt out and they would chase him from the house with blows and imprecations. Marnie could see it all!

"*Un gatto perduto!*" she announced urgently. "A lost cat. I found him on the beach this morning, and he followed me home."

"*Un gatto perduto?*" echoed the sisters, as though they could hardly believe their ears. "And you brought him in here!" pursued sister number one. "Some filthy, dirty stray, no doubt diseased and verminous. Really, *signorina*, this is too much!"

A lost cat instead of a bridegroom, Marnie thought wryly.

"He is not dirty, or diseased," she pleaded. "He is beautiful. A Siamese. He lives in a castle. His address is on his collar—the Castello di Valetta, at Monteviano."

The effect of this disclosure was electrical. "The Castello!" the sisters breathed in awe. "Home of the di Valetta family." Disapproval vanished from their faces as if by magic. They beamed, they simpered. "But this

416

is extraordinary, *signorina*! You found the cat of the Contessa on the beach this morning ... straying so far from his home?

"Quite hopelessly lost, thirsty and exhausted," Marnie confirmed. "I bought him some milk. After that he stayed with me and I had to bring him home. I couldn't very well have just left him there, could I?"

"Not the cat of the Contessa," agreed sister number one unctuously.

"Do you know the Contessa?" Marnie asked.

"Oh, yes, indeed!" The sisters could be seen gulping down their excitement.

"She called on us," sister number one continued, "last year, to question us about a girl who had worked for us, and whom she wished to employ. A charming lady. Such gracious manners. So kind!"

"She stayed more than an hour," chimed in sister number two. "Sitting with us in our private sitting room, drinking coffee with us, chatting away as though we had been her dearest friends."

"Then she doesn't live far away," Marnie broke in.

Monteviano, she learned, was a village some ten miles inland, up in the hills. She could get there by bus.

"But it would be quite simple for us to phone the Contessa telling her that her cat is here," said sister number one, who seemed to do most of the talking. "It would be a great pleasure to us to meet her again."

No doubt! thought Marnie. But it would be far more amusing if she herself were to take Chinky back to his august residence. It would be exciting to see the Castello and its chatelaine, the gracious Contessa who had so clearly bewitched the prickly Deladda sisters. Might it not be more polite, she suggested guilefully, if the Contessa were saved the fatigue of making a journey to San Paolo to retrieve her cat?

Reluctantly the sisters agreed. *Toujours la politesse!* The bus for Monteviano left the *piazza* at half past three, they disclosed. This would leave Marnie time to have her afternoon siesta before setting off.

Meanwhile, Chinky's wails continued to rend the air. "Would you like to see him?" Marnie invited the sisters. They followed her into the green gloom of the large shady bedroom. Chinky, on the bed on his favourite bath towel, greeted Marnie with a querulous cry, reproaching her for having left him. She fondled his velvety ears. "Isn't he beautiful?" she demanded.

The sisters, regarding him a little nervously, agreed that he was. But never before, they declared, had they seen an animal with such bright blue eyes. The effect was uncanny. They backed away apprehensively from Chinky's steady gaze. It was obvious that he was summing up the two twittering women, and that he didn't think much of them. From his open pink mouth there issued a vicious spitting explosion.

"*Mama mia!*" the sisters exclaimed, backing now in earnest. "He is savage. He will attack . . ."

"No, no," Marnie apologised for him. "It's just that he's hungry," she hinted.

"Would he eat a little meat? A little roast veal perhaps?" The sisters moved hurriedly towards the door. Even if he spat upon them, nothing, it seemed, was too good for the cat of the Contessa di Valetta. Marnie had a swift vision of her—young, haughtily beautiful, surrounded by luxury, playing languidly with her exotic cat in a boudoir bright with velvets and tapestries and silken hangings. The picture formed itself in her mind like a medieval painting.

The sisters reappeared, one of them carrying a plate piled with chopped-up veal in gravy. The second sister bore a newspaper, which she spread carefully on the ground to act as a tablecloth. Chinky needed no coaxing. Jumping down off the bed, he fell on his meal with zest. When he had eaten he went back on to the bed again, where, when she had finished her interrupted lunch, Marnie joined him.

Sleepy after sun, sea and food, she sank gratefully on to the pillows, Chinky nestling against her affectionately. He really was the most adorable cat. When he liked to be! Perceptively, he had not been enamoured of the Signorini Deladda, and had shown it all too plainly. Could it be that he guessed they had only accepted him because he happened to be the cat of a Contessa? She felt his quick rough little tongue licking her bare arm, then with his head on her shoulder he purred himself to sleep.

Looking down at him, Marnie was utterly relaxed and at peace. Dear Chinky! He was as warm and heavy as a baby in her arms. For the first time in days she forgot that she was lonely. Her eyelids drooped, and she too slept.

CHAPTER THREE

THE bus journey to Monteviano had its difficulties. Chinky didn't like the motion, or the noise of the engine, and he strenuously objected to being on the lead, which Marnie had borrowed from the Signorini Deladda. Relic of a pet dog, long defunct. They had seen her off fussily, urging her to remember them to *"La gentilissima Contessa"*.

"Tell her," ordered the most talkative sister, "how glad we are to be able to restore her cat to her, and that we have done all we could to feed him and make him comfortable."

Trying to grab the credit for having rescued him! Marnie thought. Currying favour with the Contessa. What blatant snobs the two women were!

The bus was crowded, mostly with peasant women returning from the market in San Paolo. Marnie was crushed into a back seat beside an enormous fat woman nursing a couple of live hens, whom Chinky regarded balefully, between his outbursts of wailing and swearing.

"Surely," remarked the fat woman, when they had left the town behind and begun to climb the mountain road, "this is the cat of the Contessa?"

"I found him wandering on the beach," Marnie explained in her stilted Italian. "And as his address is on his collar, I am taking him to his owner."

"Bene!" breathed the fat woman. "La Contessa will be joyful. It has been all over the village for the last

three days that she has been looking for her beloved *gattino*."

The two women in the seat in front of them turned to join in the conversation. The Contessa's lost cat being brought back to the Castello by a stranger, a *turista* by the look of her—what a sensation! They burst into a spate of excited chatter, which soon became general. All the passengers in the bus seemed to know each other. Marnie was able to follow much of what was being said, her knowledge of Italian having improved considerably during the last few days. Hearing it spoken around one all the time was a great help. So were her small shopping expeditions. Even her embarrassing evening with Emilio had contributed.

Chinky, she gathered, was a famous character in Monteviano, the terror of all the lesser cats in the neighbourhood. Even the dogs stood in awe of him. His courage was tremendous. *"Un bello gattino,"* a voice summed him up, "with the heart of a lion." But there was something about him that was a little frightening.

"It is his eyes," one woman suggested. "He looks at you as if he knows all."

"He does know all," another woman affirmed, crossing herself. "And he can bend people to his will. Everyone knows that Marco Morando, the butcher, is the stingiest man in Monteviano, but Chinky can march into his shop and sit there doing no more than stare, until Marco, unnerved, cuts up a slice of prime beef for him."

Chinky, who had settled into an uneasy bundle on Marnie's lap, came to life at the sound of his name and gave an indignant wail.

The woman who had just spoken muttered a nervous *"Dio mio!"*

"Have a care!" her companion cautioned. "If he

understands what you are saying about him he may put a spell on you." There was a burst of uneasy laughter.

"Are you not afraid he will claw you?" the fat woman with the hens asked, as she watched Chinky struggling to shake off Marnie's restraining hands. He had decided that a walk along the window ledge might take him to freedom and was fighting to get there.

"He won't claw me," Marnie declared—none too certainly. "I think he realises I am his friend. It is just that he does not like the bus, nor the indignity of being tied up on a lead."

"The Contessa," said the fat woman, "never puts him on a lead. He follows her everywhere, obeying her every call. She adores him; he is just like a child to her."

"There is no doubt but that he has a magic," somebody said in a half-shamed undertone. This time nobody laughed. "Look at the way he walked in the Holy Procession the other Sunday!" the shamed voice went on, more bravely this time.

One of the women in the seat in front of Marnie said, "That was only because he always follows processions. When the nuns march the schoolchildren across the school playground he marches along with them, and if there is a *fiesta* with flags waving and bands playing you will be sure to find him in the middle of it all."

"It's not natural," the nervous woman persisted. "Any ordinary cat would run a mile from the clatter of a band." Her voice rose on a note of panic. "He is bewitched, I tell you!"

"Bewitched or not, the Contessa finds great comfort in him," said the fat woman, "and it is little enough comfort she has had in her life, losing her husband in the first world war, her son in the second, and the family fortunes all the time decreasing. Things aren't what they were at the Castello when I was a young girl."

So the Contessa was not young and beautiful, but old and stricken by suffering and loss. "Does she live alone?" Marnie asked.

"Oh, no, *signorina*. She has two grandsons, the Conte Gregorio, the eldest, lives with her and sees to the farm and estate. Giulio, the second grandson, works in Rome, in a bank. But he often comes home at weekends."

A violent attack of spitting and snarling from Chinky brought the conversation to an end. Marnie had to hold him tightly as the bus shrieked up a steep incline, the road twisting and turning in an alarming series of hairpin bends on the edge of a terrifying precipice. It was all very beautiful, Marnie realised, if only she had the time to look at it; the small fields green with early summer grass, the roadside verges gay with scarlet poppies. There were hedges starred with scarlet poinsettias, and wild acacias heavy with creamy blossom. On the precipitous side of the road where the land descended to a river valley the rough, rocky land was clothed with sweet-scented thyme.

"Monteviano," said the fat woman, pointing to a distant huddle of old red roofs, topped by a church tower and grey stone battlements on the crest of what looked like an inaccessible mountain peak. It seemed impossible that the bus could ever climb up to it. With much gear-changing and engine clatter it pressed on, Chinky becoming more and more restless. Marnie looked enviously at the somnolent hens on the fat woman's lap. What had she done to mesmerise them?

They passed a hillside cemetery, guarded by a row of pointed cypresses, narrowly avoided a flock of white goats being driven by a ragged little boy carrying a flute, and swung round a bend on to a wide stony plateau of land, bounded on the one side by an outcrop of sheer granite, and on the other by a low stone wall, beyond which the land fell sharply into the river valley. Here the bus stopped, and everybody proceeded to get out.

"We have to walk the rest of the way," the fat woman explained to Marnie. "The streets are so steep and narrow that no heavy traffic can enter Monteviano."

"Are we far from the Castello?" Marnie asked as she got out of the bus, the Siamese cat clutched in her arms. Those grey battlements she had glimpsed; there was no sign of them now. But the Castello was only a few minutes' walk away, the fat woman assured her. "Take the street that turns right by the church on the *piazza*," she directed. "If you let the cat off the lead he will show you the way." With a polite, "*Addio, signorina!*" she vanished with her hens down a narrow alleyway.

Following the other bus passengers up a wider lane, Marnie came to the main street of the village, Chinky, recognising his surroundings, trotting confidently ahead of her. She looked with interest at the tall ancient houses, their tiled rooftops rose-pink in the afternoon light. The shops were small and dark, displaying a fascinating variety of wares, from strings of onions and hobnail boots, to gay hand-made pottery. Steep passageways between the houses led to shadowy labyrinths, where water dripped and old crones lurked, peering out of mysterious doorways at the people arriving in the village on the afternoon bus. An event no doubt in the tedium of their lives.

Keeping Chinky in sight, Marnie hurried on her way. Purposefully heading for his home, the cat took her across the cobbled *piazza* where old men sat on stone seats under feathery pepper trees, and women washed clothes in a trough tucked away beneath a beautifully arched cloister of honey-coloured granite.

They came to the church the fat woman had spoken of, and turned up the climbing street to the right. Suddenly the battlemented walls of the Castello were before them. With an excited cry Chinky ran towards the wicket gate that stood open in the vast main entrance, all iron-studded and barred. Passing through the wicket gate, Marnie found herself on a wide carriage drive, bordered with plane trees and limes. Neglected lawns stretched away on either side. There was a sunken wilderness of a rose garden, dotted about with weathered statuary. Ahead, the Castle loomed, a medieval pile with turrets and flying buttresses, the blank grey walls relieved here and there by mullioned windows. In the afternoon sunlight it seemed to sleep, unreal as a dream, an archaic backdrop for some ancient folk drama, or a Shakespearean tragedy, perhaps.

She came to the ornate portico, with its impressive flight of marble steps, and towering, nail-studded doors. There was a primitive bell-pull, which she tugged at tentatively. Chinky, watching her earnestly, pressed himself against the door, his tail erect, his blue eyes eager, his ears pricked, listening for the sound of footsteps within. Evidently he knew the connection between the ringing of bells and the opening of doors. When the footsteps came at last he gave a low throbbing cry, charged with all the emotion of his homecoming, and the moment the door was ajar he shot through it and disappeared, calling loudly as he went.

"Chinky!" exclaimed the young man who had opened the door, turning to stare after the flying furry figure. "Was it you who brought him back, *signorina*?..." He

425

broke off sharply, stifling muttered *"Dio mio!"* as he recognised Marnie.

Transfixed on the threshold, she in her turn uttered a small startled, "Oh!" The young man who had sat beside her in the plane the other day! It took her a perceptible moment to absorb the fact. Perhaps he was a bailiff on the estate. He was taller than she had remembered, younger looking, in an open-necked shirt and blue linen trousers of the serviceable kind worn by workmen.

He motioned to her to enter. "Do come in." He sounded politely puzzled. "We travelled together the other day, didn't we? It is an unexpected pleasure to see you in Monteviano..." But what brings you here? his inflection implied.

"I found Chinky wandering on the beach at San Paolo this morning," Marnie explained. "He was obviously lost, and as his name and address were on his collar..."

"You brought him home," the young man finished for her. "But how very kind of you! My grandmother will be overjoyed." He glanced over his shoulder at the wide marble staircase at the far end of the hall. "He has evidently gone straight up to her." A distant "Mrrow!" deep-throated as a love call, floating from the gallery above confirmed this assumption.

His grandmother! So he wasn't a bailiff after all. He was the Signor Gregorio, Conte di Valetta. Marnie's blue eyes widened.

"My grandmother thinks the world of her cat, and he has been missing for three days," the young man went on. "She will want to thank you." He was ushering her towards the staircase as he spoke. Walking with him across the vast hall, Marnie was vaguely aware of

426

dark, soaring walls, hung with archaic firearms and swords. Suits of armour loomed in shadowy corners. The cavernous hearth, engraved with a coat of arms, was flanked by high-backed oaken settles. It was all very dim and mysterious, the only light filtering through a stained glass window on a landing above the curved staircase.

Putting a hand beneath her elbow, the Conte guided Marnie up the first shallow steps. She remembered how he had held her hand that day in the plane; vividly the moment returned to her with its strange sense of inevitability. Glancing up at him, Marnie found he was looking down at her, his grey eyes whimsical and smiling. He had looked at her in the same way in the plane—as if he found her in some way amusing, but at the same time appealing. Was he glad to see her again? The colours of the stained glass window glowed before her like a great burning rose; the reflections of crimson and purple flickering on the marble steps. She felt curiously light and happy, little pulses of excitement beating in her throat. The whole thing was such an unexpected adventure in her rather dull holiday. A Siamese cat, a Castello, a Conte... they would never believe her when she told them about it at home.

"Gregorio, oh, Grego!" called a voice from the gallery above, "Chinky has come home!"

It was an extraordinarily young and vital voice. But the face looking down at them over the marble balustrade bore the stigmata of old age; the wrinkles, the lines, the sagging flesh. Yet the eyes, grey like those of the Conte's, were clear and bright, young as that lilting voice. The Contessa di Valetta, small and fragile with years, yet somehow valiant. Life, whatever suffering it had brought her, had not defeated her. "My darling

Chinky, safe and sound. It is a miracle. How I have prayed for him!" Her voice broke. "And God has answered my prayers."

"With the help of this young lady here," the Conte put in prosaically, as they reached the landing on which the old lady awaited them, the cat in her arms. He had tucked himself into the curve of her neck, his eyes closed in the bliss of reunion, his purrs loud as the simmering of a kettle.

"I cannot introduce you," the Conte turned to Marnie, "since I have not the pleasure of knowing your name."

"Marnie," Marnie supplied. "Marnie Gray."

"My grandmother, the Contessa di Valetta," began the young man, with due regard for protocol. "Miss Marnie Gray, who found Chinky lost on the beach at San Paolo this morning and has taken the trouble to bring him home to us."

The Contessa held out her free hand, her face alight. "My dear Miss Gray, how can I ever thank you!" She rested her head on the furry bundle in her arms. Tears shone in her eyes. "I have been so distressed, thinking of all the terrible things that could have happened to my poor little Chinky. I have been all over the village, looking for him. I have driven out in to the country, calling him . . . searching for him. He has disappeared once or twice before, since I believe in giving him his freedom, but never has he been gone as long as this. He has been missing since Monday. I have not slept . . ." Once more her voice broke ominously. The Conte put a protective arm about her frail shoulders.

"But it is all right now, Nonna darling. You must not worry any more. Chinky seems none the worse for his adventure."

"I know, Grego darling, and I'm so thankful!" She

dabbed at her eyes and turned apologetically to Marnie. "Forgive me, Miss Gray, if I am a little distrait. But it is such a relief to me to have Chinky back. Do come into my room and tell me all about it ... just where you found him and if he was very distressed?" She spoke with no hint of an Italian accent. However Italinate her title, this fragile but indomitable old lady was as English as Marnie herself.

She led the way into a small but beautifully proportioned room with long narrow windows overlooking the neglected lawns. In contrast to the sombre hall everything here was light and colourful, the comfortable chintz-covered settee, the deep chairs upholstered in pale rose velvet, the flower-patterned carpet, the watercolour paintings on the ivory tinted walls. Family photographs in silver frames stood about on every available space. A great bowl of lupins had been placed in front of the empty Carrara marble hearth. Save for that hearth and the oil painting of a dashingly handsome man in Italian military uniform above it, the boudoir was an English drawing room in miniature.

At one side of the hearth there was a wicker cat-basket, luxuriously cushioned. When the Contessa put Chinky down he made straight for this haven, where he curled up tightly and was instantly asleep.

"Poor little cat, he is worn out!" the Contessa said tremulously. "I don't suppose he has had any rest during the past three nights. I wonder where he spent them?"

"Probably in the Old Port," the Conte suggested. "He could have been coming from there when Miss Gray saw him running along the beach. Perhaps he got into the fishmonger's van when it called here on Monday."

"I thought of that," said the Contessa, "and phoned

the fish shop. But the man said he had not seen the Siamese in his van."

"He could have slipped in and out unnoticed, attracted by the smell of the fish."

"Only that he hates raw fish," the Contessa declared. "Nor does he eat mice or rats. So he must be starving, poor lamb!" She pressed a bell beside the hearth. "Baptiste must bring him something to eat at once."

"He had a lunch of veal and vegetables at the *pensione*," Marnie put in. "I am staying at the Primavera with the Signori Deladda."

"Ah, yes, I believe I have met them," the Contessa nodded. "Excellent women. They keep a very good table, I am told. It was kind of them to give Chinky lunch, and more than kind of you to rescue him from his wanderings."

"I am so glad I was able to, and indeed it made my day," Marnie confessed. "I was bored with my own company, lying there on the beach with not a soul to speak to . . ."

The Contessa's eyes widened. "But you are not staying at San Paolo alone?" She sounded faintly shocked.

"Actually, I am," Marnie faltered. "The . . . er . . . friend I was coming with couldn't manage it at the last moment."

"My dear, how unfortunate for you!"

"I thought you said somebody was meeting you that day at the airport," Gregorio put in.

Marnie shook her head. "Only a travel agent."

"Miss Gray and I travelled from London the other day on the same plane," he explained to his grandmother, who was looking a little puzzled.

"Our seats were side by side," Marnie contributed.

430

"Your grandson, the Conte, was very kind when I was a little nervous."

"Not that there was anything to be really nervous about," Gregorio put in quickly, giving Marnie a warning glance. Clearly, he had not told his grandmother about the delayed landing, and that nerve-racking hour spent cruising before it could be safely accomplished.

The old lady looked from one to the other in a slightly quizzical fashion. "Well!" she laughed, "it is indeed a small world, and how amazing that of all the people on the beach it should be to you, Miss Gray, with your generous heart, that Chinky turned for help." She tilted her head imperiously. "You will stay and have tea with me?" It sounded more like a Royal Command than a request. Seating herself on the settee, she motioned Marnie to sit beside her. "Will you join us, Grego?" she demanded of her grandson.

He shook his head. "I'm afraid not, Nonna, much as I should like to. But I have a tenant waiting for me in the office, and a man from the Cheese Co-op is coming to see me at four. So if you will excuse me . . ." He bowed formally to Marnie and left the room. It seemed very empty when he had gone.

"Poor Grego!" the Contessa sighed. "He has always so much to do for the estate and so little wherewithal with which to do it. Things are not easy for him . . ." She spoke in a musing tone as if to herself, and then remembering her guest, turned to Marnie. "I hope you are not in a hurry to get back to San Paolo, Miss Gray. It is such a pleasure for me to have somebody English to talk to."

"You are English, then?" Marnie remarked unnecessarily.

"My home was in Yorkshire . . . more years ago than I care to remember. My parents had a house in London

431

also, where they launched me on my first season. It was at my coming-out ball that I met the Count, Gregorio's grandfather. We were married almost at once, and he brought me here to Monteviano."

Marnie listened with interest to this briefly told snatch of the Contessa's history ... had she been happy with her Italian husband?

"Do you often visit England?" Marnie asked.

"I haven't been back since just before the last war." The Contessa passed a transparent hand across her eyes in a weary gesture. "Sometimes it seems to me as I have lived through nothing but wars and revolutions. Italy has not been a happy country during my lifetime. There have been many changes."

The fat woman in the bus, Marnie recalled, had spoken of the Contessa's bereavements in two world wars, and of the di Valettas' broken fortunes.

"To be old," the Contessa whispered, "is to look back on much sorrow. So often now I find my thoughts returning to the grey stone house in Wharfedale. The grounds sloped down to a busy little river. Wild lily of the valley grew in the surrounding woods." She broke off. "But I talk too much of myself! To be old is to become garrulous." Her smile held the same hint of whimsicality as her grandson's, the same singular sweetness. Indeed there was a marked likeness between them. It was from his Yorkshire grandmother that Grego got his fair colouring, his blunt handsome features. He was more English in appearance than Italian, Marnie thought, and found an odd satisfaction in the reflection.

"But today I do not look back," the Contessa was saying. "Today there can be nothing but rejoicing. You have brought my Chinky back to me!" She touched Marnie's arm lightly. "You will never know what you have done for me, Miss Gray. My constant companion, my faithful little shadow. I don't think I could have borne it if he had vanished for ever, leaving me wondering what terrible fate had overtaken him." Once more she checked herself. "But here I go, talking about myself again. Do forgive me, and tell me something about *you* instead. Is this your first visit to Italy? Are you enjoying your holiday?"

Marnie hesitated. "In many ways, yes. But I'm finding it a bit of a drag being on my own. Nor had I realised how conspicuous a solitary female can be in Italy."

The Contessa laughed. "You mean the young men are pursuing you? I am not surprised, you are very attractive, though indeed any unaccompanied young woman is considered fair game in these parts. For one thing, she is invariably a foreigner. Italian girls are usually chaperoned or escorted."

"Or they go about in droves," Marnie said. She gave a regretful sigh. "I've quite given up going out in the evenings, though I love seeing the crowds on the promenade and the shops lit up until long after midnight. It's all so gay, so Continental." She shook her head ruefully. "But not for me any more. The boys just seem to look on me as an easy pick-up."

"It might have been wiser if you had not come to San Paolo alone," the Contessa suggested.

"I didn't plan it that way," Marnie reminded her. "But as I had already paid my fare and a sizeable deposit to the *pensione*, I decided to carry on when my friend dropped out. I had hoped I would have found some English visitors at the *pensione* with whom I could have chummed up, but all the other guests are non-English-speaking Continentals. As I'm no linguist I just sit mum most of the time. It gets pretty lonely."

"I am sure it does," the Contessa agreed feelingly. "At my age one grows to accept loneliness, but it is all wrong for you." She gave Marnie a speculative glance. "Perhaps there is something we can do about it . . ."

A tap at the door heralded the entrance of an old man dressed in a faded livery. He was carrying a silver tea tray, lavishly laden.

"Ah, Batiste!" the Contessa greeted him. "I rang, but I see you have already brought tea."

"The Conte told me to, my lady," the old man explained. His glance went to the cat basket. "He told me, too, that the little cat has come home. *Grazie a Dio!* I have brought him something to eat. *Povero gattino*, he will be hungry." Taking a pewter plate from the tray, he placed it by the hearth.

"Rabbit!" exclaimed the Contessa. "Dear Batiste, how thoughtful of you."

"*Prego!*" murmured Batiste with a toothless smile.

The gamey smell of the rabbit pierced Chinky's dreams. He sat up, sniffing the air, and in another moment was out of his basket eating ravenously.

Dotingly the Contessa and old Batiste watched him.

"His favourite meal!" the Contessa sighed contentedly.

"Gina has made it ready for him every day since he vanished," the old man said. "She has prayed endlessly to the Blessed Virgin for his safety, and knew he would return."

The Contessa looked dangerously near to tears again. "Thank you, Batiste. Thank you both!"

Batiste bowed low, and with another "*Prego!*" a polite expletive which seemed to cover so many eventualities in Italy, he left the room.

Marnie eyed the well-stocked tea tray and discovered

she was hungry. The nervous strain of her bus journey with the struggling Chinky had taken its toll. She was quite ready for the unexpected assortment of eatables which old Batiste had brought in—Sally Lunns, Eccles cakes, plum cake, toasted tea-cakes swimming in butter.

"I always have a good Yorkshire tea," the Contessa confessed. "I have taught a series of Italian cooks to make the indigestible things which I love. Gina, Batiste's wife, can even make lardy cakes. Fortunately I am not one of those people who has to worry about weight." She heaped home-made strawberry jam on to a well-buttered scone. "Neither are you, I should imagine." She regarded Marnie appraisingly. "Do try one of these cheese cakes."

They ate for a while in companionable silence. Having finished his rabbit Chinky washed his face. Then with one of his most sociable "Mrrows", he jumped on to Marnie's lap.

"He doesn't easily go to strangers," the Contessa said. "But he knows you rescued him and this is his way of saying 'Thank you!'"

Marnie stroked the brown velvety head. "He hated the bus journey this afternoon."

"You brought him here by bus?" the Contessa exclaimed. "My dear, how ever did you manage it? I assumed, without really thinking about it, that you had come by car, which would have been difficult enough. But in a bus it must have been almost impossible."

"It wasn't easy," Marnie admitted. "The Deladda sisters loaned me a lead. But it wasn't much help. Chinky resented it."

"And he would hate the noise, those dreadful screaming changes of gear as you climb up the mountain road."

"He certainly didn't enjoy it!"

"I don't suppose you did either," the Contessa said ruefully. "I am more and more in your debt. Apart from the nervous strain of all this there was your bus fare... Chinky's lunch. You must allow me to recompense you."

"Oh, no, please!" Marnie protested. "I loved finding Chinky and bringing him back to you. It's the first really nice thing that has happened to me since I started my holiday." She hadn't meant to speak so feelingly. A confession of loneliness. Suddenly the week behind her seemed very bleak and empty. "You made me so welcome," she said. "You've been so kind... inviting me to tea..."

"It is you who have been kind," the Contessa said, "giving up your afternoon listening to an old woman's chatter. And you will not let me try to repay you. But I will think of a way. It will come to me! Meanwhile, let me refill your tea-cup."

An hour later they were still sitting over the tea tray. Chinky having paid his respects to his rescuer was asleep on his mistress's lap.

How the time had flown. But the Contessa was so easy to talk to. There was nothing simulated in her interest and quick sympathy. Marnie had found herself telling her about her work at St Margaret's about her home and family. Of her broken engagement she could not bring herself to speak, the last-minute break-up of her wedding plans. It would all be so difficult to explain, and sitting there in the small elegant room Marnie realised how distasteful in retrospect the whole episode had become. To tell the Contessa about it was somehow unthinkable. She only wanted to forget Glenn now; let him slip out of her mind as if he had never been.

Batiste came in to remove the tea tray. Marnie stood up. There was really no excuse for her to stay any longer.

"I wonder what time the bus leaves for San Paolo?" she said.

"You are not going back to San Paolo by bus," the Contessa declared firmly. "Grego will drive you there. Though he will not be free just yet, I'm afraid."

She looked up at Marnie with her most winning smile. "Why don't you stay and have dinner with us? It would give us such pleasure," she urged. Not that Marnie needed much urging. Once more she had that strange sense of inevitability, the intimation of a pattern falling into its predestined place. Murmuring her acceptance, her heart curiously light, she sat down again on the settee.

CHAPTER FOUR

THEY ate in a great vault of a room hung with faded tapestries, and darkly painted ancestors in tarnished gilt frames. The long oaken table was set with heavy silver and not very well polished glasses. Dust lay visibly on the immense sideboard with its clutter of cruets and decanters. It looked as if there were not very many servants in the Castello, for it was old Batiste who served the meal. The food was indifferent, not nearly so well cooked as the dishes provided by the sisters Deladda. But the wine was good, the cheese something to dream about.

It was made on the premises, Grego told Marnie. He was trying to establish cheese-making as an industry in the village, it appeared. "Some time you must show Miss Gray your little factory," the Contessa said, as if Marnie were to be at the Castello indefinitely. At the head of the long table she looked smaller than ever. She had changed into a black lacy frock for the evening, and wore a cape of soft white down about her shoulders. In spite of the heat of the weather it was chilly in this vast stone-paved apartment, and there was more than a hint of dampness in the air. With a suppressed shiver, Marnie wondered what it would be like in the winter, when icy winds blew in from the Yugoslavian hills across the Adriatic.

Grego sitting opposite to her was suave, but a little abstracted, drinking his wine with a dreamy air. He was

438

tired perhaps after a long day wrestling with the problems of the impoverished estate. "It is a poor village," he told Marnie, "and though it does not belong to us as it did in the old feudal days we still try to do what we can for our neighbours. They look to us for help and we cannot disappoint them."

Vines grew well in this part of the country, Marnie learned, and there was a little mixed farming. The crops were mainly maize, fruit and olives, with grain and hay grown for the animals.

What were her plans for the remainder of her holiday? the Contessa asked her presently. She had thought of going to Ravenna tomorrow, Marnie said. "There is a bus from San Paolo," she began, but the Contessa interrupted her with a hurried, "I could take you by car, which would be much more pleasant... if Grego could spare the Fiat?"

"Of course," Grego agreed at once. "I can use the estate car tomorrow."

The wine had brought little patches of pink to the Contessa's pale cheeks. Her eyes were bright. "There are so many beautiful places you ought to see," she told Marnie. "It would be such a pleasure to me to show them to you." Her voice became soft and persuasive. "All through dinner I have been thinking how much simpler it would be if you were staying here as our guest. I could take you about, show you the country." The full battery of her charms was turned on in her smile. "Would you give up the rest of your holiday to gratifying an old woman's whim?"

Marnie's hesitation was born of sheer astonishment. In the small pause which followed the Contessa's invitation Grego turned to her. "You would be doing us a real kindness if you were to stay," he assured her. "My grandmother is far too much alone. I have so little time to spare for her."

"We mustn't trade on Miss Gray's good nature," the Contessa put in quickly. "It is true that I am often alone, but I am also thinking of Miss Gray's wasted holiday. I think she is finding it rather dull at the Pensione Primavera, and there is the difficulty of her going about unescorted. I don't think she quite realised how it would be when she decided to come here on her own."

"I certainly did not!" Marnie laughed. "The Italian boys are a menace!"

"Italy is a man's country," the Contessa said, with a shake of her white head. "When an attractive girl is seen to be alone it is assumed she is looking for a protector."

"And the protectors rush forward by the dozen," Grego laughed. He gave Marnie a gallant little bow. "Can you blame them? What you need, evidently, is a protector from your would-be protectors."

Was he suggesting that *he* should be her bulwark against the hordes of importunate young men?

"Perhaps a chaperon might do," the Contessa said. Marnie felt a little breathless at the unexpectedness of it all as the old lady added, "So you will stay, won't you, Miss Gray?"

There was nothing she would like better, but the whole thing seemed so improbable that Marnie did not know what to say. To spend the rest of her holiday as the guest of the Contessa di Valetta, in this romantic old Castello! It didn't sound real. Why she had been invited? "A whim," the old lady had called it. She was too much alone, her grandson had pleaded.

I did tell her a lot about myself, Marnie worked it out. She knows I am a qualified nurse from one of the

440

best London teaching hospitals. Perhaps that makes her feel she can trust me. But there was more to it than that. In the short time they had spent together Marnie and the ageing Contessa had established one of those rare sympathetic bonds that do at times occur between the most unlikely people. Now when they looked at one another and smiled it seemed suddenly quite natural for Marnie to accept the impulsively given invitation.

"I should very much like to stay, if you're sure I shan't be in the way," she said.

"Then it is all settled!" the Contessa beamed. "My dear Miss Gray, I am delighted."

"Won't you call me, Marnie?" Marnie said. "It's really Hermione, but I keep that dark. I feel it's altogether too pompous a name to live up to."

"Perhaps so," the Contessa agreed. "You can start using it when you are middle-aged and have developed a presence. Meanwhile, Marnie is a sweet diminutive." Her grey eyes softened. "It began in the nursery, I expect. One couldn't very well address a small baby as Hermione!"

Marnie went back to the peach she had been peeling, and began mentally to work out the practical implications of her change of plans. She would have to disentangle herself from the *pensione*, explain matters to the Deladda sisters, fetch her luggage . . .

"I could run you down to San Paolo after dinner if you want to collect your gear," Conte Grego was saying.

"That would be splendid," the Contessa chimed in, before Marnie had time to reply. So, over her head more or less, it was all arranged. She was to be installed at the Castello right away, with no delay. Marnie could only marvel.

After that it was all more and more like a dream;

Grego bringing the big shabby Fiat round to the portico steps, the Contessa, tiny as a child in the vast arch of the doorway, seeing them off, the Siamese cat, erect as an Egyptian statuette, sitting by her side, his Oriental eyes aslant.

"Don't hurry back!" the Contessa called to them. "Let Miss Gray . . . Marnie . . . see something of the night life of San Paolo, the illuminations, the Casino, the cafés . . ."

"I'll take her dancing at the Savoia," Grego called back.

It was cool in the open car after the heat of the day. With the village on its mountain top behind them they swung down the twisting road through the lilac evening. There was little traffic at this hour. An old man, placidly ignoring them, drove a flock of goats before him, the bells hung round their necks making a silvery music in the quiet air. A few peasants still worked in the terraced fields, weeding, hoeing, their backs patiently bent over the ripening maize and neat rows of vegetables.

On a treacherous bend they had to pull to the side, all but hanging over the precipitous valley, to make way for an ox cart driven by a young man, naked to the waist, his deeply bronzed torso beautiful as a piece of polished sculpture.

"Why are all the oxen in Italy white?" Marnie asked when they had left the cart and its handsome driver behind.

It was a question Grego couldn't answer, but he told her how he and the villagers longed for some more modern form of transport. Ox drawn carts were picturesque, but tractors and motorised waggons would be far more useful. "It is a poor country," the young Conte mourned. "We just can't afford the mechanisation which

442

would make all the difference to our economy." She encouraged him to tell her something more about his cheese-making enterprise. Glancing at his classic profile, she noticed how the faint hint of bitterness disappeared from his expression when he was animated, holding forth on the topic so evidently dear to his heart. What sort of a life did he lead? she wondered, marooned in that lonely castle with an ageing grandmother. Were there many social occasions? What about girl-friends? Was he as unattached as he seemed?

Away below them the lights of the coastal towns stretched like a necklace of diamonds against the darkening sea; San Paolo and its adjacent resorts lit up for the long night's gaiety. The lamps would not go out until dawn. At half past nine the fun had scarcely begun.

When they came to the avenue of palms Grego slowed down the car and turning to Marnie asked her gravely if she were sure she would not regret leaving the liveliness of the seaside for the quietness of Monteviano.

"Of course I won't regret it," Marnie assured him vigorously. "It was wonderful of the Contessa to invite me to stay at the Castello. I'm very thrilled about it."

"I only hope you won't find it dull. You will miss your swimming, I'm afraid."

"I can always nip down to San Paolo on the bus if I want to bathe," Marnie pointed out. "Anyway, I haven't come to Italy just to bake myself brown lying about on the sands in a mindless heap. I want to do some worthwhile sightseeing."

"So you shall," Grego promised. "Ravenna, Forli, Cesenatica. My grandmother will enjoy taking you about. She is a competent driver, and loves a day out when she can find anyone to go with her."

Before Marnie could say how happy she would be if

she felt her companionship was being some use to the Contessa, they were drawing up outside the Primavera.

Going up the portico steps she had a momentary qualm. Would the sisters be very annoyed at her sudden departure from the *pensione*? But the announcement that she was going to stay at the Castello would probably save the day, and they would most certainly be overawed at the presence of the young Conte di Valetta. He stood by her side, tall and distinguished, as they waited for the door to be opened to them. It was Maria, the little maid of all work, who appeared. *Le signorine*, she announced surprisingly, were not at home. They had gone to see a Biblical film which had won an international award at a recent film festival.

"Which means they won't be back until well after midnight," Grego calculated. "So we can go and have our dance at the Savoia and come back later."

Could he wait a few moments while she changed her frock? Marnie asked. She was still wearing the cotton frock she had put on when she came from the beach that morning.

In the room with the purple-covered twin beds she made a hurried toilette, choosing her favourite peacock blue frock, one of the most successful items of her trousseau. Bought for the bride of Glenn Wayland, and now she couldn't be quick enough getting into it to go dancing with another man. Was she completely heartless? Marnie asked herself. Her own warmth and love of life answered her. Glenn and she had hurt one another, but it was all over now, and if the hurt had faded rapidly it was because nothing very deep had been involved. Nor could there be anything vitally significant about tonight, she reminded herself. A dancing date with a man she scarcely knew, a man older than herself, enigmatic, completely outside her orbit, an impoverished Count whose most passionate interest seemed to be in cheese-making. Yet their association tonight, however superficial, was touched with magic; the magic of a summer evening in Italy with its music and starlight and gaiety. She knew as she walked with Grego back to the car that she would treasure every moment of it.

They came again to the avenue of palms and drove down the wide main boulevard of the little town. The brilliantly lit pavements were thronged with promenading townsfolk and visitors. Here were the souvenir stalls, and open-air cafés, the smart little dress shops, the bookshops and art shops, all as busy with customers as if it were the middle of the afternoon. The amplifiers in the illuminated trees poured out a medley of music, ranging from Italian opera to the latest pop songs. The inevitable Vespas and Lambrettas screamed up and down the roadway.

"In Italy," Grego commented drily, "we love noise!" Guiding the car through the strolling crowds, who spilled carelessly from the sidewalks, he turned into a by-way that led to the sea. This was the more select end of the long promenade. The colonnaded entrance to the Hotel Savoia, golden with light, overlooked the water. The beach in the strong illumination was bone-white and ghostly, the dark sea, fringed with foam, whispering along its edge.

An impressively uniformed attendant helped them to park the car, which looked shabbier than ever among the gleaming models of the rich tourists. They entered a mirror-lined foyer. Marnie could see their reflections everywhere. She seemed small and slight beside the tall young man in his regulation white tropical dinner jacket. It made him look even more definitely blond than usual.

445

When their glances met in one of the mirrors his grey eyes twinkled, as if he were mildly amused at finding himself here, escorting an unknown English girl.

He led the way into a crowded cocktail bar, but in spite of the congestion he was instantly recognised by a lynx-eyed maître d'hôtel, who welcomed him and fussed over him, waving him to a corner table. It was too long since they had had the Conte di Valetta's patronage, the man murmured in servility. It was a great privilege to be able to serve him. "And your lady," he added, with a bow in Marnie's direction. What, he enquired, would they have to drink?

Marnie chose an *albicocco*, the delicious ice cold apricot juice she had learned to ask for in the beach cafés. Grego lifted an eyebrow at her choice, and ordered a liqueur for himself. When it came he held the narrow glass out to her and invited her to try it. She leaned forward and sipped at the sweet, fiery spirit, faintly disturbed by the intimacy of the shared glass. Would her lipstick come off on the edge of it? "It burns," she said, blinking, "but it's good."

"The best," Grego agreed. "When you have finished your fruit juice you must have some. It is a regional speciality. It is not possible to visit San Paolo without sampling it."

The apricot juice now seemed to Marnie insipid. She was aware of Grego's eyes on her as she drank. In this light they were the same golden colour as the liqueur. Their watchfulness began to make her uneasy. There was an intensity about this young man that was a little frightening. Things either mattered to him not at all, or they would become too important. There would be no half measures.

446

Now he burst out suddenly, "Whoever let you come abroad alone wants their head examined! A lamb flung to the wolves. Don't you know that you are far too young and pretty to be wandering about on your own, at least in this country? It may be different in London."

This oblique flattery made her feel foolishly confused. It was by no means the first time a man had told her she was pretty. But Grego had sounded so oddly angry about it.

"It *is* different in London," she said. "But nobody *let* me come abroad. I don't have to be 'let'. I make my own decisions. I'm a free agent. Free, white and twenty-four," she added.

"Good heavens, I thought you were about eighteen!"

She ignored the interruption. "I'm self-supporting. Self-sufficient, if you like. I earn my own living . . ."

"In an office?" Grego hazarded.

"No, in a hospital. I'm a staff nurse, if you know what that means."

"I'm afraid I don't."

Marnie explained, and Grego looked impressed. "A fully trained hospital nurse. That's quite an achievement at your age, isn't it? It is that, I suppose, that gives you your air of assurance."

"Yet you thought I was eighteen," Marnie reminded him.

"Your manner is older than your looks." He smiled. "Excepting perhaps when you are feeling scared in an aeroplane!"

Marnie grimaced. "Don't remind me of that horrible hour of cruising round and round, not quite knowing what was going to happen at the end of it. Anyone with a spark of imagination would have been scared."

"I was none too happy myself," Grego admitted. And

then, reverting to her work, "Do you like nursing?"

Marnie nodded. "I love it. It's full of interest, and there are many aspects about it that make it very satisfying."

"But you are not nursing all the time. You have a social life? A home life?"

"Oh, yes, lots of both. I have a mother and father and two young sisters."

"And there are friends?"

Marnie nodded once more. "One makes plenty of friends in hospital."

"Yet you couldn't find anyone to come abroad with you?"

Marnie frowned. Why did he keep harping on it? "As I have told you," she reminded him, "the friend I was supposed to be travelling with let me down." For a moment she was on the verge of telling him exactly what had happened. But her courage failed her. She didn't know him well enough to enlarge on the details of her painful break with Glenn. So she said instead, "It wasn't easy to make fresh arrangements at the last moment. So if I hadn't come alone it would have meant giving up my holiday altogether. I wasn't going to do that, since I had already paid for it, and had spent a lot of time last winter going to Italian classes so that I would be able to get as much as I could out of my stay in Italy."

Grego gave her an approving look. "That was very enterprising of you. It must have been a blow to you when your friend disappointed you. I think it was marvellous of you to pick up the pieces and press on alone!"

She found herself blushing at this tribute.

"I only hope all the effort will have been worth while."

"Now that your grandmother has asked me to stay

at the Castello it most certainly will," Marnie told him glowingly. "It was most unexpected. After all, I am a complete stranger to her."

"She likes you," Grego said simply. "She has a way of making up her mind about people on sight, and, as she told you, she is often lonely. It will be a great pleasure to her to have your company."

"Doesn't she have many visitors?" Marnie asked, probing in her turn.

"A few. But we are fairly isolated on our mountain top at Monteviano. The folk we know are scattered over a wide area, and Nonna is not as young as she was. She does not care for driving about alone, so that if she does have the odd caller, she seldom returns the call. It all adds up to a pretty solitary existence. I often feel guilty that I can't give more time to her, but I always seem to have so much to do. It is a relief to me that you are going to be with her for a little while." He touched her empty glass with a finger tip. "And now what about that liqueur?"

She sipped it slowly when it came, its subtle fire warming her veins.

"I've told you about myself," she said. "Now it's your turn."

"There is so little to tell." He spread out his hands, sensitive Italian hands that made eloquent gestures as he talked. "My life is uneventful. Most of it you can guess at already. Apart from my rare sorties to England to pick up agricultural implements and know-how, I live in a remote village with the vestiges of an old power, but without the money to implement it. It is not easy."

"You could find yourself a rich wife, "Marnie suggested lightly. Perhaps the unaccustomed liqueur was already loosening her tongue. But he didn't seem offended, answering in a tone as light as her own, "Perhaps I will." And then with a shrug, "Marriages of convenience are possibly the only marriages that work out."

"I wouldn't say that." Marnie took another cautious swallow of liqueur.

"You are young enough to have illusions."

Her face hardened. "You'd be surprised at the number I've shed. I've had my share of disappointments. Who hasn't?"

"Who indeed!" His tone dismissed the subject, and a moment later he was asking her if she would care to dance. Guided by the strains of a string orchestra they crossed a floodlit patio to an open-air dance floor. On a terrace hung above the ghost-white beach they moved over smooth polished marble. There were flowery arches beyond which the sea shone mysteriously, its phosphorescent gleam shimmering with the rise and fall of the gently breathing water. Little waves broke at regular intervals against the shore, making a cool and lovely sound in the quiet night.

He held her lightly, but she was almost overwhelmingly aware of his nearness. For all his slender, build there was a steely strength about him. It was not all physical, Marnie felt. Behind that dreamy, somewhat abstracted air there was a will of iron. Meeting his oddly detached yet purposeful glance, Marnie shivered. She wouldn't like to get on the wrong side of him, she thought. He would make a relentless enemy. The piercing way he had of looking at you, as if he would read your very thoughts! And whatever he was seeing at this moment seemed to be amusing him. His smile was quizzical. "If you nurse as well as you dance they are very lucky patients," he said.

Marnie stiffened a little in his arms. "Nursing and

dancing!" she mocked. "What a *non sequitur*! The two things are totally disconnected."

"But you have hospital parties," he persisted. "Dances, balls. There are young doctors, no doubt . . ."

What was he getting at now? His curiosity suddenly nettled her. She gave him a basilisk glance and firmly changed the subject.

CHAPTER FIVE

IN the silence which followed magic took over. The music, the white beach seen dimly through the archways of flowers, the sea with its canopy of stars, all this, Marnie felt, would be imprinted on her mind for ever. And Grego's nearness, half troubling, half sweet. He was holding her more closely now. She could feel the stuff of his dinner jacket against her cheek. There was no effort in their dancing, the music carried them along on a silvery tide, their every movement co-ordinated.

"I am usually all feet when I try to dance," Grego said softly. "But with you it is perfect!"

She didn't answer him. She was so happy there was no need for words. To speak you had to think, and she didn't want to think; she just wanted to go on drifting along on the tide of music in Grego's arms. "With you it is perfect," he had said.

She stood dazed for an instant when the dance came to an end and Grego bowed his thanks. It was hard to come back to dull reality again, harder still when a distinctly American voice called out: "Grego! Hi, Grego! Come on over and say hullo!"

With a muttered, "Good heavens! Sean Macreedy!" Grego steered Marnie towards one of the tables which bordered the dance floor. Three people were sitting at it; a bronzed good-looking man of middle age, an extremely elegant woman of about the same vintage, and a girl with the jet black hair and speedwell blue eyes which hints at an Irish origin.

"Eileen, how nice to see you!" Grego was taking the older woman's hand. She smiled up at him. "We were hoping we should run into you this evening. We phoned the Contessa and she told us you were doing the night spots of San Paolo and had mentioned that you might be coming here.

"Patricia, *carissima!*" It was the girl's hand Grego was bowing over now. Her speedwell blue eyes rested on him hungrily. Hard eyes, Marnie thought. She had a magnolia-pale heart-shaped face, and her hair was cut daringly short, revealing her small ears and every line of her perfectly shaped skull. Only authentic beauty could have survived such a trying style, but there was no doubt about this girl's beauty.

"Miss Marnie Gray," Grego presented Marnie. "Senator and Mrs Macreedy, and Patricia Macreedy."

The Senator, standing to acknowledge the introduction, gave Marnie a massive handshake and a cheery, "Hi, Marnie! Glad to know you." He was a large, powerfully built man with an authoritative manner. Mrs Macreedy smiled her welcome to the stranger. The girl stared impassively and murmured a casual "Hullo!"

Taking it for granted that they were joining them, the Senator fussed hospitably with chairs. "What will you drink?" he asked.

"Strega for me, thanks," Grego answered. Marnie chose fruit juice, and was aware that Patricia gave her a withering glance. Her tipple no doubt would be Vodka and lime, or whatever exotic beverage the latest fad might decree. There was an unmistakably sophisticated air about her, and it wasn't all due to that daring, up-to-the-minute haircut, or the long black and silver

453

earrings swinging from her shell-like ears. Behind that magnolia-pale face with its width of brow was a formidable intelligence. The coldly appraising eyes proclaimed it. The Irish origin, Marnie decided, was a long way back; this girl was so patently cosmopolitan.

"Are you staying in San Paolo?" she asked Marnie.

"Not exactly. I was until today . . ." Marnie looked to Grego for her cue.

"Now she is our guest at the Castello," he said.

"Indeed!" The single word came out like the click of a flick-knife. Something that might have been outrage flashed in the speedwell blue eyes.

"It is quite a story," Grego began.

"I found the Contessa's Siamese cat wandering on the beach, this morning," Marnie took it up. "His address was on his collar, so I took him back to the Castello."

"Where my grandmother," Grego went on, "overcome with gratitude at the rescue of her adored pet, persuaded Miss Gray to remain. She will be staying with us, we hope, for the rest of her holiday."

There was an odd little silence. "It was really terribly kind of the Contessa," Marnie said hurriedly. "I was here on my own and finding it a bit lonely."

"So you rescue the Contessa's cat and the Contessa rescues you," laughed the Senator, easing the momentary tension. But it was clear to Marnie that the Macreedy family hadn't been altogether pleased to hear that she was a guest at the Castello.

"That cat sure has nine lives," the Senator went on. "Do you remember the time he got himself stuck on top of one of the castle turrets, and you had to get Monteviano's equivalent of a fire brigade to get him down?"

"Shall I ever forget it!" Grego laughed.

So the Macreedys were familiar visitors at the Castello, Marnie thought with an unaccountable pang.

"Did you get my letter?" Patricia was asking the Conte.

"I did," he confirmed. And then as if apologising for some lack of response on his part, "But you didn't say which day you would be coming to San Paolo."

"I said towards the weekend," Patricia returned a trifle acidly. "And today is Thursday."

Had he half expected to run into the Macreedys tonight? Marnie wondered. Was that the reason he had been so anxious to come down to San Paolo; why he had brought her to the Savoia? She smothered the unworthy suspicion, wondering at the sense of outrage it brought. It had nothing to do with her if the Conte di Valetta had hoped to meet his friends.

"How is Rome these days?" he was asking the Senator.

"Noisier than ever! And the crowds, the traffic! It's totally impossible to find a parking place anywhere near the centre of the City any more."

"We had dinner with Giulio at the Napolitana last night," Mrs Macreedy contributed. "He asked us to tell you he will be home for the weekend on Saturday."

"Oh, good," Grego murmured—without much enthusiasm, it seemed to Marnie.

The drinks came, and the Senator, frowning at Marnie's fruit juice, ordered a magnum of champagne. "After all, it is an occasion!" he pointed out. "It's not every day Mammy and I find ourselves in an Italian night spot hob-nobbing with a member of the aristocracy."

Patricia winced visibly, and said in a low voice,

"Poppa, really! You sound like someone straight from the sticks!"

"Well, I am," the Senator declared cheerfully, "if you compare our little home town with a plushy resort like San Paolo."

The orchestra began to play a Strauss waltz. Patricia put a possessive hand on Grego's arm and her upward glance held invitation.

"Will you dance?" he responded inevitably. They went out on to the dance floor. Patricia Macreedy wasn't unusually tall, but she had a long-limbed grace and managed to be at the same time shapely yet slender. She was wearing a frock of shimmering silver, which clung to her lithe body provocatively. She held herself proudly. Marnie couldn't help envying her poise. Would this be one of the times Grego was "all feet"? she wondered, half hoping it would! But he seemed to be getting round the floor with reasonable ease.

The Senator stood over her, bowing gallantly. "Will you risk a turn on the floor with an old man, Miss Gray?"

"I'd love to," Marnie agreed, not altogether truthfully. She rose from her chair.

He turned to his wife. "Will you excuse us, honey?"

"You go right ahead!" Mrs Macreedy smiled her blessing. "I'll be only too glad to sit here and draw a few quiet breaths!"

"We came all the way from Rome today," the Senator explained, "and my wife did most of the driving. The heat on the roads was overpowering."

"You've been staying in Rome?" Marnie queried.

"For the past ten days," the Senator confirmed. "It certainly is a beautiful city, but a bit wearing. All those churches and gallerys one has to visit, the Forum and

456

the Colosseum, and so on. Pat drove us without mercy, determined we shouldn't miss a thing in her adored Rome. She's lived there for the past four years ... has an apartment near the Farnese Palace ..." He was trundling her round the floor as he spoke. Anything less like her dance with Grego—! She was glad when it was over and she was free to sit down again.

The champagne circulated; the evening went on and on. Marnie had to have several more dances with the Senator, Grego being monopolised by the two Macreedy women. When at last he got round to Marnie the magic of their earlier dance was missing. Now he seemed preoccupied, vaguely uneasy.

"I wish they hadn't turned up at this particular moment," he said suddenly, breaking the silence. An unguarded remark. It came out impulsively as though he spoke without thought, but Marnie's spirits lifted.

"Do you mean the Macreedys?" she asked. "Are they old friends?"

"Oh, yes, very. We've known them for ages. Delightful people ..." his voice trailed away. Changing the subject abruptly, he began to enlarge on the advantages of an open-air ballroom on a hot summer night, but it was all a little forced.

It was well after midnight when the party broke up. The Macreedys were staying at the Regina, a lavish hotel on the sea-front nearby. Grego and Marnie walked with them along the brightly lighted promenade. In her shimmering silver gown Patricia might have been a mermaid straight out of the phosphorescent sea. They were going to have a day of sunbathing and swimming tomorrow, she told Grego. "Is there any chance of you joining us?" Her voice held appeal.

But Grego shook his head. "Not a hope, I'm afraid.

I've a particularly busy day at the dairy factory to-morrow."

"You and your smelly old cheeses!" Patricia grumbled. "Why don't you have a manager to take care of them?"

"Managers have to have salaries."

"Oh, well, we shall be seeing you on Saturday, "Mrs Macreedy put in briskly. "It's so sweet of the Contessa to invite us for the weekend. Shall we arrive about noon?"

"That would be perfect," Grego agreed.

There was a chorus of "goodnights", and then Marnie and Grego were walking back to their car. "We can't possibly call at the *pensione* at this hour," Marnie protested, as they drove down the still scintillating boulevard.

"We can stop by and see if the lights are still burning in the downstairs windows," Grego suggested. "The cinema show is probably only just finished. This is Italy, don't forget."

The animated crowds thronging the boulevard bore out his words. This was Italy indeed, at its summer night liveliest.

Forced to cruise at a snail's pace to avoid the jay walkers, Grego lolled in his seat. "I hope you enjoyed the Savoia?" he said presently. Was this a hint that he had been expecting some word of appreciation from her for the evening's entertainment? Marnie wondered guiltily. The truth was that the Macreedys had spoiled everything, which was ridiculous. What right had she to feel resentful because some old friend of the Conte's had turned up?

"It's been a marvellous evening!" she enthused falsely. "That dance floor was sheer heaven, and it was nice meeting your friends." (Might she be forgiven the lie!) "Do they often come to San Paolo?" she couldn't resist asking.

"Sean and Eileen turn up about once a year, when they are over here from the States, vacationing, as they call it. Pat we see more often. She lives in Rome, has a studio apartment there. She paints, quite brilliantly. Some of her stuff is outstanding. There is talk of her giving a one-woman show in Paris during the autumn."

So Pat Macreedy was as sophisticated as she looked, running an apartment in Rome, sufficiently a painter in her own right to hold a Paris exhibition.

"She must be very clever," Marnie said, with an unconscious sigh.

"She is," Grego agreed. "Only twenty-one and already an established artist. Not only that, but she is a brilliant linguist and has taken a degree at the Sorbonne."

The prick at Marnie's heart could only have been jealousy, and she was instantly ashamed of it. But girls like Pat Macreedy had so many advantages. There was money behind her, lots of it, if appearances were anything to go by. Those pearls Mrs Macreedy was wearing tonight had the sheen of authenticity, and her diamond rings must have been worth a sizeable ransom. Pat would have had the best in the way of education America had to offer, rounded off no doubt by a year or two in some exclusive French or Swiss finishing school.

"Is she an only child?" Marnie asked.

"Yes. The precious solitary chick! Her parents are naturally very proud of her, and very ambitious for her."

Did their ambitions include marriage into the Italian nobility? Marnie wondered. She glanced at the patrician profile at her side. Generations of breeding had produced

459

that air of unconscious superiority. As if aware of her scrutiny, Grego turned and smiled at her, a slow and musing smile, curiously tender. He took a hand off the steering wheel and laid it lightly on her knee. "It has been fun this evening, Marnie. You're a very sweet person to be with. We must do this again some time... that is, if you'd like to?"

"Oh, yes!" It came out a little breathlessly.

"There is a *trattoria* in a fishing village along the coast road, where you eat sea-food on a terrace overlooking a beautiful little rock-girt bay. They give you crayfish as large as lobsters, and soles grilled with rosemary, over a charcoal fire—cooking it at your table. There is nothing between you and the stars but a trellis of vine leaves. On a moonlit night it is right out of this world!"

"It sounds enchanting," said Marnie, her blue eyes wide, her heartbeats quickening. It seemed hardly credible. Grego who was far too sincere a person to make idle promises had offered her a date on a moonlit terrace, "out of this world". Patricia Macreedy's intrusion into their evening at the Savoia lost some of its sting. Perhaps she was Giulio's girl. She was coming to stay at the Castello on Saturday when he would be at home. After all, she must see a lot of him, since they both lived and worked in Rome.

Grego began humming a pop number which the amplifiers in the trees had been plugging all the evening.

She felt his fingers close over her own, cool and firm, instinctively she moved nearer to him, leaning against his shoulder. If only this tree-lined avenue would go on for ever! But they had turned into the by-road now and there was the *pensione*, its downstairs windows all ablaze.

"What did I tell you?" Grego triumphed.

A heavy-eyed Maria opened the door to them once more. Was she never off duty, poor child? Marnie had heard her padding about the house in her down-at-heel slippers long before breakfast, and here she was, still on the go. And there I was envying Pat Macreedy, Marnie thought. To Maria, she herself must seem to be one of fortune's darlings. It was all a question of degree, of course. But Maria's weary, eager-to-please little face left one feeling rather guilty.

"Va bene!" she nodded eagerly in answer to Marnie's enquiry. *Le signorine* were now at home, having a late supper. She would call them. She sketched a brief curtsey, then stumbled as she turned to hurry away. The presence of the Conte seemed to fluster her. It obviously flustered the Deladda sisters also, for they came twittering into the hall, resplendent tonight in floral frocks and gauzy stoles.

"The Conte di Valetta!" they gasped in chorus. How proud they were to receive him in their humble home, they exclaimed. And how was his grandmother, *la gentilissima Contessa*?

He answered them courteously, but briefly. "I have come to rob you of one of your guests, I'm afraid," he apologised. "My grandmother has invited the Signorina Gray to stay at the Castello for the remainder of her holiday. We do hope it won't inconvenience you."

The sisters darted black-eyed glances at one another, seeming to be taken aback.

"Naturally I will pay for my room here, since I booked it for three weeks," Marnie added a little hurriedly, in case the sisters should protest. But they did not seem to hear her, gazing at the Conte in rapt admiration.

"It was so kind of Miss Gray to rescue my grandmother's beloved Siamese," he continued. "And she

461

wishes me to thank you too for helping Miss Gray. It was more than good of you." He went off into a torrent of rapid Italian, which Marnie couldn't follow. But whatever it was he was saying the sisters seemed more and more enchanted, nodding their heads in agreement, their faces wreathed in smiles, their hands clasped to their floral bosoms.

"It is quite all right," he told Marnie when this exchange came to an end. "They are quite reconciled to your change of plans. No hard feelings."

"Bene, bene!" chimed the sisters in chorus. But still they did not look at Marnie, nor did they make any comment when she said she would go to her room and pack her things. It was as though she did not exist. Probably they were glad to be rid of her, Marnie thought, as she bundled her frocks into her two suitcases. They had never liked her. And of course they had been completely overcome at having a visit from the Conte. She had heard them, as she left the hall, inviting him into their private sitting room. But what she did not hear were the words spoken by the most forceful of the sisters as they ushered him into this sanctum : "This English *signorina*, your Grace; if she is to be the guest of the Contessa at the Castello di Valetta, we feel you ought to know something of the way in which she came to us. She is not what she seems. It is the strangest story . . ."

When Marnie returned to the hall with her cases the Conte and the two sisters emerged. If the atmosphere had become oddly strained, she did not notice it, intent now on her journey to the Castello. Grego relieved her of the cases. This seemed to shock the sisters, who made protesting noises. But Grego, ignoring them, moved towards the open hall door. His face was set and stern. The Deladda women, Marnie concluded, were getting on his nerves with their twittering and fussing. He strode down the steps to the car to wait for her while she settled the account which had been prepared for her. As she had already paid part of her debt in advance, the transaction didn't take long. Slipping the receipt into her handbag, she bade the grimly silent sisters a cheery farewell.

"Thank goodness that's over!" she said, as she settled into her place by the driving seat. "And thank you for helping me to extricate myself. I don't think the Deladda girls were really upset at losing me. For some reason they've never been very friendly. In fact there were times when they were barely polite to me. I can't think what I've done to offend them. Perhaps it's that they are shocked at me for travelling about alone. Are all Italian spinsters of uncertain age as prim and proper?"

"They have some ideas you would no doubt find comically old-fashioned," Grego replied. After which he drove for the most part in silence, only speaking if he were forced to answer some remark of Marnie's, and then confining himself to the barest number of words. He was tired, she concluded. It was very late, and the twisting mountain road didn't make for easy driving. Leaning back in her seat, she closed her eyes and discovered that she too was growing sleepy. But it had been a wonderful evening. That first dance with Grego! "With you it is perfect," he had said. For her too it had been perfect. And he wanted to take her out again, to a *trattoria* overlooking a moonlit sea, so beautiful that it was out of this world. Happiness filled her heart.

They were nearing Monteviano now, passing the hillside cemetery with its ghostly white marble statutary and ink-black cypress trees; the last landmark on the way home.

As they entered the hall of the Castello an elderly woman rose from the settle by the hearth, where she had evidently been awaiting them. She wore a black alpaca frock and an old-fashioned white frilly apron.

"Ah, Gina, there you are!" the Conte greeted her. "Has the Contessa gone to bed?"

"*Si, signore.*" She bobbed a curtsey as she spoke. "Her Ladyship sends the *signorina* her apologies," there was another bob—in Marnie's direction this time, "and bade me show her to her room. La Contessa wishes the *signorina* a very good night."

"*Grazie!*" Marnie murmured, a little overcome by all this formality. There was a spookiness too about the great stone hall, where a single light burned, a flambeau lamp held aloft in the hand of the marble nymph that adorned the newel post at the bottom of the immense curving staircase. A faint smell of damp and dust hung in the air, an odour of vanished centuries. Generations of feet had worn the flagstone paving on which she stood. Armour gleamed in shadowy corners. For one fanciful moment Marnie could imagine ghostly eyes of di Valetta ancestors watching her balefully from the oil paintings on the walls. She shivered with a sudden chill.

"If the *signorina* will come this way," old Gina was saying, motioning towards the staircase. Marnie turned to look up into Grego's set, withdrawn face, she held out her hand. "Goodnight, and thank you for a lovely evening."

"My pleasure!" he murmured, and holding her hand briefly, bowed low. It was ridiculously stiff after the companionable hours they had spent together. What had come over him?

Too sleepy to work it out, she followed the old servant up the stairs. It had been a long, exciting day, and her head was slightly befuddled. Though she had drunk as sparingly as the evening's hospitality would permit she had had a bit of a mixture. Wine at dinner in the Castello, then that strong liqueur at the Savoia, followed by the Senator's champagne. She was not accustomed to intoxicants of any kind, and now they were all catching up on her. She thought longingly of bed!

Her room was large and oriel-shaped, as if it might be the inside of one of the thickly walled towers. But if so, the walls had been disguised, plastered and painted over in a delicate shade of green, which went well with the dull gold hangings hiding the deeply embrasured windows. The bed, turned down and ready for occupation, was single and blessedly modern. Marnie had half expected a vast fourposter hung with faded tapestry. The second door in the room led down a short flight of steps to a bathroom, old Gina was explaining. She hoped the *signorina* would find she had everything she needed for her comfort. "If not, please ring for me." She indicated an old-fashioned plaited woollen bell-pull at the head of the bed.

"I'm sure I have everything I need," Marnie protested. "And if I hadn't I wouldn't dream of ringing for you at this late hour." Perhaps she made it too emphatic in her inadequate Italian. Gina looked a little hurt.

"*Grazie, molto grazie!*" Marnie beamed at her. "*E buona notte.*"

"*Buona notte, signorina.*" Gina bowed herself out. Poor old thing! Ring for her, indeed ... Remembering the weary little Maria at the *pensione*, Marnie wondered if Italian servants ever got any sleep.

CHAPTER SIX

DRIVING through the hot golden sunshine to Ravenna the next morning Marnie felt on top of the world. With the Contessa at the wheel they were trundling along at a sedate forty miles an hour. They had gone even more cautiously on the twisting mountain road from Monteviano, but now they were crossing the plains that led to the coast—"the Marches", the Contessa called them; lush green pastures where the dairy cattle grazed. The wide-roofed farmhouses they passed looked prosperous and comfortable with their flower-filled window-boxes and neatly kept vegetable patches. But the Contessa said farming on the Marches was an uncertain and even dangerous life. Sometimes in winter, when the snow melted on the high mountains owing to mild weather or spells of rain, floods would rush through the valleys and inundate all the surrounding country. The wide acres of the Marches were, of course, a safeguard, for the water could spread out and do no more damage than the ruination of the crops and the land. But in the narrow valleys houses, and even churches, could be swept away, and there was loss of life.

They passed through an occasional village, with its tree-lined *piazza* and inevitable beautiful church. Cars were few and far between, but they had to watch out for straying animals and lumbering ox wagons. It wasn't tourist country, the Contessa said, making it sound like a recommendation. She was wearing a light dust coat and had twisted a sky blue filmy scarf about her head. This made her look twenty years younger than her age, and watching her swift reactions as she drove, Marnie was filled with admiration. How attractive she must have been in her youth! Even now the beautiful bone structure remained. Her likeness to Grego was very evident this morning.

There had been no sign of him when Marnie got downstairs, rather late after her night of dissipation. No doubt he had already gone off to his numerous duties on the estate. And he had not appeared to see them off when they set off on their trip to Ravenna. It was old Batiste who drove the Fiat round to the portico steps.

"I hope you had no difficulty with the Signorine Deladda last night," the Contessa said soon after they got under way.

"Oh, no, they were most amiable about my leaving," Marnie told her. "They were so pleased to see the Conte that I don't think they cared what happened about me!"

The Contessa laughed. "As long as they weren't annoyed with me for annexing you ... I wouldn't want them to be upset."

"Believe me they weren't!" Marnie said a little wryly.

"Did you enjoy your dancing at the Savoia?" the Contessa asked.

"I had a marvellous evening!" Marnie enthused. "For the first time I was really able to appreciate the light-hearted atmosphere of Italy at night; the crowds, the music, the lights. Having an escort made all the difference."

"I'm so glad," the Contessa murmured a little abstractedly, her attention engaged by a flock of goats coming towards them.

"Grego told me he met our old friends, the Mac-reedys," she volunteered a moment or two later when the goats had been safely negotiated.

"Yes, we had quite a party," Marnie confirmed. "The Senator insisted upon us drinking champagne, and it was all very gay and friendly." Which sounded a bit prissy, Marnie thought, but the Contessa might not know what she meant if she was told the evening had been "absolutely fab".

She said, "Sean is something of a power in American politics, an astute man both in business and in the Senate. I shouldn't be surprised if he had an eye on the White House. In America all things are possible, and he is immensely rich, which, I understand, helps a good deal."

It was all way out of her depth, Marnie thought with a flash of amusement. Counts and Countesses and aspiring White House Presidents, to say nothing of prodigy girl painters who held exhibitions in Paris! But she mustn't let it get her down. Ambitious politicians and people with ancient Italian titles were as human as anyone else. When Grego held her in his arms to dance she didn't think of him as a Count, an enigmatic man with a world-weary air that could at moments turn to something oddly wistful, even hopeful, as if he didn't quite believe in his own disillusionment. She wondered what had brought about that disillusionment. Once or twice last night she had had the strange feeling that he was looking to her for help, which of course was ridiculous. Saying she was "sweet to be with" could easily have been no more than a champagne reaction, a mood which had begun to evaporate by the time they were driving home.

It was noon when they came to Ravenna. Marnie fell

in love straight away with the beautiful little town. Cruising slowly down a narrow street, she had time to admire the tall old houses, their walls and fluted rose-red roofs mellowed by centuries of sunlight. When they had parked the car they went first to the church of San Vitale. It seemed vast and cool, uncluttered by pews or the usual ecclesiastical furnishings. There was nothing to distract from the mosaics that lined the octagonal walls. Light came through translucent alabaster windows, set high overhead. Everywhere colour glowed, the fragments of jewelled stone fitted together with such artistry that foliage, garments and human countenances all appeared to have their separate textures. Marnie gazed in delight at patriarchs, apostles and angels.

They went through a small door into the famous Tomb of Galla Placida, a cruciform building erected in the fifth century to the memory of the Roman Honorius. He must have been greatly loved, Marnie thought, for this was no tomb, but a small church of surpassing beauty, so old that it had sunk several feet into the ground, yet the mosaics which adorned it were as fresh as the day they had been made. White doves drinking out of a gold-edged bowl against an azure blue background; a shepherd, life-size, with lambs; stags quenching their thirst at a holy fountain; a dreaming apostle with what looked like a pair of archaic spectacles in his hand; and over it all the Cross, stark in its eternal appeal, set against a night-blue sky strewn with stars that seemed to live and twinkle. It had an air of tenderness, this building, of heartbroken love for all living things.

"I never knew mosaics could be like this!" Marnie whispered with tears of emotion in her eyes. All she had known of this art form before was the rather dull Roman pavements she had seen on archaeological sites during educational excursions when she was at school. But here was an expression of the human spirit at its most sensitive; colour, form and design, which included the structure of the church itself, had been brought together in perfect harmony. And it had all been done centuries ago, before modern civilisation had developed to any degree.

There were many other places to see, the Contessa said. But they had better leave them until they had had lunch.

They ate on the open terrace of a small *trattoria* overlooking the main *piazza*. The meal was light and delicious, ending with wild strawberries and cream, followed by cups of hot reviving coffee.

"Sightseeing is so exhausting," the Contessa sighed. "But you must see the marble in the San Francesco, and the Lombardo decorations."

"Please don't try to do too much on my account," Marnie begged. "Isn't this the hour you ought to be having your siesta?"

"But not in Ravenna!" the Contessa protested. "There are far too many interesting things to see, and I'm really not at all tired. My excellent luncheon has revived me."

She certainly didn't look tired, Marnie thought, with an admiring glance at the small animated face beneath the cloud of blue chiffon.

It was the hottest hour of the day as they left the vine-shaded terrace. Heat blistered the shop fronts, shimmered on the pavements. It was a relief to wander in and out of the big cool churches. They looked conscientiously at columns of Greek marble, sculptures and paintings, at the tomb of the poet Dante with its everburning lamp, and the Palazzo Rasponi where the illfated Lord Byron had stayed when he first came to

Ravenna at the beginning of the nineteenth century—a fairly modern item of interest compared with the antiquities of the churches.

But nothing, in Marnie's estimation, came up to the mosaics in the Galla Placida. She had, she felt, been face to face with perfection there and would happily have left it at that and seen nothing more. The Contessa, however, seemed insatiable. There was an effigy in the Accademia di Belle Arti, she declared, that they must on no account miss.

With a curiously eager air she hurried Marnie through a network of small streets until they came to an unpretentious and blessedly shady building. Firmly ignoring the ground floor picture galleries, she piloted Marnie to an upstairs room dominated by a bier upon which, immortalised in white marble, a sleeping warrior lay. He was very young, very beautiful, his eyes closed on life for ever.

"This is the Tullio Lombardo carving I specially wanted to show you," the Contessa whispered. Somehow one had to whisper in the presence of that austere reclining figure.

"Guidarello Guidarelli," the Contessa spoke the musical name, "treacherously killed in some foolish brawl five hundred years ago."

Marnie gazed at the flawless features, the sensitive full-lipped mouth, compressed in bitterness. There was no resignation on that sleeping face.

"He was so young. He didn't want to die." The Contessa dabbed at her eyes with a lacy pocket handkerchief. "Forgive me, but he invariably has this effect on me. Yet I always have to come and see him when I visit Ravenna. There is a haunting quality about him. Perhaps because

471

he bears a curious resemblance to my grandson Grego. Can't you see it?"

"Yes," Marnie murmured musingly. That beautifully cut, unhappy mouth, the classic lines of jaw and chin, the lofty brow. Grego imprisoned for ever in lifeless marble, despairing, resentful. A shiver ran through her.

They stood for a timeless interval in the sombre room. It was a relief to be back in the bustle of the streets again, to feel the heat of the sun.

"Oh, for a cup of good English tea!" the Contessa exclaimed presently, dispelling the mood of that sorrowful upper room. But it wouldn't be easy to find English tea in Ravenna. They settled for fruit juice instead, bought at a wayside stall, and stood side by side sipping it in the hot afternoon sunlight. What a sport the old girl was! Marnie thought with a glance at the dauntless old lady, who somehow contrived to look as dainty and fresh as she had done when they started out. And she still had the long drive home before her.

It was beautifully cool cruising along with the roof of the car open. "I *have* enjoyed today!" Marnie enthused. "It was kind of you to give up your time, showing me all those wonderful places."

"My dear, it was a pleasure. I can never get enough of Ravenna. It must be a whole year since I revisited those superlative mosaics . . . and my adored Guidarello. He draws me like a magnet, even though he makes me so sad."

Was it because of his family resemblance that he attracted her? A moment later she was speaking of Grego. "He would have enjoyed today, but it is so difficult to get him away from the farm. Sometimes I think he uses his work as an escape from social obligations. I can so seldom get him to relax. I was delighted when he suggested taking you to San Paolo last night. It is good for him to be in young company now and then; he spends far too much time alone with me."

What had made him like this? Why did he prefer his work to human relationships? Marnie wondered. But it would be impertinent to probe.

Fortunately the Contessa seemed disposed to pursue the subject. There is something about driving home through a sunlit evening after a shared day's outing that encourages confidences.

"Grego has always been inclined to be a bit of a recluse," the old lady continued presently. "Perhaps because he was badly hurt at a vulnerable age. He was twelve years old when his mother smashed all he believed in by taking a lover and eloping with him. The Conte, Grego's father, was fighting at the time in Africa. We were leading a more or less beleaguered existence at the Castle. Grego adored his mother; she was gay, radiant, beautiful. Her great spirit had helped us to get through those last terrible years of the war. We all relied on her—too much, perhaps. Then suddenly she was gone. It seemed to me quite incredible. I could hardly believe it. But to Grego it did the greatest damage."

"How terrible for you all. I'm so sorry!" Marnie murmured awkwardly. A feeble attempt at comfort, but it was difficult to know what to say to this intimate snatch of family history. Too intimate perhaps to be offered to a comparative stranger. But old people slip so easily back into the past. And old people are garrulous.

"At times I used to think he was getting over it," the Contessa went on, now fairly launched on this account of her grandson's shattering experience. "But a girl he fell in love with some years ago let him down rather badly and that just about finished him. It must have

473

seemed to him that love was a mockery and all women untrustworthy.

"Now," she said after a moment's pause, "there is Patricia Macreedy. A charming child, and so suitable for him in every way. It is the earnest wish of her parents and myself that she and Grego will make a match of it."

"And the Conte?" Marnie couldn't resist asking. "How does he feel about it."

The Contessa smiled. "Oh, he is attracted, I'd say .... definitely attracted. Pat is beautiful, artistic, brilliantly intelligent."

And extremely wealthy, Marnie thought. She gazed blankly at the meadow they were passing. The early summer grass had already been cut for hay and lay drying in the sun, the dying poppies scattered on the orderly swathes bright as splashes of blood. "You could marry for money," she had said to Grego last night when he had spoken of his family's poverty. And he had answered her drily, but with a purpose she had not suspected, "Perhaps I will." Marriages of conveniences, he had added, were possibly the only sort that really worked out. Had he been thinking of his mother's defection? The unhappy story made it easier to understand his aloof attitude to life. Something of warmth and spontaneity had been destroyed in him. Irresistibly she was remembering Guidarello, the young man turned to stone.

A sudden pain twisted in her heart. She clenched her hands, amazed at the wave of anguish which swept over her. Why should the troubled affairs of the Conte di Valetta affect her so deeply? The answer was humiliatingly obvious. Blindly, unthinkingly she had let herself fall in love with him. It had been fatally easy. Lost and adrift after her broken romance with Glenn, she had been caught on the rebound. It was all quite crazy, of course; absurd and impossible. The Conte Gregorio di Valetta, scion of an ancient and noble Italian house, on the brink of a union with the daughter of an American millionaire. And if it had not been so, the situation would have been equally hopeless. His world was so totally removed from her own, his background totally alien. Yet she had imagined that strange sense of harmony between them. She had been deluding herself, indulging in wishful thinking. Grego found her mildly diverting, a little pathetic perhaps; a gauche young English girl blundering about an Italian holiday resort alone. He wouldn't have met her type before, she would have a novelty appeal . . .

The car swerved as they cornered sharply, narrowly avoiding an old man riding on the back of a sleepy donkey. "If only they would learn to keep to the side of the roads!" the Contessa groaned. "But the old ones, they amble along as though cars had never been invented."

As they turned in at the castle gates Chinky came bounding down the drive to meet them. "He always knows when I am out in the Fiat," the Contessa boasted. "He sits on the portico steps watching and waiting until I come home." She opened the door for him as he drew near, and jumping into the car with a triumphant "Mrrow", he settled on her lap.

"Not very helpful to my steering!" she said, as she wobbled to a halt before the great front door.

Over the dinner table Grego was politely interested in their day's doings—more polite than interested, Marnie felt. "And what did you think of the Galla Placida mosaics?" he asked her.

"They are incredibly lovely!" Marnie answered.

"Reputed to be among the best in the world," Grego

told her. "Probably because of their extraordinary state of preservation."

"And their subjects," Marnie added softly. "They are so human, so appealing . . . so tender."

Grego glanced at her oddly and changed the subject. He had greeted her formally when they met in the hall before dinner, bowing low, with Continental gallantry, over her hand. But his touch had been impersonal, a bare brush of his finger tips, and throughout the meal which followed he had seemed to be avoiding a direct glance in her direction. Save for the exchange about the mosaics he addressed his remarks exclusively to his grandmother.

But what else had she expected? Marnie asked herself bleakly. What castles in the air had she been building on the strength of the brief intimacy of their trip to San Paolo last night? Italians, she reminded herself, were mercurial, given to swift changes of mood. Last night he had found her amusing. In the gala atmosphere of the seaside resort she had been "sweet to be with". Now he was his usual withdrawn self again and she was no more than a somewhat unexpected guest in his house, the protégée of an old lady's whim.

"What are your plans for tomorrow?" he was asking the Contessa. "Shall you need the car again?"

"No, my dear, I think I will rest tomorrow. I thought you might like to take Marnie to the home farm, and let her see something of the cheese-making."

"But of course!" The Conte turned to Marnie. "If that is what you would like?" The tone was less willing than the words, and once more there was that maddeningly formal little bow.

"Thank you," Marnie murmured, longing to say that she could do without the cheese-making demonstration

476

if it was going to be a bother to him. But her duty as a guest was clear. The Contessa, weary after her long day in Ravenna, was asking her grandson to take over the entertainment of their visitor, and Marnie could only fall in with whatever her hostess suggested.

A single chandelier burned in the great shadowy room, throwing a pool of light down on to the dining table to glint on glass and silver. The Contessa sat at the head of the long table, the Conte at the foot. Marnie in the middle, feeling small and obscure, glanced from one to the other, the dauntless old lady and the proud, aloof young man. A wave of loneliness swept over her. What had these people to do with her, or she with them? She was a stranger in a strange land, and no matter how charming the Contessa might be to her, it could not be otherwise. A fact she must keep well in mind!

CHAPTER SEVEN

THE home farm was a couple of miles from the village, situated in a sheltered dip of the land. It was another perfect morning when Grego brought the estate car round to the portico where Marnie awaited him. "I can't get used to this endlessly settled weather," she told him as she got into the seat beside him.

"You should be here in the winter," he warned her, "when the icy winds blow across the Adriatic, and snow lies in deep drifts on the hills."

"But at least you know what to expect," Marnie pointed out. "During your winters it is cold, and in summer time it is hot and fine day after day, whereas in England you can have five different climates in one week at any time of the year."

"Humph," grunted Grego in a bored way that killed the rather banal exchange stone dead. Marnie felt snubbed. Talking about the weather, she supposed, was conversation at its lowest level. But it wasn't easy to know what to say to this withdrawn, reserved young man. She glanced at his stern profile. There was no sign of the night before last's genial mood. It was almost as if she had imagined it!

The road they took was the one that led to San Paolo, but when they came to the cemetery it forked, and Grego swung the car on to a secondary road, little more than a rough mountain track, which hung perilously over a scrub-covered precipice. Naked boulders protruded from the sandy soil. As the car bumped over them Grego swore mildly under his breath. "One of these days," he prophesied grimly, "this road is going to be washed away by winter rains that would surprise you summer tourists."

"The Contessa told me about them yesterday," Marnie said, a little hurt at being called a tourist. "How the mountain streams, swollen with rain and melted snow, sweep through the villages in the valley. It must be terrifying!"

"It certainly is—for the luckless people who lose everything. You are much better off with your dull English climate, one of the most equable in the world."

Here they were harping on the weather again! Marnie racked her brains for some more original topic. Perhaps Grego would like to talk about his work. "Do you employ many people in your cheese factory?" she asked.

"Not nearly so many as I could do with. Can't afford it," he muttered grumpily. And that was the end of that. Perhaps he was one of those people who were never at their best first thing in the morning. It was only just after eight o'clock. Grego had apologised the night before for the early start they would have to make, but if she wanted to see all the processes of the cheese production they would have to be at the farm when the work started.

Bother the cheese! Marnie simmered now rebelliously. She didn't really care when or how it was made. But she had looked forward to being taken to the farm. She just wanted to be with Grego, share his interests, and if cheese was one of them, then cheese let it be.

They had come to a smoother bit of road now, leaving the precipice and the river valley it shelved behind them. As they descended the land flattened out. They passed through a vineyard, the leaves of the young vines golden

479

in the strong light. There was a roadside cottage surrounded by lemon trees, the lemons bright as little lamps hung amidst the dark foliage.

"That's where my foreman lives," Grego pointed out. He drove through an open five-barred gate and the farm buildings were before them, a huddle of red-roofed sheds and barns ranged round a large cement-paved yard. Heat was already shimmering on its surface, but the whitewashed dairy he led her through was mercifully cool. This was where the milk was kept before being processed. In an adjoining building men in rubber boots and white overalls and caps stood over steaming vats filled with greenish liquid, which they stirred rhythmically.

It was a job that had to be done by hand, Grego explained. "There is no machine which would reproduce the slow stirring which is so essential a part of the cheese-making. The vats, too, have to be heated gradually."

Marnie listened politely, more interested in the dark individualistic faces of the men than in the work they were doing. Grego spoke to them in quick Italian, and they answered him freely, laughing with him at some joking allusion, too technical for Marnie to understand. But they clearly adored him. He was completely at ease with them, his face coming alive and animated. Suddenly he looked ten years younger, interested, absorbed, utterly different from the bored young man who had sat beside her in the estate car, vainly trying to make conversation.

"The cheeses in the vats are not quite ready yet for lifting," he told Marnie presently. "While we are waiting for them I will show you my dairy herd." They were grazing in a green meadow fenced about with willows, small, delicately boned animals, with dark muzzles and pale fawn bodies. Grego enlarged on the amount of milk they gave, and how it had to be kept overnight at just, the right temperature. Refrigerators were anathema to him, it seemed, all wrong for the highly specialised job of cheese-making.

He put a hand under her elbow, helping her over a low stile. His touch was impersonal, and he talked all the time of the technicalities of Italian farming. He wasn't aware of her as a woman any more, Marnie felt.

When they got back to the room of the vats an air of excitement prevailed. The cheeses had reached their final stage. It was like being present at a birth, Marnie thought, as she watched the rubber-gloved hands groping in the green liquid of the dark vats. There was a breathless hush as the rounds of waxen cheese were withdrawn, a good three feet in diameter. "And they must not be broken!" Grego whispered, not daring to raise his voice at this critical moment. They waited in silence until the last round had been placed on a slab to drain. He took her then to a cool dry cellar where the finished cheeses were stored, while they matured.

"We are turning out some first-class stuff," he told Marnie with pride. "If only I had the capital to advertise, speed up and extend my distribution . . ." He broke off with a shrug. But surely capital unlimited was within his reach, Marnie thought bleakly. He only had to make the grade with Pat Macreedy.

He talked about milk yields and crops and cheese all the way home. "I'm afraid I must be boring you," he ended it at last. "But farming is about the only thing I am really well up in. I leave the social graces to Giulio. He will be here this afternoon and will, I know, enjoy taking you about." All this in a tone that held little apology, a declaration of non-involvement with a chance house

481

guest for whom he had no responsibility. If she didn't want to listen to his technicalities she could go elsewhere for her entertainment. He wasn't going to put himself out for her. That, at least, was how it sounded to Marnie. What about the *trattoria* on a cliff top, where you ate crayfish by moonlight? Had she dreamed it all up? she wondered desolately.

It was only ten o'clock when they got back to the Castello, and the Contessa had not yet appeared downstairs. Marnie drifted out on to the terrace wondering what she would do with the rest of the morning. Having deposited her, Grego had driven straight back to the farm, leaving her in such a hurry that she barely had time to thank him for the time he had given up to her. Guiltily she felt she had encroached on his working day —a short day at that, for it was Saturday and the Macreedys would be arriving about noon. Surely he would be at the Castello to welcome them? She herself would rather be out of the way when they came. She decided to go for a walk and explore the village.

As she went down the drive Chinky appeared from nowhere and attached himself to her, trotting purposefully by her side. It was all right to let him come, she supposed. He had seemed perfectly at home in the village that day he had led her from the bus stop to the Castello. When they reached the cobbled way beyond the Castle gates he moved ahead of her, stopping to look behind every now and then, as if to make sure she was following him. Amused at his antics, she was glad of his company. The sense of loneliness she had felt last night at dinner returned to her. Had it been a mistake to come and stay at the Castello? Or was it just that she was, in a foolish way, dreading the arrival of the Macreedy family? They were old friends. She would feel herself to be something of an intruder. Patricia with her cool, insolent air, offering herself and her beauty to the Conte. Was she in love with him?

Jerking her thoughts back to her surroundings, Marnie looked at the small stone-fronted shops on either side of the narrow street, a bakery, a wine shop, a general store displaying every imaginable kind of merchandise, from boots and shoes to groceries and strings of golden onions. There was a revolving rack containing postcards just outside the door, and Marnie stopped to examine them, choosing several views of Monteviano and the Castello to send home. She would occupy herself this afternoon writing the cards, and she would also send a long letter, telling her family the latest of her adventures. Ravenna and the mosaics, her morning with the Conte at the cheese factory—an odd enough combination! Cheese factories and Counts didn't go together.

A gentle nip at her ankle reminded her of Chinky's presence. "Mow-wow!" he wailed in a scolding tone, evidently disapproving of her dalliance. With a whisk of his tail he was off down the street.

"He is away to the butcher's," said a large woman who had appeared in the shop doorway. "Always he has to have his tit-bit of *fegato*, or liver as the English call it." She laughed good-naturedly. *"Il bello gatto della Contessa!"* She broke into a torrent of Italian in the thick mountain dialect Marnie found it so difficult to follow. But she gathered the outburst was a paean of praise for *"la gentilissima Contessa."*

"You are staying at the Castello, *signora*?" the woman asked. "The lady who found the Contessa's cat in San Paolo."

So the story had gone all round the village, Marnie

483

thought, amused. "Yes, I'm staying at the Castello," she confirmed, and paid for the postcards she had chosen.

Continuing down the street, she saw Chinky entering a shop with a white-tiled front and a window containing the cardboard reproduction of an outsize porker. Halting outside the door to see what would happen next, she watched the cat approach the scrubbed wooden counter with a confident air and a loud imperious cry. The butcher, an immensely fat man with curling black moustachios, greeted him with an exasperated exclamation. Then catching sight of Marnie he switched to an ingratiating politeness. *Il gatto* was with the *signorina*? *Bene, bene!* What could he do for the *signorina*?

"Liver, *per favore*," she answered, pointing to a slab of the unappetising-looking stuff in a glass-topped refrigerated showcase. What was the word the postcard woman had used for it? *"Fegato!"* Marnie brought it out triumphantly.

"Ah, *fegato . . . so! Subito, signorina!"* The butcher opened the refrigerator. "It is for this blue-eyed devil of a cat, no?" He cut off a small slice of the liver and using a piece of greaseproof paper for a plate placed it on the floor in front of Chinky, who began wolfing it greedily.

"Twice, maybe three times a week, he comes, this cat, and makes a noise like a lost soul in hell, until I give him the *fegato*," the butcher enlarged.

"I must pay you," Marnie groped for her purse. But the man waved away the lire note she produced. "It is nothing," he declared with a wide, moustachioed smile. "A morsel for the cat of the Contessa. It is an honour that he patronises us!" He burst into a gale of laughter at his own witticism.

Smiling and bowing, he showed them out, Chinky

pleased with himself after his gory tit-bit, running ahead of Marnie, with a satisfied and throaty "Mrrow!" Famous last words! Straight into the road he went, all but under the wheels of a bright red sports car. The young man at the wheel shouted an angry, *"Dio mio!"* and braked violently, missing the cat by a hair's breadth. Trembling with shock, Marnie gathered him up in her arms. He clung to her in terror, his tail bristling to twice its normal size.

"It's all right, Chinky, it's all right, darling," Marnie soothed him. "You're not hurt!"

"It *would* be Chinky!" said the young man in the car. "One of these days that darned cat is going to cause a serious accident."

"You might have killed him," Marnie said shakenly.

"Not Chinky," the young man laughed. "He has more than the proverbial nine lives if I know anything about him. All the same, my grandmother ought not to let him roam about all over the place. It's not safe!"

His grandmother! So this was Giulio; Grego's younger brother from Rome.

He was out of the car now standing over her. Marnie looked at him with interest. He was very good-looking, in a typically Italian way, dark, svelte, with a humorous glint in his eyes. She met their bold bright glance.

"You will be the famous Miss Gray," he said. "When I telephoned her last night my grandmother told me all about you. It seems Chinky picked you up on the beach at San Paolo." He grinned at her impudently. "I can forgive him a lot for that! Nonna said you were now her guest at the Castello and that you were young and English and charming. So I decided to get home as quickly as possible."

Lighthearted flattery, but it cheered her up, made her

realise how bleak her mood had been before he appeared on the scene. She smiled up at him. His dark eyes had golden flecks in them, friendly eyes, laughing and warm.

"Let's get to know each other," he said. "There is an *albergo* on the *piazza* where I can buy you a drink. Hop in the car and I'll take you there."

CHAPTER EIGHT

LIFE at the Castello speeded up with the arrival of the visitors. Now the great hall rang with laughter, footsteps echoed on the marble staircase. Rooms long unused were opened, windows unshuttered. Sunlight played on silver and furniture recently polished. The extra domestic helpers recruited from the village must have worked hard to achieve the effect.

On the evening of the day the Macreedys arrived cocktails were served in a long salon overlooking the stone terrace beyond which lay the neglected rose garden, a room filled with the clutter of generations of opulent living. Marnie eyed the inlaid pedestal tables, the huge chandeliers of sparkling Venetian glass, the ivory and porcelain ornaments, the oil paintings on the damask-covered walls. Couldn't some of these art treasures be sold to bolster up the family's failing fortunes?

Patricia Macreedy, glass in hand, was studying a small landscape of jewel-like colours hung to one side of the monumental chimneypiece, Giulio at her side. The painting looked like a Bellini, she said. But it was no more than a clever copy of the Master, Giulio told her. "If it had been an original it would have been sold long ago. There is not much of great value left in the poor old Castello. Two world wars have seen to that."

So the pretty tables and ornaments and paintings were so much distinguished junk, Marnie thought regretfully.

"Bellini lived in these parts at one time," Patricia

was saying, airing her artistic knowledge. "During the famous *cinque-cento*. He painted a glorious Pieta for the Malatesta family. It is now in a gallery in Rimini."

"The Malatestas are remotely connected with the di Valettas," the Contessa put in conversationally. Marnie was aware of the ripple of interest caused by this announcement. She caught the significant glance that flashed between the Macreedy parents—an eager, hungry look, tinged with hopefulness. The Malatestas, as every well-informed tourist knew from the guide books, had been a power in Italy throughout the Middle Ages, almost a royal power.

"A tyrannical lot," Patricia dismissed them, with scant respect. "And Malatesta di Verucchio who founded the family was one of the most disliked. The 'old mastiff', Dante called him. I've always felt sorry for the lovely Francesca da Rimini, who married his son, Giovanni the Lame, and all the time she was eating her heart out for his younger brother. Dante has written a poem about it."

Giulio put an arm about her shoulder and gave her his impudent smile. "She ought to have been more careful which brother she fell in love with."

Patricia laughed, colouring a little, not missing the implication. "She wouldn't have had much choice. In medieval marriages, which were invariably arranged by the families concerned, the eldest son was the most eligible."

"And where property and titles are concerned times haven't changed," her father put in.

There was a small deadly silence. Even the big sun-tanned Senator began to realise his remark had been a little too markedly related to their own circumstances to be altogether in good taste.

The silence grew suffocating. Marnie glanced at Grego, sitting on a spindly gold love-seat, more elegant than comfortable. "What is wrong with arranged marriages?" he demanded calmly.

Pat turned to him, her blue eyes ablaze. "Nothing," she said. "Nothing at all. Heads are a better guide than hearts any day."

"But a little romance does help things along," Mrs Macreedy said.

The Contessa stood up, small but regal, her silvery head held high. "Shall we go in to dinner?" she said. In her icy tone unspoken rebuke was crystal clear. An arranged marriage between this rich American girl and her favourite grandson might be in the offing. But one did not discuss such matters in public, not even obliquely. As though conferring unimaginable favours the old lady gave the somewhat abashed Senator her arm.

The rest of the evening passed off pleasantly. It was still warm after dinner and they sat on the terrace overlooking the tangled rose bushes and ghost-white statuary. The wicker lounge chairs out here were more comfortable than the baroque furniture indoors. Conversation was drowsy and spasmodic. They would go to the coast tomorrow the visitors planned. The Senator had the use of a friend's cabin cruiser which would take them to the rocky coves north of San Paolo. Marnie wondered if she was to be included in the party. She had, as she had expected, felt a little out of things during dinner, listening to the easy exchanges between the young people. And she had upset the seating arrangements, by being the odd woman present. The Contessa had paired with the Senator, Mrs Macreedy with Giulio, while Pat was inevitably partnered by Grego. Now the two of them were wandering off into the shadowy rose garden, where they seemed to be deeply engrossed in conversation. Marnie watched them with an ache in her heart.

"You are very quiet this evening, little Gray girl!" Giulio slid into the wicker chair beside her own.

"I haven't had a chance to be anything else," she might have answered truthfully. It was Pat who had held the floor all through the prolonged evening meal. Lovely, vivacious, brilliantly clever, and fully aware of her charms, she had quite obviously set herself to impress. Skilfully varying her approach, she had exerted her powers of attraction over the Contessa and her grandsons, concentrating markedly on Grego. Her chatter of Rome was sparkling. She seemed to be equally at home with the social set and the artistic set, and could even insert the odd snatch of exclusive political gossip. Her dazzled parents, hanging on her every word, had been drawn now and then into the conversational net, but Marnie she had consistently ignored, save that she gave her an occasional blank glance as if she wondered vaguely how she came to be there. When the Contessa, with a hostess's concern, had tried to bring the English girl into the flow of talk Pat had cleverly and not very politely out-manoeuvred her, by switching to Italian, which she spoke perfectly.

Now Marnie turned to Giulio with a wry smile. "I'm the proverbial good listener," she told him.

He shrugged. "There are times when one has to be." Was he mocking a little at the voluble Patricia? Changing the subject abruptly, he said, "Do you snorkel?"

"Snorkel?"

"Under-water swimming."

Marnie shook her head. "I've always been contented with the surface of the sea."

"Then I'll show you a new world tomorrow," he

promised. A snorkel and flippers were all she needed, he explained. "We shall find a supply of them on the *Bella Rosa*, and they are perfectly simple to use. Snorkelling isn't a skilled job, like managing an aqualung."

"Am I coming on the cabin cruiser tomorrow, then?" she asked humbly.

"Of course you are!" He seemed astonished that she could think otherwise.

"There are moments when I feel I'm a bit of a gate-crasher," she confessed. "You all know each other so well ... I'm the stranger in the land ..."

"A very lovely stranger!" He covered with his own the hand she had laid idly along the arm of her chair. "It is hearts you will crash, not gates. If you knew what you did to mine when I saw you in the village street yesterday!" He spoke softly, so that the rest of the party on the terrace could not hear him.

She laughed, not taking him seriously. Flattery came from his lips as easily as dew falling on the twilit garden. He had been flirting with her outrageously since the moment they met, pouring out compliments, not meaning a word of them. How different he was from his brother! Or was it merely that Grego had a more subtle technique? That grave attentive manner, the air of complete sincerity when he talked of moonlit *trattorias*, or told her she was sweet to be with—had it meant anything more than Giulio's more blatant cajolery?

"Why so sad?" he whispered in her ear. "Doesn't it amuse you to know that I adore you, little Gray girl?"

She turned to him, startled. She had forgotten he was holding her hand. Gently she withdrew it. "It would amuse me much more if you didn't find it necessary to talk nonsense to me so often." A smile took the sting out of the rebuke.

491

"You English!" he grumbled. "You make such heavy weather of everything. Love is a light, delicious game when played expertly by two people who know the rules. Some day I will teach you."

She laughed. "Is that a threat or a promise?"

"A promise, *carissima*."

In spite of Giulio's assurances Marnie still had doubts the next morning about the trip in the *Bella Rosa*. Did the Macreedys really want her along? They hadn't specifically invited her. She lingered over her breakfast—coffee and rolls and honey, served in her room—took a leisurely bath and made up her face very lightly. It was too hot for foundation cream or powder, the merest touch of skin lotion and a smear of pale lipstick was enough. The thought of the cool, blue-green Adriatic was tempting. She put on a bikini, topped with shorts and a brief sleeveless jacket, and went downstairs. The shorts and jacket were white and made her scantily clad body look very golden. She had developed quite a sun-tan during that week of idling on the beach at San Paolo. Her hair too had brightened in the strong light, smooth and gleaming it clung close to her head. Catching sight of herself in a wall mirror, she couldn't help being pleased with the result. She looked so utterly different from Staff Nurse Gray of St Margaret's Hospital!

At a turn in the marble staircase she saw Grego standing alone in the hall beneath. A strange panic assailed her. Her legs felt suddenly weak. Why should he have this power to disturb her? A man she had known for little more than a week, and who was making it clear he hadn't much time for her.

As she came slowly down the wide, shallow steps, one hand resting on the broad banister, he looked up at her, and for one unguarded moment his grey eyes held a sharp awareness of her, a hint of panic resembling her own, or so for a fleeting instant it seemed.

The great hall doors were open behind him, and she could see the cars waiting on the drive, the Macreedys and Giulio fussing around them packing picnic gear, talking, laughing. Their voices were gay and carefree in the bright morning sunlight. They were all so at ease with one another. Once more Marnie felt she had no place among them.

"Are you ready for the road?" Grego asked her.

Her palm on the cool banister was clammy and damp. "I thought I'd stay at home and keep the Contessa company," she said.

"What's all this about somebody staying at home?" Senator Macreedy stopped on his way through the hall with a bundle of beach wraps and towels. "Of course you are coming along with us. This trip on the *Bella Rosa* is going to be quite something. We wouldn't want you to miss it."

His tone was so kind and welcoming that it would be ungracious to protest any further. And she had so obviously put on her beach wear. Thanking the laden Senator, she followed him across the hall, Grego in their wake. If he was pleased she was to be included in the party he showed no sign. Out on the drive she stood waiting to find out which of the two cars she was to travel in.

"Marnie, you go with Giulio," Pat arranged it for her. She herself got into the back seat of the big open Lancia, motioning Grego to come and sit beside her. She smiled up at him as he took his place, confident, sure of herself... and of *him*, Marnie thought bleakly. She watched him turn to her with a whispered remark, at

493

which they both laughed. He was so clearly at ease with her, happy to have her there at his side.

Giulio's Ferrari was a two-seater, long, low-slung, with a supercharged engine. He drove it as though he were on a race track, cornering at breathtaking speed as they tore down the precipitous mountain road. Marnie sat with her hands clenched against her sides. Conversation was impossible. They reached San Paolo well ahead of the others The *Bella Rosa*, an imposingly large yacht with a striped sun awning spread above its well-scrubbed deck, was anchored in the harbour at the Old Town, some distance from the beach with which Marnie was familiar. A companion-way with brass-tipped steps led to a large, luxuriously appointed cabin, where a man-servant was laying the central table with silver and cutlery. So the picnic lunch was to be served in style! Marnie looked about her with interest. Beyond the dining saloon a narrow passageway, deeply carpeted in rose pink, led to the sleeping quarters, small, elegantly fitted staterooms, each holding two bunks. The miniature dressing tables were fitted with every imaginable toilet accessory. The eiderdowns on the bunks were of softest rose satin, and real roses to match bloomed in the silver wall vases. Marnie exclaimed at it all with delight.

"The *dolce vita*!" Giulio said. The soft living. "So it appeals to you? To me, also. How I hate working in that damned bank day after day, handling money I can never hope to possess!" Marnie was surprised at the bitterness in his voice. For once he was being sincere, speaking with real feeling.

"Grego is the lucky one," he went on, "with Pat Macreedy and her fortune ready to fall into his lap." He swung round to Marnie at his side, his dark eyes alight. "Do you know something, little Gray girl? You've got

494

twice the appeal of the dollar princess. She is all brains and bossiness, while you . . ." He caught her in his arms, not bothering to finish the sentence, and set about kissing her with a vigour she was powerless to resist. Pinned in his grasp, she tried to turn her head evasively. But the purposeful kisses persisted. Footsteps overhead heralded the arrival of the rest of the party. Desperately Marnie renewed her efforts to free herself, but this seemed to excite Giulio all the more. His kisses became more passionate. Suddenly Pat Macreedy was standing in the doorway, a look of scornful amusement on her lovely face. There had been no sound of her approach over the lush carpeting.

"You don't waste much time, you two, do you?" she drawled, with a light laugh.

Giulio, quite unabashed by her arrival, laughed with her. "Do you blame us?" he said, still holding Marnie close.

"On the contrary," Pat shrugged. "Go to it, my children! I'm all for a spot of quiet fun. But for the moment it might be more tactful if you were to show yourselves on deck. Pop wants to know how many snorkel outfits he should collect from the club house."

Crimson with embarrassment, Marnie followed her up the companion-way, Giulio bringing up the rear, humming to himself lightheartedly. Marnie longed to turn round and box his shapely ears. How dared he swoop on her without as much as a by-your-leave? He was a wolf of the first magnitude. She ought to have realised this and been more on her guard.

At lunch time she contrived to sit by Mrs Macreedy, pointedly avoiding the ardent glances of Giulio, who had placed himself directly opposite her. When they went on deck after the meal she continued to ignore

495

him. The sea was calm and blue, the sky cloudless. Beyond the shoreline the distant mountains were misty in the afternoon heat. The strong light drained all colour from the land they were leaving behind them. Only the sea was alive and sparkling, slapping against the hull of the moving yacht with an invitingly cool sound. It was all so beautiful, it was infuriating that Giulio should have marred the day's peace. Gradually relaxing in her deck chair, Marnie put him out of her mind, and gave herself up to the magic of her surroundings. The chairs beneath the awning were ranged in a semi-circle. Everyone was sleepy at this after-luncheon siesta hour. Through half-closed lids Marnie watched Grego and Pat. Their chairs were very close together, Pat's drooping head threatening at any moment to rest on Grego's shoulder. At the far end of the semi-circle Giulio was fast asleep. Even with his mouth a little way open he contrived to look handsome, in a lazy, sensuous, Latin way. As dark as a gipsy, and as irresponsible, Marnie suspected. It would be silly to take his misdemeanours too seriously, and quite impossible to avoid him for the rest of the day. The party was too small, too obviously falling into pairs, her partner inevitably being Giulio.

When they anchored in the rocky cove where they were to swim, he fussed over her, showing her how to adjust her snorkel and flippers. Awkwardly she clambered over the ship's side, lowering herself into the water. "Are you sure you will be all right?" It was Grego calling after her. "If you have never done this before . . ."

"Of course she'll be all right," Pat interrupted him sharply. "Nobody could go wrong with a snorkel. It's childishly simple."

Marnie, submerging, heard no more. Swimming just below the surface, she made her way through the quiet

496

sea. How cool and peaceful it was in this green translucent world. She watched fish of every size and colour darting hither and thither beneath her. Fronds of bright weed moved gently with the tide. A crab scuttled across the sandy floor of the bay, where anemones, fastened to the rocks, unfolded like exotic flowers in an underwater garden. Barely moving her flippers, Marnie glided through the water as easily as the fish she disturbed. As Pat had said, snorkelling was childishly simple, but utterly delightful.

Tiring at last, she went back to the yacht, where Grego helped her aboard. "How did it go?" he asked kindly.

"It was gorgeous!" she enthused, and wondered for one mad instant if he had been watching her progress, postponing his own entry into the water until he was sure she was safely back on the ship. His swimming trunks, she noticed, were dry.

"Aren't you ever coming in?" Pat called to him impatiently.

Marnie watched him dive over the ship's side to join her. Unlike Giulio and the elder Macreedys, they were not snorkelling. Swimming easily side by side, they made their way to a raft anchored some way from the shore, where they lay baking in the hot sun, lost to the world on their little wooden desert island. The Senator had to sound the yacht's siren to recall them when it was time to move on.

Their next stop was at Adriano, a small fishing village with a wide stretch of foreshore, where speedboats were on hire, and water skiing in full swing. Grego and Giulio and Pat gave a superb exhibition of their skill at this sport, while from the deck of the yacht the elder Macreedys and Marnie looked on, Marnie's eyes all for

Grego. Golden-haired, gold-skinned, he stood erect on his skis, every muscle and limb in perfect control. He had a magnificent body, not an ounce of superfluous flesh anywhere—an athlete's body. Giulio, who was of a heavier build, had not half his grace.

The halcyon day wore on, ending with dinner at a little *trattoria* on the quayside, with an informal dance afterwards in a big bright café where the fishermen brought their girls. Marnie, perforce, danced most of the time with Giulio, but in spite of herself she enjoyed it. He danced so well, with a faultless precision that was almost professional. It was towards the end of the evening, when Giulio was dancing with Pat, that her turn came with Grego. At his touch magic enfolded her. Glancing up at him, she caught for an instant that strange flash of pain in his grey eyes as they met her own. Then the mask clamped down and his face was expressionless. Had she enjoyed her drive in the Ferrari? he asked her.

"It was a thrill!" she told him. "Almost too much so at times. I was quite relieved when we arrived in San Paolo intact."

Grego laughed. "Old Giulio certainly steps on the gas, but he is an expert driver." He listed his brother's triumphs on the racing track. Holding her slackly, his movements were listless; it was so obviously a duty dance. Glancing at his wrist watch, he exclaimed at the lateness of the hour. "I hope we are soon on the way home," he said. "My grandmother has been alone all day. I would have persuaded her to come with us, but she is an indifferent sailor, even in perfect summer weather like this."

Touched by his concern for the old lady, Marnie said,

"I wish I had stayed with her, as I suggested this morning."

He gave her a grateful glance. "She wouldn't have wanted you to miss the trip. Probably we're worrying ourselves about her quite unnecessarily. I expect she has been perfectly happy, pottering about, with Chinky for company."

"And he *is* company," Marnie asserted.

"Yes, he's a comical little cuss, full of character. Nonna adores him ... to a pathetic degree. Mortgaging her heart. One day in the course of things; if she lives long enough, she will have to lose him."

They danced for a moment in silence. Then he said, "Why is it that the price of love is invariably pain?"

Was he thinking of his mother? Or of the girl who, according to the Contessa, had let him down? "Must all love end in pain?" she said, answering his question with another.

He shrugged. "It's a risk one has to take, I suppose, if one is fool enough to fall in love. Personally, I don't think the game is worth the candle."

Then what was he doing with Pat Macreedy? Marnie wondered. As the yacht cruised back to San Paolo he disappeared with her to a shadowy corner by the stern. It was scarcely dark even at midnight, the sky bright with stars. A young moon hung like a sickle over the landward hills. A perfect night for love. From her deck chair under the awning, Marnie could hear the muted murmur of the two voices. They sounded very happy and content. She saw Giulio approaching and hurrying out of her chair, made for the companion-way.

"What about a turn round the deck?" Giulio predictably suggested. But Marnie knew only too well what such a stroll would entail. "I was just going below," she

499

told him, and vanished down the brass-tipped steps. In the saloon the Senator and Mrs Macreedy were having a quiet drink, and invited her to join them.

When they reached San Paolo the cars awaited them on the quayside. Giulio was first off the yacht, hurrying over the cobblestones to his precious Ferrari. Marnie lingered on deck. If she lagged behind perhaps Giulio would set off without her, and she could then go home in the Lancia, with the Macreedys. Hidden in the shadow of the sail locker, she was unseen by Grego and Pat, making for the gangway. As they passed her Grego was saying, "Perhaps we ought to take Marnie with us in the Lancia. From something she said today I gather she's a bit scared by Giulio's furious driving."

"My dear, you're so wrong!" Pat's tinkling laughter rang out. "Marnie adores the Ferrari, to say nothing of its owner. You should have seen the way they were kissing in one of the cabins this morning! I stumbled upon them by accident, going below to powder my nose. Believe me, they're well away, those two—only waiting to find themselves alone, driving home under the stars. So don't go butting in and being a spoilsport."

Grego's muttered reply was lost as the couple moved on. With burning cheeks, Marnie stumbled after them, down the gangway. On the quayside Giulio was already unlocking the Ferrari, and took it for granted she was coming with him. When he opened the car door for her she got in beside him without a word. In that moment of pain and confusion there was nothing else she could do.

CHAPTER NINE

THE next day was a public holiday and there was to be a festa at the neighbouring village of Ostana. They would set out for it early, Mrs Macreedy planned; in time to see the religious procession which opened the proceedings. It would surely provide Sean with some interesting sequences on his ciné-camera. After lunch at the village inn, famous for its *stracciatelle,* a delicious chicken soup enriched with eggs and cheese, there would be country dancing on the *piazza.* Later there were to be beauty contests for the girls, trials of strength for the men, and an exhibition of painting by local artists, who might include anyone from the butcher to the village postmistress, Giulio explained. The whole thing added up to the kind of genuinely local jollification the Macreedys wouldn't have missed for the world.

Marnie too would have liked to see it all, but she was determined this time to stay with the Contessa, who once more had elected to remain at home.

Watching the others depart without her, Marnie wasn't entirely sorry. Pat's unfortunate disclosure to Grego last night still rankled. What could Grego think but that she was up to the eyes in an affair with his brother, and thoroughly enjoying it! An impression, Marnie suspected, that Pat would be only to happy to convey. She wasn't having any competition in her efforts to capture the heart of the Conte di Valetta. Not that she need have worried, Marnie reflected dryly.

Grego these days seemed scarcely aware of her existence
—and more and more noticeably aware of Pat's. Their
rapidly hotting-up courtship had been obvious enough
yesterday. Giulio had remarked upon it on the way home
last night, when, to Marnie's relief, he had been too
absorbed in controlling his high-powered car to have any
time for lovemaking. Closing her eyes, she hadn't dared
to estimate the speed at which they travelled, and conversation, for the most part, had been ruled out. But they
had slowed down at one point, encountering some road
works, and it was then Giulio had begun without any
preamble: "Old Greg and Pat seemed to be making
the grade very nicely today, or didn't you notice?"

"They were certainly very much taken up with one
another," Marnie agreed, in a small prim voice that
didn't sound like her own.

"Which is just what the doctor ordered," Giulio said.
"Everyone will be delighted to see them heading for the
matrimonial stakes.

"Excepting," he added after a moment's pause, "the
poor devil Pat kicked out of her life a little while ago;
a painter chappie in Rome whom she's been working
with for the past two years. They were crazy about one
another, inseparable—or so we all thought. Then quite
suddenly Pat ended it all. Love in an attic didn't appeal
to her. It wasn't hard for me to guess that she was playing for higher stakes, leaving the coast clear for Grego.
In fact she as good as told me so, and her parents'
arrival in Europe precipitated things. She knew they
would be tickled pink if she got herself an Italian title,
so she acted like the sensible lass she is and showed
Lorenzo the door."

"She couldn't have thought much of him," Marnie

502

murmured, rather taken aback by this unexpected confidence.

"Oh, but she did! He was the love of her life, all right. I was her confidant throughout the whole emotional upheaval. Mine was the shoulder she wept on when the final break came. But heartache was a luxury she decided she couldn't afford. Her head ruled the day, and her heart, if I know anything of her, will soon recover. She has it all weighed up, believe me. She knows what she wants, that dame, and will see to it that she gets it."

"Does Grego know all this?" Marnie asked in a shocked voice.

"About Lorenzo? Sure he does. But it doesn't bother him, since he makes no pretence of being romantically in love with Pat. Grego just isn't the romantic type. He's in this for what he can get—just as Pat is. She wants a title and he needs her money, so they will be making a fair exchange. Simple, isn't it?"

"No, it's . . . horrible!" Marnie choked.

Giulio shrugged. *"C'est la vie!"* he philosophised easily. "And I must say I shall be glad when it's all settled. It will be good to have a bit of money in the family again, to say nothing of an influential American Senator, who is also a Wall Street tycoon. Perhaps he will rescue me from my slavery in the bank, and find me a plummy directorate on one of his companies. There are, I believe, European affiliations."

Lingering on the terrace over a belated breakfast tray, Marnie mulled over this distasteful conversation. Grego's cold-blooded remark the other day about finding himself a rich wife hadn't, for some reason, shocked her so much as Giulio's disclosures about Pat Macreedy. If there were to be love on neither side what kind of a marriage could it be? A business deal, nothing more or less. How would they endure so empty a relationship year after year? Grego wasn't the romantic type, Giulio had said. Marnie wondered! There was a capacity for passion in those deep grey eyes, a hint of feeling kept under rigid control in the strong, sensitive face. Grego was no iceberg! She had felt it when she danced in his arms. The fire that leapt up in her when he held her close ... was he unaware of it? Surely it took two to produce that sort of conflagration?

Crazy questions! The answers eluded her. She only knew that her meeting with the Conte di Valetta had robbed her of all her usual common sense, left her defenceless. But there was nothing to be done about it. Blindly she had fallen in love with him. Like a physical illness the unsought emotion had descended upon her. And like a physical illness, she would get over it in due course. The madness would pass. It would have to! Meanwhile it made everything but the immediate moment seem unreal. Her past, her future ... none of it mattered. Even the upheaval of her broken wedding was remote now, unimportant. Here she was on what should have been her honeymoon, staying as the guest of an improbable Contessa, in an even more improbable medieval castle, in love with the family heir. Her whole world had gone topsy-turvy. But she would straighten it out again when she got back to England, she promised herself firmly. She would have to. There was nothing else to do. She would be Staff Nurse Gray once more, getting on with her eminently realistic job, while her Italian holiday faded away into the dreamland to which it belonged.

The day that followed was pleasantly restful. The
504

Contessa, obviously glad of Marnie's company, took her all over the castle and up on to the battlements to see the view, which was a "must" for all visitors to the Castello di Valetta. It was certainly worth the laborious climb up flights of worn stone steps. Orchards and olive groves rolled away beneath them into the plum blue distance, grasslands and ripening grain made patches of green and gold on the patchwork landscape, roads twisting up hill and down dale led to remote villages, and framing the whole the Dolomites rose in rugged splendour against a blue sky, pale with heat.

"Once upon a time," the Contessa said, "almost all the land you can see belonged to the di Valettas." She rested her hand on a small iron cannon embedded in one of the battlemented embrasures. "When lands could be defended with weapons like this. Now there are enemies against which such antiquated defences are no use : world wars, changing governments, and the pitiless encroachments of time." She pointed to the vast roof that needed repairing, the rotting gutters choked with dust, damp stains running down the thick stone walls. "It would take a fortune to put the place to rights," she sighed.

Pat Macreedy's fortune, Marnie thought.

After lunch the Contessa rested in her boudoir, while Marnie took Chinky for a walk in the Castle grounds, which turned out to be far more extensive than she had imagined. The plateau on which it stood was unexpectedly wide, accommodating stable yard, garages, kitchen garden and flower gardens—all sadly neglected. There was even a small stretch of woodland where umbrella pines filled the warm air with their tangy resinous scent. Seating herself on a convenient boulder, Marnie admired the effect of the sunlight, slanting through the dark spreading branches of the trees on to their long rose-coloured boles. Chinky, turning himself into a ferocious hunter—quite obviously showing off—explored rabbit holes and stalked imaginary prey. Until, tiring of this make-believe, he flung himself at the nearest tree-trunk, and having sharpened his claws on it thoroughly, shinned up its length to a precarious foothold on one of the topmost branches. Here he sat, wailing piteously to Marnie to come and rescue him. It was an anxious half hour before she could persuade him that if he got up, he could get down, and that there was nothing she could do to help him.

"I thought we should have to send for the fire-brigade, or whoever it is that rescues climbing cats in Italy," she told the Contessa later, when they were having a leisurely tea on the terrace.

The Contessa laughed. "You need not have worried. Next time he does that just walk away and leave him. You'll find he can descend from the highest tree-top quite easily. But he pretends he can't. He enjoys a spot of drama and so raises the alarm. Anything to attract attention!" Chinky, sitting at her feet, squinted up at her knowingly.

She spoke then of the absent guests, hoping they were enjoying Ostana and the *festa*. "They will be off to Venice tomorrow," she said. "Pat has some paintings in an exhibition there, and wants to show them to her parents." They would be remaining in Venice for a few days, Marnie gathered, before continuing their tour of Northern Italy. Pat would accompany them, returning with them to the Castello after a short stay in Florence. By which time, Marnie thought, the Senator and Mrs Macreedy would be proudly announcing their daughter's engagement. They would certainly see it all settled before they ended their European holiday.

"It is a pity you missed Ostana today," the Contessa was saying now. "But you must not miss Venice—even if there is only time for you to have a glimpse of it. Grego will be going along in his car and can drive you there, bringing you back with him in the evening."

"Won't he want to stay in Venice with the Macreedys?" Marnie asked, a little breathlessly. The prospect of a long tête-à-tête drive with the Conte filled her with foolish panic.

"It won't be possible for him to stay. He will have to get back here to see to his numerous affairs," the Contessa replied. She stooped to give Chinky a saucer of cream, which he fell upon greedily, sending splashes of cream over the terrace flagstones.

"Siamese cats have such terrible table manners," the Contessa apologised, but her voice was warm with love. Chinky could do no wrong! They laughed as he pushed the empty saucer across the stones, licking at it with unabated force.

Lying back in her wicker lounge chair, Marnie relaxed. The Contessa was so restful to be with—perhaps because she was done with all the feverish complications of being young. Marnie glanced at the small serene face beneath its coronet of white hair. The deep grey eyes were full of tenderness, following the movements of the cat—unclouded eyes, clear with truth, eyes that had looked straightly at life, accepting its ups and downs with courage. Forthright as her Yorkshire spirit. Grego had inherited those truthful eyes . . . and much of that dauntless spirit? But not enough to wipe out the hint of resentment and bitterness. Nor had he yet developed his grandmother's balanced sense of humour. If he ever would? Italian emotionalism pitted against North Country common sense. Which would win?

"Your holiday will soon be running out," the Contessa said. "We must plan your remaining days carefully —there is so much you ought to see in this lovely part of the world. When do you have to return to your hospital?"

The question brought Marnie up with a start, reminding her of the unsettled state of her affairs. Had she too easily assumed that they would be glad to have her back at the hospital? And if she did resume her old position it would not all be plain sailing. She must face the painful explanation about her broken wedding, the awkward encounters with pitying friends and colleagues. Her soul shrank from the prospect. And suddenly she found herself telling the Contessa all about it.

The old lady listened in silence, but it was a sympathetic silence, and her questions, when they came, were gentle, calculated not to wound.

"I suppose I rushed into my engagement without really thinking about it," Marnie admitted. "But Glenn is very attractive and I was very much in love with him, dazzled by the fact that he's an up-and-coming young scientist. Then one day just before we were due to be married, and we were arguing about a church wedding —Glenn didn't want that—he told me that he didn't believe in God, nor in love as an idealistic concept, that it was simply a biological trick to ensure the survival of the human species." She broke off with a rueful laugh.

But the Contessa was shocked. "What a way to talk to one's bride-to-be! Do you think he really meant it, or was he just trying to show how scientific and objective he could be?"

"Oh, he meant it all right. He had said things like that to me before, but I hadn't taken them seriously. Now, suddenly, I realised the gulf there was between us. His whole life was the atomic research for which he had been trained. People weren't real to him. He didn't want a wife, but a sort of female robot who would fulfil his material needs."

"My dear, what a monster!"

"He wasn't really," Marnie said, trying to be fair. "But science had done something terrible to him, robbed him of humanity. His education had been entirely one-sided, and he was naturally self-centred and cold, dazzled with his own cleverness." She took the sorry tale to its conclusion, telling of Glenn's arrogant disregard for all the wedding plans, and how he had accepted a post in Australia, and agreed without consulting her that they would both set off to the other side of the world at a moment's notice. "That just about finished me," she ended with a shrug.

"You poor child!" the Contessa commiserated. "I should think it did! You're well out of it all. I think you have shown great pluck the way you have come through it, and you were very wise to come away as you did, leaving the dust to settle."

"But it isn't going to be exactly easy going back, putting my life together again—eating humble pie and asking for my old job at the hospital."

The Contessa put a kindly hand on her arm. "Try to forget it for the next few days. Make the most of your time in Italy, and as you are under no obligation to begin work for a while I hope you won't be in a hurry to leave us."

Marnie gave the old lady a grateful smile. "You're so kind to me! I can't tell you what it has meant to me,

509

meeting you, being invited here as your guest. It was all so unexpected. I was feeling so lost at San Paolo."

"Like my poor little Chinky! It was wonderful how you found each other," the Contessa smiled. "We owe you so much, both of us!" They laughed as they watched the cat leap up into the air after an elusive butterfly, his long lithe body graceful as a ballet dancer's.

The sound of an approaching car made them turn sharply, and there was the Ferrari, with Giulio at the wheel. He had grown tired of the junketings at Ostana, he explained when he joined them. "I've got to go back to Rome first thing in the morning," he pointed out, "and I hoped I could persuade Marnie to come out and have dinner with me tonight. We could run down to San Paolo."

"That would be very nice," the Contessa agreed, beaming at Marnie, wholly unaware of her embarrassment. An evening alone with Giulio was the last thing she wanted. But there was no getting out of it now that the Contessa had as good as accepted the invitation for her. Giulio's handsome face lit up wickedly as she murmured her acquiescence. He had not missed her recent attempts at avoiding him, and was amused at her dilemma.

It was as they were preparing to set out some time later that Grego and the Macreedys got back from Ostana. Coming down the marble staircase Marnie saw them entering the hall, where Giulio awaited her, elegant in a velvet dinner jacket and frilled white silk shirt that made him look like one of his own ancestors. Warned that he was taking her to one of San Paolo's most glittering night spots she had put on her loveliest frock, bridal white, designed for that luckless honeymoon. Long, severely cut, it clung to her slender body, seductive, revealing. Why hadn't she chosen something simpler? Grego would think ... what could he think? Only that she was out to impress his brother, put herself and her charms across. Standing, hesitant, at the foot of the stairs she met his scornful glance.

"Now we know why Marnie didn't want to come to Ostana today," Pat laughed. "And why Giulio was in such a hurry to get home!"

"*Naturalmente!*" Giulio drawled. "Of course I was in a hurry. Can you blame me?" Giving Marnie an exaggeratedly low bow, he offered her his arm. She put her hand upon it and together they walked across the vast hall, slowly, as if to music.

"Good hunting!" Pat called after them as they reached the door, and once more her mocking laughter rang out.

CHAPTER TEN

VENICE. Marnie stood in the Piazza San Marco gazing about her with the dream-like sensation which had pervaded her ever since she entered this city of golden domes and gleaming water. It had been an early start from Monteviano that morning, followed by a long drive through not very interesting country. On the last lap of the way the glimpse of industrial Mestre had dismayed her, but soon they were cruising down the long causeway which linked the mainland to the vista of soaring palaces and ancient churches that was Venice. It had burst upon Marnie like a shout of music, the colour and light, the sparkle of water, the clamour of church bells.

At the railway station where the causeway ended they had taken a *vaporetto*, one of the little water buses which plied the Grand Canal. Gondolas, the Senator said, were the traditional mode of transport, but gondolas were slow, and today time was precious for all of them. The Macreedys and Grego had to get to the opening of the art exhibition, and Marnie wanted to see as much of Venice as she could during the few hours at her disposal.

At the quay where they disembarked she had assured the kindly Mrs Macreedy that she would be quite happy to be on her own, that she would much rather do some sightseeing than go to the art exhibition—to which, it occurred to her afterwards, she had not been invited. Nor was her eagerness to avoid it exactly flattering to

Pat and her paintings, who ignored the unintentional snub. Marnie watched the party walk away, Pat possessively holding on to Grego's arm. It had been arranged that he should meet Marnie at the car park near the station for the return drive home.

Feeling deliciously free with the whole day in front of her, Marnie strolled along the Molo, a favourite waterside promenade, thronged at this hour with townspeople and tourists. She thought the trinket stalls and postcard stands, to say nothing of the candyfloss vendors and ice-cream barrows, didn't quite fit in with the dignity of Venice, but she lingered, nevertheless, to buy a few post-cards to send home. Mentally she planned her itinerary. The Doge's Palace, the House of Gold, the Bridge of Sighs, the Rialto ... and the Frari Church, which the Contessa had told her she must on no account miss since it contained Titian's tomb and one of his largest and most glorious paintings.

Now, with all these wonders disposed of, she had come to the famous square of San Marco, the very centre of Venice, with the great golden cathedral which gave the square its name before her. She gazed at it through a haze of weariness. The glittering domes and prancing bronze horses were oddly familiar, for it was surely one of the most painted and photographed churches in the world; she had seen dozens of reproductions of it. The sun beating down on the wide, open space was merciless in its intensity. Crowds jostled her, her feet ached. All at once it was imperative to sit down and rest. She had had no lunch, she remembered, and there was hardly time to see about it now if she wanted to explore the Cathedral thoroughly. Perhaps she could have a cup of coffee and a snack at one of the rather grand-looking cafés bordering the *piazza*. Limping to the nearest table, she sank gratefully on to a hard little chair. Waiters rushed back and forth, carrying trays high above their heads, but none of them seemed aware of her existence. Somewhere behind her an orchestra played selections from Verdi, the violins sweetly sentimental. Dreamily Marnie listened to them, watching the pigeons picking their way expertly among the feet of the passers-by. You could buy little bags of grain to throw to them, although they were, according to the guide books, fed officially twice a day. Fat, smug-looking birds . . . Marnie yawned vastly, and fought back the inclination to drift off to sleep.

It had been close on three a.m. when she and Giulio got back to the Castello last night. In spite of her misgivings it hadn't been at all a bad evening. Giulio, on his best behaviour, hadn't pestered her with lovemaking. Perhaps it had begun to dawn on him that she didn't like it, and he was too much of a gentleman to persist against her wishes. He had teased her a little, however, about her English coldness. "The prim Miss Gray," he mocked. "Some day you will be Miss Rose, Miss Gold, Miss all colours of the rainbow, when somebody wakens your heart. I wish it could have been me!" he sighed romantically. "If I could keep you here in the bright Italian sunshine for a few months, teach you what food to eat, what wines to drink, how to idle on the golden sands all day, and dance to the golden music all night, you would begin to know what life is all about.

"What do you do when you are not on holiday?" he demanded.

She told him about her work at the hospital. He thought it was very sad. To be for ever surrounded by the sick and dying; what could be more depressing? They were sitting at one of the little gilt tables which

514

flanked the dance floor at the Savoia. She smiled at him over the rim of her champagne glass. Helping sick people to get well could never be depressing, she told him. She spoke of the courage and gaiety to be found in so many of the patients, the sense of achievement which inspired the medical staff. "It isn't in the least sad," she urged, "quite the contrary." But his gaze was blank. He would never understand. The ideal life for him had to be all sunshine and luxury ... the *dolce vita*.

They drank their champagne and danced on the open-air floor, beneath the stars. There was a delicious supper at midnight. More champagne, more dancing ... on and on into the small hours. All round them the golden-skinned girls drifted in the arms of their dreamy-eyed escorts. As the night wore on the dancing became more strenuous, swinging, twisting, jiving. It was hard work in its way, this *dolce vita* ... Thinking back over it now, Marnie's head sank on to her breast, and the Verdi music seemed further and further away. She slept.

She thought she was floating down a shining river in a softly cushioned gondola. There was no gondolier. The boat, shaped like a great black swan, moved of its own volition, smoothly, silently. On either bank of the river there were trees of surpassing beauty, their delicate leaves shimmering like green jewels in the brilliant light. The air was filled with music. She became aware that she was not alone in the boat. Reclining on the cushions beside her was a man, whose face she could not see. His presence filled her with a strange, aching sorrow. Tears forced themselves through her closed eyelids; she could feel them warm on her cheeks. The man at her side stooped over her and kissed her, very gently, his lips just brushing her brow. She woke to find Grego di Valetta standing by her chair.

Flustered, she wiped the tears from her cheeks. "The sun was in my eyes," she tried to explain them away. "I shut my eyes to keep out the glare..."

"And fell asleep," he laughed. "I've been watching you for some minutes."

Had he wakened her with that strange, fleeting kiss? She smothered the disturbing suspicion, feeling foolish and confused.

"Is it time for us to leave?" she asked.

"Not yet." He eased himself into the chair opposite her. "We have a couple of hours to spare. I got tired of the art gallery, since I'd seen Pat's pictures before. In fact I have watched her at work on some of them in her Rome studio."

So he had visited her in Rome!

"How did you know I would be here on the *piazza*?" Marnie asked.

"I didn't," he answered tersely. "I just thought it would be as good a spot as any in which to kill time."

She felt her cheeks grow hot. What on earth had made her think he had been looking for her... and how stupidly she had betrayed her egotism.

"It is amusing to sit and watch the pigeons and the crowds," he was continuing equably. "And here at Florian's you can get a really good cup of tea." He gave her a brief smile. "That ought to appeal to you. Shall I order?"

The waiters, who had ignored Marnie's existence, now fluttered towards them at the sight of her escort.

"Tea," Grego demanded. "Quantities of it, with lots of cream." He turned to Marnie. "Would you like some pastries? They are specially delicious here."

"If I could have a sandwich," she suggested diffi-dently. "I didn't have time to bother about lunch..."

"No lunch?" he exclaimed in horror. "No wonder you fell asleep. You must be utterly exhausted." He spoke in rapid Italian to the hovering waiter, while Marnie groped beneath the table for the shoes she had kicked off. "I walked miles in the Doge's Palace," she apologised as she struggled to get her swollen feet into them. "All those acres and acres of paintings; I didn't know there were so many in the whole world! Then there was the long walk down all those utterly fascinating back streets to the Frari. The Titian *Assumption* took my breath away—a great blaze of crimson and purple behind the high altar." She had been a bit disappointed in the Ca' d'Oro, the House of Gold, she told him. "There didn't seem to be very much gold about it. But I liked the big shady courtyard with its fig trees and doves and the beautiful marble well-head."

"In ancient times it was a real house of gold," Grego said. "The entire front was richly gilded. Like San Marco's today." He pointed to the ornate Cathedral at the far end of the *piazza*. "A poem of light and stone, somebody has called it. You mustn't leave Venice without at least a glimpse of its famous interior."

"I was on my way to see it when I more or less collapsed," Marnie confessed.

He gave her a withering glance. "No lunch, and breakfast a good seven hours away; you aren't fit to be let out on your own!"

But the sandwiches when they came revived her, and the tea was all that tea should be.

She walked with him across the *piazza* and through the great bronze doors of the Cathedral, and stood entranced. From the marble floor to the soaring domes the whole place glowed with jewel-like colour. Light pouring in through the windows of the five cupolas flowed over the sumptuous confusion of pillars and statuary and paintings, so that the whole place seemed to shimmer and glow.

"It's almost too much," Marnie whispered. "One doesn't know where to begin to look."

He took her to a small side chapel, where walls and domes and arches were all richly inlaid with gold mosaic, every inch of space filled saints and angels, with birds and beasts and strange exotic foliage. Grego murmured guide-book snippets of information in her ear. She hardly heard him. The beauty of the place oppressed her. It was too rich, too suffocating.

"It's more like a theatre than a church," she said, when at last they came out once more on to the *piazza*. "I would rather have my little Galla Placida at Ravenna. A work of love," she added softly.

"What do you know about love?" His tone was mocking.

"Only that I felt it at Ravenna . . . in the simple designs those long-ago craftsmen put into their mosaics; the drinking doves, the shepherd with his lambs, the old apostle carrying what looked like an archaic pair of spectacles in his hand."

He shrugged. "Tricks of colour, artistic illusion . . . perhaps that is as good a definition of love as any."

"What would your definition be?" she asked.

"Oh, illusion. Most certainly illusion. A dream that somewhere there might be between two people faith, integrity, loyalty. Qualities most women seem incapable of."

They walked on in silence. The music of bells filled the air. Suddenly all the pigeons rose in flight, as if at a given signal, the beating of their wings making a rushing sound.

"Why do you speak so bitterly of women?" Marnie asked.

"I have had bitter experiences," he returned. Was he thinking of his mother's defection, or of the girl the Contessa had mentioned, who had let him down?

"You haven't finished with life yet," Marnie reminded him. "There's plenty of time for you to find that things are not so black as you imagine."

He made an impatient sound. *"You!"* he shot at her accusingly. "You of all people! Are you honestly telling me that you believe all the idyllic mumbo-jumbo of a romantic love that lasts for ever?"

"It's not mumbo-jumbo," Marnie declared. "Nor are you the only person in the world who has had bitter experiences. Believe it or not, I've had my share of disappointments in love. But it hasn't shaken my faith. I'm quite sure two people can love each other truly, and go on loving one another all through a shared life. That's my idea of marriage, and the only kind I would want."

"Meanwhile," Grego said with a sneer, "you amuse yourself with types likes my brother Giulio."

Marnie coloured hotly. "That's not a very nice thing to say."

Grego shrugged. "But it's true. I have eyes in my head. If you could have seen how radiant you looked setting off with him last night in your choice white gown. Like a bridal gown. Was it, by any chance? All you needed to complete the picture was the flowing veil, so cynically a symbol of virtue."

"Just what do you mean to imply by that?" Marnie's tone was hard, her blue eyes furious.

"Nothing," Grego hastened, noting the danger signals. "My apologies, if I have been misunderstood." He gave her a mocking bow. "It is just that in these days of

519

emancipated females the demureness implicit in the white veil seems a little old-fashioned. Not that they aren't vastly becoming. And so was your satin gown last night. I am sure Giulio was as impressed as you no doubt hoped he would be."

"I'm quite at your mercy. You can taunt me as much as you like." Her anger choked her. She broke off. No apologies could wipe out that unpardonable crack about the white veil, and now he had added insult to injury, saying she had dressed up for effect. Did he think she was really trying to "catch" his aristocratic brother, worm her way into the princely family of the di Valettas?

They were walking along the Molo by this time, the Piazza San Marco behind them. "There is our *vaporetto*!" Grego exclaimed. They had to run for it. It was crowded to capacity, so it was easy for Marnie to lose herself in the throng once they had boarded it. Thankful to be rid of Grego's company for the moment, she leaned on the taffrail, nursing her indignation against him. Why did he try to humiliate her, make her feel cheap? Would it matter to him if Giulio fell in love with her? A wild impossibility, of course, and that Grego should be jealous about it was even more impossible. His remark about the wedding gown was odd. The white dress had almost been just that. Seeing it in a shop window, Marnie had bought it impulsively. Then neither she nor her mother and sisters had liked it very much, so they had made something more elaborate from cream-coloured brocade, and the plainer frock had become a dinner dress.

Getting off the *vaporetto* at the terminus, Marnie could see Grego scanning the jostling throng for her.

Perversely she let him go on searching. It would do him good!

"*Dio mio!*" he exploded when at last he caught up with her. "Why couldn't you have stayed close to me? Do you think we have all night in which to play hide and seek? It is a long drive back to Monteviano and I want to get started."

He was impossible—arrogant, ill-tempered, as well as downright rude. "I won't trouble you to drive me back to Monteviano," she said coldly. "I would prefer to travel by rail."

"*Bene!*" he snapped. "There is a slow train which would get you into San Paolo about midnight, long after the bus service has packed up. So you would have to walk to the Castello; a mere ten miles over the mountains. You would enjoy it, I'm sure!" He was laughing at her now. It was intolerable. She was so mad with him she could have burst into tears of baffled rage.

"Come on, Marnie!" His voice was soft suddenly, conciliating. "Stop sulking and let's go and find the car. I won't tease you any more about Giulio, if that's what is worrying you."

She submitted to his hand on her arm and walked with him to the car. As they drove inland she maintained her stony silence. Not because she was sulking, as Grego would obviously think, but because her hurt was too deep for words. If only she didn't love him! If at least he didn't think so badly of her. Though why he should bother to have violent opinions about her, she couldn't fathom.

"Still mad at me?" he enquired presently. His flippant tone jarred.

"I don't like being condemned without a hearing," she choked.

521

"Meaning that, in spite of all the evidence to the contrary, you are not as involved as would seem with my young brother?"

"It was the Contessa who arranged for me to go out with him last night," Marnie said. "I wouldn't have chosen it for myself, any more than I would have chosen to find myself locked in his arms the other day in one of the *Bella-Rosa's* cabins."

She felt Grego's sharpened glance. "Why bring that up?"

"Because, since we're having a showdown, you might as well know the truth. Not," she added, "that I imagine it matters to you. But Pat Macreedy saw us that day on the *Bella Rosa,* and later I overheard her telling you about it. What she said must have given you an entirely false impression of my relationship with Giulio."

"So what you are saying is that you have been more kissed against than kissing?"

"You must know your brother," she murmured desperately.

Grego shrugged. "Like most young Italians he has one idea where women are concerned. Which doesn't mean he is a heel."

"Of course he isn't a heel," Marnie defended him. "As soon as he got the message and realised I didn't go for petting, he laid off. Last night he was just . . . very good company."

"So . . . !" Grego drawled. "And now I suppose I owe you yet another apology."

"Don't strain yourself!" Marnie said.

Grego threw back his head and laughed so infectiously that Marnie found herself joining in. Suddenly the atmosphere lightened.

"I'll tell you what I'll do by way of atonement," he

offered. "I'll buy you a dinner on the way home. Remember that fishing village I told you about, Belmara?"

"The place where they cook the food in the open, and you eat on a terrace overlooking the sea," Marnie said, a little breathlessly.

"The very same. It isn't far out of our way and we are making excellent time. Not that it matters within an hour or so when we get home, but I don't want to leave Nonna on her own too long."

"If you think we ought to drive straight back to her . . ." Marnie began. But Grego interrupted quickly, "No, no. She will be all right. I promised you this dinner . . . and tonight will be as good a time as any."

So he hadn't forgotten after all! Happiness flowed over her. She was hopeless, she told herself. Her anger against him had all gone. One kindly gesture and she succumbed weakly to his charm.

It was just after sunset when the Fiat cruised down the winding main street of Belmara, and came out on a cliff top where they parked. A rose-coloured after-glow stained the sea and sky; small golden clouds like the fat cherubs in a Renaissance painting floated in the upper blue. There was a precipitous path descending from the cliff-top to the wide outcrop of rock, where the lights of the little *ristorante* twinkled. Following in Grego's wake, Marnie looked down at the clear green sea, two hundred feet below them. "If you are scared hang on to me," he invited, giving her his hand. There was strength in his grasp. The evening light was a rosy mist now through which she walked unseeingly, conscious only of the touch of his hand.

He began to hum the song he had sung that night driving home from the Savoia when everything between them had been so perfect. Or so it had seemed. Did he remember it? He had left Pat and her art exhibition today long before it was necessary. But then he made no pretence of being deeply in love with her. He didn't believe in love.

They came to a terrace, roofed over with vine leaves, set with rough wooden tables and functional benches. Lights hung in the vines among the bunches of tiny green grapes.

"In August," Grego said, "the grapes are large and purple and you pick them for your dessert." But now it was early June and in the long twilight they watched the lobster-catchers at work on the rocks below. A gipsy-dark fisherman came up the path from the sea, a bucket in his hand. When he reached the terrace Grego hailed him with a friendly *"Buona sera, signore!"* The man gave them a white-toothed grin, and stopped to show them the lobsters in the bucket; deep, inky purple, their tentacles coral and yellow, their cruel claws snapping helplessly in their captivity.

"Lobsters for the *signorina's* supper." The fisherman smiled at Marnie. "You couldn't have them fresher than that."

"I don't like to think of them being cooked," Marnie shuddered as the man moved on. "Boiled alive!"

"It's a quick death," Grego assured her. "And they haven't got nervous systems like ours."

It was to be hoped he was right, Marnie murmured, and ordered pasta when the menu was put before them. She was being squeamish and hypocritical, Grego accused her. "Almost everything one eats, apart from vegetables and cereals, means killing. But as long as you don't see the killing you don't worry." Imperiously he changed her order to crayfish, for which the little restaurant was famous. Afterward they had plump soles, cooked with rosemary on a charcoal fire on the terrace. It was all just as Grego had described it. There were no other diners, but in the shadowy room beyond the terrace men in faded cotton shirts played some interminable card game under the light of a swinging lamp. A dusky interior, rich in mystery as a Rembrandt painting.

The glow faded from the sky and the moon came up. There were peaches and figs for dessert, and the wine they drank was sweet and cold.

What would Pat Macreedy think if she could see them? Marnie wondered. She looked at Grego across the table. In the muted lamplight his skin and his hair had golden tints, even his eyes were golden. Sleepy eyes, watching her musingly as she peeled a peach.

"So you are not a flirt," he said suddenly, out of the blue. "You don't enjoy light love. Which makes you that much more dangerous. Only the impossible is any use to you . . . the dream lover who drops out of the sky to lay his life at your feet for all time."

She wiped a trickle of peach juice from her chin with a snowy table napkin that smelled as if it had been spread out to bleach on the salty rocks.

"I've met your sort before," Grego murmured softly, but with deadly inflection. "When the chips are down they don't care how many people they hurt. They break up homes, trample children underfoot, ignore every consideration but the gaining of their own ends." He passed his hand across his eyes and gave her a look of naked pain.

Harping on his mother again, Marnie thought, her compassion tinged with impatience. Granted that his mother's behaviour had ruined his childhood, it was surely a little unwholesome the way he dwelt on his injury. And a little hard that she in her innocence should be used as a whipping post.

"Heaven preserve me from idealists!" he whispered.

"And heaven preserve me from cynics," Marnie countered.

The plump smiling girl who had waited on them throughout the meal brought coffee, scalding and strong.

"The first cynics," Grego said, sipping his coffee, "were members of a Greek sect of philosophers, noted for their respect for truth, their bluntness of speech."

"In *my* dictionary," Marnie retorted, "they are described as 'persons giving to sneering at goodness, and tearing the veil from human weaknesses.' Furthermore, it says the term cynic is derived from a Greek word, *kuon,* meaning a dog."

Grego stared at her in blank amazement for a moment and then burst out laughing. "So I am no more than a yapping dog! Marnie, you baffle me. You sit there looking as if butter wouldn't melt in your mouth, then without warning you turn on your opponent and rend him without mercy. Where did you get this extraordinary dictionary?"

"It wasn't extraordinary . . . just the usual Oxford edition. I used to read it under the desk when I got bored with Sister Tutor's lectures in hospital."

"And you stored it all up in your squirrel brain?"

"I especially remembered the bit about cynicism, because I've always hated cynics."

"Thanks a lot!" But his eyes were twinkling. He was still laughing at her.

When the plump girl brought the bill Marnie said a little awkwardly, "I wish you would let me pay my share. You and the Contessa and Giulio have been so generous, taking me about, buying me meals, and I have no claim on you, after all. I'm a stranger in your midst . . ."

"Exactly," Grego smiled. "And that is your claim, and our pleasure. You are our honoured guest." It was a little too flowery and formal to be heart-warming, but Marnie could only murmur her thanks for a delightful evening.

She looked back regretfully at the little restaurant as they got into the Fiat. On its shelf of rock above the darkening sea it looked so peaceful; a vine-wreathed sanctuary her heart would remember for many a long day. "Out of this world," Grego had described it when he first spoke of it. It hadn't been quite that tonight. The magic had been missing. But Grego had been very kind and she must be thankful for small mercies.

They drove through the moonlit night. It was all so beautiful and peaceful that Marnie didn't want to talk, and Grego too seemed disinclined for conversation. It was when they were nearing Monteviano, passing beneath the little cemetery on its hilltop that he slowed down, steered the car on to the grass verge and switched off the engine. Silence descended upon them, broken only by the throbbing song of a nightingale in the cemetery cypresses.

Now what? Marnie wondered.

He slid an arm along the back of her seat and turned to her. In the greenish moonlight his face was grim and set, its bone structure outlined. In a momentary flash Marnie saw again the tranced bitterness of the young Guidarello, trapped for ever in the marble of an effigy at Ravenna.

"Why did you have to come here to torment me at this particular juncture of my life?" he burst out. He drew her towards him almost roughly and kissed her, lingeringly and with a strange tenderness. She could not move in his arms, could scarcely breathe, too taken aback to feel either resentment or response.

"I have been wanting to do that ever since I first set eyes on you," he said calmly, as he released her.

"To kiss without love?" she cried brokenly. "I don't understand you." Tears filled her eyes. "What do you want of me?"

"That you should be what I first thought you were . . . simple and sweet . . . untouched. You seemed so young, so made of truth." His mouth twisted. "I soon found how wrong I was!"

Merely because she had gone about with Giulio, Marnie thought despairingly. So he hadn't believed a word of her disclaimers. The misery in his eyes as he looked at her tore at her heart. She could still feel his kiss on her lips. Nor could she believe it was so unaccountable a gesture as it seemed. It mattered to him that she was not all he had hoped. Yet he could so grossly misunderstand her.

Sadly she turned to him. "The whole truth of it is that you don't really want me to be what you first thought I was. You like being disillusioned, disappointed in people, so that you don't have to bother with them. It's so much easier to judge and despise than to love and understand. This is your behaviour pattern. You would do anything rather than submit to love. It's too dangerous for you, too risky for your precious peace of mind." She drew in a long shaken breath. "If I would make any sacrifice for the sort of love I believe in, you, equally, would sacrifice everything, even your own soul, to save yourself from the demands of a real and lasting love."

He took this tirade in silence. His eyes, in shadow,

528

were dark and inscrutable. Slowly he turned from her and switched on the ignition. "Did you also read books on amateur psychology beneath the desk when you were bored with Sister Tutor's lectures?" he asked—a mocking question to which he evidently expected no answer. Abruptly he started the car, and a few minutes later they were drawing up at the Castello portico.

Batiste was waiting for them in the hall, and at the sight of the Conte he burst into a flood of agitated Italian, too rapid for Marnie to follow. But it was clear that something was badly wrong. She saw apprehension quicken on Grego's face as he listened. He turned to her. "My grandmother has not been well today, Batiste says. She had a fainting fit this afternoon and was unconscious for some time. Forgive me . . . but I must go to her at once."

He was mounting the stairs when Marnie called after him, "Please let me know if there's anything I can do." Would he remember that she was a nurse? Hurrying on his way, he did not seem to have heard her.

CHAPTER ELEVEN

MARNIE woke early the following morning, her first thoughts of the Contessa. She listened for sounds that might indicate crisis, but her oaken door and thick walls shut her away from the doings of the household.

Last night she had hung about in the hall uneasily until Grego reappeared to tell her that his grandmother's condition did not seem to be serious, and that she must go to bed and not worry. His manner had been distant. The Contessa's fainting fit, he said, had left no alarming after-effects and she had refused to have the doctor. He had given her one of her sleeping tablets and she was resting comfortably. He had bowed over Marnie's hand then, bidding her a formal goodnight, which came a little oddly after their evening together. If it hadn't been an entirely harmonious evening it had at least, in its way, achieved a certain intimacy. That unexpected kiss, and the strange things Grego had said about her coming into his life to torment him—"just at this juncture". What juncture? Had he been referring to his pending engagement to Pat Macreedy?

It was all pretty baffling, but beneath her bewilderment Marnie was conscious of a certain satisfaction, because she hadn't been altogether wrong about that moment of fusion between herself and Grego when they first met. He too had felt it. He had been drawn to her, liked her, and then for some reason she couldn't fathom turned almost savagely against her. Jealousy of her friendship with Giulio seemed scarcely a sufficient excuse. Even when she had explained to him how little Giulio's overtures meant to her he had not warmed to her again. She could only assume her efforts at amateur psycho-analysing last evening had hit the nail on the head. Grego, Conte di Valetta, was afraid to love. Or was it, more simply, that she had disappointed him by failing to measure up to his standards? After all, she came from a very different background from his own. Perhaps he had decided she just wasn't good enough for him. A humiliating possibility, but in the cold light of morning it seemed highly feasible.

She jerked her thoughts back to the Contessa. How was she this morning? Had she had a good night? Dressing hastily, Marnie ran down the turret stairs to the great corridor that stretched the whole length of the Castello. Everything seemed quiet and normal. At the far end of the corridor one of Gina's villager helpers sang to herself softly as, down on her knees, she polished the marble floor. Reaching the door of the Contessa's boudoir, Marnie hesitated. The door opened and the Contessa herself appeared, looking reassuringly cheerful in a voluminous silk negligee.

"Ah, there you are, my dear!" the old lady greeted her, almost as if she had been expecting her. Chinky, emerging from the folds of the negligee, added his own gruff "Mrrow!" of welcome, rubbing himself ingratiatingly against Marnie's ankles.

"He wants to go out," the Contessa said. "I was just going to sneak down and open the front door for him and was looking to see if the coast was clear. Grego made me promise I wouldn't stir out of bed until after lunch . . ." She peered up and down the corridor conspiratorially.

"I'll take Chinky downstairs and let him out," Marnie offered. "Do please go back to bed, Contessa."

"I was just about to ring for my breakfast," the Contessa said. "Shall I ask for yours to be brought up too, and we can breakfast together?"

It was a very pleasant hour that followed. Propped up on her pillows, the Contessa idled her way through two cups of coffee and three slices of crisp toast, asking questions about Venice. She seemed a little disappointed Marnie hadn't seen Pat Macreedy's paintings.

"It would have been interesting to hear what you thought of them," she said; as if Marnie's opinion mattered! "Giulio tells me they are mostly the modern kind, all those incomprehensible lines and blobs and angles. Pat is such a clever girl." She sighed as though it were something to be deplored. It was difficult to get her back to the story of yesterday's fainting fit, which interested Marnie professionally. She was conscious too of a certain sense of guilt because she had encouraged Grego to stay out later than he would have done if he had not had to entertain her.

"It was really nothing," the Contessa protested. "I was coming upstairs for my afternoon nap when everything blacked out and I just sank into a heap on the landing, where, it seems, I lay until Batiste found me. Chinky was lying across my chest, which made it rather difficult for me to breathe. He was so scared, poor little chap—he is always so sweet when I am ill. I was vaguely conscious of him giving my face little licks now and then, as if he were trying to revive me." She seemed far more interested in Chinky's loving ministrations than in her own plight.

"It is just my silly heart," she dismissed it. "A creaking gate that will no doubt hang on as long as I need it. I've got some tablets which keep it ticking comfortably, but just recently I have been a bit careless about taking them."

"And I'm afraid you've been doing too much entertaining," Marnie added. "All those week-end visitors, to say nothing of myself. I feel very guilty now at having let you drive me all the way to Ravenna the other day, and all that strenuous sightseeing when we got there."

"Oh, but I enjoyed it so much," the Contessa protested. "It is a delight to show the treasures of my adopted country to someone as appreciative as you are. We must make some more trips before you leave. There is so much you ought to see. The Rubicon, for instance, you said you wanted to see that." This was the ancient bridge, over an ancient river, made famous by Julius Caesar's legendary crossing.

"But I shall soon be going home," Marnie pointed out.

The Contessa looked dismayed. "My dear, I thought you were in no hurry to leave us."

"Indeed I'm not!" Marnie assured her. "But I ought to be getting back to see about my hospital job, and my plane reservation is for next Friday evening."

"Wouldn't it be possible to have your ticket altered?" the Contessa persisted. But Marnie was adamant. The Contessa would be better off without visitors for a while. After her heart attack she ought to rest, and all too soon the Macreedys would be descending upon her again.

She wouldn't want to be here when that happened, Marnie admitted to herself privately. Watching Pat lay claim to the Conte wouldn't be much fun. There would be the formal engagement announcement, a family celebration of some kind; she would be more than ever the stranger at the feast . . . nursing her foolish heartache. Far, far better get back to the red-brick villa in a neat suburban road that was her home, and let this Italian holiday with all its disturbing complications fade into the limbo where even the best of holidays must go.

For the next few days she vetoed all suggestions for her entertainment, and persuaded the Contessa to rest in her boudoir, or on the sunny terrace, in a comfortable lounge chair. Devotedly she stayed by the old lady's side, fetching and carrying for her, listening to her flow of reminiscenses. Like most elderly folk, her thoughts often dwelt in the past. Many of her recollections concerned Grego, whom she adored. Marnie, listening with an avidity she was careful to conceal, learned how he had been altered by his mother's elopement. It had cut across his formative years, cruel as a sword slash. From being a lighthearted, mischievous boy he had changed almost overnight to a sullen, embittered adolescent.

"Did the young Contessa make no attempt to keep in touch with her sons after she went away?" Marnie asked.

The old lady shook her head. "She was killed in a car crash before a month had gone by. It was all so tragic, so unnecessary, a crazy war-time episode. We had had quite a lot of bombing to put up with here, and everyone's nerves were frayed. Lucia, who had worked devotedly for her family and the villagers, was ill with exhaustion and strain. Her husband was away with his regiment in Africa. She hadn't seen him for years. Then suddenly the war was over and the place was full of foreign troops; English, American, French. Antoine Lefarge was a young French doctor attached to some medical unit in the district. As luck would have it he was one of the officers billeted at the Castello. He began prescribing for Lucia, giving her medical advice. What emotion sprang up between them one can only guess, but she was worn out with work, worry and loneliness, and suddenly he was everything she needed. When unexpectedly he was recalled to France she went with him.

"Grego, perhaps naturally, is hard on her," the Contessa ended the story with a sigh. "He does not remember what the war was really like. As a child it did not affect him quite as much as it affected older folk. He can only see his mother as a traitor, deserting her husband and children. I had hoped that as he grew older he would learn to judge her a little less harshly—give her the benefit of a few doubts. I am convinced that the whole thing was no more than an unfortunate episode. Lucia's heart was in the right place. If she had not been killed I am sure she would have come back to us. It was all so foolish, so sad . . ."

And it had warped Grego's whole outlook on life, Marnie reflected.

She saw him briefly at mealtimes. Since their dinner at Belmara they had exchanged barely a dozen words, save when they sat facing one another across the vast mahogany table in the dining room. And then, with the Contessa present, their conversation was of necessity superficial.

Suddenly it was Thursday; Marnie's last day. At lunch time the Contessa insisted that this final afternoon must not be wasted. They would drive to the Rubicon, she planned firmly, ignoring Marnie's protests. She was quite fit for the effort, she declared; the doctor had seen her only that morning and pronounced her to be in excellent health. Grego's approval settled the matter. His grandmother had been cooped up long enough, the outing would do her good.

535

They set off after the Contessa had had a brief siesta. For once the sun was not shining, and the air was still and heavy. Colours were accentuated in the subdued light, the young vines more sharply green, the distant mountains a rich dark blue. The way led through the beautiful old town of Cesena, where they stopped for tea. The ancient castle dominating the town had once belonged to the famous Malatesta family, Grego's renowned if somewhat infamous ancestors. The Contessa seemed proud to point it out to Marnie and talked interestingly of its history.

Back on the road they idled through pine woods, climbed a winding mountain road and came at last to a signpost marked "Savignano sul Rubicon". It was just outside the little town that they found the Roman bridge, spanning the historic river, shallow and sluggish in the dry summer weather. Leaning over the time-worn parapet, Marnie tried to visualise Julius Caesar in 49 B.C. leading his cohorts across the little stream to declare war on the Republic on the other side, an irrevocable step that had altered the course of history—so that to this day the name of the river has been used to denote the taking of momentous and irreversible decisions.

"Did you find it impressive?" Grego asked Marnie, when the afternoon's outing was discussed over the dinner table.

"I'm afraid I didn't," Marnie confessed. "It looked a very ordinary little river. But I'm glad to have seen it."

"We all have our Rubicons," the Contessa mused, thinking perhaps of her own great moment of choice, when she had left her Yorkshire home to marry her Italian Count.

"Sometimes we hover on the brink," Grego contributed, seemingly absorbed in the walnut he was cracking.

The Contessa gave him a wry glance. "Don't hover too long, Greg dear. There are some things I would dearly like to see settled before I die."

"Which gives me years in which to make up my mind," Grego returned robustly.

The Contessa shook her head. "Don't bank on it, *carissimo*. Time runs out."

An oblique exchange, obviously referring to Grego's protracted courtship of his American heiress. So the old lady was putting on a little discreet pressure! Marnie looked at Grego across the darkly polished table. For an instant their glances met. Grego's eyes burned with a strange intensity, but it was difficult to read their message, if indeed there was a message to be read. The reasonable assumption was that his thoughts at the moment were exclusively occupied with Pat Macreedy. But over coffee in the drawing room he talked endlessly of his cheese factory, the Contessa valiantly stifling her yawns of boredom.

It was a relief when Chinky joined them, intent upon his usual evening game. The Contessa produced a ping-pong ball from her pocket and for the next half hour the Siamese kept them diverted with his antics, as he leaped and cavorted, chasing the ball back and forth across the wide expanse of floor; clowning deliberately, playing for laughs. Like most Siamese he was an inveterate show-off. Even Grego enjoyed the display, forgetting his worries.

The sun shone the following morning, yesterday's clouds rolling away over the mountains. Marnie decided to make a last trip to the beach and took the bus down to San Paolo. The water was deliciously cool, and she enjoyed her swim. Drying out afterwards, stretched face down on the warm sand, she felt the sun soaking luxuriously into her bare brown back. Drowsily she thought of London, a grey city under a grey sky where she would by this time next week be looking for a job. The prospect seemed oddly unreal.

Back at the Castello she found lunch ready on the terrace, the table laid for two. Grego was away for the day, the Contessa explained as they sat down to eat. "He has driven over to Bologna to join the Macreedys who are breaking their journey there on their way to the port of Chioggia where they are meeting their yachting friends. They will be coming here again next week, but dear Grego was too impatient to wait for that. He wanted to see Pat at once." Her eyes grew dreamy. "I have an idea everything will be settled between them today. He promised me as much . . ." She gazed into the distance ecstatically.

So the discreet pressure last night had had its effect!

"I hope everything will work out for them," Marnie managed mechanically.

"Oh, I am sure it will." The Contessa's small face lit up. "Pat with her artistic flair will make an excellent chatelaine for the castle. She will restore what needs to be restored without spoiling the character of the place. Her sense of period is impeccable. For example, if she instals new bathrooms, she will see that they are unobtrusive."

"Americans are so keen on bathrooms," Marnie murmured inadequately. The delicous pasta she was eating turned to dust and ashes in her mouth. She took a swallow of wine to help it down. Would Grego be back before she left this evening? It seemed not. He had asked his grandmother to make his farewells for him. "He wished me to convey his regrets that he is not here to make them in person," the old lady finished.

Marnie could just hear him uttering the formal words, polite to the last. How she hated his empty courtesies! She choked down the lump in her throat.

"Batiste will drive you to the airport," the Contessa was arranging. Marnie expressed her thanks. This was the moment to make a gracious little speech, saying how much she had enjoyed her stay at the castle, but somehow the words would not come. It was the Contessa who was gracious, putting a hand on Marnie's arm, and looking at her with real affection in her grey eyes as she said, "Dear child, I shall miss you!"

"And I shall miss you!" Marnie said in a voice that wasn't very steady. She took the small frail hand between her own. "You've been so kind . . . so very kind!"

"I was so glad to have you!" The words rang with a poignant sincerity. She is lonely here in this great vault of a house, Marnie thought with a pang.

"Perhaps you will come again," the Contessa said. But there was no conviction in the words, and they were oddly wistful. Gently she withdrew her hand from Marnie's grasp. "At my age," she said in a low voice, "all farewells are sad."

What did she mean? Marnie shivered in the warm air.

Idling on the terrace later, while the Contessa rested in her room, she leafed through a pile of magazines, finding it difficult to concentrate. She had the suspended feeling that so often comes before a long journey—a hiatus in time when nothing seems quite real. But a photograph in the current issue of *Oggi* brought her up with a start; it was a coloured picture of Grego and Pat dancing together. Some wandering Society columnist had evidently come upon them the other evening at the Savoia. There was a wordy caption, praising Pat's skill as a painter with reference to the exhibition of her work in Venice. Here was an up-and-coming young artist Italy could be proud of, and it was rumoured that she was thinking of adopting Italian nationality in the most romantic way possible. There could be no mistaking the hint of her forthcoming engagement to the young Conte. Tight-lipped, Marnie gazed at the pictured couple, Grego looking very distinguished in his evening clothes. Making a mental note of the date of the issue, Marnie decided to buy a copy at the airport news-stand. It would be a bitter-sweet souvenir of her days in Monteviano.

Presently she went to her room to pack. Her beautiful green and gold room, with its deeply set mullioned windows, and marble floor. You could sense the thickness of the walls beneath the pastel green paint. They had stood for seven hundred years. How many brides had come to the Castello during those centuries? All gone now, dust blown down the winds of time. Only the Contessa from far-away Yorkshire remained, living out the last of her days in the alien land that had become her home. An icy hand touched Marnie's heart. The room seemed to darken with an indefinable sense of doom. It was all these morbid thoughts about dead and gone brides.

With a shrug for her fancifulness, she went down to tea, which was served in the Contessa's boudoir. There were the inevitable hot griddle cakes and newly baked scones soaking in butter, the cream, the delicious home-made jams—North Country fare the Contessa had taught a succession of Italian cooks to produce.

"I ought not to eat all these good things," she confessed. "My doctor tells me they are very bad for my heart condition." But unrepentantly she continued to enjoy the meal.

Back in her room Marnie did her final packing. Batiste would come for her suitcases at six. As the church bell in the village tolled the hour she ran downstairs to say goodbye to the Contessa. It wasn't going to be easy. Even now she could hardly believe that she was really leaving the Castello for ever. It seemed so much more than a mere fortnight ago since she had walked up the drive with Chinky, to meet the gentle old lady who had laid such a strange hold on her heart. Of Grego she would not permit herself to think.

Pausing at the boudoir door, she tapped lightly. There was no answering *"Avanti!"* She tapped again, and was greeted by the unmistakable wail of a Siamese in distress. Perhaps the Contessa had gone down to the hall to see her off, leaving the cat imprisoned. Marnie opened the door. At a first glance the room seemed to be empty. Then she saw the Contessa stretched prostrate on the settee, with Chinky crouching on top of her. Marnie hurriedly removed him. The Contessa groaned, her hand on her labouring breast. "Indigestion," she gasped. "I ought not to have eaten those hot cakes at tea-time."

But it was much more than indigestion. Marnie's experienced eye took in the ashen pallor, cyanosed lips and pinched nostrils. With a shaking hand she reached for the bell that would summon Batiste, Gina . . . anyone who would tell her how to get hold of a doctor without delay. If only Grego hadn't gone to Bologna today!

CHAPTER TWELVE

THE doctor had come and gone. The Contessa lay in her bed in the room beyond the boudoir, deeply sedated. There was nothing he could do for her, the doctor had said, but save her from the last hours of pain. He had spoken of "advanced cardiac collapse", and advised Grego to send for the priest. "You will also need a nurse," he had added more prosaically.

"The English *signorina* is a nurse," Grego had blurted, and turned to Marnie, pleaded apologetically, "Forgive me, Marnie! I am taking too much for granted. But you won't leave us, will you?"

A cry for help to which she could only give one answer.

To her immense relief Grego had returned from Bologna soon after the doctor arrived to pour out questions and instructions so intermingled with technicalities that they were beyond her limited Italian. Taking in the situation at a glance, the Conte had come to the rescue.

Now, in the boudoir, just after the doctor's departure, they faced one another. "You have missed your plane," Grego said remorsefully. "How can I thank you?"

"You don't have to thank me. I couldn't have gone away, leaving the Contessa so ill . . ." Marnie's voice shook.

"You are fond of her, aren't you?" His grey eyes softened.

"She has been so incredibly kind to me!"

He nodded. "She is always kind. But for you she had a specially warm corner . . ." He drifted over to the window. Beyond the trees the thunder clouds piled up. The evening was hot and growing unbearably sultry. "She is pretty bad, isn't she?" Grego brought out with difficulty.

"Heart cases are unpredictable." Marnie tried to infuse a little optimism into her tone.

"It's all right," Grego said gruffly. "You don't have to wrap it up for me. The doctor was definite enough . . . telling me I ought to send for the Father. I suppose I had better go and phone him right away."

"Do you think you could, at the same time, send a telegram to my mother for me?" Marnie ventured. She scribbled the address and message on the little notepad she always carried in her handbag. "They'll be expecting me at home tomorrow morning," she added as Grego took the slip of paper in his hand.

"So you are really going to stay and see us through!" His glance was warm and grateful. "It is very good of you, Marnie—changing your plans like this at the last minute . . . missing your plane. I know you wouldn't want me to keep on about it, but it means a lot to me. Nonna would so much rather have you caring for her than some stranger."

He went to the bedroom door and gazed anxiously at the drawn little face on the pillows. Chinky, who had hidden himself beneath the bed during the doctor's visit, now emerged to settle himself in his favourite place at his mistress's feet.

"Do you think we ought to leave him there?" Grego asked doubtfully.

"If we turn him out he will only wail in the corridor

543

and that might distress the Contessa," Marnie pointed out.

"You are probably right," Grego agreed. He moved closer to the bedside and stood looking down at his grandmother in silence. His lips moved. Was he offering up a silent prayer? As if aware of his presence the Contessa stirred and opened her eyes. "Ah, Grego, my dear, you are home!" She held out a transparent hand and the young man took it, bending over her to catch the whispered words.

"Did you have a good day at Bologna? Have you brought Pat back with you?"

"She couldn't come just now, but don't worry, Nonna darling."

"You mean everything is settled?"

"Yes, everything is settled." There was an odd harshness in his tone.

"Grazie a Dio!" the old lady sighed. "Now I can sleep in peace." Visibly relaxing, she closed her eyes. A half smile played about her lips, and the lines on her face seemed to smooth out. Marnie and Grego crept from the room. So the engagement was definitely "on"! Marnie smothered the pang she had no right to feel.

"Thank God she doesn't seem to be suffering," said Grego.

"She won't," Marnie promised him. "The doctor left me the wherewithal to take care of that. She pointed to the hygenically covered tray, incongruously on one of the boudoir's small inlaid tables, holding a hypodermic syringe, tablets, cotton wool and antiseptics. Already a faint hospital-like odour hung in the air.

The Conte put a hand on her shoulder. His face worked, but for a moment no words came. Then he said huskily, "I know you will do all that is possible to make it easy for her." Abruptly he left the room.

In the hours that followed Marnie felt as if she was moving in a dream. It was all so strange and quiet, so unlike the bustle and certainty of nursing in hospital. Here she was alone, wholly responsible for her patient. Sitting on the settee in the boudoir, she listened to the laboured breathing from the next room. An oxygen cylinder had arrived and been installed. Using it at intervals, the invalid sucked in the air greedily. Had she been conscious when the priest visited her? Marnie wondered. If so, she had shown no sign of awareness as the murmur of prayers rose and fell. Feeling very much an outsider, Marnie had remained in the boudoir, while Grego and the servants knelt in the sickroom. The comforting last rites with their message of hope, the anointing with holy oil, the sweet smell of incense . . . how much did it mean to the dying woman? In her own way Marnie had added her petitions, her eyes full of tears.

Later, dinner had been brought to her on a tray, Grego looking in to make sure she had everything she wanted before having his own solitary meal in the vast dining room downstairs. He was being so kind. But how chilling kindness can be when what you crave is warm, uncalculating love! Couldn't she ever forget herself and her silly feelings? Marnie had asked herself angrily, as she ate, without appetite, the food which had been sent up.

Now it was eleven o'clock; time for the Contessa's next injection. At the prick of the needle she opened her eyes and looked about her with interest, as if she were seeing her bedroom for the first time. "I've been such a long way away," she said. She seemed to have forgotten that Marnie ought to have been on her way to England, and showed no surprise at her ministrations.

"Where is Chinky?" she asked anxiously.

"Right here, Contessa," Marnie assured her, as the Siamese came trotting into the room, uttering the conversational "Mrrow!" with which he usually announced his presence. "He has been out for his evening walk," Marnie explained, "and has just got back again. Gina gave him some rabbit for his supper."

"Oh, good!" The Contessa breathed a small sigh of relief. She lifted a feeble hand to stroke the cat's velvety brown head as he jumped on the bed, to settle at her side, purring loudly. "Dear Chinky, he is such a comfort. Don't let them take him away from me, Marnie, will you?"

"Of course I won't!" Marnie promised.

"He is always so scared of the doctor, poor lamb. I think he gets him mixed up with the vet who once came to lance an abscess he had."

So she remembered the doctor's visit, realised she was ill.

"Did I dream Grego came in a little while ago and told me he and Pat are going to be married?" she demanded presently.

"No, you didn't dream it; it really happened," Marnie assured her, in a voice that didn't sound quite like her own.

"I'm so glad it is all settled." Faint pink showed in the sunken cheeks. Her eyes shone. "It has been the dream of my life to see the dear boy happily married . . ." The words trailed away as she sank into her drug-induced sleep.

The hours dragged on, Grego prowling in and out restlessly, until at last Marnie begged him to go to bed.

546

"I'll call you if there is any change in the Contessa's condition," she assured him.

The silence intensified as the night wore on. The curtains hung limp at the open windows. It was one of those stifling summer nights when not a current of air stirs. The world seemed to be holding its breath, waiting for the storm which did not come.

At three o'clock Marnie gave her patient another injection, and a drink of fruit juice. She had to prop the old lady up in her arms, holding the feeding cup to her lips. "What a helpless creature I have become!" she said with a shaky laugh.

"It's partly due to the injections the doctor ordered to relieve your pain," Marnie reassured her. "They make you drowsy and inert."

A smile flickered over the small pale face. "It's all right, Marnie dear. You don't have to invent comforting explanations. I know how it is with me." Her sunken eyes looked up at Marnie imploringly. "Don't let Grego be too much alone. Stay with him until Pat can be with him. He will be so lost at first. Help him, Marnie . . ."

Marnie nodded, swallowing the sudden hard lump in her throat. "I'll do all I can for him, Contessa."

"I know you will." The old lady put out her hand and Marnie took it. "You are a good girl, Marnie. It seems nothing short of a miracle that you should have come to us now—just when we need you so sorely. You have done so much for me. I don't know how to thank you." A spasm of pain crossed her face.

"You're talking too much, Contessa," Marnie warned gently. "And as for thanks, they're completely unnecessary. I've loved being with you."

"I know you have, dear girl. That is what has made

547

it so good to have you. You fitted in with all my little ways so sweetly and patiently. It is almost as if you were the daughter I never had."

Chinky, disturbed in his night's sleep by this conversation, gave a smothered growl of protest, stood up from his place at the foot of the bed, turned round three times, scratched the quilt into a more enticing resting place, and settling down again curled himself into a tight ball.

Watching him, the Contessa smiled tenderly. "What will become of him when I am no longer here to take care of him?" It was a very muffled question, almost too painful to bring out. A tear trickled down the withered cheek. "Don't let him fret, Marnie. Comfort him . . ."

"I'll see he's all right," Marnie promised recklessly. "But you mustn't talk of leaving him."

"It's better to face the truth. I'm not afraid." The brave words were scarcely more than a thread of sound, and the Contessa did not speak again. But death takes its time, will not be hurried.

It was high noon when the bedside vigil ended, and Marnie crept away leaving Grego alone with his sorrow.

Up in her turret room she looked at her bed, unslept in, at her two packed suitcases. Was it worth while unpacking them? How soon would Pat Macreedy be arriving? Grego would surely have contacted her last night, telling her of his grandmother's serious illness, and she would come to him at once. Now that they were engaged her place in such a family crisis was at her fiancé's side.

Weary after her sleepless night, Marnie sat down on the bed, her heart heavy with the mystery of death. The awful blank there was, the feeling of a door irrevocably slammed in one's face. In hospital she had frequently witnessed death and it had never failed to touch her with awe. But here it was more personal. Her friendship with the Contessa, brief though it had been, had forged a bond it was painful to break. Her feeling for Grego too seemed in some way to intensify her involvement with the family's sorrow.

There was a tap at the door. It was old Gina, red-eyed with weeping. "The Conte wishes to know, *signorina*, if you would like your lunch served in your room, or if you will be joining him in the dining room?"

"I will come down, Gina, thank you," said Marnie. Hurriedly she washed her face, brushed her hair, freshening up after her night of nursing. Stony-faced and dry-eyed, Grego awaited her in the great gloomy dining room, where their places had been laid at one end of the vast table. It was a difficult meal, neither of them had much appetite and old Batiste, serving them, was absent-minded and obviously distraught. They did not speak of the Contessa, nor of their mutual grief.

"You must sleep this afternoon," Grego advised, when the coffee stage had been reached. "You must be tired out."

"I'm not, really," Marnie denied. "I feel beyond sleep, strung up . . . and I ought, I suppose, to do something about my plane reservation for this evening. It isn't going to be easy to get my ticket changed."

"Must you go home at once?" He sounded desolate. "There will be much to see to here. I know I mustn't impose on your time . . ." He broke off, looking embarrassed. Asking favours didn't come easily to him.

"Giulio will come," Marnie suggested. "Other members of your family, perhaps."

"Some ancient aunts," he said disconsolately. "A few

549

distant cousins; none of them likely to be of much practical use."

"But you will have Pat Macreedy," Marnie ventured. "She will be anxious to be with you at this time."

Grego gave her a dead-pan glance. "Pat and her parents are off on an Adriatic cruise in the *Bella Rosa*. I don't want to upset their arrangements. Besides," he added, "I very much doubt if I could get in touch with them."

"I see," Marnie murmured, thinking she didn't see at all. Wasn't his fiancée the natural person for him to turn to in this sad emergency, and surely a yacht the size of the *Bella Rosa* would be equipped with radio reception?

There was an odd, strained silence. Then Grego said softly, "Please stay for the funeral, Marnie. *She* would have wanted you to."

Somehow that settled it. Remembering her promise to the Contessa, Marnie said in a rather quavery voice, "All right, Grego. I'll stay as long as you need me."

She saw the light leap up in his grey eyes. But he only said briefly, "Thanks, Marnie. And now what about that rest you ought to be having?"

CHAPTER THIRTEEN

IN the strange days that followed Marnie often found herself wondering why Grego had asked her to stay on. Absorbed by the numerous duties the sad occasion demanded, he seemed to have forgotten her existence. He was seldom visible, save at meal-times, and then they were so surrounded by visitors and relatives that any kind of personal exchange was impossible.

Death in a great house. From her place on the sidelines Marnie watched the ceremonial comings and goings; the lawyers and clerics and undertakers, the weeping retainers and villagers, the visiting cousins and aunts, with their respective husbands. All the female relations wore the deepest mourning. They accepted Marnie, in a preoccupied way, as the English nurse who had looked after poor dear Edita during her last brief illness, but they had little to say to her. It would have been almost a relief to see Giulio, but he was not expected until the actual day of the funeral, pleading his duties at the bank. The truth, Marnie suspected, was that he had little liking for the gloom in which the house was plunged, an atmosphere far removed from his *dolce vita*.

The weather did not help. Day after day the thunderclouds gathered, to roll away over the mountains unbroken. It was close and oppressive, the earth parched and dry, waiting for the rain that did not come.

So the week dragged on, while all that was mortal of the little Contessa rested in the small chapel in the garden, surrounded by candles and flowers and black-clad praying relatives. Feeling out of place in her gay holiday frocks, Marnie would keep out of sight, wandering about the neglected gardens, wishing herself miles away. This atmosphere of heavy mourning seemed to have nothing to do with the cheerful, vital Contessa. Marnie missed her at every turn. The Castello seemed empty without her. The one remaining link with her gentle presence was Chinky.

Poor desolate Chinky, who had hidden himself for twenty-four hours after he had crept from the sickroom on the morning the Contessa died. It was some time before anyone in the preoccupied household missed him, but when it became obvious that he had disappeared Marnie searched for him distractedly, reproaching herself that she hadn't taken better care of him. She had found him at last, crouching hunched and terrified in the tool shed beneath the terrace, and taking him to her room she had fed him, brushed him, petted him, until some of the fear went out of his blue eyes, and his rigid body relaxed. Since then he had clung to her, following her on her lonely walks, sleeping in her room at night. Not once had he gone near the boudoir, or cried for the familiar bedroom door to be opened to him. Uncannily, he seemed to know that his mistress had gone from him for ever. Like the rest of the sad household he went through the motions of living, but he was very subdued; all the playfulness had been knocked out of him. How would it be with him when she had gone? Marnie wondered uneasily. Old Gina was very fond of him, and he would always find a welcome in her big homely kitchen. But would that be enough? He was so used to being loved and spoiled. Perhaps Pat Macreedy would give him the sort of special attention he had come to regard as his right. Somehow, Marnie couldn't quite see it happening. She would discuss the problem with Grego before she left.

She would take the Trans-Continental Express from San Paolo on the evening of the funeral day, she had decided, having abandoned the idea of getting her return air ticket extended. At this busy time of the year a chance seat on a plane would be practically impossible. And even if she got one it would almost certainly mean she would have to pay her fare again. The train fare would come to less, and there was certain to be room for her in the great express, perhaps even a *wagon-lit*.

The day of the funeral dawned more sultry and overcast than ever. One of the cousins insisted upon lending Marnie a black silk coat, and a crêpe-veiled hat which sat oddly on her glinting gold-brown hair. Awkward in this borrowed array, she took her place in the last coach in the funeral procession with the most distant relatives. Grego and Giulio were far ahead, walking behind the massive ornate hearse, drawn by four ebony black horses caparisoned in black velvet, their heads crowned with nodding inky plumes.

There was an interminable service in the village church, punctuated by the sonorous tolling of the dead bell. Marnie glanced at Grego in the front pew, tight-lipped with grief. Listening to the soaring voices of the choir, she longed for it all to be over. The endless prayers droned on. She had had about as much of this orgy of public mourning as she could stand. Her own sorrow was a bitter-sweet nostalgia, not to be assuaged by these ponderous and gloomy ceremonies. She would take the memory of the little Contessa back with her to England, and her life would be the richer for having known her and loved her.

As for the Conte Gregorio...but here Marnie's thoughts came up against a blank wall, the wall of his indifference towards her. It would be a relief to be done with the pain of their fruitless encounters.

At last it was all over, the service in the church, the slow journey up the precipitous road to the graveyard on the hillside, where the great white marble mausoleum of the di Valetta family dominated all humbler resting places.

It was as the cortege wound its way home that the storm which had been threatening for days finally broke. Rain sluiced down in torrents, thunder roared overhead, lightning cracked in the air like whips of flame.

Back in her room in the castle Marnie looked in dismay at the streaming sheets of water beyond the window panes. This was the hour in which she had planned to slip away, with the briefest of farewells to Grego. She had finished all she had undertaken to do, and there was no point in prolonging the agony. He had asked her to stay on for the funeral as a mark of respect to his grandmother. This she had done, and now she was free to go. Only she couldn't walk to the bus stop as she had hoped to do. Batiste would have helped her with her luggage. But the heavy rain made all this impracticable. She would have to phone for a taxi, and as it was already a little late for the bus she would take it all the way to San Paolo.

Going downstairs to see about phoning for the taxi, it occurred to her that she hadn't seen Chinky for some hours. She would have to find him, and leave him safely in Gina's care. It wasn't going to be easy saying goodbye to the little cat. Grego, when appealed to, had assured Marnie that between Gina and himself Chinky would have plenty of attention. She could only hope he was right, but she wasn't wholly convinced, and it was with a heavy heart she made her way through labyrinthine passages to the kitchen, thinking that Chinky might be there.

Gina, surrounded with her helpers from the village, was preparing the evening meal for the house guests. No, she answered Marnie's anxious enquiry, she hadn't seen the *gattino* since she gave him his morning feed of rabbit and cereal. But Batiste had seen him. "He followed you out of the house, *signorina*," he told Marnie, "when you went to get into the coach at the end of the cortege. I watched him trot down the drive in the wake of the cars."

"Probably he went all the way to the church," a large woman in a gingham apron suggested. "You know how he loves processions, that little cat, especially holy ones."

"Only this time it wasn't the procession he was thinking about, but his poor mistress," Gina said, and burst into tears.

Was it possible he had followed the cars to the cemetery and was still up on the hillside in all this rain? Marnie wondered. Dismissing the unwelcome thought, she left the kitchen and searched through the house, looking in all the places Chinky most usually frequented. But he was nowhere to be found. She even dashed out in the storm to explore the tool shed beneath the terrace. He was not there. He was sheltering somewhere from the rain, she consoled herself. She had missed her bus, and now it looked as if she was going to miss her train as well. But she knew she wouldn't be able to leave the castle until she had discovered what had happened to Chinky. The picture of him trotting small and desolate at the tail end of the funeral procession haunted her as she joined the guests drinking sherry in the drawing room. Giulio, she learned, had already returned to Rome, having gone straight back from the cemetery. Grego, with the most important of the aunts and uncles, was closeted in the library with the lawyers, where, presumably, the Contessa's will was being read. A mere formality, Marnie gathered from the chatter going on around her, since the estate was entailed and everything automatically reverted to Grego—the tumbledown castle with its burden of debts. It wasn't much of an inheritance, Marnie reflected. But Pat Macreedy's fortune would restore the ancient fabric, pay off the debts, inaugurate a new era of prosperity for the Conte di Valetta and his future sons. She ought to be glad about that. She *was* glad, she told herself firmly.

After the sherry there was an endless dinner. Grego at the head of the long dining table might have been on another planet for all the notice he took of her. He looked tired and drawn and must be finding the voluble aunts a little trying. But not for an instant did his grave courtesy towards them falter.

As soon as she could Marnie escaped. There was no hope now of her leaving the castle tonight. She would get away first thing in the morning. She went up to her room, thinking she might find Chinky there waiting for her. But he was not. Reluctantly she began to prepare for bed, the sound of the rain loud in her ears. Was Chinky wailing and lost somewhere on the dark hill road? Could it be—oh, frightful thought!—that he had slipped unnoticed into the roomy old mausoleum during the committal service and got himself locked in there? It was more like a small chapel than a tomb, with plenty of corners in which Chinky could have concealed himself from the coffin bearers and clergy.

The more Marnie considered this dire possibility, the

more it obsessed her. She could not go to bed with this worry on her mind. Going to the window, she saw that the rain had ceased. The clouds had lifted and there was still a faint drift of summer twilight in the western sky. This improvement in the weather decided her. She would go up the hill road to the cemetery, calling Chinky as she went.

In the hall she encountered Batiste and told him of her purpose. "I won't be long," she assured him. "But I can't go to bed and leave the poor little cat out there in the wet and the dark. It may be that he has forgotten his way home."

"*Non possibile, signorina!*" Batiste declared. "He knows all the roads around here better than I do. Undoubtedly he hides somewhere from the rain, and will come home when it pleases him. My guess is that you will find him waiting for you here when you return."

"I hope I shall!" Marnie said fervently.

The air was deliciously fresh after the storm. Hurrying down the village street, she came to the hill road. It was darker than she had thought. In the distance the thunder still rolled round the mountain tops, echoing against the stony slopes. "Chinky!" she called fruitlessly at intervals. It seemed an interminable way to the cemetery. Would the gateway with its carved marble angels never appear? Perhaps in the darkness she had taken a wrong turning. The road she was on now was little more than a goat track, dangerously skirting what she sensed rather than saw to be a steep precipice. Soon it became obvious that she had indeed lost her way. "Chinky!" she called despairingly. If he was sheltering anywhere it would surely be among the bushes and tombs in the graveyard. And she still hadn't shaken off the idea that he might be locked in the mausoleum. So that when she heard the hoarse Siamese call, she stood peering incredulously into the darkness. The sound seemed to be coming from the void beneath the precipice.

"Chinky, where are you?" she cried. "Oh, woe!" he wailed from somewhere beneath her. Had he fallen over the edge and hurt himself on the jagged rocks? If only she had brought a torch with her. She put a foot forward gingerly, wondering if it might be possible to scramble somehow to the spot from where the cat's cries were coming. She felt loose earth and stones beneath her feet. At her touch they went crashing down into the valley. Hurriedly she stepped back on to the path, which she now realised had been undermined by the torrential rain. At any moment tons of the mountainside might come adrift. She thought of the story the Contessa had told her of whole villages being wiped out by landslides of sodden mountain earth during the winter rains. Perhaps that, in a small way, had already happened here, and Chinky was trapped under a fallen rock. She could feel her heart thudding, cold prickles of fear ran down her spine. There was only one course open to her—she must return to the Castle and get a lamp, and someone to help her.

It was as she moved farther back on to the path that the ground melted beneath her and she found herself slithering slowly but irresistibly down into the darkness. The substance on which she moved was wet and slushy, so that she was not hurt, not even bruised when after a bewildering moment she came to rest on a narrow ledge of rock. She lay still, trying to collect her senses, assess her position. It wasn't going to be easy to get back up this slippery slope. Crouching on the ledge, she wondered what to do next.

"Mrrow!" came a soft voice close to her side. Chinky!

She put out a hand and felt his arching back. He rubbed his head ecstatically against her shoulder, all the time keeping up a stream of explanations. Whole sentences of "miaows" poured from him. Clearly he was trying to tell her what had happened to him. The same thing, most likely, that had happened to herself. He had slipped over the edge of the precipice and on to this ledge and hadn't been able to get up to the road again. She held him close, glad of his furry warmth.

Where do we go from here? she wondered. How many hundreds of feet lay beneath her ledge of rock? There was a river valley, she knew, far below, with a road that led in a roundabout way to the village. But she would never be able to reach it. The thought of venturing from the comparative safety of the rocky ledge into the void below appalled her. A sharp clap of thunder right over-head emphasised her plight and a second or two later the rain was once more pouring out of the sky in a solid flood. Half blinded by its fury, Marnie closed her eyes. She was wearing a thin summer mackintosh which offered little enough protection from the deluge. Chinky pushed his way into its folds, with a grumbling cry.

"Oh, Chinky, what are we going to do?" Marnie wailed despairingly. An ominous rumble answered her as tons of earth and rock, detached from the hillside by a torrent from the waterlogged road, came crashing down, just missing the ledge by inches. Marnie held her breath. There was a sharp blow on the side of her head from a bouncing splinter of stone, stars danced in front of her eyes, and she knew no more.

CHAPTER FOURTEEN

SHE was awakened by the sun shining in her eyes. When she moved her head it hurt, so she closed her eyes again and lay very still. There was a dream in which a nurse dressed as a nun pushed a hypodermic needle into her arm. She was a very young nun and she had a sweet face. It made Marnie feel safe and happy, so that she slept deeply and there were no more dreams.

The next time she woke it was evening and the room was filled with sunset light. It dawned on her slowly that she was in her own turret room in the Castle. Trying to work out how she had got here made her feel dizzy. The last thing she remembered was clinging to the rocky ledge in the middle of a thunderstorm. The memory of the darkness and terror set her trembling; she could feel her teeth chattering, which was ridiculous, since she was perfectly warm.

"Have you had a nice sleep, my dear?" It was the nursing nun bending over her.

"You're English!" Marnie marvelled.

The little nun nodded. "I'm Sister Angelique, from a nursing order in London. I've been in San Paolo looking after a patient who is now well, so I stayed on to do a few cases for Doctor Ortese."

The doctor who had attended the Contessa.

"But I'm not ill enough to need a nurse," Marnie protested.

"Of course not," the little nun agreed, smiling. "But the Conte wasn't taking any chances and wanted you to have every care. And now you must drink this." She held a cup of warm malted milk to Marnie's lips.

"Where is Chinky?" Remembering him suddenly, Marnie pushed the feeding cup away and sat up so abruptly that it started her head aching again.

"He's quite all right," Sister Angelique was beginning when Marnie heard his familiar cry at the door. Sister Angelique let him in and he jumped on to the bed, greeting Marnie with little welcoming cries.

"He's pleased to find you're better," Sister Angelique laughed. "He's been watching over you almost as closely as I have for the past twenty-four hours. I could hardly get him to go downstairs for his necessary little trips into the garden!"

Sinking back on to the pillows, Marnie stroked his velvety head, waves of relief washing over her. Chinky was safe. Her efforts that awful night on the hillside had not been wasted. "Who found us and brought us home?" she asked.

"The Conte," Sister Angelique replied. "Batiste had told him you were out in the storm looking for the cat, and when the time went by and you did not return he became alarmed. With Batiste and one of the gardeners he set out to look for you. It was Chinky's cries that led them to where you were . . ."

"So Chinky saved my life!" Marnie exclaimed.

"He saved you from lying unconscious all night in the rain," Sister Angelique supplied, less dramatically. "But as it was his fault you were trapped on the mountain-side the least he could have done was to contribute to your rescue . . . and incidentally his own."

"It's a good thing the rescue party heard his cries,"

said Marnie, with a shudder for the consequences if they had not. "He has the most amazing power in his voice when he's agitated."

"So I've noticed," Sister Angelique agreed dryly. "His protests when I tried to keep him out of this room were more likely to disturb you than his presence."

Dear Chinky! Marnie drew him, purring, into her arms. He seemed to be trying to make her into a substitute for his lost mistress. A disturbing thought. Marnie put a hand to her aching head, and discovered a sizeable lump.

"Seems as if I've had a knock on the head!" she said.

"You've got a nasty bump," Sister Angelique agreed. "And you're slightly concussed."

"So you've been keeping me sedated?"

"Exactly. But there are no bones broken. A day or so in bed should put you right. And now," Sister Angelique ended, "you're going to have a real meal. An omelette, perhaps, and a glass of wine. Does that appeal to you?"

Marnie slept deeply that night, with Chinky at her feet. "I must go home," she thought drowsily, when she woke the following morning. But she felt too comfortable to move. It was good to lie still in the green and gold room thinking of nothing in particular. Chinky, who loved people to stay in bed making a warm nest for him, was most attentive. Sister Angelique came and went. At midday Doctor Ortese appeared and pronounced Marnie well on the way to recovery. Another twenty-four hours' rest should see her back to normal.

There were polite messages from Grego, but he did not visit her. Venturing out of bed late in the afternoon to test her legs, Marnie went over to the window and looked down at the tangled rose garden. A tall man walked there with a girl at his side. Grego and Pat. So the bride-to-be had turned up! With a twist at her heart Marnie got back into bed.

She did not sleep so well that night, and woke early in the morning from a sad dream, with tears on her lashes. She couldn't remember the details of the dream, but she had a vague impression it had something to do with Pat Macreedy. The sooner she got away from the Castle the better—she would go this very day, she resolved, and told Sister Angelique so when she brought in her breakfast tray. There were the inevitable protests, but Marnie was adamant. "The Trans-Continental Express stops at San Paolo at noon," she pointed out. "And I've made up my mind to board it. I simply must get back to England. I've postponed my departure twice already and my family will be growing anxious about me. Besides, there's my work . . ."

"Well, if your affairs are so urgent," Sister Angelique reluctantly conceded, "I suppose we'll have to let you go, but I'm afraid you'll feel pretty weak when you get on to your feet."

"I'll be all right," Marnie declared doggedly. And she didn't care if she wasn't. The main thing was to get away from the sight of Grego and Pat Macreedy. Nor would they want her hanging around!

When the breakfast tray and Sister Angelique had been disposed of she got out of bed and slipped on a flimsy dressing gown—specially seductive, designed for her honeymoon. But honeymoons were far from her mind when she dragged her suitcases out of the wardrobe. Someone had unpacked them, and trying to get her things back into them made her feel dizzy again. So she abandoned the effort for the moment and sat on the edge of the bed, fondling Chinky. How would he fare when she had gone? Would Gina really be kind to him? He had been so spoiled and petted, poor lamb, he needed so much love. If it were not for the quarantine laws, Marnie mused, she might have asked Grego if she could take him home with her. After all, she could argue, she had promised the Contessa she would look after him. But he would never survive the statutory six months' quarantine in a cattery.

Suddenly it all seemed so sad that she could not bear it. Still weak from her adventure on the hillside, her heart burdened with the pent-up grief of the past strange week, she let herself go and sobbed unrestrainedly.

It was like that Grego found her. "Marnie!" he exclaimed, striding into the room. "Whatever is the matter?" And suddenly she was in his arms. Her head was on his shoulder, he was stroking her hair. It was all quite crazy. Surely she was dreaming! Yet the hard masculine chest she was leaning against was real enough. She pressed her hands against it, pushing him gently away from her.

"I'm sorry," she offered. "I'm just being silly. Don't pay any attention . . ."

"Sister Angelique tells me you are talking of going home today."

She nodded. "I must get back. I've stayed away too long already."

"Was that what you were crying about?" He took a large clean handkerchief from his pocket and handed it to her, watching her gravely while she wiped her eyes.

"I was crying about Chinky," she said, "wondering who would look after him when I've gone away. I know he'll have you, and that Gina will be kind to him. But Siamese are very special little animals and need a lot of

understanding. The Contessa loved him so much..."
A dry sob caught in her throat. "And he adored her. He
tried to go to her funeral..." The tears were flowing
once more uncontrollably.

"I'm sorry to be making such a sentimental fool of myself," she sniffed into the handkerchief. "It must be that
I haven't yet quite recovered from toppling down the
mountain in the middle of a thunderstorm, and banging
my head on the way."

"That ghastly night!" Grego gave her a hollow look.
"As long as I live it will return to me in nightmares.
When I realised that you had been swept down the hillside in an avalanche of mud and stones..." He covered
his eyes with his hands for an instant and when he looked
up again his face was gaunt and drawn. "It was Chinky's
cries that led us to you. How we got you up through
all that debris I'll never know, nor how you escaped
with your life. Half the hillside seemed to have broken
away, loosened by the heavy rain."

Marnie held out her hand. "Don't think about it any
more, Grego. But thank you for saving me." It was
pretty inadequate, but if she tried to say any more she
might begin to cry again.

He had taken her hand in both his own. "You were
so limp and quiet in my arms. I didn't know how badly
hurt you were. I was frantic. Oh, Marnie, the relief when
I got you to the car at last and found that your heart
was beating fairly strongly!"

Lifting the hand he held, he pressed it fervently to
his lips. These emotional Italians! In spite of his mixture
of Yorkshire blood there were moments when the Conte
Gregorio di Valetta was very Italian indeed—a fact she
must not overlook, Marnie warned herself. Steeling herself against the misleading sweetness of this intimate

565

moment, she said in a brisk voice that perhaps he had better leave her now, as she wanted to dress.

"If I hurry I should just about catch the midday express at San Paolo. Did Sister Angelique tell you I have decided to make the journey by train? I'd never get a seat on a plane at a moment's notice."

He didn't appear to be listening. The intensity of his gaze was embarrassing, making her conscious all of a sudden of her unpowdered nose and tousled hair. She wished he hadn't caught her in such a state of disarray, looking her very worst after her days in bed, and with a green and blue bump on her forehead.

Drawing the flimsy negligee more closely around her, she stood up, hoping Grego would realise the conversation was at an end, and depart. But nothing seemed further from his mind. Catching hold of her arm, he pulled her gently down beside him again on to the crumpled quilt. "Don't go away today, Marnie. Don't ever go! That is what I have been trying to say to you each time you have been on the point of leaving. You helped me with dear Nonna, and for that I am eternally grateful. But that isn't by any means the whole story. It wasn't entirely on Nonna's account I begged you to stay. It was for my own sake as well." His voice was suddenly rough and broken. He jumped up and began pacing the room. "Maybe I ought not to have sprung it on you like this, but I thought ... I hoped ... you would be glad."

She looked up at him, her eyes wide with an amazement that was akin to fear. "What are you saying, Grego? I don't understand."

He put his hands on her shoulders. "Is it so hard to understand? Do you really think, as you once said, that I am incapable of love?"

"No, no," she blurted painfully. "But there's Pat Mac-

566

reedy. She was here yesterday. I saw you walking with her in the rose garden." The awkward jerky sentences came tumbling out.

"She came with her parents. They had read of my grandmother's death in the press and called in to offer their condolences. It was all a little difficult, since I am not exactly in the Senator's good books. I don't suppose I shall be seeing any of them again."

"But you're engaged to Pat . . . you're going to marry her!" Marnie all but shouted, her mystification increasing.

"What makes you think that?" Grego demanded maddeningly.

"You went to Bologna the other day to propose to her. The Contessa told me how happy she was about it. Then when you came back that night you told your grandmother it was all settled. I couldn't help overhearing you."

"So that's it!" He had taken his hands from her shoulders and thrust them into his jacket pocket. Standing over her, he looked very tall and stern. "It *was* all settled," he said, "but not quite in the way Nonna imagined. If she misunderstood me it was perhaps all for the best. I admit I was a bit devious, but she was too ill to be worried with the true facts of the case. She died believing something she had set her heart on was going to happen."

"And isn't it?" Marnie gasped.

He shook his head. "What Pat and I settled that day was the impossibility of our ever meaning anything real to one another. Pat is in love with a chap in Rome, an artist like herself. She tried to transfer her affections to me to please her parents, and perhaps too because she fancied the idea of having a title. Americans make rather a lot of that sort of thing, I understand. But it didn't work out. I could see she was unhappy." He paused.

"And you?" Marnie prompted.

He shrugged. "What I had embarked on with Pat was more or less to please poor little Nonna. I think she guessed her days were numbered, and she wanted to see me comfortably married, or at least on the way to that supposedly blissful state, before she left me. She thought Pat would make an ideal wife for me, and incidentally that her considerable wealth would help to mend the di Valetta fortunes—a notion that I must admit appealed to me for a time. I hadn't met you, you see, when it was first mooted. Lately I've been realising what an impossible arrangement it was ... a marriage without love on either side ..."

Marnie's eyes grew wider and wider.

"Darling, don't look at me like that!" He dropped down on the bed beside her. "It is almost more than I can stand. Pat and her dollars mean nothing to me."

"Then why," she asked bluntly, "did you get so involved with her?"

"I've told you. For Nonna's sake ... partly. But it fitted my book very nicely; it protected me from you."

She gave a shocked gasp.

"Do you remember the things you said to me that night we had dinner at Belmara? You told me that I liked being disillusioned in love. That I wanted to be disappointed in people so that I could keep myself free from them. That was my behaviour pattern, you said. Love was too risky for me, so I persuaded myself the loved one was unworthy of me. Remember?"

She nodded. Embarrassment at hearing herself quoted made it impossible for her to speak. And the whole conversation was so unexpected, so astonishing, she couldn't quite take it in.

"It was an acutely perceptive observation," he went on. "It stayed with me. I kept thinking about it, until I had to admit that in your summing up you had described exactly what I had done in my reaction to my love for you."

"Your love?" she echoed incredulously.

"It came so easily, like a great burst of sunlight... that night we first danced at the Savoia. Holding you in my arms, looking into your eyes, I felt you were a part of me, that in some mysterious way it had been ordained we should find one another. It isn't easy to explain... that rare moment of complete affinity, when the heart seems to find its home."

"Oh, Greg!" Marnie choked down the tears that threatened once more; tears of bewilderment and a joy too great to be contained. "Driving away from the Savoia you held my hand. You were singing a love song..."

"Then we called at the *pensione* to collect your luggage," Grego took it up, and halted ominously. "You left me alone with the Deladda sisters and they told me how you had booked to come to them for your honeymoon, but in the event turned up alone, cheerfully announcing that you had ditched your bridegroom, practically at the altar steps. They were shocked that you should have decided to use up your travel tickets, your *pensione* vouchers, going through with your holiday, occupying alone the room you should have shared with your bridegroom. It seemed to me one of the most heartless things I had ever heard."

"So you fitted me into your theory that all women are faithless," Marnie said tonelessly.

Grego didn't reply. His face was stern and sad.

Here we are back at Square One, Marnie thought. When he spoke to her of love just now it was of the love which might have been—if he had not walked into the Deladda sisters that night, when for a few brief hours he had glimpsed the happiness which must ever elude him. Why hadn't it occurred to her before that the Deladda sisters, who hated her, would most certainly have talked against her? Now she could understand Grego's sudden change of mood that ill-fated night.

"You judged me without hearing my side of the story," she said, a wave of anger and sheer misery made her reckless. "Just as you judged your mother!"

He stood up, white to the lips. "What do you know about my mother?"

Her heart beat thickly. She had estranged him for ever now, trespassing unforgivably on his private life, roughly touching the wound which had scarred him for all time.

"The Contessa spoke to me of her," she said, "told me something of her sad history. She had no anger against her. In her wisdom she found much to excuse in her conduct—war-weariness, loneliness, even ill-health. The Contessa loved your mother. She was so sure she would have come back to you all if she had not so tragically been killed."

He had turned his back to her, moving towards the window. Outside the sun shone, the world went its heedless way. Chinky on the windowsill washed himself vigorously. Slumped on the edge of the bed, Marnie put a hand to her confused and aching head. What madness had induced her to bring Grego's mother into the already too complicated conversation?

"Maybe the Contessa ought not to have talked to me

about the family's private affairs," she offered wretchedly. "But old people live so much in the past . . . her heart was burdened. She worried about you."

"Did she tell you of her efforts to get me married to a girl called Linda Danelli a few years back?" he asked in bitterness. "And how Linda let me down?" He swung round to her, his grey eyes blazing. "It didn't matter to me, Marnie. Linda's defection didn't hurt me nearly as much as the doubts I had about your integrity. I wasn't in love with her, I suppose. Not in the way I love you."

"Even though you think I've done something that seems to you heartless, unfaithful?

"Maybe you had your reasons. But whether you had or not I don't care." He had come close to her again, and was standing over her. She could feel the tension in him, the pent-up storm. "I've staked everything I've got this time. The reckless last throw. The only thing that matters to me in the whole world is my love for you —no matter what pain it may bring me."

She couldn't bear the anguish in his glance. "Oh, Greg," she cried, "we hurt each other so. All of us. Parents and children. Husbands and wives . . . and lovers. The more love there is the more capacity there seems to be for pain. We blunder along, lonely, confused, and only love, if we have faith in it, can heal the hurts we cause one another.

"There was no love in the end between myself and Glenn, the man I was going to marry. It took me a long time to find this out, but when I did discover it I knew I couldn't go through with the wedding. He had acted in a way that made it once and for all abundantly clear to me that he did not want me, the *real* me. He saw me simply as a convenient appendage to his own life and plans . . ." She broke off. Grego's stony face frightened her.

"I'm not making excuses about my broken wedding," she said sadly. "It's just that I hoped you might understand."

"I do understand." He put his hands on her shoulders. "And you needn't have done all that explaining, darling. I was prepared to take you on trust. For weeks I've been fighting the demons of jealousy and suspicion inside me. I know in my deepest heart that you are all I first thought you were . . . but I had to torture you, torture myself. The hurts we give each other; you have put it so beautifully, my wise Marnie. Only love, if there is enough of it, can heal our wounds. If you love me, Marnie, as I love you . . ."

"If I love you! Oh, Grego!" When they kissed it was as if all heaven was suddenly about them. No problems any more, no uncertainties, only the joy of loving and being loved.

It was Chinky who brought them back to earth. Having exhausted the diversion of his morning toilet on the sunny windowsill, he jumped down and strolled towards them with a soft "Mrrow". He had been left out of the conversation long enough. All this embracing! He gave Marnie a purposeful nip on her bare ankle and was rewarded by her cry of protest. It was better to be scolded by his adored humans than totally ignored by them. Jumping on to the bed, he pushed himself between them, his tail erect, his blue eyes squinting hopefully.

Laughing, Grego released Marnie from his arms, and sat back, admitting defeat. Chinky, left in possession, got on to her lap.

"Fair's fair," Grego said. "After all, he brought you here to the Castello. And now you won't have to leave him to Gina's tender mercies," His voice softened. "Nonna would be pleased about that. I've an idea she would be pleased about everything. If it hadn't been for that wholly misguided bee in her bonnet about Pat Macreedy I'm sure she would have been happy to see you installed permanently at the Castello di Valetta."

"Do you mean you're asking me to marry you?" Marnie marvelled.

"My good girl, what do you think I've been trying to get across to you for the last half hour?"

"I don't know," Marnie murmured, bemused. "It's all been a bit mixed up. And it's so unexpected. I mean I'm so unimportant . . . a mere nobody, with no ancestral background, no fortune. You need so much money for the upkeep of the Castello, the running of the cheese factory."

"We'll manage," Grego said airily. "We can live simply, shut up most of the great vaults of rooms. Or, alternatively, furbish them up a bit and open them to the public, as your English lords do. With the tourist trade on the up-and-up we might make quite a good thing of it. As for the cheese factory, with the results I'm showing now I should be eligible for a Government grant. We are selling all we can produce, ready to move into the export market . . ."

He broke off. "Why the hell are we talking about cheese?" Firmly pushing Chinky off the bed, he took Marnie once more in his arms.

It was very quiet then in the sunlit room. At the open window the green and gold curtains stirred, and Marnie had an odd feeling that someone had joined them, a gentle, beneficent presence that wished them well. It was all imagination, of course, but in that magic moment all things were possible. Miracles were in the air. Love was a miracle. How could one brief half hour have so transformed her life? And yet it had.

"Oh, Greg," she sighed, "I can't believe it!"

"Neither can I," he agreed. "But there is plenty of time for us to get used to the wonder of it. We have all the rest of our lives to work it out."